Return to Faërie

***

Book Three

Windy Hill Prayer

Return to Faërie

A trilogy comprising the following books:

Moonrise
A Delicate Balance
Windy Hill Prayer

www.return-to-faerie.com

Copyright © 2021 Jane Sullivan

All rights reserved (including all forms of reproduction or adaptation of text and images, in all forms, in all countries)

Jane Sullivan
www.calligrafee.com

ISBN: 9798558967128

Table of Contents

Windy Hill Prayer

1. Flaming Moon and Silver Leaf 1
2. The Harp of Barrywood 23
3. Samhain Eve 51
4. Brother and Lover, Sun and Moon 75
5. When the Owls Fly Forth 97
6. A Study in Mauve 119
7. Back and Forth 147
8. Miraculous Music 179
9. The Cup of Light 207
10. Eli's Journey and Erreig's Lament 233
11. Vanzelle 267
12. The Hill of the Sun 309
13. The Sailor and the Silkie 339

14. The Hawk, the Loch and the Island 367

15. Purple Wine from Black Berries 391

16. Hermits and Home-Comings 413

17. The Eagle and the Unicorn 451

18. The Painted Dulcimer 487

19. Revelations, Invitations and Reassurance 511

20. The Stone Circle 533

21. Many Islands, One Path 557

22. Morning Prayer 587

A Blessing 613

Three More Notes in the Music 615

Index of Characters 617

Maps 619

Chapter One:
Flaming Moon and Silver Leaf

li had taken a window seat on the flight home to France. Against a sunset sky, the plane circled Paris, preparing to land. From her little window, foggy with condensation or blurred by her own tears, she was unsure which, Eli glimpsed the new moon. It was following close behind the sun, and both seemed eager to dip below the richly painted horizon in the west.

"This doesn't feel much like riding my flying-horse," commented Eli inwardly. The thought made the corners of her mouth rise in the slightest of ironic smiles --- but it made her tears well-up again too.

"And this is the special day of Ævnad, the 17th of June. And on this day, in Faërie, I was swooning into a faint because the Dragon-Chieftain had stolen the Amethyst Cloth, a part of my mystical shroud on the Island of the Scholar Owls, and I --- I mean Mélusine --- had awakened to challenge him…

"And here I am," she continued, still in silent conversation with herself, "two-and-a-half weeks later, at the same date all over again. But nothing is the same. Except that I'm swooning once more, only this time it's into a 'real' life as a human-being. And that feels very much to me now like fainting or losing consciousness: losing the consciousness of who and what I really am."

The plane landed with an incredible rush of noise and a far-from-graceful bump on the tarmac of the runway.

"Nope," she nodded, her lips pursed, "about as unlike Peronne's soft and silent landings as it would be possible to imagine."

She collected her baggage and made her way from the air-terminal to the railway station, purchased a small bowl of quinoa and sweet-potato salad in plastic, and eventually found her train back home to Saintes.

"Hardly *buicuri* with Piv and Leyano," she smirked, as she began to eat her salad on the train. "And although I will be contented to see the steeples of Saintes loom into view and to find myself in my own little flat again, it doesn't really compare to an airy bed-chamber perfumed by trailing jasmine and honeysuckle in the silver-turreted City of Fantasie."

It would, she was sure, require many more days or weeks to re-adjust herself to her life, her human life in the world. It was a much more difficult process than it had been after her first Visit back to her fairy-home.

Why was that?

Perhaps, she admitted to herself, all this extra struggling and longing, filling her with over-dramatic and pathetic loneliness, came from the fact that she did not believe that --- this time --- she was going back.

"How can I, really?" Eli asked herself, over and over again. "How can I love Brocéliana as I do now, and force her to leave Garo and her beautiful home in our father's kingdom, and to come into this modern and sordid and violent civilisation here?"

But that was not where her objections ended. The other reason, more dismal and causing her much greater consternation, was difficult for Eli to pronounce, even to herself. Very privately, very silently, very deeply within herself, she repeated it once more, as she had whispered it to herself for seventeen days now.

"It's Finnir. I don't think I can go back, ever, because Finnir is there. And I am in love with him. And he is my own brother."

Her train arrived very late in Saintes, and Eli walked home to her apartment on the *rive droite* under a balmy but very black summer sky. No moon, for she was long ago set. And too much light was coming from the small city, even at midnight, to allow the stars to be very visible either. At least, they were not as visible as in Faërie.

A smile stole over Eli's lips as she turned the key in the door and then switched on the light. Clare seemed to have been waiting for her! Eli could feel the warm greeting of her harp, almost as if the instrument were smiling back at her.

The Lady Ecume's words resonated in her mind yet again: *I remind you: before your human life you were a fairy, and after it you will be one once again; but do not forget that between these two --- between past and future --- there lies the <u>present</u>, and that there, without a doubt, you are also a fairy, whatever else you might be.* Only a fairy, thought Eli now, would be able to feel the greeting and the smile of her harp!

"I may be back, and it may be for good," she added, whispering her words aloud as she ran her hand over the sweeping curve of Clare's feminine and gracious form, "and I may, therefore, never be a fairy 'once again', as the wondrous mer-harper put it. But in the present, in my here and now, though I'm a human still, I am also --- somehow --- Mélusine. I will always have a fairy's soul."

Funny that, Eli continued to ponder as her hand caressed the golden wood of her harp: Clare feels warm to the touch. My hands are a little cold, but my harp is definitely warm. Or isn't the proverb more 'cold hands, warm *heart*'? Well, maybe my heart *is* warm too, like Clare!

Reaching up, instinctively as she spoke, Eli fondled the silver ear-ring that the Lady Ecume had given her. It, too, felt warm --- almost hot. She found she could not touch it for long, as it was almost burning her hand. She went into her bathroom, to look at it in the mirror; strangely enough it was something she had not thought to do until now. "At least here we have such things as mirrors!" she laughed to herself.

How very odd, she thought suddenly, that it hadn't occurred to her to look for the ear-ring in her reflection while in California. In fact, she had hardly looked at her own face in a mirror! She had, it seemed, begun to become used to a world without mirrors.

But now, going into her bathroom in Saintes and scrutinising herself in the glass, there was no ear-ring to be seen.

She lifted her hand to her ear-lobe once again, pushing a strand of red hair out of the way. Yes, she could feel it and handle it, and it was still burning hot. But in the mirror her hand was playing with thin air.

"I should have thought as much," Eli admitted to her reflection. "That's why no one could see it. Not Leyano or Reyse, not even my father when I arrived at Dawn Rock. Not my teacher Janet either, I'll warrant, or the two other musicians at the 'healing harp' workshop these past two weeks in San Francisco. Not even the security staff at the airport when I made the alarm ring as I stepped through their metal-detection-archway! No one can see it or feel it but me. And even I tend to forget that it's there.

"It's only visible to me. To me --- and Barrimilla, and the 'other fairy who will be at my side', I suppose," she added, recalling the prophecy of the magical mermaid. *When the time is fulfilled, and you are called to use the greatest power of this gift, you will show it to a fairy named Barrimilla, and another fairy will be at your side, and will know of this gift also, and understand its properties.*

"But if I never return to Faërie, not even at the end of my human life, I won't be making use of its greatest power, the 'mighty charm' she spoke of. It may very well --- here in this world --- give me the power to heal others, as she said; and it may protect me from the dangers 'shortly to be unleashed' --- whatever they might be. But I will never be asking it to *open a passage*, one that will bring me 'through the red waters, through the Garnet Vortex, back into Faërie --- by the Fourth Portal.' Because going back, even after my human-death --- if that is what she was alluding to, rather like my father did --- will still, I imagine, mean that Brocéliana will have to leave. And even though I go back at the very end of my human life, in how ever many years that may be, Finnir will still be there. And though I grow old here --- here where age is quickly accumulated, much more quickly than in Faërie --- I will still and always love Finnir. I have no doubt about that."

Tired and somewhat jet-lagged from her long journey, Eli went back into her little sitting-room, gave Clare a kiss, opened her suitcase and pulled out her pyjamas and her shoulder-bag from Faërie. She climbed into her bed, having laid Lily's journal on her bed-side table, with Reyse's unfading rose beside it.

She gazed at her window for a moment, where the white curtains were softly undulating in the current of air passing through the small opening left when closing the wooden shutters. She could conjure, in her sleepy mind, the pretty scene of the *trompe l'oeil* painting in Banvowha's house. The eaves of a dark forest and a half-hidden castle, the rising moon and a tiny dancing unicorn, and a trailing vine of silver leaves and golden flowers curling over the sill...

****

June gave way to July, and Eli became occupied with her work: with playing for summery gatherings in gardens or for weddings, and teaching one or two of her students who were not off on their holidays elsewhere (as Annick was, in Brittany). At the tail-end of July, she remembered that the first of August, Lughnasa, was her father's birthday. And that Reyse's birthday fell soon after that, on the 10th. Her own, at least hers as Mélusine, had come and gone on the 21st of June --- but she had been happy that she was playing, all *that* day, at a medieval festival. She had let her duties keep her mind off her memories, and indeed they had helped to curb the stinging thoughts of her 'last day in Faërie', before she had stepped through the Portal of Dawn Rock and back into Santa Barbara --- back into the same afternoon that she had left, on the 1st of the month.

"I could ask a favour of Clare," she considered, late in the afternoon of the 31st of July, a Saturday. She had played in the ordered and pristine gardens, *à la française*, of a nearby *château*, for a wedding-reception, earlier. Now she was home again, and feeling relaxed with her work behind her, work which had included a nice buffet luncheon with a glass of champagne as well. "I could play Clare and ask her to communicate a 'happy birthday' wish to my father, for tomorrow."

Eli did *not* follow this idea with an intention to contact Reyse as well. She had relegated Reyse to the *very* furthest reaches of her mind, with some success, these past weeks. At the start, when she had found herself back in America and then in France, she had wondered if her fairy-suitor and champion would appear out of the blue, as he had done in May, following her first Visit. But he had not. And she found that she was relieved, somehow. For she really didn't know what to do with her affection for, or her attraction to, or her affinity with that dashing lord of the Shee of the Dove. She was certain, now, that her heart was deeply in love with her half-brother, and yet she could not define *what* her heart felt for Reyse.

And so she preferred not to think about it, for the moment.

But it would be nice to wish her father a happy birthday; though at the thought of speaking with him, even by the means of some magical form of harp-language, her chest tightened with sobs once again. Never to see him again, that was an unbearable thought. Never to see her father, or Demoran, or Leyano or … Jizay! And never, never to see Finnir, ever again.

As her tears abated, Eli reprimanded herself.

"Champagne amplifies and exaggerates your emotions --- always has," she chided herself. And her good-humour began to return.

"You are *free*, my girl," she added, speaking gently and philosophically to herself as she pulled Clare's travel-cover off and sat down on her music-stool to play. "This is a *freely*-made decision of yours, not to return to your fairy-life. You made it by your own choice and for good reasons, and you must live it with conviction and with joy. Don't make it into your life's great burden and tragedy. You are Lily's daughter, so honour her wisdom and her spirit: be firm and be at peace with your decision."

She stopped short, her hands paused in mid-air beside the harp-strings. "No, I'm *not* Lily's daughter," she whispered, her cheeks feeling suddenly drained of colour and her eyes moistening again. "I have chosen to call Lily, still, my 'mother' and even the Lady Ecume called her that; but I am --- in fact --- the daughter of Queen Rhynwanol. *Queen Rhynwanol…* And I hardly know my true mother."

Not knowing why she did so, Eli immediately began to play an air, an Irish and a very ancient one. The haunting, modal melody filled the room and seemed to turn into swelling waves of sound that refused to die away, but just continued to gently lap against the walls and to encircle Eli's slightly rocking body with warm arms of liquid sound.

Eli closed her eyes as she played, and as the melody drew to its close, she opened them, feeling now very peaceful and relaxed.

But the music continued.

Before her, on the far side of the very small room, was Gaëtanne, the Queen's tall and cob-web shrouded harp from her Music Room. But it was not cob-webby now. It was uncovered and very bright, polished as if with bees-wax; its softly-sculpted pale pine-wood form was gleaming in the late afternoon light from the window at Eli's back.

The tune that Eli had been playing was coming from Gaëtanne's strings now, for the Queen herself was seated at the harp and playing with skill and with great subtlety the same tune: a melody that Eli recalled as having been very often played to her. And, like the harp, the Queen was not hidden by any misty covering; she was *not* a phantom harpist as she had been in the Music Room of the King's Great Tower in Fantasie. She was here, and real, and utterly and majestically beautiful.

She turned her head to Eli as she, in her own time, also concluded the lovely air. Her violet-blue eyes were as Eli remembered them --- remembered them from her vision of her mother on her fist Visit home, and also, without a doubt, as she remembered them from her own fairy-childhood. As the Queen moved, and gently pushed her harp from her shoulder so that it stood solidly on the floor, the long sea of black hair moved and shimmered over her shoulders and down her back. As the sunlight caught it, glints of deep blue and sweet mauve played over its surface.

Tiny clumps of langite crystal, rich humming-bird-blue and rather angular, were set like small flowers in her ear-lobes; while all down the locks of her hair were interwoven filaments of fine silver on which were strung dozens of miniature kunzite gems, soft lilac or deep pink, and many little seashells of mottled white or green. As she faced Eli, still seated, the deep v-shaped bodice of her gown revealed an agate, set high between her breasts. And swinging from a long cord bound around her waist was a beautiful amethyst, many-faceted but seemingly natural rather than cut by any craft. As she noticed it, Eli's left hand began to tingle, just in the centre of the palm.

Flaming Moon and Silver Leaf

Eli thought she had never, in all her life, seen anything so exquisite as this woman, this fairy. And then the Queen spoke, and although the music of Gaëtanne had been wonderful, this sound was more delicious and more melodious than the voice of any harp, or bird, or ocean, or breeze whispering in twilit tree-tops.

"You have healing in your hands, when you play, Mélusine. It was always thus, even before you studied this art and deepened your gift in company with the Lady Ecume. But now that she has presented you with the Flaming Crescent Moon, you will feel this force even more keenly, and you will bring health and peace to many. I am pleased to see you wearing it."

Although feeling that she could easily drown in the sound of that voice, Eli still had no hesitation in speaking.

"You can *see* the ear-ring? No one else can." And then, as she remained entranced by the lovely vision before her, Eli recalled that all three of the 'givers' of the ear-ring could certainly see it: Rhynwanol and Morliande and the third who was, she supposed, the marvellous mermaid.

"I can see it, yes," the Queen assured her. "For I made it."

Eli reached up and touched the silver pendant, and found that it was now cool and seemed to be pulsing --- like the heart-beat of a sleeping infant.

"You made it? For me?"

The glorious Queen smiled very slightly, and her eyes danced. "I made it for others, and for myself, and also for you. It was fashioned long ago. It has come to you now, a gift --- through the kind intervention of the ancient mermaid --- a gift from your *three* mothers, if I may call us all by that name."

Eli felt herself leaning into the aura of energy surrounding the Queen, a wide and warm field of vibration, although she was on the other side of the room. She repeated the strange phrase: "*Three* mothers?"

"Myself, and Morliande --- who is your grand-mother, but may be named as your 'mother' also, and Maëlys, that is Lily."

"You grant that Lily is my mother, as you are?"

"Lily is your mother as Lily is, not as I am. And Morliande is your mother in another way. And the Flaming Moon comes from us all, from your 'maternal trio'. It has a threefold power, and each of its attributes come from one of us. Lily *protects* you with it, for she will not allow you to be shamed and violated again. I endow you with great powers of *healing and helping*, as you desired of me when you first heard me play the harp to you as an infant. And Morliande has concealed the *Key of the Garnet Vortex* in this pendant, and will help you to pass through the Fourth Portal ... when the time comes."

"When *what* time comes, exactly?" asked Eli, in so hushed a voice that she wondered if her mother could hear her.

"Your mother Morliande, your father's mother, is a seer, Mélusine. She has perceived, even since you first dreampt of coming into the human world --- and that was during your years of bravery and beatitude in the Great Charm --- that you would not return to Faërie, not at your human mother's death. She saw that you would stay, as a human, as a healer, until you could traverse the threshold of mortality, in your earthly form.

"And though, in the Great Charm --- and afterwards, in your preparations for the transformation into a changeling --- you accepted that you would thus die, and pass through the human Portal of Death into what lies beyond it, Morliande has granted you a choice. When you come to that moment, you will be able to present the Flaming Crescent Moon to the keeper of the Veil of the Vortex, and it will unlock the Fourth Portal. And so you may, if you survive that ordeal, return to Faërie via that most treacherous path and doorway."

Eli was silent for a moment, and the room seemed bathed in sea-mist, and then once again warm and golden in the July sunlight. "You *know* that I will not go back for my third Visit? And you know why, I suppose, as well."

Rhynwanol was not smiling now. She seemed to be searching for her answer, and she idly fingered the dangling amethyst as she hesitated. Finally she looked very intently at Eli, and she seemed to relax.

"I do not think that is entirely correct, for I see that you will return. You *will* go back for your third Visit," she replied at last. "Why would you not? You will be gone for three hours, and the three weeks passed in Faërie will perhaps afford you greater insight and understanding in what you are to do <u>here</u>. You will not, cannot, have all your memories and fairy-wisdom restored to you as a human; your three Visits can serve to deepen your perceptions and aid you for the years remaining to you in this world. Do not refuse the blessing of those precious days and all they can teach you."

Eli could not reply, but she breathed deeply for several moments, and then she nodded her assent.

The Queen added, "I do not know when you will choose to make your final Visit, but do not hesitate too long, Mélusine. And do not forget that Finnir has asked you to meet with him, at Gougane Barra, this autumn."

"You know that Finnir has invited me to meet him, at the Portal there? Do you know why? Can you tell me?"

"As concerns Finnir, I know many things. But they are not for *me* to speak of. He has something to give you, and he told me this when he visited my shee several weeks ago. He was in company with Morliande. What his gift is, I do not know. But I will warn you of one thing, my daughter. Do not step through his Portal unbidden or unprepared. Your *destiny* lies on its Faërie-side, and I do not deem that you are ripe for it, not yet. Barrywood is as perilous as the Vortex, and you will need great strength and no vestige of fear in your heart to set foot in it alone and unchaperoned. Yes, indeed, Barrywood is Faërie at its <u>most</u> perilous, as Finnir is Faërie at its most enchanted! Heed my words.

"And now, farewell, and when you play the harp, and when you heal with it, know that I hear you and that --- though far in distance and listening from another world --- I am with you. May the blessings of the Moon be upon you, Mélusine, and the Flames of the Sun dance about your heart! Farewell."

The room was empty, or at least seemed to be so, with the disappearance of Rhynwanol and Gaëtanne. Eli's left palm burned with a sudden and sweet twinge, and then felt normal and only comfortably warm once again. Clare's strings vibrated with a gentle humming, and then they, too, were utterly silent.

****

The next morning, over her mug of tea --- very strong tea, indeed, this morning --- Eli continued to muse over the 'visit' of Queen Rhynwanol.

Had she actually been there, in the flesh as it were? She had not seemed at all ghostly or semi-transparent, and Eli had not meant to 'conjure up' a *vision* of her fairy-mother. She hadn't even been thinking of her, particularly. She had hoped to contact, somehow, her father to wish him a happy birthday! What exactly had happened?

Eli's life had, undeniably, become more and more fantastical since learning of her true nature and beginning the round of Visits back to Faërie to make the decision to ultimately return or not. But that, in itself, did not bother her. Eli had always had a penchant for the unusual and unlikely in life: she had often preferred being 'odd' to being 'normal', in fact. Perhaps that was her fairy-nature shining through her human one!

There had been times when her inexplicable and anomalous nature had grieved her, as when she had so desperately wanted to start a family with Colm --- when being at least *normal* enough to have children had become extremely important to her. But as for following any <u>logical </u>or <u>practical</u> course in her life, in regard to work or money, social status or professional advancement, even spiritual philosophies, she had never put her priorities there. But now she felt that she had entered a chapter of her life which demanded that she become serious and thoughtful about her odd situation. For much seemed to be at stake.

For one thing, it was clear (if she believed what Rhynwanol had said) that Lily was still somehow 'there'. She had died, in January of this year; but Eli was now encouraged to accept the idea that Lily was protecting her, looking over her, from some vantage point beyond death. What was Eli to make of that?! In Lily's Christian faith, it was often accepted as a possibility: the souls of the dead were sometimes seen as 'keeping an eye' on the living, and saints were often invoked for protection and even with very mundane requests for help or guidance.

Eli decided that she would read more of her little moon's journal, over the coming days. Perhaps something would be said about what Lily herself understood about 'death' and about 'life after death'. And about the Flaming Moon ear-ring, too.

And Morliande, who exactly *was* her grand-mother? This proposed plan of Eli's dying, in human terms, and then somehow voyaging through a whirling vortex of crimson water --- wherever she was supposed to find that --- and being assisted or pulled through this dangerous experience by a magical fairy who spends half her time disguised as a seal... that was the oddest riddle of all. Oh dear! What on earth, or beyond it, was Eli to make of it?

There were so many things she would like to ask her mother, the Queen, now. But it was clear, in the vision granted her by their duo of harp-music, only certain subjects were to be discussed. Eli hadn't even had the presence of mind to inquire about her mother's feelings for Aulfrin, or for Erreig, or about what were --- precisely --- the dangers and threats in her own life that Lily was to protect her against. And how. And about

Rhynwanol's own blessing, through the charmed moon-pendant, that would make Eli into a powerful healing-harpist…

Her studies in San Francisco with Janet, the harpist whose web-site had inspired Eli when she wished to sooth Lily during that last week before she slipped into death, had been filled with inspiration and information. Eli was very grateful to Emile's parents for funding her trip to the States and making that meeting possible. But had she learned anything new, really, from that encounter? Was she not, already and innately, blessed with this potent talent to heal with music?

Of course, her gift and her long education in this domain where part of her fairy-life, so perhaps she needed this extra help to bring her abilities into focus here in *this* world. And now she had, in addition, the powers imbued by the Flaming Crescent Moon in the part of its three-fold charm that came from her true mother, Rhynwanol. But how was she to put into practice this healing art? What was she meant to do? Would her playing simply cure people who heard her, as it had evidently done for little Emile? Should she seek out persons needing her help, or should she let it all happen by 'non-existent' chance?!

Oh dear, oh dear.

Eli decided to take the notebook she intended to read with her into town, and to begin by a long walk along the River Charente which would lead her, eventually, across the bridge and back to the opposite river-bank for a late coffee-and-croissant breakfast and a relaxed Sunday-morning moment with her little moon.

The summery, tourist-season patio of the *Musardière* was rather too busy and talkative for Eli, and so she settled herself in a comfy armchair *inside* the café , near the spiralling staircase --- with a little, low table before her, just the right size for her mid-morning snack.

She sighed, for she had to admit that, much as she was missing Faërie, she felt very at home here in Saintes.

"I suppose I'm suffering from 'multiple personalities' or some such malady," she grinned to herself, sipping her coffee and watching a sparrow hopping about the doorsill which separated the café from the small garden behind it, leading to the patio with its array of wrought-iron tables and chairs shaded by generous parasols.

"I like it here, and I love it there. I could live in either. It all has to do with being completely in the present --- and not making comparisons, I guess. I must learn to be like that sparrow, that little *piaf*, hopping back and forth, back and forth, over the threshold between inside and outside. He seems cheerful whichever side he's on! A bit hesitant, perhaps, or at least edgy about his choice. But cheerful nonetheless…"

She broke off a piece of her croissant and went to the door, offering it to the bird. He was not timid or indecisive at all, and cheekily took the titbit and then piped a little call to her for more.

"So, that's also a good lesson!" Eli remarked, when she had assented to his demands and handed him a second morsel. "Ask for what you want. Don't be shy. Just ask Life for more, and you'll get it!"

She took another sip of her rich, aromatic arabica, and opened Lily's notebook. But the choice of page was not made by her, for the book-mark she had tucked into the journal chose it for her. The little journal fell open, quite naturally, where the Silver Leaf was.

Eli picked it up. As she had already noticed, it was hard to define if it were a real leaf or one made of precious metal. Impossible, really, now she studied it. Running her fingers over the soft veins in relief on the gently curved oval of the leaf-form, she still could not decide if she were caressing vegetable or mineral… or neither.

"Neither," she breathed in a whisper so soft that it seemed not to come from her own lips. "It's neither a plant nor a piece of silver-work; it's made of light."

Indeed, as she laid it back onto the open page --- which she had not yet bothered to read at all, utterly forgetting that she had meant to search for Lily's philosophies or premonitions regarding the possibility of communication after death --- Eli tilted her head to align it with the angle of the Leaf. Instantly, the silver shimmered like sunlight on water, and then became crystal-clear. A tiny window had opened in the shape of the Leaf, looking down and out beyond the page, into another world.

But it was not the picture-book forest and castle of the *trompe-l'oeil* window in Banvowha's home. It was nowhere Eli had seen in Faërie, or in the human lands she had known. Or was it?

"I *do* know that place," she thought to herself, her brow wrinkling in bemusement and perplexity. "I think I know it. Or I've seen somewhere like it. It must be in Ireland, I would guess in the south-west of County Cork."

Gazing deeper and deeper into the tiny opening, falling into it in her imagination, Eli began to look about her. The café in Saintes had disappeared, or at least had been relegated to the periphery of Eli's attention. She was in the land of the Leaf, and it was wonderful!

Everything was bathed in silver light, a soft rain, a fine mist. It made her want to dance, just like the fairies did in a downpour. The earth was stony and dark, jagged and somehow primeval. It looked as though it had been scratched and furrowed by the claws of giant dragons! But in all the crevices and cracks, tiny flowers bloomed: white and precious, more beautiful than any flower Eli had ever seen.

"Moon-flowers," said a voice she recognised. "They only grow here. In all of Faërie, in all of the eleven island-shees, this is their only home. Are they not exquisite and pristine and full of laughter? Here in the Sheep's Head Shee, they are abundant and contented; but they refuse to grow elsewhere. I tried, many years ago, to transplant some to Windy Hill, about the door of the Chapel, near to where --- long ages past --- the mighty Aulf planted the Wattle Tree. But they would not grow. They withered and turned to white ash, blown away into the waters of the Inward Sea. But here, they grow everywhere, and they will be your constant companions and attendants, my dear Queen."

"Can I come here and see them whenever I wish, Finnir?" Eli asked, silently but with a serene smile on her lips. "And can I see Windy Hill and the mimosa tree, too, in the Shee-Mor? And can I be with you?"

Finnir's voice was as lovely and laughing as the moon-flowers, but Eli could not see him, only hear him.

"Of course, my belovèd. Of course you can. You can see this shee as well as the shee of Aulfrin when you will, and you can see the sacred Isle of Windy Hill and the yellow tree, and you can speak to me --- as I can to you. But through the window of the Silver Leaf, only our palms may touch, invisible and yet warm. But when you come, finally, to dwell in this place, it will not only be the moon-flowers who will be truly with you, always with you."

"*You* will be with me…?" Eli's voice trailed off, into even more profound silence now.

"I will," came the reply, so soft that it was no more than a movement of misty air to displace a lock of her dewy red-grey hair, falling over her eyes. Eli had lifted her left hand, she was sure of it; though she had not moved. And her eyes were closed as the palm of her hand pressed forward and met Finnir's.

Neither moved for many moments. A warmth like a dozing kitten tickled her palm, but Eli felt only love. A radiating, singing love that flowed out from her open hand, and that flowed into it. The same love.

The little *piaf* chirruped again, and hopped right into the room, up to Eli's feet, asking for another crumb of her croissant.

"You're very bold!" Eli scolded him, but with merriment. "Very bold, very bold indeed."

****

Bold. I will be bold, too. I *am* bold.

Eli repeated the word she had used, spontaneously, of the sparrow, turning it over in her mind as she sat back into the deep cushions of the armchair. It would be a very good thing to be filled with boldness; because she was more and more convinced that she would need it. Quite a lot of it.

She did not read Lily's journal, not until much later. Her heart was already over-flowing and could, she conceded, contain no more emotion just at the moment.

Bold, or hesitant, she wasn't too sure which described her at this instant. She only knew that she needed to think. She needed to decide what to do. Rhynwanol had said that she *would* go back for her third Visit, to absorb more wisdom and to re-awaken further memories which would help her in her mission here, among humans, for the rest of her life.

Should she see Finnir first, at the threshold of his Portal in Gougane Barra, in Ireland? And when, thereafter, should she ask to make her final Visit?

But other questions were battling for place in her jumbled thoughts. Questions that involved her love for Finnir also. In truth, Eli admitted, *everything* was involved with her love for Finnir!

From whom had come the Silver Leaf?

It seemed unlikely that it was a gift of Banvowha, for had *she* not urged Eli to re-consider *Reyse's* suit? And this magical leaf led her to *Finnir*. Or perhaps it led, quite simply, to Love. And

Flaming Moon and Silver Leaf

the rainbow-fairy thought her lover, her husband, was to be Reyse --- and her father thought the same thing. For them both, he was her 'true love'. Even the little black fairy in the Fire-Bird Forest was intent on kindling Eli's affections for Reyse.

Did Banvowha think to open Eli's heart to the fine fairy-lord of the Half-Moon Horses by bestowing this strange little token on her: a Silver-Leaf window which would grant her a vision of her true love? Only instead of the rainbow-fairy's choice, the *real* object of her own desire had appeared: Finnir.

Another fairy now came back to Eli's mind, as she thought of those who had discussed her *proposed* marriage as Mélusine. It was the curious little Artist of Kitty Kyle, with his wings like those of a flying-fish and his audacious, confident, very tranquil demeanour before the King. He had related the opinion of his Sovereign's mother, Morliande, that Mélusine would wed the next King of the Sheep's Head Shee. And the Silver Leaf *had* shown Eli the Sheep's Head Shee, without a doubt. And Finnir had called her a Queen…

But Finnir was to be the next King of his father's shee, not of the Sheep's Head!

"I am neither bold nor timid," said Eli, almost aloud, as she left the *Musardière* and walked along the broad, bright boulevard towards the Cathedral of Saintes. "I'm just confused!

"What I need to do is to play Clare, and relax, and meditate perhaps."

It was very good to make music, as Eli had anticipated. Very good, and very calming, and very healing. As far as her gift of musical medicine was concerned, she decided that the first person she needed to heal was herself!

And so, seated near her open window with the sunshine streaming in and the swallows dancing in the blue sky beyond it, she played and played.

She did not pose any questions or invoke any mystical wisdom as to when or how she should return to Faërie for her last Visit. She did not day-dream about Finnir, or about Reyse, or about any other enchanted personage or landscape. She just played.

It *was* rather like a meditation. No thoughts, no images. It was not dramatic or transporting, as had been her meditation at the Haven of the Smiling Salmon. It did not contain encoded messages or memories or fortune-telling. It did not invite ephemeral ghosts into her airy little apartment. It was just harp-music.

And that was magical enough.

After about an hour, her fingers slowly ceased to move, and she stood Clare upright again on her three short, turned-wooden feet. She went to the window and leaned out, delighting in the whirling swallows and their flights-of-fancy aerial acrobatics.

She forgot, for the moment, that swallows were one of the three animals associated with Finnir. She was too happy just watching them to associate them with anyone or anything. Unless it were with Love itself.

"That's what it feels like for the heart," she said, at last, speaking clearly and with a peaceful smile softening the faint wrinkles of her face. "That's what it feels like, for a heart that loves: that tumbling, joyous dancing in the clear air. That's 'being in love' --- exactly."

And then, just as she had done on impulse last January, she opened her computer to look for an air-ticket to Ireland. Six months previously it had been, as it turned out, to be beside her little moon, her Lily, for the last days of her life. Now, it was to go to the doors of Barrywood, to the mossy-trunked trees of the woods of Gougane Barra in West Cork, to meet Finnir and to receive his gift --- whatever that might be.

He had said --- in his words sent to her via her lovely brother Leyano --- that she should go there 'early in the autumn'. "So I suppose that could mean September," she thought as she searched for suitable dates and prices.

Wondering if she should be conscious of the phase of the moon or not, Eli noted that the first week of September was the last quarter of the moon, from half to new.

"I don't think I should go to that strange forest when the moon is new and totally dark," was the amusing thought that came to her at once. But she tossed it aside.

"Be bold!" she affirmed, with a decisive nod of her head. "I'll try to be there on the 7th, in fact, when the waning crescent is showing its final and finest 'moon-lash'; what's more, *seven* is the number of the riddling gate called Wineberry in the Silver City. All good omens. That will do then!"

And so, with a 'boldness' that surprised even her, Eli bought her tickets, and organised herself to be in the woods that concealed Finnir's Portal at the end of the first week of September. She would hardly see the tiniest sliver of the moon on that date, unless she ventured into the Woods in the wee small hours before dawn --- and she did not think that her 'boldness' extended to that. But she could certainly go that day…

"In any case, you're very bold, very brave," she repeated to herself once more, almost as if she were the cheeky *piaf*. "Very bold indeed."

****

Windy Hill Prayer

Chapter Two:
The Harp of Barrywood

he week preceding her trip to Gougane Barra Eli had decided to spend mostly on the Sheep's Head Peninsula, a little further towards the south-west tip of County Cork.

She had worked almost non-stop throughout August, in and around Saintes and even further afield in France, playing harp for every event she could find and even spending entire days under the trees along the banks of the Charente with a straw-hat upturned on the grass beside Clare. Passers-by had been generous when she had been busking, and as for more formal gigs, such as weddings, they always paid well. Thus with all her various work, she now had enough in her bank account to enjoy the comforts of a beautiful B&B near Durrus for several days and nights, only a short drive from Bantry where Lily had lived.

The landscapes were all familiar to Eli, of course, but they were new as well. For now they were not only the glorious and wind-whipped fingers of Ireland's south-west coast and the ubiquitous patchwork of emerald fields delineated by endless stone walls, they were also the green curtains drawn over fairy-doors. These were the mysterious and magically wild lands that she now knew hid Portals into another world, into Faërie: one of them, in nearby Gougane Barra, led to her father's kingdom, and two others on the small Sheep's Head Peninsula led to the shee where her mother dwelt, and which she had seen in the Silver Leaf.

But August had not been exclusively devoted to harp-playing, and as Eli unpacked her small suitcase in the charming bedroom of her B&B, she was not thinking only of her upcoming meeting with Finnir. For among the items that she arranged on the wooden table under a large window overlooking the gardens, were Reyse's un-wilting white rose and the small phial of 'love-potion' from the black-fairy-mama of the Fire-Bird Forest. She had brought both these things with her, as well as her little moon's notebook, because Reyse was very much on her mind.

Very much, and very perplexingly.

She had, since her last Visit to Faëire, been back in the human world for three months --- but she had had no news of her father King Aulfrin or of Faërie. Lughnasa, the 1st of August and one of the four Great Festivals of the Celtic year, had been Aulfrin's birthday, and it had been marked for Eli by her mysterious communication with Finnir through the 'window' of the Silver Leaf. She had meant to contact her father the day before that event, by playing her harp; but it had been her mother, the Queen Rhynwanol, who had appeared to her then.

Throughout the first week of August, Eli had repeatedly sought to have some information about the King, about his realm, about the tensions between the Moon-Dancers and the Sun-Singers, about her full-brothers Demoran and Leyano… She had, only once more, sought to speak with --- and perhaps touch --- her half-brother, Finnir, via the Silver Leaf. But she had not succeeded in doing more than sending word to him that she would come to the Woods of Gougane Barra on the 7th of September. She had not heard his voice again, and only the fact that she could dimly see into the world of Faërie when she turned her head in alignment with the Leaf allowed her to hope that the beautiful and enchanted Prince had heard her message...

That glimpse into Faërie had been on the 7th of August, early in the morning, with a tiny and pale arc of the last phase of the sickle moon hung in the deep blue of the eastern sky. She had thought it propitious to seek to contact Finnir again on that date, and at that moment of the moon's waning. And she had fancied that his presence was somehow *tangible* in the scene revealed to her by the Silver Leaf's oval eye of light, staring into Faërie --- somewhere. It was a glade, a clearing in a wood of golden and silver trees. A little beige squirrel scampered up one of these, its sleek body making a blurred series of half-circular shapes all along the interlaced boughs.

"Finnir," she had called, very low, "Finnir, I'm coming to meet you at the gate of the Portal, in the Woods of Gougane Barra, on the 7th of September. Is that date suitable? I do hope so. Will I find you in the morning, or should I come later in the day? How will I know the place? For I have asked Clare but no image or answer has come to me... Finnir, do you hear me?"

The trees came in an out of focus in the window. As before, in the *Musardière* café, Eli did not feel herself to be looking at a picture or even gazing through a small window at all. She was *inside* the picture as well as outside of it. Just as she had felt on that first occasion, she had *fallen into* the Leaf and was no longer aware of its limiting contours or tiny form. But, at the same time, she was not entirely a part of the land she beheld.

She felt that she had reached out, with both of her hands, into the mist --- trying to touch the wavering trees or to clear an opening in the fog enough to catch a glimpse of Finnir, if her were there. But she knew that her arms had not really moved, and she could not make her fingers touch the trees or even the mist. And, of course, he had said that she could not *see* him, only *hear* him, so it was useless to try to look for his tall, noble form among the quivering trunks and branches. And there had been no reply, no sound at all.

She had decided to bring the Silver Leaf with her to the Woods on the day she had chosen, and to hope that she could contact him then. But the worrying idea had grown in her mind since then: had she created or imagined all of this about the Leaf? Had she really heard Finnir's delicious voice and his tender words of love? Or was it her own longing heart that had manifested those sounds, and the sight of the delicate little moon-flowers among the craggy rocks?

Eli tried to reassure herself, and to be 'bold'. But she had considered changing her plans and cancelling her trip more than once. Until three more days had passed.

On the 10th of August the moon had been new, 'sleeping with her eyes tight closed', as Piv would have expressed it. And it was the birthday of Reyse.

Eli had been playing all morning in the piebald shade of the tall trees that lined the riverside-walkway, between the *jardin public* and the River Charente in Saintes. At noon she paused to eat her picnic lunch. She was biting into a juicy apple when a familiar voice made her close her eyes for a second in gratitude and joy, and then open them again quickly, to see Reyse --- or Liam --- standing beside her.

"I passed my second Initiation in the company of apples and apple trees, as I think I have already told you, my dear Eli. So it's very nice to find you like this, in the midst of enjoying their marvellous fruit!"

Before Eli could answer, Reyse had seated himself beside Clare, at Eli's feet. From her low music-stool, Eli looked only slightly down into his deep brown eyes with their rings of gold. She smiled, and then laughed.

"I'm very glad to see you, Reyse," she admitted, passing her apple to him to share with her. "Yes, I recall you telling me that. It was when I asked you about the ruby in your palm. I'm afraid I can't remember its long and complicated name, though."

"As long as you remember mine, I am content," he laughed in his turn. "And I agree, her name is rather complex. It is *Blarua Criha-Uval*. I think you might translate it as something like 'The Red-Blossom Heart of the Apple'. And as we are speaking of hearts, I have come here to visit you today, to I remind you that mine is yours, dearest Princess."

Eli swallowed, and looked away. In order to change the subject, and deflect Reyse's rather surprising directness, she said, "I think it's your birthday today, is it not? Happy Birthday dear Reyse. But why are you not celebrating in Faërie?"

"Because I was missing you, and concerned for you, and because I would rather spend my birthday, and the many hundreds of birthdays that I hope to pass thereafter, in your company."

Eli could not contain her consternation at his tone any longer. "You are making very --- well --- *unequivocal* declarations of affection today!"

Reyse relaxed his regard, and laughed again. He took another bite of the apple and passed it back to her.

"Yes, I suppose I am," he nodded. "Forgive me, Eli. I have learned that you are going to meet with Finnir in the autumn. I was visiting him recently, in Barrywood, and he told me that he had invited you to the threshold of his Portal. I felt it would be advisable to remind you of my undying 'affection' for you before you receive your own belated-birthday-gift from your... *half-brother*." At the pronouncement of these final and overly-emphasised words, Reyse caught Eli's eye very pointedly.

He knows, she thought. He knows that I am in love with Finnir. Did he learn this from my father, or from Demoran, or from Finnir himself? But Eli's questions were kept strictly to herself. She nodded, and took out from her satchel the goat's cheese sandwich she had purchased at the *boulangerie* early that morning. She broke it in two, and passed half to Reyse.

They ate in silence for a moment. And then Eli ventured a question. "Did Finnir tell you when, what date exactly, he would meet me?"

"No, only that he had requested that you come to his Portal in the autumn. Don't you know the date?"

"Well, I've chosen one, but I don't know if Finnir knows. And I have no idea how to find the exact place of the Portal, in those rather magical woods."

"There *is* no exact place," was Reyse's simple response. "It will find you. Or he will, if he comes to the Portal on the date *you* have chosen."

"You think, if I interpret your tone, that I should have allowed Finnir to choose the date," Eli retorted, rather too haughtily, she immediately felt. She quickly added, "I'm sorry, Reyse. I shouldn't be bothering you with this. It's so lovely of you to come and see me. I'm sorry if I sound rude, talking to you about the choice of date."

Reyse was not frowning, but neither was he smiling any longer. He remarked, in a softer tone than he had used up until now, "Choice is an important matter, certainly as regards the Prince Finnir and you. I would say that, yes, it is probably best to allow Finnir to make his choice of… dates and meetings. And I have come to visit you in order to remind you that you, also, have choices to make. The choice to return to Faërie as the Princess Mélusine at the end of your next, and final, Visit --- for example. And other choices, also, of a more sentimental and romantic nature."

Eli looked intently at Reyse as they both continued their meal together, but for many minutes the fairy-lord kept his eyes downcast. This gave Eli the time to study, once more, his fine and proud features and his thick chestnut hair hanging in waves just down to his shoulders. His hair was shorter than he wore it in Faërie, and his ears had no points here. He was more

Liam than Reyse, in his looks. "But not in what he says," commented Eli inwardly. "Liam was my lover of two weeks. And Reyse wants to be my lover for many centuries."

As if he could read her very silent musings, Reyse now looked up again, and he almost seemed to continue Eli's own internal monologue for her.

"I have not come here to ask for *Eli's* choice to be my belovèd, as I did thirty years ago. For I am not asking for a short romance of two weeks, not now. I'm hoping you will consider carefully the choices you make as Mèlusine. For I have asked that fair, wise and amazingly beautiful Princess to accept my suit for many long years already, and I am still asking it. But I know that you cannot make that choice while you are Eli. I would like to suggest that you do not make *other* choices, of similar kinds, in your changeling-form either. Wait, please, Eli."

She breathed deeply before remarking, "Why did you desire those two weeks with me, in Kilkenny and Cork, Reyse? Why did you choose to come into the world and seduce me, as the human I was then, when you *knew* that I had refused you in my fairy-form?" Eli's turquoise eyes were flashing, and yet her voice was calm, almost affectionate, more tender than accusing in fact.

Now Reyse laughed again, warmly and with a fairy's good-humour and deeply-rooted joy. "I had no intention of finding you in Kilkenny, my lovely Eli; I had come to enjoy a harp-festival. I love harps!"

As he continued, Eli had to smile too. "I was much more surprised than *you* were at our encounter, for I knew you at once, if you did not recognise me. And it became clear to me that you were on the verge of falling in love with me then. Can you fault me for opening my arms to you as you approached me? I think, if anyone did any seducing, it may very well have been in the opposite direction. Applaud me, rather, for having the courtesy and self-control --- hmm…after a couple of glorious weeks that is --- of taking my leave of you. And of taking the opportunity to leave you a little reminder of who you really were, to be comprehended much later."

Eli's eyes met Reyse's now, and nothing was said between them for a long while. His smile was faint, but somehow more filled with the many years of his love for her than it would have been if more exuberant. Eli's was sincere, and very loving in a way; but it was the smile of a memory and not of a full heart at this time. It was also the smile of love of another kind, of respect and sympathy, and even devotion. But she did not, now, feel *in love* with Reyse. At least she did not believe so…

After many more minutes had passed, or perhaps it only seemed a long time to Eli, Reyse stood, and so did she. He kissed her hand.

"I am on my way to the Sheep's Head Shee, via its Portal near the Stone Circle of Ahakista. I have come from Demoran's Fair Stair Portal into France, to share some moments with you, dear Eli. But I must leave you now and make my way to Ireland. I shall be gone into the Sheep's Head Shee before you arrive at its Irish name-sake, no doubt. But I hope we will meet again very soon. You will be returning for your third visit, I suppose, before this year is out?"

Eli sighed, but did not answer. She continued to hold Reyse's hand as she said her farewells. Before he left her, Reyse smiled once more, and made one final remark.

"When you find yourself faced with a choice, a choice of paths," he said, very sweetly and softly, "paths that you hope will lead you to Love, remember the words of a very wonderful human whom I have always admired: the Buddha he is called I think. He said, if I quote him correctly, *There is, in fact, no such thing as a* **path to Love**. *For Love is the Path.*"

Eli's eyes grew misty and she had to close them as Reyse released her hand. When she had blinked and opened them again, her devoted suitor and long-ago lover was nowhere to be seen. Eli rubbed her hands over her flushed face, and then she sat down at Clare once again, to play lilting harp-music for the passers-by.

****

For three weeks, Eli had revisited Reyse's words, all of them, almost daily --- or more truthfully, nightly. Her sleep had been broken by memories of his coming to her after her nightmare in the great Chamber of the Seven Arches, of his vows to protect her, of his arriving at Leyano's Golden Sand Castle astride Peronne and languidly gliding back and forth in the sea-scented air before her wondering eyes, of their first shared moments in the Silver City sipping crazily-named beers at *The Tipsy Star*.

"I'm *not* in love with Reyse," she repeated, even now as she unpacked her belongings in her Durrus B&B and fingered the white rose and placed it gingerly beside the little bamboo phial. She found she harboured a fear that the rose would come into contact with the love-potion, and work some odd chain-effect enchantment on her, forcing her to shift her love from Finnir to this ardent and indefatigable fairy of eagles and apples and half-moons. The thought made her laugh at herself, but it also made her reach up and touch the Flaming Moon ear-ring.

"This powerful little jewel, this crescent-moon encircled by flames, this charm from all *three* of my mothers, has something to do with Finnir." Eli's words were spoken aloud, measured and musical. She lowered her hand, opening Lily's notebook to where the Silver Leaf marked its still un-read page. She continued to speak, clearly and very slowly. "This Leaf is linked to Finnir, but so is the Flaming Moon. I know this, but I don't know *how* I know it. And neither of them are linked to Reyse, even though Banvowha herself perhaps thought so.

"Why have I not read this page before?" she asked herself, bewildered by the fact. "I've read other passages over this past month or two, here and there, jumping through my little moon's thoughts and experiences, her love for her Sean, her visit to Faërie, her concerns for --- and her faith in --- me. But I haven't read the page of the Leaf. I've only opened it to use the leaf-window to search for Finnir. But perhaps, just perhaps, he's on the page. And maybe, as my heart is telling me, he's in this ear-ring somehow too. "

Trembling with the revelation that was now running through her and making her eyes wide and her palms rather moist, Eli took the journal up and held it almost as if it were the bejewelled and richly illuminated Gospel Book of an ancient Irish monastery. She sat on the edge of the rose-quilted bed of her B&B's bedroom and laid the open book on her knees. Reverently sliding the Silver Leaf over to the left-hand page of pencil illustrations, she read what had been beneath it. And as she read, she lifted her left hand once again to her ear so that she could touch, with the tip of one finger, the Silver Moon.

It is the sunny summer of 1991, my darling Eli. Two years ago you moved to this wonderful country of Eire, and now I have followed you here. Sean came to me this past spring (I had turned sixty-nine a couple of months before) and he urged me to leave everything behind me in Los Angeles and to come here to Bantry Bay.

He himself had found this cottage for me to rent, and I pay very little indeed. I think Sean had something to do with that! He knows the people who own this charming house, and they are --- like him --- joyful and trusting and generous and musical. Yes, Aoife and Dermot are both musicians: she a singer in the haunting, keening, ancient Irish style called 'sean-nós', and he a pianist. They don't play together, because the sean-nós songs are sung **a cappella***, as you know I suppose. But they are both very skilled artists. They remind me, in fact, of the people we met when we found our little home in the canyon north of Sunset Boulevard, when you came to me, my dear girl. Yes, they are very like that kind couple who also rented us a beautiful cottage for relatively little money. I wish I had never left it! But though I told myself, at the time, that even that reasonable rent was too much and that I would find somewhere cheaper in East L.A., it was more truthfully because I could not stay where I had been with*

Sean. The memories were too much for me. I was very sad in those days...

But then my fairy-love came back to me! And for nearly twenty years now he has been coming to visit me --- not perhaps as often as I would have wished, but quite regularly and always bringing me peace and happiness and a good dose of wonder. And now, better still, I have come here to a land he loves dearly, and which I now know is my land also --- or that of my ancestors. Ah yes, my Eli, I am, in my deepest heart and roots, Irish too! I have learned something quite amazing, and I will share it with you now. I could not have told you before, before you knew of your own fairy-life and truth. But in this journal I can.

Just before I was to leave Los Angeles a couple of weeks ago, my dear poet-prince, the dashing Leo, came to visit me once more. I have not seen him for many years, not since Sean took me to Santa Barbara to see where the threshold into his kingdom lies, and Leo --- or rather the Prince Leyano --- was there at the entrance of the Portal, to meet with us. But this time Leo came to me on his own, and unbeknownst to Sean.

And he brought me a present. A little silver leaf. It had been given to him, to give to me, by the Lady Sea-Foam, the marvellous mermaid that Sean drew for me, and who had blessed you with forgetfulness and healing after your --- tragedy, when you were a child. But this magical gift was not really from the mermaid, it came from another fairy-creature, who had made it long, long ago and imbued it with special charms and powers. And she sent it to Leo and asked him to bring it to me, to show me something very private, very secret, that she wished to share with me.

It was your true mother, my Eli, who made this, and has sent it to me. Yes, it comes from the Queen of Faërie, Sean's wife who was banished from his kingdom many centuries ago and who lives in exile in the shee of her grand-father, called the Sheep's Head --- named after the peninsula near me here in Ireland. Even Leo did not know the use or the magic of the Leaf. He told me that the Lady Sea-Foam had said that it would show me its powers itself, and that he was simply to tell me to hold it in the palm of my hand and look at it. Simple enough!

But he added that I would not receive its messages until I had moved here --- as, by then, I knew I was to do. He said to keep it safe and secret, and to bring it out when I had arrived in my new home in Ireland, and was quite alone...

When Leo had left me, I tucked the little leaf into this, my notebook, and I made a sketch of it too, here on the facing page. But, isn't it odd, if you are holding it now --- as I have been told that you would, for it would come to you not long after you were to be given this book of mine --- you will see: I couldn't draw it right! It wouldn't come out! As I tried to sketch it, my pencil went its own way. For here, you see, it isn't a leaf at all, but an island. It looks just like an island with many points and jutting cliffs or angular shore-lines: nothing at all like the shape of the Leaf.

*So, be that as it may, now I hope you have received the Leaf yourself, just as your mother told me you would. If you have not done so yet, it doesn't matter; it will come to you soon enough, for I know that the Queen is to be trusted. For she is not only **your** real mother, she is --- in a way --- mine too. In a way...*

*Yesterday, I took the Leaf in my hand, here in the garden of this lovely little cottage of mine, with the fuchsia growing all around the stone walls and the roses filling the sea-breeze-air with their delicate perfume. As I looked at the Leaf, which I thought was made of finely-wrought silver --- or maybe a real leaf that had been **dipped** in silver-coating --- it changed completely into another material. It became clear like glass, or maybe I should say invisible as if it were simply made of light. It was a window, and I could see through it and into a glorious landscape, all wild and windy but filled with colours and sunlight too. There was a rainbow over a distant headland, against a sombre and dramatic sky, but the foreground garden was bright and flowery. The ground itself seemed rocky and dark, but there were tiny white flowers everywhere, and purple ones too and blue campanula and pink clover and yellow dandelions. It was lovely.*

But more beautiful than all the flowers put together, more beautiful than anything I think I have ever seen --- except perhaps you, my Eli, especially when you were new-born and lying in your flying-unicorn cradle --- was the Queen. She was sitting on a bench in her garden, just as I was here, and she smiled at me. I suppose, now, you know your mother again, if you are a fairy once more. Probably you remember her from your childhood, or maybe you have even visited her in her Sheep's Head Shee. But I could not describe her fittingly, even if I tried. She was too lovely.

She greeted me, as *if* **she** were honoured to meet **me**(!), and told me I resembled, very closely, my ancestor. I asked her who she meant, and she told me: "My daughter," she said, "one of my twin daughters; Malmaza is her name, and her sister is Mowena. They are half-fairies, for their father was the Donegal poet called Grey-Uan. I had met him and loved him --- oh somewhat recklessly I must admit, for I was rather young and impetuous --- in the year 1112. A good while after (for my pregnancy-time was longer than that of a human but less than that of a fairy, in fact), our twins were born. This was in 1114. By then I had come back to Faërie, to the shee of my own father, called the Little Skellig. My girls were born there.

"They grew as fairies grow, quickly and then slowly, passing their Initiations in that tiny but very enchanted shee. But at the age of nineteen, in 1200, they both chose to go into the human world, ever as fairies but resembling humans. This they wished to do, together with another fairy-woman named Ceoleen, in order to bring help and enlightenment to the coming generations of humans and to encourage them to forge greater respect for plants and animals. As my twins were half-fairies, they could choose to continue to age very slowly, and this they did. And Ceoleen was and is a full-fairy, so she ages, quite naturally and normally, four years for each century.

"In the year 1700, Malmaza --- not yet 40 --- met and fell in love with an Irishman, as I had done many centuries before, a poet and a dreamer and a shepherd. They had a son, and he had a son, and he had a daughter and so did she... and so on until the year 1922. In that year, a little girl was born to a couple in Brittany, in France. Her mother was of the lineage of Malmaza and the Irishman. And on the other side of her family tree, the father of her father --- her grandfather --- was a changeling, a full-fairy, who had elected to remain in the human world. He and his wife had adopted a child, a boy (for changelings cannot produce children) and this son grew and married the mother of the little Bretonne girl. And that little girl was you, Maelys.

"So your mother was of the long line of my own daughter, Malmaza. And your grand-father was, although not your ancestor by blood, the bearer of many enchanted blessings which he bequeathed to you, his little Lily. It was he who suggested your name, Maelys, for it contained the little word 'lys' which would bring into your own life a fairy-blessing, for the lily is our most sacred flower, even as are the sweet moon-flowers --- a modest yet extraordinary variety of lily --- growing here at my feet.

"For Malmaza, I made, long centuries ago, the Silver Leaf, to enable her to remain in contact with me through its window. For many generations it remained in her family, and among her children and grand-children and great-grand-children there was always one who could look into the realm of Faërie, and visit it in vision and even in speech.

"Now, for Malmaza I had made the Leaf, but for Mowena, my other daughter, I had made a similar jewel: a Golden Flower. Thus she could remain in contact with me from the human world also. Mowena did not marry, nor ever bear children, and --- though she still lives --- the flower came back to me --- oh it is a long story --- for it had been immediately lost. Or perhaps stolen. It fell into the hands of the Dragon-Cheiftain of Quillir, Erreig; and it became the means by which he communicated with me, and seduced me. After I had been banished to this shee, in 1367, my son Demoran retrieved the lovely Golden Flower for me: a great adventure that feat was too. Since then, I have kept it for many years, for I had no one in need of it for seeing into the realm of Faërie, as was its purpose in the hands of a human or half-fairy.

"At his death, your grand-father asked your own mother for the Silver Leaf, and he was buried with it. It came back to me, through him; this was around the year 1940. And it was by happy coincidence that the Leaf and Flower could thus be reunited, for by then I had someone in mind to whom I wished to give them, someone very enchanted indeed and very important in the tale of Faërie, of Greater Faërie --- the extended realm of all the Eleven Shees of our world.

"This great personage among the fairies used, for many years, the combined powers of both Silver and Gold, of both Leaf and Flower, to weave enchantments that would further our combined plans, his and mine --- and many others, for the unification of all of the Eleven Shees into a great confederation of fairies, and of humans too.

"And then a day came, not long ago, when he spoke to me of the destiny of these two charmed tokens, the Leaf and the Rose. He said that they were readying themselves for the next chapter of their work, and that they needed to pass back into the world, borne by humans but who were also of fairy-family or who were true fairies adventuring in those lands. We discussed our plans at great length, but at last we chose a path for both of the tokens to come to their correct bearer. I asked the great fairy-lord to pass the Leaf back into the human-world by the Portal of my youngest son, Leyano. The Flower, he kept, and he will see that it falls into the hands destined to bear it.

"Thus my brave Leyano has now brought this sacred Silver Leaf into the realm of mankind, in order that I may give it to you, dearest Lily. For the Lady Ecume has told me that she will bring you, one day, to our shores. And on that voyage, you will place the Leaf into the hands of another Woman of the Moon, or at least of the family of the Moon-Dancers. She is a fairy of the rainbow; and as a true image of the rainbow, she will serve as the playful and iridescent pathway for the Leaf to come to its next bearer, as is ordained by the fairy-lord to whom I conferred it fifty years ago.

"Until that time, it is yours to use, dear Lily, daughter of mine by many generations of fairy-children. It will be your companion and your secret eye and ear into Faërie, to me, for nearly twenty years to come, until you pass it on to the rainbow-fairy when you are granted your gift of coming to this world of ours on a brief visit. Use it well until then, and allow it to remind you, always, that greater and greater wonders shall continue to come to you, as this great wonder has now done.

"Wonder leads to wonder, dearest Lily. Ever more, ever greater, forever more wonderful. That is the law in both of our worlds!"

"Wonder leads to wonder," Eli repeated, silently, in her head and heart.

For many minutes she pondered, and reread, the strange tale recounted in her little moon's journal. Her own fairy-mother was also, many generations ago, a sort of 'mother' to her dear Lily. Incredible, and very beautiful, it seemed to Eli. Like a looping, spiralling branch of that 'family tree', as curly as the withies of the cork-screw willows on the white Islands where she was educated as a young fairy. And Lily had owned this Leaf, and used it, and it had been returned to the rainbow-fairy Banvowha and then somehow it had delicately fallen from the window-sill of the *trompe-l'œil* painting back into the notebook, to be a gift to Eli. A gift from her true mother, and from her human mother, and from the great fairy-lord… Who was he?

She turned the few pages back to where she had begun reading, and moved the Silver Leaf a little further to one side. Yes, there was the strange little sketch of an island. Decidedly an island. Nothing like a leaf.

But this Leaf was nothing like a leaf either! She turned her head to align with its pointed, oval form, as she had done before. Immediately it cleared and shimmered like freshly cleaned glass in a tiny window. As it had done previously, it suddenly became the only view Eli could perceive, and all the bedroom faded into a misty periphery.

The same island-form was now in the centre of the view, but in a blink it metamorphosed, and it was no longer a drawing on a page as if it were represented on a map: now it was real and rising out of the horizon. Not the horizon-line of an ocean, but of a vast lake it seemed, for a distant and wooded coastline could be descried. The island was hilly, and densely clothed in trees and shrubs, but Eli could see that on its summit was a white chapel and through its open door, though far far away, she could see a bright yellow tree.

Suddenly she was flying, as if born up on her own wings. Peronne was not there, nor was she astride another creature.

Indeed, she seemed to be flying of her own accord. Beneath her was the lake, too wide and deep to be a lake at all: more like a land-locked sea, though there were only the slightest of wavelets disturbing its surface of ultramarine decorated with gliding swans here and there. Now she had reached the shore of the sea, and far beneath her on a wide promontory was a castle clothed in flowering vines and dark-leaved ivy, surrounded by immensely tall trees --- in fact the castle was shaped rather like a massive tree itself!

Soon it was lost to sight, and she was soaring over a winding stream, a little running river leaping over rocks and swirling about the complicated roots of very ancient oaks all along its banks. The river ended, at its beginning: for below her was the half-hidden and overgrown pool or well which was its source, no doubt.

Now, in her vision, she flew down and alighted before a truly remarkable tree. It was not very tall, but at the height of her own head it branched out in many curving arms, leaving an empty space in the centre. It looked rather like a giant's throne, encircled by many lifted and leafy branches. But the one at the back of the throne was much more consequential than the others; and it was huge and hollow, more like a secondary trunk. A fissure in its centre gaped, just above the 'seat' of the throne, and it had taken the distinct form of a heart. Cuddled into the space within the hollow of this secondary trunk were two small grey owls, staring at her.

As they flew out of the tree, the circular throne of branches opened like a hand --- reminiscent of the red hand whose palm had opened to receive her tiny raft when she arrived at the Island of the Archangel to meet the Lady Ecume. As the 'fingers' opened, so did the tree itself. The heart-shaped fissure, where the owls had been, was transformed into a tall, arched door leading to a passageway beyond.

"*The Heart-Oak,*" Eli heard whispered, as she gazed into the doorway. There, far down the dark passage, she could just make out the light of another land, another world. There were tall, mossy trees and great green-grey rocks. She could hear water flowing, not only from the source behind which fed the winding stream, but also far off in the distance, in the land beyond the passageway.

Eli tried to memorise the look of the trees she could descry. "Gougane Barra," she confirmed. "That is Gougane Barra, though I cannot see exactly where in those Woods I am being shown."

A voice spoke from among the mossy trees.

"My Mélusine," it said, and Eli's shoulders relaxed and she smiled in deep gratefulness. "I will be here in seven days' time. Here in the midst of the green glade of these merry woods. You will hear me before you see me, for I will be playing a harp. Follow the music, and follow your heart to me --- always!"

When Eli opened her eyes, which she had closed as if already seeking to hear the far-off notes of Finnir's harp, she was sitting on the bed of her comfortable room, listening not to harp-music but to birdsong in the garden of the B&B. She continued to smile as she closed Lily's journal, leaving the Silver Leaf where it was on the page with the island-sketch.

****

A golden week. It was wonderful to be in West Cork, to explore the Sheep's Head Peninsula and to enjoy, once again, Bantry town and its pubs and shops, and the many-coloured boats out on the Bay. And more than all that, it was wonderful *in the extreme* to look forward to meeting Finnir in the Woods of Gougane Barra at the week's conclusion.

Wonder leads to wonder. There was no doubt about that in Eli's mind now.

The morning of the 7th was quite rainy, which made Eli imagine Finnir dancing like all the fairies would be doing in such weather! She arrived at the Lake of Gougane Barra in the late morning, and had a coffee and cake in the tea-room overlooking the picturesque and swan-dotted waters backed by the rocky, gorse-brindled, heathery heaths of the mountain-side, streaked with dark lines where the hundreds of waterfalls fell into the Lake.

They made her think of the Innumerable Falls, the name she had heard in relation to Finnir's princedom --- where there were waterfalls that fed the Inward Sea. It was also the name of the sapphire set into his hand, which had saved her in mid-air when she had flown close to the Stone Circle: *The Eye of the Innumerable Falls*, her father had called it. The Falls and the Inward Sea near Barrywood, and *that* was where the Island of Windy Hill was located, she was now sure. Surely, that had been Windy Hill with its chapel and mimosa tree that she had seen in the window of the Silver Leaf; she was certain that she had now seen Finnir's Castle, and the Heart Oak Portal, as they truly were. And she had flown over them using her own fairy-wings!

Marvellous as were *these* thoughts, better still was her delight that Finnir would be there, in the Woods, today. She would see him, as she could not do in the Leaf. And he would give her his gift.

Eli took her time enjoying the little Oratory of Saint Finbarr on a tiny arm of land almost like a would-be-island touching the lakeshore. So peaceful and beautiful it was, with few tourists --- but those that *were* there were as reverent and silent as she was.

She continued, on foot, into the adjoining forest, maybe for about half-a-mile. The great green toes of the high trees were curled over huge stones or splayed out over the moist grass and shady, soft, almost yielding earth of these mystical woods. It seemed to Eli like the Irish equivalent of Brocéliande in Brittany. One or two other walkers could be seen in the distance, but soon they were lost to Eli's view. She seemed to be utterly alone.

Except for a brooding, attentive, listening presence.

The trees, the stones, the moss, the birds, the few blond or beige squirrels that Eli could see high in the pines or larches, all seemed to be holding their breath --- as she was now. The rainy skies had transformed into a pale forget-me-not blue, dotted with racing clouds exactly like the classic image of gambolling lambs. But they were less and less visible, for the trees were denser as she walked on and they created a dark green shade through which only occasional shafts of golden light slanted down to the springy, mattress-like ground. These columns of sunlight were so opaque that they made Eli think of pulled toffee. And they were the same colour as the squirrels, who were in abundance here.

Softly at first, and then more and more clearly, came the sound of harp music. Just as Finnir had said. And just as he had instructed her, she listened to her heart and followed the sound --- to him.

After only a dozen more steps, Eli saw the sight that she knew would remain with her until the end of her days, and beyond, if that were possible. Perhaps a hundred yards away, coming in and out of view between the maze of great, straight tree-trunks, was a rider. It was Finnir, on Neya-Voun. It was Neya-Voun as Eli had seen her on the shore of the Shooting Star Lake in Faërie --- every bit as real, as vividly clear --- and much, much more amazing; because this was *not* Faërie, but Ireland! And yet it was true: just as she was *sure* she had seen this fact in the enchanted kingdom of her father, Finnir was seated on a glistening white **unicorn**: his horse --- but complete with a silver spiralling horn.

And he was playing a harp.

Eli was convinced that she was *not* dreaming this. For she could not have come up with the 'dream' of what happened next.

Little by little, Finnir approached. Eli stood still, fingering the Silver Leaf that she had put into her pocket this morning. She watched, and she listened to the music of the harp her half-brother played, and she waited. Hardly breathing...

The unicorn tossed its head as it walked between the mossy boles of the trees, and her luxuriant, crimped mane undulated over her arched neck. Her long tail almost touched the ground as she picked her way over the knobbly carpet of over-grown stones. Finnir was dressed in deep green. His dark blue cape, as she had seen in the City of Fantasie when he rode with his company of riders out of the north-eastern Gate, was clasped at his neck by a broach of three gold-encircled acorns and it hung down over his back and onto Neya-Voun's croup. Because of his deep-hued, forest-shade clothing perhaps, his short, golden hair and his fair face and hands gleamed almost as brightly as the glistening pearl on his forehead. The amber of his ear-points sparkled and as he strummed the harp with his left hand, the sapphire set in the back of that hand shone out as well. Eli felt an answering tingle of warmth in the lobe of her right ear, where she --- as Mélusine --- wore a sapphire of the same family, the stone which had joined with Finnir's to save her from her near-fall off Peronne.

Finnir at last arrived, and Eli felt sure that she was no longer breathing at all. Time and reality seemed to have come to a graceful halt, and only the trees continued to inhale and exhale almost eternally, in rhythm with the lovely melody that floated out from the strings of the harp.

It was not Finnir's silver-wood lap-harp: it was considerably larger, and made of pale wood, like Clare. Its strings were brilliant white, except for the normally red and blue *do's* and *fa's*, and these were mauve and sage-green. But the loveliest colour of all was the blue of Finnir's eyes: that infinite blue of a summer sky, inviting Eli to fly into it forever.

The Prince did not speak. He smiled, and so did Eli, as he dismounted and walked up to her. He placed the harp on the ground, leaning it against a cushioned tree-trunk where a couple of ochre-yellow squirrels leapt and played. The unicorn nodded her exquisite head once or twice, and then she stood as still and silent as Eli.

Finnir took her hands, both of her hands which were now reaching in slow motion towards him, and held them for several instants. He stood facing her, just looking into *her* eyes.

Then, without any further hesitation at all, he placed Eli's hands open and high on his chest, and moved closer so that he could put both his arms about her. And he kissed her.

****

They had not spoken for two or three hours, not since Finnir had appeared.

They had kissed, and walked --- the unicorn following them, with the Harp of Barrywood held against her withers by a length of diaphanous scarf laced through the instrument and lightly wrapped about her neck. And then Eli and Finnir had sat by a stream, the first pure and singing water-course of the River Lee which rose from its source in the Lake, and they had kissed again, and again, and held one another. But they had not spoken at all.

Then they had continued to walk, alone --- except that they were together, and so not *at all* alone --- in the wondrous Woods.

In the early afternoon, as they sat side by side on the soft green of the forest floor, Finnir had pointed up into an opening in the branches not far above their heads, where the western sky was framed by leaves making a natural 'window', not unlike the shape of the island in Lily's sketch.

"Can you see her?" the voice of Finnir whispered. Eli moved her head slightly to rest on his shoulder as both reclined against the thick-as-felt moss covering the tree-trunk. She looked up, beyond his upturned profile, with features so fine and so intrinsically *known* to her that it made her nearly swoon. As her eyes half-closed, relaxed and intoxicated with joy, she gave a little cry, "Yes! Oh, how beautiful!"

The very tiniest line of curved white was visible in the exact centre of the space between the leaves. Eli had never seen such a fragile and thin sickle moon. Against the innocent blue of the day-time sky it was amazing to see it at all.

"It should be invisible to me, if I'm really a human," she laughed softly. "That's a moon that only a fairy can see!"

"You *are* a fairy, Mélusine. Even as Eli, even as a human, you are still a fairy. Some changelings live their human life completely human; some never relinquish their fairy-ness! Lily's grand-father was like that. He had chosen to remain a human, but --- despite that --- he was always and ever a fairy. He was a lovely man."

"You knew him, Finnir? You knew the man that chose my human mother's name and called her 'Lily'?"

"Yes, yes. He came to the threshold of my Portal, for the last time, one Samhain eve. It was in 1939, as a terrible war was brewing in the human world. He was filled with sorrow, and wanted to visit Ireland, and the borders of Faërie once again, ere the shadows deepened over Europe. I had met him before, for he was not an infrequent visitor to Ireland and to the Woods of Gougane Barra, but this time he came right to the doorsill, as it were, and was able to glance into Faërie and see a little of Barrywood, just the trees and creatures near the Heart Oak. It was a great privilege, accorded him by the Portal itself!

But he was deserving of it, for he was a kind and lovely man, ever heedful of the wisdom of trees and plants, flowers and beasts. He was a lover of all creation, all weathers, all colours. Yes, a great man.

Before we parted, I counselled him to ask that the Silver Leaf be buried with him. Using it, he was admitted into the Chapel of Windy Hill, as a ghost-fairy I suppose you might define him; and he lingered many weeks in my domain in Faërie before continuing his voyage into his human death. He did not wish to stay in our enchanted world indefinitely; no, he was content to pass, and to continue. He had become a Christian, and I think Lily's deep faith in that Way perhaps came from him --- they were very close when she was a small child."

Eli's eyes had left the tiny moon-lash, and met Finnir's as he spoke. He turned his head to smile down at her again.

"Do you think that I will be able to use the Silver Leaf, like Lily's grand-father, to return to Faërie, at the time of my human death?"

"No, no, my love. The Silver Leaf will permit you to communicate with me and with your mother, and certain others fairies, before that. To return to Faërie after your own 'death', you will use the Flaming Crescent Moon. That is why your *three mothers* gave it, presenting it to you by the webbed hands of the Lady Ecume. Morliande has blessed it with that power; you have been told about that, have you not?"

As he asked his question, he gently stroked Eli's face and hair, and his hand came to rest on the ear-ring. He played with it for a moment, caressing it as if it were an extension of Eli's ear.

"You can see, and feel, the Flaming Moon, Finnir? No one else can."

Finnir's long, white fingers returned to his lover's cheek, and then slid over her neck and shoulder. "I, and Barrimilla, we can both see it, yes. Besides you and the ancient mermaid and the three Women of the Moon, we are the only ones who can."

"Who is Barrimilla?" whispered Eli, in as hushed a voice as she could.

Finnir's two arms embraced her strongly now, and he kissed her again.

"Today is not for *all* answers. Today is for that," he remarked as their kiss ended, speaking as softy as Eli had done. He lifted his head a little away from hers and opened his shining blue eyes. "Many many answers are to come to you, and to others, soon my Eli. Be patient, for the hands are laid upon the edges of the velvet curtains, ready to pull them open and reveal the lovely scene! Be patient; it is coming --- very soon."

The couple stood, and with their hands joined they walked the short distance to where Neya-Voun stood.

Finnir faced Eli and took both her hands in his once more, and he said, "I must leave you now, my love, and step back through the Portal of the Heart Oak. When you come to Faërie for your third and last Visit, we will meet again. But in Faërie, at this time, we cannot express our love as we have done today. But we can speak when you are there for those three weeks, and we must. For it is vital that you come to know and to understand many things on that Visit, before you return, again, to this world."

Eli sighed, less with the confusion she felt about all of this information, than with the sorrow at Finnir's imminent departure. But she nodded, and then she smiled at him, because she could not possibly do otherwise. Her heart was brimming with joy and delight. It did, indeed, feel like swallows swooping and looping in the clear air.

"The Harp of Barrywood is my gift to you, my Lady," continued Finnir, turning now to Neya-Voun and undoing the wispy scarf so that the golden-wood harp came into his arms. He turned back to Eli, and passed it into hers.

"This lovely instrument is your gift to me? Oh, dear Finnir, she is beautiful! I am thrilled with her....but," Eli hesitated, and looked doubtfully at the gorgeous instrument, "but how is it I can see and touch a fairy-harp? I thought that was impossible for me, in my present form."

"This is *not* a fairy-harp, not exactly," laughed the Prince, his eyes dancing and sparkling with as many stars as Eli's. "I made it for you from a fallen pine --- a tree that had grown weak, from age and storm-wounds, a tree from these Woods of Gougane Barra. And very pleased he was to be granted a new and exciting life, like a phoenix rising from the ashes of its supposed funeral pyre!" At these words, Finnir's eyes flashed, and Eli knew that he knew <u>everything</u> --- all she had heard about his adventures, all she had claimed concerning her own. He seemed to be playing the strings of a harp that was her very mind and heart and life, as if combining the notes into chords and refrains, and making them sing.

I am a harp, in Finnir's hands, she found herself thinking. *I am Finnir's harp!*

She felt herself slipping into his eyes yet again as these silent words came to her mind, floating through her head just as the lamb-like clouds continued to move across the azure sky. A delicious warmth enveloped her, and she wanted to laugh.

But Finnir was speaking again now, continuing with these words: "It is not as mystical and powerful, perhaps, as harps in Faërie may be. But the strings that I have chosen are rather magical, I must admit," he laughed. "They will teach you, as you play them --- as you play for others --- what gifts they contain."

He took the harp back from her arms, and placed it on the green ground at their feet, between them. He wrapped her in his embrace once again though without kissing her; their heads were pressed closely together, their hearts beating in unison as if touching through the thin veil of their skin and clothing. Touching and mingling and flying like the swallows, thought Eli.

A last caress of his hand glided over his belovèd's cheek, and he stepped backwards a pace, finally turning swiftly and mounting his marvellous unicorn. Before Eli could take the deep breath she so needed, they had walked away through the ranks of towering trees, the moist and shady green giants of Gougane Barra, and no sign of steed or rider remained.

Only a sudden leaping explosion of squirrel-antics overhead, as five or six of the creatures dashed down the nearest tree-trunks and whisked away into the emerald shadows where Finnir had gone.

Eli was alone in the silent Woods. Only she had never felt less alone in all her life, or more blissful.

****

Windy Hill Prayer

Chapter Three:
Samhain* Eve

here is, without a doubt, something extraordinary about the light on the Sheep's Head Peninsula. Lily was not the only artist to have noticed that fact, but she had certainly appreciated it when she had moved to Bantry from Los Angeles.

Eli recalled her revelling in this new-found luminosity the very first summer she had arrived, in 1991. Her little moon had not done much painting in recent years, only her more 'commercial artwork' for private clients and for the Hollywood studio she continued to work for, free-lance, from time to time, until her retirement in the mid-80s. She had loved doing pencil-drawings and had continued to illustrate volumes of poetry: not Leo's poems any longer, but those of other gentle spirits and nature-loving bards. But painting, in oils or watercolours, she had left to one side of her artistic life. Until she came to Ireland.

Sitting with a glass of Murphy's stout in an old-world pub over-looking Kitchen Cove, a short drive from Bantry about half-way along the Peninsula on its southern side, Eli thought back to Lily's words; for the sunset light was glorious and golden, staining Dunmanus Bay in copper-red and shining

---

*Samhain is pronounced "sow" (as a female pig) plus "when". The "mh" gives the sound of a "w".

celadon blue, rather akin to Leyano's long chestnut hair decorated with bright turquoise gems!

"Fairy-light," Lily had called it, adding, "the air itself seems to be made of the brilliance and the laughter of fairy-folk; and all the three peninsulas near me here --- the Beara, the Mizen and the Sheep's Head --- all have their own individual *style* of light. Each place offers a different way of seeing, a different invitation, a different discovery."

Recalling those comments by Lily, Eli now knew that her human mother had learned, only just before, that she was not so human as she thought! As Eli could say of her own life now, a new world had opened to her, a fairy-land where she no longer saw herself as a mere dreamer, an outsider, no longer an unwitting trespasser into an other-world of legends. Lily had come to Ireland, with its magical light and its 'invitations' and the revelations offered her by the Queen Rhynwanol, and suddenly her own already rather *unusual* life had become even more miraculous and wonderful. *Wonder leading to wonder*: indeed, just as in Eli's own story.

"And from today," thought Eli, "I am truly come into the *fairy-light* too. For I have learned what it is to be thoroughly, perfectly *in love*. I never, ever, tasted such a thing before. I could never have even *imagined* it.

"It is like spending all your long life reading books and singing hymns about God, and really *wanting* to believe, and being quite sure that something is indeed there *to* believe in; but it's all in your head --- it's not experienced. It's not the Light, not yet. And then, when you're grown quite old and you think you maybe *have* understood but you're still not completely convinced, you suddenly receive the grace of an unmistakable **conversion**, you find yourself in a new place. A place or a dimension, in your heart, in your soul, in your experiences, where there is the breaking of undreampt-of light, the light of a new dawn. *The brilliance and the laughter*, as Lily put it. And you see differently, or maybe you *really* see for the first time.

"Final and unequivocal religious or spiritual enlightenment must be very like falling in love. It's an invitation, a discovery, but it's more than that. It's waking-up, as I have done today, and finding yourself in the arms of your belovèd, right where you belong, probably right where you fell asleep before all the nonsense of the 'not-real' life you've been living even started! But there you are, back in the brilliance and the laughter, discovering it as if it were brand new --- but knowing that it was a part of you, your roots and your very origin, all along."

The day was fading and the moonless night was beginning to twinkle with the first shy stars. "I wonder did I love Finnir before. I wonder if we were together before I became a changeling. Or is *this* the beginning, even though it would be a beginning that comes from forever, from eternity, from always?

"Piv was quite right," she concluded, taking a final sip from her glass and preparing to return to her B&B, "*Love is always the solution.* For I can't see any problems anymore. Just at the moment, I can't imagine that the fact of Finnir being my half-brother presents, or will present, any impediment to us whatsoever. I can't even doubt that we will find a way to be together, a way that will not endanger Brocéliana's happiness. I can't feel that our beautiful love could in any way lessen Finnir's, or my, powers as royal fairies. It all appears to me as being certainly and obviously *able* to be resolved, somehow or other.

"That said, I can't imagine how! But tonight, I can only imagine one thing, and that is loving Finnir… forever."

Very lovely, being in love. But when Eli arrived back at her B&B, and had carried her new and also un-dreampt-of gift, the Harp of Barrywood, into her room and stood it beside the desk near the window, she noticed Lily's journal with Reyse's white rose lying across its cover. Her face grew quite sad.

"Oh, poor Reyse," she said aloud. "He loves me, is *in love* with me perhaps. And he is a dear and close friend of Finnir's. Even if Finnir and I cannot be demonstrative of our love in Faërie on my next Visit, I know --- I just *know* --- Reyse will feel something. He will know that I have changed, that everything has changed. He will be able to perceive that my heart is never going to be his."

This thought had a very strange effect on Eli.

Aside from this wave of sympathy for him, *how* did she know that Reyse would know? What bond, what empathy, what silent language existed between herself and Reyse that would make it so clear to her that he would be attuned to such a change, such an awakening, in her heart? Was that not a kind of love, too?

"That's a very strange thought to be having, <u>tonight</u>," she had to murmur to herself.

She now turned back to the harp, and was just debating if she should play something now, or if she should go out for dinner in town, or if she should make some special plan to play the Harp of Barrywood for the first time in some significant and perhaps enchanted place, when she noticed that it was decorated. Rather odd that it had not caught her attention before; but then, she was in a preoccupied state-of-mind, to be sure, when Finnir had presented it to her!

It was not *richly* decorated, not painted, not like Clare. No Celtic interlace or tiny dragons. But high on its fore-pillar, where the Lady Ecume's Harp of Seven Eyes had its sculpted sea-horse, there was a rose. A smallish rose, open and many-petalled, like an old English tea-rose. And it was made of gold.

"I think," said Eli in a very awed voice, "I think *that* is the Golden Flower, the jewel given to Mowena by our mother the Queen. I think --- I feel sure now --- that the fairy-lord she gave it to was <u>Finnir</u>. And finally, to fulfil its destiny and mine, he has given it to me, as a part of this harp. He has reunited it with the Silver Leaf."

Samhain Eve

Eli stared at the delicate red-gold Rose. Like the Leaf, it was impossible to tell if it were vegetable or mineral, 'real' or a skilfully-wrought jewel, solid or made of warm light...vernal and shimmering.

The rest of the decoration of the Harp of Barrywood was of a very natural nature, for it was created by the well-defined and very beautiful grain of her wood. All along the sound-table, the upper curve and the pillar were rivers in the rich grain: gorgeous patterns of swirls and lines and circles, golden and beige, blond and ochre, almost reddish-brown in places and in others almost white.

"And made by his own hands," she sighed, running her fingers over its polished surfaces, but not yet daring to touch the white, mauve or sage-green strings. "Made by Finnir, for me."

But then Eli chose to do a very strange thing, and later she would question her act and re-examine it from many angles. She covered the Harp of Barrywood with a light, hand-woven shawl --- long ago made by Lily, even before she had met Sean --- and she went to dinner, but she took with her the unfading white rose.

At that moment, she really did not think about what she was doing, unless it was as a sort-of 'gesture' of recompense or apology to Reyse. She took Reyse to dinner with her, and left Finnir under the shawl, awaiting her there in her bedroom. She gave Reyse one more convivial and ordinary and informal moment with her, and she left Finnir where he was: in her heart, in her harp, in her quiet and shadowy room, in her future and in her forever. But as for Reyse, she took him with her, into her 'now'.

It was a happy and private little dinner, in a nearby pub, with some locals playing music --- not exactly fairy-music, but very Irish and very gay! And all through her meal Eli's thoughts were as calm as if she were meditating. Of course, she recalled her tender and romantic moments with Finnir earlier that day in the Woods of Gougane Barra; but she was not particularly dwelling on those thoughts. They inhabited her, but were not in the foreground of her mind's landscape.

If anything, she was more preoccupied by wondering when she should ask to go back to Faërie, and to which of her harps she should pose the question. Clare awaited her in Saintes, and the golden harp made by Finnir was here with her in Ireland. Would she continue to play both instruments in her work, her concerts, her lessons? Would Finnir's harp, and the 'gifts' he had hidden in her strings, lead her further into the field of healing or musical therapy? Would Clare feel *jealous* of that?! Eli had never owned two harps at once, and she wondered how she would balance her time and her attention between them…

She would be home in France at the weekend, for she was taking the ferry back on Saturday. She could make her decision then, choosing which harp to ask and … what to ask. Did she wish to go back for her third Visit as soon as possible? Or did she, in fact, wish to wait and think and wonder --- about many things?

All very strange ideas, Eli thought, toying with her dessert as she listened to the small group of impromptu musicians giving a touching rendition of 'Blind Mary'. Hmm….the piece she had been playing when she had met Yves. Passionate love, that, and utterly *blind*, de-stabilising, tyrannical. But, in the beginning, she had been so sure, so very sure. And then, disaster.

Eli was very pleased that 'Blind Mary' had ended, and the session continued with gigs and reels, music to make the heart dance. That was much better. Better than fear.

Was she feeling fear?

Eli felt a chill run up her spine, and an odd tingling in the lobe of her right ear. She reached up and felt the Flaming Crescent Moon dangling from her *left* ear-lobe, and it made her think of how Finnir had fondled it, and then how his hand had strayed down to her neck... And no fear remained.

But she found that, with her right hand, she had --- at the same time --- reached into the pocket of her long blouse and pulled out the white rose. She had not meant to, but she had now placed it on the table beside her dessert plate, and her hand was covering it, the tips of her fingers delicately running along the edges of the soft, fresh petals.

The musicians were finishing their session with a haunting Irish air, *Óró mo bháidín,* 'My Little Boat'. It reminded Eli of 'The Water is Wide'.

Doesn't she ride the waves with grace?
Oro-oh my little boat
And how lightly she's carried in on the tide,
Oro-oh my little boat...

Let us raise the oars and set off!
Oro-oh my little boat...

"Yes," she thought now. "Yes, I think I'd like to go back to Faërie as soon as might be."

****

On Saturday the ferry left Cork in the late afternoon, heading for the tip of Brittany in an overnight sailing. The sky was like a vast and cosmic brindled cow, all dots and splashes of cloud, white and grey-blue. Three dolphins saw the boat out of the Lee Estuary, leaping in splashing arcs out of the choppy water along the starboard side of the ferry. Eli had visions of Brocéliana's crescent-moon boat being pulled by them! As she watched the trio, the setting sun suddenly found an opening among the porridgy-clouds, and made a blazing pathway to Eli as she stood on the highest deck, bidding farewell to Ireland.

"Just like the greystone altar of the Abbey of Ligugé," she sighed. "The same choppy sea conjured out of the rough stone, the same pathway of light calling me towards the horizon. Only this time I'm not rowing a little boat that will shortly transform itself into a flying horse! But the light is still beckoning me home, revealing my secret life and my true fairy-nature. I wonder if the realm of Faërie is far, far out there in the western seas, where the sun is setting.

"Funny how such optical riddles work," she pondered, looking at that highway of golden light. "The setting sun is making a pathway just for me. When I look to right or left, the water is dark. The sun is only illuminating the undulating seas in a straight and singular line from itself to me; it's my personal path of gold! But for those people I can see further down the deck, looking at the sunset too, it's making a path just for *their* eyes, and the water before *me* --- from their perspective --- is black and foreboding. Now isn't that odd? And rather nice! We all have our own utterly personalised invitations into the light, across our unique patch of troubled waters; but it's all the same sun. One sun and many private golden roads. Whether we're fairies or humans, good or bad, merry or mad, we're all sent the same sun-invitation --- each to our own address! Yes, I like that very much."

The golden orb dipped below the horizon, and the clouds seemed to have found a little breath of wind in the end, for most of them had also dispersed and left the rich turquoise sky almost clear. All except for the bright crescent of the new moon.

As she looked upon it, the moon seemed to smile back at Eli, like the mischievous 'winking watcher' who had haunted her when those first tantalising clues to her changeling-story were being sent her.

It was reminding her of other moon-sightings also, for she could hear her father's words, when he was thinking of his newly-exiled wife: *A sudden pang of unreasonable hope flashed into my heart as I beheld the new moon in the sunset sky that evening. She seemed not to be sinking or setting, but to be sailing --- like the lovely little crescent-craft of Brocéliana, pulled by dolphins and lit with a magical lantern. That sliver of moon was bearing my Queen from me, far into the western seas, to her ancestor's shee of the Sheep's Head. A sorrowful journey, but not a disappearance. We must never forget this: the Moon returns. She always returns. Her lantern is the Sun which illuminates her with pure light, and her dolphins are the urging force of the globe itself. But her dance is a rondeau, a great and stately circle.*

"I am missing my father." Eli pronounced the words as if she were speaking to the moon itself. "He looked upon you, you lovely and ethereal ever-returning moon-lash, and missed his wife and Queen. And now I am missing him.

"And, what's more, I've hardly left her shores but I'm already missing Ireland and the Woods of Gougane Barra and the Sheep's Head Peninsula," she added, gazing at the increasing drama of the horizon-colours where a solitary low bank of cloud remained, all purples and jewel-reds. She felt that the sky itself was waving its gaudiest banners and flags, joining with Eli in bidding a farewell to the receding coastline beyond the wake of the ferry's churning and rather reluctant --- it seemed to her --- movement out into the open sea.

Even the dolphins had said their good-byes and turned back towards the Old Head of Kinsale in the far distance. Her heart felt undeniably heavy and so Eli returned to her cabin, to lie down for a while and dream and remember and hope and wonder…

They would be the recurring themes of the coming weeks.

The ferry arrived on the early morning of the next day, the 12th of September. As Eli drove away from Roscoff and began the long route back down to Saintes, she was suddenly struck by the significance of that date. And by the date on which she had chosen to meet Finnir, five days ago.

When she was a little red-haired toddler in Los Angeles, her dear Daddy, Sean Penrohan, had died on the 7th of September. That had been in 1961. This year, 2010, it had been the day when she had met her love in the Woods and he had kissed her, and given her the Harp with its Golden Flower. Death jostling with new wonderful life; how interesting that they fell on the same date.

And when Reyse had recounted the story of Finnir and the Ghostly Chapel of Windy Hill, he had noted that it was on the 12th of September that Sean, now once again the King Aulfrin, had climbed up out of the subterranean shadow-lands to Eagle Abbey, and thence to Dawn Rock on the other side of the Portal. Today was the anniversary of his 'resurrection' from human-death to renewed fairy-life.

What was more, in that year as in this one, there had been a waxing crescent moon in the skies. And now she also recalled how Reyse's strange tale had included that detail, and also the joyful assurance of the squirrels that Finnir's liberation would take place on the 12th. They had called it 'the Prince Finnir's freedom day'. And Reyse had added: *I was delighted for Finnir, knowing how he loved the 12th of September: a day that he had always celebrated, for as long as I have known him, as an anniversary of some great deed or event that he was bound by solemn promise to guard as a secret, so he said.*

So this day, for some mysterious reason, was sacred to Finnir. As Eli drove, she postulated various explanations for this. A 'great deed or event': so perhaps something in their family history, a victory in battle or a treaty being signed or some wild adventure or the home-coming of a lost hero… But Eli was not Mélusine, and had no access to memories of legends or fire-side tales from Faërie. Maybe it was like the Day of Ævnad in June, simply a holiday in honour of some famous character. But why

Samhain Eve

would any of these things be a *secret*, bound to be kept by 'solemn promise'? A promise to whom?!

Well, such a coincidence of date provided a good pretext for playing her new harp this afternoon, when she arrived back in Saintes. And perhaps to seek to contact Finnir, through the window of the Silver Leaf, as well. It was, to all intents and purposes, an auspicious day.

Nothing in all her life --- at least the only life she could remember for the moment, that is, her human one --- had been so wonderful as being in Finnir's arms and experiencing the ecstasy of kissing him. And nothing, in some sort of musical equivalent of the same grandeur, could compare with the sensation of playing the harp he had made for her.

Eli was a talented musician with a good ear and an in-born gift for connecting with the sound of her instrument and joining with it to give life to her own interpretation of each piece she played. She had long mastered the art of *listening* to her harp's personal voice, and also of *speaking* through it. With Clare, especially --- ever since Uncle Mor had presented her with her beautiful French-Breton instrument --- she had known a real 'marriage' of harpist and harp, symbiotic and alive, a pleasure to her and to her audiences also.

But now, with the Harp of Barrywood, as with Finnir himself, she had no precedent or point of comparison to gauge where she found herself. And no words could express what it was like. Folly to say 'sublime' or even 'transporting'. Ridiculous to qualify it as 'heavenly' or 'extraordinary'. No, the harp did not simply have a superior tone or timbre, neither did it resonate more or differently, nor was the balance of bass and treble strings to be held accountable in any way.

When Eli played, it was quite obvious to her that she was in Finnir's arms, as she had been when he had placed the harp on the ground between them and embraced her before he left. Their hearts beat together, were mingled. Were one.

And that is what happened when Eli played the Harp of Barrywood for the first time, upon returning to Saintes.

Later in the evening, however, Eli found that she had to play Clare. Perhaps it was because Eli was missing her father, the King: for although she had intended to ask questions of the golden harp made by Finnir, she found that she could <u>not</u> pose her questions about Aulfrin and Faërie to the Harp of Barrywood --- she had to ask *Clare*. Not only in regard to news of her father, but also touching the subject of her next Visit. For when she had been on the threshold of Leyano's Portal, coming home in June, Aulfrin had clearly said: *Play your harp,* **Clare***, soon my dear child, asking her to instruct you in your choice of date and place for your final home-coming.*

She knew, therefore, that to pose her questions, she had to play Clare. Even though her father had not known that she would have a new harp, even though he may very well have been thrilled to know that her half-brother had given her this beautiful gift (much happier, at any rate, than he would have been to know that Finnir and she had embraced and kissed!), even though the wisdom of Finnir's harp might be clearer or more profound than that of Clare, Eli could not ignore her father's instructions.

In any case, in the first rapturous hour or so of playing the Harp of Barrywood, she had not had the presence of mind to formulate any question. She had simply been soaring in sparkling skies and blissfully aware of little else. And so, concluding her improvisations on her *new* harp, she turned to her *old*. And it was, strangely enough, just as delightful to play Clare.

No, she did not seem to be jealous at all! And Clare's voice was as lovely as ever and their 'marriage' of eleven years was just as filled with love as it had been all throughout the ups and downs of their long partnership and sharing.

But the insights she received were a little alarming.

Firstly, trying to bring an image of her father to mind, she had an overwhelming sensation of some threat --- was it to Aulfrin or to herself? --- and the notes of Clare seemed to be coloured by a red anger or cold, blue defiance. Eli felt a fear and an apprehension rising through her body as she played, and it was echoed by tense minor modulations and unresolved cadences and chords. Eli could not help but connect these feelings, somehow, with the theft of the Amethyst Cloth. Was she, or her sleeping fairy-self, or her father the King, still in danger because of Erreig's crime?

Secondly, she could clearly see a vision of her father. He was standing on a low sea-wall or short, sheer cliff. Waves were beating against the dark rock at his feet, and he was leaning into a strong wind so that his green cloak was blown back from his shoulders like a mighty banner. His left hand was raised, and the white and blue light of his clustered gem-stones shone out into the eye of the wind. She thought she could hear voices in the tempest, but she could not distinguish any words or phrases.

And thirdly, and most disconcerting of all, was the following silence and calm, for it was *utter* and of such a contrast to the storm as to feel like an explosion of deafness and mute surprise. Slim trunks of white or silver trees, and some that were yellow-ochre or blatantly golden, were all about her, and one enormous oak tree just at her back. Out of the silence, *spoken* by the silence, rather like the chocolate-brown voice of the blue wolf-hound Ferglas, came a clear and direct command, though to Eli it concealed a macabre twist at its very heart --- she could not decide why. It said:

"Return to Faërie, Eli Penrohan, by the Portal of the Heart Oak, as you have so deeply desired to do. Step through the door when the owls fly forth, and do not hesitate, for to do so is perilous! Step through the darkness of the Oak from the Woods of the green-toed trees to the magical Glens, just as the unicorn has done. Step through…on Samhain Eve."

"Samhain Eve?" Eli repeated the words as if they were the refrain of some kind of incantation or spell from a Hallowe'en witch. And Samhain Eve was Hallowe'en indeed. The greatest of the Celtic festivals. It was, and had always been, the supreme *bridge* between this world and that Otherworld. Not between life and death, not exactly. But a threshold and a doorway, much more puissant than a mere portal linking humans and fairies. There was something about it --- not sinister but rather ... *terrible*; yes perhaps that was the word. Terrible as beauty can be at times, or as music, or the sea.

Eli recalled the warning given by her mother, the Queen Rhynwanol, when she had played her harp, Gaëtanne, here in this tiny apartment --- in vision or in reality, Eli still did not know.:

I will warn you of one thing, my daughter. Do not step through Finnir's Portal unbidden or unprepared. Your destiny lies on its Faërie-side, and I do not deem that you are ripe for it, not yet. Barrywood is as perilous as the Vortex, and you will need great strength and no vestige of fear in your heart to set foot in it alone and unchaperoned. Yes, indeed, Barrywood is Faërie at its <u>most</u> perilous, as Finnir is Faërie at its most enchanted! Heed my words.

She shuddered. Her destiny awaited her in Barrywood? A place as 'perilous' as the Garnet Vortex... But she would **not** be alone, and if Finnir were there, she would not be fearful. But was she ready? Her mother had thought not, not yet at any rate.

"I'm really not sure, now, that I wish to go through Finnir's Portal, at least not on *that* night! But why should I feel such concern? Finnir will meet me as Demoran did on my first Visit and Leyano on my second. It's normal, somehow, that on my third and last twenty-one days, I pass through the third Portal, that of Barrywood. I have passed the other two, and only the Heart Oak remains, so perhaps I *am*, now, ready to dare it and 'meet my destiny' on the other side of the Third Portal...

"But there is a Fourth." Eli stared blankly straight ahead of her, whirling visions passing through her mind like debris caught in the twisting wild-winds of a tornado.

"There is, I know there is, a Fourth Portal also. And it would seem that I will come back here to my human life after this Visit, and then go to Faërie again, one day, after my *death* ... by the Fourth Portal, by the Garnet Vortex.

"Is <u>that</u> my 'destiny', too?"

Eli left Clare and went to sit again, now, behind her new harp, and rested it against her shoulder. Her hands were in mid-air, either side of the bright strings.

"I will be *bold*, and go through each one. And this next Visit must be made through the Portal of Barrywood. As my last must be through the door that is unlocked by the charm of the Flaming Moon Ear-ring. And maybe Finnir will be with me for that crossing too, as he will be there for this one."

Eli noticed that her fingers were poised just above well-spaced chords, in both hands, that included *do's* and *fa's*: the notes that were marked by coloured strings, mauve and sage-green respectively. Finnir had told her, *This harp is not as mystical and powerful, perhaps, as harps in Faërie may be. But the strings that I have chosen are rather magical, I must admit. They will teach you, as you play them --- as you play for others --- what gifts they contain.*

"Are all the strings magical?" Eli wondered. "Or just the tinted ones? And why did he choose these colours? Is the mauve for the Amethyst Cloth, or cloths, that cover my sleeping fairy-body? And what is the sage-green symbolic of?"

She exhaled deeply, and lowered her hands without playing the chords.

"You are being characteristically **over-dramatic**, my girl, and you are looking for mysteries and messages *everywhere!*" she sighed, laughing at herself. "Don't let your imagination run away with itself, at least no faster than this whole incredible wonder-tale dashes ahead. You have been given an answer to your question, and now you know that you shall go through Finnir's Portal on Hallowe'en. *Allow it, receive it, welcome it* --- as the Smiling Salmon would say.

"But *why* that date…?"

****

Deciding to put these queries and dramas aside, Eli made herself a mint-and-honey infusion and sat in her rocking chair to sip it, as *thoughtlessly* as possible. Finally, feeling refreshed and more relaxed, she calmly returned to the Harp of Barrywood.

This time, as Eli played the harp with the Golden Flower on its brow, she asked two questions. Clear, specific questions. She asked if it was dangerous for her to pass into Faërie at Samhain, presumably at night, and she inquired *why* it should be at that sacred and ominous date when she was invited to cross the secret threshold in Gougane Barra.

No words were spoken or suggested by the harp, but --- as was sometimes true with Clare as well --- a face and a feeling came to her. Very unexpectedly, it was the face of Aindel.

The tall, strawberry-blond, freckle-faced fairy, Aindel. The close companion of Alégondine, the friend of Piv --- and also of Finnir, as Eli had understood. Aindel's lovely features came into focus in her mind, and his violet-blue eyes were sparkling and his hair was characteristically knotted at his neck, as Eli often wore her own red tresses.

And the feeling? A very warm and good one; not at all akin to the *anxious* sensation that the very word 'Samhain' had brought her. Eli was sure, with her whole being, that she loved Finnir; she also had no doubt that some other kind of deep and loyal love existed between herself and Reyse. But there was also love, another love, between herself and Aindel. The same image suggested itself to her now, as had come to her mind

Samhain Eve

when they first met on the terrace of *The Tipsy Star*: 'he is the missing piece of a puzzle, my puzzle'.

Her intuition was that, perhaps, he would be there too, to guide her into Faërie on Samhain Eve. He was a close friend and ally of the Prince Finnir. And he was a fairy of the Sheep's Head Shee, two of whose Portals were not far from Gougane Barra, on the luminous peninsula where Eli had been this past week, and which Lily had so loved too. Reyse had said that one of the Portals was hidden where an ancient Stone Circle --- much smaller than the one just outside the boundaries of the City of Fantasie --- had been discovered, close to the village of Ahakista. She wondered where the other lay. For it was the shee where her mother, Queen Rhynwanol dwelt; and Eli would have loved to visit her there --- or maybe to see her again in the window of the Silver Leaf, as Lily had done!

That was an idea!

She had been playing the Golden Flower harp for many minutes now, asking her questions and ruminating on Aindel and the Sheep's Head. Now she allowed the last lingering notes to die away peacefully, and she went to her suitcase, not yet unpacked on her bed. Taking out the notebook of her little moon, she reverently opened it. At first, it was the page marked by the white rose that she fell upon; she delicately removed the unfading flower and returned it to her satchel. She continued to turn several more pages until she came to the Leaf.

Leaving the journal open on top of her still-folded clothes, she held the Leaf in her left hand and went to sit again in her rocking chair. Tilting her head just a little, to come into line with the angle of the oval window, Eli closed her eyes for a second, as if praying. She *was* praying, in a way: requesting to see her mother, to ask her some of the great and burning questions bubbling in her mind's Hallowe'en cauldron!

And her prayer was granted --- but not as she might have wished.

When she opened her eyes, she was already well and truly in the land of the Leaf, and her apartment was dim and hardly visible at the corners of her field of vision. She was not in a garden, not in a landscape at all: she was in a room more shadowy than her early-evening flat and filled with a pungent odour, like violets or great amaryllis lilies. 'It must be the Concocting Cell, thought Eli. I am in Fantasie, not in the Sheep's Head Shee where my mother lives.'

But she did not recognise the room, in fact, and neither could she find the Queen's Head Vase on its low table. But the Queen herself was indeed there.

Dressed all in violet, a rich plum-colour like the cloak worn by Alégondine, Rhynwanol stood, facing Eli but at a distance. Eli knew, instinctively, that she could not approach any nearer than she now was. But she could hear her mother's voice, though her lips did not seem to be moving. Ah no, it was not the voice of Rhynwanol! It was the voice that Eli had heard when she had gone to the Concocting Cell with her father, the voice which chanted the poem that explained why she could not love her own brother. The voice of breaking waves and sea-breezes and crying gulls. The voice of Morliande.

"Twenty-one days," said the oceanic and majestic woman, now visible beside the Queen. A Queen herself, but so different to Rhynwanol! Morliande was only slightly less tall than her daughter-in-law, but she was just as regal and enchanted, possibly more so, and powerfully filled with moving and dancing energy, like water itself. Perhaps she was standing still, but all Eli could perceive was endless, wavering motion.

'She is a shape-shifter, like Garo,' thought Eli. 'She is a seal, a silkie, and the mistress of invisible and moving islands, and a sailor in whale-bone boats…'

The voice of Morliande continued:

Samhain Eve

"She must return to the human world on the twenty-first day of her Visit, at the same hour. It will be the first night of the full moon on the twenty-first of November. *This* is not permissible."

"I will delay it," said the woodland, twilight voice of Rhynwanol, "if needs be…"

"That will not be necessary," retorted another voice, and this was a man's. He was cloaked, also in deep purple, and his hood was pulled up over his face. But Eli knew the voice. "The full moon will rise at sunset, and Eli will be gone through the Portal at the same moment. For Samhain Eve commences at the *setting* of the sun on the 31st of October, and for her return through the Heart Oak twenty-one evenings later she will be deep in the shadows of Barrywood. The moon will *not* appear over those dense and towering trees before she has passed back through the Portal." Eli recognised the voice as that of Aindel.

"It is dangerous," came the liquid voice, once again, of Morliande. "The Moon rose early once for Eli, on her first Visit, and it may do so again. And the Unicorn Glens touch the glade of the Heart Oak, and there is no knowing what the Moon may do there."

"I will protect her," said a soft and gentle voice. The voice was of the fourth person in the scene before Eli's wide eyes. "I will protect her, and so will her brother." Between Morliande and Aindel stood another woman, even slightly smaller than the silkie-seal fairy. But this was not a fairy.

This was Lily.

"Then let the decree stand," proclaimed the Queen Rhynwanol in conclusion. "Let Eli come on Samhain Eve."

Eli wanted with all her heart to speak, to cry out, to move closer. But she could not. Her eyes were overflowing with tears and her sobs were shaking her so that the rocking chair was making it impossible for her to hold the Silver Leaf without closing her hand around it.

She clasped the Leaf tightly and brought it against her breast. And she cried and cried.

"Lily is *there*, she is alive," wept Eli. "She's not dead, she's not gone. Those were my *three* mothers, together and all three alive. And Aindel was there as well, and my little moon said that my *brother* would protect me too, and that must be Finnir. She knows them all. She is somewhere in Faërie, my dear mother, my dear moon, my Lily…"

From the dimity of that part of the apartment where the two harps were standing side by side, came a reverberating sigh, as if a wind were playing in and out of the sound-boxes of the two instruments, or as if they were conversing together in a humming language of whispered music.

Eli heard the sound, and it stopped short her weeping. In the next instant, she nearly expected to see a huge and full moon shining at the window, reprimanding her for being, once again, so over-dramatic and so easily moved to tears.

"With all I have learnt, with all I have been through lately, with all the miracles and blessings and surprises and delights, *why* would I be so shaken by such a vision?! Why should *not* Lily, part-fairy and befriended by fairy-queens and magical mermaids, once a wife of the King of Faërie, and part of the trio of 'givers' of the Flaming Moon charm, NOT be alive?! How could she not be? Really, my girl, you need to pull yourself together and begin to believe **everything**, with your whole heart. There is no other solution except that!"

Having thus chastised herself, even *without* an 'impossible' moon appearing at her window, Eli shook her head with a smile, and rose from her rocking-chair to put the Silver Leaf back in her Lily's notebook. She pulled out the other things from the rough-woven satchel to put beside it on her bedside table: Reyse's white rose --- lifting it gently once again, almost hesitant to touch it --- and the phial of 'love-potion', and also the moonstone pendant on its long silver cord which had been

Reyse's 'birthday gift' to her as she left Faërie three-and-a-half months ago. She had not worn it since going to Gougane Barra.

It was the same gem, a moonstone, as those set into Reyse's ears. The same precious stone that Mélusine wore embedded in the skin over her heart: the token of her second Initiation passed when she, as the Princess, had been eighteen. Banvowha had told her that she had spent that Initiation in Reyse's company, riding with him and the horses of the Half-Moon. It was in that year --- it must have been sometime in the fourteenth century! --- when she had refused his love for the first time. As she had done again in the year 1500, and at *that* rebuttal he had left to face the ordeals of his own Great Charm.

For three-hundred-and-thirty-three years he sought to escape his heart-break and to soar beyond the pain, as an eagle might. But you were his sun, and his moon as well. And he could not forsake you in his longing and his love. So the rainbow-fairy had said.

"And now I will be rejecting him yet again," Eli remarked, turning the moon-stone pendant over in her hand. "He will be heart-broken again, and even more so. For Finnir is his friend and as dear as a brother to him, and to lose me to *him* will be very, very hard."

For some reason, Eli was suddenly reminded of the date. "This is still the 12th of September, and Finnir's freedom day," she said aloud, as if addressing the moonstone, glistening in her hand. Strange that it should shine, for her appartment was quite dark, with only one little lamp switched-on, beside the harps, casting its light onto her music-stand. But shine the stone did, as if with an inner light, glowing deep in its centre.

"I wonder if --- as Reyse played so vital a part in Finnir's liberation from the Caves of the White Cats, bringing his unicorn to him over a carpet of yellow blossoms --- I wonder if Finnir's harp would help me to ease Reyse's pain, by liberating *him*. By freeing him... from *me*?

"What a peculiar thought," Eli admitted at once, laughing as she did so. "But how good it would be to soften the pain that my love for Finnir will bring him. How I would love to take that dagger out of his heart, even before he learns enough to feel its sting. Finnir is *in* his harp, my harp, the golden harp he made for me. He will help me. If I play for Reyse, it will be my first act of 'healing' with the Harp of Barrywood. And maybe the Lady Ecume will lend me power and support, too, and the Golden Flower that was wrought by my mother, Queen Rhynwanol.

"Oh but it must be getting very late. I hope it is not after midnight already. I hope it's still the 12th!"

As Eli took the moonstone with her, over to her new harp and into the light, another part of Reyse's tale, the story of Finnir's liberation, came back to her --- word for word, so clearly that it was like the lines from her own juvenile poem which re-surfaced in her mind last spring, just when she needed to hear them:

It was not midnight after all, but only twilight; and there, in the midst of the sunset palette, was the fragile arc of the waxing crescent. But what was even more beautiful was that the entire moon was visible, for even the unlit regions of her roundness were clearly painted for us to see: deep grey, almost violet-blue. She was lovely!

Eli glanced at her clock. It was, indeed, just coming up to midnight. She breathed very deeply, and went to her window and opened it onto the quiet, late-night street. Her window, which faced east.

But as the buildings had playfully tricked her once before, so they did now. The sky-light in the roof of the apartment across the street was reflecting the *western* sky. Eli knew what she would see before she saw it.

Midnight or not, there, reflected in the facing window like a school-painting made by a child --- it was so colourful and vivid --- was the sunset sky with a crisp right-hand sickle moon proudly gleaming in the midst of the paint-box hues, sailing down in the wake of the sun. And as Reyse had remarked of that moon nearly fifty years ago, all of her rich orb was somehow visible as well: it was the same violet-blue as the robe of Rhynwanol or the cloak of Aindel. The same violet-blue as their eyes.

"Oh Finnir, what does this day stand for in your heart? What memory of magical wonders do you celebrate on this date? Whatever it is, please, please, help me to help Reyse. Whatever magic for healing and freedom is contained in this special day, let it flow into him, because he is dear to both of us."

Eli's words were spoken, almost intoned one might say, as though she were praying to the God of her Christian religion and not to her fairy-lover. But whichever of the two harkened to her prayer --- so filled with the desire to avert terrible hurt and heart-break for the noble Lord of the Half-Moon Horses --- some power surely responded to it, for its intention was for good and therefore it sprang from Love. She was sure of it.

Eli left her window and returned to the Harp of Barrywood, sat down, and placed the moonstone pendant on the music-stand before her. With a delicate movement of her hands, she gently invited the harp to lean against her shoulder, and then her arms enveloped it. She looked once more at the moonstone before she closed her eyes, and then she began to play.

****

Windy Hill Prayer

Chapter Four:
Brother and Lover, Sun and Moon

he could not know what her playing had done, what grace it had procured, what blessing or healing it had bestowed, but Eli had faith in its effects. She released any need, in her own mind, to understand immediately what may have transpired, or to learn what Reyse might have felt. She did not doubt that *something* beautiful had happened on the night of the 12th of September.

And this became characteristic of how she would play for the few weeks remaining in Saintes, before she returned to Ireland and to Gougane Barra at the close of October. All throughout the autumn, she took the Harp of Barrywood to hospitals, retirement homes, day shelters for the homeless, even to the animal-society refuge to play for the cats and dogs. She never wondered or asked herself, or inquired of her audience, if anything had happened to them, if any 'healing' had taken place. But she always knew that it had.

Eli realised that, when she played, she could feel the energies of the harp flowing outwards, in the vibrations of the strings perhaps, but also in the *intention* behind the sound, the generosity and the kindness of her heart as she played. She did not play for herself any longer, not even for love of the beauties of harp-music in general. She played for others, for everyone, for anyone.

Windy Hill Prayer

In any case, the Harp of Barrywood left her no choice. It *only* turned outwards. It was an open and loving harp, and no sound from her strings could do otherwise but fly to some waiting and needy listener.

Eli did not take her other harp, Clare, on her trip; she only took Finnir's harp with her to Ireland. And it looked very right and comfortable in the corner of her room in an Inn over an old-fashioned tavern in Inchigeelagh, less than half-an-hour's drive from Gougane Barra. She thought it wise to have this harp with her, for communication or guidance just before Samhain Eve. And it gave her the feeling of having Finnir beside her, too.

She had played Clare once again before leaving France, but the same triplet of insights repeated themselves: the red and blue waves of anger and defiance, and some threat or danger --- perhaps to the King; the vision of her father at the stormy margin of the sea, with his hand raised and the bluish-white light of his jewels streaming out into a tempest alive with voices; and the invitation, or the decree, for her impending visit: *Return to Faërie, Eli Penrohan, by the Portal of the Heart Oak, as you have so deeply desired to do. Step through the door when the owls fly forth, and do not hesitate, for to do so is perilous! Step through the darkness of the Oak, just as the unicorn has done. Step through…on Samhain Eve.*

Eli had not contacted Finnir again using the Silver Leaf, nor had she used it to try to see her mother (fairy or human), nor to voyage further into Faërie. These past weeks had been for her <u>human</u> life, she had decided, and for the healing she wanted to engage in, and for coming to know and love her new harp better and better.

She had decided that it needed a name, not just a formal title such as 'the Harp of Barrywood'. All harps need names! So she had called her *Róisín**, the 'little rose' in Irish. The harp

---

Róisín is pronounced "raw-sheen".

seemed pleased with her new name, and the Golden Flower had gleamed contentedly when she first pronounced it --- as Eli had noticed that it had done, just briefly, at the end of every recital or concert she had played so far.

Perhaps it was because of her golden harp and its name that Eli choose to have a meal, the evening of her arrival in the little town, at a pub called *The Briar Rose*. She had glanced around the pub which was downstairs from her B&B, but she had not seen what she was looking for. Both establishments served good Irish fare, but Eli was not regarding their menus: she was hoping to find Brian, the human (raised as a fairy) whom she had met with her father, just to the north of Shooting Star Lake. He was to return to his life in this world last June, when the 'changeling' who had replaced him in his cradle came back to Faërie; and it was to Inchigeelagh that he had planned to come.

No, at *Creedon's* she saw no one who might have been a young man recently arrived by way of Finnir's Portal into a human life which had been interrupted at birth! Eli wondered if she would even be able to recognise such a creature, instinctively or by some tell-tale signs of his seventy years in an enchanted parallel world, so at odds with modern civilisation. But when she arrived at *The Briar Rose*, her eyebrows lifted and her smile broadened: here he certainly was!

Of course, Garv-Feyar, as he had been called in Faërie, had no memory now of his many years in Aulfrin's realm. But he was easy to spot, even before one of the locals hailed him as 'Brian'. As he had said himself: *I'll be a wise and happy twenty-year-old, with no memories of any past to weight upon him and all the music and joy of the fairy-folk hidden somewhere deep inside.* He had the straw-coloured hair of his fairy-form, and his eyes were as sky-blue as Finnir's --- only, to Eli's mind, not as sparkling or inviting or infinite! But they were still the eyes of a fairy, or at least of one who has known and delighted-in great beauty and deep, joyful peace and a close, loving, respectful relationship with all of Nature for seven decades.

Windy Hill Prayer

How Eli wished that she could ask him about his passage back through the Portal, and what Barrywood had been like, and how he was managing to navigate his way in this new chapter of his existence. But as he had no memory of all that she would speak of, it would no doubt be a rather perplexing or ridiculous conversation. And he was less than half her age, and at this moment busily engaged in an animated and earnest discussion with a group of friends on the merits of a particular beer that they were sampling. Perhaps he had brewed it himself, as this had been one of the skills that he was pleased to be bringing back with him to the human world.

Eli hoped that he would, in some way, bring many other sparks of fairy-knowledge and glints of the light of that land into the years ahead of him here. She blessed him with a silent toast of '*sláinte*' and continued her meal in a quiet corner of the pub.

****

Eli had arrived in Cork on the 30th, a Saturday morning, and a very rainy morning too. And all the weekend, the rain continued. It would be a very dark Samhain Eve, very windy and very wet, evidently.

She could have hoped for slightly better weather conditions for her trip, alone, to the mystical Forest this Sunday evening. Her consolation was that she would go at sunset, and so it would not yet be utterly black night. But with a thick roof of endless clouds --- although in motion and careering along in the very blustery winds --- the light of a setting sun would not be very evident, even at the twilight-hour. Samhain Eve, by definition, did not begin until the sun sank to his rest. She could not pass through the Portal any earlier.

But, for the moment, it was still only late afternoon. Eli was making her way to her 'appointment' in Gougane Barra, but she was taking a *very* circuitous route to get there. For she had decided to go to Glengarriff, not far from Bantry, on the morning of Samhain Eve. It was a spot that Lily had loved to visit, given that she was so fond of sketching and painting trees, for the Forest of Glengarriff contained some of the oldest oaks and birches in Ireland. So Eli had driven there, despite the pelting rain, and --- as was common with the Irish weather --- she had been rewarded with one or two moments of sunshine and even a glorious rainbow. But now it was tea-time and she was having an excellent pot of Earl Grey at *Casey's*, in Glengariff town, watching the silver rain streaming down the window-panes and thinking how, most probably, all of the fairies of her acquaintance would welcome such a cloudburst and would be out dancing in it.

As these thoughts were bringing a smile to her face, despite a rising feeling of trepidation mingled with tantalizing nervousness --- not dissimilar to 'stage-fright' --- in anticipation of seeing Finnir once again this very night, a voice greeted her with a warm chuckle.

"I thought to find you in the tea-room looking out over Gougane Barra's Lake, and --- though I was right about the beverage --- here you are, at least ten miles away!"

Eli laughed with delight. "Oh Aindel, how glad I am to see you! How wonderful that you found me --- and that you're here! But it's even further than ten miles, I think, at least by car."

"True, true; I imagine it could be *much* more in such a nonsensical contraption," nodded the tall, fair gentleman --- looking for all the world very like a human as he stood before Eli. "But I was thinking of the distance 'as the fairy flies', with his or her own wings, I mean. May I join you?"

Aindel sat beside Eli, and she could see that --- just as when Reyse was Liam --- he had no pointed ears or shining gem-stones. He still looked far from ordinary, at least in Eli's happy eyes; but he did not look as though his wings would sprout from his back at any moment."

They regarded one another for a few minutes without speaking. Eli could imagine him, as he had appeared in the window of the Silver Leaf, cloaked in purple and standing beside her three mothers. She wanted to ask if he had seen her on that occasion --- or if it had truly been only a 'vision' granted to her, when another question superseded that one.

"I thought you told me, dear Aindel, when we met at *The Tipsy Star* and you recounted a little of your incredible changeling-story, that you had never been to this human world --- or, at least, only for an hour, as an infant. But here you are… Is it just to meet me and share a pot of tea?!"

Aindel laughed heartily, and his blue-violet eyes twinkled as he did so, in a very fairy-ish manner, Eli thought.

"That's exactly right, dearest Lady Eli; I've not returned since that hour-long 'holiday' in a cradle in the year 1321, also on the Feast of Samhain I might add. I have not come back --- until today. And indeed, it is in *your* honour, and I was using what little magic I possess to find where you would be exactly. For it was clear that I could not let you brave the threshold of the Portal on your own, at least on this side, before Finnir would meet you on the doorstep of the Heart Oak in Barrywood. It can be rather treacherous, and so it seemed wise to *us* that we should *both* be there."

"How very kind of you," said Eli, pouring a cup of tea for her guest, as the patron had hastened to bring a fresh pot and another round of scones to her table. "I am very touched, and very relieved, that you and my…brother have decided to protect me, both of you, as I cross over."

"Finnir will be very glad to see me there, I think, but as surprised as you to find me on the human-side of the mysterious Oak. We have often met in Faërie, both in the shee of Aulfrin and in my own, and we have adventured together in far-flung errantry in our youth, but he knows that I do not come into this world. He will be unexpectedly pleased, I think, that Lily persuaded me to come."

Eli's eyes grew large. "It was *Lily* that asked you to protect me as I go through?! Oh Aindel, do you know that I *saw* you together, you and Lily, and the two Queens also…?"

"Of course, I know you did; we saw you too," rejoined Aindel, enjoying his scone with mounds of jam and cream. "These are very nice; I feel as greedy as Piv here! Not quite fairy-fare, but really quite delicious." Eli had to chuckle. All fairies seemed to be so full of fun, and so slow to fall into melodrama or even worry.

"Aindel, may I ask you: where is Lily now? Is she *alive*, somewhere in Faërie?"

He wiped the strawberry jam from the corners of his mouth, and looked with great tenderness at Eli. "She is. She dwells in my shee, for the moment. But not for long. She was invited to linger among us, with the fairies that are her distant kin, after her death, and she wanted to --- how can I put it? --- *watch over you* while you hesitated between the two worlds. But soon now she will continue her voyage, for she has not chosen to reclaim her links to our enchanted realm. She wishes to follow her own path, through Death… and into Light."

Eli nodded as she sipped her tea thoughtfully. "She is a Christian," she agreed. "She will walk that path right into the final and eternal Presence." Aindel nodded as well.

"Will I be able to see her, on this my last Visit?" added Eli, looking intently into the wonderful mauve eyes before her.

"You go to the Shee Mor, not to the Sheep's Head," Aindel replied. "No, you have been granted the sight of her through the window of the Silver Leaf, but you may not see her face to face. Still, that is already a great blessing, is it not?!"

Eli smiled. "Yes, yes it is. A wonderful blessing. And I've been given others lately too, so amazing that they make my head spin. I'm so glad to be seeing Finnir again tonight." She added this last phrase without meaning to --- spontaneously, almost as if talking to herself. She lowered her eyes, and wondered what Aindel would read in her enthusiastic tone of voice.

"That's another reason I've come," he said softly. "Finnir and I are…very close. I feel the rings of ripples across any distance between us, when great emotions or important events come to him. His heart is as filled with love as yours, dear Eli."

Eli gazed straight before her, and then she closed her eyes, in gratitude, exhaling deeply. Finally she turned again to Aindel.

"I don't believe there could be any problem in our love, Aindel, no problem that we can't overcome. I know that Finnir is my half-brother, and our father has told me that it is not permitted for consanguine *royal* fairies, at any rate, to be together. But my heart tells me that we will find a way. I believe we will; I can't help but believe it."

Aindel smiled again, not at all dramatically --- really quite calmly and happily. And he finished his second very laden scone.

"The heart is incapable of falsehood, Eli. That is certain. You should always listen to your heart. And, as Lily likes to say, 'it is very good to *believe*'.

"Now, I think we should be going forth into the storm, to find the Portal and to be ready when the 'owls fly forth' and the moment comes for you to meet Finnir once again and begin your third and last Visit. You will have to 'drive' me in this ignoble chariot of yours, this *car* I think you called it, for I will not risk the use of my wings any further, now that I am in this human-guise.

"What an idea," he shuddered. "A motorised box made of metal machinery! Have they no horses, even without wings?!"

****

"You did not bring your harp?"

Aindel had spoken little during the drive, not seeming to like the motion of the car very much, and only making the odd comment --- in a somewhat disparaging tone --- that this must be what it felt like to be trapped in a cage. Now they were arriving at the Lake-side to find a parking place, and to begin the final part of the road into the Forest on foot.

"Róisín is at my B&B; I didn't like the idea of leaving her in the car, even though it will only be for three hours --- though I'll be visiting for three weeks," explained Eli.

"It might have been prudent to have her here to guide us. No matter, I have a flute."

Very like Aulfrin, Aindel seemed equally at ease on both instruments. At Leyano's Sand Castle, he had played a harp --- a tall white-drift-wood harp strung with gold --- but now he produced, from his coat pocket, a small silver whistle very akin to the King's. The rain had abated, but the sky was still heavy, very low and sombre. When they left the car and began their long walk, Aindel began to play a low, peaceful air, like a lullaby.

As they passed under the eaves of the Woods, he stopped playing and stood, listening and looking deeply into the shadowy ranks of immensely tall trees before them here.

Eli had a sudden thought, and asked, in a whisper, "Aindel, If you became a changeling at Samhain, and were stolen again from the crib by the Sheep's Head fairies, as a babe, to be raised by them in their shee, then do you think of *this* as your birthday?"

The tall, regal gentleman beside her seemed much more fairy than human again, as if just being in these Woods had changed him back to himself already.

"Yes, Samhain Eve is my birth-date, both as a changeling and also in my previous life; for years earlier, in my own shee, it was the night of my birth as well. I was eighteen when I made my decision, and I chose to become a changeling on the same date as my first birth. So, you could say that tonight is my double-birthday, or rather night! And, of course, it is Finnir's too."

"Finnir was also born at the Feast of Samhain?" exclaimed Eli. "Well that's a nice and rather magical coincidence."

Aindel smiled bemusedly at her.

"Ah, over there! Look, I see one of the pale squirrels, so the Portal has materialised somewhere nearby no doubt. Oh but the little fellow looks very frightened. Rather strange that, for the storm is not so intense as it was. Perhaps others, besides ourselves, are planning to cross into Faërie on this exceptional and mysterious night. But then, Samhain is *ever* an evening of fearful mysteries and other-worldly secrets, is it not?" With these words, Aindel winked at her.

"Come, Eli, and stay close."

A rogue gust of wind had swept into the Forest, and was whining about the boles of the trees. Rain had begun to fall again, softly and almost musically; but Eli did not feel like dancing in it. The clouds had closed overhead so that not even the tiny gaps in the branches showed any spots of twilight-coloured contrast to the slate-grey nimbo-stratus sky. When she and Aindel had advanced to where the nervous squirrel had run up a mossy-trunk and into a giant knot-hole, no sky at all was visible. The ceiling of the forest had shut them in, so dark a green that it was nearly black.

How Eli longed to see the glistening white of Neya-Voun's ethereal form, with the spiral of silver on her forehead and Finnir mounted upon her bare back, coming towards her as she tried to keep up with the sure, long strides of Aindel.

Her companion lifted his flute to his lips again, now playing with urgency, like someone calling from an oar-less boat adrift in a foggy sea. Unable to restrain herself, Eli reached forward and wrapped one arm around Aindel's waist as he played, snuggling against him as if to find shelter from the intensifying rain. He lowered the flute and the dying notes of his music were snatched up by the wind and shuttled off through the labyrinth of trees. He, also, wrapped a strong arm around Eli's shoulders.

"There is a problem, I think, Eli," he murmured, his voice calm and steady, but very hushed. "I saw a wink of light, undoubtedly where the Heart Oak had opened its doors to us; but immediately it went out. Let us wait here and see what Finnir does.

"He is an excellent Guardian of such a Portal, but Samhain Eve is the most challenging of the entire round of the whole, sweet year. Even for such a Prince, this night calls for all his reserves of courage and skill; but I feel that there is more danger, tonight, than usual. I think he is holding the Portal closed by force, by magic, against some other traveller --- or some other power.

"Samhain is the supreme moment for the foolhardy and the reckless to try to find the passage into Faërie. Ah, in the early centuries of his guardianship, Finnir had many dealings with difficult trespassers, wandering imps and hob-goblins (or worse) as well as humans, and even some unusual beasts. But my intuition tells me that he is holding the passage from *his side* of the threshold, against something wishing to come out *into* the world, rather than against an unwanted worldly visitor. Wait, look.... There he is!"

Eli's heart rose to her throat, for Finnir was too beautiful to believe. She had never beheld him in his 'armour', if that was what it was. She had only ever seen him in flowing cape and long tunic, loose trousers and soft clothing. Now he was dressed as the Guardian and Prince of the Portal of Barrywood.

She could not guess the material of his apparel: whether of some fine metal or woven of thistles and moonbeams! His doublet and mantle were luminous and richly covered in arabesques of embroidery or tracery designs studded with diamonds and pearls perhaps. He wore high cloud-grey boots over deep blue leggings and in a grey-gloved hand he carried a staff or spear of what seemed to be pure gold, though it may have been highly-polished wood, like that of her harp. The pearl in his forehead was blazing, as were the tiny points of amber in his ears. Eli could feel that the amber of Aindel's own ear-points and those set beside his eyes had reappeared and were gleaming too, sending out a warm and answering light from just above where her head was pressed against his chest.

Finnir's short mantle-cape was billowing out behind him in the wind, and its lining of sapphire blue was shimmering like lake-water, defying the darkness all about it. But the blue of his piercing eyes was more brilliant. Those eyes were keen and bright and brimming with power, and yet they also contained such tenderness and gentle patience and reassurance that Eli felt all of her fears evaporating and fleeing like the ringing notes of Aindel's flute had done.

"He's like a guardian angel, or a guardian *archangel*," she thought. "He is wonderful and terrible and kind and loving, all at once."

However Finnir was clearly as anxious as was Aindel.

"It is a joy and a blessing to find you here with... Eli, my gentle Aindel. But there is strife in Faërie," said the shining Prince, an aureole of light trembling all about him and now answered by a similar light emanating from the other regal fairy. Eli released her arm from around this equally noble fairy, and stood more erect, facing Finnir from a short distance, and smiling as she breathed deeply and regained her composure.

He smiled back at her, and inclined his head. It was a courteous and rather formal greeting, but Eli noted that his sky-blue eyes were sparkling as if filled with stars and fireworks. She returned his *reverence*.

"Erreig is in the Unicorn Glens, not thirty miles from the Portal," said Finnir, without further greeting, but regarding Aindel intently. "And his six lieutenant-dragon-riders were seen passing over Barrywood this afternoon.

"The King is presumably in Quillir still, or it may be that he has even gone to the coasts of Star Island --- or beyond; he has not been seen in the Silver City since he met with Alégondine just after your last Visit, dear Eli. I came back to the Shee Mor after my quest with Brea was completed, and I arrived in Mazilun several days after you had left Faërie, my Lady, but I did not cross paths with the King. Until recently, I believed him to be in Fantasie.

"We have had little news, and the Moon-Dancers are becoming increasingly agitated. I have never witnessed such anxiety, at least not since I felt the trembling energies in the very soil of Faërie when I was detained in the Caves of the White Cats. Demoran and Leyano are now holding their Portals and their domains on alert, and many fairies are flocking to the regions around their Castles.

"But I do not know where Reyse is, and this troubles me almost more than all the rest," Finnir added, in a quieter voice.

Eli's eyes were very wide and worried, not only as concerned Reyse, but primarily for her father, and for his realm. She recalled the sensation of some *threat* that she had gleaned from her harp Clare, a menace to her father: *a red anger or a cold, blue defiance*, was how she had perceived it. The two colours, red and blue, now seemed to combine in her imagination as Finnir spoke of the King being, perhaps, 'gone to the coasts of Star Island itself'. She had a momentary glimpse of Aulfrin encircled by the angry red and the defiant blue of swirling mists --- but they melted together, into a rich and imperial purple... She felt her heart pounding quickly, though she continued to stand still and upright beside Aindel, his hand still laid lightly on her shoulder.

"And so I must tell you," Finnir resumed at last, "my most precious Eli, that I cannot allow you to come into Faërie at this time. I do not think the King would wish it, and I myself do not deem it safe, with Erreig haunting the threshold between the two worlds. I am not sure if he knows that you are planning to pass the Portal, or if he is seeking to leave Barrywood to venture into human lands himself. If this latter is in his mind, I will not permit it, not while you are so near to the doorway."

Finnir extended his free hand to Eli now, and she left Aindel's side and went to him. He hugged her close to his breast and then held her beside him as she turned, with him, back to face Aindel.

The tall, fair fairy was smiling warmly, his freckled face almost like a lantern in the profound green shadowland. There was no hint of surprise in his expression, Eli noted. He simply said, in agreement with Finnir:

"Yes, I believe you are right, my darling Finnir. Eli is safer, as a human, in the human world, at least for tonight. Until we know more of Erreig's position and his plans, we should do all we can to keep the two apart. I feel, in my heart, that he is hunting for you, Eli; and I perceive that this insight comes from Lily, for some reason."

Finnir turned to bestow a gentle kiss on Eli's head, before he spoke. "Yes, I believe you see aright, Aindel of my heart. Faërie is unstable tonight, and Aulfrin unaccounted for; indeed you should remain where you are, Eli. But I must request that Aindel comes to my aid, I think, as soon as he may, on *this* side of the Portal. And that is a worry to me as well, for it will leave you alone, to await further news in your Irish lodgings --- with no fairy protector beside you."

Eli shivered, but her strength of character, her love for Finnir and her confidence in him and in Aindel, won out over her fears.

"I'll be fine. I am <u>not</u> afraid, not if you and Aindel are holding the Portal. I will be safe in Inchigeelagh, until you can send word to me of what I should do. Will I be able to make my Visit…later?" she asked, turning her head to look up into her love's eyes.

It was Aindel, however, who replied, speaking slowly as if he were considering, carefully, the various possibilities.

"There is the problem of the full moon, Eli. We had agreed that I would help you to come back through the Portal just before she appeared on the night of the 21st, at sunset. You cannot come into Faërie later than tonight, if you are to remain for three weeks. You may have to make your third Visit at another time of the year, my dear sister."

"Your...*what*?" hissed Eli. "Why do you call me that?"

There was a breathless pause, not only in Eli's breathing but --- it seemed --- in the wind itself. Finnir's embracing arm tightened around her, and she could *feel* him smiling. But it was to Aindel that he spoke, in a whispered tone of relief and thankfulness.

"You have made this exceptional voyage, coming to the human-side-doorway of my Portal, my beloved Aindel, from that of the Sheep's Head Shee, to release me from the bond of this secret?"

The Woods remained absolutely windless and silent, except for the rustling movements of two beige squirrels, twining about Finnir's ankles and then sitting still beside him on the arch of a large, ferny, fungusy tree-root.

Aindel stepped closer to the couple, and placed a hand on each of their shoulders.

"Here we are on the margins of the two worlds, in danger and mystery, filled with questions, yet filled with hope and love as well. Let us create a little space and time here, a little invisible hermit's cell, where none may enter but ourselves. And therein we will have honesty and light, a calm eye in the storm that threatens us, that surrounds us, that awaits us. A brief and concise moment of pause and of peace, and of explanation, which must not go further than we three --- not yet. At least, let us reveal to Eli the truth, to ease some of her worry and suffering, and yours also, my sweet Finnir."

Eli could sense that Finnir was weeping. But, when he turned to look into her own glistening eyes, his face was radiant. Radiant with gratitude and longed-for lifting of some burden. He spoke softly, but with great contentment:

"You have heard Aindel's tale, Eli. How he became a changeling, like you, but was snatched away by the fairies of the Sheep's Head, and raised there as their Prince?"

Eli nodded. Finnir continued.

"And he has told you that the mother of the human babe was in league with those fairies, and so had agreed that they could take the changeling-fairy-infant if she could keep her own. But she had to give some gift to the fairies of the original shee of Aindel, so that instead of leaving with her human child, they would have another…"

Aindel now took up the tale. "And so, my dear Eli, the Sheep's Head Fairies were granted their fondest wish: to plant in the royal family of the Shee Mor one of their own Princes, the new-born eldest fairy-son of the recently established royal line of their shee. A little true-fairy who would play the role of the human babe --- in this case the human child was not really a *human* but a *half-fairy*, for the father was of course Aulfrin, who had come into Ireland in the early Middle Ages to woo Daireen of West Cork, as he would later do in Brittany to wed Maelys. But clever Daireen secretly kept her child, the son of Aulfrin, who was named Ardan. And so, in his place and unbeknownst to Aulfrin, the fairy-company --- coming from Aulfrin's own Shee Mor --- found the little Prince of the Sheep's Head Shee, disguised to resemble the golden-haired half-fairy babe.

"That babe was none other than Finnir, born on Samhain Eve in the year 1321 to the new King and Queen of the Sheep's Head Shee. The stolen changeling was Aulfrin's eldest son Timair, and he would now replace the new-born as the Prince of the Sheep's Head Shee; he was renamed Aindel so that his identity would remain concealed from the King Aulfrin --- remain concealed, in fact, from *practically all* save the King and Queen of his new home. Very soon, the Sheep's Head Prince, growing up in the Silver City of Fantasie, would also be reminded of his true lineage.

"And so now I reveal it also to *you*, Eli, that I am that stolen-changeling. I am Aindel but I am also Timair of the Shee Mor, your eldest brother. And Finnir is *not* Ardan, given a fairy's name though only a half-fairy. And he is *not* the son of Aulfrin at all. Ardan was the half-fairy son of Aulfrin, and he remained with Daireen; and as Aufrin thought him to be *me*, he was given *my* three Visits, and by agreement with me --- for he and Daireen knew all, of course --- Ardan chose to remain in the world, and was very content to live out his life in a monastic order in medieval Germany. Poor Aulfrin mourned the loss of his son, but Ardan --- though half-fairy --- was not at all the changeling-child that the King believed him to be. For I was that changeling-prince and I was ever since, as now, happily installed as the next-in-line to the throne of the Sheep's Head Shee; just as Finnir --- the true Prince of *that* shee --- was happily made the eldest son of the royal family of the Shee Mor.

"Happily, until he fell in love with the Princess Mélusine, with you!" concluded Timair.

Eli was cold with shock, and then flushed with revelation, and then trembling with joy and bewilderment and hope and even some vestiges of doubt. After a very long and silent moment, she looked up into the sky-blue eyes of Finnir.

"You're not my brother at all?" She intoned the words so quietly that they seemed a continuation of the deep silence.

But Finnir, stroking her damp, long, dishevelled red hair, just kissed her --- long and lovingly. And then he answered.

"No, I'm not your brother at all. Timair --- alias Aindel --- is your brother, and Ardan was your half-brother. I am only the fairy in love with you. That's all." And he kissed her once more, but this time rather hastily.

"And so much in love with you, that I must send you away from here," he said, softly but with insistence.

"Yes," agreed Aindel. "We cannot delay longer. I have joined my own charms with those of Finnir to strengthen his hold on the Portal as we spoke, but we cannot keep a doorway to Faërie locked on Samhain Eve; that is contrary to our laws. And Finnir must deal with Erreig, on the threshold of the Heart Oak or further off in the vales of the Unicorn Glens. And I must make sure you arrive safely at your lodgings, in Inchigeelagh at least for tonight, before returning swiftly to assist your *not-at-all*-brother! Tomorrow we will see what our next step may be. For now, we must go, and with all haste."

As he turned to go back through the passageway of the Heart Oak, Finnir brushed the back of his left hand across Eli's right ear, where her own sapphire would be, were she Mélusine. As she had felt it when nearly falling from Peronne, a surging spray of energy seemed to unite the two for an instant. She smiled at her love; but in the very same moment he was absorbed into the shadowy form of the tree-trunk with only the glint of a disappearing squirrel-tail flashing among the giant roots before all was still and utterly dark.

But, in fact, not all was dark, for the beautiful and bright face of Aindel, or rather Timair, looking with love and pleasure at his sister, was shining. Without another word, he took her hand and led her, with long, sure, swift strides, back out of the Woods.

****

Timair went with Eli back to her B&B. It was not late, and so they found a private nook in the crowded bar downstairs and spoke together over their frothy, dark beers.

"If we should meet in Faërie," cautioned Timair with a grin, "please remember to call me Aindel!"

Eli acquiesced, but added, "Why this strange, centuries-old secret? Why did the fairies of both of these mighty shees wish for such an exchange of Princes, and why cannot Aulfrin know?"

Timair sipped thoughtfully, still smiling slightly. "Well, it is a complex and delicate situation, indeed. And it goes back much further than us, than myself and Finnir. It is a long tale, and we do not have all the time we need for it this evening, for I must go back to your beloved Finnir's aid, and soon. But I can tell you the bones of the beginning of the story."

A session of music had begun on the other side of the pub, and Eli noticed that Brian, whom she had seen at *The Briar Rose* yesterday, was among the players. He was radiantly gay, filled with laughter and youth, and also with peace, and he was a fine fiddle-player too! She sighed happily, for him, and turned her attention back to Timair's tale.

"The Alliance of the Eleven Stars is not a new one, dear Eli. But for a long age now it has remained but a dream of very few and far-flung fairies across the whole constellation of our island-shees.

"I was thirteen when I undertook my second Initiation, in 1288, and for that challenge I was hosted by the folk of the White Deer. They are a very magical race, with many clans inhabiting most of our shees, or travelling sometimes between them. You have heard the tale of Garo's education, perhaps? He is a protégé of one of the greatest lords of that family, the Lord Hwittir, the Red-Eared Hart, a creature of profound enlightenment and great powers, the ruler in fact of his shee. Well, as an adolescent fairy, I thus came into contact with the deer-people, and I learned that they looked forward to a time when all the lands of Greater Faërie would be one; this was not so much a 'dream' as a premonition, almost a prophecy among them.

"But at that time, great kings ruled several of the shees. Our grandfather, Aulfrelas, had passed his kingship over to his son,

Aulfrin, at the dawn of that century; and in those years, our father was a very proud and very powerful monarch already. But strangely enough, he was also very fearful. In fact, those traits often go together! Pride is generally linked to the ego, to a desire to be separate and to wield power over others --- and such desires can only spring from *fear*. I think that the King has changed; he has matured and grown greatly in this respect in these last centuries. He has seen, I believe, that fear engenders anger and aggression. He has also begun to look with great honesty at his *own* anger, his pride and his desire for vindication of his personal ideas and his often rather stubborn positions. Yes, he has changed much in the years I have been visiting his realm, and watching him from my own. And Finnir has told me of many positive developments in his foster-father's thoughts.

"But it is not we, the Princes and children of the great kings, who move the pieces as yet. The Great Ones who are at the origin of our dreams, they are older and much wiser than we are. But we are *one* Alliance, a blending of youth and age, of many races of fairies and of many marvellous beasts. All of us, together, must work with subtlety and with patience to nourish the growing compliance between the rulers of the Shee Mor and the Sheep's Head, the Little Skellig and the Red Lizard, the Bull, the Red-Eared Hart and the White Kangaroo. Those are the seven shees which are governed and guided by royal fairies, very powerful beings, very magical. You have already learned some of this in our meeting at Leyano's Castle. The shees of the Dove, of the Goats and of the Dragon-Bats, they have no kings or queens, though there are wondrous fairy-lords with many gifts and skills among their great families --- high and noble fairies such as Iolar MacReyse. And the tiny Shee of the Bells, the Shee Beg we name her, is under the wings of a mother-fairy, the Abbess. She is the most powerful of all, for she has no ego. She is transparent and boundless, like air and water. She is our great inspiration and our hope…"

Timair closed his eyes, and breathed very deeply. When he opened them again and looked at Eli, the colour of those extraordinary eyes seemed to have intensified. Still a violet-blue, they were no longer a peaceful mauve hue; they had become like an alien sky of purple clouds studded with unknown stars and planets in spots of scintillating white like secret, sacred fires. Eli recognised, now, that Timair had the eyes of their mother.

"As I grew, dear Eli," he continued, "I followed the deer in many adventures, and Finnir was often by my side, and Reyse, and even --- in the beginning --- Demoran from time to time. We forged many friendships and we saw and learned much: all in preparation for the time when we would give our full-energies to the plans and projects being put into place by the leaders of our cause. For the very Ancient Ones, the very great fairies, are working tirelessly to see these flowers come to blossom and then to fruit. But they tell us that, while it is vital that the Alliance grows stronger, it must --- for now --- grow stealthily and cautiously. They believe that Aulfrin is on the brink of joining us, and will soon do so, and then our secrets can be shared with him and with others. But they cannot yet be shared with *all* of the players in the great drama. The sap is rising, but it is not yet springtime.

"For the Great Ones, they do not conceive of this as merely a *fairy-harvest* of the fruits of unity and light and strength and harmony. It is not only the longing to see the Moon full, *ever*-full and illuminated by the burning life-giving force of the Sun. They are working to unite Faërie with this strange and fragile world of human-kind as well. And they believe that it must happen simultaneously, for the two worlds are knitted together, mingled since their creation, linked and intertwined like the colourful interlace practiced by the snails."

Timair looked very lovingly at his sister, as he concluded. "You were at the very spearhead of all of these projects and dreams, my lovely Mélusine. You left us to use what you had learned in the Great Charm to further the readiness of the humans. You have one Visit left to Faërie, and then you must judge if you are to continue in your role as a human or if you can be of greater effect as the fairy you truly are. If you choose the latter now, it will be with Finnir by your side, I suspect. You would be a powerful pair.

"But," he added, very thoughtfully and with a heightened sparkle in his wise eyes, "if it is not deemed, by you, to be the best choice for these *coming* years --- if you choose to come back here --- then you will be a powerful pair...later!"

He rose, and ushered Eli to the stairs leading to her bedroom.

"I must go back to the Woods, and go through the Portal --- as *you* may not tonight, sweet Eli. I will bring, or send news as soon as I may. Play Róisín tomorrow morning, and listen well. And look with the Silver Leaf, too, if you feel drawn to it: for the insight given by that charm may bring you guidance also, from many of the highest and most luminous among the Alliance.

"May the blessings of the Moon-Dancers be yours, my brave and beautiful sister, and those of the Sun and her true attendants also, for both are filled with music and merriment, might and majesty. Good night!"

The laughter and melodies, the *craic agus ceol*, in the pub was increasing to a crescendo with the final strains of 'The Road to Lisdoonvarna' giving place to the 'Swallowtail Jig'. But sweeter than those lilting tunes was the singing of the rain outside. There were voices in it, and in the wind, thought Eli: majestic and merry voices, the voices of Faërie.

She watched as Timair draped his long plum-purple cloak over his shoulders and covered his blond head with its ample hood. And then he crossed the threshold of the pub and seemed immediately to disappear up into the silver curtain of raindrops.

****

Chapter Five:
When the Owls Fly Forth

wonder who else knows the truth about Timair. Does Garo know, or Demoran? Or Reyse? Even if these friends adventured together, was my brother's identity known to any other companion save Finnir? But Alégondine, who is so often with Aindel --- I suppose she, at any rate, *must* know..."

Eli was pondering these questions as she covered Róisín with a loose-fitting protection of faded burgundy-dyed Indian cotton, like a small bed-spread. This was her harp's 'travel-garment', for she was taking her to the Woods of Gougane Barra.

Her musical interrogation of the harp had taken place at dawn, for Eli had found it hard to sleep any later. She had only played for several minutes, when the sound of Finnir's own voice had replaced the equally sweet tones of Róisín's vibrating strings.

"Come now, my Eli. Come this morning, for Aindel and I, we are both at the Heart Oak. Follow the swallows: several are awaiting you in the Woods to guide you to the threshold. And bring the Harp of Barrywood, which you have rightly named Róisín. Bring her to the Portal also. Come soon, my love."

Eli hastened to put her belongings together, into her shoulder bag, for her Visit home to Faërie. Obviously, she slipped in Lily's journal with the Silver Leaf hidden between the pages containing her little moon's surprising island-sketch and the entry about Leyano, or Leo, bringing her this gift from the Queen Rhynwanol, via the Lady Ecume --- and all the wonderful news that the Queen had given her.

And then Eli hesitated for a moment. There remained three other things to put back into the bag: the bamboo phial, Reyse's white rose, and also the moonstone pendant on its silver cord. She had not worn it for several weeks... But she had kept it with her, and always had it on her night-stand near her bed.

She realised, as she lifted it before her and then let it rest in the palm of her hand, that having it beside her at night was a comfort, almost like having Reyse sleeping nearby in the alcove of the great Chamber of the Seven Arches in Fantasie, and playing a lullaby to her on his *vielle*. Did she so need, or desire, his presence? Did she wish to retain him as her champion and protector, even though now she knew that her heart would never be his? For the moonstone, where it had appeared when he offered it to her, hung just over her heart --- where she, as Mélusine, evidently bore a similar jewel. And Reyse wore moonstones as well, in his ear-lobes and ear-points...

She kept his pendant, but did not wear it now: was she afraid of the connection between herself and Reyse, the communion of their shared jewels --- like the sapphire in Finnir's hand that communicated with that of Mélusine's right ear-jewel?

Rather odd that she did not wear it, but kept his gift close, especially at night. She could not, herself, imagine why. She closed her eyes for a moment and sought to be honest with herself, but she could not divine the exact answer. When she thought of Reyse now, what --- truthfully --- was she thinking?

"I have no time to dwell on it at the moment," she remarked aloud. "I must go, right away, to Gougane Barra. My belovèd Finnir and my brother Timair are waiting for me. I must begin my Visit."

"But take me..." whispered the moonstone. "Take me with you..."

No, there had been no sound in the little bedroom of her B&B. Eli shook her head at herself.

"You have too vivid an imagination, even for a human-cum-fairy, my girl," she remonstrated, pursing her lips at herself.

But she packed the pendant into her bag, nonetheless. And, with it, she also put in the white rose and the phial of love-potion.

The waning crescent moon was already high in the clear, rain-washed sky. It seemed to insist, rather mischievously, in remaining visible all through her drive to the Woods, staying framed in the rear-view or side mirrors of her car. Although very pale and fragile-looking, it persisted in grinning at her as she drove westwards. For the first part of her road, she was beside the beautiful Lough Allua, following the River Lee upstream between Inchigeela and Ballingeary.

She could not refrain from stopping for a moment beside the lovely Lough, stepping out of the car to taste the early morning breeze and to delight in the calm of the scene being elegantly disturbed by the flight of a large congregation of ducks, flying rather low and in a ragged formation, with their usual urgency and insistent calls. They seemed to be in a 'hurry', as she now was too! She returned to the car and continued on to her destination.

Eli drove for only ten or fifteen minutes more, and came to the Lake of Gougane Barra as the sun was just peeping over the shadowed rim of the high hills with their dark traces of myriad waterfalls and their crags of grey stone covered with blankets of green. A lingering mist hung about the lakeside boulders and over the surface of the water, though it did not hinder the contemplative morningtide tour of the shallows by a pristine pair of white swans.

There was still no rain in the air, but Eli kept Róisín's cover draped over her as she carried her along the trail into the Forest. Though easily as large as Clare, this harp was much lighter --- impossibly so, in fact. Eli could carry her with ease, and for several hundred yards.

No one else seemed to be about, not near the humble Oratory beside the Lake, nor at the Tea Room, nor anywhere to be seen along the woodland track. Gougane Barra seemed to be given over, wholly, to Eli's presence and to her invitation from Finnir.

Though she was happy to be alone while seeking the entrance to Faërie, Eli nonetheless found that she was a little nervous. The woods seemed to be in listening-mode, hearkening to her very footfalls and her somewhat heavy breathing, and their high heads of dim and agitated leaves were muttering together and peering down at her in curiosity or maybe even animosity --- she could not tell which. The air around her became very still as she left the footpath and plunged into the ranks of huge trees, straight and green-skinned and hoary-toed --- their short branches seeming out of proportion to their unguessed height.

But it was bright daylight in the Woods, not dark and eerie as it had been at twilight yester-eve. It just seemed, to Eli, that every blade of grass and every leaf and twig was inordinately *alive*, so alive as to be ready to explode. As she continued on, deeper and deeper into the Woods, she would not have said that the place felt exactly *sinister*; only that it felt bursting with anticipation and with vigilance.

Suddenly, instinctively, Eli stopped. She could not go another step. Róisín had become incredibly heavy, as if demanding to be put down. Eli did so, and removed the cotton blanket. Instantly, the Golden Flower on her harp's forehead blazed out like the beam from a light-house across a stormy seascape of tempestuous green waves. Eli's fingers were drawn to the strings, and with one hand --- just standing where she was beside the instrument --- she began to play: broken chords, rolling arpeggios, but always including the subtly coloured strings as well as the pure white ones.

Answering notes came to her ears, but from high up: the cries of swallows, perhaps seven or eight of them, tumbling about in the dusty, diagonal shafts of sunshine far above her. Lowering her eyes, Eli saw, at a short distance, the purple cloak of Timair; he was walking towards her along an alley of trees, his fair face bright under his hood, the amber points beside his eyes glinting as if to complement their violet-blue with their own rich golden-ochre.

Eli threw the burgundy cloth over her shoulder and picked up Róisín, now airily light once more, and walked quickly towards her brother.

Not ten steps from where Eli had first seen her brother, a massive oak tree was now visible. It looked incongruous here, amid the rows of pines in this part of the Forest, for she could see no other oaks around it. It had relatively short and stocky branches, and very few of them at that; they were already bare and leafless, and yet they did not look at all wintry or withered. Quite to the contrary, she had never seen a tree look *so* alive, unless it were the Great Trees themselves in the centre of the City of Fantasie!

As if space itself were playing tricks on her, Eli spontaneously had a vision of the tree from the *other* side. It was the view she had seen when she had looked into the Silver Leaf and beheld Barrywood and the Heart Oak, with its pair of small, grey owls in the hollow trunk and its branches like a cupped hand.

Even as her eye fell on the owls, or the strange vision granted her of them on the other side of this oak tree, they took flight and flapped noiselessly out into a haze of golden and silver light.

"Quickly, Eli, step through," Timair urged. "You have only one breath to do so!"

Windy Hill Prayer

The doorway was wide and welcoming, but it appeared, indeed, for only the blink of an eye. With a loud 'thump' like the bang of a door being closed by a gust of wind, Eli found herself standing on the far side of the Portal. Timair was beside her, his arm still around her waist as though he had just lifted her over the doorstep. And facing her, only a yard or so away, was Finnir.

Behind her was the huge oak, its branches in the form of an open hand like a woodland throne, roughly at the height of Eli's head. She had turned from the beauty of her lover's face to glance back over her shoulder, to see the wondrous tree as she had done in the vision accorded her by the Leaf. The opening in the widest branch at the back of the throne was like a heart-shaped window into the hollow trunk, and the two little owls were already alighting --- once again --- within it.

She turned back to Finnir, passed her harp into Timair's hands now, and stepped forward into the arms of her Prince, the Guardian of the Portal of Barrywood.

****

But Eli's fairy-prince was *not* radiant with power and enchantment this morning. He looked decidedly tired.

Finnir was no longer dressed in his finery, the regal raiment of last night. He was in comfortable and 'ordinary' fairy-garb: a long beige tunic and off-white, coarse-woven linen trousers, with a short cape of dusky blue pushed back over his broad shoulders. The pearl in his brow was dim, the amber gems in his ear-points were covered by his short, blond curls. Even the golden skin of his smiling face seemed somehow in shadow.

"Was there a battle last night?" whispered Eli, her voice filled with concern.

"A defeat, but no battle," replied Finnir with a wry smile. "And the defeat was mine. I lost the trail of Erreig in the Unicorn Glens, for I could not venture too far from the Portal ---

as I'm sure he knew. Since just before the first glints of dawn I have sought to rediscover his whereabouts or his escape-route, but I have found nothing. Just before beginning my search, I returned briefly to my Castle to send word to you, in the music of Róisín --- as soon as you would play her --- to come through the Portal in all haste. For I fear that Erreig has slipped past me, and crossed into the human world.

Eli emitted a little gasp of fright.

"At least here, you have the protection of various fairies. There, you have none --- unless Reyse has appeared?" concluded Finnir with a tone of hopeful inquiry in his hushed voice.

Eli shook her head. "No, I have not seen Reyse. You think he may be on the other side, the human side, as well?"

"I do not know," rejoined Finnir, sighing. "The valiant Reyse is wont to come and go, in and out of Faërie, on Samhain Eve --- as at other times," he added with a curt laugh. "I thought he might have wished to visit you, but then I guessed that he might very well have known that you were to come back to us last evening. I really cannot sense, at this time, just how much he knows … about anything! But I feel in my heart that he will turn up, and soon. That said, if he is in the human lands, I do not know what Portal he may use, or when…"

Finnir's voice had trailed off into silence. Indeed, Eli thought he sounded almost overcome by fatigue and disappointment. It was Timair who spoke now.

"I was here, beside the Heart Oak, for most of the night as well, and especially vigilant when Finnir was required to search further afield for the intruder in the Glens. But at one moment, one very dark moment, possibly about midnight but it could easily have been a bit later, I felt a menacing presence off to the north-east, in the direction of the Jolly Fairy River. I left my 'post' for perhaps ten or twenty minutes of time --- but time is very playful at the feast of Samhain. When I returned here, just as Finnir was reappearing as well, we found that the ground was scorched as with fire and the two owls were nowhere to be seen. Dawn came swiftly then, as if hours had passed rather than a handful of minutes."

"Erreig is cunning, almost mischievous, and also quite skilled in time-charms --- or he has allies who have such powers," murmured Finnir, but he smiled again as he added, "though to send a fairy and a huge white dragon into the modern human world is a rather comic idea, and I do not think that Erreig's allies are at all comical in their strategies. If he has gone there, he and Bawn, I think it was a rash and very independent idea of *his*, not prompted by another."

"Let me remain here now," said Timair, "while you take Eli to your Castle. She must be led away from the Glens. Peronne is waiting there for you, Eli. He arrived yester-eve. There is good news as well, you see! Our father has returned, and is in the Silver City. He sent your flying-horse here, knowing you were to enter his kingdom by this Portal. But his message, brought to Finnir with Peronne, was brief. *When Eli steps through the Heart Oak, reunite her with her steed promptly. Peronne will bear her to me here forthwith. She should not linger in Barrywood.* And he is right. Your life as Mélusine is bound-up with the mighty Glens --- and you are not equal to that force and not ready to face them, not in your human form."

Timair sighed rather philosophically, and then he spoke in a somewhat lighter tone. "Now, take a moment of peace together both of you, and say your farewells at the Castle. There you are fully under Finnir's protection, and far distant from the Unicorn Glens. And Eli, please remember, to no one at all am I *Timair*. I am Aindel, if you must mention my name at all. Don't forget!"

"I'll not speak your true name," promised Eli. "And thank you, *Aindel*, for sharing your story, for allowing Finnir to share your secret with me. Thank you so much."

The freckled and kind face softened with a broad smile, and he kissed his sister's head. His smile was even more radiant as he nodded to Finnir, and as the two Princes parted Eli could not help but think how alike they seemed, or maybe how intertwined they had become by the threads of their curious history. And both were so…enchanted and mysterious, still, to her.

She had this 'proof' that she had come back into the realm of Faërie, for enchantment seemed completely normal here. How marvellous to be going to meet Peronne, and 'turn again her wind-horse feet to the silver turrets of Fantasie'! Yes, it was very wonderful to be back to this astounding place, and very good that her father was safe and back home again, too. Very good indeed, that --- though Eli hoped that he was not vexed that she had come into his realm by Finnir's Portal.

Swallows were, as ever, swooping about the Prince's head and a large beige squirrel was curled up, sound asleep, in the prow of a curious shell-shaped boat moored in the miniature haven adjoining the pool of the river's source, where Finnir now led her, just beyond a nearby line of golden-leafed trees with shining silver bark.

To be honest, Eli had rather hoped that they would be riding, together, on unicorns! But she had not seen Neya-Voun, nor any other unicorns, or even horses. As they floated along the narrow, swift stream, Finnir played on his silver lap-harp. Róisín had been placed, by him, in the stern of the little boat, delicately wrapped, once again, in her wine-coloured cloth. Eli did not dare to propose a duet with her lover; in any case, she was contented just to listen to the rippling notes of Finnir's music and the voice of the lap-harp --- which seemed very akin to the sound of the running river.

And the river *did* 'run' and quickly, and many miles of its graciously curved route flowed under the shell-boat in what seemed to Eli only a few minutes --- though it was, in fact, surely closer to an hour. With only the gentlest of a cascading drop over its wide, ultimate mouth the river tumbled into the northern bay of the Inward Sea. The little boat hardly felt the fall at all, and continued on as if dancing. Finnir did not need to steer or guide it, for it turned to the left of its own accord and skirted the shoreline for another ten or fifteen miles before it came to the feet of the promontory where his enchanted abode stood.

The Castle of Barrywood was as Eli had seen it in her vision, too. But in that imagined moment of swift-flight she had caught only a glimpse of its beauty. Now, as Finnir helped her out of the shell-boat and onto the pathway leading up the sloping lawns, she could look upon it at leisure, and it was certainly a fantastical feast for her eyes. The morning light glistened on dew-drops strung on endless vines of flowers; the blossoms themselves were like necklaces of rubies and pearls, yellow diamonds and pale peridots, woven back and forth over the towers and walls. Interspersed with these garlands were patches of dense, dark ivy, or rich red Virginia creeper, or thick masses of jasmine. The walls, when one could see them at all through the vegetation, were nowhere straight or vertical, but rather sloping or irregular --- as if they were not sure, themselves, if they were masonry or tree-trunk!

Bedazzled by the sight of the Castle, Eli could not immediately look elsewhere; but at last she turned her head to the south, just as she and Finnir had reached the broad terrace welcoming them to the great Entrance Doors. Their hands were clasped, and Finnir carried Róisín in his other arm. Eli's free hand was now raised to her mouth, muffling an exclamation of wonder.

Not twenty miles from the point of the promontory, was the Island of Windy Hill.

It was not simply its loveliness that made Eli catch her breath; though lovely it was, assuredly. A large island, it was wooded and green, softly rounded, decked with flowers, serenaded by birds, surrounded by white-lace wavelets and the vast indigo water of the Inward Sea which was alive with sun-stars and rippling in the morning breeze. Yes, it was very beautiful. But what fixed Eli's eye was not the Island; it was the Chapel.

From this distance it should have been hardly visible, encircled by un-seasonable blossoms and verdant shrubs, shaded by tall and statuesque trees: for the Chapel itself was humble and plain and quite small. But it *was* visible. Very much so. It had almost *flown out* over the water to meet Eli, as it had long ago approached Reyse across the Whale Sound when he and Dinnagorm had stood on the Point of Vision. It rushed to meet and mingle with Eli; it sang to her, filling her senses... and her heart.

And *its* heart was visible too, for its low-arched door faced the Castle. And there, --- deep, deep within the Chapel, protected and cocooned in its shadowy interior --- was a throbbing heart. A yellow heart, soft and flowery, alien and yet perfectly at home there: the mimosa tree planted by Aulf the Mighty, the wattle-flower flame of the altar of the Chapel of Windy Hill, the fire-charm of Finnir's resurrection from the phoenix-pyre of his imprisonment...

Eli's voice came out of her *own* heart, and she found herself pronouncing a very strange remark. Without taking her eyes off the magnified view of the far-distant Chapel, she quietly said:

"I thought there were no mirrors in Faërie. But there I am; I can see myself. That is <u>me</u>."

Finnir had released Eli's hand now, and he stood behind her, having placed her harp on the jay-blue paving-tiles just between them. He wrapped his two strong arms around Eli from behind her and crossed them over her shoulders, holding her close against his own chest. He whispered, "It is you, yes and no, my Mélusine. Or, rather, it is not *only* you. It is **us**."

When Eli at last released her gaze from the Island of Windy Hill, and turned to face Finnir, his arms still encircling her, they kissed long and passionately. His weariness seemed to be lessened, perhaps by his harp-playing, or the sight of Windy Hill, or maybe --- Eli hoped --- by being with her.

It was bright mid-morning now, and they turned, holding one another close still, to walk up the steps and into the splendid Castle. But there, standing to one side of the Entrance Doors, was Peronne!

Eli ran to him, and Finnir laughed with shared joy as she embraced her steed's broad, arched neck of soft moon-dappled grey, his long white mane mingling with her own red hair --- now fallen loose about her shoulders and in delicious disarray from her love's caresses. The lily-lights deep in Peronne's dark eyes shone and sparkled. He greeted her, silently but with resounding warmth, his voice ringing in Eli's ears as she continued to stroke his head.

"Welcome, my blessed and happy mistress! It is good that you were able, at the last, to pass into this land, albeit delayed by one night. It will require that you take great care when your time comes to go back…if, indeed, you choose to do so."

Eli inhaled deeply, and she realised that the fragrances in the air were a complex mixture of all the flower-scents, fresh sea-breezes, ancient odours of tree and stone and also something akin to spices --- like the inviting smell of mulled wine.

"Oh, my darling Peronne, it's true that I don't know for sure yet," she replied, speaking in a low voice, but aloud. "My heart seems to be overflowing with faith in all things, impossible or unlikely, natural or obvious, wished or dreampt or desired. But I don't know, yet, what I will or should do about my life here."

"You have three weeks to decide that, lady of my heart." Finnir's voice was relaxed and tender. "For now, come into my Castle and let us take some refreshment together."

"And then we must hasten to the City of the King," commented Peronne, still in his silent speech. "I have instructions to bear you there as soon as you have broken your fast with the Prince. I must urge you not to delay, dear Princess. You are in the 'cocoon' of this Castle's vibrations here, but the Glens are not far off, and their energies are tangible even in the breezes. You should not linger over-long within the range of their rippling force, at least not without other fairies, friends or family surrounding you."

Both Eli and Finnir nodded, and they entered the Castle to find, to Eli's immense pleasure, that the wafting odours had not lied: chalices of hot and richly spiced wine awaited them, as well as dark bread filled with morsels of dried fruits and chunks of nuts oozing with honey. It was a lovely, and *loving*, breakfast.

"It seems we have not the time to converse overlong this morning, my love," said Finnir as they ate. "But you have learned much since last evening that will be occupying your thoughts for today --- or many days! Dwell on the joy of what Aindel has permitted to be revealed, for the knowledge of my true lineage, and his, offers us the freedom to contemplate our future together.

"And as for the more worrisome questions surrounding Erreig, they will be solved soon; and you are here and well-protected --- and Róisín is with you. I would not wish Erreig to find the Harp of Barrywood, for he is as skilled a musician as any in Faërie and would gain great insight into many things with that sweet instrument in his hands.

"Now, you must fly to your father, and happily he is *there* to fly to, home once again in the Silver City. I do not think I shall be able to come to him in the days ahead, as I would have liked to do. I will not be able to abandon the Portal soon, even with Aindel keeping guard with me. And Aulfrin does not need to know of Aindel's presence here, if you will agree to refrain from revealing that, please."

"Yes, of course," agreed Eli. "I understand. I will be glad when no more secrecy is needed; but I realise it is not you or Aindel who decree that."

"No indeed. There are great hands fingering the pieces on the board, and they are wise and trustworthy. We will have faith in their judgement, and in the interpretation they bring to the music which is being played out in our lives and in our Alliance. We are all members of the orchestra, my sweet Eli, and each note has its importance and its contribution; so let us be patient and play with skill, and in love and unity. And we will follow the indications and the inspirations of the conductors' many and beauteous batons!"

Eli smiled, and as they stood to leave their table Finnir once again took her in his arms.

"We will find a time to be together, later in this your third Visit, my Lady," he assured her. "And before us lie the years and the centuries of our love, their days and nights. At this time, you are Eli still; I am keenly aware of my boldness in having expressed my love, our love, while you are yet in human form. I would not have done so save for the troth that was plighted between us during your Great Charm --- though I am aware that you have no memory of that, save as a resonance of our affinity that you have felt since our rediscovery of one another in the course of these your changeling-Visits. I would not venture to exhibit our love, our romance, our true union before you are once again, fully, my Mélusine. No, not yet. We will have to exercise our patience in this matter, as we do in the other great and universal matters of our two worlds!"

Eli's turquoise eyes, wide and wondering, tearful and joyful, were gazing into Finnir's crystal-blue ones so intensely that she did, in truth, have the sensation of flying out into the infinite sky they had always suggested to her. She breathed in the heady aromas of the Castle of Barrywood yet again, and kissed her love 'farewell'.

Finnir led her to Peronne; she mounted in a graceful bound and he fastened the feather-weight Róisín on the proud horse's neck as he had done on Neya-Voun's. Eli laced her fingers into the long strands of crinkly white mane, and smiled back at her fairy-prince once more. Peronne trotted in a spritely gait along the balcony for three or four strides and then stepped up into the air, spreading his wings to climb slowly over the northern-most reaches of the Inward Sea.

They flew high and fast into the west, following the southern margins of Barrywood, keeping the Unicorn Glens far to their right; while to their left the imposing heights of the White Hart Mountain and later the ruddy slopes of the Feather Mountain filled all the view. As they reached and passed over the Salley Woods, Peronne veered to the north-west and decreased his altitude to rush along over the plains of sunflowers and cornflowers, now faded and brittle-brown --- but somehow still lovely even in their early-winter garb. And so they crossed the River of the Grey Man not too far from its source in the Stone Circle, perhaps fifteen miles off. Gliding over the south-eastern Gate of Wineberry, they entered the City of Fantasie, just after mid-day.

Over two hundred miles of flight, without a pause, but in haste and grace, were now rewarded by the sight of the silver turrets and the coloured haze undulating about the Great Trees, in pulsing mists of mauve and soft yellow-green. Eli was home, again, in the heart of her father's kingdom; and every fibre of her being seemed to be tingling with a further and still keener dimension of life which she had not known for over fifty years. For this, her third Visit, it was evident that she had been granted even more sensation and memory of her true nature than she had so far experienced.

Was it the Great Trees who ordained this? Or the King? Or was this, simply, how a changeling's home-coming Visits functioned?

Whatever the source of these sensations, Eli threw wide her arms, as Peronne soared more slowly over the wide lake and on to pass just above the Fountain of Lyathel. As she closed her eyes and opened her arms out to embrace all the glorious aliveness of her true nature and her true self, Eli heard her father's voice, loud and clear inside her head. She opened her eyes, and there he was, standing far off on the great circular balcony half-way up the King's Moon-Tower.

She could hear the words as if he were sending them out to greet her on a rippling wave of laughter: "Here is my third home-coming gift to you, to welcome you for this final Visit, my dear girl. Breathe deeply the air of Fantasie, and fly home to me!"

Eli's arms were still out-stretched, but as she inhaled and felt herself rushing into her father's equally enthusiastic gesture of arms flung-wide, Peronne descended, to land in the courtyard of the Entrance Court.

But Eli did not descend with him.

The feeling of exploding **life** was concentrated, for only a split-second, in both her shoulder-blades. And then she felt them: her own wings! Her body arched like a high-diver's before he turns to plunge, and she held her head up with chin lifted and a wide, beaming smile on her face. Her laughter joined with that of Aulfrin. Behind and above her she could feel the powerful beating, though almost in slow-motion, of great but delicate wings. She knew herself to weigh less than a feather, and her whole body became one with the rhythmic movement of her wings' waving through the bright air.

A few glorious moments later, she landed with a very poised and graceful bend of the knees in front of the King.

"Well done!" he cried. "One would think you had last flown only yesterday! Bravo!!"

Eli was giddy with laughter and delight. She turned her head, and almost cried out with astonishment, though at the same time she felt a confident recognition of what she was beholding.

"I'm like a butterfly, a giant butterfly!" she piped.

"*Polygonia gracilis zephyrus*, I believe, is what humans call this lovely species, yes," nodded Aulfrin. "You chose it as your wing-form very early on, oh at only the age of three or four, I would say. Most fairy-infants go through multiple pairs of wings before they find those that will satisfy their tastes and complement their characters --- but you seemed sure of yourself right away! You changed the colours, though, I must stress. No butterfly in the human world is painted in those extraordinary tones and tints of watery blues and alizarin crimson softening to lavender. I always found them very nice, indeed, your wings, my Mélusine. Welcome back to them, and to Faërie.

"By the way, you may retract them at will --- quite so: just decide to. They will appear again whenever you call them forth. That's excellent."

As she 'thought' of pulling them back into her shoulders, so the wings were instantly absorbed. Eli's bemused expression made her father continue to chuckle, but he took her in his arms as well, and the feeling was --- to Eli --- almost as wonderful as her *zephyrus*-wings.

****

During their lunch together, Aulfrin mentioned his slight surprise at Eli's decision to return by Finnir's Portal this time; but he could not fault it, he conceded. Had it not been permissible, it would have been denied. And not necessarily by him.

"The right of passage, for a changeling," he explained as soon as the attendant fairies, serving them generous slices of some rich tart made of pumpkin and chestnuts, cranberries and sour apples, had withdrawn, "is accorded by a force even superior to that of the King." His eyebrows danced a little as he said this, and the corner of his mouth lifted in a half-smile. "It is, one could say, the fairy-spirit which waits in its state of limbo who really decides if such a date or place is suitable for a Visit. In your case, your true-self seems to have desired to pass by all three Portals, one after another. And so, of course, the Heart Oak had to be among them. The choice of Samhain Eve, that is another matter."

Aulfrin poured a second cup of sweet cider for Eli and for himself. His deep green eyes glinted at her over the rim of the little pottery bowl. "That's your typical and incorrigible desire for drama and daring, as ever demanding to have its say. You are a lover of danger, in some ways, Eli --- at least when you are Mélusine. You seem to have a character trait, which I could never restrain, of seeking-out --- at all costs ---where your limits lie, and then pushing them further! The very best way to get you to *do* something, is to tell you that it would be more prudent *not* to!"

Eli had to laugh. She certainly recognised herself in this description, even her human self.

The King sounded a little more serious as he continued. "But your desire to pass the threshold on Samhain Eve failed, and this is a slight complication. You have now, officially, arrived here today, on the 1st of November. By rights, you must return --- if you return --- to the human realm on the morning of the 21st: the twenty-first day of your Visit, at the same hour as you arrived. But the full moon falls on the 21st, rising at sunset and setting with the dawn. Now, here in Faërie --- as in the world, also, I believe --- the moon is not just 'full' on one date, but on *three*. We count as 'full' the moon on the day arriving at fullness (if you like) and the one following it. For she *appears* full for all of those three nights. So you will find yourself in Faërie on the first night of the full-moon, just preceding your return; and that is, officially at least, *not* permitted.

"Yes, you are required to pass through the Portal of Barrywood roughly two hours after sunrise, if I have correctly understood when you were greeted by *Finnir* this morning."

Eli glanced sidelong at her father. His eyes were sparkling, as were the emeralds and peridots in his crown. His jewels always seemed to echo his thoughts in their glinting and glowing, Eli affirmed inwardly. What did he know? How much did he guess? As ever, impossible to be sure...

"Well, we will have to reflect upon this slight *moon*-problem. But we have three weeks to do so!"

As he concluded, Aulfrin arose and gestured for Eli to follow him to the southern window of their dining-room. Father and daughter looked out together from the high turret, enjoying the beauties of the Silver City and the coloured mists about the mighty Trees.

Suddenly, a shrill sound rang out below them, in the diamond-shaped Courtyard beyond the Entrance Doors. It sounded like trumpets.

Aulfrin leaned out over the balustrade of the high, open window where he stood with Eli. The clarion call was repeated. Eli leaned further out also, close beside her father, and looked down.

Two tall fairies, clad in the blue-grey capes of Fantasie, (embroidered with the emblem of Faërie in orangey-red and yellow-ochre) were indeed blowing into long horns: like slender and finely crafted lengths of brazen pipe with upturned bowls, similar to Roman tubas.

"Is it an alarm of some kind?" whispered Eli.

"It is, yes; an alarm to inform me of 'suspicious tidings'. Not usually of woe or of great danger, just of concern. Look, there is the reason, I suppose."

Eli squinted in the bright, low, wintry sunlight. Landing on the trellises of wisteria and on the edges of the high walls, on the railings of balconies and now circling many of the silver turrets, were dozens of owls. Huge owls, like those that she had seen before in the Dappled Woods and at Demoran's Castle, and like those who were watching over her and her half-sister Brocéliana when they slept in the Fair-Faced Flower Beds near to the Whale Sound. They were obviously Scholar Owls.

"I haven't fainted," Eli thought to herself, "so this can't mean that my slumbering fairy-body, the wraith of Mélusine, has been awakened again…"

But she hadn't the time to ask anything of her father, for a giant black and silver Owl had just alighted on the balustrade before him, and the King had stepped back a pace to give it a little room and to listen to its news. The Owl inclined its head quickly to both the monarch and his daughter.

Whether it was that the bird spoke in Eli's own language or that her ear was now attuned to the speech of this realm or of these creatures so intimately involved with her transformation and her human adventure, Eli did not know. But she could clearly understand what the Owl said.

"The Amethyst Cloth," it began, "has left Faërie, Sire. We have been reinforcing all of the charms that guard the Princess Mélusine since it was stolen in the summer. Help has come from many quarters to do so. We exercised constant vigilance, for all of these past four months; but even though it was no longer on our Island, we could at all times feel its existence still in Faërie, even far-off on Star Island. But now, it is gone.

"It left this shee, in whose hands we do not know, in the darkest hours of last night, in the very middle of Samhain Eve. We can perceive it no longer. It has passed out of this realm, Your Majesty.

"We fear that the Princess is in danger of fading, perhaps even --- in her fairy-form --- dying. Some among us perceive that it is possible that her life-force will be given entirely and irreversibly to her human-form."

Aulfrin's face had turned ashen white and his hands were slightly trembling. Eli looked from her father to the great Owl. Her thoughts were racing.

"Is *that* why I felt so alive?" she said to herself, not daring to speak aloud, hardly daring to breathe. "Did I feel so much more real and aware and completely *alive* because my fairy-self is fading? I thought it was because I was, at last, truly in love! But if *her* life-force goes completely into *me*, then I'll have to be a human, only a human, forever --- if Mélusine fades and disappears, I'll only ever be the *human* me!

"Or will I die too? If she <u>dies</u>, I will certainly die also, with no hope of coming back through any secret doorway or Portal or Vortex... For I won't be a fairy at all, not in any way.

"Am I more alive, or less?! What is happening?

"Oh, I wish Finnir were here…or Reyse."

****

Windy Hill Prayer

Chapter Six:
A Study in Mauve

aturally, Aulfrin's first response and reaction to such news was to consult a wise and trusted instrument. His Music-Room, where his small silver harp awaited him, was adjacent to the great Council Chamber of the Seven Arches. He and Eli went swiftly from their dining-room up a spiralling staircase connecting this lower level to the upper storey of the same part of the King's Moon-Tower.

"Wait for me, my dearest Eli, in the well-fortified Chamber which offered you protection and sanctuary on your last Visit. I will not be long."

"Yes, father, of course," Eli replied obediently, but she added, "I will wait here, but I *would* first like to just ask you if I am in imminent danger of dying!"

Aulfrin stopped where he was, and smiled.

"Do you know, my changeling-daughter, you sound more and more like your true self. Your directness and your tone --- rather defiant and almost amused --- belie Mélusine's character. You are a very strong and regal fairy, and this pleases me much."

Eli relaxed a little, as Aulfrin now had done, and she smiled back at him.

"I'm not sure that I feel particularly strong or defiant at the moment," she admitted. "But I feel curious and, well, yes, ready to 'fight for my life', as a *human* might say in, if needs be!"

"I don't think it will come to that," said her father, breathing deeply as he continued to smile, now taking both her hands in his. "I don't think fighting will be needed and, in any case, I don't believe it would solve anything. Life usually thrives *best* when fighting *ceases*!

"It is clear that the life-force of Mélusine is bound-up with the Amethyst Cloth which Erreig stole. Now perhaps, in the charms of your transformation which were worked in such complexity by the Scholar Owls, among others, the cloths which constitute your shroud are imbued with such a magical link to your very life. Or perhaps this 'spell' comes directly from you; for you orchestrated much of your own transformation-music, I understand.

"What puzzles me is that the Owl-messenger said that you, as the Princess, are in danger of *fading*, or perhaps *dying*. Why not <u>awakening</u> to face and challenge this occurrence, as you did when Erreig himself was before you? I feel that such a fairy as Mélusine would not sleep through such an effrontery nor such a threat. But, my Princess-daughter may have had other things in mind.

"In fact, it's always the same question: what do we mean by the word 'death'?! It is a many-faceted jewel, *death*, and can mean many things. That is what I need to inquire of my harp, at least to begin with.

"And then, I need to know where Erreig is, and if it was indeed this troublesome Dragon-Rider who has taken the Cloth out of Faërie. For I have been long in Quillir, but I did not *directly* encounter Erreig there. That said, I would suspect him over, for example, the Sage-Hermit himself …"

Aulfrin exhaled with a short, slightly derisive huff. "I will be quick, and then we shall know more." He winked at Eli, his eyes full of green stars. "You don't *look* as though you are about to die, my darling girl. In fact, I've never seen you look more radiant! So I am not worried. Are you?"

Eli had to laugh. "No, not really. A bit confused, but not worried. I don't feel like I'm dying either!"

With a last caress of his brown hand across her cheek, the King turned and strode off into his nearby Music Room.

And Eli went into the Council Chamber.

Waiting for her there, standing on the sill of one of the southern windows and looking out at the Great Trees, was Piv.

"Oh!" cried Eli, her smile now broad and her tone not merely relaxed, but utterly delighted. "Periwinkle! My dear Piv, I'm so very glad to see you!"

The pixie turned where he was, and flew across the room to Eli, hovering before her face to meet her eyes and then kiss her forehead. But he was not smiling.

"My little Eli-een," he cooed, his bright green wings all a-buzz and his tiny hand grasping her sleeve to pull her to a nearby settee so they could sit side by side. "I followed the Owls from the Dappled Woods, where I was finishing-up, that is tidying-up, the remnants of our feasting of last night. Oh a great host of my cousins living in France had made the journey through Demoran's Portal to spend Samhain with myself and my family here. It was such a gay gathering; I do wish you'd been there! Pixies and little green dragons, brownies and wood-sprites, whirling mushrooms and an excellent choir of spiders... it was a treat!

"But then the Owls passed overhead, early this morning, and I flew with a pair of them for a few hundred yards and, oh, their news was strange and terrible! I went to Castle Davenia straight away, where two or three of the Owls were speaking with Demoran and Ruilly. Jizay and Ferglas were both there as well --- they both proposed running all the way across the Star-Grazing Fields to try to get to Scholar-Owl Island and to the vault of Mélusine, but the Prince dissuaded them; I imagine because he knew that they could not get to the Island over the wide waters of the Sound.

"Demoran and Ruilly, they told me the same as the Owls I'd met. The Amethyst Cloth, they said, had been taken from Star Island and --- while the Portals of Faërie were open for Samhain Eve --- it had been transported through one of the doorways, and was now in the human world. I thought it was you, maybe, who had called for it somehow. I didn't know yet that you were one of the brave beings to cross the threshold last night, or was it this morning? Oh, the reports are all a bit muddled, or is it my head?! But here you are, and you're alive. I'm so glad, so relieved, because they said that the Princess was possibly fading into fairy-death, because the Cloth contained some magic that kept her alive, I suppose...

"Oh, my little Eli, I don't understand, and neither does Demoran, I think, because he couldn't tell me more. I don't *want* you to leave us, not yet. Please come back to Faërie, Eli, so that Mélusine can wake up and you'll be *her* again, I mean *you* again, and don't die, and tell me why the Amethyst Cloth is so important as all that!"

"Dearest Periwinkle," said Eli, trying not to laugh at his high-speed-locomotive-paced discourse, "*please* don't be so anxious. I'm alright and I feel in perfect health. I don't know what the Owls meant either --- but we will find out. The King is inquiring of his harp, and my brothers, that is all three of the Princes, they will be discovering more too, I'm sure. And maybe Reyse will turn up; I know he would be able to save the day.

"Do you know where he is, Piv? Have you had any word of Reyse?"

There was a very marked silence now, in stark contrast to the pixie's accelerated monologue of a moment before. Piv came to rest on the ground at Eli's feet, and continued to look up at her for a minute, but then he lowered his eyes and stared down at his feet. He wiggled his pointed boots and sighed, still not looking up again. His words were intoned softly, and sadly.

"He's gone. Darling, dashing Reyse, he's gone from the Shee Mor."

Eli furrowed her brows, bent down and touched Piv's shoulder with her hand. "He's gone…for good?"

Piv looked back up, into Eli's questioning eyes and decidedly paler face. "Yes, my Eli, maybe for good. I don't know that either; no one does. He passed through the Portal of the Fair Stair in early August, and he told both of us, myself and Demoran, that he planned to go from France to Ireland, and into the Sheep's Head Shee from there. Now maybe he did and maybe he didn't, but no one knows anything more of him. Beautiful blue Muscari doesn't know, and neither does the sweet Prince Demoran, and not even the mushrooms have any news to give me."

Eli hesitated, still perplexed and feeling oddly anxious, but also --- in her heart --- feeling somehow implicated in this situation and in Reyse's silence and absence. She recalled their last conversation, on his birthday, in Saintes, when he had said words which now haunted her:

*I have asked you to accept my suit for several centuries already, and I am still asking it. But I know that you cannot make that choice while you are Eli. I would like to suggest that you do not make **other** choices, of similar kinds, in your changeling-form either. Wait, please, Eli…. When you find yourself faced with a <u>choice</u>, a choice of paths, paths that you hope will lead you to Love, remember: There is, in fact, no such thing as a **path to Love**. For Love **is** the Path.*

"He's been away from this shee for much longer periods than that, and no one --- I suppose --- ever thought that he wasn't coming back. Why do you think that now, Piv?"

"Because of the strife there, in the Sheep's Head Shee. There's such unrest, as hasn't happened since the old King left, and all his family, to go to the Little Skellig. I think it's because of the humans, that's what I think. They get into that shee at times, and not just at Samhain. They've found one of the Portals, not many years ago, and some of them use it, or try to. But Reyse, dear Reyse, he loves that shee, almost as if it were his own, and he's very good friends with Aindel, the fair and moons-wise Aindel, Prince of the Sheep's Head fairies. I asked, and my heart told me --- in September it was --- that he and Aindel there together, side by side. But then, so suddenly, my heart went very cold, very cold and silent, for Reyse. The tall and fair Prince, I don't know, for I've not seen him, but my heart has *no* shadows when I call *him* to mind. But when I think of Reyse, the *Iolar*-eagle and the Horse-Lord, I only find tears and wells of silence in my very core. I think that the news is not good…"

"It *is* not good, you are right, my dear Periwinkle." The voice was that of the King, who had just entered the Council Chamber and was walking purposefully to where his daughter and Piv were talking. "The news, both of Reyse and of Erreig, is not good at all."

Eli started, and turned quickly. Her heart was beating fast, but whether for the threat of Erreig to her own life, or the well-being of Reyse, she was not too sure.

Periwinkle flew up and paused in mid-air at a respectful --- but rather informal --- distance from Aulfrin's eyes, kindled with an emerald fire at this moment.

"Your dear kind Majesty, is it true that Mélusine is passing from us? Please say it's not that! And my red-jeweled Reyse, tell me his is *not* dying or dead --- too."

"<u>Death</u> is not to be feared, Periwinkle. Not Mélusine's, not my strong and wild Eli's, and not Reyse's either, not yet, I deem. Not for many long years. But such freedom from the fear of death does not banish all evils, nor all dangers.

"Now, as regards Erreig it is clear, he has indeed crossed into the world of humans --- the first time he has done so for many centuries, I feel certain." Eli raised her eyebrows at this remark, but did not interrupt her father. "And the Amethyst Cloth is there also; so I can only surmise that it was Erreig who bore it thither. But Bawn is not with him. Moreover, he has gone *as a fairy* --- not as a human, that seems certain. But maybe he is transformed into some other creature, for he has that skill, I think, from the Sage-Hermit or another of the Great Ones. In any case, he left Faërie at midnight or thereabouts, but by which Portal I am not yet informed. I have sent messengers to all three of my sons, so I hope to know soon.

"The danger to Eli, and to Mélusine, I will counter also, and swiftly. The Lady Ecume is informed, by my harp-song, and she is gone to the Island of the Scholar-Owls now, even as we speak. I will fly, in all haste, to join her there --- and to present her with the amber-token. With the Black Key, the life of Mélusine will be safe-guarded. You will fly with me as far as Davenia, my dear Eli. And await me there at the Castle of your brother Demoran."

Aulfrin paused, and his voice became less decisive and confident somehow.

"As for Reyse, he is indeed engaged in the strife of the Sheep's Head, and it has recently escalated. He is involved and deeply occupied in that situation; but I do not sense that it threatens his life. But that is *not* why your heart sorrows for him, I think, my kind and insightful pixie.

"It would seem, judging from the lament of my harp's final air, that a tragedy of another nature has befallen him. It resembles a broken heart; moreover, my ear --- well-attuned to the keening of my harp --- tells me that you have, Eli, by means perhaps of your own harp Clare, communicated to Reyse a final and definitive refusal of his love. I cannot help but sympathise with that noble fairy's disappointment, and I add to that my own paternal discontent that you pronounced such a resolute and conclusive decision while yet a human, not waiting to be --- once again --- your true fairy-self and aware of all of Mélusine's memories and desires, scruples or, perhaps, re-considerations.

"Be that as it may, we must go swiftly now: you to the Dappled Woods, Eli, and myself onwards to the Whale Sound. Piv, do you accompany Eli on Peronne? We do not fly there with our own wings, for Eli is not yet well-enough practiced, again, in that art."

Eli had never seen Piv look so sad, or perhaps --- she thought --- he was disgruntled with her.

"No, my darling Majesty. I want to ask the mushrooms of the Inner Garden for news, and maybe even the Great Trees themselves. But I'll come to Davenia very soon, as soon as I can."

And then Piv brought a tear of great relief and joy to Eli's eyes, for he turned to her and added, "I love you, my precious Eli, and also you as the mauve-swaddled soundly-sleeping Mélusine, whom I'm sure will not die now that the King and the great mermaid are hastening to strengthen her, maybe even with the magic of the Black Key. And I must tell Reyse what I know in my heart --- I must find a way to tell him --- that Love *always* finds a solution, for it *is* the solution. And it always finds us, too, because it *is* us, all of us. I have to tell him not to despair, for his love will surely find you…and bring you home."

The King was leading Eli, urgently now, to the door, and thence to the high-courtyard where their flying-horses were at the ready.

"I would be glad of your help, in both of those endeavours, dear Periwinkle," he said. "We will see you soon, then. Come, my daughter; and farewell, Piv!"

****

The Harp of Barrywood, Róisín, was still held against Peronne's neck by her lighter-than-air scarf. In fact, the harp herself seemed lighter-than-air and no greater weight to bear, for Eli's strong steed, than a daisy-chain necklace. But what was even stranger, to Eli, was that her father made no remark about it. He didn't seem to have noticed the harp there at all.

"Is it invisible to him, like the Flaming Crescent Moon?" she mused, as she mounted and followed the King, at a gallop, across the court-yard and up over the balustrade, circling and rising quickly into the chill November breezes from the north.

In little more than an hour, such was their speed, Cynnabar and Peronne were above the Dappled Woods between the River Navid and the shorter stream which connected the Golden Water and the Red Triskel Lake. Aulfrin motioned to Eli to descend and alight at the Castle, while he soared away towards the first great loop of the River Ere, heading due north in his swift sky-route to the Whale Race Sound.

Peronne landed in the midst of the lawns where the company had been gathered to celebrate the Day of Ævnad. Eli well-remembered falling into unconsciousness here, and re-awakening with Reyse sitting beside her in her tower-bedroom, tenderly welcoming her back to health and hopefulness, and then playing his *vielle* to lull her into normal sleep and rest.

She sighed, and undid the scarf securing Róisín to her horse's neck. Demoran was jogging down the broad steps from the Castle-door. A leap and a bound ahead of him, Jizay was running towards his mistress. Ferglas remained at the top of the steps, just in the shadow of the high, arched door.

Eli greeted her beloved hound and Demoran took the harp from her, carrying it with one arm, the other around Eli's shoulders, rather as Aindel had done. As they walked back across the grass and up the steps together, the sky turned cloudy and sullen, and darkness seemed to be coming early. The tall trees about Castle Davenia were bending and creaking in the growing wind.

"Well, you arrive on the wings of a storm, dear Eli" he said, almost cheerfully. "But I think you will weather it! Many of the Scholar Owls have returned to their Island, and one descended to give me the tidings that Aulfrin was going to meet with the Lady Ecume and request the Black Key, to avert your ... *death*. Well, rather too dramatic that word, at least in the tone it was spoken by everyone today. I think it more likely that you were simply casting-off for a short voyage of sorts."

They were in the hallway of the Castle and Eli was removing her cape and handing it to Calenny. Demoran ushered her into the little room which she knew from other meetings, such as that with him and her father when she had arrived by the Fair Stair for her initial Visit --- and later, in June, when she had met with Garo and Piv. They were alone in the cosy parlour now, and Eli sat opposite her brother and looked searchingly into his leaf-green and sunlight-flecked eyes.

"You think that Mélusine is *not* dying, Demoran? You think that she was --- I mean that I was --- about to ...slip away on a *voyage*, did you call it?!"

"Well, you are a true child of this family, and members of this clan always seem to be like colourful balls in the hands of a juggling court-jester, and so I just thought that a little jaunt somewhere or other would not be out of keeping with your royal character," replied her calm and riddling brother.

Eli scrutinised his incredibly handsome face. Since the first moment that she had beheld her brother, she had found him beautiful. But there wasn't any real 'attraction' to that beauty, not as there was with Finnir, or even Reyse. It was like looking at a masterpiece, a portrait or a sculpture, but even more than that. "No," she thought, "it's like looking at everything I ever longed for, sought after, dreampt of in men --- and realising that it's not the same as what I imagined. I've exhausted myself running after dazzling eyes and chiselled features, wisdom and enlightenment, sincerity and serenity and humour and kindness. All my life, all my human life, I've been chasing those qualities, those elusive and laudable character traits and gifts and beautiful jewels in a man's nature. But they *can't* be pursued, or ever attained, or ever possessed. They don't even need to be *admired* really. They just need to be **experienced**, like a waterfall or a rainbow or a field of flowers or a galloping horse. When I look at Demoran, I have no desire that's crying out to be satiated, no emptiness to fill. I feel full, and yet much lighter. And I always feel like smiling at him!"

Aloud she said, "Is making a *voyage*, that seems like *death* to all those around one, something I have inherited through my family tree?!"

"It's what your grand-father did," remarked the lovely fairy, simply.

"Aulfrelas? But of course! You told me how his body was carried away into the ocean from the Great Strand; but now, he is the Sage-Hermit! So he didn't die, all those centuries ago --- I think it was in the year 1300, was it not? --- but he was transformed into something else, because of his sea-voyage. Is that what you mean?"

"Sea-serpents and whales and dragons, they are amazing creatures," nodded Demoran, serving Eli a cup of some heady tea that had just been brought in to them. As the attendant fairy withdrew, he continued. "And purple ones are especially gifted at such rites of passage. They like helping fairies to cross over strangely insubstantial dividing-lines in their life-stories. Yes, yes, purple --- or more correctly *mauve* --- sea-creatures and dragons, they're very good at that.

"But as I've told you before this, my dear sister, there are dragons…and dragons!"

Eli smiled incredulously, more at finding herself in a 'serious' conversation about sea-serpents and dragons, mauve ones at that, than at what Demoran might now be hinting at. She sipped her tea, and shook her head slightly.

"Am I to understand, then," she began slowly, "that our grand-father, the King Aulfrelas, was snatched from the sands of the Great Strand by a mauve monster who then transformed him into the Sage-Hermit? And why doesn't our father know about this, and Reyse? Because they both seem to think that the

Sage-Hermit is named Maelcraig, and they have not mentioned Aulfrelas being still alive."

"I would guess, given the profound vision and patience and enchantment with which the Sage-Hermit is always endowed, that Aulfrelas doesn't <u>want</u> them to know, yet. Otherwise, they would. And I would venture to guess, too, that his wife is implicated in all of these plans and secrets and transformations. For, next to the 'monsters' --- as you so oddly name them! --- there are few creatures in Faërie so wise and wonderful as *seals*."

"Morliande?!" whispered Eli. "Demoran, I saw her --- recently. I saw her in a vision, with our own mother, the Queen Rhynwanol, and with my little moon, my human mother, Lily, and with…Aindel. And I remember thinking, as I looked upon Morliande and heard her voice: *She is a seal, a silkie, and the mistress of invisible and moving islands, and a sailor in whale-bone boats.* I don't know why those words came into my mind at that moment, but I seemed to know, then and there, that she had powers over transformation and voyaging."

"She has, indeed, such powers, and many others. But I don't think that anyone *snatched* Aulfrelas from the Strand, or *caused* him to be transformed by their own powers, at least not exclusively their own. Aulfrelas was and is a seer, like Morliande, and he was also very beloved of the whale-folk, as he was of the Great Trees in Fantasie. I think that the transformation from King to Sage-Hermit was one which he had been preparing for many a year, and it was also a part of his love for the ocean-fairy Morliande, the most sublime silkie-seal of the far islands in the south-west of Quillir. Together, they wove this tale of metamorphosis and sea-change, and together they are working still."

"You seem to know so much, dear Demoran," sighed Eli, smiling and continuing to delight in the beauty and wonder of her middle brother.

His eyes were laughing and sparkling, and the circlet of twisted gold that he wore on his head of long chestnut hair was shining too, rather as Aulfrin's emerald crown seemed to echo and mirror its wearer's thoughts and moods. Demoran said with an amused grin, "Isn't it good that *someone* knows almost *everything* that's going on!"

Eli laughed. "Yes, that *is* good! Because there are so many moving pieces at the moment, it's making my head spin. It must be nice for you to have a clear idea about what's really happening."

Demoran was laughing now too. "It's rather tricky, that, my darling sister. I'd like everyone else to know too, and it's not yet the time. A little frustrating, I can assure you. And then there are 'moving pieces', as you say, like our fine father. And no one, not even the wisest, knows exactly what, or how much, *he* knows. He often speaks, in private council, with me --- and yet I still can't be sure, not quite sure, whether he knows more than he says to me or if he, maybe, leaves my Castle having learned almost all I know, but not saying so! But he and I are very alike, and I think we both enjoy the game, and the juggling."

Jizay and Ferglas, lying either side of Eli's chair and listening intently to all that was said, both rose suddenly, for a sound was heard in the hallway near the Castle's entrance.

"Speaking of...sea-serpents and mauve... *monsters*," smiled Demoran, rising too and going to open the door of their little parlor-room, "I believe this is someone who will be able to give much greater insight even than I can, into the voyage you *may* have been contemplating in your nearly 'death-like' sleep on the Island of the Owls."

Eli stood to greet their guest, and with great pleasure discovered it to be Alégondine. The youthful, dark-haired, dark-skinned fairy seemed to float into the room, her huge eyes like glittering and unfathomably deep well-water --- reminding

Eli of Peronne's. The sea-green emerald set in her forehead was modestly glinting; Eli realised that she had rarely noticed it at all, it was so much a part of her half-sister's face, and almost the same depth of colour as her own skin. Beside her eyes --- from the locks of her long, black hair with its intermittent strands of pink and silver pearls --- the triple-points of her delicate ears peeped out, the red tourmalines set into those points sparkling like glowing embers among the grey ashes of a smouldering fire.

Both women bowed their heads very slightly in mutual greeting, and then Alégondine said, "I am very glad to find you here, dear Eli. And to find you well."

All three sat around the small round table, and Jizay lay, once again, at Eli's feet. Ferglas remained beside Alégondine, his head with it sea-shell collar resting in her lap. The deep, musical voice of Eli's half-sister was soft, but filled with a calm tone of relief.

"I was at Kingfishers' Temple for Samhain Eve, where I had moored my boat and was communing with the sacred blue bird-priests, when I heard the news of the Owls --- relayed to us at the Temple by the turtles on the northern shores of the Bay there --- that Mélusine was…fading. Moreover, Aindel had told me that you were to come into Faërie at Samhain-tide, Eli, and so I was greatly relieved that *you* would be under his protection, and Finnir's also. A dangerous date, and place, you chose for your entry; but it was better than remaining in the human-lands, with my father there."

Eli looked quickly from Alégondine to Demoran, and then back at the lovely, rather exotic Princess. "Do you know why Erreig crossed into the world last night, Alégondine, bearing the Cloth he took from Scholar Owl Island?"

"I do have an idea, yes, Eli. But I would prefer that our mother, the Queen, discuss this with you. Aindel tells me that you have the Harp of Barrywood with you; thus, he says, you have both the Silver Leaf and the Golden Flower. It seems to be arranged that Rhynwanol will be able to come to you, tomorrow, in vision. She is still an exiled Queen, but she may appear to you here, much more clearly than she has done before, by virtue of these charmed tokens: the Harp, the Leaf and the Rose."

"You have seen Aindel, then? Is he here? I thought he was staying with Finnir in Barrywood."

"Indeed, he is with the Prince Finnir for the moment. I saw him in the Sheep's Head Shee several days ago. I was visiting our mother, and Aindel was preparing to pass the Portal into Ireland, to guide you through the Heart Oak."

"I was so happy that he turned up," Eli admitted. "I felt more at ease having him there, for it was a rather frightening evening! And I was happy to…speak with him."

Eli found herself on the verge of disclosing all she had learned about the hidden-identity of her brother. She caught herself just in time, and took a rather nervous sip of her tea.

Demoran smiled warmly. "Don't worry, dearest Eli. You said yourself that I know everything!"

Eli's eyes widened. "What, exactly, do you know?" she asked, speaking very slowly and softly.

A strange thought now crossed Eli's mind, as if it were being transmitted from her brother or sister, like an unspoken message or an invisible epistle. It simply said: *The dogs are here, and they do not know all that we do. Neither should they. Especially the King's hound, for he would surely tell him.*

Eli nodded, and took one more sip of her tea in silence.

As if to gracefully change the subject, or to go back to another, Demoran turned to his half-sister and began, "Sea-serpents and mauve dragons, these are subjects that I assured Eli you could speak knowledgeably about. I propose that we adjourn to my sitting-room upstairs, where there is a cosy fire; for the winds have brought a chill to the early evening now, and I think we could continue our chatting more comfortably there.

"May I ask you," he continued, addressing Ferglas as they all stood to leave the dining-room, "if you and Jizay would make a short tour of the Woods to the north, to learn if any of the Owls have had further news from the Island? I would be most grateful."

Ferglas, Eli thought, twitched his eyebrows, as if he guessed that he was being sent off in order to allow the conversation to take a more private turn. It seemed very like a highly intelligent child being asked to leave the room so that the adults could talk of 'grown-up' subjects! He and Jizay exchanged glances, and they left by the doors at the far end of the Entrance Hall, leading into the gardens.

Eli felt absolutely certain that both hounds knew, most probably, at least as much as Demoran. But she said nothing.

"It's really to do with your fairy-self, my dear Eli," began Demoran, when all three were comfortably settled on soft chairs around the hearth of a fragrant peat fire. "I said that you were probably setting off on a little voyage, not dying at all. And that is the *specialty* of certain mauve creatures."

Demoran winked at Alégondine, and she took up the thread of his discourse.

"Our mother, dearest Eli, the Queen Rhynwanol, is a *violet* fairy. This is a certain sort of fairy, which can exist as part of any fairy-family or race. You can recognise a violet fairy by physical characteristics, or by other details in their behaviour or talents. In the case of Rhynwanol, one sees it in her hair and in her eyes. Her eyes are violet-blue, and her hair glints with that colour also, in certain lights, as does mine --- for I have inherited those highlights of violet from her, and the powers that go with them. You do not have her eyes or hair, but you are linked to her 'violet' nature and her powers in other ways, which will become clear to you later, if they are not yet, I expect. And as our brother Demoran says, it is a 'speciality' of the mauve-ones to be able to displace themselves…rather unusually! Not exactly shape-shifting, this talent --- more a playful elasticity in their very substance, a blurring of solid and subtle, if you like. And I firmly believe that it was by using your violet-fairy gifts, and those of another mauve being, that you were most likely planning to take action against the impetuous --- one could even say impudent --- decision of my father, Erreig, to go into the human world with the Amethyst Cloth.

"My guess is that the sleeping fairy-form of Mélusine was well-aware that you, the human-form of her spirit, was on the threshold of coming here and that you would be safe --- well, relatively safe. And so, when the Amethyst Cloth left Faërie, Mélusine decided to give chase.

"Now, I must explain something rather complicated. It is a *very* magical act for a sleeping chrysalis-fairy, the true fairy awaiting her re-awakening when her changeling-form returns, to *leave* her bier without herself actually *awakening*. You experienced the effect of Mélusine coming **out** of her slumber, last June. That was not what Mélusine was proposing to do this time. Certainly it would have been very unwise to repeat that and to risk your human life or health once again. But another feat was possible for her, particularly because it was Samhain-tide. While **still in her trance** as it were --- and not *awakening* as she had done on the Day of Ævnad to confront Erreig face to face in her very vault --- she *could* depart into the world. It was also best for her to do this while you are here in Faërie: for then she would be replacing you or exchanging places with you, in a way, in order to retrieve the Cloth. At least, I believe that this is what she may have had in mind.

"Now, to invisibly flee Faërie would not be straightforward. She could not do so by way of a Portal, that would have been preposterous; for she would surely be perceived and even hindered by the many other spirits, fairies, and even humans who have the possibility of passing between the worlds on Samhain Eve. And she, though invisible, would have been detected by the Prince guarding whichever Portal she chose. However, she *could* pass into the world as a ghost, a phantom-fairy --- that is, not at all revived or awake --- using other routes.

"For *that* could be facilitated by her connection to the creatures who *serve* the violet fairies: the sea-serpents, whales and water-dragons, who are, also, somehow *purple or mauve* fairy-beings. These creatures are among the mightiest of all the ocean-dwellers, at least they are among the most magical and those most easily able to swim through the veil of 'death', as it is sometimes called.

"For in such a phantom-form, Mélusine would have been, in a way, 'dead' --- leaving you, as Eli, fully alive and very human. This seems to have been what was sensed by the Owls. It is quite the *opposite* of the state of affairs engendered by her suddenly arising, fully awake, in her vault, as she did in June! The risk, this time, would have been that Mélusine might <u>not</u> succeed in coming back to her empty body --- for that would not have moved --- and in such a case, if she did not return, she would ultimately fade completely, unable to rejoin herself to her chrysalis-being; and then her human-form would become the full and definitive *version* of herself."

"You see," interjected Demoran, "on Samhain Eve the thresholds of the worlds, all of them, are blurred. The doors between Faërie and the human-world stand open, but also those between some of the forms of physical 'life' and supposed 'death' purely in the world of mankind. For in the human world, many spirits are abroad on that night --- nothing to do with Faërie. It is a moment when their vibrations waver and oscillate, and they can be perceived by the 'living'. I think that Alégondine is right, for in the same way you --- that is Mélusine --- may have been considering a *voyage* in a ghostly-guise, to confront Erreig, just for the period of that one exceptional night.

"But, thankfully, you have been, we have now learned, restrained and turned back. Our father, when he arrives on

Scholar Owl Island, will find you asleep on your bier, and *not* dying, not even temporarily absent in spirit. He will not need to call for the Black Key."

"Yes, you are asleep again now. I received a very reassuring report," confided Alégondine, "by a trusted messenger, shortly before I arrived here."

Eli looked at the fairy-woman, now bathed in the wavering glow of the fire which illuminated her shadowy skin, making the red tourmalines dance with renewed light and her black hair gleam with streaks of blue and rose-pink and very deep purple.

"Yes, Eli. As I said, when I was at Kingfishers' Temple last night, in company with the sacred birds for the rituals of the solemn festival, we received word from the turtles across the Bay of what was passing on the Island of the Owls. I and the birds, we all wished to learn more, and so we called upon some of the greatest of the turtles, the leatherbacks, to swim further out into Sun-Slumber Bay to seek news. They did this for us, after the middle-night, and came back with news which relieved our fears somewhat, though I still decided to come here as quickly as I could today. It seems that a mighty sea-dragon had passed along the Great Strand in the darkest hours of Samhain Eve, not long before dawn this morning. I would conjecture that the sea-dragon in question was heading towards Star Island --- at least, that is my guess. In any case, several of the huge leatherback-turtles went into the coastal waters near the Strand, and that is where they met the wondrous aquatic-worm, and were able to converse together.

"Now this sea-dragon was recently come from a meeting with the Princess Mélusine herself, on the Island of the Owls. She normally inhabits a small island in the Lizard River of Margouya, an isle called Mauve Dragon Halt: the place is named for this very great and beautifully-coloured dragon, who had been summoned by you, by Mélusine, it would appear. But once arrived at the northern cove of Scholar Owl

Island, called the Cusp of the Heart Cockles, it seems that this wise worm *flatly refused* the request to bear you, as a ghost, into the human oceans! Why, or with whose advice, I am unsure; but happily the dragon countered your intentions.

"I have an inkling that your grand-mother, Morliande, may have been implicated, also, in thus dissuading you. She is among the most illustrious of the violet fairies, knows the Mauve Dragon well, and is often to be seen in the Whale Race Sound. I think she may have intervened, or even others among your family or protectors. Your father would surely have also prevented you, if he had arrived in time --- but in any case, it was a boon that this friend of long-acquaintance, the Mauve Dragon, had the sense to counsel you to remain asleep and on your Island."

"You are as head-strong in your slumbering state as you are when wide-awake, it would seem, my wild little sister!" concluded Demoran. "I am glad that, at the least, you have the sense to listen to purple dragons and like-coloured-fairies --- sometimes!"

"I remember hearing of that dragon," Eli commented, shaking her head slowly in response to this incredible tale and all its strange information on her violet-fairy nature. "It was mentioned in the reports I heard of Finnir's mission with Brea and Aytel."

Demoran concurred, "The Mauve Dragon is an ally of Prince Finnir's, it is true, as are most of the more enchanted creatures of Faërie. For Finnir is as enchanted as a fairy gets, I can assure you."

"Though he does not have mauve or violet eyes, like the Queen," muttered Eli. "His eyes are blue, like the infinite summer sky." Her thoughts were turning dreamy as she stared into the firelight, and she felt all her body becoming softly infused by her sweet memories of Finnir's affection. She sighed.

Her brother cleared his throat gently, making Eli start, and tickling her with the embarrassment that she was slipping into sentimentality over her lover --- who was, as yet, thought by all to be her half-brother.

Though her embarrassment was to be swiftly replaced by pure amazement.

Demoran was not, evidently, clearing his throat to signal that this was too romantic a remark, but rather that he knew more about Finnir than he had, as yet, revealed.

"No, Finnir's eyes are the same hue as all of his clan, for the present royal family of the Sheep's Head Shee hail originally from a far-distant and extremely sunny corner of Greater Faërie, and there *all* the members of their highly magical royal tribe have clear summery-blue eyes. He is *not* a violet-fairy, not even a blue one; he is pure white. But Aindel's, that is Timair's, eyes are certainly violet --- just like his mother's."

Eli opened her own green-blue eyes *very* wide, and her mouth fell open as well; and she turned to her brother. Then she looked at Alégondine, who was wearing a very soft smile also.

"So, it's true. You... you *both*, know that Aindel is Timair? How is this? For how long have you known?!"

Demoran's smile increased, and he gently reached over and placed a loving hand on Eli's shoulder for a moment. He said, "I learned it from our mother, for she has always known. This is why she chose to go the Sheep's Head Shee in her exile: to be near her true son, Timair. And it is why she accepted, long before that, the babe reputed to be the child of her husband and Daireen, accepted him contentedly as her own. For she knew Finnir to be the rightful Prince of her grand-father's shee, and very happy and proud she was to foster him."

"And she told you this --- recently?" insisted Eli.

"When you went into the world as a changeling," replied Demoran. "When I was imprisoned in the Red Hoopoe Mountain. I was held captive by Erreig and his dragons in a strange *cage*, a dwelling like a crystal lantern, which opened in seven triangular segments that swung downwards --- when it opened at all! But its form, in seven icy wedges, was identical to a *miniature* version of the same lantern-shape: a gift which had been offered by Erreig to his illicit lover, Rhynwanol --- but a gift which had been wrought by Morliande in fact, and passed into the hands of the Dragon-Cheiftain by her, to give to his exiled lover."

Alégondine took up the tale: "It was I who delivered the little treasure, Erreig's gift, to my mother the Queen, that very winter when he had overthrown the Scholar Owls and the Blue Hounds and his dragon-riders had seized the Silver City. You were already preparing for your transformation, dear Eli, when I took the news to Rhynwanol, telling her that two of the Princes had been imprisoned. Finnir was held in the Caves of the White Cats, while Demoran had been placed in his odd ice-lantern cell high on the snowy slopes of the Red Hoopoe's summit.

"The miniature and intricately wrought casket delighted Erreig, with its tiny jewel-flowers and insects housed in the various sections, for it was a cunningly-wrought work of very fine artistry. In fact, the small jewel-casket was carved from a dragon's egg-shell. It was the shell of an egg from the Mauve Dragon, and it was extremely enchanted: a *mauve*-dragon's dusky-pink shell intricately carved by the charmed hands of a *mauve*-fairy-queen, and presented to just such another *mauve* Royal!

"But Erreig thought only how the wondrous music sung by the flowers and insects of each segment would delight Rhynwanol, such a talented and consummate musician and harpist. He did not guess that through his gift, Morliande was giving her daughter-in-law a powerful tool of communication with her captive son, Demoran. But for over a year, this is how they exchanged news and also how Demoran was nourished with invisible and potent food and drink, kept warm with mauve-dragon-breath spells, and given great insight into many matters by the songs of the tiny creatures in the jewel."

"It was an important time for me," Demoran interjected, "a difficult and painful time --- for no fairy can easily bear any sort of cage, as no animal or other creature can either, for that matter --- but it was a time of great instruction and profound contemplation. I had lived many adventures before that, heroic and arduous and exhilarating, involving long travels to very remote lands; but this adventure --- mostly in silence and always in meditative stillness --- was as exciting and as impressive as anything I had dared in my youth.

"And one of the tales I heard from Rhynwanol and from the insects was that of Finnir and Timair. So I have known for roughly fifty years, my sweet Eli, to answer your question."

Eli was more than ready to accept a small, bulbous chalice containing a walnut wine or elixir. Demoran poured a glass for himself, and for Alégondine a paler, perhaps less rich, fruit *cordial*.

"You see," said her brother, clinking his own delicate glass with hers, "your fears --- and you had a string of them chasing their tails inside your head at the end of your second Visit --- are beginning to look like the tiny spider hanging in front of the leprechaun's eye. Your perspective is changing, and that's always a good thing."

Nodding her agreement, Eli had to add, however, "But they are not yet *so* amusing as the leprechaun's little spider-fears. For our father does not, I think, yet know that Finnir is *not* his son, and so we must be very secretive about our love for one another --- which I do not really like, and which is not at all easy, as concerns the King... And even the fact that Finnir is of no relation to me does not solve the problem of my coming back here at the end of this my final Visit. For if I return, Brocéliana must leave. And that I find very sad.

"And then, there is this business with the Amethyst Cloth, and Erreig," Eli said, adding, "for I don't yet understand if there is a <u>danger</u> in his having taken the Cloth away, a danger to me as Eli or to me as Mélusine, and I have no idea what must be done about it."

"Those are questions to ask our mother," advised Alégondine. "Play your harp tomorrow, play Róisín, and place the Silver Leaf before you while you play, where you can see into its window. She will explain, and guide you.

"And do not trouble your sleep, tonight, with fears little or large in regard to my father, Erreig. For I have asked friends of mine to follow him into the world, and to watch him from a safe distance, reporting to me what he does and where he goes. I will most probably have word this night for I return beneath the tender light of the diminishing sickle moon to my sail-boat moored at the feet of Kingfishers' Temple. From there it is but a gust of wind to the stony shores of Quillir's coast, where the land of the White Cats borders the murmuring waters of the Bay of Secrets. There I will receive messages from my friends, and I will communicate what I learn to Demoran tomorrow by one of the swift-running kits of King Isck. If needs be, you will informed --- or supported and accompanied --- by my friends also, dear Eli. And Aindel and Finnir will receive news too, for others of my messengers will hasten to Barrywood as they see fit."

"Are they some of the huge Cats, then, that you have sent to track and observe Errieg?" whispered Eli, finding the notion wonderful and exciting.

Alégondine laughed gently, and placed her tiny shell-and-crystal *cordial* glass on the low table before them. "Not Giant Cats, no, but rather several dear companions of mine, descended from the clever creatures who hosted me in my second Initiation. They are moths, some are the large, grey *mormo-maura* moths, lovers of water and shore-lands as am I, and faithful observers of my father, for they have provided such espionage-services to me before! And the others are of the clan of the elephant-hawk-moths, who greatly admire the blossoms of the honeysuckle --- a plant I love as well --- and whose colouring of olive-brown and yellowish-white and soft pink reminds me of that flower. But they are even more closely linked to the Dragon-Flower, a rare and exquisite plant, difficult to encounter even here in the realm of Faërie. It is a lily, dark purple, almost black, and related to the *common dracunculus* of the human-world. But the human-world variety is not exactly the same plant, for the Dragon-Flower which sometimes grows here is a lily, a sacred flower, descended from those of the earliest gardens of the Sun-Singers. The hawk-moths of Faërie are devoted to this flower, and as in awe of it as are the fairies of Quillir, the province where almost all of the Sun-Singers now dwell."

Eli stared into the fire's dying embers. "I would like to learn more of the legends of the lily here in Faërie, but I suppose I knew all about it when I was Mélusine."

Demoran was gazing into the flickering orange and red glow in the hearth as well. "You did, but others perhaps knew even more than the Princess Mélusine. Malmaza would be the fairy, or half-fairy, to ask about the lily. They are our half-sisters, she and her twin. And in the world, where she became the mother of a long line of humans bearing fairy-lineage in their blood, a descendant of hers married the son of a changeling who was a full-fairy. The changeling had no children, of course, for a changeling cannot, but he had an *adopted* son. Now, the changeling I speak of, he choose to stay in the world, but even in his human life he remained a disciple of the High-Priestess of the Lily, here in Faërie. For in his original shee, which was the Shee-Beg or the Shee of the Bells, there is a great Abbess, a serene and luminous fairy who is the keeper of all the secrets of the Lily. However, Rhynwanol's daughter Malmaza, by Grey-Uan of Donegal, the matriarch of a branch of that great family bearing fairy-blood, she was deeply devoted to that blessed flower also; and that is probably why the gentleman-fairy I mentioned found his way to her human family, for his adopted son married into it."

"But I have heard this tale!" cried Eli, recalling the entry in Lily's journal, but not wishing to reveal the source. "For that was the grand-father of my human-mother, of Maelys, and he used to call her Lily, as our father later did. That 'adopted son' was Lily's father, but Lily's mother, she was descended from Malmaza. But how can I ask anything of *her*, for she and her twin, Mowena, they live in Scotland now…"

"Eli," smirked her brother, "you are forgetting that fairies are fairies, and not humans! Malmaza and Mowena, born in 1114, and educated in the Shee of the Little Skelling, did indeed choose to go back into the world of their poet-father, the human-world. And they retained the gift of their fairy-aging; so they are now, in the year 2010, let's see, I would calculate their age to be about the same as yours. Yes, I think that's right, they would be fifty or fifty-one now and, as you say, they reside often in Scotland. But besides that fairy-grace of slow-aging, they have also retained --- of course --- the permission of free-passage through the Portals."

"And you have seen them, on two occasions already, dear Eli," added Alégondine, now rising to leave for her moonlit flight, for which she would use her own great wings, to rejoin her sail-boat at the foot of Kingfishers' Temple.

"I have *seen* them? Where? When?"

Alégondine, stroked the head of Jizay who had now reappeared, trotting into the dim room and sitting close before the dying fire.

"When you first met Aindel at *The Tipsy Star*, earlier this year in May, dearest Eli. I was there too, or at least I arrived and lured Aindel away from your conversation. And on your second Visit, when you went with him to the very edges of the Stone Circle, the twins were there also."

"The *silent* twins, do you mean? But I thought they were called Begneta and Belfina?" exclaimed Eli.

"One and the same, or rather *two* and the same," laughed Demoran.

"Oh dear," chuckled Eli. "Does <u>everyone</u> have *pseudo-noms* here?! But I will have difficulty in asking Malmaza, because she never speaks! And which one *is* she?"

The answer came from Jizay.

"She is Begneta, and if you can hear *my* words --- as I know you can, my dear mistress --- then you can very likely hear *hers*!"

Eli smiled broadly, and nodded her head at her dear dog, just as Ferglas came into the room. The wise blue wolf-hound shook his slightly damp, wiry coat and shivered.

He then remarked, as silently as Jizay but every bit as distinctly, "If the kind Prince Demoran has finished discussing secrets behind our wagging tails, then I would like to request, politely but firmly, that the fire be rekindled to warm us after our...*tour of inspection* of the Dappled Woods."

Jizay barked his assent, and Eli joined in her brother's laughter, as they all bid farewell to Alégondine. Demoran summoned attendants to stoke the fire for the dogs and to serve dinner for himself and his sister.

****

Windy Hill Prayer

Chapter Seven:
Back and Forth

wo conflicting and contrasting dreams criss-crossed Eli's slumber that night. They came and went, interchanging and interwoven, like Celtic knotwork.

In the first, she was re-living the indescribable and glorious sensation of flying: not seated on Peronne's broad back between his feathery blue and butter-yellow wings, but flying with her *own* wings. Her beautiful *zephyrus*-butterfly-wings in shades of azure and alizarin and lavender. She soared across the Entrance Courtyard of Fantasie in her dream, as she had done when her father called out to welcome her; but she also flew over other landscapes and seascapes. Sometimes these were known to her, such as the Rhododendron Woods with their blossoms of pink and mauve and wine-red; or the glistening lily-crested wavelets of the Shooting Star Lake or the vigorous seas of the Kitty Kyle resounding with crying gulls and conch-blowing mer-men. Sometimes she was above stranger lands, unknown or nearly-so: the golden and silver trees of Barrywood, with spiral-horned unicorns weaving in and out of the shadowy groves; a sinuous river parting to embrace a tiny, sun-drenched isle where a huge mauve dragon basked on the rich amber earth; a sunset archipelago with ragged red rocks rising out of the thunderous seas and the multiple arches of an aquatic serpent's scaly back looping in and out of the water like a roller-coaster ride.

In general they were exciting, exhilarating, delightful dream-moments. But not so the other, contrasting nightmares.

In those tortured slices of her sleep, she was distressed and despairing. For they were all the places and scenes which she had shared with Reyse, but he was no longer there.

Confused and solitary, she sat at an empty wooden table on the terrace of *The Tipsy Star* searching for his face among the cloaked and hooded clients of the Inn; she waited, under a crab-apple tree, for her companion, but no one came and she looked down at her hands open in her lap wondering why there was no white rose to hold; she played her harp and then ate her picnic lunch under the tall trees beside the River Charente in Saintes or she sipped a cappuccino at the *Musardière Café* or she strolled in the *jardin public*, but he was not there to share any of it. Nearly frantic with aggravation, she turned and re-turned the pillows of their empty bed in Cork --- over and over, but she could not find the little slip of paper with its lines of poetry written in Liam's hand. It had been there a moment ago, she was sure of it. Where was it now? Where was <u>he</u>?

She awoke with a start.

"It's only the echoes of your guilty feelings, because Aulfrin's harp said that Reyse was heart-broken," Eli tried to repeat to herself, her hushed voice trembling slightly.

She reached out and felt for Jizay beside the bed; finding his soft fur under her hand was somehow an instant reassurance.

She sat up. Her room in Demoran's Castle was warm and comfortable, despite the persistent howling of the winds through the Dappled Woods all around it. But there was no rain. Alégondine, she thought, will have her tender sickle of moon-lash in a clear, windy sky, to share her flight to Kingfishers' Temple. Eli tried to conjure up an image of the beautiful violet-fairy confidently and courageously flying through the blustery night. And she tried to visualise the place, the high and holy pinnacle of rock, which she had only seen from far, far off, looking down the King's Rise to glimpse it --- like a tiny needle --- silhouetted against the sunset. The memory of the bright blue birds in huge, fast-flying flocks on Beltaine morn, retrieving the May-wands from the water and the fire, appeared in her sleepy mind now too...

"Through the water and the fire, reborn, like a phoenix," she mumbled, and closed her eyes again.

Partially asleep, or still imaging, Eli saw Finnir, as Reyse had described him, lying on the white altar of the Chapel which ignited into his funeral pyre, and then --- risen somehow from the ashes --- standing at the cave-opening in the trembling plains of the White Cats, King Isck above him on the red rock, thunderously purring as the Prince road off on Neya-Voun along a yellow wattle-way...riding off to his freedom.

"Finnir..." she sighed, and now she was deeply asleep. And all her dreams were only of loving him, his sweet and ardent kisses, his strong limbs, his noble and fair face, the infinite sky of his blue eyes.

It was the 2nd of November, and the morning was very dark, the sky heavy with clouds. There was still no rain to make a fairy's heart dance, but the wind was weaker now. Only the occasional chill breeze sighed from time to time through the trees, so that twigs and fallen or fading leaves rustled and creaked, as if their teeth were chattering.

Standing at the high balcony of the sitting room, the same room where Garo had first encountered Brocéliana, Eli looked out to the south over the lawns running down, beyond the trees, to the short river between the two Lakes. Demoran was talking with Vintig as they approached the Castle steps below her.

The pines and cedars, oaks and beeches were filling the air with their whisperings, but fragments of phrases floated up to her where she stood.

"The horses...exchanging the news ...stables this morning..."

"He will…later today…ah! the Owls saw her?"

"And the King …never known, in all my time, such…well, thankfully!...spectres, and dragons!"

"What can be done?…but no one seems….Where is he?"

Eli turned from the balcony as the pair below her entered the Castle. She wondered if --- among kings, spectres and dragons --- there had been a reference to Reyse in their fragmented and cryptic exchanges: *Where is he?* The same question she had asked in her nightmares.

Eli went down to the small breakfast-room to meet her brother. Jizay had gone out into the gardens with Ferglas, evidently wishing to speak with Vintig and the horses…

Demoran was already there, and he gave his sister a rather unconvincing grin, then he kissed her hand as he ushered her to her chair. But his face seemed as sombre as the sky.

"It's now you, dear Demoran, who seem to be worried. But I have no story of leprechauns to ease your fears!"

His expression brightened with a little laugh. "Well, you may have a good story to tell me later, when you've seen our mother. There are reports, from the Owls and the Moon-Dappled Horses, of Aulfrin's visit to the Island, but nothing is clear to me about where Erreig is, or what he is up to. At least your sleeping form is peaceful still, or so we have heard from the Owls. Ah well, our mother the Queen undoubtedly has the clarity of vision that we lack --- pertaining to many matters.

"I was seventeen when our noble mother was banished," he continued, pouring Eli's tea and then his own. "We were very close, especially in my second Initiation, when I won the blue tourmalines."

Eli regarded her brother's ears, where both in their lobes and their subtle points were set finely-cut jewels, their pale blue colour reminiscent --- now for her --- of Finnir's lovely eyes.

"They are wonderful," she remarked, "and make me feel rather wistful and peaceful. And strangely enough they make me think, not only of Finnir's eyes --- which is what came first to my mind --- but also of someone else. I was very passionately in love with a man, when Jizay came to be with me in the form of the sickly puppy whom I nursed back to health..." Here Eli stroked, with gratitude, the golden hound sitting beside her. "They don't recall to me *his* eyes, which were very dark indeed; but rather they make me want to finally **let go** of all of the hurt and hatred that I ended up feeling for that man, a truly twisted and tortured soul. I can almost see them bearing that entire episode away, like the glistening blue currents of a silent river carrying dead leaves downstream... Oh my, what *has* made me say all that?!"

Eli chuckled at herself in surprise. She had certainly not meant to talk about Yves.

"Exactly," nodded Demoran. "That is their power and their delight. They are very rare, and come from a far-distant shee. It was Rhynwanol that procured them for me, and the blue-flowers and blue-birds with whom I worked, in my sixteenth year, who then blessed them and set them in my ears. Among other gifts, they have brought me, also, the gift of *release*, the blessing of freedom from past sorrows, as well as peace and a certain talent for harmonious communication --- or the wisdom to choose silence! For they have great healing skills, as has the Queen.

"But only a year after their coming to me, our dear mother left. And Alégondine, the 'little flower of Faërie' as she was known in Fantasie, was also taken away --- even as I looked on, helpless, when the Sage-Hermit bore her off to Star Island. I fled Fantasie soon after, and the ensuing years were spent in wandering and adventuring, seeking to assuage my bitterness.

"I would have been grateful to have had the Silver Leaf, or an amethyst set into my palm or some other form of magical amulet, in order to communicate with the Queen. I had to wait nearly six hundred years before such a gift, in the unlikely guise of the ice-crystal cage devised by Erreig, would unite me --- unknown to my captor --- to the singing dragon's-egg casket-jewel of my mother. *Terrible* to be imprisoned; *wonderful* to be re-united with her! But then, life is always made of two-sided symbols, is it not?! Two sides of a leaf, of a mountain-peak, of a question or of our life-story itself: birth and death, waking and sleep, climbing higher or falling lower, success or failure, here or there ---- coming or going. We often seem to be as you are now, Eli, two selves in one, two seasons of the same year, two faces of the Moon --- the visible and shining, the invisible and dark."

Eli regarded her gloriously handsome brother in a new light as he spoke now. Yes, all she had ever sought-after or admired in men was there, but beyond the certainty of feeling *no* need to chase after it or possess it, an even deeper sort of 'experiencing' of it was dawning on Eli. It was as Calenny had said to her on her first day here in the spring, when she had made her young fairy-in-waiting giggle by asking to look at herself in a mirror. *It **is** true, is it not, that it's always nicer to look within than without, at the heart and spirit? Even the loveliest flowers, colourful and gay as they may be to the hasty eye, are really enjoyed and appreciated only when you see their hearts, and then breathe with them, sharing their light and energy….*

She felt that she was seeing Demoran now with her heart, looking within and for the first time glimpsing, truly sharing, his essence, his 'light and energy'. And he was even more beautiful *within than without*, decidedly.

"I will be glad to speak with our mother, yes, for I know her very little, or at least I remember her --- so far --- only vaguely. Should I go now, to play my harp?"

"I have the intuition that you should perhaps wait until the moon peeps out again --- if she will do that today --- for at the moment she is cloaked by thick cloud. That said, even if she appears between the tattered edges of the cloud-wrack, she will be very slim. In only four nights from now she will be dark, her face turned from us and her eyelid closed as she prepares to return to us in the fine arc of the young crescent.

"I suppose she may elude us all day; so perhaps, yes, you *could* play this morning, and see if the Queen appears to you, or if you can at least hear her voice."

Demoran and Eli continued their breakfast in silence for a few minutes.

"So, it is as I thought,' he remarked at last, smiling a little more earnestly now, "your harp is Róisín, the harp which Finnir made this summer! I learned about his harp-making when Aytel was convalescing in Fantasie and when Finnir and Brea had concluded their quest to seek for Morliande --- filled with surprises that voyage, but assuaging much strife, I think, thanks to their journey with our grand-mother to the two mystical and neighbouring shees. Yes, I had heard that upon returning the Prince had gone, not to the Lustrous Willows of the Salley Woods, but to Gougane Barra to seek the material to fashion a harp, and that he had named it the 'little rose'. So indeed, *that* harp was his gift to you... You see, dearest Eli, I don't seem to know *everything*, after all! For the gift of the Harp of Barrywood to *you* surprised me --- as did the love that prompted it.

"I knew that Aindel was our brother Timair, and I knew that Finnir was the Prince of the Sheep's Head Shee, and I might even go so far as to say that I knew that he had fallen in love --- and that, oh a century or more ago. But it was when you said, last evening, that your 'love for one another' had still to be kept a secret from our father that I realised that the Prince's passion was for *you*. Well, now I think about it, it does not surprise me at all. And so, he has offered you this harp, and it has --- no doubt --- many and remarkable powers. It can heal, I suspect, especially in the hands of Mélusine, the protégée of the Lady Ecume. And it can obviously open a path to see and hear Rhynwanol, as Alégondine says, unified with the Silver Leaf, for it bears the Golden Flower on its brow."

"It *is* very powerful, I'm sure also, though until now I hadn't really thought how it might be *doubly potent*, when it is united with the Leaf" confided Eli to her wondrous brother. "For it's true, I have not only the Leaf that was wrought for Malmaza, but the Flower given to Mowena. Or is is Begneta and Belfina?! Why do they need secret names, Demoran?"

"For the same reason as Timair does, to shield them, for the moment, from the perception of Aulfrin. And others. But how marvellous, that Finnir had come into possession of the Rose, and placed it on your harp. I was startled, when I carried the harp to your bed-chamber. For I could see that some gem or other was shining so brightly that its glow traversed the crimson-coloured cloth you had wrapped her in!"

"Where may I play her, Demoran?" asked Eli now, as they left the table together. "Where would be the best place?"

Her brother reflected on the question for only a moment. Then he simply beckoned for her to follow him. They left the breakfast room, and Jizay joined them, coming in again from his conversations in the gardens and stables. All three now mounted the stairs to Eli's bedroom, where Róisín had been placed, still covered by the rich wine-red cloth of Indian cotton.

"We will bring her into the room which I call my Conversation Room, whose very name will reinforce the open channels of communication between you and our mother! And I think, as I have often held deep and private discourse with our father there too, it may retain some other layers of listening resonance in its acoustics."

Eli carried Róisín down the hallway, past the room where she had looked out from the balcony earlier and from there down the tower's winding passage-way. At length they arrived before a low door carved of dark wood, sculpted and inlaid, covered with repeated motifs of double-figures joined in pairs by knotted interlace or twirling acanthus leaves. There were humans or more probably fairy-folk, dogs and cats, horses and birds --- all face to face in couples, as if dancing in stately formation to some unheard music.

Brother and sister entered, together with Jizay, and Demoran indicated a place for the harp on a round rug of spiralling design, made from knobbly, thickly spun-wool. He lit several candles, for the room was quite dim and only one tiny, slim window with thick diamond-shaped panes allowed the scant light of day to filter in from the west.

As soon as Eli had removed the cloth from the harp, the small Golden Flower blazed with what seemed a greeting, or a laugh.

"Ah!" exclaimed Demoran, stepping back and admiring the bright Rose as well as the well-formed harp itself. "She is altogether lovely. A fitting gift, a bouquet of love, from a Prince to a Princess, or from a fairy to a human."

His tone became slightly more serious for a moment, and he added, "Eli, may I give you some brotherly advice?" Eli stood very still, regarding him. And she nodded.

"Please remember that, whatever words or promises were spoken by yourself and Finnir *before* your changeling-transformation, whatever declarations or preludes were played out by you long before your human experience in the hopes of becoming lovers in the future, you are now, *here and now*, Eli Penrohan. You are not yet again Mélusine, and you have but the sickle-moon light of her full-moon wisdom and judgement.

"I do not doubt that you and Finnir are sensible and careful," he added with a warm little laugh, "but you are in love. It is not a state of mind, or of heart, renowned for its common sense or its restraint! Of course, Finnir is very wise and very, very enchanted. I do not think he would lure you forward on a path that was as yet uneven or unclear, hidden by the fog which lies before your human feet. Love with your true and trusting heart, I would say, but do not open that heart fully nor plumb the depths of that love, as the human-woman you are today. Measure your steps in the dance, dear Moon-Dancer, so that they do not falter in haste or make you lose your equilibrium."

Eli nodded once more, a little less confidently, for she felt quite taken-aback by his words. But she smiled as he withdrew from the room, and she herself turned to Finnir's beautiful harp.

She had brought her shoulder-bag from her bedroom so as to have Lily's journal, the Silver Leaf still concealed between its pages, with her as well. She ran her hand along Róisín's gentle curves for a moment, and then emptied the contents of her bag onto a small, square, prettily-tiled table not far from the harp.

Lily's notebook, the Silver Leaf, Reyse's white rose covered in impossible dew-drops, the bamboo phial, and the moonstone on its grey cord. All these she extracted from the satchel, and arranged on the table. But in the bag was another item. Eli glanced at Jizay, who was sitting behind Róisín and who had cocked his head sideways. He barked once, and then emitted a low growl.

Soft and silky, made of what precious fabric or infinitely fine threads she could not guess, the article now tumbled out of the coarse-woven little shoulder-bag and was gently gathered up in Eli's hands .

It was a semi-transparent cloth, like a wide scarf or veil: mauve or lavender-blue in the warm candle-light. Eli fingered the soft fabric, and she heard Jizay's voice, hushed and deep, as if he were uttering words which were reverent and riddling, awful and holy, angry and questioning all at once.

"The Amethyst Cloth," were the words that came to Eli's ears, or heart, in Jizay's voice; but then they continued to vibrate and ring about the small room like a yodelling echo trailing off into silence.

And then another voice repeated Jizay's mute announcement: "Yes, here is the Amethyst Cloth. Or a part of it…"

It was a voice that Eli knew; a voice filled with pathos and poetry. At the sound of those words, the Cloth which Eli held in her hands slipped from her grasp and fell at her feet. She shuddered, bent and picked it up again, and examining it more carefully now, found that it was roughly torn across one side of its length. Was this how it has been when stolen, or had Erreig himself torn it asunder --- here, in this room?!

"*Erreig!*" The name was like an intake of breath or the clicking of a rusty key in an ancient and ornate lock. "Erreig," Eli repeated in an only slightly clearer voice than her first utterance. "I would recognise that voice anywhere. Was he here --- is he here still?"

Jizay had risen swiftly to his feet, approached his mistress and was now leaning his golden body against her leg, looking up into her questioning face. "He is gone, if indeed he was ever here. But I heard his voice clearly too. Play, play Finnir's harp, play *your* harp," he seemed to say. "Bring Rhynwanol here, now. She will know…"

Eli's hands were shaking, but she sat on the three-legged stool behind Róisín, placed the Silver Leaf on her left knee, and gently leaned the harp against her right shoulder. Jizay sat close beside her, his liquid brown eyes, so like a baby seal's, gazing up at his beloved mistress.

Eli played: an introductory arpeggio, the sweet and bell-like notes of an Irish air high on the treble octaves, a deep chord on the bass strings, another watery series of notes rising and falling… The candles flickered once, as if the door or window had been opened momentarily. And then they were steady and glowing very brightly again.

Eli looked at the Leaf, which was aligned with the Golden Flower on the top of the harp's curved front pillar. A silver light rose from the Leaf, a golden one descended from the Rose. And where they met a huge window opened before Eli, as if double doors made of silver and golden wood were being slowly pushed back.

They revealed an airy and well-lit room, large and richly decorated, with the sound of splashing coming from a small, shallow pool in its centre where a gurgle of water from a tilted amphora emptied into the beautiful basin from the edge of one of the surrounding pink tiles. On the settee facing her, which was a soft couch covered with rhododendron petals and hemmed with living fuchsia, sat Eli's mother, the Queen.

She was dressed in a deep purple and pale rose gown. Her black hair was glinting with gems of lilac-kunsite and tiny shells like stars; her lavender eyes --- too --- were sparkling as was the large amethyst pendant suspended from a cord of braided seaweed which encircled her waist. Eli turned her left hand over to look at her palm, which was tingling with heat. There in its centre was another amethyst, set directly into her flesh. As she looked, it shone out suddenly, and then disappeared back into her skin.

"Mélusine," intoned the twilight-breeze voice of Rhynwanol. "I am very glad that your slumbering form accepted our advice, that of Morliande and myself, and the Mauve Dragon. I am thankful that you did not pursue Erreig into the world, by ocean-paths and in phantom-form! But he felt your threatened voyage, as the Princess --- and he felt also that you were still in the world, as Eli, on Samhain Eve.

"My messengers, the great basking sharks and the green-eyed night-fishes whom I had sent into the Whale Race to join their pleas to those of Morliande --- the pleas that you remain --- returned swiftly to my shee and from there, in the darkest hours before dawn, I sent others of my servants into the Sheep's Head, in Ireland, to seek news of Erreig. These were nimble root-dwarves, well-accustomed to the dark of caves and under-tree-tunnels, and they are cousins to the leprechauns of all those regions about Gougane Barra. Alive the earth was with the movements of the Little People for Samhain! But the dwarves and leprechauns do not always remain underground, and their night-vision is as sharp as those of the kits of King Isck!

"They did not find Erreig, but they met with many bats who had indeed marked the passage of the Dragon-Lord through

Finnir's Portal, and had followed him. Oh, Mélusine, my servants tried to recover the Cloth, but without avail. Erreig eluded them all, for he knew you would seek it and his fear was urging him into folly --- as it is ever wont to do.

"I have learned, from my returning dwarves, coming back through the Portal near Ahakista's Stone Circle at mid-day yesterday, that Erreig sought you out, drawing near to the town of Inchigeelagh, in the county of Cork. But the Dragon-Lord is not at ease among humans, and has scant experience of the world of men. He could not approach more closely than the wild lands about Lough Allua, and so he lingered there all the night.

"Early in the morning, on the day of Samhain, he felt you approaching --- but not on foot, for you were travelling quickly and, as my dwarves tell me, protected from him by a moving metal construction. But it seems that you hesitated in your swiftness, and stopped for a moment beside the Lough.

"With the help of a common frog, for he could find no salamaders (his loyal accomplices in Quillir), he decided to place among your belongings a *part* of the Cloth. It is as if he wished to lure you towards him with this trickery, of course. But I will say more of that in a moment... Therefore, as your attention was captured elsewhere --- by a flock of ducks taking flight, I believe --- the frog entered the metal chariot you had left and slipped a 'gift' from Erreig into your satchel.

"He had torn the Cloth which he had stolen in *two*, my daughter. He left a portion of it, together with the echo of his voice, as a message to you --- to find when you would open your satchel."

Eli's right hand was still laid on the harp-strings as the Queen spoke. Now she emitted an anxious moan, regarding the torn Cloth visible on the little tiled-table just at the periphery of the room where the vision of Rhynwanol was presented to her.

"Mother, why did he steal it in the first place? And why has he taken it into the world? What must I do now? For he still has a part of the Cloth, and you say that he is trying to 'lure' me towards him...."

"As for your first question," began the Queen, shaking her head sadly, "he was sent by the Sage-Hermit, *not* to your Island vault, but to the gathering being held here at Castle Davenia that day in June, to honour the legend of Ævnad. He had been charged by the Hermit to come before King Aulfrin, at last --- and before the assembled company --- to seek a treaty of peace, to begin the discussions and negotiations for unity in this realm, and between others.

"He could not do it. His fear, his pride, his ego, they are all *so* weighty, and so disabling... The Sage-Hermit obviously had thought that he was ready, and why that is I cannot know. My guess is that it may have had something to do with the quest of Finnir and Brea to meet the Queen Morliande. But be that as it may, the Hermit's instructions were not carried out; and Erreig followed another prompting from his impetuous and wild heart. He flew to you, to Mélusine.

"Alas, he had learned, with the rumours of your home-coming Visits circulating throughout Faërie, of your adventure as a changeling; and it would appear that he thought to find your slumbering fairy-form more receptive, and less defensive, than the strong-willed Princess in her wakeful truth and power.

"Ah, Eli, his love is so very boisterous, rogue and reckless. Beware it, and his capricious behaviour! But be on guard not only as regards his 'love', for his *fear* is by far greater --- and much more dangerous.

"Once inside your vault (and by what charms he penetrated that hallowed place puzzles me still), his plans faltered and failed, for your chrysalis-form arose before his very eyes and challenged his presence there, as you know. Amazing that, and yet I am aware that you acquired many mysterious skills during the Great Charm --- as is evidenced by such a feat. And thus, unable to approach you or to cajole you into some longed-for promise of union with him in the future (yes, I know well that he desires that), he fled with a part of your shroud. What a brazen act on his part, for this could have been deadly! As he must have known.

"But your father's father, Aulfrelas, the Sage-Hermit, recalled him to Star Island immediately, for he had perceived the theft of the Cloth. On Star Island, the Amethyst Cloth would be, at least, under the eyes and the protection of the Hermit. Thus you were drawn out of a great danger; though a lesser danger still remained, while the Cloth was not in its correct place with you. But more than that, even the Hermit could not accomplish: for none may touch the shroud of a chrysalis-fairy but the fairy herself, or the guardians and attendants at the time of her transformation. How Erreig himself was able to do so, without causing you great and immediate harm, is baffling --- and that he *dared* to is altogether distressing to me!

"There on Star Island, Erreig was himself imprisoned, and his life suspended --- for no fairy may step freely onto the Island of the Hermit, except the Hermit himself or the Hermit-to-be, or his immediate kin, and this latter only in great need and with his express permission and invitation. But Erreig, by his felony and in payment for his theft, forfeited his life-force and his spirit, fading into a phantom-fairy much like that which he beheld on the Island of the Owls: a being suspended between waking-life and dream-death, as you are upon your bed of mauve crystal.

"As the weeks passed, the spell of the Hermit relaxed ever-so-slightly, and on Samhain Eve --- so magical a point in the seasons of the year --- it seems that Erreig found a tiny chink in the spell's strength and, using perhaps his own magic or talents or the triple-force charms of the ruby he bears, he escaped, aided by Bawn and others of his servants, I believe. He flew to the Portal of Barrywood, somehow knowing that you had determined to enter Faërie at twilight by that doorway. Did he plan to confront you, in a weaker form than that of the slumbering Princess, as a human-changeling? Did he seek to hinder your passage or to do you harm, or to beg or seduce…? I wonder, did he think to lure you to the heart of the Unicorn Glens --- a place that is weighted with peril for you, as Mélusine. We, none of the wise, are sure. But he was countered in his plans, whatever they were, by Finnir and by my dear Timair.

"Now Finnir's magic is very great and so also is his wisdom: the Portal was held against Erreig and you were advised to delay in your returning here --- though alas, Erreig's out-riders and his mighty dragon drew the Guardian away. But panic was his pursuer as much as the two royal fairies, and in his terror and confusion --- it seems, though perhaps it was his intention --- he stepped *through* the Portal into Gougane Barra, just after midnight. And the Amethyst Cloth went with him. Bawn, so we have learned, refused to accompany him. She bolted and fled, though we are not certain where.

"For the space of a few hours that night both you (as Eli) and the Cloth were on the same side of the Portal, the human side; and this small piece of your protecting shroud was in the hands of Erreig, not far from you.

"At the moment when the Cloth left this realm of Faërie, Mélusine, though sleeping in enchantment, drew her spirit out of her slumbering form, for she desired to seek Erreig in the world and to retrieve the Cloth. She proposed to confront him and challenge him, there, as a ghost: a sleep-walking and shadowy vibration of her empty body left on the Island. Inscribed in such a charm --- and it is a very daring one --- is the effect that you, her human changeling-form, would absorb, little by little, her true life-force. If she could return before dawn, she could re-enter her sleeping fairy-body. If not, she would come to exist *only* in you, as a human. It is a very dangerous spell to use, and very rash. Ah, well, that is very like you!

"But Mélusine hoped, it is clear, to gain a *swift* victory over Erreig in the phantom-projection of herself which he had already glimpsed for one terrifying moment: at last formally and finally abasing him, I suppose. So, at her call and command, the Mauve Dragon went forth to meet her ghost in order to bear her through the seas, along the routes used by the mer-folk, into Bantry Bay.

"But the Queen Morliande appeared in the Whale Race Sound and vehemently counselled against this desperate project, as did Banvowha and my own basking-sharks and fishes. They spoke with the Mauve Dragon, there in the waters of the Sound, who thereby came to see their wisdom and so went to meet the wraith of Mélusine on the shore of the Cusp of the Heart Cockles in order to stop her, rather than to aid her. The Dragon convinced the wraith to return to her bier. We must be grateful for that, and impressed --- for it is not an easy thing to counter the will of the Princess Mélusine!

"I do not know if the great mermaid, ever your counsellor and guide in your transformation, was in accord with the interdiction of the ancient Queen and the rainbow-fairy --- for she was not present, or not yet arrived. All we know is that, at the last minute, Mélusine abandoned her 'voyage'. However, as you now know, a part of the Cloth is still in the hands of Erreig --- and it is in the human lands.

"But another plan has been proposed, my dear Eli; and I must present it to you now, and hope that your courage and resolve will be equal to its accomplishment.

"You are a *violet-fairy*, as Mélusine, and this is why you are wrapped in cloths of mauve; and as such, you possess certain remarkable powers. Normally these powers belong only to the true-fairy, as do the skills you evidently gained in your Great Charm; but unlike the graces acquired in those three-hundred-and-thirty-three years of intense study, it is possible for the human-changeling to access her *violet-fairy nature*, under certain circumstances. Assistance is required, and charms and tokens.

But it is possible. And with the blessings of that fairy-nature, the changeling can do **wonders**.

"Thus, all three of your mothers, whom you saw together when last you looked through the Leaf, are in agreement now. Morliande and myself, we have been convinced by the faith which Lily has in you, in <u>you as Eli</u>. For it was Lily who persuaded us, declaring:

Allow **Eli** *to seek and reclaim the Cloth in the human world, and to confront the Dragon-Lord as the human woman she has grown into; for fifty years of life in that world have rendered her strong and resolute, great-hearted and filled with light, equal or surpassing the force of Erreig's confused desires, his fears, his rash and selfish plots. She will find the Cloth, and she will know why he has acted thus, and she will learn the truth of what he is, as well as testing her knowledge of who and what she is herself.*

"Lily is very wise, Eli, and so are you. And she is right, you are grown strong, both as violet-fairy and as woman. Your destiny is approaching, as regards Barrywood and the Unicorn Glens, as regards Finnir, as regards the great work of the Alliance and your own sacrifice and the realisation of what you have so fervently desired, designed and planned for many centuries now. But this crime of Erreig's is threatening all you have put into motion. You are not yet Mélusine again, but I agree with Lily, you have some great deed to accomplish *as Eli*, before your changeling-adventure draws to a close. Lily will not leave until it is achieved. She will protect you.

"And so we join with her now in urging you to step back across the threshold and find Erreig.

"Will you go, before the Moon is new and hidden, while there is still time? For when the night of the New Moon arrives, the peril will be too great, we deem, for you to pass between the worlds on such a quest. We all see the opportunity for you to go forth in order to find and confront Erreig *before* that date, for you will have need of the Moon. Will you go, now, and return with the missing part of the Amethyst Cloth, to restore its wholeness and return it to the Island of the Owls? Only you, yourself, may do this --- or the thief, of course. But it is not desirable that Erreig return to the Island of the Scholar Owls! Therefore, it is for *you* to replace the Cloth upon your own sleeping form: thus Mélusine will not be weakened and you, as Eli, not robbed of your fairy-nature."

****

Aulfrin pushed open the small, thick door covered with decorations of conversing couples. He found the room very dark, for the candles had burned low and most had gone out and though it was mid-day there was practically no sunlight passing through the thick, diamond-panes of the small window.

Eli had returned the Silver Leaf to its place in Lily's little journal. And possibly because of the dimity of the room, the King failed to see the Golden Flower on Róisín's brow. In fact, Eli herself would have had difficulty to see it, for it was dull and unremarkable, blending into the faint blond hue of the wood from which the harp was made.

What her father did see was Eli, sitting with her head bowed, very still beside her harp, and Jizay standing alert at her side as if 'on duty' to protect her --- his ears redressed and pointy, his deep brown eyes the brightest things in the room. And in Eli's lap was the Amethyst Cloth, or rather half of it.

Aulfrin walked slowly to his daughter, and placed a firm but tender hand on her shoulder. She did not look up.

"I thought it was Clare that you had brought into Faërie, with Finnir's help and approval, in order to have insight while you were here," he said, softly and with such warmth in his tone that tears began to trickle down Eli's cheeks. "I only saw the harp, covered, tied by a length of scarf to the neck of your flying-steed. But now Demoran has told me, and so has the Lady Ecume whom I met in the northern seas: your half-brother, the Prince Finnir, has gifted you with this new instrument. A healing harp, and a harp of vision."

At his words, Eli glanced up into his face. It should have been almost invisible in this light, but the emeralds in his filigree silver crown were pulsing with a green glow, as if they were breathing very deeply. Her father's features were bathed in their colours; he looked as though he were standing in the shade of a leafy forest on a summer's day. By the term he had used for Finnir, Eli realised that he still had no notion that they were *not* related, she and her love; but she did not detect any remonstration in his remark, either --- for why should a brother not give his sister a harp?

Aulfrin continued. "And with this enchanted harp, made of Irish wood rather than Faërie-wood as I learned, you have been able to see and hear your mother, more clearly and more directly than you were able to do in her Music Room in the City of Fantasie."

Eli nodded, and then looked back down into her lap. Aulfrin sighed.

"Yes, I understand what she has asked of you, for the Lady Ecume had just arrived at the shore of the Island of the Owls, and we both learned of Mélusine's summons of the Dragon-Dame, her mauve and mystical worm-friend. The great mer-harper assured me that the Black Key would not, now, be needed --- as I had presumed it might, if Mélusine had been truly 'departed'. But though that fear was abated, another challenge presented itself in what I learned then.

"For now I know, not only that this 'Harp of Barrywood', as they named it, has allowed you to converse with Rhynwanol, but that you have somehow come into possession of the Cloth stolen by Erreig --- and that *before* you left the human lands. When I arrived here in Castle Davenia, it was Ferglas who told me what he had sensed, even from his place at Demoran's side while you and Jizay were here: that the Dragon-Chieftain's voice was heard in this room, telling you that the Cloth is *torn in two.* So, he has returned to you only a tantalizing *half* of the Cloth.

"Even as merely the lingering echo of a voice he is insolent! Mischievous and cunning, and quite powerful --- but wholly insolent. " Aulfrin shook his head in disgust before continuing.

"And now, instead of the Princess Mélusine re-awakening or voyaging in a ghost-form to confront Erreig, it is clear to me what my wife the Queen has come to you to propose. She has asked *you*, as Eli, to go back into the world and seek for the missing part of the Cloth, has she not? To depart from Faërie once again, even now when your third Visit is in its very earliest days, to retrieve that portion of your vital and protective shroud?"

Eli made no reply, but there was an unspoken affirmation in her silence.

The King sighed again, more audibly and profoundly. Walking to the chimney-piece and then around the room to one or two nooks and to a largish table, he lit the candles by renewing their heights and kindling a flame atop each one, using his outstretched hands. Eli watched him, as she brushed her own hands over her cheeks to wipe away her tears.

Her magical, wondrous father returned to face her, sitting on a chair which seemed to displace itself across a part of the timber floor to arrive in place just as he bent his knees. Eli had to smile. And the King smiled back.

The room was filled with a gentle light now, and Eli felt less cold than she had done. She shrugged her shoulders with a hint of a laugh escaping her lips.

"I don't feel very brave, just at the moment," she admitted. "It seems to me a very dangerous and lonely mission, to seek out Erreig, a phantom-fairy who seems intent on causing trouble, and face him with no weapon and no champion beside me to challenge him, and take back the missing part of the Cloth he stole. He'll do all he can to hinder me, I'd imagine, won't he?"

"Interesting that you think of being weapon-less and alone," commented the King, after only an instant's reflection. "As regards the first of those fears, do you not recall how your courage rose when you learned that he had stolen the Cloth on the sacred Day of Ævnad? You said then that perhaps it could give *you* an advantage over *him*, rather than the other way around. In that way, it might be considered as your own, personal, *secret-weapon* against him --- if you actually think that *weapons* are a good way to resolve conflict, that is!"

He winked at Eli as he added this, and she raised her eyebrows.

"And as for not having a 'champion' with you, it's just *that* which I had thought of proposing, if you decide to go on this quest. I think it would be very wise to have --- well maybe not exactly a *champion*, if you mean by that a knight-in-shining-armour --- but perhaps a *companion*. Knights, you know, can be cumbersome accomplices: they look so threatening, and they creak and rattle a good deal too --- all that metal-mongery!"

Eli was laughing outright now, and Aulfrin was smiling to see her more relaxed.

"I was thinking more along the lines of your 'hound of joy'; **joy** being by far a more effective…hmm….*weapon* than, well, than a weapon. If you understand me."

"Jizay can come with me?!" Eli's voice was that of a child promised an undreamt-of and luxurious Christmas present. Her hound of joy, himself, was already barking and jumping in place.

"You would need to go soon," added the King, a little less jovially. "The Owls and the wise Mer-Harper all agree that you should not be confronting Errieg when there is no moon-light at all."

"Yes, the Queen told me that as well, though I don't exactly understand why."

"Quite simply, because you are a Moon-Dancer, even when you are a human," said her father. "And Erreig is a Sun-Singer.

Back and Forth

If there is no moon, he will have an advantage that might equal yours, your advantage of having the Amethyst Cloth."

"But *he* has the Amethyst Cloth, not me…at least not *all* of it, yet!"

"Yes, but that's the whole point, my darling girl. He has a part of you, of your energy, of your magic as Mélusine, in his possession. Because of that, you can find him and feel him, you can perceive dimensions of how he is playing his game in a way that you could not without it *in your opponent's hands*. But you need strength and *moon*-music and *moon*-light. And for those you need the Moon. And for friendship and encouragement and unquestionable love, you'll have Jizay."

The golden hound barked again, and Eli wrapped her arms around his neck --- just the right height from where she sat --- and kissed his furry head.

But it did seem strange to her that, even in the generous candle-light that now filled the room, the Rose atop her harp was no longer visible and did not respond to these plans in any way.

"And may I take the Harp of Barrywood," asked Eli, looking up at her father, who was now standing to invite her to go with him, presumably downstairs to find Demoran. Eli put the torn Cloth into her woven satchel, where her others treasures were already stored, and hung it over her shoulder.

The King looked very intently into her turquoise-green eyes, and inclined his head a little as he replied.

"That's an idea. Do you think to use her for healing, or for vision? Or will your brother Finnir be with you in that way, if not as a knight-in-shining-armour at least as a prince-in-a-harp?"

Eli hesitated. Not because she wished to avoid her father's line of thought, but because she didn't really know herself.

"I think for a means of *communication*. Yes, I think I would like the harp with me in order to see and hear my mother again, if I feel it necessary."

The King wore an expression that was difficult to define.

"I would have kept the Harp of Barrywood safe for you, in my Music Room in the Silver City, had you not asked to take it with you. And I would have probably hoped for the same thing from her. To see and speak with Rhynwanol again."

His voice was very hushed, almost as if the words were meant *not* to be heard at all.

He and Eli left the Conversation Room, with Jizay. As they closed the door behind them, all the candles died down and silently went out, and the only light in the room was that of Róisín: for the Golden Flower was blazing now as if she were made of pure sunlight.

****

When Eli and her father had descended one flight of stairs and entered the great Dining-Hall where Demoran awaited them for a meal that could have been described as a High Tea --- for it was the dark and stormy middle of the afternoon by now --- they found that he was not alone.

Not only was Ferglas with him, rather expectedly, but Periwinkle was there as well. Eli was delighted.

As all six of the company settled themselves around the table (or nearby on the rush-woven carpet, in the case of the hounds), Aulfrin addressed them.

"Yes, my arrival and Periwinkle's coincided: me flying back from the Island of the Owls, he from Fantasie and the Great Trees. I must admit that I monopolised the conversation at that point, relating what I had learned from the Lady Ecume about the Mauve Dragon, and I apologise my dear Piv." The pixie inclined his head graciously, accepting the King's kind words and also filling his mouth with another slice of cake as he bowed, having begun his 'high tea' as soon as he was seated.

The King continued, "Demoran and Ferglas have, I trust, brought you up-to-date on all that we know, Master

Periwinkle?" Piv nodded, his mouth once again full, very solemnly.

"So now," continued Aulfrin, "we must discuss, together, how we may organise the days ahead. Tomorrow, the moon will be a delicate 'lash', and she will rise a couple of hours before dawn. I think this would be an excellent moment for Eli to pass back into the world, for she would have the sickle above her for most of the day --- possibly invisible to humans, for it will be very slim and very faint, but it will be there. Thereafter, only two full days remain until that 'moon-lash' becomes a closed eye and, as I have explained to her, I think it would be well if she returned before that dark moment of the New Moon. At least, she should not be on the threshold *between* the worlds at such a time."

Demoran had been looking, with great compassion, at his sister's face. It was not anxious, but it was not entirely serene either. He smiled, as if he could see the two complementary aspects of her character dancing hand-in-hand, neither one too sure which was leading the other. There was Eli, a strong-willed and resourceful and resilient human --- though still harbouring hurts and doubts from her life in that challenging world; and there also was the Princess Mélusine, who in her already long life had been courageous and defiant at times and at others deeply introspective and contemplative, but ever an enchanted and royal fairy, confident and filled with unquenchable joy. How interesting that her changeling experience was now presenting her with this unique and ambitious quest, as much a trial and rite-of-passage as had been her Initiations or even the Great Charm itself.

Eli caught her brother's eye and seemed to see these thoughts there, or feel them joining with her own.

"And by what Portal should Eli pass back into the world," Demoran asked, not taking his eyes off his sister.

Piv shook his green-caped little head before the King could answer. "No, no," he said, now wagging a small, empathic finger at no one in particular, "she can't use a Portal at all. Not this one of the fine Prince Dem's, the Fair Stair, leading to France; not that of Finnir for when she passes back through *that* she has concluded her third Visit and cannot ever come back here --- because that's the one she used to *enter* Faërie; and the Portal of Dawn Rock is very far from us here and is very, very far from where the Dragon-Lord is lurking, for he went through the Heart Oak into Ireland. No, she can't use a Portal at all."

Aulfrin looked with his customary deep respect at the tiny pixie, now burying his face in a frothy bowl of creamy-sweet tea that he had lifted with both hands, it was so large. The King's respect was mingled, however, with perplexity.

"You're quite right, Periwinkle," he agreed. "I had not thought of that, strangely enough. She could go by boat, taking the mermaid's sea-road, as Mélusine had planned to do on her sea-dragon. Do you think that would be best?"

Piv replaced his bowl of tea, half-emptied, on the table and flew once around the room, his lime-green wings blurring and his head cocked to one side as if he were considering and weighing the possibilities.

"I don't think a changeling can," he sighed, returning almost to his place, to sit cross-legged on the table-cloth rather than on his chair. "During her third Visit, she can't go back across the outer-borders, even the sea-frontiers. I'm sure it's not allowed --- though only the Sage-Hermit would know for certain. But I've never heard of such a thing. The mer-folk and the silkies, they can use the sea. But when humans use it, they are usually already dead; or, at least, they will never be seen among living humans again. Such is the fate of the sailors that follow the music of the harpers and sirens, the mermaids with flowing hair and eyes of doom. She might be able to *leave* like that, but she couldn't come back that way, if you ask me."

"I think Piv is right there too," said Demoran, and the King nodded as well.

"Yes," he affirmed, "it is true. Only when they have drowned, or passed through the doors of death by other means, can the humans come to Faërie by any of her sea-passages, unless they are led here by a mermaid with...other intentions."

Eli looked wide-eyed at her father as he pronounced these words. She was recalling what she had learned of Lily's visit, sailing from Bantry Bay in the enchanted boat of the 'Lady Sea-Foam'. Their little moon was not dead then...but neither was she a changeling; and it was, indeed, a very unique invitation, for Lily was not entirely 'human' in any case. But was he *also* alluding to her own proposed or pre-destined sea-route, as foretold to her by the Queen Morliande and by the ancient mermaid as well, to return to Faërie after her own human death by the perilous Fourth Portal, by the Garnet Vortex? Did he know about that?

But she did not make any remark, nor had she the opportunity to do so, for Piv was proposing a solution. Or at least, he was reciting words that Eli already knew, as if they provided the answer:

Here am I on threshold bright,
On one side the cup of light,
On the other berries black,
Hesitating I look back,
Night and light and moon and sun,
Sip my wine and all is one!

"The Seventh Gate of the Silver City," he announced, as if its riddling-rhyme gave a clear explanation of what could be done. Eli did not see, at all, what he was suggesting.

"Wineberry, yes..." acquiesced the King, seeming to comprehend what Piv, or the enigmatic verse, was pointing to.

"Indeed, there may be an answer in the rhyme of the mysterious Gate in relation to our dilemma. *Night and light and moon and sun*. Yes, yes! If she is willing, that could work. Do you think she would agree?"

"Do you think I would agree to *what*?" asked the bewildered Eli.

Aulfrin turned from Piv to smile at his daughter. "Not *you*, my dear girl; I meant Wineberry. If *she* would agree to let you pass, while there is 'night and light and moon and sun', as there is in the final days of the waning crescent, then you could use that 'threshold bright'. But it must be done with her permission and at her decree, for the Seventh Gate opens into many lands besides the plains to the south-west of the Silver City. Yes, many strange and alien lands, known and unknown. She would have to agree to lead you into the human world, and close to where Erreig now is. And to bring you back again.

"We could indeed request this of her. We should go to Fantasie this evening," concluded the King.

Piv looked very pleased with himself, especially as he added, "I've been to the Inner Garden, and to the ring of the blue flowers, and all along the mushroom threads and thoroughfares I've heard the voice of Rhadeg and of Bram --- Mélusine's friends, and wondrous wise friends those Great Trees are to have, as any would say! And *they* told me that they would help my little Eli 'in her mission' --- so they must have known about it already! And they said that the Stones know too, that she will need special help, and they've been conversing, back and forth, in the Chamber of the Seven Arches, thinking about what could be done. For they know that the Cloth was taken, and they seem to know a lot about Erreig too --- for I could hear his name being whispered, but the fungi spoke in their own mouldy, mulchy tongue then. At least, I understood that the Trees would help Eli, and that the Stones also want her to go on some sort of *quest*. It must be *this* quest! And I think it quite clear that Wineberry will say 'yes', because Rhadeg is the *third* Tree and Bram the *fourth*, as they count criss-crossing across the central-source, and three and four make *seven*, and so I think that Wineberry will be very pleased to help too. You see?!"

All were laughing now, even the dogs. But Ferglas at last rose and shook himself, making his sea-shell collar dance and jiggle.

"Let us go then, for it will not be easy to fly or run against this wind. Let us hasten to the silver-turrets of Fantasie, you by air and Jizay and myself by land, and ask the Seventh Gate to give her blessing and aid to our Lady Eli."

Agreeing with the wise blue wolf-hound, they all stood to leave.

"Am I to fly with my own wings, or on Peronne?" asked Eli of her father.

"I do not think your wings would be as strong as those of your flying-horse, not in this storm and with the scant practice you've had with them so far. You will be back in a day or two, and there remains plenty of time for you to enjoy them then. I hope," ended the King, not offering quite as much reassurance with his words or tone of voice as Eli would have liked.

"I will get …your harp," offered Demoran, pointedly not using her name, Eli realised. It seemed clear that Aulfrin was not meant to see the Silver Leaf or the Golden Rose, or to know that they had come to his daughter from the twins of his Queen. Just as with the name "Timair", or those of the twins, it was obviously best not to use the name Róisín…

As her brother mounted the stairs to the Conversation Room, and Aulfrin pulled on his long, dark green cape and fastened it with the obsidian-broach, Eli looked down at Jizay. They exchanged a few silent words.

"It's all becoming very complicated," was Eli's comment to her dear dog. "I'm so glad you're coming with me."

"Ferglas and I will outrun the storm, my sweet mistress, and I will be there in good time to step across the 'threshold bright', between the 'cup of light' and the 'black berries'. I am glad to be coming with you also, and to be beside you --- although I cannot sip, in your place, the wine --- for that is reserved for you only, I think."

Eli looked with a puzzled glance at her hound of *joy*, wishing she felt more of that lovely 'excuse for a weapon' than she did at the moment. Demoran passed her, carrying Róisín, covered in her wine-dark cotton cloth, out to the stables. As he reached the doors at the far-end of the long Entrance Hall he turned and winked at her, the blue tourmalines in his ears glinting for a moment in the faint glimmer of fading daylight that coloured the sky.

Feeling somehow comforted, Eli swung her own long blue cloak around her shoulders, covering her shoulder-bag and holding it close against her.

"*To the silver turrets of Fantasie I must turn again my wind-horse feet...*"she whispered, under her breath. *To the arms of my moon and my sun.*

"**My** sun? I wonder what *that* means," Eli added, almost speaking aloud.

"May I ride with you, Eli-een?" Piv asked brightly, flying back in from the open door where he had accompanied Demoran to the stables. "And, to respond to that rather odd question," he whispered in her ear, "that's your motto, the writing over your bier on Scholar Owl Island --- as you've seemingly forgotten! You claimed that you were both Moon-Dancer *and* Sun-Singer, and so you wrote that, saying you would be held in both their loving arms. Oh, you never told the dear King your father *that* --- but me, I saw the words!

"And now he's been to your vault I suppose, to meet with the Owls and to make sure that his sleeping Mélusine was alright and not troubled in her slumber --- so he's most likely seen it too, the writing you wrote there above your crystal bed, in your pretty calligraphy:

> *Return Gypsy, Princess, Artist, Queen ---*
> *Your tears are the source of the rainbow's sheen;*

Through spiralling waters when all is won
To the loving embrace of both Moon and Sun.

"But I wonder if he understands it. Ah, perhaps not yet. But he will, when you come back."

Eli wished that *she* did. In any case, she and Piv joined the King now, already mounted on Cynnabar and awaiting them just down the steps. Demoran helped his sister to mount, as Peronne was rather laden already, with both harp and pixie.

"May all the blessings of the Dappled Woods go with you, little sister," he said, smiling, "and those of the Moon-Dancers and all those fairies who drink from the Cup of Light."

Eli's expression was no less perplexed than it had been earlier, but her brother's voice seemed to convey such a rich benediction, far beyond what she could yet glean from his words, that she found she was smiling, and feeling much lighter in heart.

More rain-clouds were racing up from the south-west and covering the washes of pinks and blues painting the twilight sky. Aulfrin and Eli, with Piv leaning forward over Peronne's blowing mane, trotted their winged-mounts up the garden's pathway to the north, rising on the hands of the wind and then turning full-circle above the Dappled Woods and the Red Triskel Lake before increasing their speed and their altitude to fly to the Silver City before nightfall and the breaking of the gathering storm.

****

Windy Hill Prayer

Chapter Eight:
Miraculous Music

espite their urgency and the strength of the mighty wings of both Peronne and Cynnabar, the high flight to Aumelas-Pen took the better part of three hours. The wind increased to a gale, pushing against them from the south-east; and its breath was strangely chill, even for early November. On two occasions, they were forced to alight in the rolling fields or among the white stones of the upper heaths, just to draw breath. It was well past sunset, the sky so black that it seemed deep mid-night, when they at last arrived within sight of the Silver City, its dark outer ring of proud trees and the twinkling lights in the many windows of the King's Moon Tower a welcome sight to all five of the travellers.

Beyond the lofty grey silhouettes of the silver-turreted towers and the many slanting roofs of the royal residence were the pulsating and glowing mists around the Great Trees, in shades of cranberry-red, deep yellow and tender pink, with occasional tiny scintillating-flashes of electric blue or green. Above the colourful ring of the interlaced branches rose the heads of the Seven Trees, never entirely dark for they were always inhabited by patterns of shimmering light, like the stars shining in lovers' eyes.

Eli felt a sudden, overwhelming desire to fly straight towards one of the Trees, that to the north-east of the ring. It was one of the two which had already captured her attention on her last

Visit; one of the two with whom she had enjoyed a privileged and mysterious 'friendship' in her fairy-youth. She recalled his name: Rhadeg. The other was Bram, further down the western side of the circle of great beings.

Peronne felt her urging him to fly on, past the King's Tower, to the Tree; he whinnied and shook his great head once or twice in his flight, clearly replying that he could *not* bear her thither, but that they must land in the high courtyard of the King's Palace. Piv evidently could feel Eli's desire too, for he called to her, his tiny piccolo-voice almost lost in the roaring wind: "He is longing to talk with you too, my Eli-een, surely; I can feel him calling out to you! But we must go down, and not to the Great Trees, not yet."

Decidedly against her will, if not her reason, Eli nodded her agreement and Peronne circled downwards like a cork-screw, still managing to land gracefully and gently in the wide courtyard just beside Cynnabar. Eli dismounted and untied Róisín from her place against her steed's neck. The harp felt very light and airy in her arms, almost as light as its Indian-cotton covering in fact.

"These wild winds are coming from Quillir," commented the King as the horses trotted away to the far balustrade to leap off again into the air --- only for a moment --- and find their stables beside the diamond-shaped Entrance Court at ground-level. Aulfrin and Eli, with Piv flying low over the ground and into the open doorway even before the King, passed under the arch of blowing vines and tousled ivy which seemed to be desperately clinging to the trellises and grey walls about the door.

There had been no rain on their flight, but that might have been more gay and less exhausting than the tempestuous winds. Attendant fairies took the King's and Eli's cloaks, and then the three breathless travellers made their way along the winding corridor and up the stairs to the great Council Chamber with its Seven Arches. In the huge room, with its soaring and glass-less windows, the candles spluttered slightly in their brackets and in the swaying lamps hanging from the vaulted ceiling; but the wind seemed to have less power here than one would have expected. Eli placed her harp against one of the pillars of a side-alcove, and finally she began to breathe normally again.

Indeed, she found that the Seven Arches rendered the room calm and welcoming, protecting it from at least some of the intensity of the storm. It was possible, also, she thought, that it represented a final place of sanctuary and repose --- if only briefly --- in her own mind, from what lay ahead for her. She understood that she would be expected to pass through the Seventh Gate, Wineberry, in the early hours of the morning to come. She was not wavering in her resolve, only feeling very tired and just a little apprehensive about her quest to meet with the Dragon-Lord.

Aulfrin called for a warming quince-brandy to be served to himself and Eli, and a cup of less potent mulled-pear-wine for Periwinkle. As they awaited the return of the attendants, the King reaffirmed his earlier remark.

"From Quillir, and more precisely, I think, these gales take their biting force from the Caves of the White Cats. I can hear the yowling of the great felines in them. The King Isck is seeking to protect his over-lord, Erreig, perhaps, by sending these doleful draughts to delay us!

"Though it's an unlikely scenario, for how could Isck have learned of our plans?" Then he added in a hushed voice, "Unless he, or others among Erreig's servants, came to the same conclusion as Master Periwinkle as to the best route back into the world for our brave Eli."

Piv received his mulled wine from the hands of the servant bearing the bejewelled oaken platter of drinks. He looked just a small bit disappointed to be missing the brandy, thought Eli. But when they were all three alone, once again, the pixie clinked his mug with Eli's pretty blown-glass globe of golden liquor.

"Here's to the wise Cat, then," said Piv, unexpectedly. Both Aulfrin and Eli looked at him with raised eyebrows. "For he's a good friend to the true children of Faërie, both the Singers and the Dancers, those of the Moon *and* the Sun, and I agree with you, my darling Majesty, that it's probably that kingly Cat who has sent the storm --- to tell Eli to wait another day."

"Do you, indeed, Periwinkle," replied Aulfrin. "And what makes you think that?"

"Well, what Isck can know and how he's learned it, that's as much a mystery to me as it is to you both. But I'll say this: he has a great and grand family, and all his kits have wise whiskers that can read and interpret much that is said and much more that is not. He's a mighty and magical Cat, but he's not so malicious as some of the legends recount. And I think maybe he's sent us a stormy-message to say: *Allow Eli to rest for this night and not leave on this adventure in a risky-rush, for she will need her wits about her and her wakefulness and her wide-eyed energy and quick reflexes.*

"And he's right," Piv continued, "for she's had quite a day already, and to go back into the very-much-odder-than-here world of humankind, with only an hour or two of sleep…well, a fairy could perhaps do that, but a human-girl could not. She has **two** further nights to go before the one when the Moon has closed her bright eye to sleep like a new-born babe; and I think my little Eli should do *her* baby-sleeping *tonight*. She'll be better prepared and better advised, rested and ready, to set forth in the deep dark of tomorrow's night, and there'll still be the very tiniest of a moon-lash left. And that's all she needs to have the strength to pass through."

The King considered these remarks as he sipped his brandy.

"I wonder if you are not every bit as wise as the Smiling Salmon himself, my dear Periwinkle," he said at last. "But will you do me a service, if you are not too tired yourself, and fly to the Blue Flower Garden and inquire if the Trees have more insight to give us on this matter? I would go myself, but I would rather remain closer to Eli --- though I will certainly go to confer with my harp, in order to confirm Wineberry's willingness and to have some deeper counsel as well. But I would be glad to have your further help and the Trees' approval of such a delay. I think they will agree with what you have said, though, for it *rings with rightness*, as the saying here goes."

"I will, my darling King, and I'll be back as swift as a stripy bee, to keep my Eli-een company while you play and listen to your royal harp." With that, Piv drained his cup and clapped it happily on the table, rose into the air, and whizzed out into the darkness beyond one of the southern arches.

The wind seemed, already, to have died down considerably; at least within the oval of Fantasie it was much quieter now. The candles were burning calmly and casting a lovely, warm glow over the huge Council Chamber.

With the increased clarity in the vast room, parts of it were illuminated which had been in semi-darkness a moment ago. One of these was the alcove where Reyse had slept when guarding Eli, and where he had played his *vielle* to her from his hammock stretched between two of the pillars. A cloaked figure was standing by one of those pillars now, just beside a fluted column marking the entrance to the alcove, and Eli gave a little exclamation of hope. She was sure it was Reyse.

But even as she started and called out, she knew she was in error. Her heart told her that he was far, far away. She and the King looked with curiosity at the figure, and it was clear that this was someone of lesser height than the Lord Reyse, and also of a feminine grace.

Aulfrin, probably aware immediately of who was there, was smiling as Eli glanced at him and then back to the advancing form. As the figure approached, Eli saw that the cloak was cobalt blue and embroidered with sprays of lavender and tiny white moth-motifs. She smiled too, even before the small, delicate hands were lifted to pull back the hood and uncover the lovely face.

"Brocéliana!" she enthused, "Oh, how good to see you again!"

Her half-sister was beside them now, and bowed her head slightly to her father, who lifted a loving hand to caress her flushed cheek. He added his greeting.

"My dear girl, yes, it is very good to see you --- for I have not done so since Eli's last Visit either. But what brings you here to Fantasie, alone and unannounced and silently lurking in alcoves?!"

"I am not alone, my dear father, but I had not the possibility of seeking your permission to bring someone with me here. I am hoping you will not be annoyed with our coming… together."

The King smiled. "Join us, and be welcome, Garo! I should have invited you to Fantasie myself, and many weeks ago at the least. But I was….occupied elsewhere. I now invite you *and* welcome you in one breath!"

From the alcove, Garo stepped forward to join Brocéliana.

"Thank you, my Sovereign," said the young dragon-lordling, bowing low with his hand over his heart.

The King requested that his servants prepare extra places for the couple at his supper-table, in the adjoining and intimate dining-room. He smiled warmly --- surprisingly warmly, Eli noted --- at the young lovers.

"You will both sup with us? We had planned to be somewhat on the rush, but as I'm sure you overheard, our agenda has seemingly relaxed now. We will have the time to talk a little before going to our beds, perhaps."

Eli continued to feel relieved and somewhat amazed by her father's welcome to Garo; even to the point of his remarking on the fact that the foregoing conversation had obviously been overheard, and making the remark without the slightest edge of effrontery in his tone.

"But," he continued, "it puzzles me that you should be admitted to this, of all rooms, to present yourselves to me; I don't mind, but it is rather, well, unprecedented!"

"I come from the Stone Circle, my Liege," responded the sandy-haired fairy, whose eyes were exactly the same colour as Brocéliana's cloak and glowing with intelligence and good-humour in equal doses. "It was the Stones themselves who urged me to bring Brocéliana, awaiting me at the Great Gates, directly to this your impressive and well-protected Chamber of Counsel. I flew in by one of the arches (so as not to be detained by your guards), while Brocéliana mounted the stairs. The Stones knew of the Lady Eli's arrival tonight, and of her proposed mission to seek for my father in the human-world. They gave me messages for both Your Majesty and for Eli, and they also indicated that your daughter Brocéliana would be safest here, in this blessed room. Naturally, since *you* are arrived, Your Majesty, anywhere in your palace and in your company will now assure her of protection."

"Is there some threat to her, because of Erreig?" Eli interrupted, unable to restrain herself in her concern for her sister.

Garo breathed deeply, and looked from Eli to the King.

He then turned back to Eli and said, "There is good reason to retain Brocéliana here, in this safest of all places in the kingdom of Faërie, yes. It is not Erreig that threatens her, but another who is, shall we say, uneasy that she and I have become acquainted. In any case, now that she is here, my heart is reassured and I know that no harm can come to my lovely lady. I felt a rather menacing force moving at will in Faërie during all of Samhain Eve; the Stones confirmed my apprehensions, urging me to lead Brocéliana to the King's Moon Tower, and into the King's company. I am honoured to be thus of service in guiding her here, and I will continue to protect her to the furthest extent of my powers --- just as you, Eli, are protected by those who love you."

Not understanding fully this somewhat 'formal' explanation, Eli nonetheless felt appeased and nodded to both her sister and the gallant Sun-Singer. Garo then redirected his discourse to the King, whose thoughtful expression was very difficult to interpret.

"Since my father so rashly stole the Amethyst Cloth, when I had the pleasure of sharing the festivities of Ævnad's Day with you in Davenia," began the beautiful Garo, his charming and rugged (but very noble) features as ever well-complemented, to Eli's taste, by the spar-sunstones dangling from his ear-lobes in their delicate casings of gold, "I have been trying to unravel certain strands of the tale."

"Well," nodded Aulfrin, "let us go in to the dining-room where we will shortly share a warming soup, and hear more of these strands of the story. I will be glad to have your insights, and Piv's too, when he returns. But I must leave you first, to consult my harp. Walk beside me and tell me what you will, or what you can, at least in brief. I will hear in full your messages from the Stones when I return. And we may have more time tomorrow, before Eli's passage back into the world."

Garo spoke as he walked beside the King, and the two sisters followed, arm in arm, behind them.

"After leaving Castle Davenia in June," Garo began, "I remained only a short while with Aytel, at the White Dragon Fortress, Your Majesty. He was swiftly borne back here to Fantasie, as you know, I suppose. He is, I imagine, now once again in his own dwelling, in Barrywood. But as for me, from the Beldrum Mountains I went immediately to the pine forests along the shores of Holy Bay. I was not permitted, nor have I ever been, to step onto Star Island. And so I conversed with my master the Sage-Hermit from the coast. He told me that my father had been detained *on* the Island --- which is extraordinary, to say the least. It seems that he was now in a phantom-form, but that he had not relinquished the Cloth to the Hermit; he clung to it still."

"This is not news to me, my dear Garo. I knew that Erreig had been admitted --- quite incredibly --- to the Star, and the Cloth with him. I, too, stood long upon the shores of Holy Bay and conversed with the Hermit, though I positioned myself on the rocky northern point of the estuary, rather than at the foot of the pine-forest. It is the greatest mystery of all, to me also, that your father --- even as a wraith --- could be admitted to that normally inaccessible sanctuary and stronghold. But as for relinquishing the Cloth to the Hermit, that would not be possible. Even Maelcraig would not be permitted to handle it, or to go to Mélusine's vault to restore it to her..."

"But now," sighed the King, "Erreig has absconded with a part of the Cloth, once again, carrying it into the world from Finnir's Portal."

As her father had pronounced the name --- as he thought it to be --- of the Sage-Hermit, Eli glanced at Garo, but no change came over his face. He only nodded once, and said, "Indeed, I learned this also, as you say Sire, that he has escaped, with it, from Star Island, and taken the Amethyst Cloth with him through the Portal of Barrywood."

"Yes, your father has tripped over the threshold into Ireland," sighed Aulfrin, "and now Eli must go after him. For, it seems that she is destined to retrieve it, the torn portion that your audacious father has retrained. But I have another question, and that is regarding the whereabouts of Bawn. For Erreig has not, thankfully, ridden through the Heart Oak on the great matriarch dragon! Where is *she*?"

"That I can indeed tell you, my King," Garo replied, as the company entered the dining-room and stood around the oval table, not yet sitting but for now simply finding their places. A space for the crystal dais of Aulfrin was evident at the far end of the well-laid dining-table, but it had not materialised for the moment. The King was obviously preparing to leave them to play his harp. Before turning back through the pointed and carved doorway, he hesitated, looking at and listening intently to his guest.

"She is on Mermaid Island," Garo concluded, with the glint of a smile flashing across his blue eyes.

The emeralds in the silver crown of the King seemed to dance and shimmer. "Aha! So! I had noted that she was well at-ease with my youngest son, many months ago now, shortly after Beltaine. She has gone there in peace, I presume?"

"Yes, yes, certainly not in any aggression. There is, might I suggest, a deep and mutual respect between the Prince Leyano and Bawn. I hope it is *contagious*, for it would be delightful to see such compliance and trust spread and 'infect' many other fairies and beasts of Moon and Sun."

Aulfrin smiled broadly at the muscular, courageous and yet so gentle fairy before him. He nodded, and his eyes were twinkling as playfully as Garo's.

"On that harmonious note, I will take my short leave of you all," said the King. "And when I have heard other and I hope equally optimistic cadences, I will return to you. And I expect that Periwinkle will have rejoined us by then, and the hounds will have arrived also."

As he turned and walked back down the winding corridors towards his Music Room, Eli and Brocéliana took their seats. Garo remained leaning on the intricately carved back of his chair, smiling warmly at the two ladies before him.

"It is such a pleasure to see you together," he whispered. "You are both very lovely, and very love-filled. The energy between you is like a lapping ripple of pure love across a pond filled with water-lilies."

Eli thought it was a perfect simile and image, especially as it included lilies. She smiled back at him. But before she could make a comment, a whirr of green wings marked the arrival of

Piv, flying in from the Council Chamber and down the hall, and spinning around the doorpost and into the dining-room.

"Have I missed supper? Oh! It's my darling Garo! And there's the twilight-eyed Brocéliana! I heard that you were coming, but I wondered if you'd arrived. And oh, how nice, for you haven't dined yet!"

Everyone laughed, as the pixie whirled once around the room and came to rest, cross-legged as usual, on the table between Eli and her sister. Garo now took his seat as well.

When Eli had regained her composure, and patted Piv's green-capped head with affection, she asked him, "It was the Trees, or the Blue Flowers, or the Mushrooms, which told you about Brocéliana and Garo being here?"

"No, no, it was Aindel," Piv remarked nonchalantly.

"Aindel is here?" hissed Eli, not wanting her father to overhear the name, even though he was --- by now --- far away and well-occupied with his harping. "I thought he was with Finnir."

"Well, it seems he knows that you're planning to go into the world by the Seventh Gate, and so he came to be there when you did."

"Aindel is coming with me?" Eli's tone was one of wonderful relief. But Piv did not allow her to enjoy the idea for long.

"I shouldn't think so. He doesn't go much into the human-lands, hardly at all, I think," replied Piv. "Will dinner be long, do you think?"

Brocéliana, still chuckling at the pixie, turned to Eli. "I saw him at *The Swooping Swallow* as we passed, my dear sister; and yes, he knows you must go through Wineberry, for he had been to the Inner Garden of the Great Trees, and also into the Stone Circle earlier today. He told us that he thought you might need him at the threshold of Wineberry's Gate, in order to find your way through. Perhaps he will even step over with you, onto the other side, though he did not hint at going further."

Periwinkle looked quite amazed at this idea, but he accepted it and added, "Well, it would be a great help to you, my dearest Eli, if he *did* step over with you, right through the enchanted Gate."

"I think it would almost be *necessary*," Garo commented. "The Moon will be such a slender little sickle, and you will need more of her light, perhaps, before your encounter with Erreig is completed. Perhaps that moon-light will be offered by Aindel, without him having to actually go into the world with you…"

Eli's expression was slightly less joyful now, and decidely more confused. "I don't know what help or protection I'll be needing in such an *encounter*," she admitted. "But how can Aindel's presence on the threshold grant me more moon-light, exactly?"

"Because he is one of the fairies who drink from the 'cup of light', from the Full Moon." It was the voice of Brocéliana. Eli gazed at her.

"Like in the rhyme?" she asked. "Demoran blessed me with that phrase as well. There are certain fairies who can conjure up the light of the Full Moon?"

Garo narrowed his wonderful eyes at this description. "Not 'conjure' it, my Lady Eli. He *drinks* from it. It's not quite the same thing."

Eli shook her head, but she was smiling again. "Well whatever that mystical imbibing of moon-wine might be, I'll be very happy to have my… I mean to have Aindel with me." She was suddenly aware that it was unlikely that her half-sister or Garo knew of Aindel's true identity. She was glad she had caught herself in time.

"Yes, he will be there, but your father must not know that, Eli. He has not *recognised* him yet, and it is not something for us to reveal to the King. It cannot come into his understanding that Aindel is here until… the right moment. Please be careful. But Aindel will be there, on one side or the other."

Eli looked long and hard at Garo, but did not know what to say or ask. "So," she thought, "he knows, and Brocéliana too." But in the next moment, her knowledge of what, or how much, they knew faltered.

"Aindel works very closely with us, dear Eli, in the Alliance. But the King does not yet know that he is so often here in this shee, and has not formally accepted or recognised the presence of fairies from the Sheep's Head Shee among us. As well as that, Aindel himself has asked that we do not reveal that he will assist you, as you cross through Wineberry. For some reason, he wishes to give his explanations, and to present himself to the King, at a later time --- but not yet."

Eli nodded, but decided not to ask anything further, for the moment. It was a good decision, for her father's footsteps were heard in the corridor and he came into the room, his face very contemplative, and took his place on his throne --- which appeared now on its dais of light to receive him.

He greeted Piv with warmth, and mentioned that the two dogs had just arrived as well, and would be joining them momentarily, to share a cosy supper of deep-orange sweet-pumpkin soup.

"Hooray!" giggled Piv, slapping his tiny hands onto his kness; and everyone knew it was *not* because the hounds were soon to appear!

****

For the most part, the company ate in silence, for Aulfrin's interrogation of his harp seemed to have presented him with some subjects of deep reflection. He said as much, but added that --- as it was clearly the wisest decision to await the following night to 'send Eli forth', as he put it, on her quest --- he proposed that they exchange their news and messages on the following day.

Garo assured the King that the insights given him by the Stones could be told tomorrow, and that it was preferable; for the advice to Eli which they contained was not propitious to a sound night's sleep. He would prefer to discuss their *warnings* in the light of day, he concluded. This did not exactly reassure Eli, but she agreed that discussions of the dangers lying ahead would not be conducive to restful slumber and sweet dreams.

Piv said that he, too, had messages to transmit, his being from the Great Trees via the filaments of fungus and the honeyed voices of the Blue Flower Beds. But aside from concurring with the King's certainty about the delay of one night, his words were for Eli's ears only. He announced that he would request a private audience with her in the morning. As his short, chubby arms were crossed in a very decisive fashion over his colourful tunic of bright designs, and his chin was held high giving him an air of great importance, no one dared to contradict him --- although the King was hard-pressed to conceal a smile.

Eli, very sleepy now, bid everyone a good-night and walked back along the corridor with Jizay to find the spiral-staircase to her tower bedroom. As they went, she turned and stepped into to the great Council Chamber to collect Róisín; for she had left the harp there, near another of the alcoves from that where the young lovers had taken refuge.

Aulfrin had retired, with Ferglas, to his personal apartments, while Piv had remained behind in the dining-room to talk with Garo and Brocéliana, and to ask the attendants if there would be a small dessert to 'round-off' the *light* supper they had shared.

Jizay stood at the door of the vast Council Chamber with its seven soaring arches, and Eli took two or three steps only, just to retrieve her harp and to breathe deeply, for a moment, the fresh and vibrant and yet very comforting air that circulated in this room. Indeed, just to inhale the *personality* of this place seemed to bless one with renewed vigour and courage!

But her harp was not where she had left her.

Eli glanced around her and saw Róisín immediately. She was leaning, not against the vaulted entrance to the small alcove, but against the curtains of the central column of the room wherein lay the powerful heart of the great Chamber --- a well or cauldron or shaft of energy which no fairy was permitted to access unless expressly invited to do so (by the King or by the forces themselves which bubbled and swirled behind the heavy veils of draperies).

Róisín was, however, clearly indulging in a normally-forbidden contact with the potent lights, for she was uncovered --- the wine-red cotton cloth lay at her feet --- and where she touched the central pillar, the curtains were open, though only by an inch. A gentle light shimmered around the harp's body.

Jizay joined Eli now, and standing beside her with his mistress's trembling hand on his soft head, he seemed to murmur words to her in his own silent language.

> *Sun and star and stone and tree,*
> *Meet together, are born in me.*
> *Full the cup and full the moon,*
> *And filled with light the tower's womb,*
> *Here is born and here is blessed*
> *Miraculous music for your quest.*

Eli wondered, for a moment, if it were really Jizay speaking, or if she were capturing sounds coming from her harp, or even from the radiance all around the instrument and the rich glow beyond the curtains. As she stared at Róisín, she knew that it didn't really matter --- for the rhyme came from them all. She imagined that she could hear, in the silence following the equally silent words, a post-script or a 'colophon' (like the 'afterword' at the close of an ancient manuscript): *I have given light and a powerful blessing to her, poised on the bright threshold.*

When her breath was more steady and regular, which took a couple more minutes to achieve, Eli noticed that the curtains had closed, and that Róisín was standing upright, no longer leaning against the pillar at all. Stirring herself out of her trance-like state, Eli walked towards the harp, planning to cover her and carry her away. But a voice, very like the one of the 'colophon', greeted her in a whisper.

"I will be with you tomorrow, when you step over Wineberry's threshold with Jizay and your harp."

"Aindel!" Eli hissed, trying to contain her surprise and joy, and trying to keep her voice down as well.

From where he had been standing, in the shadows beside one of the great arched windows, Aindel came forward, smiling. When he was beside her, he added, "Go to your rest now, my dear sister. Finnir urged me to procure this benediction for the harp, and for you. And he is content, too, that I'll be beside you on the 'bright threshold', the doorsill of *hesitation*. I cannot come further, but I can ease you through that hesitation, as you look back. I'll be the mid-wife of your birth out of the womb of light and into the land of the black berries!"

Not minding the riddling words of her brother Timair's declaration, Eli felt only relief at his presence and the promise of his company tomorrow night. He bent and collected-up the red cloth and draped it over Róisín; then he lifted the harp and placed it in Eli's arms.

"Restful, dreamless, profound sleep, little sister," he said softly, as he kissed her forehead.

He returned to the arch where he had been standing, and his great gold and violet wings sprung from his shoulders as he rose out of it, into the midnight velvet of the sky and the weaving pastel colours coiling around the distant Trees.

"Thank you, Finnir," whispered Eli. "Thank you, my love." And she and Jizay and the harp all went, as bidden, to their peaceful night's rest.

****

The following morning, Eli was pleased to leave her late breakfast unfinished, as she had little appetite, and to follow the already well-fed Piv out onto the lawns of Fantasie, walking towards the Fountain of Lymeril in the north-west.

When they arrived, and had stopped to enjoy the antics of the little water-serpents, Eli's memories tugged at her heart, for she could imagine looking up and seeing the brown and golden eyes of Reyse and hearing his friendly greeting to her when they first met here, exactly six months ago.

Yes, she mused, that had been the 3rd of May when Reyse invited her and Jizay to *The Tipsy Star* for an astronomical beer! She sighed. And here she was, on the 3rd of November, sundered from him and worried about his state of mind (and heart), and preparing to face a very strange new chapter in her changeling-adventure. Piv seemed to sense that Eli's mood was sombre and her thoughts sentimental. He flew up and stroked her head, tucking a little strand of wavy red hair back behind her ear and then another into the coral-clasp fastening the rest of her long tresses at her neck.

He piped in a cheery voice, "My dear little Eli, I have to give you my news from the Trees, so maybe we could go a little nearer to them to do that --- what do you think? Would you be able to go into the Inner Garden, just a little way?"

Eli's eyes brightened at the idea. "I don't know, Piv, but I'd like to try. I seem to be better able to look at the Trees on this Visit, without having to turn away from their energy too quickly. Let's go and see if I can enter further inside than I've done so far."

They walked across the lawns to the south; the vegetation was a bit more faded than it had been in May and June, it was true, but it was still filled with its own force and spirit, and seemed much more alive --- to Eli ---than any grass or flower, tree or bush in the human-world. Jizay trotted beside them, as they veered to the left and so came closer to the first Circular Garden of flowers, all yellow.

"Strange to see so many flowers blooming in November," Eli commented, as they all three paused on the margins of the wide ring of plants.

"There's always something in bloom here, and even some fruits growing and ripening, all the year long. The Inner Gardens, all three of them, can never be barren, as very few places in Faërie ever are --- unless they choose to be, of course. I recall that two rings of the Gardens went to sleep, very sad that, when the dragons and bats came and seized the Silver City, just before you went into the world as a changeling-babe." Piv reached down and stroked the back of a yellowish-green frog who was hopping by. "But otherwise, there's always animals, always flowers, always insects, always wondrous fruits, yes, all the time here.

"Come, my Eli-een, let's go in and see how the Gardens make you feel!"

Many overgrown paths wound about in a tangle of directions, it seemed to Eli, but they all gradually led further in and closer to the Trees. This Yellow Garden was easily three-hundred yards wide, and she continued to weave her way forward, almost on tip-toe, wondering if she would feel the tingling, electric charge of the Great Trees' proximity at any moment, and have to stop or retreat.

But she seemed to be welcomed and to have more of a fairy's nature about her, for she only felt happier and lighter as she went on.

"Good, good!" chuckled Periwinkle, "I can hear the little flowers, and some of the pimply-gourds on their spiky vines, and they all say you are at ease and at home! And there, can you hear him? That's Bram hailing you."

Eli stopped and looked up. Over the heads of the yellow-flowered bushes and the tall, exotic grasses with feathery, lemon-bright clusters of hairs, Eli saw --- much closer than she had yet done on any of her Visits --- the mighty Trees. Beyond the Yellow Garden, and the Blue one (which was slightly less wide), and the White one (which was the narrowest) the distant Central Garden of Fantasie filled a circle over half-a-mile in diameter. Evenly spaced around this, as if dancing a roundel, were the Seven Giant Trees. Eli had not ceased to be impressed by them at any time when in the Silver City, for their presence was palpable and their beauty breath-taking; but here, so much closer to them, even though not yet very near nor even quite in their shadow, she was mesmerised.

Their trunks were like indomitable towers, while their incredibly long branches were reaching upwards but also descending downwards in a jungle-growth of slender, curving cords like thick, brown arms or twisted and matted locks of hair. Far, far above the flower-filled Gardens was the intertwining ring of their more horizontal branches, not very leafy but wearing a halo of surging, flowing coloured mist. Above this, the heads of the Trees continued to soar upwards, impossibly high. All had their variously shaped leaves intact, though among the seven different shades of green there were mingled some red leaves, some orange-brown, some bright golden-yellow.

From where she and Piv and Jizay stood, two of the Trees were more evident and visible than the others. One was the Tree of the north-west, whose name Eli had not been told. But the one full-west was Bram, whom Eli knew to have been a close 'friend' of hers as the Princess Mélusine. And it was Bram who was greeting her now.

She could not make out any words, nor actually hear any sound. But there was no doubt at all in her heart of hearts that

Bram was warmly welcoming her. As well as this, she could understand an invitation, not to come right up to him, but to 'fly from the Yellow Garden to the Blue'.

Piv heard this too, for he clapped his tiny hands and flew up into the air and around Eli, crying, "What a wonderful idea! I'd forgotten you have your own wings now, my Eli! Yes, yes, let's do as Bram says, let's fly to where the blue flowers are, and then I can tell you what they told me yesterday."

"Did you hear the same as I did, then, Piv?! Did Bram just say we should *fly* closer?!"

The pixie nodded excitedly. "Of course he did! Come along, call out your wings and we're off!"

Jizay barked his applause, or so Eli interpreted it, as she closed her eyes for a second and simply *willed* her wings to appear. And they did, as easily as though she were telling her toes to wiggle!

With her gorgeous mauve and blue butterfly-wings beating slowly and elegantly, Eli joined Piv in mid-air and they made a touring-flight above the yellow plants, back and forth, up and down the curved beds and over the crazy paths, until finally they crossed the border into the Blue Garden. Below her, Eli could see masses of pale and dark blue flowers, but even more generous growths of berry-bearing bushes: deep ultramarine fruits, rich purple currents, bright cerulean-blue and violet-mauve berries and some others almost black-indigo, like Peronne's eyes. Here there were little fountains and pools of dark water, not so many very high bushes or tall grasses, but one or two benches carved from pale grey-blue stone. Near one of these, she and Piv came to land, and Jizay bounded up to meet them.

"Excellent, excellent," exuded the little pixie, his rosy cheeks redder than ever with joy and pride. "When you come back, we should go for a wonderful flight together, just us!"

Eli was laughing, and it made her forget her looming quest for a moment. Now, with the words 'when you come back', she remembered what she must do this very night. She sat next to Piv and sighed resignedly, but still with a philosophical smile on her lips.

"Well, my darling Piv, what did the mushrooms and the flowers and the wondrous Trees have to say to you about my trip planned under the waning sickle moon?"

The two friends sat on the low, stone bench surrounded by deep blue flowers of a variety Eli had never seen in the world to which she was going back in the darkest hours of the coming night. They looked, at first, very exotic to her eyes; but after only a moment, they seemed to become much more familiar, as if she remembered them from happy occasions in her previous life here. They almost seemed to have faces, as she had seen in the Flower Beds on the northern coast that she had visited with Brocéliana. *That* garden of sweet-faced flowers had overlooked the Whale Race Sound and had offered a view of Scholar Owl Island. Eli sighed again.

Before Piv could answer her question, she spoke her thoughts aloud. "Isn't it odd, really, all of this? Erreig has taken a Cloth from the 'me' that lies asleep on a guarded isle in the northern seas of Faërie, and the other 'me' must go after him to demand its return! He stole it from a fairy, and it's a human who must retrieve it: very odd that, don't you think, Piv?"

"I think you're always a fairy, my Eli, even when you're not completely Mélusine. You can't <u>not</u> be; it's not possible for you. Didn't you feel that, when you were growing-up and living-out your changeling life? Didn't you feel *different* from the humans?"

"Oh yes, did I!" snickered Eli. "I was always aware of not belonging, or of looking for something that was lost, or of trying to remember something I'd forgotten."

"Exactly, my darling one. And now you've almost remembered it! Well, you've been *told*, and you've been given a little *taste* of the Truth --- but you haven't come back into your skin yet, not completely. But the Trees are holding out their arms to you, especially Bram, and Rhadeg too, I'm sure of it. And you can fly, and normal humans don't know how to do that (strangely enough). And you start to think and see like a fairy again, even before you're Mélusine once more. Imagine how it will feel to be her! You've only the sweetness on the tip of your tongue, so far, as the saying here goes: soon you'll know it in your heart and soul and body and thoughts, through and through. Won't that be grand?!"

Eli laughed. "It would, to be sure, my dear Piv! Thank you, for you make me feel better already, and less worried about tonight."

"There's *no* need to worry, my little Eli-sine, not at all! That's what the message of the Trees was all about: just as you said it. For you've echoed what they told me, in a way. You're going on your voyage as Eli tonight, but you're home here on your third Visit too; so in a way you're halfway between Eli and Mélusine when you step through the Gate of Wineberry.

"It's not as if you are meeting Erreig when *fully* there as a human, or even as a human-fairy-changeling; and it's not like being the sleeping Princess, either, waking-up wrapped in her amethyst shroud to frighten him or floating over the cold seas to face him as a ghost! They want you to know that it's a special kind of 'you'. And that's very important for meeting Erreig, and it's very important for taking back the Cloth, because no one can touch that but you, and the fairy who stole it. Even the Sage-Hermit, he never took it away from Erreig, for he couldn't lay even <u>his</u> mighty and magical hands on it. No other of the fairies here could bring it back, only you.

"And even Mélusine herself, as she is now, couldn't have done it, in fact --- even if she thought of trying --- because it's filled with the charms of her *transformation*. It's as if the Cloth itself knows that Mélusine is not quite alive, not quite strong enough to face Erreig there in that human world where he's gone. And I expect he knows that too --- and hopes that Mélusine herself, much too weak to scare him or resist him *there*, will turn up to seek it. Aha, but **no**! It will be *you*, the human-and-fairy you; and he doesn't expect that, I'll wager. For *that* you **is** strong enough, because you're *really* alive, and you know what it is to be alive in the human-lands; and you're not afraid of having a foot in both worlds at the same time, because you've done that for months now, and you're only getting stronger and stronger --- all the time: more and more *wonderful*!"

As Piv spoke, Eli's back redressed itself and she seemed to take on an air of inner strength and confidence. "Oh, Piv, how splendid to hear all of this! You *do* make me feel braver. Thank you so much!"

"You should thank the Trees, thank the great and kind Bram, for the message comes from him."

Eli looked up and she noticed that the bench where they were sitting was in the shadow cast by Bram. She smiled. And, without a doubt, Bram smiled back.

"Thank you, my great and good friend," she whispered. There was a sudden gust of autumn wind, and fallen leaves blew up in little whirlwinds all about the stone bench, making Jizay bark and leap after them in a daft game. High above them, where Eli's gaze now returned, the thick garland of foggy colours encircling the Trees glowed mauve, shot through with tiny sparks of gold and rich burgundy-red. Eli smiled very broadly and breathed deeply.

She looked back at Periwinkle, swinging his short legs over the edge of the blue-stone bench, his little hands on his knees and his cheeky face aglow with love and happiness.

"And do you know, my treasured friend, why I should take the Harp of Barrywood with me? For I know that she is coming too; Aindel told me."

"When did you see Aindel?"

"Last night, on my way to my bed, I met him in the Council Chamber when I went to collect my harp. Don't tell the King, please Piv. I think it's a secret."

"No need to remind me of *that*, my sweet Eli!" chirped the pixie. "I know that Aulfrin mustn't know when our dear Aindel of the sunny hair and the violet eyes comes to Fantasie! But soon he will, my Aindel-een told me that. Soon the King will meet him, face to face, and maybe he will begin to build lovely bridges of love, over all the oceans of Faërie, even to the Sheep's Head Shee, and beyond!"

"I hope so, Piv. That's my dream too."

"But about the Harp that the Prince Finnir fashioned for you," continued Piv. "I suppose it's to keep in contact with us here, or with your brother himself. Did you ask Aindel about it? Did he say more?"

"Well, no, not really. I heard words that mentioned 'miraculous music for my quest', and so I suppose that's to come from the harp."

Periwinkle looked up at Eli with wide-eyed astonishment. "<u>That's</u> not Aindel speaking," he said, slowly and almost with reverence. "Those words come from the Light, the wild Light at the heart of the Chamber, behind its curtains.

And very solemnly he recited the verse that Eli had heard:

> *"Sun and star and stone and tree,*
> *Meet together, are born in me.*
> *Full the cup and full the moon,*
> *And filled with light the tower's womb,*
> *Here is born and here is blessed*
> *Miraculous music for your quest.*

"Did you *hear* the chanted verse of the Light, like that, my Eli? Did the harp touch the curtained pillar? And did the curtains *open*?!"

Eli was staring at Piv with eyes as wide as his. "Yes, they did --- well, only an inch."

"An inch is enough!" And the pixie gave a short laugh. "Then the Harp of Barrywood will have the seven notes in her strings and in her heart, and you can invite her to sing them when the time comes."

"What seven notes? What is the *miraculous music*, Piv? My harp has received a secret melody from the Light in the centre of the Chamber, do you mean?"

"Oh, my Eli, you have forgotten much, and I think it's good that we have time to talk today, before you go: it's not by chance, because that doesn't exist, as you used to say to me! I must teach you again the seven notes, because it's you that must play them; a harp can't play itself, you know. So listen and concentrate, because if you've forgotten the melody or cadence, what good will the blessing be?"

Eli turned and looked at Jizay, sitting beside them again. The late morning was cool and crisp, but not stormy, and her hound of joy seemed to be glowing like molten gold. Bram's shadow had lessened now and moved to the White Garden with the mounting sun, and they were all three in a pool of butterscotch light slanting down between the high branches.

Piv stood up, and seemed to adopt a 'school-master' pose, with one hand on his hip and the other used to gesture emphatically, reinforcing his words.

"I have told you already, have I not," he began, with great dignity and one finger raised as if declaiming a speech, "that the Gates of the City of Fantasie are seven in number, and arranged like this: South, north-west, north-east, due west, due east, south-west, south-east. And I've told you their names: *Ioyeas, Dwitherum, Treytherum,* --- *Quatherum, Setherum, Rhex.* Plus *Wineberry*, with her riddle-rhyme, who is the seventh."

Eli nodded, trying to be a good student, and paying close attention. Piv nodded back, breathed very pointedly and pursed his lips, and then went on:

"There are *seven* Gates, as there are *seven* Trees and *seven* Standing Stones. And they are all counted in similar kinds of orders, in a criss-cross, between all the directions of the winds of Faërie. With the exception that the first Gate is in the south and the first Tree is in the north and the first Stone is in the north-east, but otherwise they're all in the same order. So, if you've been heeding my words, you will know that, for example, in the circle of the Great Trees, your friends Rhadeg and Bram are numbers three and four, like Treytherum and Quatherum for the Gates. Do you follow?"

Eli took a moment to make the criss-cross in her mind, and then said, "Yes, alright; Rhadeg is the Tree to the north-east, and Bram due west --- yes, they're like the Gate up by the nice bakery where we arrived with Muscari and Eochra after meeting Garo, and like the other Gate far out to the sunset-side of the City's oval --- where I've not been yet."

Master Periwinkle smiled. "Good girl. Now, rightly and very obviously, each of the seven Gates, Trees and Stones, each of the seven points designating fairy-winds, correspond to a note of music."

"Ah...? How lovely!" enthused Eli.

"*Please,*" remonstrated Professor Piv, "listen carefully, Miss Eli."

"Sorry," murmured his student, and fell back into silent and attentive listening.

"Let me see, hmm. I will try to find the equivalents for a human musician like yourself, Miss Eli Penrohan --- but mind, I don't claim that it's exactly the same for fairy ears; but then, your harp is not a fairy-harp, really, so this should work. The notes go up the 'scale', I think that's what you'd call it, starting from --- let us see, yes --- *la*; seven notes like this: *la, si, do, re, mi, fa, sol.* You see?"

Eli nodded...

"Now, it becomes a little more complicated. There are different cadences, different ways of going 'round, of course. But here, because it's Wineberry that is taking you on your quest, we must use the order of the Gates. Therefore, you sing the notes as you imagine walking around all the numbers starting from one and then going *left-wards*, like this: 1, 6, 4, 2, 3, 5, 7. Do you understand?"

"Not too clearly, but I think I'm getting the hang of it," grimaced Eli, as if faced with an impenetrable mathematical equation. "So, let's see, it's as if each Gate were a note in the scale of *la* or *A*, but you arrange the scale, with its numbers from one to seven, around the Gates of the oval of Fantasie in their criss-cross order, and then you walk around anti-clockwise --- oh dear, I mean 'leftwards' ---- singing or playing the notes as you come to them, starting from **one** and ending at **seven**..."

"You are as brilliant as you are beautiful, my Eli-sine," chimed Piv. Eli laughed. "So, you're a good musician; now sing me the melody, going from the Great Gates, *la*, left around the City's borders till you get back to Wineberry, for you need to know the tune for tonight."

Eli cleared her throat, and then she hummed very softly: "*La, fa, re, si, do, mi, sol.*"

"Go **up** to the *do*, not down an octave, please," corrected Piv. "And don't forget the *F-sharp* as the *sol* is actually the root: we're in the key of *G* here, not in *la* or *A* in fact."

With a brief huff, and then a smile at her rather demanding singing-professor, Eli recommenced: *La , fa#, re, si, do (just above the si), mi, sol.*" As her little melody in *solfège* concluded, Eli jumped where she sat. <u>All</u> the birds in the Blue Flower Garden began to sing, <u>all</u> the flowers to wave madly in what was only a very slight breeze, and the Seven Great Trees themselves seemed to send up a momentarily *booming* chord of profound peace and satisfaction, almost akin to a room full of meditating yogis chanting an *aum*.

The entire Inner Garden went very silent once again, and Eli directed the bemused expression on her face, first to Piv and then to Jizay. Both were grinning.

"*That's* the 'miraculous music' of the Gates," came the sweet canine voice of her dear hound, resonating in her head.

"And *that's* what you must play on your harp when you step through Wineberry, **and** when you meet Erreig," added Periwinkle.

****

Chapter Nine:
The Cup of Light

n the early afternoon, Eli was once again in the King's Moon Tower, this time in an intimate but very beautiful room she had not seen before, near to the upper-courtyard where Peronne and Cynnabar had landed last night.

It resembled a slightly smaller version of the Reception Chamber in Demoran's castle, where Eli had met her father on her first day home in Faërie, and where she had, at the close of her second Visit, received from him the little tear-stained notebook of Lily. Though the room was not so large, it was certainly airy and bright, open to pleasant views on both sides --- but here to east and west, rather than to north and south as in Davenia. Like the great Council Chamber where her harp, Róisín, had been 'blessed', these high windows had no glass in them, only trailing ivies and fragrant (even at this time of year) honeysuckle. All among the leaves and flowers, Eli could detect tiny fairy-beings, almost transparent, with wings like bees or wasps and with furry antennae like those of night-moths. And about the honeysuckle were the surprising forms of two or three large pink and olive-green elephant-hawk-moths, but these flitted out one of the eastern windows almost immediately.

Seated around a lovely and --- to Eli's human tastes --- rather Victorian 'Arts and Crafts Movement' pool of clear though beautifully green water surrounded by ornately painted tiles in tones of sage and terra-cotta, were her beloved fairies and animals. Jizay and Ferglas lay beside the pool, their noses resting on their out-stretched paws; Garo and Brocéliana sat, side by side as lovers should, on a settee of carved cherry and pear-wood; Piv had a comfy little stool piled-high with tapestry-cushions; and Aulfrin sat on a very elegant chair of interlaced oak-twigs, which had materialised between the pool and the western window. Eli herself had taken her place on a similarly luminous little throne of silver birch, rather like the one she had occupied for the ceremonies of Beltaine morn.

"We have one or two matters to discuss before this evening's adventure begins, my dear girl," Aulfrin pronounced, commencing the meeting with gravity. "For I must tell you what my harp told *me*, and Garo will recount the news he has received from the Stones. Well, he and I have already discussed, privately, their messages which were addressed to me; but the Stone Circle had --- I understand --- counsel for you too, my dearest daughter."

Eli was feeling less confident than she had in the Blue Flower Garden, but she was trying to recapture the feeling of strength and courage that her moment alone with Piv and Jizay had afforded her. Also, during the hour or so when she was supposed to be resting after lunch, Eli had been improvising various interpretations of the 'miraculous music' on her harp, using the seven-note cadence or little musical-motif that she had learned from her dear pixie-professor.

Rehearsing once more, in her mind, the last composition she had invented, she allowed the melody made of seven different pitches, in the winsome key of *G*, to infuse her thoughts and her body; and she relaxed and closed her eyes for an instant. When she opened them, she saw that her father was smiling at her.

"When I received the communications of my silver harp, my dear Eli, I was a little apprehensive. But now, seeing you and feeling the force of your poised resolve, I am less hesitant to share the words of my instrument."

Eli smiled back at the King, and even in the act of such a simple gesture as calling a sincere smile to her lips, she felt a wave of optimism and --- as he had called it --- *resolve* flowing through her.

"I feel ready to hear them," Eli said.

Aulfrin stroked his short beard, and his emerald and peridot crown twinkled slightly, as if the insightful notes and words he had heard from his harp were percolating upwards through his thoughts and into the jewels.

"First and foremost," began the King, "I communicated with Wineberry. She is, as I did not doubt, willing and even very 'honoured' --- so she said --- to help you. So, that is formally settled, and you will be able to pass through the Seventh Gate. But once I had concluded my discourse with Wineberry, other themes rose to my ears.

"I heard *three* other distinct voices in the music that I shared with my instrument last evening," he said, rising now and striding slowly around the gathered company, his hand gently caressing the smooth wood of all the chair-backs and even the wavy red and auburn hair of his two daughters.

"One was the oceanic and tidal voice of my mother, the Queen Morliande," resumed the King. "She spoke to me in the language of the silkies, recalling to my ears the accents I remember from my infancy, when she would sing to me her haunting seal-lullabies and sea-shanties. Her message was this: she told me that other meetings awaited you beyond Wineberry's doorway --- as well as that with the Dragon-Lord. She foretold that you would make the acquaintance of a friend of hers, and that he would provide you with a means of voyaging while in the human-lands. He would be singing, she said, a sailor's song, rather like those her own voice had reminded me of. When you hear that sea-shanty, Eli, you must not hesitate, but go to him and willingly travel with him --- from one place to *two or three* other important destinations in your travels there. If you are in danger, he will surely bear you to safety. But, if I understand the subtleties of her instructions, he will provide you with much more: information and insights, meetings and valuable friendship, to touch your heart and to hasten you forward in your 'quest'.

"The second voice came to me in a musical movement at once *allegretto* and yet also pensive, cloaked in sombre, minor modulations of purple and blue intervals. It was a beautiful but variable voice, the voice of the Queen of the twilight and of the sunset, the wild love of my youth, the faithless foe of my family's tranquillity and stability, the tender and joyful mother of my four royal children. Rhynwanol, with whom I have not spoken for six centuries."

Aulfrin closed his eyes momentarily. As he opened them again, he continued. "She said to remind you of this: that all dreams are like Life itself, using *symbols*, often in poetic or riddling scenes, replacing one character or event with another --- not to confuse or to lie, but to draw you into deeper understanding of the heart's fragility…and of the heart's ultimate victory. She said that you would understand, in the moment when you came face to face with Errieg, to what her words pertained, in your case.

"But she added that they were as true for *me*, and that I should not forget to listen to them with *my* heart, as well."

A soft and pensive sigh escaped Aulfrin's lips, and he returned to his throne by the western window. He sat slowly, his eye fixed on emptiness, and was silent for some minutes. And then he concluded.

"And the third theme of my harp was a *finale*, a ringing and rippling cavalcade of notes. Spring flowers and running canals of steady, peaceful waters. Laughter and dancing, dulcimer and flute, merry pictures painted in luminous colours and starlit nights of songs and kisses. Crazy travels and cosy homes, then high waves breaking on golden sand and gulls calling through the balmy sky, bringing strange stories and tall tales to trouble lovers. Sudden sorrow turning the bright paints to hard, cracked memories in a palette kept as a souvenir; and falling stars in the late summer night and falling leaves in the early autumn; clouds of inescapable grey fading...fading, and floods of tears. And then farewells..."

As he finished, Eli's tears echoed his final phases, for she knew that he spoke of Lily. She rubbed her hands across her eyes, and cleared them enough to look up at her father and ask, "You heard *Lily's* voice...?"

Aulfrin's cheeks were wet also. But he wore a very faint smile as he shook his head.

"Beyond all hope, beyond even my most daring dreams, she lingers somewhere still; and yes, I could hear her. It appears that she is awaiting the accomplishment of your quest, this strange mission that will draw you away from us here in the very midst of your third Visit. She is ready to go, to take the ultimate step in her life's long voyage, but she is hesitating --- at least to see the unfolding of these coming days.

"Yes, it will be *several* days, it seems, or so she has told me. For I heard her words when the panoply of those images had passed. She said that she would look over you, and that your brother, your eldest brother, would join with her to illuminate your path and guide you back to Faërie, for the moon would be hidden or only very thin. And when she would see the resolution of this chapter of your adventure, then she would continue, free at last, into the Light that she is so longing to experience.

"I was so happy to learn that Finnir will join Lily in blessing you with this magical protection. I deem that it is predominantly *his* magic at work, a charm from my most mysteriously enchanted child, and that it will combine with Lily's maternal love for you --- in your human-form where she was, in every way, your veritable mother for half a century. Together she and Finnir will weave a guiding-gift for you while the moon is absent or frail: a lamp-star perhaps as brilliant as that which appeared to you as a beacon of light in the vision you were granted on the surface of the greystone altar of the chapel of Ligugé in France, the meditation-vision which heralded your being led back home to us last spring. I think that the starlight will shine on the tempestuous waters before you, and your sailor-guide will row you back to our shores --- or back to the threshold of Wineberry, back into Fantasie."

Eli knew that Lily's message did *not* speak of Finnir, but rather of Timair --- or Aindel, who was truly her eldest brother. And that he would, indeed, work some magic to allow her to stay the extra days in the world, even when the moon had grown dark. But she wished it *could* be Finnir, and that he could actually be with her there.

Or was she imagining someone else? Faces and fairies were changing place in her whirling thoughts, and she found she was steadying herself by gripping the arms of her chair. "I'm overwrought by the emotion of thinking of Lily and her finally going forth into her death. I lost her once, in a small hospital room in Bantry, in Ireland, last January; and now I'm losing her again, from the Sheep's Head Shee into the holy Light of her longed-for --- and fantastically delayed --- ultimate union with Christ. And my first impulse is to mourn and weep; and my second is to long for my own lover Finnir --- or for dear Reyse --- I don't know which. But my third impulse is the best, for in that one, which is winning out over both of the others now, I just want to blow her a kiss that will float out and mingle with the winds that fill the sails of whatever boat *she* will sail in to go where she *must* go, and where she *wants* to go, and where it is good and right and beautiful that she go."

Eli's thoughts were private and silent, but they brought colour back into her cheeks and made her lift her head high, as

The Cup of Light

she had done when Piv's discourse had bolstered her confidence and courage in the Garden.

"May God bless Lily," she said aloud, not really directing her words to anyone in the room. "Blessings to her and to all *my three mothers*, and all my thanks to them for these messages."

At that odd formula of 'my three mothers', Aulfrin's expression changed swiftly from sentimental to *startled*, and then to a happy comprehension. He nodded, and his smile returned as well.

Garo now prepared to tell his news, at least the part of his message received from the Stone Circle that concerned Eli. Aulfrin invited him to explain to his daughter what he had heard, for evidently he had already spoken with the King earlier this morning of the tidings that concerned his monarch.

The strong, agile, athletic fairy always seemed to Eli younger than she had heard his age to be, for he did not look to be in his early forties --- not her idea of what a forty-one-year-old should look like, in any case! But then, age and the count of years did not work, in Faërie, as it did for humans. In his cobalt-blue eyes, yes, there shone maturity and experience which testified, not to forty-odd years of life, but to centuries. Garo had been born, Eli recalled, in the twelfth-century. He had, as well, dared the Great Charm, as she had. And, she thought, watching him stand and move toward the green pool in the room's centre and kneel beside it, caressing an affectionate gold-fish who had just poked his head out of the water, he had been blessed by one of the Great Trees and by the Light of the Council Chamber's central pillar when he was an infant --- according to Piv's tale.

"He is a part of the *miraculous music*, like my harp," thought Eli, "and I wonder if that blessing will help him in his own 'quest', which I suppose is that of being the next Sage-Hermit, and a wonderful one."

As these interior reflections crossed her mind, Eli felt --- once again --- the pinching in her heart, remembering that a cruel separation from her lover lay in the near future for her sweet half-sister, Brocéliana. She sighed, for she had not yet found the right moment to reveal to Brocéliana that, in all probability, this third Visit of hers would *not* result in a decision to remain in Faërie, but that she thought now to go back into the world until her human-death. At least *that* would give the couple the prospect of many years in the same enchanted land. However, it was not very likely that they would be <u>together</u> after Garo went to live on Star Island. It would only give them just under another two years of freedom to share, most likely. But for lovers, even two years could be an eternity…

She would have to talk with Brocéliana later, or perhaps when she returned from her mission to confront Erreig. That encounter was drawing nearer now. Aulfrin had told her that she would be stepping through Wineberry about two hours before dawn of the next day, for then the tiny waning crescent-moon would be just rising in the eastern sky.

Garo had stood up again now: he was not very tall, but his carriage was so noble, so filled with a profound *felicity* welling-up from somewhere deep inside him, that he seemed to fill the whole room. Eli glanced at her sister, whose eyes were shining with love.

"The Stone Circle, together with its mysterious ring of bubbling waters flowing now one way now the other, has been my school-room for many years," Garo began. "It is there that I often hear the wisdom of my master, the Sage-Hermit; and there that I learn --- among other things, and from many teachers --- the arts of shape-shifting. Among these various teachers is the creature who gave me a message yester-morn." Here Garo paused, and turned his regard from Eli to the King. Aulfrin looked back at him with amicable patience and yet with a question glinting behind his deep green eyes.

"Yes, my Liege, Eli's message comes from *another* being than those who sent their advice and insights to you. For it was the Lord Hwittir who spoke a warning to Eli in the gurgling of the circular brook, the Red-Eared Hart and ruler of the shee beyond the great Portal of the Waterfalls of the Seven Sisters in Norway and another even more secret Portal in Finland. The shee of my mother, Vanzelle."

"Was the wondrous Stag in my realm?!" interjected the King. "I met him once, many long years ago, before I came to the throne here. I would have been happy to speak with him again."

"I do not think that he was, himself, present, Your Majesty. Many of my guides and tutors, for my role to come, are only present in spirit and in voice. And this was only shortly after Samhain, as well. My Lord Hwittir was most probably far away; but his wisdom and his instructions came to my ears through the threads of the water-ways that lie deep beneath this your realm of the Shee Mor, and connect it with all the others. Those liquid threads which are the warp and woof of the tapestry of the Eleven Shees, of the Spiral of the Eleven Stars."

Aulfrin's eyes were blazing now, and it seemed to the others present that a gentle but scintillating ray of light extended between himself and Garo, linking their eyes and also the thoughts and meanings running deep beneath the words of the younger fairy. But the King said nothing, and broke the cord of light by nodding his head with a slight smile.

Garo resumed. "The marvellous Hart gave me this message for you, Lady Eli. He said to tell you that Vanzelle, my mother, had also gone forth on Samhain Eve, shortly after Erreig did so, into the human-lands --- but from her own Portal of the Seven Sisters. The near-opaque mists of midnight still swathed the ice-dragons who guard that doorway; but their eyes are closed on Samhain Eve, and many folk come and go, fairy and human, gnome, *tonttu* and *haltija*. So it was that Vanzelle left her home, and voyaging among the fjords and through the forests which I knew and loved in my childhood, she came quite near to the oak-grove adjacent to the secret Portal of Lapland; and it was there that she encountered the Lord Hwittir.

"Vanzelle informed the Great Stag that she had just learned of my father's crime and also of his escape from Barrywood into Ireland, and that she had determined to seek him out and confront him. She asked the help of the mighty Hart, for she did not know where Erreig might be. The Lord Hwittir confided to me that he was glad they had met, for it gave him the occasion to <u>calm</u> my mother's anger before he would agree to assist her in finding the Dragon-Lord! The theft of the Amethyst Cloth had enraged her, and this fury was added to the anger she already felt concerning her former lover's illicit affair with your Queen, my Liege, many centuries ago. Happily, the Great Red-Eared Hart is very skilled in bringing peace to win-out over passionate ire!"

Aulfrin breathed deeply and audibly, and then he interrupted Garo's tale by asking, "And how did the silver-haired Vanzelle discover this news concerning Erreig's theft of the Cloth, and so rapidly?"

"She is a great dragon-tamer and dragon-lover, Your Majesty. And particularly beloved of Bawn, the beast who suckled her own son."

The King readjusted his position on his throne, propped one elbow on its arm and leaned his head against his hand with a short laugh. "Ah, yes! I had forgotten, dear Garo, that detail of your rather exceptional upbringing. Dragon's milk and dragon-friendship run in your family, on both sides! But how was Vanzelle in contact with Bawn?"

"Because Bawn did not go with my father into the world; she flew to Leyano on Mermaid Island, as you know. And from there she sent a swift messenger, very swift indeed, to relay her report to the ice-dragons of our own shee, and thus to Vanzelle."

"What messenger could possibly carry Bawn's epistle across more than a hundred leagues of the eastern seas of Faërie, to the Shee of the Red-Eared Hart, in a matter of an hour or so?!" retorted the King in a tone of disbelief.

"A *tursa*, Sire."

Aulfrin sat up, and Piv squeaked, unable to contain himself any longer.

"There are *tursa* in Sea-Horse Bay?! Oh, my Garo of the splendid surprises! Are there really?"

"<u>What</u> is a *tursa*?" Eli querried, confused and fascinated.

Garo turned to the astonished Eli and the excited Periwinkle. "Yes yes, my dear Piv, they frequently voyage there to play with their sea-serpent cousins and to hearken to the mermaids' music. And to answer your question, Lady Eli, they are rather like an octopus or a squid, but much larger, and they have the wings of an aquatic dragon. They are very common in my shee, and even in the lakes and fjords of the human-Nordic lands. And they are extremely fast, for they can swim and fly --- both under and above water --- more swiftly than Bawn herself.

"But allow me now to pass on the Lord Hwittir's message to you, dear Lady Eli. Vanzelle learned from him that *you* were to go into the world as soon as possible to seek for Erreig --- for the great Hart well understood that the Princess Mélusine could not be deprived of even a small piece of her sacred covering and remain at peace for long. The Lord Hwittir therefore asked my mother a boon: to remain nearby when she had found the Dragon-Lord, and to be present when *you* arrive. It is not so much to assist you in your confrontation," clarified Garo, seeing the mystified expression on Eli's face. "It is to *accompany* you when you leave him, or so I understood. The splendid Stag asked that you do not leave Erreig's company without Vanzelle's presence, for together your departure will be less dangerous. Indeed, without her, you cannot find the singing sailor or the ship you must board."

Torn between gratitude and renewed anxiety, Eli remained silent for a minute or two. No one else spoke either, and Garo knelt again on the ornate tiling and now tickled a small striped frog under its chin. The frog croaked happily, and then leapt back into the pool.

Garo returned to his seat, and Piv flew to hover before him.

"But where, in the vast human-world, is this meeting to take place, my dear Garo-boy? I thought that Erreig had gone into Ireland, for that's where the Heart Oak Portal opens. But your mother is in Lapland, is she not? Is that next door?"

"No, not at all." It was Eli's hushed voice, and she shook her head as she added, "And I was wondering the same thing. Does anyone know where I will *be* when I step through Wineberry in the small hours of tomorrow morning?"

"Yes, my dearest Eli, someone knows: Wineberry herself. And so you mustn't worry. She has offered to *help* you, not to trick you, and not to lose you." The comment was uttered in a sweet and calm and utterly trusting tone. It was Brocéliana. Eli turned to her sister with a look of surprise, but also filled suddenly with renewed hope.

"You only need to sip her wine," concluded the resplendent young half-fairy.

"To *sip her wine*?" repeated Eli. "What do you mean; what does that line in the riddle mean?"

"I don't know, at least not in your case," smiled her sister. "But if you 'sip her wine', then 'all is one'. And I think that could be true on many levels. Maybe it could mean that places which are far apart become close. Or perhaps that could be true of people, too. Maybe you'll find yourselves all together, even though you're not. I don't know, but I'm sure that all will be well, and just as it *should* be."

There was another rather long silence, but not an uncomfortable one. Eli was finding that she continued to feel lighter and more confident. Garo was now looking at his belovèd lady with the same adoration that had earlier been in *her* eyes. And the King wore an expression that was, as usual, impossible to define.

Periwinkle, who had settled himself on the arm of Garo's chair, now tugged at the fairy's sleeve.

"The next time I visit the Prince Leyano, I'm going to ask to see the *tursa*. Are they friendly, Garo? Could I meet one face to face? Do they like *buicuri*?"

Garo laughed at his little friend, but Ferglas stood and shook his head, making his collar jiggle. His chocolaty voice hummed in Eli's head, and she knew that all the others could hear it too.

"On that note, may I suggest that we take our tea? I doubt if there will be *buicuri*, but there will surely be something tasty to refresh and strengthen us all for the evening and the night and the morning which lie ahead."

He looked lovingly at Eli, as if he thought that she, at least, was more than ready for a pause and for a small but fortifying collation, in preparation for her journey.

****

Thus, Eli had now been told that the permission of the Gate of Wineberry had been secured, by the King himself, through the voice of his harp. This had been granted even before he had heard the messages of Eli's 'three mothers'. Explaining this in greater detail during their tea-time pause, he said that he had spoken to the Seventh Gate of Fantasie in harp-notes that were, in fact, a part of her own magical language. Before Piv's complicated musical explanations of the special order of the seven notes of the scale which corresponded to the criss-crossing numbering of the Gates, the Stones and the Great Trees, Eli would not have had the vaguest idea what this could mean. But now she did. She simply nodded.

At her father's suggestion, Eli had tried to sleep during the late afternoon --- and had succeeded for one or two hours --- in anticipation of a sleepless night to come. She and he had dined together, quite silently for the most part, later that evening. And then Eli had returned to her own apartments, to dress and prepare herself for her adventure, to meditate, to play her harp: to rest and relax, if that were possible.

It was now a little past the middle of the night, possibly only about three hours before dawn. Eli and her small troop of fairies and hounds, were walking down the Great Staircase, just arriving at the diamond-shaped Courtyard leading to the broad Entrance Hall. Before them were the high, open doors of the King's Moon Tower Palace. Clocks did not exist in Faërie, but Eli guessed it to be about three or four in the morning, on the 4th of November. They walked in silence. It was very cold, and she drew her cloak tightly about her.

The night-air was crisp and clear as they passed through the great oaken doors and looked up at a sky so filled with stars it was more white than black. Before them, the waves of moving lights around the Great Trees appeared to Eli just like the aurora-borealis. Except that among the greens and blues and pinks were flashing darts of mauve and deep scarlet.

They turned to the left now, roughly in the direction of the Fountain of Lyathel, but passing her well to the south in fact, mid-way between Fountain and Trees. High in the cold sky to their right was the north-eastern Tree, Rhadeg. Eli glanced up at him, and felt him bless her with an arboreal wink. She laughed to herself.

"A thousand-foot-high Tree, more ancient than my human civilisation at home in France or in Ireland, and certainly vastly older than my American one, is unlikely to 'wink' at me," she chastised herself silently. But when she looked back up at Rhadeg, she still had the impression ---- the undeniable *certainty* --- that he was winking. "Alright," she said to herself. "I suppose that primeval plants can wink. Why ever not?!"

They were seven going to the Seventh Gate: herself and her father the King, Garo and Brocéliana hand in hand, Piv ----

flying silently and steadily at the head of the procession, his head held high and his expression one of dignity and importance --- and the two great hounds, Jizay and Ferglas. And, beyond that count of seven there was another member of the party, of course, for Brocéliana was carrying Róisín, at her sister's request.

Eli had hesitated in her bedroom, but in the end she had decided *not* to carry with her the satchel containing Lily's journal and her other treasures. She had only extracted the Silver Leaf, for she felt that it should not be separated from the Flower which was borne on the brow of her harp. She wore, invisible to all save two or three absent fairies, the Flaming Crescent Moon ear-ring. That was enough. And, of course, safely concealed in the same inner-pocket of her cloak as the Leaf, she carried the torn segment of the Amethyst Cloth.

They continued on for a few yards, and then Aulfrin turned to Eli, whose arm was linked with his. He placed his brown hand on hers.

"Let us fly the rest of the way," he suggested. "It will give you a pleasant and euphoric breath of the night air, and a taste of your true fairy-nature before you step over Wineberry's threshold."

Piv overheard, and circled back to come beside Eli's ear. "And you fly *so well*, my Eli-een! Remember the Blue Garden, and keep the miracle-music in your head too!" It was clear that he sensed Eli's growing nervousness, despite her strong resolution and the promise of support and help from several quarters.

"I'd love that," she replied to her father, and simultaneously, at a gesture from Aulfrin like a conductor's baton signalling the opening chord of a symphony, Eli and the King brought forth their broad wings, glistening in the starlight. They joined Piv only about a dozen feet over the long grasses and made a languid and wide circular flight around Brocéliana and Garo walking below with the two hounds.

"I can match your pretty flight with another wonder," laughed the comely young dragon-lord. As his words were blown away in a sudden cool breeze that swept over the grass and turned its delicate blades into a wavy sea of shadowy green, a sparkle of tiny white lights shot out from Garo's entire body, concealing him in a whirling explosion of silent fireworks.

The points of light vanished as quickly as they had arrived, and there stood a huge white wolf, twice the size of Ferglas or Jizay. The three flying fairies hovered just above him, their wings beating to keep them aloft and in place --- like those of a hawk spying a field-mouse cowering below --- while the wolf smiled and shook his sleek head to make the sunstone pendants hanging from both his pointy ears dance and jingle in the silvery light. And that light was not only cast from the mists of the Great Trees looking down on the company from the Inner Garden a mile or so to the west, it was also coming from the first faint glimmer of a needle-fine scimitar of a moon, rising over the eastern walls of Fantasie near to the isolated Star-Tower which stood beyond the large lake.

"Ah, well-done, brave Garo! Magnificent!" cried Aulfrin, even before Periwinkle could erupt into gleeful applause. "And now, too, there is the moon to dance Eli through the Gate; let us go swiftly!"

Brocéliana, still carrying the feather-weight harp, climbed up onto the furry back of the giant wolf who gracefully leapt into a cantering stride. Eli thought to herself that her sister looked like a Princess from a Scandinavian folk-tale: her shining chestnut hair flying out behind her over her rippling cobalt and finely embroidered cloak, her deep blue eyes sparkling like the fireworks of Garo's transformation, and a mysterious harp wrapped in dark red cloth cradled in her arms.

The two hounds ran alongside the white wolf, and the trio of winged-fairies flew above them. They covered the two miles which separated them from the south-eastern Gate in only a few delicious minutes, it seemed to Eli. She could have flown through the late-autumn night like this forever: the sickle moon beside her, an enchanted wolf below her, her father and her sister, her friends and her belovèd hound of joy all there with her, and a million stars dancing over their heads.

****

Here am I on threshold bright,
On one side the cup of light,
On the other berries black,
Hesitating I look back...

Hesitating, indeed.

Eli had alighted, with her father just behind her, in front of Wineberry. Two beautiful rowan trees flanked the open Gate and, unlike most of the other trees of the Silver City, these were very wintry-looking: leafless, stark and silvery in the star-and-moon-light. But they were very beautiful, nonetheless, with here and there just a few clusters of red berries still clinging to the twisted fingers of their branches. Piv had landed on one of the trees, and was standing on a fork of its trunk, smiling encouragingly at his dear friend.

Who was certainly <u>hesitating</u>.

She had not seen him changing back into his fairy-form, but Garo now stood beside Eli and --- taking it gently from Brocéliana's hands --- passed her the Harp of Barrywood.

"How does Jizay manage to come with me?" asked Eli of her father. "Does he remain, umm, 'real', or is he to be an *imaginary* dog, as he was in my childhood?" As soon as she had spoken, Eli realised that she should have asked Jizay directly! She looked down at him, standing at the ready by her thigh.

"I am Jizay, *and* Laurien," he said, in a silent but laughing voice. "As you are both Mélusine *and* Eli!"

"Find and confront Erreig," came the calm and authoritative command of Aulfrin. "Retrieve the part of your chrysalis-cloth which has been taken from you in an act at once villainous and pathetic. Wait for Vanzelle to appear, and go with her to the seashore or port where you will find a boat, recognisable as yours by the lilting sea-shanty sung by its sailor. Somewhere, somehow, your brother Finnir will be aiding you. And your 'three mothers', as you call them, are with you, Eli. As am I, and as are all of the Moon-Dancers."

"And the Sun-Singers," added the sweet voice of Brocéliana. Her father turned to her in surprise, but then nodded his head with a smile.

"Yes, *night and light and moon **and** sun*," recited Aulfrin. "Yes, all of Faërie is with you, changeling-Eli and Princess Mélusine, so you and Jizay are not alone at all. Be of good courage, and do what you must do. *Bon voyage* my dear girl."

Eli knew that it was not Finnir who would be helping her, at least not in other guise than the harp he had so skilfully wrought for her. It would be Aindel; and he was probably there already, just on the other side of the Gate. She stepped up to Wineberry.

As she passed Piv, he whispered to her: "Play the 'miraculous music', my Elisine! Don't forget that it is the key to unlock the doorless Gate, on both sides. Hurry back --- and farewell."

Eli was on the threshold. Above her, the high and interlaced branches of the two rowans followed the same curve as the pillars and key-stone of the Gate's arch. Behind her was the shining City of Fantasie. Before her was utter darkness.

She took the harp in her trembling hands and removed its covering, draping the fabric over one arm.

"Why am I *trembling*?" she reprimanded herself. "Stop that at once!"

Holding Róisín with her left hand against that same shoulder --- as an ancient Irish harp might have been strummed --- she began to play with her right hand as she took one, and then two, and then three steps forward, Jizay close beside her.

La , fa#, re, si, do, mi, sol... she played, just as she had hummed the notes to Piv. Once through she played them singly and simply, and then she stopped and placed the harp on the ground, kneeling behind Róisín on the burgundy fabric that had been her covering. She still seemed to be directly under the arched branches. With both hands now, Eli skilfully embellished the seven notes with intervals and broken chords, grace-notes and glissandos, as she had done in her little 'composition' invented in her bedroom earlier today and practised again after her evening meditation.

In the wake of the vibrations of her final arpeggio, Eli realised that the arms of the trees were no longer overhead, they were well behind her. And as the harp-music died away completely, she heard another sound. There was still the *suggestion* of silence, as profound as the darkness around her and her dear dog, but it did not endure. It gave way, almost instantly, to a woolly and throaty voice --- not at all unpleasant: rather rustic, gruff and earthy.

"My brothers, Dwitherum and Treytherum, have already met you, Eli --- brave little human moon-shadow cast from Mélusine with the sun in her eyes! I am happy to welcome you here, to the passage afforded by the Seventh Gate. I am Wineberry."

Eli stood up beside Róisín and placed one hand on the top curve of the harp's golden wood, the other on the golden head of her hound. There was a faint light beginning to glimmer all around her and she could feel that Jizay's tail was wagging. She relaxed and breathed deeply.

"Thank you, Wineberry; I am honoured and very grateful that you have agreed to help me go back into the human-world."

"You travel with the Silver Leaf; that is good," remarked the fuzzy voice. "And, of course, I see that the Golden Flower is with you also, on the harp crafted by the Prince of the Unicorns.

"You will be glad of both. But it is not all that you need," remarked the slightly rasping voice.

And then another voice, more masculine but, like Wineberry's, coming from everywhere at once, as if it were an echo caught in the dim corridor or cave where Eli now found herself, added, "You will need what I bring you as well."

"Aindel! You are here!" The light in the passageway or cavern --- whatever this place was --- grew and spread so that Eli could clearly see Aindel standing not two yards ahead. She exhaled with relief and pleasure. "Thank you for coming."

Aindel stepped forward a pace, smiling. "One of us had to, for a human would need both the Cup of Light and the Berries, in order to cross over and to come back. Either myself or Finnir or the Queen Rhynwanol would have had to be awaiting you in this shadowland, to give you this."

As he concluded, he extended his hand to Eli, and in it was a flower, just six pure white petals and a tiny group of equally white bobbles at its centre, lying modestly in the hollow of his palm. It looked as though it were made of mother-of-pearl. It was small, much smaller than the white rose that Reyse had offered her, but it made Eli shiver with a sudden ecstasy that she could not explain.

"Is this the Cup of Light?" whispered Eli, wondering if she was meant to take it from him, or touch her finger to it as if it were holy water.

"Ah! What is the Cup of Light?! Now, that is a fine question, dear changeling-fey," chortled the voice of Wineberry. "And it would be just like Mélusine to inquire, and to seek it! But no, no, it is not so simple as that.

"Here the High Prince of the Sheep's Head Shee, and the elder son of the line of Aulf the Mighty, has come to give into your keeping, just for this short voyage you must make, a pretty moon-flower, the pearly-white lily."

Eli looked around her, but could still not see from whence the voice of Wineberry came. She turned back to Aindel.

"This is a lily, and a moon-flower? The sacred flower that grows only in the Sheep's Head Shee? But if I need the 'Cup of Light' and the 'Berries', where are they ---- and *what* are they?"

Aindel opened the collar of his heavy purple cloak, and untied the laces at the neck of his embroidered shirt of grey and pale green. There, over his heart, was a small but astounding gem. Eli gasped with a sudden intake of breath.

"What is that?" she muttered almost inaudibly.

"It is a blue geode of *celestite*, Eli. Its miniature pyramids of powerful and peaceful crystals were given me by the white stags and does, the deer-folk with whom I completed my second Initiation when I was thirteen, over seven centuries ago. But it was not chosen for me by the deer; it came ultimately from the Abbess of the Shee of the Bells, and by her hand from the Archangel whom we evoke on the tiny red island in the far east of our father's kingdom, in Sea-Horse Bay. Finnir's pearl shares these angelic origins, as does the agate set between our mother's breasts.

"By the virtues of these, our most sacred stones, we three have been granted an affinity with the Cup of Light, and therefore we may help those humans or fairies who are lost, or lunatic, or who need punctual protection or guidance in extraordinary tasks. For you to interrupt your third and final Visit home in order to venture back into the human-lands on a quest of some danger and daring, and to recover an enchanted Cloth vital to the very life-force of the Princess of Faërie, Mélusine --- well, that has seemed to us worthy of our aid!"

"So then, little human, listen well," interjected the woolly voice of Wineberry again. "My dear moon-child-Prince of the watery, windy shee in the west, he will now give you this little flower, filled by his precious heart-gem with the grace of the

Cup of Light, to connect you to me, to him, and to her. Keep it safe and secret until you have need of moon-light. Now, you may go on."

Aindel was no longer beside her. The grey corridor was empty and still. Eli's right hand had left Jizay's head and was outstretched to where Aindel had been standing a moment before; and in that open hand was now the tiny moon-flower.

Not wanting to crush it, for it seemed so delicate and humble, Eli chose *not* to put it into the pocket with the Silver Leaf and the partial Cloth. Instead, she decided to tuck it into the bodice of her clothing, where the v-neck of her knitted tunic covered an under-shirt of lacy open-weave linen. Wondering why she had the instinctive certainty that this was the best place for the little lily-flower, Eli felt along the seam at the point of the v-neck. The fold of the cloth concealed a tiny, interior pocket. She slipped the lily into it, and then placed her hand over it, over her heart, for a second or two. She felt another wave of the same ecstasy which had thrilled her when first seeing the flower in Aindel's palm and when he had revealed his blue celestite geode. Her finger-tips were tingling and warm, and her breathing very deep and slow.

Jizay's company had never been more precious to Eli. She had delighted in his 'imaginary' presence when she was a child, and she had found enormous solace in his proximity when she lived with Yves, but now she knew that she could not go forward another step without her hound of joy at her side.

For the passage-way had become, once again, completely dark and fearfully quiet. Eli carried her harp clutched against her and kept her other hand on Jizay's head as she walked tentatively forward on what felt like the cushioned leaf-mould of a forest floor. Slowly, somewhat relieving the utter blackness, the Golden Flower on the brow of her harp began to emit a pale beam of soft and comforting light. It didn't illuminate much of their surroundings, but Eli felt less nervous.

And then there was a faint sound also. Echoes of footsteps rang far-off, but were growing closer. Eli stopped walking, and strained to see or hear more. She turned to glance back over her shoulder and saw two amazing sights. First, high in a sky that she was sure was no longer visible --- for she could *surely* no longer see through the arched Gate to the City of Fantasie --- was a full moon. Wisps of ghostly cloud strayed across the moon's face and then a darker patch of cloud covered her entirely. When she re-emerged, only a second later, she was not full, but only the tiny waning 'moon-lash' that truly existed on this night; however, all the remaining dark area of the moon was strangely visible also, a mottled map of grey craters and lunar landscapes.

Was this the rising moon of this November night, or was it another night? Was it not, rather, the waning crescent of last June?! For the second sight Eli saw was a trio of riders: two fair, blue-cloaked fairies on dapple-grey steeds, with a handsome pack of eight cream-coloured wolf-hounds running at their heels. But the third fairy was more beautiful than all the rest of the vision, at least to Eli: it was Finnir. His own cloak blew out behind him in the summery sunlight and his short blond curls gleamed almost as brightly as the pearl in his brow. Neya-Voun bore him with prancing, dancing steps and Eli saw very clearly the spiral of silver on the unicorn's head.

The riders continued to gallop across a prairie of high blue and yellow flowers, purposefully but light-heartedly racing towards a line of willows in the distance. Eli could see it all as if it were an illustration in a child's picture-book, magically come to life.

And as she watched, she heard Finnir's endearing voice, as soft and sensuous as it had been when he had held her in his arms in the woods of Gougane Barra, reclining on a huge, mossy tree-root and speaking together between their tender kisses.

"I passed this way five months ago, my darling Eli. And it was the final phase of the thin arc of the moon in that summer season as it is for you in this wintry one. We were setting out, myself and Brea and Aytel, on our mission to meet with Morliande, do you recall? And we left the Silver City by the Seventh Gate, as you have. This is my gift-echo to you, here in this sacred passageway.

"For you, my love, the moon will grow dark and then newborn while you are in the world of humans. For me, she was also an infant-moon, a silver-white crescent, on another date: a 12th of September many centuries ago. Indeed, the 12th of September is a very precious day to me, for that was the date, in the year 1293, when Timair, our dear Aindel --- the fairy-youth who had been blessed by the white deer and by the abbess and the archangel --- met with the Lord Hwittir, the most enchanted of all the people of the forest, and conceived the idea of becoming a changeling and thus initiated my own great adventure. That was the exchange of Princes which would prove pivotal in our great cause, for the Lord Hwittir is the beloved friend of Tree and Stone, of dragon and mage. And on that date, too, many centuries later, I accomplished a part of my own destiny of liberation and new life, born out of yellow blossom and unicorn fire.

"Eli, you go to meet with Erreig now. I, too, have met with him --- in many wordless interviews and contests of wills. I come to tell you: he is not to be feared, but he is not to be trusted either. No, he is not yet become *trustworthy*, but neither is he become --- nor will he ever become --- a <u>threat</u> to you. Your wise and passionate and *com*passionate mother once became enamoured of the subtle blend of dreams and sorrows, music and melancholy, which flow in Erreig's blood, the red blood of the standard of the Sun-Singers. You, my Princess and my Queen, are a child of the yellow blossoms of the Moon-Dancers, the Flaming Crescent Moon, the ever-renewing cycle of the phoenix-fires of the lunar unicorns. And your own destiny is bound-up with them all.

"Behind you has appeared the Cup of Light --- granted by the moon-flower you bear. Before you have been planted the Berries Black. Erreig awaits you, defiant and distressed --- as ever. And he holds the remnant of the Amethyst Cloth, calling you to this meeting with it and with him. But it is *you* who verse the wine in its goblet, you who mix it and mingle in it all the colours of the rainbow. Do not waver, Eli: neither in your mission under a moonless sky, nor in your certainty of who and what you are. For the moon will return, newborn and noble in the sunset sky; and you will be faithful to yourself, as renewed and as noble as the moon.

"And, please, do not waver in your love for me, in your faithfulness, in your faith in our love, though you must go back into a world far from Faërie.

"May the blessings of Night and Light, of Moon and Sun, be upon you."

"We have arrived," said another voice. It was that of Jizay, humming inside Eli's mind like a favourite and familiar melody.

"But I do not know *where* we have arrived, at all."

****

Windy Hill Prayer

Chapter Ten:
Eli's Journey and Erreig's Lament

here was a very slight sensation of dawn in the chill air. Eli could sense the imposing mass of a mountainside behind her, even in the almost complete darkness. She did not know if there was a doorway that had closed at her back or if the final way out from the Gate's passage still lay ahead. In any case, she and her hound of joy were going forward, not backwards, so she did not need to look. She just needed to continue advancing.

Róisín no longer had her wine-red cover over her, and there was certainly not enough light to look for it now. She held the harp close to her, and walked forward.

Suddenly, Eli recalled the words of Periwinkle: *Play the miraculous music. Don't forget that it is the key to unlock the Gate, on both sides.*

There, sensing that she was at the foot of a dark mountain behind her and yet still not completely out of Wineberry's cavernous passageway or final ravine, she placed the harp once more on the ground and knelt on the peaty earth. Again she played her seven-note composition. As she concluded, she heard a cracking sound coming from rocks behind, beside, perhaps before them... Jizay barked once.

The air seemed fresher, and Eli could no longer feel anything resembling a mountain or rock walls to either side, or anywhere in front of them. It seemed clear that the Gate of

Wineberry had closed behind them, but Eli was as ignorant as her dog as to where they had come out.

The thinnest sickle moon she had ever seen was hung in the sky over another mountain facing them at a great distance, outlined in slightly darker black than the already very black heavens. But at least the skies were starry, and so the bulk of the mountain, obviously in the east, was just a solid and starless shade of ebony velvet. There were other mountains too, and smaller hills, and the sound of running or falling water.

"A glen or a valley," thought Eli. "But where?"

Although there was a sensation of imminent dawn in the air, everything all around them was still painted in various tones of deep grey and black. Black as well were the berries. All about her and Jizay were bushes, congregated all around them like a crowd of natives who had rushed up to greet a pair of aliens suddenly dropped into their remote habitat. Berries and bushes, all black but vaguely discernable in their shadow-shapes, and all richly fragrant as if ripe with early autumn fruit.

Eli waited, not daring to continue walking until she could see a little more clearly. After what seemed like an hour (but was probably only a quarter of that), the sky turned the colour of a new-born seal and their surroundings began to take shape. The bushes and the hills, the surrounding mountains and the wide river running between them, all began to come more into focus with the growing light.

They were, effectively, in a majestic glen, with --- just here --- a dense grove of high, thorny bushes all about them. Jizay and Eli agreed that they had been wise to stand still, even though the cold wind was biting; for the path was narrow and winding and they would surely have found themselves caught in the brambles and thorns. The bushes were a mixture of blackberry, blackcurrant and a variety of wild bramble unknown to Eli --- but wound in among them were decorative but poisonous nightshade, with purple-blue hats of curled petals and golden stamens like tiny dragon-heads with white tongues.

"We have seen the two sides of Wineberry, my dear Jizay," Eli said, scratching her hound's head. "We met Aindel and received the lovely lunar-lily and saw the full moon behind us for a moment too. So that was the 'cup of light' on the Faërie-side of the Gate. And now, here, we are surrounded by 'berries black', and very late in the year to be seeing them over-ripe and so abundant. Are there no birds to gobble them up?!

"I hope that the wine that Finnir and Brocéliana both referred to, and that the riddle-verse speaks of, is not made from *these* fruits; for sipping a black-bramble-brew laced with nightshade would, for a human at least, indeed make all things 'one' --- but in a very deadly and final sense!

"But now, where do we go? For we are not in Gougane Barra here, and I have no idea *where* this imposing glen *is*, whether somewhere else in Ireland or in another part of the world. And I have no idea where Erreig is either…"

The morning was steadily creeping up into the sky and spilling into the vast vale where she and Jizay found themselves. Eli drew breath, and smiled. What an adventure, and what a place! Wherever this was, it was gorgeous: all that she loved most in nature, in fact, seemed to be spread out at her feet.

As the scene became more colourful and clear, though a bit chill and hibernal, Eli saw a magnificent lake or loch between high, rocky hills and towering mountains, many of which were already topped in snow. The glen was immense, with many streams feeding the slate-grey expanse of water and many forested slopes and gorse-covered heaths and moorland. Not far below where she stood, Eli could see a regal red deer stag, his huge antlers looking like the branches of a bare tree. He bellowed, but it was *not* a mating call to attract the hinds. This was, Eli felt sure, a greeting. Or a warning. He jumped away into a thicket of pines, oaks and hawthorns, white-beams and huge holly bushes.

Eli glanced at Jizay and smiled. "Well, better to move than to stay still, for our feet will take us closer to our destination and just staring at this beautiful picture will not!" They began to descend the small, winding path and soon the berry-bushes had been left behind, and the terrain became a mixture of bog and rock, heather and tussocks of dry grass.

"I thought, at first," remarked Eli, speaking in a hushed voice to Jizay, as though reticent to disturb the natural stillness of this place, "that Wineberry had perhaps brought us to a Norwegian fjord near to where the ice-dragons guard Vanzelle's shee. And then I thought that it could be a wild part of Ireland, in Donegal perhaps. But now, do you know, I think we may be in the Scottish Highlands."

"I have never visited those human regions," replied Jizay in his silent language. "But I have heard the Lord Reyse speak of them, for his own shee has Portals opening into two places in Scotland. One is near to some sacred gardens which he names 'Findhorn', in lands where his first lady-love --- before he gave his heart to you --- has now gone to live. And the other, he has told me, is in just such a valley as this. He calls it a 'glen' and has often told me of the beautiful lake, or 'loch' that it contains. Do you not remember him speaking of such a place, when you were his child-fairy-student?"

Eli shook her head as she walked on beside her dear hound. "No, I can't recall any of our conversations, or my *lessons* with my dear tutor. It would be very nice, though," she added winsomely, "if Reyse were here now, for I have been worrying about him and no one seems to have any news of him."

Jizay looked up at his mistress, and then further off into the brightening skies. And his voice came again to Eli, deep within her own head or heart.

"*There's* a creature who might have word of Reyse, if this is indeed anywhere near to one of the Portals of the Shee of the Dove."

Eli followed Jizay's eyes, and saw a white-tailed eagle, flying in elegant circles over the water, now feathered into endless lines of thin ripples by the rising wind. Just above the eagle was the fading moon-lash. Ah…she would soon be quite invisible in the blue sky --- but she would still be there, Eli thought.

Watching the eagle, she wondered how she might be able to ask it for news: perhaps news of Reyse, but also for some idea of where to find Erreig and how long it would take them to do so. They were arriving at the level of the loch now, for the opening in the hillside amid the crowd of berries had not been very high up, poised on an outcropping of the long toes of a much greater mountain behind.

The eagle continued to fly in lazy circles, as Eli and Jizay now found a twisted rowan-tree, very like those marking the entrance to the Seventh Gate or the one in the stony foothills to the north-east of Fantasie where she had first met Garo. She and her dear dog now settled themselves under the tree: Eli sitting on a mossy stone seat of tumbled boulders beside one of the myriad streams and Jizay 'standing guard', it seemed, just beside her.

Aulfrin had told Eli, at their dinner the evening before, that Wineberry herself had sent word --- by her own messengers --- that the daughter of the King of Faërie would be wandering in the wild, into the human-world where the Gate would open for her. The King had therefore been assured that whatever fairies or nature-sprites were in the place would help her to find food and drink during her adventure, both for herself and for Jizay (though her hound was --- of course --- a fairy-dog and not a worldly one, and so might easily be able to look after himself!). Therefore, as Eli seated herself --- thinking she might play Róisín for some guidance --- she glanced down between the stones and tree-roots and was not surprised to find a willow-wood basket, no bigger than a loaf of bread. And it contained just that.

Was it bread? She inspected it and smelt it a little suspiciously, but it had a lovely and fresh fragrance and seemed to be like a traditional Scottish bannock: round and rough, oaty and a bit salty to the nose. She nibbled a corner, and then shared some with Jizay --- just to be polite, for he seemed rather uninterested in eating. She complemented her impromptu breakfast with a handful of icy water from a silver thread of a brook no wider than her foot, passing just the other side of the boulder; and then she began to play her harp.

And as she did, the enormous white-tailed eagle flew down to join them.

****

"This is not *quite* like being a human," thought Eli. "I have found myself, somehow, magically transported to a glorious glen in Scotland (I think), where I am joined for an unlikely breakfast --- found in a basket at my feet just as I was getting a little peckish --- by my wondrous hound from Faërie and the largest eagle I have ever seen."

She smiled as she completed the musical phrase she was playing, and stood the Harp of Barrywood upright once more. Jizay and herself were both regarding the impressive bird who had alighted on a low stone before them. He was easily three-feet tall. And he was magnificent.

Eli spoke in Jizay's own silent language now, asking her hound, "Is he a 'real' eagle, or a disguised fairy? He has amazing eyes!"

Jizay was grinning. "Fairies rarely take the shape of animals when they come into this world, except for *pookas*, who delight in such charades. But this is no *pooka*. No, this is not a fairy-man or woman in eagle-robes; but it is *not* an eagle of these lands, either, dearest mistress. I recognise him, if you do not!

He is indeed a fairy-*animal* who has taken the clothing of a bird familiar to this place, as I did when I stepped into the tiny body of a dying puppy several years ago --- to be found and saved by you and thus bring you comfort and company. I would venture to suggest that this fairy-creature is up to the same sort of trick!"

Eli turned from the eagle to look at Jizay, who was literally laughing. And, herself smiling also now, she turned back to the great bird.

She looked again at the bird's eyes. In fact, she had secretly been hoping that this was Reyse, transformed into an eagle --- his namesake, as *Iolar* MacReyse-Roic. But the eyes were not the hazel-brown and amber-ringed ones of Reyse. They were, for an eagle, very much too dark and very large, and indigo rather than 'normal' eagle-eyes of gold with piercing black pupils. But they did have *remarkable* pupils: silvery white, and formed to resemble arum-lilies.

Eli blinked. "*Peronne*?!"

The huge bird closed his eyes, lifted his head backwards in a throaty guffaw of laughter, and stretched his wings out to either side, flapping them and splaying the 'fingers' of black feathers at their tips. The span of those wings was easily six feet, if not more.

Jizay barked a warm welcome, as Eli simply sat where she was, mesmerised. Peronne spoke, using the fairy-creatures' interior language and in just the same voice that Eli had heard from him as a flying-horse.

"When I learned you were to come through Wineberry, I took it upon myself to speak with Rhadeg --- a Tree with whom I, too, share a deep affinity --- two evenings ago now when we first arrived in Fantasie," he explained, folding his wings and hopping closer to Eli to settle himself on an exposed root of the rowan tree. "He knew, of course, that Erreig had moved on to Scotland, having swiftly fled from the woods of Gougane Barra for fear of the Prince Finnir. I suppose he travelled by night, and often under the cover of cloud and storm, to fly here to the Highlands of Argyll with his own wings. Very brash behaviour," he huffed, and shook his head.

"At Rhadeg's suggestion, I hastened to Barrywood and passed into this human-world by the Portal of the Heart Oak --- with the dear Prince Finnir's approval. And there I was given help, also, to affect this splendid transformation into an eagle. From Cork I flew to Tipperary, and passed into the Shee of the Dove, and them out another of its Portals into Loch Ness. It was not too far, from there, to fly to *this* beauteous loch, and it gave me the chance to meet many other charming eagles on the way. In any case, I find that flying as a white-tailed eagle is *most* delightful --- wonderful balance and silky wind-resistance! Really quite a contrast to equine-flight. It was indeed a most pleasant journey here, to this lovely loch were Wineberry has elected to situate her doorway amid the dark and deadly berries."

"My dearest, loyal, wonderful steed," sighed Eli. "How kind of you to come to my aid."

"Ah, perhaps not your *aid*, my Lady," corrected the eagle, tilting his head slightly to scratch his beak with one enormous talon. "Neither Jizay nor myself can *aid* you, not directly as regards your meeting with Erreig. But it is always good to have support, friendship, company for the route, and two extra pairs of eyes --- one of those pairs being air-borne!"

Eli smiled with gratitude. "But you say 'the route', dear Peronne; is there more 'route' to come? Are we not arrived? I thought Erreig would be somewhere near here."

The eagle cleared his throat, and continued, "I gather that Wineberry did not desire to drop you into Erreig's *lap*, exactly. The Dragon-Chieftain is in the Highlands, and not far to be sure, but not here in Glen Etive. He is hoping to lure you to him in another very mysterious and isolated glen, near to another loch only a few miles from this one. There are so many in this glorious country! I have seen him, in my early morning flight. And I can lead you to where he is."

"Peronne, does Erreig know I am *here*?"

"I imagine he expects you, and very soon. He has come here, with the Amethyst Cloth, expressly to lure you to him. But I do not suspect that he knows of your *exact* whereabouts, no. But still, we must be cautious.

"He is a little north of here, in the Lost Valley of Glencoe. It's only about half-an-hour, as the eagle flies --- but on foot, your two and Jizay's four, I would say it will be several hours of rather rough hill-climbing. Rough, but beautiful. Beautiful, but cold. There is snow already in the high passes."

"It's rather a pity," reflected Eli a bit dreamily, "that you're not a winged-horse. That would have been a better way to travel!"

"The Scots are marvellously sensible folk," conceded Peronne, "for they have little difficulty in accepting that there is an ancient monster in Loch Ness. And the mer-horses of Faërie tell me that she is a charming sea-serpent, too. But to see a flying-horse, well, that might be just one step too far! Now, it is true, in the Highlands in November, there are not *crowds* of visitors; but, that said, this is a people who don't mind walking and climbing, boating or even playing the bag-pipes in any and all weathers --- so they *may* venture into even these remote places. No, no, I think it is not wise to have a flying-horse with you: too startling and fantastical even for the most august and whimsy of the kilted Caledonians! And, in any case, Jizay has no wings and I cannot carry him: the same problem we always encountered in our adventures together in the realm of King Aulfrin...or even further afield."

Eli thought that the eagle shot her a glance at once knowing and cryptic. It was true, of course, even in Faërie it had been complicated to travel all three together. But she and her winged-steed *had* made amazing voyages together, just the two of them; for Peronne had been with her, she was sure, when she had discovered the Fourth Portal and the Garnet Vortex. She had seen and felt it in her vision at Leyano's Castle, and she was sure it had really occurred. And maybe would occur again…" She fell silent for several moments.

The wide-winged eagled ruffled his feathers once more, and brought her back to the present. "A long road lies ahead, then; so perhaps we should begin? And we may have to break our journey from time to time. They say that, here in the Glens, it is common to encounter all four seasons of the year in the same day. I'm not sure, but I wouldn't be surprised if we have a good bit of at least autumn *and* winter on our trip."

"What is the first leg of the journey?" Eli asked, standing and lifting Róisín to cover her snugly with one long fold of her cloak. "Do we continue along the loch's shores; is that north?"

"Four or five miles, yes, north to the head of Glen Etive, and near to Gualachulain."

"To *what*?"

"To an ancient and once very magical cairn of white stones, near to where the River Etive rises, I believe, to feed this majestic loch with its mythical waters. Come!"

So saying, the mighty sea-eagle rose into the sharp breeze that was beginning to blow over Loch Etive. Mingled with the wind-song was the far-off but strident bellowing of the red-deer stag they had seen earlier.

It sounded, to Eli, like trumpeters signalling the start of a tournament between jousting knights. She hoped the image was not premonitory.

****

After perhaps two or two-and-a-half hours, Jizay indicated the outcrop of white stones marking the ancient cairn. Nearby, he also directed his now rather weary mistress's eye to a clump of holly bushes. Peronne had already landed in the small, secluded space inside the circle of red-berried, prickly-leafed shrubs.

Eli followed both eagle and hound into the concealed coppice, and found them sheltering against a particularly large holly which broke the wind. She joined them on the thick carpet of deer-nibbled grass, where they had found a flat stone to serve as her seat between them. From behind the thick curtain of dark, shiny leaves, the great eagle pulled, with one enormous black-hooked and bright yellow foot, a little bowl woven of oak-leaves and hawthorn twigs. It contained a rich assortment of nuts and pieces of apples, plus raw finely-cut rutabagas --- or neeps --- with some of their leaves too.

"Wonderful restaurant," quipped Eli, "though it lacks a warming glass of crab-apple brandy!"

"You will have to make-do with river-water as your wine," responded Jizay, and added, "or a handful of snow as we go on. The Herdsmen have heads of white hair, and there is surely more snow on the way."

"What herdsmen?" asked Eli. "Are there shepherds and flocks nearby?"

Peronne answered her. "The Buachaille Etive Mor, and the Beag also, are the great and little 'Herdsmen' of Etive; they are two of the mountains here." Eli looked out over the tops of the holly, but she could no longer see any of the hills or peaks. All was wreathed in fog.

"Don't worry, dear mistress. I will be flying low, and Jizay is beside you. Now, *play your harp* to warm us all!"

Eli raised a quizzical eyebrow, for she had never thought of using a harp to warm herself or anyone else! To heal, yes perhaps --- but to change the temperature, never... Still, the idea appealed to her, and so she reached for Róisín and began to play softly. Her fingers were rather cold already, and the stone seat was making her entire body feel chillier too.

The eagle nodded. "Now, quicker and with *intention*!"

Trying to heed his instruction, Eli closed her eyes and accelerated her improvised melody. She allowed images of a blazing fire in a cottage chimney to come into her mind, and then a memory of hot baths scented with essential oils. She felt like laughing at herself, but after a moment or two, her hands felt distinctly warmer.

"I'm playing quickly, so my fingers are warming-up, obviously," she thought. But she had to admit that it was not just her hands. Her bottom on its cold stone was no longer chilly or numb, but deliciously warm --- just like sitting in a bath of hot water.

She changed her imagined source of heat again, still delicately calling forth a lively tune from Róisín's strings. Now she was scantily dressed in a bathing-suit and a flowery sarong, splashing along a white beach, her bare feet in the shallow ebb and flow of the breaking waves, her body warmed by a Californian sun. And then, as if creating a hybrid climate, she interchanged some of the elements from both places: the snowy, foggy glen and the sunny Malibu coastline. She actually *willed* the warmth to seep into the landscape around her!

As Eli played, the music became hybrid too: now Celtic, now almost Tahitian or Hawaiian. She created a setting for herself and her music, in a vision even more eccentric than the places she had visited in Faërie. The holly bushes shone in the brilliant sun, the snowy flanks of the Herdsmen-mountains glistened forth from the parting fog like sequined bride's-gowns in the glinting sunlight, summer flowers --- exotic and highly unlikely --- burst into bloom along the banks of the loch: hibiscus and birds of paradise, frangipani flowers and mauve jacaranda trees like those in the hamlet of Shepherds' Lodge. Parrots called and stags bellowed, icy mist swirled around rays of sunlight as yellow as ripe bananas!

"This is absolutely crazy," Eli cried aloud. "I love it! And," she added, opening her eyes as she finished her concerto with a flourish, "it works!"

Peronne and Jizay, eagle and hound, were laughing with her. The Golden Flower was gleaming on Róisín's head, and Eli felt light-hearted as well as very comfortably warm. She stood, and sighed happily.

"I thought I would be needing the moon, not the sun," she remarked. "I have the moon-flower concealed in my clothing, charmed with the forces of the Cup of Light. But I suppose that's not intended for increasing body-temperature on a wintry hill-walk!"

Before he took flight, to sail low and steady in the once-again thickening fog just before Eli, the mighty eagle looked intently at her with his lily-and-indigo eyes. "You'll be needing the Moon before the end. But it's good to be reminded that you need both Moon *and* Sun. Very good."

With that, he opened his vast wings and soared over the hollies, as Jizay trotted out of the circle of sheltering bushes and Eli, with her still softly vibrating harp hugged against her, followed them both up the trail into the very head of the glen.

"We will be following a road known as the Pass of the Deer, beautiful but quite rough in places," signalled the sea-eagle as he flew close beside Eli. She had been walking, climbing, stumbling occasionally and progressing slowly against the wind for two more hours or so, at least. It seemed much longer to Eli, but she could feel that it was not yet twilight, only mid-afternoon. The sky was a single cloud, or a single sheet of dense fog, but it was not dark, only pale grey. So, she thought, it must still be day-time, even if there's precious little day-light.

"I'm very tired," Eli murmured to Jizay, still walking close beside her.

"The moon has set," he nodded. "You will feel greater fatigue without her. It is only an hour or so before sunset now, and the tiny sickle --- well hidden as it was beyond the white blanket of the cloud-cover --- has gone down into the west. Soon it will grow dark."

Eli looked a little concerned, though she immediately realised --- as Brocéliana had so confidently pronounced --- that 'all would be well', even as she asked, "What do we do for the night, up here? Is there somewhere to take shelter?"

"There is *always* a solution," replied Jizay, without hesitation. And he smiled again.

Time had become immeasurable to Eli. She felt she had been walking for days. And now it was certainly dark and the curtained sun had long ago set, for she could see only a step at a time, thanks to the faint light provided by the Golden Flower on the harp under her left arm. Jizay she could no longer see at all, but that did not matter: he was like an extension of her own body, unquestionably still beside her aching legs as she climbed. An encouraging and eternal presence…

The fog was all about them, like a tunnel of dark grey cotton-wool and a ceiling of moist cloud, barely moving except when it was disturbed by the low flight of the white-tailed eagle regularly appearing like a huge, black angel ahead of them. Leading them onwards and upwards.

Eli closed her eyes, involuntarily, and stumbled on a stone. When she opened them again with a start, the eagle was perched just ahead of her, at eye-level, on the long branch of an ancient alder tree crossing the path. Or *were* they still on the path?

There seemed to be several trees nearby, for bare twig-fingers poked through the mist. And in places the grey mass to either side was not mist, but stone. There were great boulders here, tumbled helter-skelter in some primordial avalanche or left in the wake of some ice-age glacier's slow passage. The fog was lifting quickly and Eli could clearly see the huge eagle a couple of yards before her, and Jizay shaking the falling snowflakes off his golden fur, just to her right.

"Where are we?" asked Eli sleepily. "Are we lost?"

Jizay seemed to urge Eli forward a step or two, and so they drew nearer to Peronne on his low branch. Now that she had stopped walking, Eli felt the cold very keenly; and the snow was coming faster now, but with it a phenomenon of illumination and peace…and silent holiness.

"Are we back in Faërie?" Eli found herself muttering. She thought she was on the verge of fainting, or of slipping into a dream. Confusion and a rather comfortable and welcoming exhaustion were stealing over her.

"In a way," came the rich, interior voice of Peronne, "you never left. In a way. For you are still, somehow, on your third Visit home. This is just an interlude in that musical composition: a moment to slip back into the world you came from, but remaining a changeling coming home to her fairy-realm as well. You did not come through a Portal to arrive here; you came through a Gate of the Silver City. You are your human-self, but as she is when in Faërie. You are between the worlds, and in both."

The words of the wondrous eagle were falling into Eli's mind like the hushed, tickling snow-flakes on her silver-grey cloak. She smiled, but she swayed as she did so.

"Hold onto Jizay," commanded Peronne, "and follow me."

Behind one of the largest boulders, almost the size of a small cottage, was a narrow opening into a hidden grotto of tumbled rocks and ragged, course grass. Above them, the alder tree extended some of its larger branches, more or less covering the opening between the fallen rocks and the mountainside itself.

"Do you remember," whispered the eagle, settling himself beside Eli where she knelt on the damp grass, "the story of fair Ævnad?"

Eli had tucked her harp into a cleft of the stones, and was cuddled into her cloak, pulling it close about her where she sat on her heels with Jizay lying against her leg. She yawned, and looked into the eagle's indigo-lily eyes. "Ævnad? The woman in the snows, the 17th of June…?"

She felt her head nodding, but she tried to blink and look into the strange, wise eyes. One great wing had opened now and the eagle was wrapping it around Eli's shoulders.

"Fleeing with her newborn babe, she would have perished in the midnight snows," recited the calm, gentle, singsong voice of the sea-eagle. "But a huge white dove came to mother and child, melted the snow around them, and covered them with its wings --- keeping them warm and safe until the morning."

A second long, dark wing was wrapped around Eli now too. And she thought she could see other eagles, golden eagles, alighting in the alder tree above her. Or were they giant doves… or Scholar Owls….?

In only a moment, Eli was asleep.

When she awoke it was bright morning. Peronne was stretching and flapping his wings beside her, and practically filling the entire space of the tiny, secret grotto by doing so. Jizay barked, clearly saying 'good morning', and she rose to follow him out into the snowy mountain pass.

"Forgotten by the squirrels, or left on purpose for you, I'm not sure which," he smiled, leading Eli to a knothole in a nearby pine where there was a large hoard of hazelnuts to crack with stones and wash down with snow-water. Eli felt oddly warm, deeply happy, free and faithful, confident and calm. She said this to her two companions.

"You'll be requiring all of those gifts for today's challenges," remarked the eagle, philosophically but with good humour. "Ready?"

Eli nodded, and went back to the stony shelter to collect Róisín. The rising wind made the strings vibrate, as if the harp were wishing her a 'good morning' too.

"Thank you," returned Eli. "I think we will have interesting things to do together today."

Rested and in good spirits, the company began the final march to their destination in the Lost Valley of Glencoe, taking the several miles of the Pass of the Deer at their leisure and enjoying the splendid views over a wintry and enchanted corner of the Highlands.

There were no clouds this morning, but Eli searched in vain for the last wisp of the moon. Indeed, she admitted, the moon was too tiny for human eyes, even a human with one foot still in Faërie, for she was nearly new. Tomorrow there would be no moon at all.

"But she will be back," smiled Eli, to herself, remembering her father seeing the moon-set on the evening that his Queen was banished. "For the moon always comes back."

And then, echoing words of Reyse's spoken in the great Council Chamber of the Seven Arches, she added, "And some of us see her ever-full." She immediately wondered why she had said those words, but they would not go away; they continued to repeat themselves in her mind, in the rich tones of Reyse's voice. *There is always a moon, Eli. Always. She is always somewhere, and always where she should be. And some of us see her always, and ever-full.*

As she walked, Eli had the strong impulse to place her hand over her heart, where the tiny pocket in the lining of her tunic's bodice held the moon-flower of Aindel --- her brother Timair. Even through her cloak, the pocket seemed to be purring like a contented cat. She smiled, and noticed that the white-tailed eagle, far ahead and flying high, had been joined by a pair of golden eagles.

"Were those other eagles with us last night?" she asked Jizay as she continued to look up. He made no answer for several seconds. And then he said, softly, "I thought I saw other birds too. But no, I don't think they were eagles. Those are real birds of this land, and what I saw was something else."

"Scholar Owls?" suggested Eli.

Her hound of joy turned his head to smile at her as he walked. "Here? That *would* be something! Even more astounding than you and me and Peronne! No, I only saw faint forms, as if in shadow. Strange, for I have very excellent vision at night; but then, I was as sleepy as you, and lulled by the beautiful legend of Ævnad that Peronne had conjured up for us.

"But, if I had to identify the creatures, I think I would say they were *not* birds at all. Bats, I believe. Yes, three or four bats. Very odd to see them sitting still like that, rather than whirring about. But then, Errieg is near. So maybe it's not that odd."

Eli fell silent, and felt a sudden shiver run up her spine. She closed her right hand a little more tightly over the moon-flower in its hidden pocket, and held Róisín closer against her side too.

"Erreig is near," she repeated, under her breath. "Please be with me, my own little moon Lily, and my *other* two mothers...and Finnir, please."

****

They had reached the Lost Valley probably at mid-day, and had now begun to descend into its heart. But it was not what Eli had imagined. For one thing, the snow was gone.

It still resembled the Scottish Highlands, majestic and wild. There were high and imposing walls of grey rock to their right, and slightly softer --- only very slightly! --- crags and hills and steep, narrow, stony trails through the hardy vegetation on their left. Eli could see some deer among the evergreen trees, as she had seen in the Pass as well, and there was also a small congregation of snow-buntings and even a ptarmigan, but they looked as perplexed as she was.

Why was there no snow here?

Eli stopped to admire the view, for the long glen was home to a sinuous river and it stretched for miles under a sky of pale blue decorated by cirrus clouds like wisps of thin, wavy hair.

"It's not winter here," remarked Eli, her hand resting on Jizay's high-held head. He was surveying the landscape too.

He gave a short laugh. "I'm not sure it's even Scotland here!"

"Is that possible?" asked Eli, as Peronne reappeared, having flown on down the valley for a mile or so and now coming back to give his news.

"Anything is possible now," he replied, landing beside the golden hound. "I was wary of Erreig spotting me --- though seeing an eagle here is not a surprise --- so I flew quickly and did not stay to take in all the details. But I think you will agree that it was an excellent idea my coming to join you; for having a 'bird's-eye' view of the situation is a boon. He is about three-quarters of a mile ahead, beside the river, near a mass of yellow gorse and purple thistle."

"Gorse may very well bloom most of the year here, but thistles --- that's surely a summer flower. I have the impression that it is *definitely* not winter any more." Eli retorted. And then, noticing that she was reacting more to the inexplicable change in the weather and even in the season than she was to Errieg's proximity, she smiled. "I don't seem to be as anxious as I thought I would be," she admitted to her two companions.

"It is wise not to be anxious, for worry is always a useless endeavour and moreover fear usually leads to blindness or folly, or even anger," conceded the eagle in a whisper. His hushed tone of voice reminded Eli that the acoustics in such a valley could bring the sound of their conversation to Errieg's ears. "But do not let your *courage* make you less *cautious*.

"It may well be that this odd change of climatic conditions is a charm worked by the Dragon-Lord himself; or it may be that he has secured help from another and more magical fairy, such as the Sage-Hermit. I cannot say. But it is a good reminder that very soon you will be confronting a powerful fairy and a quite unpredictable one, and one who has --- in the past --- shown himself to be capable of tricks and treachery and unexpected manoeuvres. Be wary, dear Eli."

Eli felt immediately more careful and sensible, but --- to her surprise --- still not at all nervous. She began to walk forward, Jizay beside her and Peronne just over her head. When they had gone perhaps half a mile, she stopped and spoke in silence, in her heart, for both eagle and hound to hear.

"I will go on alone from here. And I will leave Róisín here too, I think. Will you please keep an eye on me, dear Peronne, from those crags above us, and send Jizay, and come yourself, if you think I'm in trouble?"

"Of course," replied the great bird, and Jizay added, "I would take your harp a little closer, dear mistress. Leave her among the gorse-bushes, but not too far from you and the Dragon-Chieftain."

Eli looked down into her dog's large, tender, brown eyes. She nodded. "Yes, alright, I'll keep Róisín close. Thank you, thank you both."

"The blessings of the Moon in all her phases and the Sun in all his seasons be upon you," Eli heard, deep in her heart. But whether the words came from bird or hound, or from somewhere else, she could not be sure.

She touched her hand, once more, to the hidden pocket of her tunic where the moon-flower was. Then she reached into the larger side-pocket of her cloak and pulled out the portion of the Amethyst Cloth that she carried there. She extracted the Silver Leaf from its folds, and replaced that precious item in the pocket once again. Then, clutching the Cloth in one hand and bearing her harp with the other, she walked confidently down the heather-and-thyme-bordered path, to meet Erreig.

The waters of the swollen river were running swift and full, as if the magically melted snows had amply fed them. Or perhaps it was just the joyful vigour of a normal stream in springtime. If they were in a fragrant Scottish glen on a sunny early afternoon in spring, Eli thought there should be other visitors and hill-walkers nearby. But she was quite alone, except for one thoughtful figure sitting beside the noisy waters of the river as it flowed over the many angular stones in its bed.

Erreig, where he sat, had not heard her approach; or if he had he did not choose to turn and face her. Eli had not been so close to him when she had seen him at a distance in the Salley Woods, speaking with Alégondine beyond the grove of pussy-willows.

She now concealed her harp only a few yards away from the Dragon-Lord's unmoving form, so that Róisín was safely nestled in a patch of thick, glaringly bright gorse bushes which were beautifully complemented by the high and gaudy thistles beside them. Eli took a few more steps, until she stood only about ten feet from the Dragon-Lord's back. His dark cloak, almost black and hemmed in red and yellow interlace-appliqué, hung from his broad shoulders and was spread out over the boulder behind him. His hood was thrown back and revealed his very short-cropped deep golden hair and his sombre-skinned head and pointed ears. Eli could just see one of his ear-lobes, and in it was a huge chunk of labradorite, the same pale blue as the sky above them.

"I have come for the Amethyst Cloth, which you took from Scholar Owl Island, Erreig," she heard herself say, but she almost wondered if it were her own voice.

She also wondered if the Dragon-Lord had heard her, for the river was running with a very loud voice and had perhaps drowned her words in its own passionate music. Eli also found herself wondering if Erreig would understand her, or if he spoke only the language of Faërie and could not translate it into human language as could all the other fairies she had encountered. But then she recalled that she had understood his words, when he had spoken with Alégondine. She hoped they spoke the same language here too, at least…

As these thoughts swirled in her head, rather as the loud waters were swirling around their grey stones, Erreig seemed to draw a deep breath, as if he were about to answer her.

But instead, he began to sing.

It was the same deep baritone --- but oddly feminine --- voice that she had heard in the Salley Woods, but now it was amplified by being used to make music. Its warmth was greater: easily able to melt all the snows of winter, Eli thought, and bring springtime to this valley. And its sorrow was more profound.

"If I could only play the harp like that," Eli thought, "I would wring the hearts of my listeners and fill their eyes with sweet tears and heal any and all ills they might have and move them all to fall instantly in love with one another!"

These were the words that Eli heard, but they may have been sung in the language of Faërie and transformed on the wind that was dancing down the Lost Valley so that Eli could hear in them in her own tongue: a ballad and a lament and an echo of the longing in the heart of Erreig.

> *I vowed, "She must be proud and bright,*
> *Strong as the Sun, fragile as spring,*
> *Beauteous as stars, wise as the night,*
> *Worthy of contest, born to bring*
> *A throne to a king."*
>
> *I sought her in snows and dragon-fire,*
> *In forest, in flower, in sea, in stone;*
> *I wrestled with phantoms of phoenix-fire,*
> *Betrayed by beasts who were my own,*
> *Forsaken, alone.*
>
> *Moons wax and wane, love wakes and sleeps,*
> *Suns set in the west, in the east they rise;*
> *But my longing, eternal, waits and weeps*
> *And rain bejewels the twilight skies,*
> *Soft as her sighs.*
>
> *Daring all dangers, desire will take*

A treasure, a token, a trophy to hold;
Once hers, now mine. Will she awake
And choose the sun o're moonlight cold:
Red, rich and bold?

The strains of his song were so tragic and heart-rending that Eli was overwhelmed by an urge to approach Erreig where he sat, his back still towards her, and to place her hand on his shoulder. To touch him, to comfort him, to allow all the empathy of her heart to reach out to him. She took one step.

But then she stopped. Was this the same tidal-wave of empathy mingled with desire which swept away her own mother's loyalty to her husband the King? Was this how Erreig had seduced the Queen Rhynwanol: with music and pathos?

Another thought now blossomed in Eli's mind, or two thoughts in one. The first was of the Flaming-Crescent-Moon, for it brings protection. Rhynwanol herself said that *Lily protects you with it, for she will not allow you to be shamed and violated again.* "Erreig has disgraced you and stolen from you, he may have violently attacked you," Eli reminded herself ... "The ear-ring will keep you safe."

And with that thought came the second: "You bear the moon-flower and the moon-flower bears the virtues of the Cup of Light. The moon is overhead, though frail and invisible in this bright sky. She is there. And for you, Moon-Dancer and Princess of Faëire, she is full, *ever-full*, even though she is only a tiny sickle today. Know that she is there; that the Cup of Light is there. They are there, and they are yours. Keep that certainty in your heart."

She breathed very deeply, and stood still. But Erreig had not remained motionless after his song. He had risen to his feet also; and now standing in the shallows of the flowing river, beside the great boulder, he had turned to face Eli.

He was perhaps Garo's height, and had roughly the same athletic and solid build. His skin was almost as dark as Alégondine's, but his eyes were blue like his son's. But not the same blue.

In the incredibly beautiful and rugged face before her, Eli had the impression there were two holes or windows, for the eyes of the Dragon-Lord were exactly the same pale blue as the sky beyond him.

"No," thought Eli. "Why am I seeing blue sky behind and all about him? There is no sky directly behind Erreig, only high mountains and grey ravines, dark patches of forest and soaring eagles ---- or are those bats, or dragons?"

Now her own eyes were caught and held in the piercing regard of Erreig. She saw clearly where he and she actually stood, she heard the river's white-water song, felt the cool breeze of spring lifting her hair and billowing her cape out behind her, smelt the heather and the thyme and the pine-trees on the slopes. But at the same time she was far away: soaring on the scaly back of a huge dragon and flying proudly in company with many other such wind-worms, flying in an azure universe which belonged only to herself and her companion. She was free and bold and new-born: a red-robed queen of a land forgotten or unknown to all but herself and the Chieftain of the Dragons. A land beyond the human-world or even that of Faërie. A land that would one day be theirs, only theirs…

Eli swayed where she stood. And Erreig advanced.

Now he was only a very few feet from her, almost within reach of her hand. He halted, and suddenly, leaping from the shadow that had lain upon it until now, the white diamond in his forehead, *Kalvi-Tivi*, flamed out like a blinding star. Eli closed her eyes, but as she did so she involuntarily lifted her right arm to shield them. And in her hand was the Amethyst Cloth.

The light of *Kalvi-Tivi* shot against it as if this was truly the jousting-tournament that Eli had heard heralded by the trumpet-bellows of the red-deer! Its beam of white light shattered against the mauve fabric, small and soft and crumpled as it was, and was instantly dispersed all about Eli in fleeting crystal shards.

A soft beam of violet light emanated from the torn fabric and seemed to reach out towards a similar light --- softly radiating from a concealed inner pocket of Erreig's cloak. She opened her eyes, and smiled.

She did not step back, but Erreig did. Only one or two paces, but it belied his concern and his uncertainty. There was silence for only a moment, and then Erreig spoke. His voice was the same heady mixture of heart-ache and dreams, masculine strength and feminine sensitivity, like a cadenza on a harp rolling from the depths of the bass-strings to the chiming bells of the treble.

"You are like your brother, Mélusine. You are two eyes in the same face, you and Finnir. You have come to inflict upon me the same brutal shame and fear. And I had thought to lure you to me… to speak in sweeter tones."

Eli was still smiling as she lowered the Amethyst Cloth, and now held it at her breast, just where the moon-flower was concealed.

"If you feel *fear*, we will find it difficult to speak at all; for fear is a wall, or a cage. And I would be glad to speak with you without it, even though I cannot promise that our conversation will be sweet."

Eli was surprised by her words, but --- as she concluded them --- not so surprised as all that. They seemed to come from her own heart, from a place deeper within her breast than the exterior Cloth or the concealed Flower. Perhaps, she mused, the Cup of Light has spilled its contents into me!

"Let us speak together, then," said Erreig after a moment's reflection.

Further up the bank, near to the gorse and thistles, was a second great stone similar to the one at the river's edge, suitable to use as a seat and large enough to allow Eli to keep a safe distance from the rather enchanted, and enchanting, fairy.

The breeze had fallen and there was a hushed stillness, as if the birds and trees, bushes and aromatic herbs were pricking their ears to listen. The clouds had dispersed, and the sunlight was warm on their stone seat. Erreig threw back his cloak as he sat. No light came from any pocket, and Eli's half of the Cloth was now replaced in its own hiding place too.

The deep red fire-opal in Erreig's chest, *Gurtha*, glowed modestly: it was a sleeping dragon whose nostrils nonetheless exhale a coiling smoke like incense, to remind one that his slumbering bulk contains greater fire not yet rekindled. High on Erreig's left arm was a twisted band of thick gold, of the same skilfully-wrought design as the torc about his neck. His bare chest was sculpted in muscle and about his hips was a loin-cloth of soft lizard-leather decorated in Celtic knots like his cloak. The labradorites in the lobes of his very pointed ears were exactly the same pale, piercing blue as his eyes. But, for the moment, those eyes were not working any magic on Eli, for they were filled with despair and defeat, it seemed.

"I do not know what occurred between you and Finnir, in the White Cat Caves," began Eli, in as gentle a tone of voice as she could muster, "but I have no desire to aggress you. I have only one purpose in seeking you out, and that is to request the return of the portion of the Cloth which you retain."

Eli felt that her discourse sounded like that of one government to another; it was indeed similar to very formal war, or pre-war, negotiations! She decided it may not be the best place to start.

"Erreig," she said, very slowly, "will you tell me who you are, really? I am, at this moment in fact, visiting the realm of Faërie, still as a human. I am here, but somehow still in the kingdom of my father King Aulfrin --- for I have not come here to Scotland (if that is really where we are) by a Portal, as you have. I'm on my third Visit home, as a changeling. I have learned, or re-learned, much about Faërie and its inhabitants, but this is the first time I have met *you* face to face. I'd be glad to learn more about the Lord of Quillir."

The Dragon-Chieftain glanced at her, studying her eyes for an instant as if questioning her sincerity, but then he returned his gaze to the far side of the glen.

He said, sulkily Eli thought, "I have lived nine centuries in Faërie, and for most of those in only one corner of it, in wondrous Quillir. But I am, I think, like you: a visitor, or so I often feel myself to be. I am homeless, even when I am in my White Dragon Fortress in the pass of the Beldrum Mountains. I am a Lord and a Chieftain, but even my own subjects fly in the face of my authority, taking sides with those foes who would submit me to their own wills. I have sought respect and renown, which I merit; but it has been stolen from my grasp."

"As you have stolen the Cloth?"

Erreig's eyes flashed as he turned them suddenly to Eli once again. But they were veiled, immediately, with weariness and regret.

"Yes," he admitted. "As I stole a piece of your shroud, Mélusine. As I stole the love of your fair mother, the Queen of Faërie, and as I have stolen a moment with her daughter, here in the human world."

"*Are* we in the human world?" smirked Eli, shaking her head. "I thought I was, yesterday. Now I don't know! Is it you that stole away the snow, too?!"

Erreig had to grin at her word-play, and he looked upon her again, evidently with less discomfort now, for he looked long.

He nodded. "Yes, I *stole* the snow. I poured the sunlight of my much-loved province of Quillir into this hidden valley. Just for us."

"That was very kind of you," chuckled Eli outright now. "I'm warmer than I was coming over the pass from Loch Etive. Thank you. But are we in Quillir; or are we in the Highlands of Argyll?"

Erreig still looked into Eli's face. It was clear that he found her company and her conversation engaging. Eli felt the wave of attraction, stronger even than when he had been singing and proclaiming it in verse. What troubled her was whether it was only *his* attraction for her, or if she were feeling it too. She banished the thought.

Erreig replied to her question: "Our surroundings, our perceptions of reality, are like our romances. We conjure them out of ourselves, and paint them to our own taste. All the canvas is white, in the beginning. We are artists, sometimes inspired, sometimes mad."

Eli recalled the similar discourse of Banvowha, the rainbow-fairy. She nodded with a smile. "Yes, you are right," she said. "And so, if I can enter into your sunny landscape it must be because I retain none of the ice and cold of the previous one. It is a shared conjuring-up of spring, in a private valley, between adversaries --- or perhaps allies?"

"So began my encounters with the Prince Finnir, with just such condescending and deceiving words --- though in silence," growled Erreig, his mood changing swiftly to resentment and his lips pursed in anger. "But he sought only victory, and to paint his *own* pictures, to paint in the yellow and white of the moon, on my red page! A battle of wills, and his was the greater; I admit that. He is his mother's son."

Eli did not deem it her place to inform Erreig that Finnir was *not* the son of Rhynwanol, nor of Daireen, if he knew that tale --- which seemed unlikely.

But she remarked, more coolly that the Dragon-tamer beside her, "Were both of you fighting a battle to gain a <u>victory</u>? Or was it only you, Erreig?

"It's possible, I suppose, to try to contend with someone who is at *peace* with you," she continued, "and to *call* it a battle; but in fact it is one-sided, for the other party is *not* your enemy. A famous teacher, in this human-world, once called this 'kicking against the thorns'. It is not a *real* battle, not when one seeks to aggress a spiky thorn-bush! It is as much an invention of the artist, the *mad* artist in this case, as this our charming vernal composition of flowers and a sunny, glinting river."

Erreig looked intently at her. "The mystical Prince subdued me, vanquished me," he retorted, with emphasis and bitterness.

"You are mistaken, I believe. I truly do not think he wished to humiliate you." Eli exhaled with a long sigh, and then she added, "But you are right in one thing, I think. Finnir and I are two eyes in the same face. And so I can tell you, with some certainty, that if I am not your enemy, then neither is Finnir. And I am not. I refuse to be. We may not be friends, but we will never be enemies --- for that is *more* than a one-sided battle against a humble though prickly plant, against thorns that are just being thorns. To be real 'enemies', we must be two to fight. And I am not here to fight with you."

Erreig seemed to struggle to regain his composure, and he did so after a minute or two. He said, very softly now, almost as if his voice were made of richly flavoured forest honey, "I proposed friendship, and more than friendship, to Mélusine, long years ago."

It was Eli's turn to have flashing eyes. But her voice remained diplomatic in tone, if not entirely pacifist. "You may cast it in those terms, but I think you deform the truth. It was *not* friendship that you offered, and it was not what you call 'more than friendship' --- by which I suppose you mean *love* --- for such an affinity as love, or even friendship, is not linked, at all, to taking. Only to giving.

"It seems to me that you have sought, in your seduction of my mother and in your pursuit of me, to take or win some renown for yourself from the fact of having a high and noble consort, a Queen or a Princess. And more impressive still if it could be the wife, or the daughter, of the ruling sovereign whom you wished to challenge. But I would like to remind you that love *never* seeks such celebrity or such status from the loved-one; it does not *use* the belovèd to increase the worth or the self-image of the lover. It only gives. Like the Sun itself, Erreig, it only *gives*."

He glared back at her now, quite transformed by desperate misery. "But the children of the Moon, like the Moon itself, they take! They take my light, reflecting it back for all to see as if it were their own. They are false; *they* are the wily conjurers and the mischief-makers!"

His tone was heated, and Eli felt a warning in her heart that this fairy was very volatile and not at all given to self-control. She breathed the fragrant air, and tried to send out some conciliatory vibrations of peace.

At last, she spoke very soothingly and almost in a whisper. "I would venture to guess that Finnir sought to present another perspective to you, as I do; to suggest another fashion of looking at the interplay between the Sun and the Moon, Erreig. Does it have to be taking and tricking? Could it not be more like two strands of counterpoint in one and the same composition, a marriage of music?

"Might we try that, here and now?" she concluded, simply.

To Erreig's obvious and immense surprise, Eli rose and stepped in among the high, yellow blossoms of the gorse bushes near their stone seat. She emerged with Róisín in her arms. Without another glance at the baffled Dragon-Chieftain, she sat on a smaller, mossy stone facing Erreig, and embraced her harp in her arms. She had pulled out the Amethyst Cloth once more and hung it over her right wrist as she played.

If Eli had any clear idea of what she was doing, she was not conscious of it; but it seemed that her hands and her spirit did. For she began by playing an air based loosely on the seven notes of the 'miraculous music'. The same tune she had used to traverse the Gate of Wineberry, but in a very different rhythm and tempo. But after only a few measures it changed, and she suddenly *recognised* this second melody that naturally flowed from her fingertips. Or would it be more correct to say, perhaps, that her fingers *released* this tune from where it slumbered in the strings of the Harp of Barrywood? Certainly, it was a melody that seemed to be coming from somewhere beyond herself and her own intentions.

It was the tune of the haunting song that Alégondine had sung at the Golden Sand Castle of Leyano, at the close of the council of the Alliance of the Eleven Spiralling Stars.

It was a song which had, on that occasion, caused Eli to drift into so enchanted and profound a sleep that she had not even noticed going to her bed, or being carried there.

But here, as Erreig listened to it, the melody had a slightly different effect. For Erreig knew the words of this song; or perhaps they were verses of his own and not at all what Alégondine had sung, for they were --- as hers had been --- unintelligible to Eli's ears. Both Erreig's daughter and Erreig himself sang, in equally mystical and powerful voices, words in the ancient language of Faërie and not translated (and probably not translatable) into Eli's human tongue.

Early, pale blue afternoon seemed to pass, in timeless hours of magical measures --- so beautiful a 'musical marriage' that Eli was hardly able to keep from weeping, or laughing aloud --- until the sky turned as mauve as the Amethyst Cloth and one high star began to shine into the Lost Valley. Eli felt the sudden realisation, even as her fingers started to tire of their playing, that the last wisp of the moon-lash had set.

A wave of fatigue broke over her. She was sure that Erreig felt it, felt that she was about to faint, fall into a trance or collapse into an unnatural sleep. If she did, he would surely come to her, and sweep her up into his strong arms… Did she, in fact, wish for just that? Her eyes were closing…

She blinked once or twice, as her harp-music and his song ceased simultaneously. Everything around them fell silent: wind, trees, water and bird-call. Yes, she could see Erreig coming towards her. He was coming, slowly and yet with strength and daring, with strides at once passionate and presumptuous.

She could not stay awake. One more blink of her heavy, closing eyes --- just one more…

And then, high above Erreig --- or no, now very close and moving fast --- was a white-tailed eagle. His huge wings were as mighty as a dragon's, and his voice, though utterly silent, was clearer and brighter in Eli's confused mind than the hot flames from a winged-reptile's open jaws would have been.

"The moon-flower! Bring forth the moon-flower, and hold it up!"

Not aware how she had managed to tell her hands what to do, Eli found that she had leant Róisín against one of the yellow bushes and had reached into the tiny pocket of her tunic and extracted the delicate little flower. Erreig, as soon as the eagle had swooped down to join them, had halted where he was --- in wonder or fearful alarm, Eli did not know which.

In her right hand, the Amethyst Cloth still draped over the wrist, she held the moon-flower. She raised her hand, slowly, towards Erreig. With her left hand she reached up and touched the Flaming Crescent Moon that hung from her ear.

She took one long, deep breath, and then her vision cleared and Eli could see Erreig standing before her, staring. Jizay was once again beside his mistress, and he was staring too. And so, when he landed on the great stone seat, was the sea-eagle.

But they were *not* staring at her.

Eli turned to look, with the others, up the slopes of the darkening glen just behind them. She could see very clearly now, too clearly for human vision in a twilit Scottish glen, be it winter or even springtime. But the vision provided its own light.

A woman was there.

Eli had thought her mother, the Queen Rhynwanol, to be the most beautiful creature, human or fairy, that she had ever seen. But such a verdict had to be questioned now.

And fully as beautiful and wonderful as the woman, was the beast she rode. A stag, or hart --- not a red-deer, but a *reindeer*. A red-eared one. He was huge and almost pure white, save for his ear-tips; and his massive, triple-branched antlers were of a greater span than Peronne's eagle-wings.

Astride him was a woman; indeed, she was a fairy, for she bore tall and magnificent multi-form wings like the torn banners around a heraldic coat-of-arms. Only these blowing strands and ribbons and frayed flags were not made of cut fabric, but of iridescent insect wing-membrane and frosted cobwebs, embellished with dazzling light.

But even her incredible wings were pale and dull beside her own beauty.

Her long, straight hair was of pure silver, shining like moonbeams, and her eyes had the same metallic hue. Her skin was golden, or made of gold, or perhaps drenched in molten gold. And gold and white and ice-blue were her robes, hanging in their ribbon-like tatters --- tatters as eccentric and beautiful as the petals of an extravagantly scalloped and irregular, utterly *outlandish* peony --- all about her lithe body.

Riding on the Lord Hwittir's back, and smiling with a twinkle of defiance in her silver eyes, she came down the slope of the rocky, forested mountainside. Fairy and Stag halted a couple of yards from their on-lookers.

Silently regarding Erreig for a long moment, looking down upon him from her high seat astride the enormous reindeer, the fairy then turned towards Eli.

"Greetings, Princess Mélusine," came a voice that could only have been uttered by a creature made of gold and silver, of snow-flakes and frosty moon-glow and ancient dragon-force.

"I am Vanzelle."

****

Chapter Eleven:
Vanzelle

azing still at the glorious fairy, Eli overcame the temptation to believe that she had, in fact, fainted and that this was a vision or hallucination of her troubled and tired brain. She dismissed the idea, for her breathing and eyesight seemed perfectly normal to her now. It was just that this entire place and scene before her was not, in any way, normal. Well, not if one were a human.

Vanzelle was still mounted on the Red-Eared Hart, the Lord Hwittir. And they were still about two yards away from Eli and Erreig, Jizay and Peronne.

"*That* was a truly splendid entrance," was the comment Eli made to herself. "Really, even having grown up in Los Angeles and Hollywood, I couldn't fault it. Spectacular."

The white fairy-Stag was larger than a deer of any species Eli had ever seen or heard of. He was roughly the size of a Canadian moose. He was as pure and gleaming a white as virgin snow, his coat thick and furry, the red all about the edges and tips of his ears shining like holly berries, and his cloven hooves giving the impression that they bore a dusting of diamond-chips. His triple-branched antlers resembled a bare, wintry tree and he had enormous eyes as kind and deep as Jizay's, as enchanted as Peronne's and as wise as Aulfrin's.

Vanzelle modestly retracted her incredible wings and swung her right leg over the withers of the mighty Hart, jumping down from his lofty back as though she were well used to dismounting fantastical beasts much, much larger than the Lord Hwittir. She stepped, or glided, down the few feet of coarse grass to the stony place beside the twilight purple thistles and the shadowy-yellow gorse bushes.

Really, she was altogether amazing, thought Eli once more. And she added, still silently and only to herself, "I could say of Garo what Erreig said of Finnir: for the handsome dragon-lordling who has won the heart of my half-sister is certainly *his mother's son*. I see where he comes by his magic and his beauty."

Erreig stood at one side of the golden fairy, Eli the other. Up close, Vanzelle was very *petite*, but she exuded dignity and nobility, unfathomable depths of courage and wells of experience. Eli wondered how old she might be, in fairy-centuries that is. If she had met the Dragon-Lord in his youth, bearing Garo in the early twelfth-century, she was at least nine-hundred-years old.

Eli also wondered when Erreig had last seen her, for he was regarding her now with utter fascination. The expression on his face reminded her of her own astounded breathlessness when, as a teenager visiting Mount Pinos near Los Angeles, she had seen snow falling for the first time in her life. She had been so wonderstruck that she had danced! The boy-friend who had taken her there on the back of his motorbike had thought she was crazy; but she hadn't been able to help herself. Well, now she knew that, as a fairy and a Moon-Dancer, it was perhaps a very normal response to such a miracle as snow!

In any case, Eli smiled, looking at Erreig looking at Vanzelle. But then she herself had to return her gaze to the resplendent gold-and-silver fairy. She was about to *attempt* to find her voice and politely greet the wondrous apparition, when Vanzelle turned to address the Dragon-Chieftain.

Vanzelle

"I *know* the song you were singing, Erreig. You used to sing it to *me*, in the Bay of Secrets."

"Indeed, Vanzelle," he nodded, his voice as hushed as the snow that was now beginning to fall once again. The sky had once more become a single, thin, pale-grey roof of cloud, the setting sun a ruddy disc behind it --- glimpsed for a fleeting moment far down the valley, and then only a memory. But the night was not yet cold, nor utterly dark. Vanzelle and the great white reindeer were gently glowing, and the lacework of the delicate snowflakes accumulating on the stones and bare bushes shone pale and luminous.

"It is true: I sang it to you, and *for* you," continued the deep, sorrowful voice. "It was our love-song."

Vazelle's silver eyes glistened like the diamond-hooves of the Lord Hwittir. She exhaled very audibly, evidently annoyed.

"You should <u>never</u> sing the same love-song to more than one woman, Erreig. Singing those words to the harp-music played by the Princess Mélusine, or which you perhaps drew forth from her harp, was incorrect of you. That is an act at once forbidden and destructive. It is *un-aligned*. So says the Tradition. You must never woo two women with the same song."

"The Tradition does not take into account the estrangement of lovers, the winds that blow them apart, the <u>choices</u> that divide them." Erreig had squared his broad shoulders and lifted his chin defiantly. But his voice was still sad.

"The Tradition takes *all* into account," returned Vanzelle. "It springs from the understanding and the 'accounting' of all, from the wisdom of that accounting and from all the experience of the Ancestors. As a legend cannot grow from *nothing*, but only from the seeds of truth, so the Tradition grows from our most ancient wisdom. And the Tradition decrees that it is *folly* and *danger* to sing the same love-song to various women."

Eli felt the temperature of the dialogue rising while that of the glen fell to freezing. She interrupted as gracefully as she could.

"What do the words say, the fairy-words which I could not understand? The song is very beautiful and profoundly touching, even without comprehending the lyrics, though…"

Vanzelle turned to Eli once again, and smiled affectionately. Her voice became somewhat gentler, as a gust of wind may dwindle to a breeze.

"They speak of unity, of honesty, of reconciliation. They say that, even though I may wander and we may part, that I shall turn and *re*turn, going forward and upward, until we meet again on the same climbing path. They speak of a spiralling, soaring flight. They say that the impulsion of love is always a spiral…"

"Like the Alliance?" ventured Eli, whispering the words, but audibly enough for Vanzelle to hear her question and for Erreig to widen his eyes in response to it.

"Yes, Mélusine, yes. For we *are* the Alliance, when we love," nodded Vanzelle, her voice now like the caress of northern winds among the long needles of towering, incalculably old pine trees. "We are the Alliance in miniature, or perhaps in amplification, when we are lovers. This is the true wisdom of the Tradition, for the sacred spiral is constantly shown to us, time and time again --- indeed, this is how nature is, how nature works. This is the art of nature's progressing: season in love with season, insect in love with flower, bird with seed, wind with leaf… heart with heart. We *are* the spiral, and we are the Alliance. All of us, all fairies, everywhere.

"But we must respect it, this wise and sacred Tradition of the Ancestors. As we must respect one another. The passion of lovers is useless and even perverse, without the *respect* of lovers."

"Is it *respect* to abandon one's 'lover'?" muttered Erreig, the fire-jewel in his chest smouldering with an angry orange light.

"I did not *abandon* you." The glistening fairy's voice was firm but still as soft as the deepening snow around them.

It was not Eli that stemmed the tide of the discord this time, it was the white reindeer.

"My children," said the Lord Hwittir, to Eli's surprise not speaking in an interior fairy-voice, but rather moving his mouth and pronouncing the words in a very charming though somewhat guttural Finnish accent, "let us move to the shelter of the forest, for the Princess Mélusine is human-and-fairy combined perhaps, but not as you are, Vanzelle-*yala*, nor you Erreig-*herra*. She will be cold. Come, little Eli-*lapsi*, for I have brought food and drink from my shee and from the forest-dwellings in Finland near to one of its hidden doors."

As the great Stag concluded his invitation, he turned his head and emitted a sonorous, quite gentle bellow, as if chanting in a strange and forgotten tongue. Immediately, both Jizay and Peronne made ready to follow him; the golden hound trotting happily up to the reindeer and respectfully bowing his head, while Peronne, landing close-by him on the stony ground, opened his wide wings slowly, and then closed them with his noble head slightly inclined in similar recognition of the honour due the sovereign of the Shee of the Red-Eared Hart.

Obediently, if somewhat sullenly, Erreig followed Vanzelle and Eli, who climbed after the Lord Hwittir back up the short slope toward the trees. Jizay and Peronne followed close behind.

Under the cover of the pines, from whence the Lord Hwittir and Vanzelle had first appeared, Eli found two pixies waiting, roughly the size of Periwinkle. They were introduced to her, by the great Stag, as royal gnomes who had ridden with them from the hidden oak-grove Portal of his Shee. Their names were unpronounceable to Eli, but Vanzelle translated the foreign words as 'pine-cone' and 'penny-grass'.

While Pine-cone lit three or four large, squat candles, Penny-grass quickly laid out a soft quilted rug, like a bedspread in

Scandinavian star-block 'bear-paw' patterns. On this 'picnic blanket' he then arranged tiny wooden drinking-bowls and what looked to Eli like presents from a Christmas stocking: little packages of folded leaves tied with golden and white, red and green ribbons and bows.

The *kuksa*, as Vanzelle called the wooden cups with compact handles carved from the same continuous piece of birch-wood, were filled by Pine-cone with *glögg*. This was an extremely 'fortified' mulled wine, as purple as if it were a *liqueur* made from the berries that had surrounded Eli and Jizay when they arrived in Glen Etive. As Eli sipped it, her whole body was warmed by the rich alcohol tasting of raisins and ginger, clove and cardamom.

Penny-grass then smiled and passed Eli her little leaf-package, nodding enthusiastically for her to open it, his button eyes closing as he grinned and his red cheeks becoming even more round and shiny. Untying the ribbons, Eli found --- to her delight, for she now realised she was very hungry! --- not one, but two types of pastries.

The larger, oval, savoury ones tasted of rye flour and were filled with a mixture of barley, caramel-sweet carrot and a few blueberries. Like the mulled-wine, these delicacies were steaming hot. Together with these *karelian* cakes were found two or three tiny versions of *pulla* cinnamon-rolls, no bigger than French *petits-fours*.

Erreig and Vanzelle sat side by side, silently sharing their meal, with the Dragon-Lord furtively glancing at the dazzling fairy-woman from time to time. The hound and the huge eagle occupied another part of the patch-work quilt and ate the same foods as the other guests, though they did not drink any *glögg*. Eli sat closest to the mighty reindeer, who had descended --- as it were --- to her height and was lying with his legs tucked under his great body. She was three or four feet away from him nonetheless, owing to the span of his antlers.

Vanzelle

Of course, Eli had brought Róisín with her into the woods and the harp stood beside her, next to the trunk of a large Scots pine. From this tree, two very inquisitive red squirrels joined them, and were as delighted as Eli was with the pastries! When everyone had dined, the two gnomes quickly cleared the cloth, and disappeared behind the nearby tree-trunk, or possibly climbed up the pine to continue their visit with the two squirrels.

The Lord Hwittir, remained 'seated', breathing deeply, and making clouds of vapour-swirls rise from his nostrils, like an old man blowing smoke-rings from a great pipe.

"My children," he repeated once again, "your paths were severed many long decades ago, and you have both grown and matured since your youthful love-affair. But now comes the time when your paths re-cross. Weave well that crossing of life-treads, and you may yet make a pretty garment of them!"

Erreig spoke immediately, obviously wishing to defend and vindicate himself.

"I would have kept you by me, in Quillir, Vanzelle. You were bound to return to your own shee to complete your Initiations. But you might have returned."

"Or you might have joined me there," came the silver fairy's quick retort.

"*Might* is a useless word, in all of its costumes," laughed the Lork Hwittir, dispersing --- as he did so --- the building tension of the atmosphere in the pine-clearing. "Of course, I have always disliked the concept of *might* as 'force' or 'strength'; we must remember that water is wiser, stronger, slower but working greater change than a 'mighty' boulder or mountain. *Might*, as force, is an odd and elusive concept at best. Ah yes, force is usually folly when it is preoccupied with its own might! Whereas a gentle brook or a slow but steady flutter of timid, soft snow will one day change the face of the hardest landscape.

"And 'might' used to mean 'what could have been' is even greater nonsense. What *might have been*, was not what *was*! And what *might be*, is not yet manifest, and may turn out to be quite otherwise!"

"But I had my province of Quillir to defend and my lordship to establish," protested Erreig. "My lady should have come back to me; she should have been at my side."

"*Should* is not much better than *might*, I think." The comment came from Eli. The great reindeer turned his massive, antlered head to her and nodded his assent.

"Quite right, my dear. Worse, in my opinion. But I will indulge in a little of your 'what might have been' and 'what should have happened' game, Erreig-*herra*. Though I will say 'could' rather than 'should' or 'might'!

"You *could* have chosen to follow your lady, the noble Vanzelle-*yala*. You could have left Quillir and the realm of King Aulfrin. I *would* (ah, not a bad word either, that!), have welcomed you in *my* shee. As I was happy to welcome your son, the dragon-lordling beloved of the Great Tree, the friend of wolf and bear, my sweet sandy-haired Garo. The White Dragon Family *would* have been a splendid jewel in my kingdom's treasure-chest!"

Vanzelle's tone was slightly bitter as she said: "Erreig was occupied with his own ambition and with disharmony and dissonance, driving a spear into the heart of Aulfrin's realm to separate Sun-Singer and Moon-Dancer, confusing the music of Faërie with the tiny bugle-calls of his own ego."

"Please…please," murmured the Stag, his voice as soft as the velvet on a young buck's summer antlers. "Allow the ice to melt, Vanzelle-*yala*. Allow it to melt. Ice upon ice becomes destructive, for it has been known to crack and fall upon our heads in an avalanche of recriminations!" The reindeer was laughing warmly now. The candles blazed as he did so, and Eli had to chuckle with him.

"It's never too late," she mentioned, "if I may use a motto from the humans, and one that I have also heard spoken in Faërie. It's never too late to change, and nature does so all the time. The page *before* us is blank and white, and --- if I'm not mistaken --- sometimes we *need* a part of the path to be folly and disharmony, so that we can see more clearly how to construct their opposites."

"You are wise, little Eli-*lapsi*, very wise --- for a human!" the Stag affirmed, still with amusement in his voice. "But then, for many centuries the fairies have been coming and going, back and forth into the human world, like sweet water over hard rock, and so they have changed many human ideas, and they are still changing them!"

Eli was continuing to smile, too, as she looked at Erreig rather pointedly and said, "Yes, it has been a great blessing to have the doors open between the two worlds, and it is now more needed than ever. It would be a pity and a shame to see them closed."

Erreig grimaced.

"Love never closes doors," said the fantastically beautiful voice of the fantastically beautiful silver fairy. "It only knows how to open them."

There was a short silence, where one could have almost heard the snow falling.

"Let us sleep, my fair ones, my little ones," said the Lord Hwittir, rising. "Pine-cone and Penny-grass will build you a pretty fairy-*kota*, Eli-*lapsi*. We, the fairies and gnomes of my shee, sleep in the snow and the pine-trees. And you, my defiant Erreig-*herra*, will you try our snowy beds too? I know you come from a land of sun and scorched earth and that you have a fine fortress for your dwelling, but it is sometimes as profitable to change your sleeping-habits as it is to 'change your mind'! I will see you all with the light of morning."

Chuckling, the great Red-Eared Hart trotted off into the darkness beyond the first row of tree-trunks and out of the glow of the candles. Eli followed Pine-cone and Penny-grass, with her hound and her eagle and her harp, to another clearing and an amazing and comfortable *lavvu*: her 'pretty fairy-*kota*', as the kind reindeer had called it.

What choices and changes of mind were made by Vanzelle and her former lover, Eli did not know. Though she had her ideas.

****

The day of the new moon dawned cold and crisp in the Scottish Highlands, although Eli felt herself to be in a scene form a Nordic fireside tale. The two tiny gnomes were waiting for her at the door of her *lavvu* with a hot infusion of some sort of frothy mocha-coffee and several more of the delicious cinnamon pastries of last evening, plus berries and a minuscule serving of sweet porridge.

"The Lord Hwittir awaits you, further down the glen," announced the familiar voice of her flying-horse, though still in his disguise of a white-tailed eagle. He was sitting on one of the bare branches of a nearby oak tree. Jizay, emerging with Eli from her fairy-*kota*, stretched and yawned. They had both slept well.

She asked her hound of joy, "Why am I not weak and dizzy, with the absence of the moon and the theft of the Amethyst Cloth draining my life-force? I feel fine. I don't understand this at all."

"Both parts of the Amethyst Cloth are here in this valley, and so --- in a way --- it is whole," replied Jizay. "And you have passed through the 'berries-black' upon leaving the Gate in the moutainside. Thus all is gradually converging and coming together at last. *And* you bear the moon-flower."

Eli still looked perplexed as she finished her breakfast and the two adorable gnomes trotted off with the *kuksa* as she gave her last two *pulla* to Jizay.

Peronne flapped his wide wings, and added, "Your suspended form, the veritable Princess Mélusine, is slumbering, but is also with you here. When you have the Cloth, you have a part of Mélusine --- more of her fairy nature, and perhaps her powers, than you have as a human-changeling, dear Eli. This is perhaps one part of the reason why Erreig took it. And it is why you must retrieve it.

"But, please remember, that taking the Cloth or keeping even a part of it, does not equate with 'possession'. The Cloth is yours and is *you*, in a small but vital way. He can steal it, handle it, dishonour it --- and you --- but he does not become its, or your, *possessor*."

Eli smiled and felt a surge of relief and confidence rising through her body.

Jizay remarked, "You have strong support from many fairies, but --- in the end --- you need only your own belief in the Princess, and also the human-woman, that you are. I think the King alluded to a moment when you had realised that, when Erreig first stole the Cloth. "

She stroked her dog's head, and smiled at his seal-wise, loving brown eyes. "Yes, I remember the conversation with my father and Leyano." She thought quietly for a moment, and the words floated back to her, as they had been spoken in her brother's Golden Sand Castle on Mermaid Island:

"I am greater, higher, more noble and more powerful than Erreig," she had said. *"I am more loving and more honest. He may think to have stolen a prize or a sort of talisman that can work some charm of possession over me, but I think it much more likely that I myself can use the fabric, which has been in contact with my enchanted form for fifty years, to gain some insight or magical power of surveillance over him! He may, in fact, have made a tactical error by indulging in such a theft, for I might very well turn it back upon him and see into the depths of the heart against which it is clutched."*

*Aulfrin had then said, with pride: "Now, **that's** my Princess talking! Aha, there you see with the eyes of the heart; you invoke your* *own power and you turn his mischief to your good and true advantage!"*

And Leyano had added his very beautiful conclusion: "You have seen this, Eli, as our father says, with the eyes of the heart, and thus you begin to dilate the half-face of the Moon to become full at last. For with the eyes and the heart of the Sun we shall one day see the Moon ever-full; just as with the eyes of your own heart you, Eli, will one day know the fullness of your own power."

She looked back and forth, from Jizay to Peronne.

"And so," she said, very softly, "perhaps it is good that Erreig still has the Cloth, and has not returned it to me….yet. For maybe I can use it to see into 'the depths of the heart against which it is clutched'. Maybe I can still help turn his mischief to my advantage, and maybe I can also help to 'dilate the half-face of the Moon to become full', seeing it with the eyes of the Sun. Maybe I have that power, already, even before I become the fairy-Princess I truly am."

"Or maybe," remarked the deep voice of Peronne, "you have *more* power here and now as Eli-the-human, than a full-fairy would have."

Jizay added, "If all is one, as it is, then you are *both*. And the Cloth is whole, and your sight of Erreig's heart is clear. And the Moon is already full, even if she is new and dark and invisible. I think the Lord Reyse would agree with me, for he has the gift of seeing into the Sun, and thereby of seeing the moon ever-full."

Eli shivered, but not with the cold. "Let's go further down the glen, then, and find the enchanted reindeer, and the dragon-lovers," she said, lifting her harp and holding the torn portion of the Amethyst Cloth gently, and confidently, in her hand.

Although still late autumn, this morning seemed a moment poised between winter and spring: a marriage, a mixture, a threshold. Snow lay once again on the slopes of the Lost

Valley, icy-cold water threaded down the slim, cascading waterfalls and flowed lazily in rocky stream-beds. There were brown, curled ferns and hardy grasses, dark pine trees and graceful, naked silver birch, hoary oaks and sequestered alders, wise and knowing trees. And all of them seemed part of a *winter* landscape.

But in the air was a breath of new life, of tender green, of buds and shyly opening first flowers, subtly infusing the valley with perfumes that were not suited to autumn or winter at all. Eli remembered her Lily's recollections of springtime in the forests of Brittany; she had often spoken of the exciting and sacred moment when one could feel the first stirrings of the change of season. How lovely, ruminated Eli, that she had met her darling Sean on just such a spring day…

Peronne flew above and a little ahead of Eli and Jizay. A ptarmigan crossed their path again, manifestly content to have some snow back under his feet, croaking a song to himself. Among the trees to their left, Eli saw the occasional faces of red-deer does, their large eyes as dark as the obsidian brooch on her father's cloak. There were mountain hares, squirrels, and also a pine marten, who --- like the deer --- all seemed to be watching her and asking questions as to her business there, especially as it was clear that she had something to do with two fairies and an enchanted white reindeer, further ahead.

Eli stopped and closed her eyes for a moment, silently extracting her portion of the Cloth. She imagined, rather than playing or even humming, the 'miraculous music' as she visualised the other half of the mauve fabric, hidden in Erreig's cloak-pocket. In her mind she saw the pocket sewn into his dark cape --- directly over his heart. Like a prayer, she allowed her imaginings to include that troubled heart; and there, in its sorrowful and blood-red-dragonfire depths, she visualised the Cloth whole again. As well as other sundered and separated things brought together once again also.

Finally Peronne swooped lower and whispered, "They are just beyond that boulder, not far from the shallows of the passing stream."

Eli opened her eyes very peacefully. She looked up and shook her head.

"Boulder, indeed! It's the size of an elephant," she remarked to herself. "And what a primeval landscape this is! One has the impression that one is treading on millennia of history, right under the soles of one's boots. Stark and august mountains, sublime and almost unearthly ravines and tumbled heaps of gigantic rocks: and many of those rocks look as if they were quarried and cut smooth by giants. This is a *mythopoetic* land. It would be absolutely perfect for dragons!"

As she turned the corner of the pachyderm-sized boulder, Erreig was saying almost the same to Vanzelle.

"I am sorry that Bawn did not accompany me here; this is indeed a playground worthy of that prodigious beast!"

Vanzelle, who was walking back from the river's edge with her hands and face wet and dripping crystalline droplets of icy water, smiled.

"Ideal for dragons, yes. And the beauteous Bawn would surely love to fly here, exploring the movements of the winds down these glens and canyons, wheeling and diving over those crags and snowy peaks. It would make for wild riding, would it not?!"

Erreig regarded her wordlessly.

It was Vanzelle who noticed Eli first. "Ah, greetings and good morning, Princess Mélusine."

As she spoke, Erreig rose to his feet, for he had been tending a small fire sheltered from the wind in a crevice of the rock-face. A brazen jug was perched on some stones just touching the flames, and he lifted this to pour a cup of warm liquid for Eli. He held out a rustic, pottery mug painted in red and yellow designs of suns and triskels. He said nothing, but his pale blue eyes shone almost warmly, Eli thought.

"Amazing what love can do to people," she smiled to herself. "There is a calm in the eyes of the Dragon-Lord, since last night, that I would guess has been absent for many centuries."

"What exactly *is* this drink?" she asked aloud, accepting the pottery cup with a curious grin.

Erreig hesitated only a moment, then --- in a voice that was at once strong as the surrounding rocks, warm and alive as the orange fire, and reposeful as the shallows of the running stream --- he said, "It is a peace-libation, Your Highness. To aid us in our conversation and in our ... mutual understanding."

Eli held it before her face, trying to catch the scent of what it was made from.

"Do not worry, Eli-*lapsi*. It is very safe to drink this brew!" The almost jovial voice was, of course, that of the Lord Hwittir. He had trotted, or airily skated, across the expanse of cropped grasses, patchy snow and myriad stones stretching away to the wooded foothills. "It is not a *potion* to make you sleepy or to transform you into a dragon yourself! It is simply a drink which promotes docile and conciliatory discussions."

"Well then, I'm happy to taste it, and I wish we had some on tap here in this human world," grinned Eli. "It would be an excellent cordial to serve in meetings and parliaments, households, schoolrooms and back-alleys alike!" She took a sip, and raised her eyebrows. "Delicious. A blend of herbs... and fruits?"

"Among other ingredients, yes. One could say it is a mixture of plants and peaceful intentions, thoughts and petals." Vanzelle's voice was as strong and sure as Erreig's, but filled with colours which his did not possess. His accents belied the *fragility* even of mountains, of fire-breathing reptiles, of monstrous felines or armoured warriors. Whereas the voice of the Nordic fairy Vanzelle was all blues and whites, and as strong as tiny flowers growing quietly beside thundering waterfalls, or the daring flights of tempest-tossed snowflakes as light as butterflies but as cold and mysterious as the Arctic vastness itself.

"If I may say so," commented Eli, as she continued to take short sips of the delightful beverage, "you make a very wonderful couple. You seem very complementary. It's just a feeling I have when I see you together…"

Erreig and Vanzelle were silent, but the latter was smiling.

"Sit by me, my children," instructed the Lord Hwittir. "That's right, you there dear Eli-*lapsi*, with your golden hound. I see your eagle-horse is with you too, just up on the edge of this small stone beside us; good, good… And the 'wonderful couple', as you call them, yes, just here on either side of me. Hmm, indeed, as you say, they are filled with… wonder. Yes.

"And do you have other feelings, when you see them together?" The elocution of the huge reindeer was charming, thought Eli. As she settled herself on a low slab of rock near where she had placed Róisín, she smiled at him, and at the two fairies sitting either side of the Red-Eared Hart.

"Well…," began Eli. She closed her eyes for a moment, as if she were seeking to see, not with her normal sight but with her heart.

You will invoke your own power and turn his mischief to your good and true advantage. Those had been her father's words to her. And Leyano had added: *With the eyes of your own heart you, Eli, will one day know the fullness of your own power.*

Eli considered the idea of 'turning Erreig's mischief to her own advantage', but the image rang false, in a way. She really didn't want to have the *advantage*; she simply desired <u>respect</u> for her own truth and her own life. Furthermore, she was sure that the power her brother had spoken of was just that: not a power of force or of might or of superiority, but one of respect, mutual respect. Lily had written something like that in her journal. What was it? *Love is endless, just as it is beginning-less. It is noble and worthy of respect, and our loves, our romances, must be* filled with <u>respect</u>. I'm respecting love itself in my realisation that I cannot, again, be Sean's lover.

"What I'd like to say is this," Eli stated, coming out of her reverie and regarding Vanzelle and then Erreig, and then the very patient Red-Eared Hart. "The Dragon-Lord has stolen a piece of my shroud, from where my true fairy-body lies on the Island of the Scholar Owls. It seems that this is a serious crime, for it weakens or somehow threatens the life of the Princess, the fairy I truly am, or will be again, when I decide to step back into her form at the end of my human-changeling sojourn. I thought, at first, when he did this, that it was to have some sort of *control* over me, like a magical charm or a spell, so that he could see into me or manipulate me."

"I had no such intention!" Erreig's large, tanned hands were gripping his own knees as he sat cross-legged and now with his back suddenly redressed and his eyes filled with effrontery and injury.

"Allow the tale to unfold, Erreig-*herra*, and hold the fire of your heart in check. I do not hear accusation in Eli-*lapsi*'s tone. You too, have need of the peace-libation. Drink!"

"I have tasted it, my Lord Hwittir; at dawn I drank of the libation with Vanzelle."

The reindeer nodded, adding, "Peace is not needed punctually and is not to be applied only to *certain* of our discourses or our relationships. Peace is a way of living and a way of exchanging with all things. It is not selective. It is like the light of ... the sun."

Erreig's wide blue eyes glistened, but Eli was not sure if it was with defiance or with mounting tears. She decided to continue.

"Indeed, I do not accuse you, Erreig, this morning. For I have searched in my heart, and in yours too I think --- perhaps having a part of the Cloth in your hands allows me to see and understand your intentions better. What I have seen in our *two* hearts is <u>fear</u>. I believe that you feared me, have feared me for a long while, because as Mélusine I tried to defy you in your policies towards my father and his realm. And I feared *you*, because I have confused you with a vision or a memory that I had of a great and terrible violence done to me when I was a child."

"I did you no violence, not ever...."

Before he could finish his exclamation, the Lord Hwittir snorted, once, very markedly.

Erreig coughed and breathed deeply, and then he said, "Excuse my interruption, once more, of your tale, Mélusine. But I have not committed any violence against you in your childhood."

"Then I'm glad to hear that I am right," smiled Eli, "because I have just come to that conclusion too. I had a terrifying dream, or the dawning of a recollection in my long-buried memory from my human life, of a brutal attack. I think it *did* occur, but I do not think it was, or could have been, you. My mother, the Queen Rhynwanol, explained it in these words: *All dreams are like Life itself, using symbols, often in poetic or riddling scenes replacing one character or event with another --- not to confuse or to lie, but to draw you into deeper understanding of the heart's fragility...and of the heart's ultimate victory.*

"I think I may have cast you, Erreig, as a villain in my dream, unintentionally, because you were the symbol of some great fear deep inside me; perhaps that was because I associated you with the separation of my parents so many centuries ago. You see, although I begin to see that my dream was not an *exact memory* of the event, it has much to teach me, I believe. The fear sown by my mother's banishment has perhaps haunted me and made me refuse to believe in love and fidelity, somehow. I'm not sure yet, but I am sure that it is in *facing* that fear and the 'fragility of the heart', that I will win through to the 'ultimate victory' she spoke of. There are probably still many interlaced strands of fear in me --- but I am beginning to *wake up* from my confusing dreams so that I can, at last, eradicate them.

"At least I now see that to *fear* you will never serve me in any of my goals or plans; as for you to fear me, or my father, or Finnir, will not serve you either. We need to unravel the knotted stands, perhaps, if that is possible, of our respective and intertwined fears; but we must begin by banishing fear itself. And replace it with respect."

The eyes of the Dragon-Chieftain were wide with surprise, but Eli thought that a faint and foetal smile, like melting snow, played at the corners of his lips.

"I am so saddened to hear of this aggression done you as a human-child, Mélusine," Vanzelle said, with maternal or sisterly tenderness. "This is a grievous scar to bear, and I think that the Great Ones of Faërie should be able to heal you and help you, now you are coming home."

"I think I have already received some kind of help, though I cannot know exactly in what form. I believe that the ancient mer-harper, the Lady Ecume, learned of the violence done to me, and since she knew my human mother as well as the King, she used her...skills, to remove the <u>vivid</u> memory of what actually took place. At least, I think that is what she did. In any case, my greatest joy today is to know, in my heart, that it was not you, Erreig, who committed this crime. Beside it, stealing the Amethyst Cloth is perhaps less serious; though it seems to involve a danger to me, both as Eli and as Mélusine."

"May I speak?" Erreig --- speaking in a rather hushed, almost humble tone of voice --- seemed to be asking this permission from everyone at once. He looked at the white reindeer, at Vanzelle, at Eli, and even at Jizay and Peronne.

But the first to answer, was Jizay.

"You may, of course, Lord Erreig," said the golden dog, sitting up where he had been lying beside Eli, and speaking in silence --- but very clearly to all. "But allow me to say, first, to my mistress, that she has well-heard the truth of her heart. I was there when you were attacked and dishonoured, my darling Eli. I was not as I am here, part-fairy and part-worldly dog; I was invisible and purely insubstantial. That morning, when you were only eight years old, I wished with every fibre of my being that I had chosen to enter into the body of a 'real' dog. But as it was, I could do nothing to avert the attack --- and it broke my heart.

"It was me, thereafter, who spoke to your father the King, even before he once again ventured into the world to visit Lily. I beseeched him to seek a means to erase that memory from your human mind and body; but he told me that such violence could be considered as part of the experience you had desired when you embarked upon your changeling-adventure. He would try to learn if he had the right to intervene. It was a difficult process, I later learned, for him to secure the charms of the Lady Ecume and to dull your memories and some of the scars the crime left on your youthful human sensibilities.

"Later, alas, such violence --- or other crimes as perverse --- would again manifest in your adult life, and at that time I came as a true dog. But, alas, I was equally impotent to avert the brutal attacks upon you; for as a dog, I could be confined and separated from you. When you were aggressed by Yves, I was not present --- I found myself once again howling with empathy and anger, but now beyond closed doors!

"But, how wise your father the King was, and how filled with <u>respect,</u> in knowing that such incredibly brutal experiences might very well have been part of your courageous intention in going forth on this adventure in the first place. Only Méluisne knows, and so we cannot unlock the answers now. But today I am wondering if it may also be true, as regards the experience of this crime of the Dragon-Chieftain's, that there is a reason and a plan behind it. For how else, ever, would you have contrived to sit face to face with Erreig, with Vanzelle present, and with the noble Lord Hwittir to guide your peaceful conversations towards their destined reconciliation and resolution?

"Nothing arrives by chance, for chance does not exist, as you have oft said! And without our sorrows and sufferings, it is hard to see how we would grow and spiral upwards; for they teach us and strengthen us so wonderfully."

Of all the company, only one was weeping outright. It was Erreig. "My heart is breaking for you, as did Jizay's," he wept. "I would never have done violence to you, Mélusine. I sought only to love you. It was a poor love, I will grant, for it was confused perhaps and surely founded upon *seeking* and not *giving*, as you have said. I begin to understand, since we have met... I begin to see. It was perhaps a shadow of true, respectful, upwardly-spiralling love; another love which I had once glimpsed, long ago. But in my confused, no doubt fearful state, yes, I loved you, as I had loved your mother the Queen, the wife of the King whom I so envied... But I would *never* have done harm to you, or to any child or to any woman be she human or fairy! I would have willingly done harm to the villain, had I been there. I would have sought, as Jizay would have, to protect you. But to attack a child or a woman, I could not believe this possible of any fairy.

"I did commit one act of violence," Erreig confessed, very softly, between his sobs. "I did not mean to, but I was in the heat of conflict and, as ever, fear. Terrible and blinding fear. And in that moment of dreadful timidity and panic, I wounded your brother, the Prince Leyano. I wounded him, and my heart bled as did his. And I mingled our hearts in song, in Sun-Song. And he lives.

"But your elder brother, the Prince Finnir, he very likely learned of that violence against Leyano, and perhaps he did not, and does not, forgive it. Though he never spoke of that episode, nor did I, in the humiliating encounters imposed upon me in the Caves of the Cats in my own realm; I often wondered if he were seeking to punish me for that unintended blow to his younger brother."

Eli rose, and found herself doing what she had desired to do when she had heard Erreig's first song. She walked to him, stood before him, and put both her hands on his shoulders, his broad and powerful shoulders which were still rocking as he wept.

"Finnir would not *punish* you, Erreig. And what you did to save Leyano --- yes, I have heard the tale from his own lips --- was valiant and good. It absolved you, I believe, on the spot. And Leyano has since forgiven you, as I'm sure you know. And Bawn has become a visitor to his isle, and Garo has become his friend. And now you have healed Aytel also, and that is a further absolution and a great act of skill and kindness on your part. And here and now, I thank you for it."

Erreig visibly relaxed, and Eli redressed herself and stepped back a pace, smiling. The Dragon-Lord lifted his eyes, and looked into hers. Eli could see a certain apologetic change, almost true humility, perhaps even a courageous awakening and openness flitting across those eyes; but other emotions and doubts remained. His regard was like a stage crowded with many players, a mingling of tragedy and comedy --- but not *laughable* at all. She felt that she had to use this opportunity to further their communication, but she wondered if he would be truly receptive to more of her philosophising or reconciliation. It would be much to ask, all at once.

Nonetheless, after a moment, she said, speaking slowly and softly, "But I must remind you of one thing, Erreig. As you spoke, you called Quillir, where the Cat Caves are found, *'your own* realm'. And yesterday, you also referred to it as *'my* province of Quillir' and you use the term *'my* lordship'. None of these qualifications are valid, are true. I am the daughter of the King of Faërie, and I must emphasise this to you: *Quillir is a part of the realm of Aulfrin*. He is the king of both Moon-Dancer and Sun-Singer, and you have taken upon yourself the role of a

Vanzelle

rival lord or chieftain in his kingdom. This is a fraudulent division of the Shee Mor that you, and you alone, have devised."

"Not entirely alone." The voice of Vanzelle was also rather tearful, although she had not wept outright. "I lived with Erreig, my lover and the father of our valiant son Garo, in the Bay of Secrets. We were the 'White Dragon Family' for Bawn was our pride and our emblem, and we believed --- together --- that to tame the great matriarch dragon and to gather about us a force of great worm-riders permitted us, or even *entitled* us, to declare Quillir our duchy.

"I saw, long centuries ago, the folly of that illusion. And I urged Erreig to return with me to my own shee, and to abandon his designs to be a petty-king in a corner of the Shee Mor. I longed for him to fly the arctic skies with me, where he could be free and happy, in the Shee of the Red-Eared Hart, the shee of the Lord Hwittir."

Erreig was very silent now. Eli guessed that, indeed, too many emotions at once had fallen on his shoulders, and into his heart.

After a long moment, the Lord Hwittir spoke, very calmly and with a gentle sigh like the wind carrying the two golden eagles who were circling high over the heads of the assembled company.

"I led you, Erreig-*herra*, on your third and final Initiation-quest, for you sought to pass that great trial with the polar-dragons whose eyries, concealed to all but the boldest, cling to the crest of Mount Saana in Lapland. And I remember you told me of your other Initiations as we travelled together. Ah! those were splendid tales!

"Your pale blue gems, set into your ears as pointed as a young fawn's, those you received from the pretty pincers of the blue crabs, living along the southern shores of the Shee Mor, if I recall correctly…"

Erreig, his tears abated but his face rather stern now, nodded to the reindeer.

"Yes, yes, the crabs...," continued the great Hart, "as tenacious a race as exists anywhere in all of Aulfrin's realm! You surely became more, shall we say, *resolute* --- with their aid. And your second great trial, let me see, ah yes! Drawing closer to dragon-fire, you were then, brave youngster of fourteen winters. For to win your prize of *Gurtha*, great fire-opal of the Ancestors, you sought out the tallest of the waterfalls of the Mountains where the dragons nest, the range of the Beldrums, did you not?

"To win *Gurtha* from those tumbling giants, that was a feat! A great stone of magnification that, tripling your already impressive powers. Ah, well --- waterfalls, like dragons, are normally untameable, are they not? And it is required to have skills and force greatly amplified, especially if you seek to become a master of wind-worms!

"Hmm, but I seem to recall that, even then, you had heard tell of my shee, far to the east across many icy oceans. For not yet another year passed before you began to tame and ride the great dragons of the Shee Mor; and so flying, one late autumn day in the year 1126 I believe, to the farthest isles of Sea-Horse Bay, did you not encounter a *tursa*? Aha, I have not forgotten your stories, you see! And you rode him by sea and sky-paths to Norway, and saw my pretty fjords, and the snow on my sparkling mountain peaks, and the ice dangling like frozen tears from the fingers of the unfading trees.

"Was it not then, I believe you told me, that you conceived the idea of requesting that your third and final Initiation be passed with the polar dragons? Oho, you were not yet eighteen winters old when you dared that! I was your guide and companion, dear Erreig-*herra*, as I say, but your own heart also lead you into other adventures.

"For after your challenges with the Saana-worms, you voyaged from Lapland back again to Norway, and there I recall you saw my seven *vannfall*-daughters, the veil to my greatest Portal. Ah it must have stirred you in your deepest heart, you who felt the force of waterfalls in your own breast, to look upon the Seven Sisters! Do you remember seeing them, then, in your youth, for the first time?

"And perhaps you remember seeing more than that..."

Erreig straightened up, and then he rose to his feet. Eli had returned to her own place, beside Jizay, so she was not a hindrance to the Dragon-Lord as he walked around the broad antlers of the Lord Hwittir and came to stand before Vanzelle, who rose to her feet, now, also.

"I saw the most beautiful wonder in all the eleven isles of Faërie or in this human-world," he said, his rich baritone voice almost chanting the words. "And I do not speak of the seven wondrous waterfalls. No, I beheld Vanzelle. And she is still, though nine hundred autumns and winters have flown like dragons across the winds of time, more lovely even than those colossal cascades with their dazzling ice-dragon guardians."

Between the labradorite-blue eyes of Erreig and the silver eyes of Vanzelle, there shone a softly vibrating field of coloured lights like dust-specks in a sun-beam. Some of the lights were an orangy-red, like the sparks from flames; and some were opaque white like grains of sand or tiny hail-stones of pure ice. Eli, sitting once more beside her hound of joy, smiled and caressed his furry back.

"Before we go to our mid-day meal, up in the slopes between the pine-trees singing in the breeze," said the Lord Hwittir, "I think you have an important deed to accomplish, Erreig-*herra*."

It took Erreig several more moments to tear his gaze away from Vanzelle, but when he at last succeeded in doing so, his expression was questioning, and rather dreamy.

The white reindeer had risen to his feet too, and towered over all the company. But he was still smiling.

"The *Amethyst Cloth*," he whispered.

Erreig suddenly blinked, and then he nodded and turned to Eli. Without a word, he walked past her and back to where the fire had now dwindled to a red rose of warm embers. A tree, not very large, grew from a crack in the boulder's sheer face; defying the lack of soil and the harsh elements of such a home, it had sprouted almost horizontally and then turned to grow towards the sky. It was a young rowan.

And hanging on it, unnoticed and unfelt by Eli until now, was the torn half of the Amethyst Cloth, matching her own.

The Dragon-Lord took it down --- with great respect Eli noted --- and bore it to her.

"I ask your pardon for this theft," he said clearly, not in a whisper but with sincere and candid courage. "I put you in peril, I now realise. It was not my desire, but it was foolhardy and... disrespectful. I ask your pardon," he repeated, looking her squarely in the eye.

Eli took the Cloth, and felt a strange pulsating shock-wave of energy rising from her toes to the crown of her head. Jizay barked; and Eli could feel herself glowing slightly.

But the ripples of mauve light soon faded and seemed to be *inhaled* back inside her own body, into all the pores of her skin and into her ears and eyes. Her left palm burned, hot and startling for an instant, and then was cool once again. Simultaneously, the moon-flower hidden in its tunic-pocket over Eli's heart sent out a bright gleam, right through the knitted frabic --- like the ray of a miniature light-house --- and the Golden Flower on the brow of Róisín answered it with a similar brilliant glow, as if she were calling or singing to it.

"You have my pardon," said Eli, holding Erreig's eye as he had done hers. And then releasing it, and --- with a warm smile and a very relieved sigh --- turning to follow the Lord Hwittir up the stony incline and into the woods.

****

After their meal, Vanzelle and Erreig wandered off together for a long walk, and --- in another direction --- Jizay and the Lord Hwittir did the same. Her hound of joy explained to Eli that he had never before had the pleasure of meeting the famed sovereign of the Shee of the Red-Eared Hart, and it was a blessed opportunity to converse with him. They had crossed the shallow swirling waters of the stream-bed and trotted off together into the woods on the far side. As for Peronne, he had excused himself much earlier, to cast an eagle's eye over the land, as he had said, in company with the two mighty golden birds still impatiently circling overhead.

Eli was very pleased to have her privacy this afternoon. She found a comfortable spot for herself and Róisín, and spread her cloak over the pine-needle carpet beneath them. On this grey cloth she laid the mauve ones: side by side, with a gap of only a few inches between their torn edges, she positioned the two halves of the Amethyst Cloth. And in the space between, she carefully aligned the Silver Leaf to be a pointed, oval, arched 'window' into Faërie.

Following her instincts, or a mute message deep within her own heart, she left the moon-flower where it was, tucked into her bodice. And now, she began to play.

About her, just beyond the frontiers of the grey cloak, an audience assembled to hear the opening measures of her fluid and haunting music. Many red squirrels were there (bringing Finnir to her mind), a group of snow-buntings who had difficulty to fall completely silent but continued chattering for many moments, a mountain hare, and --- keeping a timid distance --- five red-deer does with huge black-coffee eyes.

But most remarkable of all was the appearance of a rare capercaillie. He paraded up and down, his wide black tail with its curious white motifs held open like a Chinese fan, his beak clacking in time with Eli's notes, and his bright black eye blinking under its eyebrow-arc of berry-red.

Eli played Scottish airs and Irish ones, the 'Lament of the *Blanche Biche*' from Brittany, 'The Ash Grove' from Wales and 'Scarborough Fair' from England. Dozens of melodies flowed through her fingers, and her mind felt at ease and at peace, her heart full of images and sensations of reconciliation and of spiralling love.

As the animals began to retreat back to their own occupations, Róisín seemed to invite Eli into improvised figures and flourishes, long strands of arpeggios like garlands of flowers, descending glissandos like slow-motion waterfalls. She even found herself playing snatches of the song that Erreig had sung, his love song to Vanzelle, Alégondine's starry lullaby for her...

And finally Eli repeated once again the 'miraculous music', gently releasing the seven notes one by one, and then improvising around them for a moment or two. Alone and deliciously emptied of everything but pure peace, she and her harp drifted into silence. Now Eli knelt beside, rather than behind, her instrument. Near her head, the Golden Flower pulsated with soft light, like a candle. Looking intently at the delicate Silver Leaf lying before her, Eli now relaxed her vision so that everything around her, trees and harp and the Leaf too, became a little hazy. She took a deep breath, and then exhaled very slowly.

Perhaps she had closed her eyes. Or perhaps she had not needed to. The window was opening.

Eli had thought to see her three 'mothers', and probably Aindel with them. Perhaps even Finnir would appear to her. And all of them would be so pleased, so proud, so relieved that she had won her victory and that the Cloth had been returned to her.

But, to her surprise, none of these fairies appeared. Instead, she saw Leyano. Pallaïs was with him, his betrothed, playing plaintively on her golden-wood oboe. And on the shores of the

Island on which they stood, on an isolated point of rock, was the Lady Ecume.

"A victory you have won, yes," said the ancient mermaid, though she was not facing Eli. "But be wary, it is not conclusive, not yet. For the moon is new and dark, though you have the moon-flower, the Cup of Light, to protect you.

"You are between the worlds, Eli, and so is the Dragon-Lord. You are changeling-fairy and visiting-human, not 'returned home' to one place or the other, not yet. As for Erreig, he has fled his imprisonment on Star Island, very cunningly. But he has not regained his full life-force. He is still *part*-wraith, though it be only a small part; as you would have been *partly* alive, though *mostly* wraith, had you departed your vault to seek him in fairy-form. As you had planned.

"I myself would not have hindered that decision, as others did. But I came too late, for the Mauve Dragon had departed and your father the King had arrived. He, as well as your mothers, countered your intention, and mine. So be it. I will not say they were mistaken. For when we take any decision, another is always possible as well. And Life can use, to our good, whatever path we follow --- strangely enough!

"I knew that Mélusine wished to confront Erreig in his lingering-phantom form, and as a phantom herself, and I saw the rightness of that choice. But, of course, other roads were possible too. And it was the word of your human-mother, Lily, which won the confidence of the fairy-Queens --- for she saw that you, as Eli, could prevail in human-form and thus set into motion many forces for change, and for healing. I do not doubt that she was right, for she is wise. But she is human, more human than fairy. As you are also, I grant, today. But I am full-fairy, and sea-fairy. I see as Mélusine would see, and not as Lily.

"Therefore I come to bring you a timely message. Your sea-brother Leyano --- who is a strong link in the chain of love between yourself and your little moon, Lily --- together with his belovèd, Pallaïs (herself a wondrous sea-fairy, even as I am) will become part of your adventure here… in shadow and echo only, but supporting you with their combined blessings. We, will offer another layer of victory to you, or at least the opportunity for you to win it.

"Erreig is wavering already. Wavering between many paths. You must meet with him once again, but it will be but a brief encounter. It is needful this further confrontation. But we await the moon's return, here in these lands.

"Vanzelle will be with you, and others will come to your aid also. You have retrieved the torn Cloth; so much is excellent and already worthy of great praise. But it is not finished, your sojourn in Scotland, nor your dealings with the Dragon-Lord. The Cloth is still sundered. The music is not yet resolved into its final chord.

"Be vigilant, and bold, and listen to your heart's wisdom and verity. Farewell."

Before the window before her closed, the scene changed. Pallaïs' melodious oboe-keening was still in the air, and resembled the Irish tune 'My Little Boat'; but the vision of the various sea-fairies had faded. She briefly saw Finnir, at his Portal, with Peronne --- in his white-tailed eagle guise --- taking flight through the Heart Oak. But before Eli could speak to her love, or hear any message from him, he had gone and there were only eagles: her own 'eagle-horse' (as the Lord Hwittir had named him) and two noble golden ones. The skies were rain-washed and breezy, but besides the three birds, nothing else was visible. Strangely, she was convinced that she would see, if only for an instant, Reyse's face. But she did not.

Soon, even the three eagles faded and were gone.

The window closed as if white curtains of snow were being drawn over it. Eli looked up. Indeed, it was snowing now, and the two pieces of the Amethyst Cloth were already covered in a delicate layer of snowflakes, like icing on a lavender cake. She rose, and put the twin Cloths and the Leaf back into the pocket of the grey cloak; then she moved the harp to one side, and covered herself. She stared into the falling snow for a moment, but she could not decide what she felt, anxiety or courage, encouragement or longing.

Peronne was perched just above her, in the arms of the pine tree.

"I've spotted a little cave among the fallen stones, just beyond those trees," he indicated with his long, black-fingered wing. "Roísín will be safe and dry there."

Eli carried her harp there, and Peronne alighted on the ground beside her.

"Erreig and Vanzelle are returning now, coming up the glen. And Jizay and the Lord Hwittir will be here before nightfall. I have been down to the village of Glencoe, and I think it will be wise to begin to make your way there this evening, all of you. There are heavy snows coming. The Lost Valley will become dangerous for you Eli, even if the fairies can *weather all weathers*! Ask the Lord Hwittir to carry your harp, for you will need your hands as well as your feet. And urge him to lead you down the glen as soon as he arrives, for there is no moon to light the snows or to guide a Moon-Dancer on her way tonight."

Eli nodded, and Peronne --- after such a warning --- tried to encourage her with an optimistic conclusion.

"You have done well so far, and I think the worst is behind you. And you will reach the village safely and swiftly, no doubt, for you have friends to help and guide you now!"

As he finished, the Lord Hwittir and Jizay came leaping up the slope of the wooded hillside, laughing together like old friends. Appearing from another direction was the floating figure of the golden-and-silver fairy, just calling her frosted wings back into her ribbon-robed body as she landed. She looked rather thoughtful and subdued, Eli thought.

And Erreig was not with her.

Peronne's observations and words had already reached the ears of the giant white reindeer, or he had had similar misgivings for Eli's well-being in the gathering storm.

He instructed Pine-cone and Penny-grass to fasten the Harp of Barrywood to his neck with braided cords of coloured string, like the handles of the knap-sacks in which they carried the food and drink. He apologised to Eli that she could not mount and ride him, for he was --- he confided --- merely in his illusory fairy-dream-form. Asking, cheerfully, what that might mean, Eli was told that he had *also* remained in his own shee, for he was its *king* and so he liked to "keep one eye on my fanciful and frolicsome subjects", as he said. The vision she was seeing of him here was just that, a vision, but also a presence…

"Ah!" he chuckled. "Our dreams are often so lovely that we dream them to be true! But they are also, sometimes, oft-times, truer than we could imagine --- if you take my meaning!" He chortled, again, to himself.

Eli smiled too, and then queried, "But Vanzelle rode you, did she not?"

"Exactly," nodded the triple-antlered head of the enormous stag. "Exactly!"

Realising that she did not have the time, or the fairy-logic, to continue to seek further clarification, she simply asked, "Then Jizay and I follow you? Will you guide us down the glen, and through the snow?"

"Of course, dear Princess," said Vanzelle, coming --- it struck Eli --- out of her own troubled and far-away thoughts. "I am quite at ease flying in snowfall like this. Sleet and hail are trickier, but I have other powers at such times to complement those of my agility in flight.

"It is a pity that Erreig is not here to soften the season's chill," she added, in a more hushed tone. "But he can only do so during the day-time, in any case; a Sun-Singer cannot call forth the sun's warmth when there is no sun overhead."

They started off, with the two little gnomes seated comfortably on the Lord Hwittir's antlers, Jizay and Eli following the flight of Vanzelle --- who had once again sprouted her glorious and tattered wings looking like lace and frosted webs, and Peronne gliding slow and low before them all. They left the shelter of the trees, and Eli realised that her sea-eagle's warning was timely. Everything was already white: stone and grass, tree and bush. The slopes and ravines of the Lost Valley made a wide cleft before them, but the high heads of the hills and mountains were invisible, cloaked in deep whitish-grey cloud.

It was, most probably, Eli calculated, roughly the twilight hour of a very snowy night to come. She rather wished that someone had thought of offering her a hot drink before setting off, to warm her blood and --- were it sufficiently fortified --- bolster her courage as well.

In fact, they were not far from half-way down the great glen, and it was surely only early evening still, 'twilight' as Eli had imagined. Vanzelle flew just ahead of Eli and her hound, glowing slightly, almost twinkling --- like a star, thought Eli. Peronne was no longer visible. Nor was the Lord Hwitter, most of the time. At odd moments he would appear, to one side of them or the other, bounding along with the two coloured gnomes holding tight and sometimes with their short legs sailing out behind them in the air! The red-tips of the stag's ears shone slightly, as did the golden glow from the Flower on Róisín's brow. But most of the time they were invisible to Eli. She surmised that the great Stag was coming and going, ahead and behind and off on his own sidetracks, running much more quickly than she and Jizay were walking. Despite the silent and fairly even carpet of snow, her lightly-booted feet were tripping on barely covered stones and tufts of grass or even small, brittle bushes of faded heather or gorse.

One hand was often on Jizay's back, but the other was sore and scratched now, with trying to keep her balance by grasping

Windy Hill Prayer

taller stones or the branches of bare, half-white trees, or the mischievously snow-hooded prickly holly bushes.

Finally, just when Eli was sure she could go no longer or further, Vanzelle stopped and turned back to land before her.

"Do you need to rest, Mélusine? It is not an easy terrain, it's true." The silver fairy's voice was faint, blown away on the wind.

Eli was breathing like a marathon-runner, but at least she was not at all cold. The effort was keeping her warm!

"I heard a story," she called into the whistling wind and whirling snow, hoping Vanzelle could hear her. "About Garo, your son. Didn't the Lord Hwittir help him once, him and his wolf and bear friends, by conjuring-up a *sled*? Couldn't he do that now?"

Vanzelle came close to Eli, and her wings wafted and curled about her tired human charge. "No use to us here, for the path is treacherous and narrow now, climbing and falling, and there is a gorge coming up, still running with deep water. We must take the road along its edge, clinging to the rock wall and holding onto the kind trees, when we may. But I think we should rest perhaps. Your strength is not quite that of a fairy."

"But my desire to arrive at Glencoe is what will get me there, not my physical strength," declared Eli, surprised at herself, but quite in agreement with the words bubbling up, unexpectedly, from her spirit and resolve. "Let's go on."

As Eli heard herself saying those last words, a memory sprang up in her mind. It was the voice of Wineberry. *My dear moon-child-Prince of the watery, windy shee in the west will now give you this little flower, filled by his precious heart-gem with the grace of the Cup of Light, to connect you to me, to him, and to her. Keep it safe and secret until you have need of moon-light. Now, you may go on.*

"Aindel," murmured Eli under her breath. "Timair. The moon-flower…"

She parted her cloak and reached her hand into the fold of her bodice, to the seam of her tunic, where the little flower lay hidden. Holding it in one hand, she reached into her other, larger pocket with her other hand, and touched for a moment the two soft, torn, but at least closely re-united pieces of the Amethyst Cloth. Withdrawing that hand, she now held her cloak closed tight again, against the howling wind.

She closed her eyes for only a second, and then opened them into the full force of the snow-stormy gusts. "Timair," she repeated, still speaking lowly but with utter faith and confidence. "Wineberry, and you my brother, and Lily my little moon, I have need of moon-light on this moon-less night. I have need of the Cup of Light. For the moon is always there, and to me, indeed, she is ever-full."

Her hand was filled with such radiance that it almost rendered her very human flesh-and-bone quite transparent and translucent. But that was not the *only* light that shone forth on her path.

"I may not be able to conjure up the Sun, but I can request the Moon," she said, smiling at Vanzelle. Jizay jumped and sent up a delighted volley of ringing barks.

The snowfall and the furious wind seemed both to sigh and exhale, as if they were as exhausted as Eli had been. And then they ceased. In the sky above, the low and menacing clouds had become high, fast-moving, wraith-like filaments; and they now parted to reveal a starry expanse of velvet black.

The golden-skinned fairy was shining and glowing and Eli's closed hand was illuminated like a torch, but these two were outdone by the Moon. Passing like a sailing galleon across the glittering sea of stars over their heads --- passing much too quickly, in fact, across the wide space left by the fleeing clouds --- was the full moon. Its light was as bright as day.

For one hour at least she gleamed and guided the trio, following the hoof-prints of the leaping stag, gone before them along the narrow and rolling pathway. They were out of the Lost Valley now, and clambering along the Pass of Glencoe towards the village.

The landscape was as silver in the moon-light as the long, thick hair of Vanzelle. As they arrived at the furthest outskirts of Glencoe, the clouds floated together again, and the dream-moon was gone.

Vanzelle said, softly and quite simply, "You are blessed by enchantment and you are a true Princess of Faërie, whether human or not." After a moment she added, "I will see you in the morning, for my guidance on your path is not quite at its end. But for tonight, sleep well and warmly, little Full-Moon-Dancer of the Shee Mor!"

Though it was late, the charming little hotel before her tired eyes had one room left, and a hot dinner to propose as well. Evidently, the staff could not see Jizay, so Eli simply invited him to her well-appointed room to sleep by her tartan-quilted-bed on a thick rug.

"Good night, *Laurien*," she whispered to him with a broad smile. "And thank you, my little Moon and my dear brother." And, thoroughly exhausted, she was immediately sound asleep.

****

It wasn't until the morning, over a very Scottish bowl of porridge ('the oatmeal in the Highlands', thought Eli, *'that's* where they get the strength to blow air into, and music out of, bagpipes!'), that she realised she had brought no money with her into the world. How was she to pay for her downy bed and delicious food?!

When she had finished her breakfast, Eli approached the whiskered gentleman at the front desk of the little hotel.

"Och, ye cannae be leavin' oos so soon, lassie?" he beamed at her, deep concern in his eyes and both his large hands placed squarely on the counter before him.

Eli hesitated, firstly to try to follow his accent, secondly wondering how to deal honestly with her situation. She could hardly say that she was just visiting Glencoe from fairy-land.

Well, perhaps she could --- this was a sensible Celtic county --- but it really didn't excuse her oversight; for she should have thought to bring money.

"No, well, I may be staying another night, in fact…" she began, hoping an idea would occur to her as she spoke. But a small, snowy-white lie seemed the only immediate answer. "I've left my pack behind me, up in the glen, when I was forced to hurry back here because of the storm. I need to retrieve it before I can pay you, I'm afraid."

"Ochone! If it's oup in a bothy in the glaen, it's safe!" he chuckled merrily. "Ye'll get it soonar or laytar. Ye didnae waint to geit it the day, ye wad dee of the coold. Aye, ye'll hae yerself another dae ar twa in ma hoom here; there's a céilí the nict in the bar, and ye'll be welcome."

Eli nodded, wondering how she would resolve the problem. And if she would ever fully comprehend the Scot's accent. Fresh air, she thought, would be a good first step. Jizay, still quite invisible to all and sundry, was by her side as she slung her cloak around her shoulders and went out to visit the port of Loch Leven.

As it turned out, the hotel Eli had found was a very old Inn, quite far from the loch, in the hills bordering the River Coe in Ballachulish, Glencoe, and it was a good five mile walk to reach the centre of the actual village and the banks of the lovely loch.

The day was chill and bright, but the crisp cold was revitalising and the snow was no longer falling, only decorating all the landscape with a silent coverlet of pristine white. The rising sun was not visible yet over the glen behind her, but it would be there to warm her back before she arrived at the loch. She hoped she would easily find Vanzelle once more, and especially the Lord Hwittir --- as he still had her harp! But she had no doubt that all would fall into place, even her problem of money.

She and her dear dog had only gone a few hundred yards when Peronne swept down out of the heavens to join them.

And just as he arrived, Vanzelle also appeared, descending through the powdery snow on the hillside to Eli's right. Eli glanced up and down the roadway, to see if there were other 'tourists' such as herself; though she doubted that they would be able to see the fairy. But there was no one.

"I'm pleased to see you rested and radiant, dear Princess Mélusine," the silver-haired fairy greeted her.

"Good morning, Lady Vanzelle," replied Eli. "I hope you have slept as well as I have. I had a very comfortable bed and warming food too. And the tea here is every bit as good as in Ireland."

"I'm glad to hear that! I have slept, but not serenely. After Erreig and I had spoken, yesterday afternoon, he desired to be alone. He was ever someone who broods overmuch, and this has not changed from the time of our youthful… interlude. But it is possible that he is still nearby, reclusive and reflective, though I hope not too sullen. My only worry is if he should rekindle some anger or arrogance, some petulant mood arising from your words. You were right to say them," Vanzelle hastened to add. "Quillir is not Erreig's realm, and he should be reminded of that. But for many centuries he has built a false dream-kingdom for himself, a phantom loyal-land of Sun-Singers that is 'under his control'. Ah, dear… It is a place made from vapours of dragon-breath, a smoky vision as insubstantial as those fumes --- and potentially as noxious. He is poisoning his own mind with his longing for grandeur and power.

"If only he would come to my glistening and glassy shee, filled with water and woods, with snow and ice, with strange flowers and fantastic beasts! There he would be *my* king, if no one else's.

"But, alas, he has so long cherished his dream, nursed it in his poignant and weary heart, clung to his red-rock corner of the Shee Mor, that he is probably finding it hard to imagine who he would *be* without that suffering and sorrow, those ambitions and all that wounded pride."

Vanzelle

Eli nodded, saddened by Vanzelle's sadness, and not a little anxious about what Errieg would do next. At least she now had *both* pieces of the Amethyst Cloth. She left unspoken her concerns about what the Lady Ecume's message could presage. She could not imagine, at all, what might lie ahead.

"Come," smiled the beautiful ice-fairy. "The wind from the sea bears a song, and my purpose --- according to the counsel of the Lord Hwittir --- is not yet fulfilled as regards your voyage here! For you must return to Faërie. Come, we must hasten on!"

Eli did not like to say that she must find some way to beg or borrow money to pay for her lodging of last night, and so she must come back here later today. Nor that she now knew she would be remaining in Scotland until the waxing crescent moon once more appeared. But, for the moment, both Jizay and Peronne were already jogging or flying in the wake of the fairy's swift footsteps along the white road. Eli followed as quickly as she could.

She did not have the keen ears of the fairy, but after an hour or so --- still passing no one at all, even in the village of Glencoe which seemed to be fast asleep --- they arrived within sight of the shores of Loch Leven. And then Eli heard the song that Vanzelle had said was borne on the sea-wind:

Tiens bon la vague, tiens bon le vent
Hisse et ho, Santiano !

"I know that tune, and those words," Eli said, softly but aloud, as she and Jizay stopped beside Vanzelle. "And I know that voice!"

Her amazement knew no bounds. There, all alone and anchored only a stone's throw from the shore, was a sailboat or small yacht, perhaps eighteen feet long. Its deep russet-red sail was being fastened into place by the singing sailor, and from a shorter mast, aft, floated the black-and-white ermine-motifs of the flag of Brittany.

> *...D'y penser j'avais le cœur gros*
> *En doublant les feux de Saint-Malo*
>
> *Tiens bon la vague, tiens bon le vent*
> *Hisse et ho, Santiano !*

"*Uncle Mor*?!" whispered Eli. Then she called the name again and loudly, out over the short stretch of cold, lapping water, into the wind. And he heard her.

He turned and waved his arms as if he had been *expecting* this utterly unlikely meeting. And with a burst of laughter he called back to her.

"*Bonjour, bonjour ma petite, et bienvenue*! Welcome my dearest Eli! Ah, it's been years and years. Aha! I've a tale to tell you, a very tall-tale, of how I knew I'd find you here! Look, isn't she a lovely lady, by new little Longboat. She's only a small yacht, but she'll do the trick! I've just bought her… Wait now, and I'll come ashore. Ah, Eli *chérie*, how glad I am to see you again, and just as I was told I would. Oh but the sea is full of surprises, even after all my long years loving her!"

More confused, delighted, flabbergasted, Eli had never been. She watched as Morvan paddled across the few yards of icy water in a tiny, inflatable dingy. But her awe and astonishment only increased as she waited for him, for the silver fairy beside her touched her shoulder and pointed to the prow of the bobbing boat. And thus, even before Uncle Mor could arrive to embrace her and explain the mystery, Eli saw for herself the name --- freshly painted it would seem --- that had been given to his new boat.

She gazed, and blinked, but it did not go away. Painted in a terra-cotta red to match the sails and outlined in silver, the named seemed to wink back at Eli. She read it, and then murmured it aloud, shaking her head.

"Vanzelle," she whispered, completely bemused. And then she repeated it again, as she turned to run the few steps into Uncle Mor's arms. "He's named his boat… *Vanzelle!*"

****

Windy Hill Prayer

Chapter Twelve:
The Hill of the Sun

hough now in his early seventies, Morvan, Yann's child from his first marriage before he had wedded Maelys, was certainly still hale and hearty. A sailor's life seemed to have agreed with him, as Eli had noted when she had lived with him for six months, just over ten years ago now.

As they stepped back from their warm embrace, Eli struggled with her choice of question: so many were dancing around in her head. Her beloved 'Uncle Mor' seemed to see the perplexity in her face, and laughed as he looked her up and down.

"We've both crossed a lot of wide water, my dear harper, since last we met, and there's tales to tell! We'll get around to it all. I'll say this, though: you're even lovelier than you were, my dear Eli. You've got a special light about you that you didn't have then. But of course, when I saw you last you were at a great cross-roads, and coming out of dark days. Maybe your days have been brighter since?"

"There were other dark ones that still lay ahead, Uncle Mor, but I've gotten through them," Eli said philosophically. "And yes, I do feel much brighter and lighter now, and my life is full of wonder and new possibilities. But I'll not start telling you all of *my* story here beside a chilly Scottish loch! Though I must admit, it will be good to hear your news, especially about how you come to be *here*."

"It's a tale of wonder, like yours, I suppose. And it merits a pint of good ale or an excellent whisky, and I imagine neither will be hard to find in these 'bonnie' lands. Oh, I've always wanted to sail to the Highlands and Islands, and I thought perhaps my chance had passed me by. But the sea is a magical *grande-dame* with many tricks up her sleeve. And she has wonders in her depths that we haven't ever fully understood, nor shall we ever, I'll warrant.

"Do you know a good *bistro* here, Eli, for a coffee to warm us this morning? And then maybe later on we'll find a pub and lift our glasses to the Lady of the Sea!"

"Well, if I haven't completely lost count, it's the 7th of November today. But that would make it Sunday. We'll see if the Scots allow for coffee-shops to be open, or *bistros* as you so charmingly call them, on their sabbath. Let's hope so!"

As they strolled back up towards the village of Glencoe, Eli commented, "That's an....*unusual* name for a yacht, 'Vanzelle'. You'll have to tell me how you came up with it."

"Oh, it's a part of my tale," her Uncle Mor assured her. "Don't you worry about that!"

The fairy Vanzelle --- having led Eli to her 'namesake' --- together with Jizay (communicating in their habitual silent language) told Eli they would remain nearby while she took a moment to talk with the sailor. Morvan could not see either of them, as was clear by his concern that Eli was there to meet him, "all on her own", as he said. Peronne, it seemed, he *could* see, for he commented on the beauty and grace of the white-tailed sea-eagle circling high over the little haven, and said he had seen others on his way here, swooping over the water and catching their meals by skimming quick and low and "snatching a fish up without wetting more than the tips of their talons"!

Over their hot drinks, in a delightful café (with not only very convenient Sunday-opening-hours but also an array of woven crafts on sale --- bringing Lily to Eli's mind) they talked mostly of Morvan's life in Brittany, near Concarneau, and also about music. He asked Eli if she still had Clare, the harp he had given her. She told him that Clare was safe and sound, at home in Saintes, but that she had another harp now too, which she had brought with her and whom she had named Róisín.

"Ah! The *little rose*," Mor had exclaimed, "that's very good. I thought you might say you had named her after your mother, our Maelys, that is Lily. But the rose is important too, did you know that? The Lily is the queen, but the Rose is the princess --- that's what she said."

"Who said? Did Lily say that to you when you were young.?"

"Oh-ho, Lily said many wise and pretty things to me, when I was a babe, and after. But no, that bit of knowledge came to me from another lady. Lily was enchanting, but this lady was, well, literally *enchanted*. But she's a part of my tall-tale, and I'm saving that for our dinner together, and our toast to our meeting once again in this magical place."

"Alright, that will suit me," laughed Eli. "You still know how to spin-out a story, my dear sailor-man! Will you come with me back up to the Clachaig Inn for a meal tonight? I hear there's to be a session of music, a good *céilí*. We could dine there, perhaps…oh dear, but I *can't* invite you: I've no money with me!"

"Ah, my dear Eli," chuckled Uncle Mor, "you've not changed a bit in that respect! You were always a dreamer and never had a hold on the coins in your pocket, as I've told you before. I'll be very happy to invite *you*, of course, and I would have insisted anyway. I'm a good Breton gentleman, as you'll no doubt recall!"

"Indeed I do! Thank you, dear Uncle Mor," sighed Eli, very relieved.

"And don't forget to bring *Rozennig*, your 'little rose', and then I can hear her voice and compare her to Clare!"

"And you can sing in Breton," rejoined Eli. "Though I enjoyed your song earlier, in French; *Santiano* I think it was. You used to sing that when I lived with you, did you not?"

"Ah, I did, possibly. Though I think in those days I usually preferred my own Celtic language and songs; but I've since softened my hard edges a little, and now I sing many a song in foreign tongues --- such as French!"

Eli laughed again, remembering that Lily had always called French a 'foreign language', even though Brittany was, to Eli's mind, certainly a part of France. "Well, then, I'll meet you later this evening at the Inn. Do you go back to *'Vanzelle'* now?"

"Indeed I must. My lady-love, my new 'wee' boat, as I suppose they might say here, needs a little attention before she's ready for our voyage."

"*Our* voyage?" Eli raised her eye-brows hopefully.

"Of course! And isn't that why I'm here in the first place?" Morvan stroked Eli's cheek affectionately, rather as Aulfrin would have done. "It will all be told, all be told... *Ken bremaïk*, my little Eli-ig, *à tout à l'heure*, see you later!"

Morvan returned to *his* 'Vanzelle', and Eli to find hers. In her case, it was not complicated, for Jizay was awaiting her, very much in his imaginary likeness of Laurien --- invisible to all save his mistress --- at the gate of the coffee-shop's snow-covered patio. He said he knew where they would find Vanzelle, for Peronne had just passed by with the news of her whereabouts.

The snow was beginning to melt now, as the sun rose higher into the cool, clear sky. Eli followed her dear dog as he trotted along the road, in the opposite direction taken by Uncle Mor, and then, just outside of the village, turned up a climbing path into a wooded area of oaks and pines.

And there, indeed, they met with Vanzelle. Who was not alone.

But it was not --- as Eli would have expected --- Erreig that stood beside the shining golden-skinned fairy, nor even the great fairy-reindeer. It was two *other* fairies that Eli had already met: silent and cloaked, as she had seen them at the Stone Circle, and yet --- to Eli's part-human, part-fairy eyes --- recognisable nonetheless. Begneta and Belfina.

Eli, extremely surprised, nonetheless greeted all three fairies with the customary hand-on-heart nod used in Faërie. The twins returned the gesture, but Vanzelle simply inclined her head with a smile. As the twins both pushed back their hoods with movements made in unison by their graceful hands, Eli could appreciate, once again, their beautiful clear blue eyes, their fair complexions and yellow hair. But they did not look *quite* the same as in Faërie.

Apart from their flowing capes, rather like Eli's, they were dressed as humans --- which was also true of her: warm jeans and a double-layer of knitted sweaters. In Eli's case, these were slightly sturdier copies of the clothes she had worn when stepping through Finnir's Portal into Barrywood; they had been given her, for her adventure here, the evening before she traversed Wineberry's Gate. As for the outfits of the twins before her, they seemed to be old and comfortable garments with years of wear in them. But they did not hide the lithe bodies and pretty figures of the two women, who seemed to be roughly her own age.

And women they surely were, not fairies, or so Eli decided now. Their ears were not pointed, and though they were clearly the two ladies that Eli had met in Aindel's company at *The Tipsy Star* and later coming out of the Stone Circle with Garo, they were now somehow not quite so 'other-worldly'. And, to further underscore the contrast, they now spoke with voices --- and very lovely ones, with the gentle music of Scottish accents or even lilting Irish brogues ringing in them.

"Good day to you, Eli," said one of the twins. "I am Malmaza, and this is my sister, Mowena. We are your half-sisters. It is very nice to be able to say that word to you at last, and to use our true names."

"We couldn't before, not on either of our previous meetings," chimed the second twin, "and I'm not even sure you could hear our 'hellos' on those occasions; although we *did* say them, I assure you!"

Eli was delighted. "Yes, I've now learned the story, so I know who you are. And I know that the names I'd heard used for you in Aumelas-Pen are not your only titles. How nice to meet more of my... extended family. It's so pleasant to learn that I have brothers and sisters, and not only in Faërie it appears! But may I ask what you are doing here?"

It was Vanzelle who interjected, "Well, I would venture to say that it was thanks to the eagles we saw earlier --- but it seems that word of your visit here reached the northern coasts of Scotland and the fairies who live and work there. And so, when you left with Morvan to find your morning refreshments, Peronne brought the twins to me, giving me the joy of making the acquaintance of fairies I had not previously encountered."

Peronne was perched, not far above, in an oak tree whose branches were not yet quite bare, framing him with a very lovely garland of rustling, scalloped, brown leaves.

"Indeed, the golden eagles, having met with your own sea-eagle, *did* bring news to the coasts near to Findhorn, where we often make our home," agreed Mowena, "but it was also, in our case, the presence of the Silver Leaf and the Golden Flower, so near to us, that caught our attention and invited us to seek them out, and you."

Malmaza added, "We had felt them together earlier this summer, but far away, in France. Having them here in Scotland, we could not deny ourselves the pleasure of flying here, and of meeting Vanzelle also. Garo has, of course, oft spoken of his golden-skinned, silver-haired mother."

"You *flew* here?" asked Eli, surprised. "You look to be in human form now. Do you still have wings?"

Mowean nodded, "We do. Though we mingle and blend with the inhabitants of this land, we have kept our fairy-natures, our fairy ages, and many of our powers --- though not all. We are hybrids and cross-breeds!" she laughed. "But we flew in the dark night, with no eyes to see us, far above the storm-clouds. And here, we are again dressed as we are in Findhorn, when we are among the folk of that hallowed community. For unlike Vanzelle, who is a full-fairy visitor to Scotland and so invisible to human eyes, we are not."

"I see, or I think I do," grinned Eli. "But though I have the Silver Leaf here, in my pocket, the Flower is on the head of my harp, and *that* I have not yet recovered from the Lord Hwittir."

"He is only a little further up the path," indicated Vanzelle with a graceful gesture of her extended arm, "and we may go and join him now. He awaits you, dear Eli, to say his farewells."

"He is returning to Lapland? And do you ride with him, dear Vanzelle?" Eli inquired, as the four ladies, Jizay and Peronne, all began their ascent through the ancient oak-wood.

"Yes, yes, I will go too," said the silvery fairy, almost in a timbre of voice frosted with sadness. "I have enjoyed meeting you, and I hope that the spiralling stars, all eleven of them, will bless us with other and frequent meetings to come."

The twins and Jizay were walking a little behind Eli and the silver-and-gold fairy.

"And have you found the Dragon-Chieftain again, now?" Eli ventured to ask, whispering her words for Vanzelle's ears only.

The Nordic fairy's tone grew even sadder. "I have not seen him, not since yesterday when we spoke in the Lost Valley. He may be sulking nearby, or he may have fled further. I will consult with the ice-dragons upon my return; but even the Lord Hwittir has no tidings for me of my Lord Erreig. I must wait… and hope."

After a moment's silence, with only the sound of the crunching snow and crackling twigs beneath their feet, Mowena came closer to Eli and spoke again.

"I am very pleased, dear Eli, that you have met Morvan once again. He is a fine fairy-friend, and a wondrous good sailor too."

"You know Uncle Mor? Ah," exclaimed Eli, "that is so very nice! He gave me refuge many years ago, and he has turned-up once more now like a guardian angel. I haven't heard the full story yet, but I shall do tonight. Vanzelle, I suppose, has told you that she guided me to him in the harbour on Loch Leven; but how is he known to you as a fairy-friend?"

"Many years ago, I visited Brittany," continued Mowena, "just to walk under the boughs of the Forest of Brocéliande in the late spring-time. I was ever a rather reclusive fairy, and as a hybrid-human I am too, I suppose. I loved to spend time alone in woods or mountains, and also in chapels or chant-filled monasteries. But to go to Brocéliande was a special treat for me. And while I was wandering there, I met a little child, who had strayed from his parents, also visiting that mystical and mysterious forest.

"I led him back to them, and we talked a good deal on the way. Though he was only six or seven, we found that we had much in common, for we loved the legends and songs of the Celtic lands and, even at that young age, he could recite some of the lays and also sing splendidly! In any case, children of six or seven are generally extremely intelligent and interesting, I always find. They may become less so, unfortunately, in later years --- but not all of them.

"As I say, I guided him back to his family, but I didn't stop to introduce myself to little Mor's father and his step-mother, for I was very shy of them. But it was a pity, in a way: I later learned that their names were Yann and Maelys, and that the latter was a descendant of my sister's! Well, fairies are drawn to fairies, we always say. And chance does not exist."

Eli was laughing. "How wonderful! It's a lovely tale, and so good to know that children don't just *imagine* fairies; they sometimes really meet them!"

"And not only children," said Malmaza in her turn, and also smiling. Her blue eyes danced. "But, as with most children, many adults don't know it! I met and married an Irishman, oh three hundred years ago it must be now, and I don't think he ever imagined for an instant that his wife was *fey*. But little Morvan, according to my sister, had an eye for the enchanted."

"Did he know you were a fairy, then?" inquired Eli of the other twin.

"Not me, no, I don't think he did. But as we walked and sang, and drew closer to where Maelys and Yann were searching quite anxiously for their little boy, he was telling me that he knew that the legends of the famous Forest --- telling of Viviane, Merlin and Morgan and other famous fairy-folk --- were certainly true, whatever others might say, for he'd *met* a fairy, a real one, and so he *knew* they existed. I asked him where they'd met, and he told me that he lived with her.

'A haunted house, is it, that you live in?!' I laughed, and he giggled with me. 'Maybe that's how to say it, but she isn't a ghost, she's a fairy-queen. I saw her one night. I'd had a nightmare and woken-up crying, and my step-mother came in to comfort me, only it wasn't her at all. It was a fairy, all in white, with a yellow crown and wings like flower-petals. It wasn't an angel, or a ghost. She was as real as you, but all shining, just like that.' And as the little fellow finished his phrase, he pointed to a lily-of-the-valley peeping through the mossy grass between the roots of a huge tree. So I realised, later, that he had recognised the *fey*-light in Maelys, or Lily as we call her now."

Eli stopped for a moment, and studied the face of Mowena, and also that of the other twin. She felt a mounting warmth, not linked to the snow-melt and the rays of the pale sun filtering through the branches overhead. She sighed happily.

They had arrived at where the Lord Hwittir awaited them. Jizay was already beside him, or more precisely beside the two gnomes, who were feeding the happy hound *pulla* pastries and reaching up to pet his silky-soft head. They then offered Eli a *kuksa* of mulled wine, not quite as strong as what they had served to revive her in the Lost Valley two days ago, but delicious nonetheless.

"Thank you Pine-cone, thank you Penny-grass," she said politely, and both little gnomes beamed and bowed. She turned to the mighty Stag, who addressed her with his throaty, Finnish-lilting accents.

"We take our leave of you here, little Eli-*lapsi*," he said slowly, "and I return your harp into your keeping, for you have much good work to do together. She has been talking with me this morning and she sang an Irish *suantrí*, a lullaby, to me last night… She is very skilled, as are you too, or so she assures me! But she spoke of another matter to me, at dawn of this very day, and I'd like to say something to you regarding it."

"Yes, of course, my Lord Hwittir," replied Eli, returning her *kuksa* to the two miniature attendants and looking inquisitively into the huge, dark eyes of the white Hart. "I'm very pleased to hear that you are able to converse with my harp --- I think that's a lovely idea. And I'm happy to learn what she shared with you."

"This beauteous harp," began the giant reindeer, "was made for you by a great Prince, a being of Faërie as magical, or perhaps more so, than I am myself. And he loves you. It is a gift of love, and she --- Róisín --- knows this well. But she bears, also, a great and powerful token, the Golden Flower, her eponymous Rose. And you have also been given, by another of the great ones of your own shee --- ah, but in fact, ultimately by this same Prince --- the Silver Leaf, its counter-part and sister jewel. Both were wrought by your mother, the Queen, and both had been given to these excellent half-fairies with us today." He nodded reverently in the direction of the twins.

"Now the Circle of Stones near young Aulfrin's Silver City, it has told me quite a bit, and my sweet sandy-haired Garo-*poika-puun* has told me more, concerning *you* --- you as the Princess you truly are, the Princess asleep more soundly now since the bold Dragon-Lord has returned to you her purple Cloth! You are Mélusine, of course, <u>but</u> you are also Eli, and at this moment you are more the one than the other: you are a pretty fugue, a song where both themes are played and are interwoven, but Eli is in the melody-line and more easily heard. You realise this, do you not?"

Eli nodded, and remarked, "The Prince you speak of, who loves me --- and whom I love --- used almost the same words when I met him, when I returned to Faërie as a changeling. He said to me then: *You are like Mélusine, and yet you are not her: you are Eli.* And that is how I feel it to be also, of course."

"Very good," continued the Lord Hwittir. "But I agree with what your harp mentioned to me at sunrise, for she said that the Leaf and the Rose are great and prodigious gifts, and to bear both, together, is --- not exactly a burden --- but, to use her words, a *weighty responsibility.*

"Eli-*lapsi*, Eli-sine, I and your wise harp, we spoke of this: it is hard, in the strong winds, for a tiny sapling to bear a heavy, ripe fruit; and rare it is that a young fawn carries the antlers of a full-grown stag. But you are doing this, and such challenges, I think, were your desire, even as you undertook to voyage on this path of changeling-life that you have lived now for half-a-hundred years. Ah, and it is not over! For many years lie ahead of you, and you will be neither fairy nor woman, not entirely one or the other, but somehow both. You will be your own riddle, Eli-sine. You will continue to be a lilting duet!

"Our warning to you addresses this interesting state of affairs, for the brave and wise heart of Mélusine sleeps with *her* on an Island in the northern seas of your Shee Mor, and the heart of Eli is young, very young, and bears deep scars already for such a short span of time. And so we say: *Make no vows, no more promises than Mélusine may already have pronounced, and bind not your <u>human</u>-fairy-heart to that of the great Prince, not until your true-fairy-heart re-awakens. For to join together the Princess Mélusine and the Prince Finnir, that is a very daring and auspicious act, epic and enigmatic and filled with consequence for all of Faërie. Eli cannot partake of that decision; only Mélusine may.*

"We are advising you to be patient, patient as the trees, the snows, the stars. The years will seem long to you, Eli-*lapsi*; they are not. They pass like the grey-lag geese, and like those great and gregarious *merihanhi*-folk, the years of your exile will end with a migration home, and then you will have the wisdom demanded for your choice. Then only.

"Yes, be patient, and do not *promise*, but simply *pray*. Pray... and wait. Róisín has reminded me: there is a very singular and sacred place near to the dwelling of the Prince Finnir --- ah yes, a place filled with magic as potent as the Prince's. It is a chapel on a hill, on a windy hill. When you pray, as you shall, see yourself there. And your prayers will thus be kindled into yellow moon-flame as soft as flowers!"

Eli inhaled very deeply, as if the cold and invigorating air of the snowy woods would allow the words of the magical Hart to penetrate deeper. Something else was there, though, in her heart, in her very respiration. A thought? A dream? An uncertainty? Or perhaps it was the embryonic form of the Windy Hill prayer that she would pray for all the rest of her human life. Perhaps. Her lungs felt the chill of the crisp air; but her heart felt the burning of her wordless questions.

"I will remember your warning and your advice, coming from both you and my harp, great Lord Hwittir. And I thank you."

Vanzelle touched Eli's head with her open hand, and Eli wondered if this were a ritualistic blessing or the way that fairies bid farewell in her shee. As she smiled, the shining fairy intoned:

> *Ice and dragon, snow and fire,*
> *Moon and Sun in endless day,*
> *Secret door in northern oak,*
> *Seven Sisters water-play,*
>
> *From northern fairies and Lapland-folk,*
> *Bear and wolf and doe and hind,*
> *I bestow, by frost and flame,*
> *A benediction intertwined:*
>
> *Wander whither you must go,*
> *Chill or sunlit be the way,*
> *Our protection on you rests:*
> *Though seeming lost, you shall not stray.*

Vanzelle was standing beside the Lord Hwittir one moment, and the next she was astride him. Eli hadn't even seen her move. Hugging the Stag's antlers were the two Periwinkle-sized gnomes.

"A safe and sure return to Faërie, dear Eli-*lapsi*," called the giant reindeer as he turned in the powdery snow and leapt away between the hoary oaks, with Vanzelle's hand raised in a final farewell.

Eli heaved a profound sigh, and collected her harp from where it was leaning against a nearby hazel tree --- a beautiful tree complete with a scampering squirrel, as if to further emphasise the presence of Finnir in Eli's thoughts.

"We shall be leaving too, before nightfall, Eli," said the gentle voice of Malmaza. "Let's go for a walk together first, to the Hill of the Sun. It's not far from here, and it is a beautiful and blessed place. If we find ourselves alone --- on this sunny

*Sun*day --- it might be nice to make a little music, for the Sun *and* the Moon! She, the new crescent moon, is overhead today, but so slender as to be nearly invisible. But as the sun sets, you might catch a glimpse of her."

And so, with Jizay beside her and Peronne above, and taking up Róisín in her arms, Eli followed her half-sisters on white, winding, woodland paths until they reached the Hill of the Sun, not very far from the road leading back to her hotel.

To Eli's great joy, the place they found, private and still in the frail sunlight of mid-day, was not unlike the Fair Stair. A dark grey boulder stood beside an ancient tree, and along one side of the great stone's fern-flourished and heathery bulk ran a series of steps, all uneven and cracked. Eli almost expected to see Demoran appear, or to be serenaded by a singing spider in its dew-flecked web!

Instead, it was the trio of sisters that did the serenading, to an appreciative audience of golden hound, white-tailed eagle, two foxes and a grouse. Eli played Róisín, and Malmaza and Mowena took from their back-bags a small fiddle and an Irish wooden flute. Their playing, curiously enough, brought no other visitors to listen --- only small animals, including an assortment of songbirds just brave enough to pay them a visit before the late afternoon chill set in and they found their ways back home to their snug nests.

When they had finished their 'session' of several haunting and slow airs, and one or two sprightly jigs and reels, Malmaza asked, "Could I *see* the Silver Leaf, Eli? The Flower is proud and bright before us, on the forehead of Róisín; but the Leaf lies hidden --- in your cloak, if I'm not mistaken. I can feel it there. Would it be possible to take it out?"

"Of course, of course," Eli replied, almost embarrassed at not having thought to present it to its former bearer immediately. "I'm so sorry. In the pleasure of meeting you both, and playing music together, I hadn't even thought of it! How silly of me."

"Not at all silly, dear Eli," Malmaza assured her. "You should really only bring it forth or use it when prompted by your own heart, and keeping it safe and hidden is a very good thing. And I don't suggest using it myself, for I no longer have need of that. I and my sister are often in the Shee Mor these past years, and also in the Sheep's Head Shee --- so we can sometimes visit our mother in person."

Eli extracted the shining Leaf from her pocket, leaving the Amethyst Cloth's two pieces where they were. She remarked, with a tinge of longing in her voice, "I would love to visit her there. But I don't suppose that is possible for a returning changeling, not until I become a real fairy again anyway. I would very much like to see that shee, though, and our mother. And also my human mother; for she is there with the Queen, I believe. Unless she has already left..."

Both Malmaza and Mowena were regarding the Silver Leaf with affection and appreciation, where Eli had placed it on the great grey stone. It looked very pretty there, on a bed of moss surrounded by mushrooms and framed by brittle, brown ferns. Mowena looked back and forth between the Leaf and the Flower once or twice, and smiled contentedly. As did her twin.

"We met Lily, on our last visit to our mother's pink-brick Castle on the northern coasts of the Sheep's Head Shee," Malmaza confirmed. "I do not think that Lily is often with her there, but she had made the trip from her other, temporary, lodgings in that wind-swept and wonderful shee, expressly to meet with us. It was wonderful to see her, for she resembles in every way the 'fairy-queen' that came to Morvan's bedside when he was a child."

"Does she?" exclaimed Eli, her eyes wide and shining. And then she added, after a moment's reflection, "So she should, for she *is* a queen; just as the lily is the queen of flowers, even the humble lily-of-the-valley of the human world. I think all lilies are regal, enchanted and somehow holy."

Without taking her eyes from the Leaf, Mowena said, "All <u>flowers</u> are enchanted and sacred. All plants. All of nature. Enchantment and divinity, these are their birthrights, as it is for us all. We are all 'divinely enchanted' by the gift of Life itself, which gives us the possibility of creating the world around us, thought by thought, word by word, dream by dream. The beauty of flowers is the manifestation of their own dreams.

"But the Lily, she dreams grander dreams than the others! And next to her is the Rose. They are the most enchanted of the dreamers. But there are many others…"

Eli mused for a moment, and then hazarded another question that was tickling her mind. "You know Aindel, and Garo, and Alégondine, and I suppose many others of the Alliance. Do you also know Finnir? And…Reyse?" Eli's voice had fallen to a murmur, as if she were not really sure that she wished to add that last name to her list. At least, to put it beside Finnir's name seemed somehow to bother her.

It was Malmaza who replied. "We have never met Finnir, neither of us, I think." Her sister nodded in agreement. "We had left Faërie to come into the world before he was born. Of course, we know *of* him. Among the great leaders of the Alliance, he holds a very luminous place."

"Does he?" inquired Eli, almost shyly.

"The exchange of infants, of Finnir for Timair, is not fully comprehended by all in Faërie. We know of it, from Timair, or Aindel as you call him --- and you call him by that name quite wisely and guardedly, for you have been, recently, visiting Aulfrin's realm, and his identity must still be protected. And we know of his story from our mother also, of course."

Malmaza fell silent, and it was Mowena who added, "Yes, he is very great and very enchanted, in the same way that I said the flowers are. None, not even Garo or the Sage-Hermit himself, are so filled with the enchantment that brings dreams into being as is the Prince Finnir. That is his role in the Alliance, and his purpose in coming into the Shee Mor."

The Hill of the Sun

She said no more, and it seemed that both twins became composed and silent, as if the subject had been fully explained. Eli waited a moment more, and then, still in a very hushed voice, she reiterated her other question.

"And the Lord Reyse? Do you know him?"

Both the twins smiled and their eyes sparkled. "We work side by side with him, and have done so for many centuries!" Mowena was almost laughing. "And now, we are so happy to have him more often with us, at Findhorn and in other places here in Scotland, Wales, and England. He, and also Ceoleen, contribute more and more to our efforts with the humans now. It is an exciting and passionate time in the world."

Eli nodded slowly. She did not know what to say or if she should ask more. She rather wished, now, that she had asked less.

She received the Silver Leaf that Malmaza now lifted reverently and handed back to her. Still preoccupied with her thoughts, Eli simply held it in her closed hand, and smiled --- a little wanly --- at the twins. It seemed they were preparing to leave, as they packed away their fiddle and flute.

"Thank you, thank you so much," Eli found the courtesy to say. "It was lovely to play together. I hope we'll meet again, and play again, in Faërie, or here in the world."

Both twins nodded their blond heads and continued to smile radiantly.

"I'm sure of it, dear Eli-Mélusine!" said the first, and the other added, "And may your voyage with Morvan the sailor, the little fairy-queen-seer, be blessed and bright, guided by sun-rays and moon-beams!"

Both of the twins bowed their heads to Eli, their fair hands over their hearts. Eli wondered if she would one day see what jewels they wore, as fairies, in ears or foreheads, stranded in their long yellow hair or set into their hands... She inclined her head in like fashion, and watched them descend the pathway.

On arriving at the Hill of the Sun, the twins had previously pointed out to Eli the way to return to the Clachaig Inn, but she felt herself in no hurry to go there right away. She ran her hand over Jizay's back, as he stood beside her now.

"While we're here," she said silently to him, "here on the Hill of the Sun, I think I would like to have a look in the Silver Leaf --- as we're alone. Perhaps I will be allowed to see where Reyse is, and send him a greeting."

The dim, deep voice of her hound of joy reverberated within her. "You have already discovered, darling mistress, that those whom you *seek* or *expect* to see in the Leaf are not always those who appear. Are you feeling strong enough, in this moment, to look and face *whomever* might be on the other side?"

She turned to Jizay's seal-soft eyes, looking deeply into them and letting their love and protection flow over her as if she were swimming in a warm lagoon. Her smile crept back to her lips, but a certain sorrow passed over her own eyes at the same time.

"Yes, I think I'm strong enough," she said, to herself or to Jizay, she was not sure which. "And I believe I'll see the fairy I wish to, I *ask* to see. I think I'd like to try, anyway. I feel very anxious to know how he is."

She left her harp next to the old tree, as dark a grey as the huge stone beside it, and walked up the strange, stony stairway. She turned around the far side of the sombre boulder and descended a short slope into a little dell. There, looking out to the west --- if she was not mistaken in guessing her orientation --- she sat on a smaller rock that was exceptionally dry and snowless. And she opened the hand where she held the Silver Leaf.

****

Two, perhaps three hours had passed. Eli did not know, and was even unsure how far she had strayed from the grey boulder, and from her harp.

The vision she had seen in the Leaf had not lasted very long --- why was it now past sunset? Where had the time gone?

She was kneeling in a puddle of melted snow in a dingle of bracken and brambles, coarse grass and trampled ferns. At one side of the little bay the sky was dyed crimson and orange by the sun's last disappearing rays. And in the wake of the flaming orb was the fine, impossibly fine, new sickle moon.

On all the other sides of the dell were clouds, blowing up from nowhere and everywhere, covering the colours, forewarning icy rain or even more snow. Yes, filled with forewarning, as Jizay had been. Why had she not listened? Where was *he* now?

Her left hand was trembling violently, but the Silver Leaf had not fallen from it. Was she trembling from fear, or from the increasing cold now that the twilight had come? Where, oh *where*, was Jizay?

She rose slowly, her eyes still rather dazed, and slipped the Leaf back into her pocket. There, on the ground at her feet, were the two halves of the Amethyst Cloth; but stranger still was the fact that, posed delicately atop them, was the moon-flower. Eli snatched it up quickly, as if she thought it would be whisked away by the howling wind, and with her violently shaking hands she tucked it back into the fold of her bodice. The two pieces of the Cloth she returned to her cloak-pocket, with the Silver Leaf.

"I'm crying," she whispered, speaking only to herself. "Why am I crying? Why should I be crying, at *that*? Oh, oh dear... And why is the wind moaning and crying too? What's gone wrong with the world?"

She turned, and saw, at a short distance, the high boulder, now in shadow. Jizay was sitting on its summit, like a lone wolf howling at the moon.

"But the moon's just set, right after the sun," muttered Eli, her teeth chattering. "And she was tiny and frail."

There, behind Jizay's outlined form, turning him into the classic silhouette of a great wolf, was a full moon so huge that it encircled her hound like a silvery-white disk, an aura of mottled gray light.

Eli's tears were coming, once again, in a torrent, and she bowed her head and hid her streaming eyes in her hands. When she at last calmed her sobbing and lifted her face, Jizay was leaping down the side of the gully and rushing to her. The full moon was gone, and so was all light. The clouds had closed over the sky, over the woods, over the Hill of the Sun.

Holding her cloak close about her with one hand, Eli kept the other on Jizay's back as he guided her up the slope and out of the dark little dell. Passing the looming rock and finally coming to the ancient tree, Eli could see Róisín vaguely, for the Golden Flower was glowing. It represented the only light, Eli thought, for miles around. And very glad she was to have it.

She did not want to take out the moon-flower again, to ask for moon-light, or for the Cup of Light, or for any vision or any more *enchanted* aid. She wanted to take her harp, her gift from her beloved Finnir, in her arms, and holding tight onto Jizay or Laurien or whichever dog he was at this time, to return to her hotel, to the cosy Inn. There would be warmth there, and a fire in the hearth, and amber ale or a tumbler of something stronger. And there would be other people --- human, *not* fairy.

Eli tried not to teeter as she lifted Róisín, and Jizay moved closer to her, to support and lead her along the pitch-black paths with one of Eli's hands laid on his high head. Just before her was a tiny spot of illumination, as if her harp were shining a torch or a head-light onto the ground only a foot or two before each of her faltering steps, to guide her back to safe shelter.

It wasn't a long road, and Eli was breathing slowly again now; she felt she could walk quite quickly, despite the uneven track. A small bridge crossed the River Coe, and the sound of the running water seemed somehow to be filled with encouraging voices. It even sounded a little like applause! Was she delirious, she wondered.

Her face was frozen with the tears she had wept, for they had changed to ice on her cheeks. She didn't want to let go of Jizay, and she didn't want to put down her harp. She just wanted to keep walking. The cold didn't matter. The dark didn't matter.

She continued for what seemed much too long a time, for she could not be far from her destination. At last, there, in the distance, she could see the lights of buildings, homes perhaps, and a little farther the Clachaig Inn. She wondered if Uncle Mor would have arrived yet. But she could not go to him right away, or even warm herself at the fireside and have a glass of something to revive her.

No, not yet.

She did not feel cold any longer, even though her face was covered with frost and her feet were wet and her limbs tired. No, not cold in the least. Maybe the blessing of Vanzelle was warming her. Maybe the Lord Hwittir had bestowed some special hardiness on her, making her resistant to snow and ice.

Or maybe there were invisible wings sheltering her, like those of the angelic dove from Reyse's shee that saved the life of Ævnad and her babe in the snows. Like the wings of Peronne, and other eagles perhaps, who covered her in the grotto at the head of Glen Etive and allowed the image of warmth that she and her harp had conjured up previously to return and heat her body all the night long…

Or maybe it was the hot gust of a dragon's breath, or the balmy winds of a sunny island in Faërie, or her own inner fire, her royal and regal pride and confidence, her own victory…

Or maybe it was that the cold simply did not count for anything compared to the loss of her little moon. Lily had died eleven months ago, and then she had --- oh, how Eli wished she could stop crying --- then she had come back to her, in a little tear-stained book, in visions, in words. Eli knew her human-mother still existed, still 'lived' --- somewhere. But she could not be with her again, could not see her again --- not really. And very soon now, finally and forever, she would be gone. Again.

And Eli felt so keenly, just at this moment, how she would miss her, for the rest of her life. Why had her vision resulted in *that* realisation for her?

Eli had found a fallen tree-trunk, or it had found her. She sat and waited, waited for her tears to abate once more, waited for the stars to come out --- because the clouds were blowing away and with them the threat of snow or rain, she thought.

"Rain isn't a threat," she smiled to herself. "It makes the fairies dance!" She continued to cry, but she added, "That's why there's no rain, for I don't feel like dancing. I just feel like looking at the cold, silent, beautiful stars. They're like the lilies-of-the-valley that I saw on the wavelets all along the Shooting Star Lake…"

As the black heavens became populated with twinkling, mute, infinitely distant points of brilliant light, Eli relaxed. And now she could remember, calmly and without fear or tears or delirium, what she had seen.

Loch Eil, that was the name she had heard someone say, though only in her heart, in silence. "It's almost like my own name," she remembered thinking. "But why has he gone there, and why is he appearing to me now, in the window of the Silver Leaf?"

Not to be trusted, that was what Finnir had reminded her. Erreig is not to be trusted. *He is not to be feared, though not to be trusted either. No, he is not yet become trustworthy, but neither is he become --- nor will he ever become --- a threat to you.*

"But Finnir, my love, he did threaten me! I <u>did</u> feel threatened. I <u>did</u> feel him menacing me with… with *what*?"

Suddenly, Eli could not think exactly why she had felt such trepidation.

"The difference now is this," she said to herself, aloud, slowly, under the dancing stars. "I'm *looking* at it now: I am the **witness** of what has just happened, what I saw. I'm not the **victim** anymore.

"And once I make that distinction, once I change my perspective, he can no longer harm me, or even threaten me. My father agreed with that wisdom, he said that *that* was the key. Become the witness, and not the victim. And now, I can see it all, but I am no longer a part of it."

The island was small, but there were some trees on it, a little grove of trees. The Silver Leaf had taken Eli there immediately, there to a little island in the sea-loch called Eil. And Erreig had been waiting for her there.

"But no, I don't think it was *me* he was awaiting." Eli's eyes grew large as the truth dawned on her. "I was afraid, as soon as I saw him. My fear of him was re-kindled, and his of me. Fear was in the air all around us. But I was mistaken, right from the first. It wasn't *me* he expected to meet. It was Vanzelle!"

Eli shook her head at her own penchant for drama. "Why didn't I think of it when I saw him in the Leaf? He was hoping to see his lover again, for he was brooding and sulking and confused and lost. And he needed Vanzelle to come and help *him* to change *his* mind.

"And instead, I arrived! Oh, poor Erreig!"

Eli sat up straighter, and Jizay looked into her eyes from where he sat at her side. The deep pools of his kind eyes were filled with reflections of the stars. Eli smiled slightly.

"All I could sense, all I could capture of those waves of energy as I perceived Erreig there on that strange little islet, was longing and desire and a smouldering passion and a well of confusion in his sad, troubled heart. But as soon as I felt all of that, I believed it to be for *me*. Oh Eli, your *ego* is much larger than your *good sense*. And much, much larger than your heart.

"As soon as I unleased my own towering wave of terror, breaking over the scene in the magical Leaf like a *tsunami*, Erreig's own fear was awakened too. And two beings facing one another, entirely overwhelmed by their fears, are in a sorry position to see clearly or resolve any difficulties."

Eli continued to relive her vision, speaking aloud to herself up to this point, but now commenting and comprehending more in silence than in words. Her breathing was quick, reliving the encounter, but her eyes were shining with the blessing of greater comprehension now. Her hands were no longer trembling, and one of them moved from the upper curve of Róisín's frame down onto her strings.

Slowly, as if coming from far, far away, a series of sounds, like beads on a thread, came from the harp's vibrating strings as Eli caressed them, releasing them one by one. *La, fa#, re, si, do, mi, sol*. She hadn't had her harp <u>with</u> her when she had looked into the Leaf, but now --- reinventing the anxious scene she had beheld earlier --- Róisín was within reach, and could be played.

And so Eli liberated the 'miraculous music', just as Piv had reminded her she must do, when she would encounter Erreig.

She looked again at the Dragon-Lord --- now only in her own mind and memory, but at last experiencing herself as a *witness*, with <u>understanding</u> instead of <u>fear</u>. And the notes of her harp rang out in the starry, cold, merry night. For, as Eli could testify at this moment, as the rainbow fairy had reminded her, *with our limited perceptions, our expectations, our fears or our dreams we create our reality*. Or re-create it, when we have mistakenly fashioned it from our nightmares!

In her vision, Erreig had once again worked his magic and had transformed the winter into spring, or even high summer. For the island, Eli's vision of the island, was verdant and filled with colour. The trees were in full leaf, and there were wildflowers among their roots: yellow, pink, purple, blue, white. The sky was clear and cloudless, the air was very hot. But not only with the warmth of the Scottish Highland's summer-time. A dragon was there.

Could that be possible? Was Erreig a master of phantom-forms? Or was there really a dragon on the island in the loch?!

In her panicked state, beholding Erreig and the dragon from a Leaf-window which had expanded and evaporated, leaving her truly face to face with these two impressive characters, there had been no doubt.

Eli was no longer, even then, on the Hill of the Sun. Or was that the true name of this dream-island? It would be appropriate. For the mighty Sun-Singer was there, and seemingly an even greater dragon than the huge white matriarch of the winged-worms of Quillir…

She lifted her chin higher. And she came back into the present --- where she was sitting on a chilly stone under a starlit sky, somewhere in the woods and foothills near Glencoe and almost within sight of the cosy Inn where her Uncle Mor was probably already singing with the assembled musicians.

"Oh, dear me," she sighed, almost laughing at herself. "How terrifying it was to find myself on the shores of the island, right beside the glowing furnace of those open jaws, with the Dragon-Chieftain challenging all I had said of my father's kingship, of his misappropriation of Quillir as his *own* realm, of the illusion and folly he had spun for centuries trying to assert his pathetic lordship in a land that would never be his, *could* never be his."

It had all happened so quickly; but even as she thought that, Eli realised that it had been in 'slow-motion' too. Each detail had unfolded in dream-like lethargy, each moment more worrying than the last.

First, at the very start of her vision-scene, there had been thunderous *silence*, when she had found herself alone on the Island. For that moment of 'prelude' to their encounter, even her imagined aggressor was only a vibration, a shivering arpeggio of fright and impending doom rising up her spine. Just as in her nightmare in the Chamber of the Seven Arches, she had looked around anxiously and called for her mother, and for Jizay, or *Laurien*; but they were not there.

Then there was the sight of the dragon, or dragons; or *were* they dragons at all? Flying in formation, high up over the tiny island: six, no seven. Ducks, geese, bats, eagles…dragons? Were there riders on their backs? But mounted or riderless, what was certain was the panic that they brought to Eli. Freezing fear, but not of their imminent attack: fear of another kind of violence, for these had become the dragon-formation which had been the herald --- in her awful dream --- of the worst crime she could possibly imagine.

But now they were only memories; and they flew away like shards of a splintered spear, an angry explosion --- with all their potential for harm and violence simply and naturally blowing apart…

And, then, finally had come Erreig's appearance. Enraged, desperate, indignant, scornful, and tormented by the collapse of his dreams, his hopes, his very *identity*. A true ghost, an empty shell; but a hollow and haunted form that was seething with fury. His eyes --- no longer blue, but red.

No, those were the eyes of a *monstrous* dragon!

In the very midst of her re-living of her encounter with Erreig, he was gone. Had he been there at all? For the entire scene before her now was completely given over to this incredible dragon.

Crashing through the low clouds, tearing them into tattered grey-blue shreds as it descended, the wild worm flashed through the skies like a searing bolt of white-hot lightning. Eli had cowered for an instant in the smoky, spark-filled air, dropping almost to her knees as she bent and buried her eyes in her hands --- blinded by the explosion of flame and deafened by the roaring and the earth-shaking screeching. The entire island seemed to rock and rumble in the dark shadow of that immense wing-span. Dark, leathery wings, as thick and impenetrable as the over-lapping scales on its body, wings more powerful than steel and tipped with blood-red claws. Eli could see them as she lifted her pale face from her hands and straightened her back to watch the dragon wheeling away.

The dragon's jaws were gaping like the brazen doors of a furnace. The heat was almost unbearable...

Steam and smoke, mist and fog, confusion and terror. But it was all swirling in circles in her mind again now. Nothing seemed clear.

Eli breathed deeply, breathed in the cold air wafted down from between the timeless stars. The vision had utterly dissolved, and even her memory of what had happened was drifting apart.

No, she still recalled one thing.

"Vanzelle," someone had cried, "Vanzelle is here!"

Was it the phantom voice of Erreig which had called out for her, or was it someone else? Oh, if only she *had* been there.

Eli spoke her thoughts aloud, even as the re-play of her vision evaporated; and her fingers wandered over the strings of her harp.

"How I wish Vanzelle, his true love, had indeed been there, had flown down out of the burning skies on the back of the marvellous reindeer, to turn his hot anger into a gentle snow-fall of calm and new beginnings. To convince him to flee with her to the Shee behind the Seven Sisters in Norway, or through the magical oak-tree in the far north of Finland."

Eli continued to stroke the strings of her harp, and now she took the instrument between her two hands and skilfully re-interpreted her composition based on the seven notes. She re-interpreted the 'miraculous music' as she was re-inventing the scene on the island in her memory.

Finally she saw it, clearly, gloriously. Created anew. Recast in a breaking light, it was not a terrifying scene, but a pageant of apocalyptic revelations. This was the vision-scene that Maelys had seen when Sean had proposed the name of their child and spoken of the famed fairy Mélusine. This was the scene that Eli had been shown, of herself --- beautiful and proud and defiant and queenly --- with a dragon wheeling away, vanquished… This was her own victory.

Was Erreig, like the retreating dragon, vanquished? What had been the outcome of *their* confrontation? Surely, he had done her no harm; no one had --- this time. Her memory was gone, completely gone now; at least it was no more realistic in the present than the faint, fleeting remnants of a chilling nightmare.

Surely the mighty dragon *had* departed from the island, and Erreig too, and only Eli had remained. Or was someone else with her?

In her search for some recollection of the spectacle, yes, there was a man, or an armoured knight. Or a king. But now it was not at all clear. Had Leyano been there? Or Finnir? Who *was* this shadow on the fringes of her memory?

Eli stopped playing the notes of the 'miraculous music', and the night became very still and silent all around her. Peronne had landed in a naked tree beside the road, as if he had just returned from seeing off the great dragon, too.

"Oh Erreig, make a 'Hill of the Sun' with Vanzelle in the Shee of the Red-Eared Hart. And give your burning fears to the ice-dragons to melt into *peace*. That will be your own phoenix-fire rebirth. Oh, how I wish you could find the courage to do it."

And then, in a very low voice, she added, "How I hope that I will find such boldness also, when I need to…"

As Eli came back fully into the present moment, sitting under the starry sky with the final notes of her music fading as they flew off into the darkness of the trees, she realised that both her earlier vision in the Silver Leaf, and this re-visiting of it under the twinkling stars, were neither of them --- yet --- come to pass. Nothing had been real; but all was true. In vision and in echo.

So clear and intense, both scenes had been to her. And yet, now, without a doubt, she knew that the encounter with the Dragon-Lord was *before* her, not behind.

Was this, somehow, the 'further layer of victory' promised by the Lady Ecume, that she and Leyano and Pallaïs were to 'offer' her? She heaved a sigh of resignation; but then a half-smile took form on her lips, and she looked high and far --- up into the starry sky.

"I've yet to do this," she said aloud, and Jizay licked her hand as it fell from Róisín's strings back onto her knee. "I haven't met Erreig yet; I haven't met him for the last time --- I haven't faced him on the island.

"But I soon will. Very soon.

"And **now** I'm ready."

****

Windy Hill Prayer

Chapter Thirteen:
The Sailor and the Silkie

␣t was not as late as Eli thought it should be. The bar of the Inn was busy and convivial, and there were a few tables left unoccupied --- as yet --- in the adjacent dining-room. Uncle Mor had been playing on a borrowed accordion, changing now and then to his own tin whistle, and more usually occupying his hands with his glass of beer while singing intermittently and lustily in French, Breton or English as the mood took him. He hailed Eli when she appeared, and asked if she'd like to play first and dine later, or the reverse!

Eli was happy to relax and have some dinner, she said. She now realised she hadn't eaten all day, only the good coffee and cake of this morning with Morvan at the craft-café. She was very tired and hungry, but also feeling quite 'emptied' of many and various emotions and memories and worries. She was thus delighted to sample the fare on offer at the Inn, and also to share in the jovial mood of her companion.

"It's so nice to be with an *ordinary* human," she smiled to herself, and continued to muse silently: "But then, I think I may be about to hear a story that will contradict that adjective! If Morvan has arrived here in Scotland --- just in the nick of time --- to offer me passage on his new yacht, which he has named 'Vanzelle', I think I might be in for as tall a tale as I've ever heard."

Their supper concluding, her 'uncle' asked where *Rozennig* was hiding, and Eli said she would be happy to fetch the harp from her bedroom where she had taken her. But, she interjected, she would be even happier to hear the explanations of why and how he was here in Glencoe.

Calling for two drams of Islay single-malt as their dinner-plates were taken away, Morvan smiled. His red cheeks and stubby white beard were both shining in the warm fire-and-candle-light of the room, but it was his perky little eyes which outshone all.

"Settle yourself for a sailor's story, as I've never before heard tell of in all my years," he winked. Before they clinked their tubby glasses, Morvan looked Eli in the eye for a moment.

"That charming gentleman over there, in the red and black and yellow kilt (which he told me was the true and ancient --- mind you, not modern! --- tartan of the MacDonalds)," he chuckled, "he rattled off a long toast to me when we took our beers together earlier. Now I didn't catch all of it, for his accent is not too easy for me to follow, but it began with a lovely line, and so I'll use that tonight for you and me and for the yarn I'm about to spin for you!

"So here's to us, and as Monsieur MacDonald said: *May those who live truly be always believed.*"

Eli was silent, and slightly misty-eyed for a moment. "Ah, my dear Eli, now why has that made you sad?"

"I'm not sad, really," she said, touching his arm and smiling. "It's just that it reminded me of Lily. She used to say, '*It is good to believe*', and it made me think of that. It's very good to believe, and to be believed. I think she would agree with extending her little motto to that toast."

"Now isn't that odd, for I recall her saying that to me, too, when I was a very little lad. Funny, but the occasion that comes back to me was one night, oh I was only a child of four or five, and I'd woken with a start from a bad dream. I was sure, absolutely sure, that a beautiful fairy all in white and looking just like a flower, had come into my bedroom to sooth me back to sleep. When I told my sweet step-mother about it in the morning, she seemed very amazed, but not at all incredulous. And that was when she said those words. *It is good to <u>believe</u>.* And I can assure you, from my point of view, as a child and throughout my life of wondrous and surprising events, it has always been a blessing to believe, and very *very* good to *be believed*, also.

"And now I'm glad that you brought that image back into my mind, for it fits snugly into my tale. And with Lily's blessing upon us, I'm hoping you'll be ready to believe me and my story; though I'd be heartily surprised if you did not!"

With that, Uncle Mor began.

Morvan's Mermaid --- or The Sailor and the Silkie

I'm a good Breton-Celt, as I'm sure you'll agree, my dear Eli-ig, and so you won't find it odd at all that my story starts on la nuit de la Samain, *what you would call Samhain Eve. It's a strange time to up-anchor and make a long voyage, perhaps, for the seas are rough with winter just beginning and a week ago Concarneau was buffeted by gales and soaked to the bone with the pouring rain. But, it's always been true for me: I love the rain. Can't get around it, and can't make any one of my friends or fellow* marins *think me anything but stark mad, but I just love it. It always makes me want to dance and click my heels!*

Now, for a good while I'd been thinking to sell my own boat, which is a hard thing for me; for selling a ship is like ending a love-affair, and I've never been gay about either in my seventy-three years. But I had a short nap after my lunch, as usual, that afternoon before the evening of Samhain began, and in my dreams I saw myself at the helm of <u>another</u> boat, a new one, with lovely red sails. 'Well, the time is ripe,' I said to myself when I awoke and made myself a tea. 'She's somewhere waiting for me...'

*So there I was, on the late afternoon of the eve of Samhain itself, looking through a magazine about yachts and sailboats as I sipped my tea, when I saw an advertisement for a Drascombe Longboat for sale, up here at Fort William to be precise. And didn't she have **red** sails?!*

'Ma doue!' I said to myself, 'I've always wanted to visit Scotland!' And so I called the person selling the boat. A lady it was, and she was fully my own age --- who'd been a sailor-lass all her long life, like me, and had thought to continue with this splendid new craft, when her ridiculous family had intervened and asked her to stay ashore and convinced her to sell her Longboat. A sad and tragic thing, as I told her; but a blessing for me if she'd sell me her boat --- *if* I could find a buyer for mine. But then and there she laughed, and said she'd only promised her land-loving kin that she wouldn't take to the seas in <u>this</u> yacht she'd just bought, but she never said she wouldn't do so in another! So didn't she up and suggest that we could make a trade and that she'd take my sail-boat in exchange for hers?!

Well, I had a pretty Swallow yacht, and that swift-sweet sea-dame and I had had a passionate affair for several years; but of course I didn't know if the Scottish lady would see it as a fair trade.

'Oh' she piped into the phone excitedly, "but I **dreampt** of that sail-boat last night, a Swallow Cruiser, and what's more there were real *swallows flying all around her!* We have a saying here: 'Whit's fur ye'll no go past ye' --- I think you'd translate that into normal English as 'Whatever is meant to, will happen to you.' And somehow I'm sure it's **meant** to be.'

'Well, I'd agree,' I told her plain, 'what comes to us, is meant to. And we sailors, we're the best in this wide world for spotting a sign and a symbol, for there's none so superstitious as we are! And I think it's clear that your red-sailed Longboat is waiting for me, and your Swallow is here for you. Do you think I could sail her to you right away, so we can make the trade?'

'Indeed, I think you're obviously supposed to! How long will it take you?'

'Looking at the winds and rain today, I'd say a fortnight if I'm lucky.' But then I laughed. 'Unless there be mermaids and dolphins to help me along, that is!'

She laughed too, and a musical and infectious laugh she had. 'I'll send you some dolphins from our loch here,' she giggled. 'We've plenty today. But you'll have to find the mermaid yourself!'

Curious that she said that, and even that I'd come up with that quip about being helped by such creatures. But it's quite true, I've always loved the songs and stories of mermaids! And, just as I'd always cherished my dream of sailing one day to Scotland, so I'd always kept in a deep and fantastical corner of my heart the idea that --- some day before I died--- I'd meet a mermaid...

And now, it's happened!

There, you don't look too surprised, dear Eli, and that's just as I thought would be the case. For she's known to you, isn't she? Ah, yes, I knew it. Well, to continue...

I left the next day, so that was the 1st of November, and you'll say --- if you know anything at all about the nautical miles that lie between my home in Brittany and this fair land --- that it's barely possible to imagine sailing here in three days! For it was on the 4th, three days ago now, that I met the sailor-lady of Fort William and we exchanged our boats. But what's possible for me and what's possible for **them**, *well, it's not the same thing at all.*

I left as soon as the tide allowed me, and I made right good speed, for by twilight I was passing between Ouessant and the Île Molène, with Lampaul-Plouarzel smiling at me from the coast afar off. The weather was improving, and though I'd had cloud and some fog in the morning, the afternoon had been clear and now I could even see the sunset painting all the water in pretty colours just for me.

And then I saw her.

She was just how I expected a mermaid to look, and for that reason, I thought at first that I'd made it up or was hallucinating with the cold and wind and how I was trying to put haste in my sails to take me to my new Longboat waiting for me in the Highlands. But as I passed close-by, I could see she was real. And I could hear her too, for she played a harp!

Well, I slowed, and tended to my sails, and then I could use just the motor to inch in closer to the rock she was on. Absolutely amazed, I was, but even greater than wonder was my sense of gratitude; this was my prayer answered, for I was really seeing my mermaid! I didn't dare come too nigh to start with, but I could see her plain as the rocks and islands all around, and she didn't flee nor dive into the waters nor anything. She just kept playing.

Her hands made marvellous music on the little golden harp she held, and I could see that her fingers were webbed like the feet of a seagull. But strangest of all was her long white hair, for it was all made of feathers. Then I knew I hadn't made her up, for I wouldn't have thought of that! But in all other respects, she was my very notion of what a beautiful mer-lady should be: bare-breasted and tanned the colour of rich honey, a long tail with scales of blue and green that swished in and out of the waves around the base of her little rock, and what seemed a very fair face. But she never lifted her eyelids. She just kept looking down at the strings of her wonderfully painted and bejewelled lap-harp.

Oh, the melody was sublime! But though I've a head for a tune, I'd be hard-pressed to hum it to you now. It wouldn't stay in my mind, even the moment after she fell silent. Well, not silent, but not playing anymore; for instead of harp-music, I now heard her voice --- even more lovely it was than the chiming and rippling and ringing of her instrument. Her words, however, were only in my head, or so I think; for I never saw her move her red-lipped mouth at all.

'It is our habit,' she said, right inside my own head, 'and our delight at times, to lure sailors away with us, to our own lands. Many say they drown, but that is rarely the case. We are not usually so cruel in our invitations, but rather generous; for we find it not too unkind to share our realm with some doughty men of the sea, those who love our music and our voices. Our own mer-men are rarely to be found among us --- they are solitary for most of the round of the year, and come to us only by brief seasons! We like the company of human men, and though they do not live as long as we do, for we are many hundreds of years old, their short lives are passed with us in pleasures they could not know in the human lands or seas.

'But I am not come to lure you away forever, I'm come to meet you, Morvan, little step-son of Maelys, because you are a friend to the folk of Faërie, or a potential friend. For you can recognise us, even since your childhood... And at this time, we need your help.

'A very great Queen among us will meet with you, near to the Isle of Man, as you pass northwards. She will take you to another land, on a voyage of privilege and wonder. As the waning moon diminishes, well before she falls into darkness, you will meet the fairy-woman who will ask a great favour of you. From there, you will return, with our help, to seas which dance against Scotland's shores --- lovely they are! Filled with seals and dolphins, whales and mer-serpents! There, you shall become the skipper of your blessed craft, on the very eve of the new moon. For thereafter, from Fort William, you will have a very important mission to undertake and accomplish, if you have accepted to fulfil our request.

'Do you understand, and believe all I say?' she concluded.

I answered her, and with my heart full to bursting, that yes I did, and that I was honoured to help the fairy-folk, if indeed I could. I've always loved the legends of fairies, and I have never doubted their existence, nor that of all the splendid creatures in our mythologies and traditions. Why should they be unlikely?! What could be more unlikely than our own life, our birth and our growing, our amazing bodies and talents and minds and souls, or the sea itself for that matter? I ask you, why should we find it hard to believe anything?! And I'm sure I learnt that wisdom from Lily herself, now I come to think of it.

So I said my 'yes' of course, but I mentioned one thing --- not wishing to offend the lovely creature, but not really sure if she understood the ways of modern boats. For two days to get to the Isle of Man, crossing the lively Celtic Sea, and St George's Channel, and then up into the Irish Sea, with the waves very great and strong and the winds as wild as November could make 'em, well, that was a tall order! I said so, as politely as I could.

And then she almost looked at me --- I think, for I sort of felt her knowing little glance. She asked me if I trusted her, even though she was a mermaid, if I trusted that she was not going to lure me away underwater to her kingdom in the ocean of fairy-land. Well, I said, I had no reason not to trust her, and even if she did take me to her aquatic realm, I supposed I'd be happy enough to discover that! She seemed to laugh at my answer, and then --- quite contented, or so it sounded to my ears --- she said I should just relax and travel comfortably in my boat, and sleep soundly at night on all the nights to come, and she and her sister-mermaids, together with the dolphins and sea-monsters, would steer my boat forward in safety and through all the waves and winds and fogs and dangers. She said I wasn't to worry, but just have faith in her.

And, do you know, Eli, I didn't hesitate an instant. Those are rough seas, and though I'm a salty old sea-dog, I knew I couldn't do it on my own. So I was glad, and very curious too, to have her help.

We parted then, for of its own accord, my pretty Swallow flew off, even before I could hoist her sails again. I jumped to the helm, to avoid the rocks, but when I looked back at where the mermaid had been, I only saw a flash of a large and bright blue tail-fin as it disappeared under the swell.

Eli, my lass, that was the start of some very amazing and sublime days and nights!

The evening fell quickly and it was dark just after I'd left the mermaid's rock; and before me lay the open waters of the Celtic Sea, just where she meets the Atlantic Ocean. The swell was stronger than before and the winds were far too much for my sails. But not for a moment did I waver in my faith. My prayers had been granted, and I'd seen a real and beautiful mermaid! If I were to drown that night, that was well and good --- but I didn't think I would, not in my heart.

The heart cannot lie, Eli, of that I'm sure. I listened to my heart and though it was beating fierce fast, it was open and full of trust --- in the mermaids and in God. So I battened-down my hatches, and I just went into my little cabin below deck.

I never slept so sound, not in all my life. Anyone should have been terrible sick with the rolling and rocking, even a seasoned sailor; but I was not. My dreams were all of the luscious mer-lady, and her feathery hair and her shining, wet skin the colour of bees-wax, and her sweet music --- though I couldn't quite hear the melody, not exactly as she had played it.

When I awoke at dawn, I was snugly tucked up in the port of Penzance! How I got there, I can never tell you. I laughed all the way into the town, where I found a nice English breakfast and a few supplies to take with me. And then, as soon as ever I could, I set sail again.

That day at dusk, I came to the shores of Ireland --- to Kilmore Quay on the coast of County Wexford. Now I never meant to, for I thought to follow the coast of Wales northwards. But there I was when the evening star came out to chuckle at me! I went into the village, and some lovely songs were sung in a very hospitable pub --- and I was feeling sleepy when I returned, very late, to my boat as she lay tossing a bit in the soft rain and the gentle Irish breezes.

I'll swear to anyone, I clean forgot to cast off, even though I knew that the mermaid had told me she and her sisters would guide my boat. I'd certainly intended to do so, for they'd led me safely, just like it were a miracle, the night before; but I'd had a Guinness too many, and my head was heavy. I just found my berth and knew no more... until the next morning.

It was long after the rising of the sun when I poked my throbbing head above deck, and there off to larboard was the great town of Dublin, far across the green water. I had only a hundred miles or so to go to the Isle of Man!

My sails had been hoisted high --- by whom, I couldn't tell you --- but now they lowered themselves, with not a bit of aid or interference from me, and the boat moved forward smoothly of its own accord. And me? Well, I simply sat myself down on the breezy deck and ate my breakfast and drank my coffee. Sure it was, I was like a passenger on board a lovely little cruise-liner!

Well, my Swallow flew along through the strong currents, graceful as the family of dolphins beside us, with nary a worry in the world, just like me. And at sunset, there was the Isle of Man before us.

Now, I was not at all sure where on the Island the mermaid thought I should be making for, but as it turned out, I had little say in the matter. Suddenly, they were all around me in the purple, twilight waters: dozens and dozens of seals. Oh, gorgeous they were, with their eyes as big and round as demi-tasses of espresso coffee! They barked and played and gyrated in the soft swells, just as if they were thrilled to see the arrival of a long-expected guest. And before I knew it, we were in a little secluded inlet on the southern island, called the

Calf of Man: all rocks and kittiwakes, manx-shearwaters and seals, and me and my sturdy sail-boat.

I watched the lovely grey seals for a long moment, and many of them continued to crowd around me and my boat. It was incredible that I'd taken no harm coming up to the shore, for the rocks there are very treacherous and many were hidden right under the dark surface of the waves. But all was looked after by the mer-folk and the fairies, I suppose.

But now, my dear Eli-ig, I'll probably offer you another drink --- for my tale becomes stranger still, and I think even you will have to admit that wonder begets wonder, very often, in our marvellous lives!

Morvan called for refills of their excellent whisky, and Eli --- not making any comment --- simply smiled and touched her glass to his as he resumed his tale.

Climbing up out of my bobbing boat to tie her to one of the pointed rocks and have a little look around, I met the Queen that the mermaid had told me I would. Oh Eli, never was the little child deep within the old man happier than that evening! I'd read, or heard tales, of those creatures, but I couldn't even imagine what they could really be like. But here one <u>was</u>, right before my eyes: **a silkie**.

Now, you'll know from your love of Celtic and Nordic mythology, dearest Eli, that a silkie is a shape-shifter, for she is a seal in the ocean, but when she comes ashore and sheds her skin she becomes a beautiful lady. But I think that the word 'beautiful' is ridiculous here; for as a lover finds it hard to call his 'dulcinée' merely **beautiful**, *because the word falls short of all he sees in her, so I cannot use that word of this Queen.*

It may have been the shadowy sunset hour, but I didn't lack light. There was a glow all around the woman, and around me and my boat too. I could clearly see all of the 'real' seals, and far off the bright ray of a lighthouse, and overhead the first of the stars in a clear, cold sky.

And before me was the Queen: her seal-skin lay at her feet, like a crumpled bath-towel, and her small, perfect body was draped in grey and silver clothes as fine and delicate as moon-beams and sea-foam on a white beach. Her hair was grey like the seals, with strands of white in it. She looked very very old and inestimably young at the same time. Her eyes were changing colour as I gazed: one moment lavender-blue and the next as green as the Irish Sea as I'd seen it that morning at dawn. And they were laughing eyes, and filled with knowing and loving.

'Greetings, Morvan; I am Morliande,' she said, in a voice like undulating wavelets. 'Are you ready for your voyage with me?' She seemed to be giggling like a girl, and yet solemn and regal as a great monarch. 'I and my sisters, violet ladies of the Moon, ladies of Faërie, invite you to come with me tonight on a long sea-voyage. Tomorrow you will be received and entertained in the lands of the fairies, where you will meet a very special fairy-woman who will make a request of you. And then you will be brought back here to your boat, and from this island guided to the Scottish loch you seek, and the new boat awaiting you there.'

I hesitated to speak to the majestic silkie, but I took off my cap and bowed to her --- and that seemed to amuse her, for she laughed once, and her purple and green eyes twinkled like the stars overhead. Finally, I found my voice, and I said,

'I'd be honoured and pleased, Your Majesty. But why should you give such a fine gift to me? I'm no one very special or important.'

Her eyes glinted and many of the seals barked, as if they were laughing too. 'Fairies, perhaps, see things differently than humankind. To us, everything is special and everyone important! Now many of us have great gifts or possess wondrous qualities, but rare is the fairy that would doubt for a moment his importance in the dance of Life. It is not for any of us to say that this flower or this star, this leaf or this mountain, is more or less special --- the very idea is nonsense to us. You are the <u>ideal</u> person to accomplish the deed we shall ask of you, for many reasons; and in return, we wish to bless you with a rare gift --- rare, but not unheard-of --- to venture into our realm for a short visit. We have an idea, growing more and more present in all of our thoughts these past decades, that if certain humans could glimpse our world, and come back here with a memory of it, that it might contribute to an openness, a bridge between us. And the time is ripe. Ah, we have been waiting for many centuries!

'Now, one of my sisters whom I spoke of, she became aware, long years ago, that you were just the right kind of human to help us: she says that you have an eye for fairy-truth, a child-like capacity for belief in the enchanted, and an open heart. The deed which needs to be done, cannot be done by a fairy, in our opinion. It needs the human touch. She will ask this favour of you, when you meet; but first, if you are ready, let us take to the seas!'

I bowed again, and replaced my cap, and I was now smiling as broadly as her ladyship. I followed her over the crest of the rocky cove and down into another, and all the stars were jigging and dancing as if the great BonDieu, the dear God of the world and the sea and the sky, was himself a fine musician, playing hornpipes and reels in the heavens!

There in the next little inlet of dark water, reflecting those capering stars, was the Queen's boat. Eli, will you credit it?: it was fashioned of a single, white bone! The jaw-bone of a whale, I suppose, it was but a larger whale than him that swallowed Jonah. However, the boat was not immense, more like to a long canoe: maybe only a foot or two longer than my sail-boat, but very narrow and shaped like a basket-weaver's curved bodkin. But I didn't doubt that she could float, not for a second. The Queen stepped aboard and me after her, and she sat on a neat little throne near the fore-castle, which was itself very cunningly carved and rose to a sort of a point with a lantern, like a flickering candle inside a lace-work shell. And as for me, there was a thick blanket in the stern, where I could lie down, or sit-up and look out into the black night, if I preferred.

We must have sailed many hours, all through the night. The tiny waning moon showed herself, I recall, but I think I'd dropped-off to sleep for several hours before that. It was still very deep night, though, when I sat up again, and we were skimming through an ocean as calm as a lake: still and flat, showing a perfect reflection of the starry dome above us as if in a mirror.

And then, just as I was feeling a weariness come over me again, I looked up to where the Queen still sat, high and regal on her little throne in the bow of the jaw-bone boat. And she lifted-up one of her white hands before her into the night, and a light shone out of it, out *across the dark waters ahead of us. I sat up straighter, and I could see an answering light, like a lighthouse maybe or another extended and unseen hand that could send forth a glimmering ray of light, like the Queen's could.*

The rays of light held steady, and seemed to be pulling themselves together, right across the still waters. I couldn't see aught on the horizon, just the point of light. And then I think I may have nodded and slept again. For next thing I knew, dawn was brightening the sky at our backs, and the wake and wash of the whale-bone boat was all gold when I turned to glance at it. Ah, but then when I faced into the west once again, an island was before us, lit by the rising sun.

In the pale seal-grey light I looked around me, but I didn't know these waters at all. There were some waves now, and to nor-nor-east - -- just on the farthest point of the horizon a little behind us now --- I thought I could see the outlines of another island, huge and jagged as if there were great mountains not far from its coast. Ahead of us was the island with the shining-and-pulling ray of light; and a little off to the right of it, further north and west, was a another and slightly bigger island, too. But when I looked a second time, at both of these <u>other</u> lands, I could see nothing at all, only the endless sea. All that remained was our own island destination. But that sufficed for me, for she was altogether lovely!

I'm not a poet, dearest harper-Eli, so I can't paint my picture in words. I can only say that the island we made for was wild and rocky, forested and flowered, singing with birds and running water, and shining like a jewel in the clear, bright blue morning. The Queen lowered her hand, and the light was gone from it, and so was the other ray of light from the land.

On the shore, as we arrived in the shallows, I could see a man, and I wondered if it might be the King, the husband of the Silkie. I think she heard my silent thoughts, for the lovely seal-Queen turned to me and smiled.

'This is not the King who is my husband, Morvan; but he is a King also, so you are right in that. This is Durnol, the King of the Shee of the Little Skellig. Beside him is Rhysianne, his Queen, and the bright light you saw welcoming us came from a great jewel set into her palm.

Later today you will voyage to the shee where dwells their daughter, Rhynwanol, also a Queen, though a Queen in exile --- at least for the time being.'

We stepped out of the whale-boat and onto a low pier made of shining green stone. I didn't know if I should kneel or bow to their Majesties, but before I could decide, the silkie intervened. 'No formalities are due the royal fairies here, dear Morvan. We touch our hearts and bow the head in some of our island shees, while in others we simply incline our head with an inward blessing. Here in the Little Skellig Shee it is customary to open the hand, like this.' Whereupon, she made a gracious movement before her, with palm uplifted. The King and Queen did likewise, and so I followed suit.

'You are many to hold the titles of King and Queen,' I remarked, when everyone was simply smiling at me. 'Or perhaps everyone is royalty here?' The fairies all laughed, but in a delightful way, not making fun of my ignorance at all. In fact, they seemed to like the idea.

'As I said,' agreed Morliande, 'to fairies, everything and everyone is important. So in a way, you are quite correct: as a human might understand the titles of royalty, we're all as high in honour! But here, what makes a fairy 'royal' is that he or she possesses certain powers or qualities that are more, shall I say, 'enchanted' than those of an 'ordinary' fairy. We're all enchanted, of course, but Kings and Queens have more magical gifts, or they are seers, or they are shape-shifters like myself.

'Now we will go with King Durnol and Queen Rhysianne to break our fast of this night.'

The regal couple led the way, and I followed with the wondrous silkie-Queen. A pavilion made of thick cloths, green and yellow, earthy red and glittering gold, was awaiting us further up the shore, filled with tables and soft chairs. There were attendants to serve us delicious food and drink, and musicians strolling about playing little harps and fiddles, flutes and horns, guitars and lutes.

'I hope you enjoyed your voyage, Morvan?' asked the Queen Rhysianne, who was dressed in lavender and pale green, shimmering like the scales of fishes and subtly changing hue as she turned or moved.

'Very much,' I replied, 'though I've no idea where I am, or what seas we've crossed!'

'You are in Faërie, dear man,' said the rich voice of the King. 'And though the seas do, at times, connect our worlds, there are other doorways also. The Lady Ecume, whom you met, the most ancient and revered of the mer-harpers of our eleven island-shees, agreed with the Queen Morliande that to come to us by the sea-paths would suit you best. No human sailor has ever discovered them, not yet!' He laughed merrily, and bid the attendants refill my tankard of excellent --- though sea-green --- beer.

'But it would be wonderful, literally filled-with-wonder,' interjected the dark-haired Queen Rhysianne, 'if one day there could be a free and open passage between us. That may be much to wish for, but it is our dream that humans could enter into true friendship with us, understanding our tenderness towards Life and nature, and usually towards one another!'

I ventured an odd question, then, but her comment sparked my curiosity. 'Are there then, sometimes, disputes here in Faërie? Are there battles and even wars? Or do you always live in peace --- for a civilisation that could claim that, I think that would provide a good example to humans!'

Morliande, the silkie, seemed to grow a little sad, or at least reflective. 'Alas, we are not always at peace. There are not open battles, that is very rare indeed --- some ancient tales tell of such things --- but there is strife, and the play of various wills and the ambitions, or illusions, of certain fairies among us. War, in the human sense, in the sense of companies of combatants seeking to do harm or even bring to the frontiers of death their adversaries, no. That we have never known.'

'Although, once, many ages ago,' recounted the King Durnol, his voice even more pensive and sombre than Morliande's had been, 'a great people of the Shee Mor, our largest island-shee, experienced something akin to war. Well, they themselves did not fight, not in any way similar to their aggressors.

'In those times, ah millennia ago now --- why, my own father was only a fairy-lad then --- many, many of the folk of the Shee Mor went often back and forth between the two worlds; yes, they were as at ease in the country of Ireland as in Faërie, and no wonder, for Ireland was then a dense and magical forest for the most part. Ah, my father remembered, even as an infant, visiting the oak-woods of ancient Ireland and conversing with the wise and merry trees!

'But one day, an army of human-men --- known as the Sons of Míl --- arrived and moored their sleek boats, with figure-heads of snakes and lions, far up the estuaries of the wide rivers or at the very feet of the high cliffs. They came into the land, and not for one moment did they entertain the idea of conversing with either fairy or tree. The people of the Shee Mor were astounded.

'It was evident that the new-comers were not well-sighted, and could barely see the flitting, flying forms of the fairy-folk, and it appeared that they were also quite deaf to the voices of the oaks. Why, they did not even listen to the animals! The Shee-Mor fairies, who were subjects of a glorious queen then, called Dana, sought to show the wonders of the leaf-dancers and flower-singers to the invaders, sought to share with them the music of the deep sources of the magical waters and the profound wisdom of the fishes therein. But the human-children --- very young and brash and inexperienced in all music and magic they seemed --- had no intention of harkening to the voices of the fairy-tribe of Dana. And worse even than their disinterest, blindness and deafness, they showed them fierce aggression.

'That beauteous tribe of Dana they chased with iron! --- unbearable that metal to all fairies. With iron swords and spears, and also with fire. Groves of meditating oaks they burned, and others they hewed with iron-axes. It was an abomination! At last, all that the fairies could do was to pass back into their own realm, using the myriad doors, or Portals as we name them, set in hills and mounds of stony or grassy earth.

'They were many, those Portals, and had ever been left wide open. But now they sealed them, and wept, and many cursed the killers of the oaks and the fishes, the hunters of the deer and the playful hares

and rabbits; calling them humans of bloodshed and pain, of disharmony and of terror.'

I found I was weeping as the King Durnol told his tale. I cried not only with anguish for the fairies, for the trees and animals, but for shame. For I well-recognised my own human-race in the face of those invading men of Míl.

His wife the Queen concluded with these words, and sorry I was to hear them: 'And since that time, many of the fairies have harboured resentment, though I do not say hatred, of the humans. They mistrust them, and dismiss the possibility that there may yet be those in your world who would behave better. In all of our island shees, save one, there are still Portals into the human lands, but they are not numerous, not as they were. And they are kept locked, and guarded, secret and hidden. Spells and charms lie on them, and cruel tricks are sometimes played on the unwary human who crosses those thresholds unbidden. The sea-paths are concealed by magic, also. A few of the birds of Faërie use, at times, the sky-ways; though they are also generally closed by enchantment, save for the playful pathways of the tempest-winds which unite our two lands.

'For nature is not sundered, but is ever one thing only, the same here as there. And though the magic is very, very strong that separates us still, there are fairies who dream of re-opening the passages, and there are trees and fungi, strange creatures in the deep waters and mysterious insects, who communicate between the two worlds and urge us not to despair, but to continue to dream.'

'But,' *added the voice of the silkie, like a wave breaking on a white strand,* 'our dreams are vivid in our restless sleep now, for some among us become impatient to see them realised, and we hope that the day is not far when our two races will once again mingle, and this time with respect and upwardly-spiralling love. We have begun, certain among us, to **act**, to move towards our goal. For the first thing to do, dear Morvan, if one desires to make a dream come true, is to awaken out of sleep!'

I was silent for a long while, and we continued our little feast and the music of the minstrels around us echoed many of my own thoughts and prayers. And then I asked another question, as the meal was obviously ending and it seemed that Morliande was preparing for us to continue our voyage together.

'And between yourselves, between fairies, you say there is sometimes…strife, also?"

King Durnol sighed, as his wife commenced her reply to me. "The Queen Morliande, of the Shee Mor, would be able to tell you of the rivalry and the antagonism in her own shee, where her son is now the reigning sovereign. But my husband and I are also saddened by turmoil in our own shee."

'There is turmoil here? But it seems a paradise of peace and beauty," I exclaimed.

'Ah, it is not <u>here</u> in the Shee of the Little Skellig. Happy we are to have come here, and it is many centuries that this lovely island --- with its pinnacle Portal opening into the rocks of Skellig Michael in Ireland and Saint Michael's Mount in Cornwall --- has been our adopted home. But we have relinquished the rule of our native shee to another fairy-clan, welcoming them as part of our proposed alliance of all eleven of the shees and delighted to have their extreme gifts of enchantment to contribute to our dreams and our efforts. But, unfortunately, the new royal family which we invited to take our place has not been firmly accepted by all of our subjects. Most are loyal to the new King and Queen, but some have expressed the opinion that we go too far, and too quickly.

'The family we have installed in the place of our own, the new royal fairies of our original home, the Sheep's Head Shee it is named, come from a very distant shee --- with a culture and with many traditions which do not feel familiar enough to some of our own fairies. It is, I have heard, the same in your human-lands: to bridge the distance between certain cultures and beliefs, certain practices and deep-rooted traditions, <u>that</u> can pose problems. Even where there is a sincere desire to do so.'

'Ah yes, it's like a cross-cultural marriage, in a way,' I smiled. 'We have the same difficulty, sometimes, between certain societies or races, or colours of skin or gods that we believe in. And I've always thought that it's comparable to when two lovers, coming from very different *backgrounds, decide to marry. Oh, they may very well have rough seas, in such a case! More than likely, that. But it's always the same thing that sees them through the storm: <u>love</u>. And if it works for a man and a woman, well, I think it's the solution for tribes and clans and nations, too.'*

Queen Rhysianne looked long and hard at me, but her expression was as soft as a rose-petal.

'I think that my 'sister', the fairy-woman who has invited you here, the friend of Morliande and of our daughter Rhynwanol, I think that she has made an excellent choice. I believe you are <u>just</u> the right human to assist us, dear Morvan of Brittany. To assist us to make many humans, and fairies too, realise that the only solution is Love. Ever.'

'Now, we must go the Sheep's Head Shee, Morvan," whispered the silkie, rising and bidding farewell to the handsome King and Queen. I said that I hoped we would meet again, and they smiled at the idea and said that they believed it would be possible, one day. And so we, myself and the Queen Morliande, we returned to our whale-bone-boat, and set off once again.

****

We sailed for a very long time, but I couldn't count it in hours and nautical miles. I watched the gulls overhead and the great fishes beside us in the clear water, and the clouds that sailed along with us, high in a sky more blue than I've ever seen anywhere. It must have been late in the afternoon when the silkie-Queen said to me, 'There, before us, is the Sheep's Head Shee. We will meet the new King and Queen first, and then we will visit the fairy-woman who was our advisor in choosing you to help us. And she will explain to you what we ask.'

'If she is like you, dear Majesty, or like the two fine royals we have left in the Skellig Shee, well, I don't imagine I'd be able to deny her anything!' And Morliande smiled very warmly at me, which made me feel like I was swinging in a hammock between palm trees on a tropical isle!

But a 'tropical island' was not at all the style of the place we next came to. For the Sheep's Head Shee is well named --- though the silkie told me it is named for where two of its Portals open, and not for where it really is. Well, to my mind it was as Irish a landscape as I could dream-up!

Where we moored resembled more closely the photos I've seen of the Aran Islands than the peninsula in south-west Cork, it's true. Windswept, almost bleak, that's what I'd say. But very thrilling, too, in its way. As we walked from the haven or port to go to our meeting with the King and Queen, I saw that the landscape was all dark rock, divided by crevices and gullies, cracks and ravines, all filled with roaring, flowing streams and rivers. Impossible as it seemed to me, the giant slabs of rock and the dramatic hills of boulders and twisted, stunted trees shared their habitat with huge colonies of flowers! They were all small and pretty, like those of an alpine garden perhaps: blue campanula and pink heathers, little white-and-rose daisies and yellow poached-egg flowers, violets and buttercups, cyclamen and periwinkles. All out of their seasons and places; but all very happy and vivacious!

There was another flower, too, but I couldn't name it. It was white, with six petals and six little white knobbles in its centre. Shy and pure, it seemed, like edelweiss, but with an exotic personality that made me feel sure it came from another planet! Morliande told me that it only grew here, in this shee. But she cautioned me that I was not allowed to pick any flower here --- though I hadn't had the slightest intention to do that*: why, it seemed to be forbidden by the flowers themselves!*

The royal couple we met on this island-shee, they were not at all like Durnol and Rhysianne --- my word, no! Now those two, the King and Queen living on the Little Skellig, why you could mistake them for human-beings quite easily, except of course for the jewels they wore in their foreheads or hands or in the very un-*human points of their pretty ears. But their Majesties Tirrig and Bowarry were not at all like them, nor like us.*

Well, I say that, but they were and they weren't! They were a bit like the most elegant and amazing tribal people of Africa or even the natives from 'down under': more like ancient paintings of gods and goddesses on the stony walls of prehistoric temples or tumulus than like living people. They didn't seem to be made of flesh and bone, but rather of lights and colours that wouldn't stay still in any certain form for more than a breath. Ah, but they were beautiful to behold! As lovely as the saints in a stained-glass window, with the sun shining through the dazzling paintbox-coloured-panes so bright that you couldn't keep your eye fixed for long.

I didn't talk with them, not longer than to salute them – and the silkie-Queen Morliande told me that I didn't need to bow, for their form of salutation was done with heads held high, and just a very kind look with the eyes, very intense and brilliant, but filled with caring it was. So I did that, and both of them smiled, and we drank a cup of clear water together, from a large bowl with lovely designs of animals and suns and moons running all around its outsides --- and when I say 'running', I mean just that; for the pictures moved while we drank and they all seemed to be dancing! There was music too, but I couldn't see the players.

We were outside, standing before a great 'castle' that was like a tree, like a house made of a tree: it had branches going up and others going down, and all so winding and thick that it was like layers of leafy-branchy woven curtains. There were up-stairs stories and rooms like in a tree-house on many levels, all made of the twined branches. But we didn't go inside, and so I could only hear the notes of the many strange instruments floating out to us on the flowery carpet in front of the tree-palace. Singers there were too, behind the branch-curtains, but they sang in a language I couldn't recognise. It was like bird-calls and laughter and strong winds among reeds and rocks. Altogether marvellous!

But better even than the sight of the King and Queen, shining like the sun and the moon, and the haunting music of their hidden people, was the fairy-woman I was permitted to meet there. The silkie took me to her, in a real little cottage not far from the tree-palace of King Tirrig and Queen Bowarry. There were so many of the other-worldly six-petalled white flowers around the door, that I thought we wouldn't be able to walk over them without crushing their beautiful, starry *faces! But didn't they seem to just welcome our feet, and not bend or break at all?*

And inside the cottage, dearest Eli, I found your own little mother.

Yes, indeed, it was **Maelys**. But then and there I realised my mistake, my mistake when I was a little lad of about five: for I had thought then that a fairy had come into my bedroom after my nightmare; but all along it must have been my step-mother herself. For here she was, Maelys, or Lily as her grand-papa and your own father too had always called her, and she looked just like the fairy-queen that had visited me all those years ago.

She was shining and happy, but her skin was as white as if she'd just died. Truly, she was white all over, for she was dressed like one of the little flowers, like a fairy **made** of flowers! The only other colours about her, other than pure white, was the yellow of her delicate crown --- set atop her wavy white hair like the stamens of a blossom --- and the bright sky-blue of her eyes. Her eyes were rather like those of the King and Queen, in fact, for they had clear blue eyes too. But for all that, I think Lily's eyes reminded me more of the royals of the Little Skellig. Yes, yes; they truly had the same eyes as Lily, though a bit darker, like a twilight sky.

So there I was, with a magnificent Queen who was really a seal, and with another fairy-woman, who looked to be a queen as well, but who I knew from the human-world too. But you know, Eli, I'd stopped questioning it all. Everything had become so amazing, that my brain had just decided to say 'yes' to the whole kit an' caboodle!

Notwithstanding that, I had to ask the wonderful being standing before me: 'My darling Maelys, are you real? And aren't you **dead** these ten months?!'

She laughed, and that was as beautiful to hear as the sighing, singing music of the tree-palace.

'I've lost the ability to define that word, dear Morvan,' she said, still giggling like a young girl. "From a hospital bed in Bantry Town, I floated through light and dark, colours and sounds, nothing and something and almost everything...and found myself here. Treated like a high and honoured guest I am in this place, seemingly because I am descended from a half-fairy, named Malmaza, who came into the *world --- centuries ago that was. And it seems that Malmaza, my ancestor, was particularly devoted to a great high-priestess of the fairies, a keeper of a sacred lily, called a Dragon-Flower. It's an altogether delightful tale!*

'But now, my dear Morvan, I've spoken to some of the great and wise fairies around me in this shee where I've been lingering since my passing from the human-lands, and I've even met Malmaza and her twin sister and many other wonderful creatures and folk here. They've all agreed that I could ask your help... so listen carefully, my dear step-son, for I have a question for you, a favour to ask of you.'

'I'm listening my dear, white Queen Lys!' I cried. 'And what a wondrous adventure this is! And of course, I'll help you in any way I can, and with pleasure. Just tell me what you'd like me to do.'

'It's this, dear sailor-Mor: my daughter Eli, she's been to visit this fairy-land, rather as you are now. Of course, she is --- like you --- a human. Well, that's not altogether true; for, in fact, she's not exactly who or what I thought, these past fifty years. That's a long story, and all I'll say at this time is that Eli was here in Faërie recently, and something precious of hers was stolen by a great Chieftain of the Shee Mor, the biggest of the islands in this great realm, and he took it back out *of Faërie and into Ireland and then to Scotland. So Eli has decided, very bravely, to go after him.*

'Three of the great fairies that I have met here, they are seers: they can look ahead into time and glimpse some of the events that await us. In Eli's case, they have seen that she will have to travel quite far, across parts of Scotland, to reach the Chieftain and to reclaim what was stolen from her. She'll succeed; I've no doubt. But her adventure will not end without a confrontation, a very important one for her, on a tiny island in one of the Scottish lochs. And this is where your help is needed. For she'll be needing passage to reach the place...

'Eli will be in Glencoe, not far from where you are now bound, which is Fort William I think, to exchange your present sail-boat for another one. Morvan, I ask you to **meet** *Eli there, in Glencoe, on the night of the new moon or the morning after --- I don't know how quickly she will be led to the shores of Loch Leven --- and take her to*

the meeting with the Chieftain on the little island, back to the north of there, in Lock Eil. Are you following me?!'

'I am, dear Maelys, but might I ask you a question? Is this 'confrontation', as you call it, a danger to Eli? Who and what is this Chieftain? Will he be armed, and do you need me to **fight** him as well as just give Eli passage in my new little yacht?'

Maelys was silent for a moment, as if collecting her thoughts or wondering how much she should tell me. It was Morliande who answered, after a minute or two.

'It is rather complicated, sailor-Morvan,' said the silkie, very soft and low. 'We, myself and the mermaid you met and the Queen of the Shee Mor, we are the seers of whom Lily spoke. We see the vision of Eli's meeting with the Dragon-Lord, but we do not know if she will have regained what was taken by him before their encounter, or what mood he will be in, or if the silver-and-gold fairy Vanzelle will still be with her or not…'

'Wait just a moment, now, your lovely Majesty!' I exclaimed, all of a dither. 'Did you say that Eli's opponent was a '**dragon**-lord'?! Is he some kind of mythological monster, then? Is Eli to fight with a dragon?!'

'Ah, no, no, my wonderful Morvan,' smiled Maelys. 'He's a lord of dragons, a dragon-rider. But he has no dragon with him in the world. That said, when Eli encounters him, <u>she</u> will see a dragon, in a very real and terrifying vision. She will be seeing with the eyes of a fairy, with the eyes of her heart as a Princess of this land.'

'Eli is a Princess here?'

There was a pause, a hiatus in the replies of both the beautiful ladies before me. And now I was smiling too, for the thought of you, my dear Eli-harper, as a Princess pleased me very much. And, I must add, I thought it right and fitting!

At last, Morliande said, 'Yes, Eli is a very great Princess, of the Shee Mor.'

I wasn't smiling now, for another thought had crossed my mind, seeing Maelys all in white and transformed into a fairy-queen.

'Is Eli…<u>dead</u>, and turned into a fairy like you?' I whispered.

Maelys shook her head, her expression all compassion and concern. 'She is not dead, no, but her life as a fairy is in danger, her life in this wondrous realm. For the thing that was stolen is charmed with great magic, and she <u>must</u> retrieve it and bring it back to the Shee Mor in order to continue on to live as the royal fairy she is. Without it, she will surely fade or even, possibly, die. But we do not doubt that she can and will fulfil her mission. It is a great and daring quest, but she is equal to it, and it is very good that she must achieve it in the human-world and not here in Faërie. For the Dragon-Lord is pure fairy, and Eli is --- at this time --- still a human. There in Scotland, she has a greater strength, in many ways, than the Chieftain she must face.'

'But it would be well if she were not alone,' interpolated the silkie. 'And she needs a boat to reach the island, and a boat to leave it and sail back to her doorway into the Shee Mor. And that doorway is in Loch Etive. Do not worry for the encounter between Eli and the Dragon-Lord, Morvan, for another fairy will be there to support her, in case the conflict should become aggressive.'

'But I think it will not be aggressive or dangerous to Eli,' said Maelys in a very soft, rather winsome voice now. 'For the Chieftain will have met, on this flight of his into Scotland, his own true love: Vanzelle --- whom the Queen Morliande mentioned --- a golden-and-silver fairy from a far-distant shee who will join Eli and the Chieftain. And I think that his heart will be filled with confusion and longing, and perhaps doubt and even repentance. For love solves many riddles and may soften the heart of even the fiercest champion!'

'And these fairy-lovers, the Cheiftain and his lady... Vanzelle, are they visible to the humans, or are they visions, like the dragon?'

'No, I shouldn't think they will be visible,' replied Maelys. 'Only Eli will be real to your eyes. I do not think that you will be able to see the Dragon-Lord Erreig, or the fair Vanzelle.'

'What a lovely name that is,' I said --- though I don't know why. It just struck me as very pretty, musical and even a little Breton-sounding. 'I'm sorry I won't be able to see a fairy with a name like that! And did I understand aright, did you and the Silkie-Queen say that she is golden-and-silver?!'

'Yes, so she is,' smiled Morliande. 'An exquisite creature! But it may be that she will not even go the meeting on the island, for I do not see her there in any vision or premonition in my heart. And that is a pity, for her presence would perhaps turn the encounter into a gentler occasion --- as Maelys suggested --- were she there with the Chieftain to remind him of the love still living in the depths of his heart.'

I had a sudden idea, and so I said, 'Well, a thought has just struck me. What if I were to call my new boat by her lovely name? Then, in a way, she'd be with us on the little island, and it might contribute to the peaceful outcome of Eli's confrontation. A boat, like a harp, embodies the likeness of her name, for she's a real and unique being, with a personality and --- I've always firmly believed --- a soul of her own. My 'Vanzelle' would be less exquisite than a fairy, no doubt; but she'll be a lovely lady nonetheless!'

The two queens looked at one another, and both were smiling and nodding now.

'That is an excellent initiative and a very beautiful idea,' beamed the silkie, and her mauve and sea-green eyes were all aglow. 'I am so happy that you will help Eli, and I think you will help the Dragon-Lord also, with your sail-boat named 'Vanzelle'. But the time grows late, Morvan, and I must bear you back to the Isle of Man, and from there my seals and many of the dolphin-folk will accompany you to Fort William.

'And now, before we leave, Lily will give you a token, also, to assist and protect you, to bring further blessings to your boat, and to pass on to Eli when you find her. It will allow her to find her way back to Faërie from the Scottish Highlands. For you are deeply linked, now, brave Morvan, to both Lily <u>and</u> Eli, and so you are doubly blessed by the most noble of flowers: for the Rose is the princess, but the Lily is the queen.'

We left the glimmering white fairy-queen Maelys, or Lily; and I knew I couldn't kiss her or touch her, but I wished her love and joy as we left, with tears in my eyes. She said that you, Eli, knew about her being in the Shee of the Sheep's Head, and would be able to explain it all a bit more to me --- perhaps as we voyaged together.

The silkie and I, we returned to the slender whale-bone boat, swaying in the little port where we'd left her, the candle in her carved prow flickering in the dusk. I didn't see the King Tirrig and the Queen Bowarry again, nor any other fairies or creatures. All was very quiet and still, as if the whole place were holding its breath, or simply contented to shimmer and sparkle in the deepening night, like the strange, foreign constellations of stars that were above us and reflected all across the black water of the hidden ocean-paths.

*I fell asleep as we sailed, and didn't awaken until dawn. And there I found myself curled up in soft blankets from my **own** sail-boat, though I was lying on the shore, amid the rocks and tide-pools of the Calf of Man, surrounded by wide-eyed seals. The silkie-queen, Morliande, was nowhere to be seen.*

But clasped in my hand was this, Eli-ig, and I suppose it's that, the token that she spoke of and that Lily somehow gave to me --- though I didn't see her do it.

Morvan had finished his tall-tale, but not yet his second glass of whisky. Eli hadn't seen him reach into the pocket of his heavy tweed coat, hung over the back of his chair; but he was extending his hand to her now, across the table, and offering her the token from Lily. It was a dark purple flower. Eli could almost hear Lily's voice giving its name: a Dragon-Flower.

Eli took a deep breath, and then she received the exquisite gift from her Uncle Mor's hand.

She looked around the pub and dining-room, wondering if anyone would be left at the tables or playing in the *céilí*. They must have been talking long into the night, as far as her reckoning went... Morvan glanced around too, surely with the same idea.

"That's funny," he chortled, and raised his glass with Eli's. "They're still playing the same jig as they were when I began my yarn, unless they've come back to it again. "

"I think it's the same one, Uncle Mor," murmured Eli. "Those people at the next table had just finished their meal when you began, and look, the Inn-keeper has only just walked over to take their plates and offer them a choice of dessert. I don't think any time at all has passed while you spoke!"

Morvan nodded, and scratched his white whiskers thoughtfully.

"Well, and it doesn't surprise me somehow," he said at last. "For I sailed up to Fort William from the Isle of Man that very day, the day I arrived back from my escapade in fairy-land, and I met the sweet woman who took my Swallow in exchange for my new lady-love 'Vanzelle'. But, Eli, it was the 4th of November when it should have been the 5th, for I'd been with the silkie-queen two nights and the day between visiting the two island-shees. But only one night had passed from the evening I met her to the early morning when I got back, if you'd believe that!"

Eli held her glass against Mor's, in mid-air between them, repeating --- with a grin --- the very apt toast of Mr MacDonald.

"*May those who live truly be always believed*," she pronounced, with aplomb.

Uncle Mor laughed with her, and when they had drained their glasses, he asked with a wink: "So shall you be getting your shy *Rozennig*, and playing for us, Eli-harper? I'd like to hear a rendition of the Silkie-Song, *An Mhaighdean Mhara* from County Donegal. Do you know it?"

"I do indeed, and it's a mystical and mysterious melody. Very appropriate indeed! I'm sure it will sound splendid on Róisín."

"Well, the night is young, or so it would seem. Let's join the party!"

So saying, Eli brought her harp down and sat beside Morvan in the pub, playing and singing silkie-songs and many other airs, with both of their hearts light and filled with hope and courage for the trip tomorrow to the island in Loch Eil.

****

Chapter Fourteen:
The Hawk, the Loch and the Island

*he **céilí** concluded* very late, and Morvan --- who had taken a room at the Inn rather than walking the long and chilly road back to his 'Vanzelle' --- bid Eli a good night, assuring her that they could take their time in the morning. No need to make a particularly early start.

Eli was pleased by that news, for she felt she would be happy to enjoy a good porridge and some delicious toast with Dundee marmalade to complement her tea before setting off. As he had already told her, Uncle Mor also reassured her that he would pay for both of them, for their rooms and meals. Eli thanked him profusely and promised to visit Brittany and invite him to dinner when she would be back in France!

She lingered a little longer, after Morvan had gone upstairs, taking the deep purple lily out of her shirt pocket to look at it for just a moment before carefully slipping it back and sighing with a poignant and yet deeply contented smile. Then she lifted Róisín into her arms and went towards the door, where the last of the musicians, also, had just disappeared, going back to their own homes or their beds at the Inn, laughing and still singing snippets of song.

Ah, no, not *all* of the guests had departed. As the bar-man made his rounds, filling a tray with empty glasses and blowing out the few candles which had not entirely burned away, one man remained. The inn-keeper nodded to him as he passed through the low door towards the kitchen.

But Eli stood and stared.

She had smiled when she had first noticed him, for he was half-hidden in a shadowy corner of the room and, though he was not smoking a long pipe, he was wearing a deep green cloak with the hood up to hide his face. Just for a moment Eli had smirked, and said to herself, "That fellow looks just as I always imagined Strider at the 'Sign of the Prancing Pony', in *the Lord of the Rings*!"

But her amusement, buoyed-up on the pleasures of playing and singing and enjoying the camaraderie of other 'trad' musicians this evening, was suddenly extinguished like the candle-flames.

This was not Strider; it was Reyse.

Eli walked the few paces to the door and, so, coming opposite to where he sat, she stopped and placed her harp on the floor. Reyse stood, and slowly pulled back his hood. His eyes were shining, despite the dimity of the pub, but his slight grin was rather hesitant.

"Beautiful harp and beautiful playing," he remarked, coming a little closer to her. "And a beautiful Golden Flower to shine its greetings across the room to me --- and I imagine to me only, for I doubt that anyone else here could see it. Or can Morvan-the-sailor perceive the tokens of Faërie, such as the Rose?"

"Hello Reyse," said Eli, very softly. "I've been wondering and worrying about you. I'm very glad to see you. Surprised, but glad.

"And no, I don't think Morvan can see the Rose, for he said nothing about it. But I suppose you can, of course, for you know the twins very well, I understand."

"That's not why I can see it," he replied, and he smiled a little more warmly, but just briefly. "I can see it because it is now *yours* and not Mowena's. And it graces the head of the harp that the Prince Finnir has made for you, as I understand. So the Golden Flower is touched by the energies of the two beings dearest to my heart: my friend Finnir, who is closer to me than a brother, and the Lady Eli --- whose brother Finnir is not, after all."

There was a breathless pause as both regarded each other.

"When did you learn that, Reyse?" asked Eli, speaking slowly and still in a whisper.

"When I was in the Sheep's Head Shee in August. And then --- when I received the message you 'sent' to me, by way of this same lovely harp, on September the 12th --- I was able to make the *connection* between the two."

Eli closed her eyes for an instant. When she opened them again, she sighed --- but could not find any words.

Reyse continued. "Thereafter, as I think the twins may have told you, I came into the world, here in Scotland, to busy myself --- even more industriously than I have done for many years --- with our shared work."

Eli found her voice, and nodded, "Yes, they told me that you were often with them now, and with…Ceoleen, your former lover, I believe."

The golden rings about the dark pupils of Reyse's warm brown eyes glowed brightly for a second. He hesitated, and then said, "I work with *many* fairies, and *many* humans, as I have for *many* years. Yes, Ceoleen is among them, together with Malmaza and Mowena. But my heart and that of the singing-fairy Ceoleen, from the Dancing Goat Plains of Karijan, have been sundered for many centuries, Eli. As you say, she is my *former* lover. Not my present one."

"I wasn't suggesting anything, nor accusing you, Reyse," retorted Eli, in a tone more than merely candid.

"Were you not? Excuse me; I thought I read a certain defensiveness between your lines."

Eli looked very sad. She had the strange sensation of speaking with herself in a mirror, so close did she feel to this fairy before her. Confusion, attraction, regret, sympathy --- all those sentiments were mingling in her mind. But stronger than all of them was the genuine pleasure of just seeing Reyse before her, just being near him. She felt protected, and embraced by unconditional caring, and thoroughly known and understood. She felt at home.

"I *am* glad to see you," she repeated once more. It seemed to sum up all she was feeling.

Reyse looked rather sad too, she thought. He simply concluded. "I'm pleased to see you too, Eli. And I will see you again, on this journey of yours, I'm sure."

Eli's eyes brightened, and she looked up into Reyse's face with curiosity, and with hopefulness too. "Will you?"

He pulled his hood up over his long, wavy hair as he turned to go. "Scotland is a small realm --- much smaller than Faërie, even smaller than France; though it is magical beyond its spatial limitations. I think the... *chances* of our paths crossing again are very good. I think so, yes."

And, with that, he ducked under the lintel of the doorway, and was gone.

****

By the time Eli and Morvan had reached the shores of Loch Leven, it was already mid-morning. Eli smiled as she handed her harp up into Mor's hands and climbed out of the small dinghy into 'Vanzelle'. The skies were clear, and the tiniest arc of the new sickle moon was poised over the mountains in the east.

"Uncle Mor," she asked, as her dear sailor made ready to cast-off, "you said it was the 4th when you arrived at Fort William to make the exchange of the sail-boats, did you not? Today's the 8th, and I think you'd only arrived here yesterday morning. Have you been sailing elsewhere in the meantime?"

A very charming grin stole over the old man's weathered face.

"Oh, yes and no," he chuckled. "Yes and no. Gavenia and myself, well, we struck up an excellent friendship right away, you could say. We visited the neighbourhood of Fort William together, even went to see Ben Nevis. But in the main, we simply enjoyed each other's company, talking of sailing and ships and the sea, of our long lives and some of our many adventures.

"Now, I didn't tell her all that had happened to me to get to her; but I think it's fair to say that I didn't need to. She seemed to know that I'd been off on a very extraordinary voyage. She maybe has, herself you know, had some contact with fairies --- I wouldn't be a bit surprised. She's a fair and free spirit, is Gavenia, a 'bonnie lass' I suppose is the term. And I believe that I've not seen the last of her."

Eli was quite satisfied with this explanation of her uncle's whereabouts for those three days. And very happy for him, and for Gavenia too.

But Morvan now continued. "I suppose it's not impossible that we pay her a visit, but I think it will be on the way back from this little voyage, if you're willing, dear Eli-ig. For I feel I must *begin* by taking you to your island --- for that was what the lovely fairy-queen Lily asked me to do."

Eli inhaled deeply, filling her chest with the freshness of the breeze sweeping over Loch Leven. They were moving away from the shore now, and Jizay was beside her --- still quite invisible to Morvan --- and evidently occupied with thoughts similar to his mistress's. He spoke to her in silence.

"Yes --- as I heard from your Uncle Mor's tale, listening from my place unseen under the table in the *Clachaig Inn* last evening --- he knows he is to sail you to Loch Eil, and to your island-*rendez-vous* with Errieg. Fill your lungs with the sea-air, my darling Eli, and your heart with courage. You have the Cloth, and both the Moon-Flower and the Dragon-Flower, and I think other forms of protection also. It will go well, I've no doubt…"

Eli was not sure if her dear hound of joy was referring to the Flaming Crescent Moon, for she did not think that he could see it. But she well knew that she had --- indeed --- myriad 'forms of protection', as her dog had said: two parts of enchanted Cloth and two magical Flowers, her harp crafted by Finnir, the Leaf and the Rose. And over and above these, she had the love and protection of Lily, of the Queen Rhynwanol, of Morliande the silkie and of Lady Ecume the mermaid, and also of her brother Timair or Aindel, who --- like their mother --- had an 'affinity with the Cup of Light'. As did Finnir evidently, also, according to that beauteous brother. Somehow, they would all be there with her. Even Leyano and Pallaïs seemed to be implicated in this predestined meeting.

Eli wondered if Jizay had also overheard her conversation with Reyse last night. She thought not, for she had seen him go out with Uncle Mor and trot up the stairs to her own bedroom. She did not mention the meeting to her dear hound now, but simply nodded and squared her shoulders. Glancing up, she could see Peronne, high above the russet-red sails, gliding along with them.

Morvan had said that they would go gently, and be at Loch Eil in the afternoon. That said, neither Eli nor himself knew where, exactly, they would find the island they sought.

They stayed aboard, and still going along steadily, during their lunch. This was taken not long after they had passed Corran harbour and its slender strait where a ferry-boat crossed to Ardgour. The day was clean and cold with a light wind, and besides their little sailboat there were quite a few other craft on the loch, and a great many birds above it as well. Around 'Vanzelle' were several dolphins and porpoises, and seals were now beginning to make an appearance as the graceful little yacht continued north toward Fort William.

Morvan pointed out the town as they passed it, and even indicated where Gavenia had her home and the place in the port nearby where his former boat, *his* Swallow and now *hers*, was moored. Sea-birds were everywhere, crying and tumbling through the sky in rag-tag dances and dips. But among all the swooping and looping gulls, kittiwakes, gannets and guillemots, Eli could see eagles too. The two great golden eagles were there, as well as her wondrous white-tailed sea-eagle Peronne, and also --- rather incongruously, Eli thought --- a bright white hawk.

The eagles made her think of Reyse, the 'Eagle of the Clan of the Half-Moon Horses'; but the hawk simply made her wonder...

They turned into Loch Eil and passed the Island of the Trees, just off the coast from the village of Achaphubuil. Morvan glanced at Eli, but they both simultaneously shook their heads. No, this was *not* their island --- somehow they knew it would not be quite so easy and obvious.

Following the narrow loch further west, they finally emerged into wider waters. Eli had risen from her seat and, with Jizay beside her, had come to stand beside her Uncle Mor, to look out into the expanse of playful, juxtaposing light and shadow over the loch. The afternoon had passed quickly, or so it seemed, for the sun was descending before them, painting the water's wrinkled, liquid canvas in hues of apricot and deep purple tinged with gold.

A ray of sunlight escaped the bank of cloud which was now gathering over the horizon of hills before them, and it created a similar pathway of light across the water to that which Eli had seen from the deck of the ferry leaving Ireland --- reminiscent of her meditation in the chapel of Ligugé as well...

"That's very curious," muttered Uncle Mor, glancing round with a strange, but somehow very knowing smile stealing across his mahogany face and making his bright eyes even brighter. "I didn't notice, before now, that you had a lovely dog with you."

And before Eli could find her tongue, he added, "He's a fairy-hound, I'll warrant; and I can see him now because we've left Scotland."

"What do you mean, *left Scotland*?!" asked Eli, in a hushed voice, but almost ready to share Morvan's smile. "And do you mean to say that you can actually *see* Jizay now?"

"Ah, is that his name. How do you do, Jizay! Glad to have you aboard --- I suppose you're here to help and accompany your mistress, just as I am, somehow. Well met!"

Jizay barked joyfully, and licked Morvan's outstretched hand. Eli was nonplussed, but felt also very happy that her dear sailor-angel could see her golden dog, and that he was now surely able to share the changing landscape before her. For changed it had.

The young 'moon-lash' was setting in the sun's wake, between two mounds of cloud in the western sky resembling prussian-blue meringues. And directly before them, across perhaps only another half-mile of rather dark water (for the glistening sun-pathway was gone) was the silhouette of a small island.

No, clearly, this was no longer Loch Eil, or even Scotland. For that island had not been there a moment ago, nor had the dozens of seals swimming alongside their boat, nor the dolphins leaping in gay arches out of the water far off to either side of their course. Peronne was still above them, as were the two golden eagles, and also the gleaming white hawk.

And before them, inching nearer now, with no motor to push 'Vanzelle' forward and not the breath of a breeze to fill her still, red sails, was the island of *all* of Eli's visions.

It was not merely the island where she had encountered Erreig and the dragon in the scenes shown her yesterday evening. It was where she had stood, in all of the previous 'apparitions' of this place, with hair floating out on the wind and with her arms opened wide; where she had seen a knight or king in the background and a huge winged-reptile wheeling away from her. This was **the** island. But whether it existed, truly, in the past or the future, in memory or as a prophetic premonition, she did not know. But here it surely was --- in the present.

The sleek and elegant sailboat moored itself, with no help from her captain, against a little rocky finger of heathery land extending primly from the island as if wishing to test the temperature of the water.

Eli stepped out onto the rocks, and quite silently --- in her heart --- she suggested to Uncle Mor and Jizay to remain where they were, for she wished to go on from here, alone. They both understood clearly, and agreed with smiling nods. Morvan passed Eli her harp.

"I see why you called her *the little rose*," he commented, also wordlessly. Eli raised an eyebrow and smiled back at him.

As she walked up the gentle slope, the sky --- so lately darkening into indigo evening --- grew pale with dawn and then quickly luminous in the rosy blush of a clear morning. Had an entire night passed? Or was this a day in another land and from another time?

About her were many assorted colours of heathers with high, yellow gorse bushes behind them. And when she reached an area where the ground was soft with lush green grass, she could see tiny wildflowers too, opening their delighted faces to the warm breeze and welcoming the attentions of the numerous bees and butterflies.

Eli turned to look back at the stony finger extending from the shore and reaching into the brilliant blue water, and Morvan lifted a hand to her in salute. Jizay had left the boat, and was now sitting on a great rock beside 'Vanzelle'. They seemed far away already, but Eli felt comforted by their presence, and by that of the crowd of grey seals also, congregated around the sailboat and even climbing up onto many of the rocks beside her hound of joy.

Before she could turn again and continue walking further into the rich, colourful scene on the island, Eli's senses brought her new tidings. There was a sudden waft of fragrance, certainly honeysuckle. And flying around her and right before her eyes were several glorious, giant moths. Olive-green and pink elephant-hawk-moths and very large specimens of grey *mormo-maura* ones. Eli recalled that both were used by Alégondine as observers of her father, and informers of his movements and adventures. For that reason, and for many others, Eli was not too surprised by what she could now hear.

Singing, filled with melancholy and longing: a melody of loss and loneliness, of love and yearning, of resignation mingled with a wavering hope deemed to be foolish and futile.

She turned at last, and saw Erreig before her, standing in the midst of a bare plateau of grassless golden ground not a hundred yards above and before her. His song came to her ears and then floated out over the vast waters beyond the seals and dolphins.

The sea,
Cradle of clouds, spent rivers' tomb,
Sundering the islands, sundering dreams,
Singing stolen songs that were once our own;
The sea,
Wherein my heart has now foundered and drowned.

The sky,
Vague palace of wind and stars,
Resounding with furtive, retreating steps
And love-lyrics echoing between cold peaks;
The sky,
Plundering the songs from my heart…and hers.

"The sky has stolen her, and the sea lies between us. And our hearts are lost in both."

Erreig's voice was low and lovely, Eli thought, even though his words, both sung and spoken, were so despondent. She was nearly beside him now, as he murmured his final phrase.

"You were hoping that she would come here, were you not? You were... waiting for Vanzelle?" asked Eli, not looking at the Dragon-Lord, but rather gazing, with him, out across the encircling lake or ocean.

He breathed very deeply and --- it seemed --- with an effort to keep at bay his tears. "I am ever *hoping*, ever *waiting*. They are the two words which define my life. In the past I tasted bliss and knew grand prospects; in the future I sought to imagine even more glorious delights and all our dreams fulfilled. But between the two, between past and future --- you are right Princess of the Rose --- there is only hoping and waiting. And both are barren and bitter."

Eli had placed her harp beside her on the golden earth, but not between herself and Erreig. Her hand was on its curved, blond wood and now she lightly caressed it, her fingers finally coming to rest on the delicate Golden Flower. She spoke slowly.

"To brood on past and future is indeed, and always, barren and bitter, and quite useless Erreig. The heart cannot live on love-songs remembered or day-dreams of what is to come; it can only live, truly *live*, in the present. You could, perhaps, sing your love-songs *now* --- to Vanzelle."

"She is not here."

"She is... in a way. The sail-boat there, moored against the rocks below, she is called 'Vanzelle'. She could symbolise, for you here, the presence of your belovèd --- like a metaphor for your love, for your romance. It is certain, in any case: if you *truly love* the golden-and-silver fairy, she is always with you, and she will hear you."

Erreig looked straight ahead, and Eli could feel the mood of the Dragon-Lord changing, but not for the better.

"You speak of symbols and of metaphors, Princess of Faërie, as did the Prince Finnir also. Everything meant many things, in his parlance. Dragons, Great Cats, even the Sun and the Moon. To my tormentor, everything was wavering light, refracted through our own perceptions, distorted by our weaknesses, and never ever truly ours --- for light cannot be held. It slips between our fingers and continues on in its own impervious beauty. Like a boat, named 'Vanzelle," he sneered, "inevitably borne away on the tide. Away, away. Like love.

"I know what you desire, Mélusine. You wish, like your father, to chase me from my --- from his --- kingdom. I am to become an exile, sent forth from Quillir, from the Shee Mor, to live in lonely disgrace --- banished and disgraced, like your mother the Queen."

"It was not my *father* who disgraced my mother," remarked Eli, as coolly as the petulant fairy beside her. She felt, immediately, that it was perhaps unwise.

"I did not disgrace her, nor chase Rhynwanol from the Shee Mor!" retorted Erreig. "I loved her."

Eli stood her ground, but tried to sound more conciliatory than accusing. She turned to face Erreig and said, "You <u>loved</u> *Vanzelle*. You *desired* my mother. It is not the same thing.

"There was a *reasoning* behind your seduction of the Queen; that seduction was a part of your frustration and your ambitions. Your love for Vanzelle was without design or strategy --- your only intention was to share your heart and your life with her. You were not seeking to better yourself or your identity by *that* union. Even the founding of the 'White Dragon Family' was spontaneous and natural, I think, not premeditated as a part of some plan. But your affair with Rhynwanol was, I think, based on <u>other</u> motives than sharing or love.

"Was it not, Erreig?"

The warm air had turned very chill. Eli awaited a response, but it did not come for what seemed many minutes. She had the feeling that the Dragon-Lord was vacillating in his mind and heart, in his stance before her and before himself too, in all of his defences and in all of his pathetic refusals to alter his point of view. Finally he turned to face her, his pale blue eyes aflame.

"I do not know what were my *motives*! I knew nothing more than the wild passion I felt for the violet-Queen, as I also felt for you, Mélusine. I did not examine my heart's promptings, asking myself if they were noble or lunatic. I was helpless before both of you!"

His lovely, quite feminine voice had become strained and shrill. Eli did not step back, however.

But in the silence --- a very tense silence --- which followed, she slowly allowed her fingers to reach down onto the tops of Róisín's strings. She could hardly pluck them with any hope of creating a clear sound, not from this angle nor so high on them. She could not hope to find the right notes...

Or could she?

She had already set the *fa*'s to be sharps, lifting the tiny levers at the heads of those strings. She could feel where those notes, those strings, were. And, moreover, she knew that the *do*'s and the *fa*'s were coloured strings, not glistening white like the other notes. On a normal harp, these would have been red and blue; but on the Harp of Barrywood they were mauve and sage-green. In her mind's eye, Eli visualised the colours of those strings, almost as if their hues would give them a different feeling under her fingers. She partially closed her eyes, and the tips of her fingers lovingly and lightly wandered over the tops of each string, slowly seeking the correct order: *La, fa#(green), re, si, do(mauve), mi, sol.*

As her fingers found the strings she sought, the sounds were released, liberated. Miraculously. *Miraculous music... for her quest.* The cadence of notes, so harmonious, so sweet, so mysterious, rose from the harp like incense. The golden Rose glowed warmly. Giant moths fluttered in profusion around Eli and Erreig, and then they returned to the high bushes further off, among them a towering bank of honeysuckle.

From far out in the bay or ocean, beyond the sail-boat, on a rock surrounded by seals, came an answering melody --- very like the composition that Eli had invented based on those seven notes. It was played by the Lady Ecume. Even from this great distance, Eli could see the mermaid with her small golden harp; and she could hear the ringing, chiming notes blown inland to where she and Erreig had met. She fancied that a second melody-line overlaid the first --- yes, the notes of a sonorous oboe were weaving themselves among those of the harp…

But Erreig was gone.

Eli turned to where he had been standing, but she saw only a flash of black and yellow wings in the distance. The moths of Alégondine whirled away after him, but his flight was riotously fast. He disappeared over the trees to the north of the island.

But to her immense relief, there, against the background of trees, Eli could see someone else.

Finnir! And he was astride Neya-Voun, and she was a splendid unicorn now, and the Prince was dressed as she had seen him at the Portal of Gougane Barra: with high mist-grey boots and deep ocean-blue leggings, and doublet and short cape of embroidered and jewel-studded cloths in all the tints of twilight or of running water. In his lifted right hand was his golden spear, from his left shone the sapphire, the *Eye of the Innumerable Falls*. And from his forehead blazed the light of his precious pearl.

But even as she beheld him, he vanished. Finnir and his unicorn were gone also.

What had felt like a day in early springtime, now turned to that of a suffocating and sweltering summer. Eli instantly thought of the smog-polluted summers of her Los Angeles childhood. Her eyes stung and her throat was choked with the heat and the fumes. Was she about to relive the attack of her nightmare? She swallowed hard but could not find her voice to call out for Jizay, or Laurien... or Lily.

But this was not the heat of the Californian desert-winds; this was Dragon-fire! This was Bawn --- and other winged worms.

Crashing out of the smoky skies above the woods they came: the six lieutenant-riders of Erreig's household, and their Lord. All seven in formation, in a streaking, screaming chevron; and then suddenly breaking apart and shooting to right and left, diving, spinning, searing the clouds and leaving bands of black fumes in the wake of their aerial acrobatics.

The skirmish was upon her, but --- unlike in her nightmare vision on the Hill of the Sun --- she did *not* cower before the threat of some approaching violence. She took Róisín up into her left arm, she lifted her chin high, and with her right hand she played loudly and defiantly, but also very calmly amid the storm of ear-splitting dragon-bellows and blasts of spark-filled breath as they passed so close that she could see their eyes. They were eyes of serpents, yellow and green and black. Save for the albino Bawn, for hers were flaming red.

And in an instant, Bawn had landed.

Not ten yards from Eli, the huge monster lay crouched on the scorched earth, so lately smooth and golden --- now a blackened field of rutted and fire-stained rubble. Erreig was astride her, his gleaming white spear held aloft, and in his muscular chest the fire-opal, *Gurtha*, glowing like a tiny red-furnace. From the Cheiftain's forehead shone forth *Kalvi-Tivi*, diamond of ice-blue and arctic-white.

Eli recalled Leyano's account of the attack at Dawn Rock, and what he had said of the three-fold-powers of *Gurtha*: "*it can triple a fairy's strength, or insight, or his seductive charms, or his magical skills.*" And from the keen and cold glance that the Dragon-Lord had turned upon her now, Eli imagined that he would try to use all of these devices at once!

He had vowed to her that he had not harmed her as a child. Nonetheless, without a doubt, she felt that he intended to do her harm now.

Suddenly, in the midst of that certainty and the wave of terror it sent through her, Eli also remembered other words said to her by Leyano. For her brother bore a diamond also, the yellow stone named *Tohtet*, won from the eagles and falcons and white hawks, won under the guidance of Reyse, formed from the white-hot, yellow-hot core of true dragon-fire. *Erreig's diamond was icy and filled with blind defiance... a desire filled with the force of his own fears. Mine was hot as the heart of a true earth-dragon... leaping forth into utter honesty and revelation, demanding to tear open the heart and to turn it to the heavens, to look into the eyes of the sun with the sovereignty of the eagle!*

Eli looked straight at Erreig, and she saw him --- no longer dark-skinned and powerful but ghostlike, cold and white as death, white as his dragon-mount, white as his stern and unyielding diamond, though a red fire still blazed from *Gurtha* in his chest. Now she detached herself from the scene for an instant and witnessed her place in it; she beheld herself --- glowing and yellow as Leyano's *Tohtet* --- like a great golden harvest-moon of seeing and of sovereignty.

She was no ghost or phantom-form; she was Eli Penrohan, human woman with the heart and spirit of Faërie as her birthright. She breathed deeply, flooding her lungs with life, her human life as well as her own truth and her own power. Her power, here and now. The power, the eternal force that opens flowers, that grows trees, that hatches birds ... and dragons! The life-force that is --- by its very nature --- trust and faith and confidence and belief. Life that is love at its most powerful, and also at its most gentle.

Erreig had lowered his spear, and his expression had changed. He was no longer white and ghost-like. But he had *not* dismounted and he was *not* coming to attack her.

Beside the gaping jaws of Bawn, filled with white and yellow flame exactly the colour of Leyano's diamond, Eli conjured in her mind the form of Leyano himself, in his crab-and-shell armour.

In her momentary visualisation, he stood beside the immense head of Bawn, and he placed a slender and cool hand on it, right between her twisted horns. The mighty beast closed her red-toothed mouth, and thin coils of silver and black smoke rose either side of her jowls. She seemed to be smiling, or purring. In the air was music, the wistful notes of an oboe. Eli's imagination continued to interpose Leyano's calm presence with the sweet music played by Pallaïs.

Softly and gracefully the vision receded and Eli sighed, and then smiled.

Errieg's shoulders were heaving with sobs, and before he could allow Eli to see the tears streaming down his tanned faced and onto his bare chest, he pressed his knees firmly against the dragon's flanks, where his legs were held and protected by the huge scales at the base of her leathery wings --- giant wings which were now splayed wide and held high over her now docile head.

Bawn responded to her master's command, and rose almost vertically into the air, turned swiftly sideways, and sped away. As she did so, Eli replaced her harp on the earth and opened wide her arms, like an invitation to be embraced, her red hair billowing out behind her in the wind of the dragon's flight.

Only the hawk-moths remained, hovering in a quivering cloud over the spot where the dragon had been. Eli closed her eyes for a moment, and breathed very deeply, now that the air was clear and clean once again.

But when she opened her eyes and looked at the company of moths, she thought she could hear Alégondine's voice: *It is a lily, dark purple, almost black, and related to the common* dracunculus *of the human-world. But it is not exactly the same plant, for the lily which grows in Faërie is a sacred flower, descended from the lilies of the earliest gardens of the Sun-Singers. The hawk-moths of Faërie are devoted to this flower, and as in awe of it as are the fairies of Quillir, the province where almost all of the Sun-Singers now dwell.*

Eli took from the pocket of her blouse, beneath her blowing cape, the Dragon-Flower. Immediately the moths were around it, flying, dancing, drunk with delight! She took it to the place where Bawn had lain, where the earth was scorched and blackened. There she placed the Lily on the ground, and then she reached into the fold of her bodice and took out the Moon-Flower. She laid it beside the purple one. Sun-flower and tiny white lily of the Moon.

Slowly, she recited, for Erreig, now departed in despair and defeat and confusion, some of the lines of the blessing of Vanzelle:

> *"Ice and dragon, snow and fire,*
> *Moon and Sun in endless day...*

> (All is one, all is one, Erreig.
> Moon-Dancer and Sun-Singer,
> Fire and ice, here and there...
> All is one.)

> *I bestow, by frost and flame,*
> *A benediction intertwined:*

> *Wander whither you must go,*
> *Chill or sunlit be the way,*
> *Our protection on you rests:*
> *Though seeming lost, you shall not stray.*

"You will find your way, Dragon-Lord. You will find your way, and your heart, and your courage. The courage to love.

And when you can love, you will have no more fear. They cannot exist together.

"You may seem to be lost now, but you are not. You simply need to know that you *cannot* be lost, you cannot stray, if you truly love. For as Reyse reminded me, there is no path that *leads* to love --- because love itself *is* the path. You will find it --- and that love will find you."

Eli's heart was full, but she felt very tired as well as exhilarated. She lifted the two flowers from the burnt earth, and as she did so the ground's golden colour returned and any and all signs of Bawn's presence there were removed. She returned the Moon-Flower to its place in her tunic.

She shook her head, almost laughing at herself. They were Reyse's words to her, the words she had said to Erreig about love. And she knew that they were true.

And, what's more, she knew that Reyse was near.

Eli turned and walked the few steps back to Róisín and placed one hand on the harp, her fingers touching, once again, the Golden Rose. With her other hand she hid away the Dragon-Flower in its pocket --- caressing, as she did so, the Silver Leaf and the two pieces of the Amethyst Cloth.

She glanced down to the shore, and she could see Uncle Mor, his white-whiskered face beaming and his tiny, dark, bright eyes dancing like the sun-light on the water around 'Vanzelle's hull. Jizay was standing on a high stone, wagging his tail. But the Lady Ecume was gone, as were the seals.

Eli did not go down to the boat right away. She turned, and looked back up to where Finnir had been.

She was not surprised to see exactly what she sought. Not Finnir. She saw what she sought now, *just* what she knew she would. A knight, a king --- perhaps. An eagle, assuredly.

Two other eagles were there also, circling close overhead: the white-tailed eagle Peronne, and one of the two golden eagles, and also the white hawk. Ah no, the hawk had landed…on Reyse's shoulder.

He walked the short distance towards Eli.

"Thank you," she said simply.

"What do you thank me for?" he asked, warmly and rather light-heartedly. The moonstones in his ear-lobes and ear-points were twinkling like day-stars. "You did it all yourself, and it was well-done, Lady Eli. Or should I say Princess Mélusine?"

"Neither," replied Eli with a very inviting and also quite cheeky smile.

"You're right, I have a better name for you. Well done, I say again… *Licorne*."

When they reached the sailor and his sailboat, and the exuberant Jizay, Eli asked, "Are you coming with us, Reyse?"

"If I may, just as far as Gavenia's home. She'll be very happy to welcome you to stay there tonight, as I understand. And then, tomorrow, lovely lady, you must return to Loch Etive, and to Faërie. But I shall *not* be coming on *that* trip."

"How do you do, sir," said Morvan, with a very polite bow of his head, which the Eagle-Lord returned graciously as he climbed aboard. "I don't know *you*, I must say, but I know that hawk on your shoulder, I'm sure. Isn't it the bird that my dear Gavenia keeps close? Almost her 'pet' I think you could say."

"It is, yes," laughed Reyse. "She is a lady of the hawk, of the white hawk. I am Reyse, of the Shee of the Dove. And Gavenia works very closely with us, many of the fairy-folk in these parts, and has done for years. A very wonderful woman."

"I wouldn't fault your taste in saying that, to be sure," agreed Morvan. "And I'm not at all surprised that my Gavenia knows you and your kind, Monsieur Reyse. I rather thought she should do. She's very fairy-like in her own way.

"But will I still see you, and this beautiful hound, when we've left the enchanted waters here, that's what I'm wondering," continued Eli's Uncle Mor, as 'Vanzelle' drifted away from the shore.

"As for Jizay, I'm not sure, but I would think it likely. But as far as I'm concerned, yes, you'll be able to see me, for as long as I stay," Reyse assured him with a kind smile. "Though a fairy, I'm in human-guise when I'm in these parts, and so I'm quite as visible as anyone! But some of the other fairies that were here on this island, a phantom-island which was brought into being by the Queen Morliande and the ancient mermaid, they were not truly transfigured and solid in this human dimension, and perhaps they remained invisible to you. Did you see anyone else, Morvan?"

"Well, I saw, just for a twinkling, another splendid gentlemen, certainly a fairy for he was shining bright as a star, just like the luminous king and queen of the Sheep's Head Shee. He was standing up the hill by the dark trees, but he vanished as quick as he had appeared. And I heard the harp of the mermaid whom I'd met when I set out from Brittany, but I couldn't see where the music was coming from at all."

"And did you see … dragons?" ventured Eli, inclining her head as she asked her question, while Reyse helped he to stow her harp safely.

Morvan wrinkled his brows and gave Eli a rather wounded look.

"Now, you're not saying that I missed the dragon, oh my dear Eli-ig?! I knew you were to be meeting with a dragon-tamer, a Dragon-Chieftain they called him. But was there a real dragon too? Oh, I would have liked to see such a creature, and that's a fact! But I didn't see a dragon at all, nor any threatening 'warrior' near you."

Eli was not sure what to say now, as she could see that Morvan was disappointed to have missed such a wondrous part of the spectacle. Luckily, Reyse responded to him.

"I wouldn't worry about missing the Dragon-Lord or the dragon, dear Morvan. Only a fairy who has *need* of dealing with a dragon will see one, you know; so be grateful that you do not fit that description! For to have dealings with dragons and their masters means that you have some <u>very</u> great and weighty issues to overcome, to deal with, to vanquish in your life. I would say that you are blessed with a less complex and fiery nature than, well, certain folk. Certain wilful, red-haired, over-bold and extravagant folk."

Eli shot Reyse a piercing glace, but she was gently laughing.

Morvan now hoisted the russet sails of 'Vanzelle', for the wind was in the west and would guide them neatly back into the centre of Loch Eil, wherein they soon found themselves.

"We should reach our port before nightfall, if I read those pale stars correct, just beginning to peep out," said the skipper. "It seems we're back in the late afternoon or early evening of when we sailed into this enchanted loch. Though I'm sure I've seen all the hours of another day race past us, and even a couple of different seasons. Well, there you are: I won't say there's anything left for Life to come up with, that I couldn't believe!

"Next stop, Fort William," he added, "and the fine table of an excellent Caledonian cook, as I'm proud to say of my dear Gavenia."

"Oh dear, I hope there won't be *haggis*!" intoned Eli in a mock-woeful tone.

Morvan laughed heartily. "I should think not! Why didn't I already tell the gentle lady that my niece was a vegetarian?! She said that she was too. Well, myself I'll miss sampling the fish of these parts; but that said, once you've met a mermaid it's a trifle difficult to imagine gobbling-up a *filet* of baked salmon or a plate of haddock-and-chips ever again. Ah well, it can't be helped…"

Reyse and Eli laughed heartily, and Jizay barked to the giddy dolphins who were once again cavorting alongside the yacht.

Peronne circled overhead, making figures of eight with the remaining golden eagle, in a joyous *pas de deux*.

Eli spoke in a whisper to her fairy-companion. "Was it you, Reyse, who sent a suggestion to Peronne to come to Scotland? Did you communicate with him, telling him that I might need… an eagle?"

"Peronne, your wondrous flying-horse, was raised and educated by me, for you, at your father's request, my dear Eli; as I'm sure you'll recall. It was for your 500th birthday, in 1857. And in 1960, Peronne and I carried the infant Eli across the northern oceans to Dawn Rock, so that she could be exchanged with the beautiful Brocéliana. So I think it safe to say that your winged-mount and myself, we have a close bond of friendship and have been accomplices in the adventures of Mélusine for a long time. *Naturally*, we communicate easily and over long miles, and even between the worlds… So it is quite obvious that I was *somehow* involved in his decision to come to you.

"And, I might add, I have always thought that you needed an eagle."

"I think I will not get a straight answer to my question," Eli interjected, still laughing. "But that suits me. I'm happy just to have your company, dear Iolar MacReyse, even without too many answers, for tonight."

The white hawk was still sitting comfortably on the Eagle-Lord's shoulder. His other arm was around Eli's own cloaked shoulders --- just to keep her warm, no doubt.

"No more questions, or answers, for tonight," she thought to herself. "I don't really mind *why* his arm is there, for it's very nice. And that's quite enough for me at the moment."

****

Windy Hill Prayer

Chapter Fifteen:
Purple Wine from Black Berries

It wasn't absolutely clear to Eli how 'real' or not had been her encounter with Erreig on the phantom-island --- a place, as Reyse had said, *brought into being* by Morliande and the Lady Ecume. But what she felt sure of was that her intentions, her lack of fear, her compassion for the plight of the Dragon-Lord, had all been *very* real, and that --- compared to such things as the material solidity or spatial existence of an enchanted island in a mysterious Scottish loch, or anywhere else for that matter --- *they* were of greater importance!

Another thing was clear to her, also. She felt free: liberated of some duty or charge, liberated of some strange responsibility. It was more than the accomplishment of her 'quest', for she had already recuperated the torn fragment of the Amethyst Cloth. It was more than the final playing-out of the long envisaged scene of herself and the fleeing dragon. It was even beyond her spoken exchanges with Erreig and the justice or honesty of her words.

It felt more like forgiveness.

She recalled the sensation which had filled her heart when she had beheld the blue tourmalines in her brother Demoran's ears. She had, at that moment, felt something flowing away from her; she had experienced a cleansing and releasing, a letting-go of old resentments or anger, of hatred even. *That* had been in regard to Yves.

Today, it had been in regard to Erreig. Or to someone else.

The ancient mermaid --- who had played a duo with Pallaïs today --- had, according to the entry in Lily's notebook, assisted Eli long ago by somehow burying or cloaking the painful memory, the unbearable memory, of what had happened in the garden of that grubby Los Angeles garage-apartment. Why that crime had become linked to the Dragon-Lord in her mind and in her sub-conscious and even in her nightmares, Eli did not know. But it was clearly bound-up with Erreig in her psyche; for perhaps the violence and the inappropriateness and the complete un-alignment of such an atrocious act, such a perverse and horrible attack on an eight-year-old girl, was not disassociated (at least far as Eli was concerned) from the many centuries of wayward and insolent behaviour --- dictated by fear and aggression --- that had brought tragedy and shame and loneliness to several members of her family, and tension to an entire realm.

But today, in some strange and almost 'sacramental' sense, Eli could say that she had arrived at a crossroads --- of **pardon**. The conscious letting-go, the exhaling relief of allowing all the 'wrongness' to simply drift away --- or fly away.

One monk she had spoken to, years ago on one of her cherished 'monastic retreats', had reminded her that to forgive was *not* to forget, or to belittle the gravity of some wrong or misguided behaviour; it was simply the act of taking your strangling hands off another person's neck.

"Just let go," he had told her. "**Pardon** doesn't add up to anyone being right or wrong, or failing to see justice done. Justice isn't your business; it's God's. But when you stop shaking that neck in your angry hands, and release it, you can start to relax --- as can your victim. Because if *you've* been someone's victim, making him *yours* won't solve anything; it's adding fire to fire --- a useless way to quench any blaze. By contrast, if you pardon, if you forgive, if you let go, then you clear the decks of all that victim-hood and hatred, accusation and punishment --- on both sides. You put out the fire, by allowing the skies to rain on it. And in its wake, in that clear and rain-washed air, you might even find that the sun is shining --- on both of you: on the 'just and the unjust'.

"What's more, like that unconditional and non-judgemental rain and sunshine, you might even entertain the idea that cleansing and cooling, light and healing, new directions and unexpected blessings could now come more freely to *both of you*. Because both the person who's done the wrong and the person who hates him for it, *surely* are in need of blessing, and quite possibly of new directions too."

New directions. Today had been a crossroads of intersecting and quite opposed pathways, where there had been cleansing and liberation, and sunlight after the storm. It had been a release and a beckoning invitation, a calling to go forward from one life into another. She felt like exclaiming a resounding 'Amen' to that!

Eli was sitting in the charming home of Gavenia, on an over-stuffed sofa crowded with cushions and shared with two cats and a delightful collie. Jizay was lying at her feet, quite visible to everyone including the gracious and friendly cats and the easy-going sheep-dog. Reyse sat in a high-backed arm-chair beside the settee, a snoozing Scottie-terrier on his knee. Beside him was a bay window looking out over the town of Fort William, with snow-draped Ben Nevis in the distance. While on a bare oak tree close by the window sat the white hawk with Peronne beside him, chatting or reminiscing together.

Reyse smiled at Eli, and lifted his thick crystal glass of some local blend of whisky and heather-and-herb-honey, with a wink. She grinned back, relaxed and tired. Morvan and his Gavenia --- a warm-worded and sweet-natured woman with braided white-grey hair and girlishly sparkling eyes --- were seating themselves at the low table too, having finished clearing the dinner things and now setting out a little plate of home-made short-breads to go with the celebratory night-cap.

The ensuing and convivial conversation was not at all along the lines of Eli's rather philosophical thoughts about Erreig and today's encounter. Uncle Mor and his new lady-friend were discussing the best seasons to enjoy Brittany's coast, and balancing those dates with others when they wished to be in Scotland together. It appeared that they were both, already, busy filling-up their agendas with plans for sharing and sailing, making music (for Gavenia was evidently a singer) and enjoying anything to do with wandering and wildlife, waves and wind-swept lands.

Eli sighed happily, and with one hand covered a long yawn.

Gavenia smiled at her, and mentioned that they might all of them be ready for their beds soon now. Reyse had earlier said that he had organised his own lodgings, and would be biding them farewell at the close of their amicable and delicious evening together. Eli's room was awaiting her upstairs; and her harp was already installed here downstairs, nearby in the hallway, safely and prettily wrapped in a new tartan blanket-covering and ready to set off, with her and Morvan, in the morning. Ready to return to Loch Etive, and to the Gate concealed in the mountain-side behind the berry bushes.

Uncle Mor and his new companion retired to the kitchen again, just to finish tidying-up (they said), leaving Eli and Reyse a private moment together to say their good-nights and good-byes.

But there were no words to say. Or if there were, they were uttered in silent fairy-language, peacefully mingled with the star-song above them as they walked out onto the patio-deck of the cottage. Of course, Reyse kissed Eli's hand, as was his custom. And, as she had done once before on Mermaid Island, Eli lifted her face to his, and kissed his cheek.

More filled with nuance than their innocent kisses, though, was the long moment wherein they simply looked at one another. In those few minutes it seemed to both of them that myriad themes and subjects were broached and discussed.

But, still, nothing was said aloud.

Eli watched the cloaked and hooded figure descend the wooden steps and walk off along the dark street, his tall form looking very regal and elegant, with a golden eagle flying high over him. The white hawk left Peronne and flitted off to follow him too, coming to rest on his shoulder for just a second, and then flying swiftly back to Gavenia's oak tree before Reyse had turned the corner and was lost to Eli's view.

****

Feeling impatient, now, to return to Faërie and to continue the days of her third and final Visit there, Eli was glad that Morvan was content to set off for Loch Etive bright and early the next morning.

For much of the first leg of the trip they were silent, both occupied by their respective thoughts, memories and dreams. In fact, those exact terms turned in Eli's head.

"Those three things --- *memories, thoughts and dreams* --- are a good mixture of past, present and future," Eli said to herself as the sail-boat left the port, with Morvan waving and blowing a final kiss to Gavenia on the pier. "And you should concentrate on the **thoughts** of today. Stay in the *now*, my girl," Eli added, still communing with herself. "It contains quite enough to entertain and educate you, without adding any more *before*s or *after*s!"

Being a man of few words (except when recounting tales of mermaids and silkies!), her Uncle Mor did not ask any further questions, nor did he seem inclined to talk about their adventures. Eli was sure that he *was* thinking deeply about it all, though, and that he was filled with understanding and perception in regard to all of the magic around them. Jizay he could still see --- perhaps because his eyes were more and more open to fairies and fairy-creatures; or perhaps because Jizay permitted it, or because the dear sailor had been gifted with such heightened clarity while their journey lasted.

Eli had expected that Morvan would ask her about Reyse, but he did not. It occurred to her that Gavenia had perhaps supplied information about the fairy-visitor whom she obviously had already met, perhaps many times. A woman who could be described by Reyse as 'a lady of the hawk, of the white hawk', was obviously well-known to the Lord of the Eagles, falcons and hawks of the Shee of the Dove, especially if he were passing a good deal of his time in Scotland these days.

And Eli was happy that the subject did not come up. She found that she did not, in fact, wish to talk about, or even to think about, Reyse. And that was not from a lack of affection for him. She just preferred him in her silent heart than in her oft-confused head, that's all.

In any case, it seemed that Morvan was concentrated on his navigation and on the safe-passage of his dear Eli to Loch Etive. He was enjoying getting to know his new and enchanted boat, 'Vanzelle', too. But he admitted, over their luncheon-*en-route*, that tackling the rocks and challenging waters around the isle of Lismore in Loch Linnhe, and then going through the Lynn of Lorn and into Ardmucknish Bay, and from there up into the fjord-like loch beyond the narrow strait at Connel, would require all of his skill and maritime know-how. The winds were rising, and not in the direction he would have chosen, he admitted.

And then, laughing, he remarked, "What we need are mermaids! Mermaids and dolphins and seals, dear Eli. They'd come in mighty handy just now!"

No sooner had he spoken, than a grey seal came into sight, gracing one of the larger rocks near the northern-most point of the Island of Lismore, with Port Ramsay in the background. In the next instant, the seal was gone, but two figures were standing on the shingle shore of the island, and on the sheep-cropped stretch of grass beyond was another very imposing creature.

The daylight hours being rather short in a Scottish November, and the skies already filling with rain clouds for the night ahead, it was not too easy to make out the details of any of the three beings who were now regarding them from the shore of the island.

Eli inquired, "Uncle Mor, can you *see* those fairies, all three of them? It's already quite dark...and I don't even know if they're *visible* to you as well as me."

"I wouldn't say dark, exactly, my dear little Eli," he said, cutting the boat's engine and then returning both hands to the helm to keep 'Vanzelle' from running foul of the many stones hidden by the steel-blue swell. "It's a purple twilight under clouds the colour of black-berries. Not so much 'dark' as 'richly coloured'; that's how I'd put it! And, yes indeed, I *can* see two vague forms that could be fairies --- but do you mean that the beast there beyond them is a fairy too?"

"He is the Lord Hwittir, a fairy-Stag of great renown," explained Eli. "I suppose you recognise the Queen Morliande, the silkie?"

"Ah, now I do indeed," Morvan nodded, but his features wore an expression of wonder and joy. "But who or what is that woman beside her? I've never seen or heard of anything so beautiful in all my three-score-thirteen years! She's truly stepped right out of a fairy-tale!"

Eli smiled, as the yacht drifted quite safely ever-closer to the shallows of the shore-line. "She is the fairy you have named your boat after, dear Uncle Mor. She is Vanzelle. And yes, I agree with you, it is hard to imagine more amazing feminine beauty than that."

Morvan had no need of the dinghy to pass from boat to strand, for he leapt over the ship's railing as soon as the pebbly sand hissed its grating welcome and an unequivocal invitation to come ashore. Eli and Jizay followed happily.

It was evident that, although the regal Stag and the beauteous Vanzelle had *planned* to return to their own shee, both of them had now decided to become once again visible to the travellers. Morliande herself was perhaps simply a fairy-phantom --- as the others perhaps were too. In any case, everyone was clearly visible, and seemed substantial and solid.

Morvan was quite ceremoniously presented by the Silkie-Queen to the stunning Vanzelle, who thanked him for his gracious part in Eli's adventure and also for naming his boat after her --- referring to it as the 'previous sail-boat of the white fairy-friend, the Lady Gavenia'.

For many minutes, Morvan was speechless with wonder, and could only stare with grateful eyes at the golden-skinned, silver-haired fairy with her tattered-ribbon robes blowing about her slight but perfect body. She did not have her wings on show, and Eli felt rather relieved about that --- seeing her with that accoutrement as well might easily have sent her uncle into a swoon!

At last, Morvan was able to say, very softly --- as though afraid that he might awaken himself from this dream, "You <u>know</u> my dear Gavenia, *madame* …Vanzelle?"

"I do," replied the snow-fall voice of the silver fairy. "I met her only recently, however. She is a friend of twin fairies who in their turn are known to the Lord Reyse whom you met yesterday, I understand. Yes, the twins introduced me to Gavenia of the White Hawk.

"And now myself and the Lord Hwittir have flown here in our shadow forms to greet you on your way to the loch where the doorway into Faëire is concealed. We wished to thank the Princess Mélusine, Eli that is, and to bid her a final farewell. And I offer her my thanks for her wisdom and all her efforts to bring love back… into a very troubled heart."

The giant white reindeer approached them, and Morvan bowed to him, sweeping off his woollen cap in an old-worldly gesture which made the great Stag smile. The Red-Eared Hart then shocked Morvan even more profoundly, by speaking quite audibly to him and to Eli in his Nordic accents.

"Our congratulations to you, little Eli-*lapsi*. And to you, Morvan-*merimies*, whom I name faithful friend and blessed yachtsman, and ever now shall you be granted the keen vision to see the people of *my* shee, if ever you cross their paths! Here, on this island --- which once had close dealings with the folk of Norway, and where one of the tiniest Portals of my realm is still situated --- you may often find my subjects.

"And, as Vanzelle-*yala* has said, our thanks for your caring and courage, dear Princess, as regards your meeting with the trouble-hearted phantom of Erreig-*herra*. Do not worry any further for him, for he sought me out, just last evening, and has requested the right to return to my shee. We spoke long together, and he is beginning to hear the trickling of melting icicles! Ah, it is a sweet sound, that.

"He has heeded my decree and the conditions for his return to dwell with the fair Vanzelle-*yala*; and so before coming to my snowy shee, he will return to your verdant one. However, this time *not* by one of its Portals, but rather by using the sea-routes and riding upon a swift *tursa* --- a flying dragon-squid that he has not mounted for many-a-year! There in the Shee Mor of your father, he will meet with the great matriarch-worm so dear to him, who awaits her master's return (when she is not busy appearing in your dramatic visions that is, Eli-*lapsi*!). She is on an isle in the east of that realm: Mermaid Island, I believe it is, yes. I hope that he will also present himself, *and* his fervent apologies, to the King Aulfrin --- but we shall see. Let us not look too far into the dark trees of the forest before us, as we say. For there may be wolves and bears, you know, lurking in the shadows that we call *the future*. But then, some wolves and bears are very, very charming!

"Now my children, we will grant you shelter and keep you warm and dry, for it will be a night of dancing rain-storms; and so we shall lodge you in a cosy *kota*-house. My gnomes will provide you with soft beds and fine fare, sheltered from both the tempest and from the eyes of all humans. In the morning, you will go by swift sea-paths to your destination, Eli-*lapsi*. And Morvan-*merimies* you will continue at your leisure where you will... returning to the ancient kingdom of Brittany in the northern corner of fair France, or perhaps choosing to turn your own pretty 'Vanzelle' back up the long fjord here, to the Woman of the White Hawk. Who can say?!" He finished with a chuckle and an amused shake of his wide-antlered head.

To Morvan's continued amazement and delight, Penny-grass and Pine-cone ran down the dim slope of the grass from the rocks beyond, and bid the sailor and Eli and Jizay follow them to their supper and sleeping-quarters in a spacious and colourful *lavvu* or fairy-*kota*.

"We will be here again tomorrow morn, on the shore, to wave you on your way," said the Queen Morliande as Morvan returned to his yacht to fetch Eli's harp and pass it into her arms, and then all three guests made ready to follow the gnomes. There was a faint tear in Morvan's eye as he stood for a silent moment before the Silkie-Queen, and glanced back at the tumbled seal-skin that lay a little further down the shore. He sighed, and simply said, "Thank you, a thousand times *merci beaucoup*, your Majesty. To your lovely self and to the exquisite mermaid too. You've made me a very happy man with this privileged adventure in my old age."

"You were always a very happy man, dearest Morvan," smiled the silkie. "And you will be so to the end of your days, and beyond. If this had not been the case, and happiness had not been your very nature, I think that this adventure would not have come to you. We are always presented with the experiences suited to us. Always!"

Morvan smiled broadly, and bowed low to Eli's grandmother, and then followed the company up the slope as the Queen turned back to the sea-rocks in the gathering darkness.

Before she left, she spoke in a low voice to Eli. "Mélusine, I think it would be advisable for you to find a moment to be alone tonight, and to use the Silver Leaf. Your mother wishes to speak with you."

"The Queen Rhynwanol? Yes, of course, I will do as you suggest," agreed Eli.

"Not your fairy-mother, no," whispered Morliande. "It is *Lily* who would like to meet with you."

Eli's eyes were large, but she nodded and smiled to the grey seal-queen, whose mauve and sea-green eyes were the brightest things still visible, now in the first soft haze of the coming rains.

She kept Gavenia's tartan blanket close about her harp as the drops became larger, and she hurried up to where the *larvvu* was already fully materialised and lit from within by many golden candles.

When Uncle Mor, well-fed and very red-cheeked (with two or three *kuksa* of strong mulled wine to wash down an excellent meal), had fallen asleep, Eli stole out into the dark night. The rain had nearly stopped --- just for her, or truly, she could not tell --- and she found a stunted hazel-tree which seemed just the right shelter under which to sit on a mossy rock and place the Silver Leaf before her on her lap.

She struggled to hold back her tears, so that she would be able to discern the scene clearly when the window into Faërie opened. For she knew what she would see.

The cottage that Morvan had visited on his magical voyage with the Silkie-Queen appeared in the tiny oval space where the Leaf lay on her knee. And then all of the island of Lismore was swept away, and Eli could see only the Sheep's Head Shee, and a carpet of moon-flowers at the feet of her human-mother.

Suddenly, the picturesque cottage was gone, and only Lily remained, surrounded by the tiny white flowers and the dark rocks, and the sound of the sea. Her little moon was as white and pure as her namesake, most probably just as Morvan had seen her: a fairy-queen. But to Eli, she was simply the tender and brave and wise mother of her fifty years of human life. Her twilight-blue eyes, identical to Brocéliana's in hue and form, were nonetheless unique: they were the kind eyes of her own lovely and belovèd Lily.

But there were shades like transparent spectres of other people or fairies around her. Timair was there with a delicate crown on his strawberry-blond head. Morliande was present, as was Rhynwanol; Eli could even hear the far-off harp-music of the Lady Ecume. The skies were a mixture of blue and grey; there was a rainbow, and honey-dense rays of sunlight, and deep cerulean clouds.

It was Faërie and the shee of the Sheep's Head, but it was also a place that was only Lily's. She was its central character, or perhaps its only one. For now she was again alone, quite alone, and she seemed to be standing on the jetty of a port, a small pier reaching out into an unknown sea --- the widest waters that Eli had ever seen. The widest waters that we, any of us, will ever face...

Lily smiled in the vision, and she slowly began to hum lines from a folk-song, a song she had always loved Eli to play for her and that she had often sung along with. The same Scottish folk-song which Eli had played when she had asked Clare when she might come back to Faërie for her second Visit. Lines which had, then, made her wonder and dream...and decide. And now, it was Lily who chanted them, very softly:

The water is wide, I cannot get o'er,
And neither have I wings to fly.
Give me a boat that can carry two,
And we shall row, my love and I...

Her murmured song blew away, and she continued in a clear, gentle voice. "I know, now, my Eli, what the 'wide water' really is, for I can see it before me."

Lily's voice was so sweet and soft, so calm and deeply happy, that Eli could not help but smile. But her mother's form was already receding, already fading, as she added, "It is death, and it is also *Life*. All my experiences, all the wonders, all the sorrows, all the loves, the places, the faces, the blessings --- they are finally to be left behind as I traverse it.

"The crossing of these waters is part of a beautiful invitation, for this is a sea that I cannot cross of my own will or by my own strengths, and not on my own. For it's true, unlike you, my dear Eli, I'm not *really* a fairy --- with wings! No, I have no wings with which to fly: but I have Christ. And so my boat *will* hold two.

"I have seen that you have succeeded in your quest, and you are whole and strong. You will be fine, more than fine. I know that you have love and even a family around you now. As I know that your destiny is unfolding as it should, as it must. I have no more concern or worry for you.

"I have learned so much in this magically-gifted time that has been granted me here. I am so grateful for it. But I am equally grateful to go on.

"Keep my little journal, and read it sometimes. You may not yet have read all I had to say to you! But perhaps my most vital message to you is that I believe your own story will continue to be filled with wonders --- wonder upon wonder, for many years to come.

"Now I am becoming restless for my own story to continue, and to discover more of *its* wonders. *He* is with me, but He is also awaiting me. And I am impatient to be before Him, with Him, in Him. I have longed for this voyage, all of my life in a way, and I will be happy to row across the wide water with

Him and with the light of His star shining on the waves to guide me home. Home at last.

"Farewell, my little Moon-Dancer. We have already said our good-byes once, months ago in Bantry, and now I say another one. But that is how this amazing story has turned out; what a tale it has been, our fairy-tale, my Eli!

"God bless you, daughter of my heart. *Bonne continuation* and *bon courage*! Keep me deep in *your* heart, as your 'little moon' --- as I have asked Sean to keep me in a corner of his, as his Lily. God bless you, I say again. And good-bye my darling girl."

Eli's tears were hot on her cheeks now, but she had no desire to dry them. They were for her mother, Lily.

"Good-bye," she mumbled, and then she was able to say a little more clearly, *"Bon voyage,* dear queen of the flowers of both Sun and Moon, dear *mother of my heart* and always my own precious 'little moon'. My love and blessings go with you.

"*Adieu.*"

****

Their last sight of the fairies, as Morvan's sail-boat slipped out into the Lynn of Lorn in the morning, was of an enchanted assembly on the gravely shore: Morliande was in grey-seal form --- rather than queenly fairy; Vanzelle was astride the Lord Hwittir; and the two tiny gnomes were seated high up on the Stag's antlers, either side of his proud head. Vanzelle lifted her hand in farewell, and Eli thought she could catch the sparkle of jewel-light --- though she had not seen where her gems were set, whether in palm or fingertips, or perhaps they shone from her forehead or ears. Though the rain-clouds had drifted away, mist hung over the water and around the stones and the island's shore; so the fairy-company was soon shrouded in paisley-swirls of white fog.

Although the conditions this morning were not ideal for sailing, Morvan had no misgivings; for the silkie had assured him that his craft would be guided and protected. In full faith, therefore, he hoisted his sails --- more for their beauty, he said to Eli, than because he felt they would be needed to catch the wind! --- and he stood with his arm around her shoulders and his free hand gently laid on the helm, rather enjoying the sensation of its independent movement under his light grip.

Late in the morning they crossed the Falls of Lora and entered Glen Etive. The sun danced out from behind a bank of cloud in the east and shone full onto the rippling loch. A red deer bellowed from the woods, and Peronne at last appeared beside the boat, swooping low across the glistening surface of the waves streaming out from the easy movement of 'Vanzelle' through the green and blue water.

Eli had recounted Lily's farewell to Uncle Mor when they set off, and both had remained quiet and thoughtful for a long while. Eli had the impression that she was able, with her uncle, to share the same silent communication which she enjoyed with fairy-animals. He told her that it was that way for him with Gavenia, too. And that she had said that the fairy-folk dreamed of a time when many other humans would receive that gift, or cultivate it out of the deep sensitivity that she believed we all possessed for understanding and listening.

Eli now explained to him that she and Jizay would be returning to the place in the foothills of the mountains, on the east side of the loch, where they knew they would find their secret gateway. She told him that she would get in touch when back in France, and share more of her tales with him.

"Shall I stay nearby, dearest Eli-ig, until I've seen that you're gone?" he asked, with almost paternal concern in his voice. "It's a wild and cold land, and the snow is low on those mountains. Are you sure you'll find the doorway where you think to? If it's a fairy-door, it may have moved!"

Eli smiled. "I'm in good hands, dear Uncle Mor. I have Jizay with me, and Peronne is back too --- though where he's been since last evening, I'll have to inquire one day! And I <u>believe</u>

that I'll easily find my gateway and go through without difficulty. And, you know, *it is very good to believe*!

Her dear sailor-uncle laughed and squeezed her tightly.

"And I abide by that too, and I think that's the best way to live all of our adventures," he confided.

She indicated the place where she thought the pathway to her berry-bushes ran closest to the shore, and Morvan gently steered the boat towards the little inlet. He didn't really need to, for 'Vanzelle' was making her way there of her own accord; but he enjoyed that very slightest sensation of being her skipper still!

They said their farewells and shared a long hug. Jizay received a kiss on his golden head, and returned this affection with a generous lick on Morvan's cheek and two or three hearty barks. The sailor waved to Peronne, now high overhead, who dived and looped for him before heading up beyond the line of gorse bushes at the loch's brink and into the more forested regions leading to the mountain.

Morvan passed Róisín, still wrapped in rich tartan, into Eli's arms. The lovely Longboat glided away immediately, and turned back to retrace her course.

Eli waved once again, and turned her own feet, now, to the climbing path.

Peronne was waiting for her at the head of the path, as the gorse and heather gave way to the masses of berries, intertwined with night-shade. He sat on a crag of the grey rock-wall before her, beyond the congregation of bushes.

"I will return by one of the Portals, my dear Eli," he said silently, "and not by Wineberry's Gate. I have not her agreement for that, though she might have granted it had I asked. But I have come into the world by a Portal, and I'll go home by one also. My new friend, one of the golden eagles --- with whom I have enjoyed such delightful flights these past days --- has Irish cousins that we thought to visit together, and so we will return to Gougane Barra, and myself to the Heart Oak from there. I will come, as flying-horse and not bird, to meet you once again in the Silver City as soon as I may."

"Very well," smiled Eli. "Thank you, my dear companion, for coming to me. Your help and your protection were vital to me, and I'm very grateful."

Peronne lifted a large, curved talon rather as a human might have held up a finger to emphasis his words. "You should thank the Prince Finnir, who aided me with my transformation. But also, you owe great gratitude to the Lord Reyse, for he indeed gave me the idea, saying you would be glad of the guidance and love of an eagle."

The phrase echoed in Eli's heart.

"Yes," she said with a rather serious nod. "I will thank them both, when I see them next. For I begin to think that it is a precious blessing to have the love of an eagle... indeed." Peronne spread his six-foot-arc of wings and was lifted into the arms of the wind.

Eli's hand caressed the head of her hound of joy, as she surveyed the mass of deep violet and near-black fruits all about her. The tiny, bright yellow stamens of the nightshade made her think to herself that these flowers were not, in fact, those of the most *deadly* plants in their family. "Still, all nightshade is poisonous," she thought. "More or less... anyway. Well, there must be a good reason why it is here. It's certainly not by *chance*!"

As she looked at the berries she again thought of the rhyme of Wineberry, inviting her to 'sip my wine'. Was that a metaphor or symbol of some kind, or was she actually meant to squeeze some of these berries into juice, in order to fulfil all of the parts of the riddle?! Was that necessary, in order to open the Gate and to be able to go back to Faërie?

In any case, she knew that she had to play the 'miraculous music', both to pass through the Gate *into* the human world, and to go *back*. So she placed Róisín on the rather peaty ground, lifted off her covering of Scottish tartan, and prepared to play. It was only now that she noticed that it was a plaid-motif with **mauve** in it. She found it very lovely, and feminine, and quite unusual. She recalled that Gavenia's family name was Craigie, and wondered if it were the tartan of her clan.

But her thoughts were quickly invaded by clear words, resounding softly but insistently in her head, as soon as the Harp of Barrywood was uncovered. It was the beautiful voice of Finnir: *Please, do not waver in your love for me, in your faithfulness and your faith in our love, though you must go back into a world far from Faërie.*

Eli was on the verge of beginning to play, but she stopped short. Yes, into a world far from Faërie, but filled *with* fairies nonetheless. A world where she had met, again, Reyse. And had been so happy to do so…

She sighed, her thoughts hovering between the two noble fairy-lords, and then she lifted her hands to Róisín's strings.

As she began the cadence of the seven magical notes, the Golden Flower on the brow of the harp began to shine, much more brightly than was usual. This was not the warm glow of the Rose when Eli was playing for healing or when sharing melodies with other musicians, nor was it the torch-like guiding light that the Flower had provided when Eli had left the Hill of the Sun. This was a strange, smoky light: grey and flecked with golden sparks, winding and twirling, writhing and spiralling. Eli continued to play, and to watch forms taking shape in the drifting coils of dense light streaming out before the harp.

Jizay had stepped forward, into the play of the misty arms of grey and gold. The smoky vapours were encircling him, and in the glowing iridescence of the sparks, he appeared even more golden than before. He turned and glanced back at his mistress, and she heard him say, "The Dragon-Flower, the purple lily… Bring it forth now!"

With her right hand, Eli continued to release the slow, sonorous notes from her harp, and they rang through the air and seemed to fly around her like lazy swallows. With her other hand, she reached into her pocket and pulled out the dark violet lily.

Immediately, two of the swirling strands of smoke twisted and rushed back to her, embracing the lily like cloudy hands. They bore it away from Eli and held it aloft, just before the Golden Flower on the head of the harp. And there and then, it was no longer a lily at all.

A beautiful goblet or chalice took form, all in gold and studded with precious green stones, peridots or even emeralds, very like those in the crown of King Aulfrin. Growing out of the chalice were two peach-coloured, living roses and three wild blue cornflowers, and hovering just at its rim was a butterfly with scalloped tortoiseshell wings.

Eli did not know what was symbolised by all of these images; but she had the certainty that she would, one day, understand them. Or that she had understood them, long ago, but had now forgotten their meaning.

Suddenly, however, she knew exactly what she must do.

She had concluded a musical phrase, and so, lingering for only a moment on the ringing, final *sol*, she passed Róisín into her left arm, and extended her right hand to take the chalice. The magnificent butterfly flew away from it and alighted on the rock face where the path came to a *cul-de-sac*, and where Jizay was already waiting. The roses and cornflowers fell to Eli's feet, where they instantly became glittering jewels, and in a twinkling of an eye were swallowed into the earth and gone.

Looking into the depths of the ornate, grail-like cup, Eli saw the wine. It was rich purple, swirling like the smoky gold-flecked light, and fragrant as Queen Rhynwanol's 'love-potion' from her Concocting Cell. Eli lifted it to her lips, and drank.

The light of the Golden Flower was extinguished as the last echoes of the harp's notes faded utterly away. But another light shone before Eli, beaming down from over her shoulder, shining from behind her and far, far away. Eli looked quickly back up to the east, and caught sight of the small, fragile waxing crescent. As if in answer to her sighting of the thin moon, crisp and clean in the blue-bird-hued sky, the Flaming Moon Ear-ring became heavy and burning in her left ear-lobe -- for only a spilt-second; and then it was cool and light once again.

Eli turned back to the mountain's foot and its smooth rock-face --- which now had become an arched and welcoming doorway. Particularly *welcoming*, for Aindel was standing in its shadow, his fair and freckled face alight with love and contented relief.

"Well done, my dear sister," he beamed. "Come, the silver turrets of Fantasie await you!"

He extended his hand to take hers, for the beautiful goblet was gone, though Eli thought she could see the flicker of the butterfly's wings down the dark corridor before them.

With Aindel's hand firmly clasped in her own, she looked back once more at the moon-lash. But instead of a crescent, she now saw *all* the moon --- not exactly a full moon: the unlit part of the orb was a silky seal-grey against the sky, but very visible and it even seemed to suggest the features of a smiling face.

She turned back to the tall, violet-cloaked fairy and to Jizay, who was wagging his tail vigorously. His huge, dark eyes sprinkled with stars.

The passage-way suddenly became pitch black now, for the doorway behind them had closed with a 'snick' and the distant sounds and scents of the Scottish Highlands were irretrievably lost. All that remained was the rich fragrance of the purple wine, which hung in the air like the odour of an ancient church, harbouring centuries of cherished memories of chanted prayers and swinging thuribles.

Here am I on threshold bright,
On one side the cup of light,
On the other berries black,
Hesitating I look back,
Night and light and moon and sun,
Sip my wine and all is one!

Eli could hear the woolly voice of Wineberry, chuckling and singing her rhyme. And now she was muttering other words, every syllable like a berry on a slender stem, like a note from a harp, like so many tiny and very far-away dragons whirling out of view:

"Now you know, child of lilies and follower of unicorns. Now you know! You have sipped the wine, you cannot keep them apart any longer: *night and light, moon and sun*. No, no, nevermore apart! All is one, little Princess of the Rose, all is one. Don't forget me --- I am **seven**; yes, remember me --- and the music, and my wild-winged wine! My purple wine for a violet fairy; my wine from the black berries and the fearful, friendly flowers!" The voice chuckled cheekily.

"All is one, all…is…one……"

The mid-day sky was dappled with tiny clouds like the coats of the horses of Finnir's companions when they had ridden out of this Gate of the Silver City in June. Far to the west, Eli could see Lysadel's high column of water sparkling in the sun, and reminding her once again of the silver horn of a unicorn. Just before her --- every bit as glittering as the high jet of diamond-bright water --- were the eyes of her father. Aulfrin came to her as she placed Róisín on the carpet of soft grass. Jizay bounded around them both as they embraced.

Aindel was already gone, having simply laid his long-fingered hand on the centre of his sister's chest for a moment, before he had inclined his head with a loving smile and disappeared back into the shadows under the rowan-tree gateway..

It seemed that only her father and Ferglas had come to meet her --- but that suited Eli very well.

"I shall be very pleased to bear your wondrous harp for you, my darling daughter," he said with a proud and resplendent smile. "Then you will have your arms free to enjoy the freedom of your fairy-flight, if you like. Jizay will run back to the Great Tower with Ferglas, and we will fly there together. Periwinkle awaits us --- somewhat impatiently, I'm sure --- for a celebratory luncheon!"

Eli laughed as she handed Róisín, again draped in the Clan Craigie tartan, to Aulfrin. She drew her lavender and turquoise wings out from her shoulders with one deep breath of gratitude and home-coming joy. With a tiny leap as if she were playing a child's game of hop-scotch, she rose into the skies of Fantasie beside the King. They drifted and zig-zagged over the streams and coppices, lawns and late-autumn flowers of the marvellous City, Eli's heart over-flowing with delight and with wonder and with peace.

Though there remained much to understand, and to resolve and to decide, right now it was enough --- more than enough --- to be here in her true home, with her dear father, flying lighter-than-air to the silver-turrets and the rippling red and yellow banners which were unfurled and flapping gaily from all the pointed rooftops of the King's Moon Tower.

****

Chapter Sixteen:
Hermits and Home-Comings

Piv was ringing bells, just as if it were the birthday of the Princess Mélusine on the 21st of June, when Eli entered the luncheon-room. Well, they were not *exactly* bells this time, and not even *bell*-shaped flowers; but they did produce, in his tiny hands, a very sweet, jingling melody. He was flying about with a small bunch of red rose-hips combined with a spray of beautiful flowers outstretched before him, shaking and waving them as he circled 'round the room. The rose-hips and the blooms combined to produce a delicate and sweet song.

Eli laughed at the smug pixie, and when he had alighted on his high stool beside the laden table, she kissed his green-capped head.

"Those are gorgeous," she enthused. "I love the plump rose-hips, but the blossoms I don't recognise. What are they? I don't think I've ever seen such flowers in the human-world."

The King replied. "Ah, yes; they do exist there. Not as lovely as the specimens here, of course," he added with a little grin. "They are a variety of *ademium*, but normally and very aptly they are called, in those foreign-lands, 'Desert Roses'. Not *correct* to call them <u>roses</u>, really --- but as is often the case, humans can strike a note of truth by mistake! Here we name them 'The Heralds of the Royal Rose'; and so they were sent to *you*. For you are a Princess of roses, my darling Eli, and I think that this fact may have been what prompted the choice of this appropriate and exotic flower, sent you by a very wise, and generous fairy…whom you already know."

Eli raised her eyebrows, and then smirked at her father while she tried to think of a fairy to fit the description of this guessing-game of his.

"Hmm, wise, and generous…" Eli considered. She glanced at her little friend, but he simply whistled and looked the other way, and then he filled his pink cheeks to bulging with some delicacy from the table which he had taken while buzzing over it.

Her father laughed merrily as they all sat down to formally commence their meal.

"The generosity of this particular fairy is not limited to flowery gifts," remarked the King, sampling the preferred cakes of Piv now, in his turn. "When you last met, it was a gift to inspire great love, as I recall, which you received." He chuckled again.

But now it was Periwinkle who gave the answer away.

"Oh, my Eli-een, look at them! They are much too tropical to be growing even in magical Aumelas-Pen in November. They aren't to be found even in the Inner Garden around the Great Trees, as far as I know. So it's as clear as a squawking parrot that they come from the sunniest and strangest neighbourhood of the realm: the Fire-Bird Forest!"

"Ah!" Eli exclaimed, "then they are a present from the little black fairy-mama? But how kind of her; they are marvellous! And," she added with a sidelong glance at her father, "I prefer them to love-potions, however generously offered!"

Piv rocked back and forth with merriment, and his button-eyes almost disappeared behind his smile.

"I went to visit the happy black fairies while you were away," he said, when he had swallowed his third mouthful of treats, "with their dresses of sunset-and-sea-shell colours. And that was when Mama Ngeza gave me these for you and for your home-coming and said to tell you that you had done everything very well."

Aulfrin smiled proudly. "Yes, I must agree with Mama Ngeza. All that has come to my ears from my musical instruments, and relayed by creatures of air and ocean, confirms her words. Well done, dear girl; and worthy of the chiming fanfare of the rose-fruits and especially of the tropical blooms of the 'desert roses'.

"Now *adenium* exists in a huge palette of fire-work colours, but as these are deep violet ones," he added, "they most probably celebrate your victory in retrieving the *Amethyst* Cloth. Though there may be other reasons for this choice…"

Eli caught her father's eye, but she nodded rather than making any comment. She was still smiling as she examined the large petals of the flowers which Piv had placed on the table before her; they were in gradated tones of pastel-mauve to imperial-purple, with frilly edges rather like the wings of the butterfly she had seen in the Dragon-Flower chalice.

Her father continued, as he and Eli now savoured their steaming chestnut-perfumed soup, "Yes, I think it is not *only* an allusion to that trophy, that vital part of your sacred shroud, my dear Mélusine. I think that Mama Ngeza may have also recognised, in this gift, your link to certain purple, or violet, fairies. Or fairy-friends.

"The cloth which is covering your harp, I note, is also of a heathery-mauve hue. So I would venture to guess you were given shelter by a member of the Craig dynasty, while in Scotland, and the purple *adenium* may also bear witness to that. A pleasant little 'wink' to both your hostess, and to Maelcraig the Mauve, from Mama Ngeza."

Eli's face registered her surprise, and she glanced at Róisín standing in the room's corner, still partially draped in her pretty plaid blanket.

"Then it *is* the tartan of her clan; I wondered if that were the case," nodded Eli. "Her name was Gavenia *Craigie*, I believe, not Craig. But I suppose it's the same root. I thought it unusual that the pattern was predominantly mauve; but are you saying it's because of some link between Gavenia's family and the, umm, ... Sage-Hermit Maelcraig?"

"I think it may contain a reference to that," Aulfrin nodded. "But it goes deeper, no doubt."

They all ate in thoughtful silence for a moment or two, and then he added, in a rather serious voice, "Unquestionably you were protected during your quest by many fairies, and with many purple and violet tokens, for you are linked --- by that colour --- to your mother the Queen Rhynwanol and also to my mother Morliande. This is why you bear an amethyst in your left palm, bestowed by the roses of your first Initiation but not without the profound and very loving intervention of Rhynwanol also. The line of the violet-fairies is the strongest *royal* bloodline in all of Faërie, usually passing through the women of a given family, with only a very few exceptions that I know of."

Eli's spoon was poised in mid-air as she regarded her father's bright, forest-green eyes.

"Violet queens, purple flowers, mauve dragons, and the amethyst-coloured Cloths laid over a sleeping Princess...," mused Aulfrin, breaking a chunk of bread from a long, braided loaf --- spreading it with bright rose-hip jelly --- and handing it to the beaming and eager Piv before serving Eli and himself with similar morsels. "All generally very feminine, yes. The most notable exception being the great magician, Maelcraig the Mauve. As you say, the...*Sage-Hermit*."

This last title, the King spoke very slowly, almost hesitatingly, Eli thought. Did he know, now, that the present Sage-Hermit was actually none other than his own father? Or did he still believe him to be Maelcraig, as he had named him before recounting to Eli his eerie journey through the subterranean lands of the fungus-folk?

But the King continued, "And so I am not surprised that you were given shelter, and a pretty tartan for your harp, by one of the Clan Craig...or Craigie. Among that family have often arisen friends and disciples of Maelcraig, the Servants of the White Hawk they are sometimes named."

Eli paused and slowly wiped her mouth with her serviette. She looked at her father. But his slight smile made her think that he knew much more, not only about Gavenia, but also about the Sage-Hermit.

"The Servants of the White Hawk?" she repeated at last.

Her father smiled indulgently, and amusedly. He poured some water from a fluted carafe into their glasses, and bit into a shining red apple very thoughtfully.

"I think we have much to discuss, my dear Eli, now that you are back."

"But for now, suffice it to say that I am very glad that you were supported or accompanied in your task, by many fairies and … birds."

He rose with her and they walked to the western window of the luncheon-room. They looked out together at the towering white spray of Lymeril dancing in the wind. Leaves, red and yellow and orange, were floating through the air, and the early afternoon sky was covered with fluffy clouds like a lumpy quilt. Piv continued to enjoy the remains of lunch, and to share some small walnut biscuits with the two dogs. Aulfrin placed his arm over Eli's shoulders.

"As for the Sage-Hermit…" he murmured, sighing and looking far beyond the fountain or even the bounds of the Silver City, Eli thought, "I have come to understand much in these past weeks and months. As I still call Morliande 'queen', although the present Queen of the Shee Mor is Rhynwanol, so I call Maelcraig the Mauve, Master of the Servants of the White Hawk, 'sage-hermit', although I know --- now --- that he is *not* the magician living on Star Island. Yes, and I realise that you learned this before me, I imagine from *your* mother."

Eli was silent, not knowing if she should divulge the source, or sources, of this information in her case: Brocéliana, Garo, Demoran, Leyano, Alégondine, even Aindel --- all had revealed this to her. But her father continued.

"When I journeyed to Quillir, after you left us from Dawn Rock at the close of your second Visit, I met with Alégondine first; but thereafter, I spent long days and nights communing with the Sage-Hermit from the shores of Holy Bay. I did not go *onto* Star Island; but I did not need to. I discovered what I wished to of Erreig's situation.

"But even then I did not have the ears to hear, to hear clearly enough to discern the unveiling of the deep secret kept from me --- and for good reason --- for so long. It was not until you were in Scotland these past days, my dearest Eli, that this revelation came to me. I had gone to the Inner Garden of the Great Trees, to ponder and to pray, and to commune in my heart with my mother, the Queen Morliande. And thereafter, having heard her counsel and her sea-sweet encouragement --- even as I remembered her gentle wisdom from my childhood --- I had reverently, really quite humbly, flown the few miles to the Stone Circle, to silently but tenderly call upon my father, the King Aulfrelas, to be there with me --- in some ghostly and miraculous apparition from the further side of the bounds of fairy-death.

"But lo and behold, he appeared before me! Not in a vision from the ethereal and glimmering Isles of the Blest beyond the furthest oceans, ah no! The vibrations before me were not substantial, it is true, but they were wafted there on the rippling winds from no *far-distant* paradise! They came from the Island of the Star... in Quillir!

"Yes, yes. We spoke long and lovingly; and thus I know, now, that my own father, the King Aulfrelas, became the Sage-Hermit at his 'passing' in the year 1300. He was borne from the Great Strand to Silkie-Seal Bay, where his belovèd wife Morliande had already dwelt, on and off, for many a year. And from there, as had been arranged and ordained for a hundred years at least, he took up his residence and his sacred role on Star Island.

"I will not tell you, today, all I have discussed with my father. That will be for another time. But I *will* say this, that in those moments of revelation wherein I was obliged to face my <u>ignorance</u> regarding my own father's presence on Star Island --- I was faced with a *choice*: effrontery or humility.

"My ego is yet very strong in my mind and my character, Eli. I know this. I believe that kings, and also queens, have need of a good measure of 'ego', or at least of some form of pride and distinction and independence. I may be mistaken; but at least I *concede* that my ego is strong, though perhaps now it is becoming --- shall we say --- a little more tame! I felt, at first exposure to this news, only the sting of my confusion --- even to the point of considering myself 'idiotic'; yes, I was deeply offended and I saw myself as ridiculous --- in my own eyes! I felt *anger*, a red passion of deep denial and burning resentment. Anger, my dearest child, is always as untrustworthy as a mad dragon-lord; and it makes a pathetically poor counsellor.

"When my ire had passed --- which it did, with the help of my wise and patient parent --- I found that I could instead feel humbled, rather than duped by all I had learned. Humility, I discovered, is not unpleasant: quite the contrary, it is a rather delightful state. And I chose that path. I felt *smaller* and less 'in control' and less 'knowing' perhaps, but also I felt myself to be in my right place, the place appointed and appropriate to me. For the great good of Faërie, of all of the Eleven Shees, and even of the world beyond our own enchanted one, my part had been played-out for the best. My part in the choreography of the Moon-Dance was, and is, as it should be --- even though it was necessary that it included this temporary ignorance on my part.

"Accepting that, I could reclaim my dignity, without being haughty and without any residue of wounded pride or bitterness. Some elements of the situation still puzzle me, or perturb me; they will come to light in their own time, and as they should. And if I can keep my ego under control, then I will be able to continue to govern and guide my realm with grace and good humour."

He squeezed Eli's shoulder with affection, and with a generous dose of his cherished *good humour* too.

"Now, before I say more of all these sages and mages, and of fairy-friends and mauve tartans and white hawks, we must make plans. For you now possess the prize which you have so successfully retrieved --- a tale I would like, in my turn, to be told in all its interesting details, by you! But this leads us to the fact that the Cloth must be restored to its rightful place.

"Only you or one of the creatures guarding the sleeping form of Mélusine is permitted to bear the Cloth to your chrysalis-bier of amethyst stone, my dear girl. I expect it will fall to you, yourself, to go to the threshold of the vault and pass this treasure to one of the Keeper-Owls, or even to enter the still and sacred tumulus. It is a delicate mission.

"However, it is not required to do this in any *panicked* haste. For now that the Cloth is in *your* hands, there is no risk to your life, nor is your slumbering form in any immediate peril. But it must be taken to Scholar Owl Island during this, your final Visit. For, as you know, within the space of these twenty-one days, you must formally declare your decision to stay here; and at that moment --- which is usually near the close of the twenty-one days --- the *changeling* is once again *changed*. Mélusine will begin to awaken then, and you to fade.

"And the Cloth should be *in place* before that formal declaration is made."

Eli was very quiet, and looked out into the far distance even as the King had done a moment ago. She hesitated, but finally asked,

"How many days remain to me, father? It is the 10th of November today, is it not? I have shortened my twenty-one days by a night, I think --- for I was hindered in my passage through the Heart Oak on Samhain Eve. But I suppose I must still go back before the full moon rises, on the 21st day of my Visit, which will also be the 21st of November. How long do I have...to *decide*?"

The room seemed very cold suddenly. Eli's tone of voice pronouncing that last word had created a shivering vibration, like an icy breath of wind, which circled father and daughter for an instant and then blew away. Aulfrin breathed deeply.

"Do you mean to say that you are not sure to stay, to return to us?" he whispered, in a voice that seemed filled with sorrowful memories. "I have lost one of my sons to the human-world, my brave and beloved Timair. Will I lose my daughter Mélusine also? Has your love of my kingdom, of *your* kingdom, not yet been sufficiently re-kindled by your Visits home?"

Eli forced herself to turn and look into his deep green eyes, though she knew it would bring tears to her own.

"I am not sure," she said, her tone of voice tentative at first, but then sounding slightly stronger. "I am not sure where I can do the most good, father. Of course, I love it here; I love it with all my heart. And I love you, and all my family and friends here. But I did *not* go into the world on a *holiday* --- I went to pursue my dream, if I understand it correctly from all I have re-learned during my Visits. I wanted to help, to help Faërie, and to help the humans. I wanted to use the wisdom I had gained in the Great Charm to further the causes of the Alliance, or so I begin to believe. And I'm not sure that I can do it from *here*."

Aulfrin's eyes were blinking and moist, and his delicate crown was alight with points of pulsating white-green light like glow-worms.

"Think very seriously about this choice, my daughter. *Can* you do the good you wish to do, as a *human*, my Eli? The Princess Mélusine is graced with profound wisdom and enchantment. She is among the greatest of the players in the

Alliance you speak of, though you do not recall that yet. You are *not* Mélusine again. You cannot have access to all of her sagacity and enlightenment, all of her centuries of study and her courageous challenges and her full strength of spirit and character, until you are once again alive in her fairy-form. If you choose to remain a human, you will --- as I told you at the start of your first Visit, and according to your own desires at the time of your transformation --- recover *some* of your fairy-memories; and of course you will recall *all* of your three Visits here. But you will <u>not</u> recover the full wisdom or heart of Mélusine."

Just as she had thought, looking into her father's eyes had released a river of tears down her cheeks. He was not far from weeping either.

Eli exhaled very deeply.

Aulfrin finally concluded by saying, after a deep breath, "Another eleven days remain, or nearly. Yes, you must leave, that is *decide*, before the full moon. In nine days, at the latest, you should return the Cloth to the Island of the Owls; for from there you will need a day or so to return to Barrywood, to prepare yourself to pass through your brother Finnir's Portal, if you choose to make that irrevocable step. You have, thus, in all, eleven days to make your decision.

"But I warn you, my darling daughter, I will do all in my power to persuade you to remain in Faërie."

****

That evening and for most of the following morning, Eli kept to herself. She played her harp in her own bed-chamber, and lingered long on the balcony there --- simply looking out at the misty lights about the Great Trees, or down onto the lawns and gardens of this part of the Silver City. She was not sorrowful, only thoughtful. But rather than meditating, or walking about Fantasie with Piv and Jizay, she simply chose to be alone.

As the morning wore on, she found she didn't even wish to *think* about anything; she just wanted to breathe the air of Faërie and fill her eyes and her heart with the view from her open window.

Eli felt her father's presence at her back before she turned to greet him. He was standing at the door of the bedroom, smiling warmly and serenely. A very different expression than that which he had worn when saying good-night to her last evening.

"Is it time for lunch already?" asked Eli, coming abruptly out of her silent staring and stillness. "I didn't feel the time passing."

Aulfrin laughed. "Time doesn't pass," he commented, his eyes and also his emerald crown glinting almost cheekily, "**we** do! But before we pass any further through this bright autumn day, I would like to invite you --- no, not to lunch, not yet --- but to an important meeting.

"Earlier this year, dear Eli Penrohan, a dream was sent to you by one of your Tree-friends, recounting the aerial battle between myself and Erreig, and the banishment of my Queen. Aside from the fact that the full content of its tale was cut-short, I think it was very telling that such information formed a part of the messages recalling you to your true life here, recalling you to the silver turrets of Fantasie. For you are closely bound to that day and that decision.

"Life is not circular, my darling Eli. It is a spiral. But from certain angles the curves of its looping seasons do seem to rejoin, to come back together. Not exactly in the same place, but almost! You will return here --- oh, I do hope you will --- to be our Princess once again. But yours is not the only curve of the spiral to come back, somehow, to where it was before.

"Come, and see for yourself."

They made their way to the staircase leading to the floor with the branching corridors, one going off into the heady perfumes of the Concocting Cell, the other winding around to the right, with paving tiles of polished powder-blue and obsidian black. Father and daughter followed this twisting hallway --- now to the right, now left, now back to the right --- and finally arrived at the slim, dark, arched door with a crystal knob. Even before Aulfrin invited Eli, with a nod, to open the door, she could hear the music.

Her mother, the Queen Rhynwanol, was playing Gaëtanne, her harp. She understood, now, that her father wished to show her a vision of her mother, beyond the embroidered veil of thin fabric of the last door into the Music Room with its seven slender windows and its phantom, cob-webby figure of the exiled harpist. Eli recalled how she had seen her on her first Visit, and how much more real her mother and the sonorous harp had appeared to be when they materialised in her own little flat in Saintes; and that she had since seen Rhynwanol, with the help of the Silver Leaf, in other visions --- so real, so vivid, that her mother had seemed to be truly just before her.

Oh, the music was sublime! Eli paused before the wispy curtain of the last door. The notes of Gaëtanne were ringing and singing just like swooping swallows, like hearts in love! She glanced happily at her father, and noticed that his shining smile was being touched by a stray tear, rolling down his cheek and into his red moustache and beard.

He lifted the veil of fabric, and they entered the Queen's Music Room. But no vision of Rhynwanol was there to greet them.

The music had ceased. And there, standing beside her harp, was the Queen herself. *Not* a phantom, not a vision.

"Welcome home, my Queen," whispered Aulfrin. And he walked up to the beautiful violet fairy, with her long black hair glinting with jewels and ineffable star-light and her robes shimmering like burnished silver flecked with purple and her violet-blue eyes dancing, and he took her in his arms --- right there before their daughter! --- and kissed her long and tenderly.

When their kiss had ended, the King extended one arm to Eli, keeping the other about the shoulders of the Queen, and she joined them. Her mother embraced her, and the rippling energy of that touch was even sweeter than the harp-music had been.

No vision or ghost-form had done justice to the loveliness of the Queen; and Eli felt she could stand and gaze at her for hours. She also noted, with great delight, that she could clearly remember the feeling of being in her mother's arms --- though it had been over six-hundred-years since she, as a fairy-child of barely ten, had last experienced it.

Aulfrin remarked, in a soft voice, "I came here last night, just as the crescent moon was setting, with my own harp. And it was not the first time, in these past days, that I have done this. I played, humbly and hopefully, and I repeated my request, asking my exiled wife to forgive me and to return. And to my great delight and relief, she agreed.

"She came home to Fantasie with the rising moon, late this morning. She had desired to rediscover this part of our home first, on her own, even before we met once more: to visit the Queen's Head Vase in her Concocting Cell, and to play her lovely harp. And thus, I am received with music, and --- as she further ordained --- *you* are here to share these first instants of our renewed joy. For, as your mother has said to me through my own harp-playing, you were the herald and the harbinger of this event, dearest Eli, or Mélusine."

Her mother added nothing, but she stroked Eli's face, and the deep happiness in her mauve eyes was magical to see.

Then the Queen kissed Eli's forehead, and she lifted her daughter's left hand to her lips and kissed her palm. Suddenly, with a sensation like a droplet of cool water falling into it, Eli felt the jewel there. It materialised and shone, an amethyst of many tiny facets; and with its appearance, the room was flooded with the scent of roses. Shining on its cord of seaweed and twisted vines, the sister-amethyst of Rhynwanol swayed slightly as the Queen's gown undulated in the slight breeze from the windows.

"And now" announced the King, "we can all *three* go downstairs together, and dine as a family should!"

In fact, they were more than three for their meal, for both the hounds were there, and Periwinkle also. And one could say that all of the Silver City shared the occasion too: for the King had proclaimed the 11th of November to be a festival, with the trumpeters blowing a bright and braying fanfare to announce that the Queen had returned to the Shee Mor!

As they raised their glasses of bubbly violet ambrosia in a toast to the radiant Rhynwanol, another fairy joined them in the dining-room, hung with the banners of Faërie --- russet and ochre --- and also with garlands of purple flowers, among them many *adenium* and even several dragon-flowers. It was Alégondine.

Evidently, it had been the dark Princess who had brought the Queen up the River Dragonfly, passing the stately pinnacle of Kingfishers' Temple in her coral and abalone boat with its five-pointed sail. And the King had been happy to invite his 'little flower' to return to Fantasie also.

Eli felt overjoyed and not a little amazed by the turn of events. She expressed this with a simple questioning look at her father, who understood her confusion and with great warmth explained some of the story to her over their meal.

To begin, Aulfrin shrugged his shoulders in contented resignation. "It was high time, was it not, my dear Eli? High time for me to reflect upon the 'earth-quake' faults at my feet, as the Mushroom Lord had termed them. For I had shaken my realm and splintered it with cracks and crevices in my pride and anger in the year 1367, when the treachery of Erreig had been discovered. Yes, I call it *his* treachery, and not hers at all.

But I was not ready, then, to see through my blind and wounded pride, not until Garo, the son of Erreig, brought me tidings from the Stone Circle.

"It was the day before your journey into the world to retrieve the Cloth, you recall, Eli, when Garo and Brocéliana arrived here. Garo had been to the Circle, and had brought messages for you, but also for me --- and those to me he delivered to my ears and in private. For it was my mother Morliande who had sent me information and advice, delivered by Garo.

"Had I not the eyes to see, she asked, that on the head of your harp was a Golden Flower? I had noticed it, in fact, so much is true; but I did not think it of greater importance than the lovely decoration it was, and a fitting emblem to crown the harp made for you by your brother Finnir, for you are a Princess of Roses. But now I learned that it had greater significance, that it could teach me certain... lessons.

"I learned that it had been wrought, long ages ago, by my own Queen --- to be a means of communication between herself and one of her twin daughters, Mowena. And *that* half-fairy, living in the human-world, had long used it to converse with her mother. But alas, it had been stolen.

"It was in the year 1300, and Mowena and her sister Malmaza had been in the Celtic realm of Scotland for one hundred years already; they were only twenty-three --- for their aging was that of fairies, and not of humans. In this same year, my father the King Aulfrelas was taken from the shores of the Great Strand and carried, as I then thought, to his death. But what I heard from Garo's report was that the previous Hermit, Maelcraig the Mauve, had left Faërie for a brief tour of the human world wherein dwelt (already) many of the Servants of the White Hawk. As was his wont, he took the ocean paths --- rather than passing by a Portal of our realm --- and came first to the Islands of the Hebrides, where the twins were then living. And in his wake, secretly and audaciously, flew the young Erreig, then only twenty-four years of age --- not much older than your twin half-sisters. He was spied and his passage marked by many of the hawks of the Hebrides, but Erreig eluded them at every turn.

"Did he know beforehand what he sought? Had he been informed that the Queen had borne daughters to Grey Uan, before her marriage to me, who had gone into the human-lands? Did he know about the Leaf and the Flower? I cannot answer these questions, and the white wizard-birds could not learn more either. But the Mauve Mage of the Hawks, he was followed by the crafty young dragon-rider and --- though Maelcraig could not hinder the crime, he was vigilant enough to perceive it. He told my mother that Erreig had beheld his clandestine meeting with the half-fairy twins and that he had shortly thereafter returned and had *stolen* the Golden Flower. For in observing Mowena the bold dragon-boy had surely discovered its power to behold and converse with Queen Rhynwanol, its maker.

"Almost two hundred years earlier, Erreig had won the fire-opal *Gurtha* which was now embedded in his chest. This gem is renowned for its power of tripling the gifts of its bearer: gifts such as physical strength and perception, but also passion and the skills of seduction. With both the Rose and the opal of the Ancestral Fire in his possession, Erreig was now well-able to win Rhynwanol from me --- if only for a brief interlude. An interlude which I now comprehend with greater and broader understanding than I did then; and an interlude with a very precious outcome for my realm. For from the impudent and scandalous seduction of my Queen came another flower --- not a golden one, but a dark and mystical one: the exquisite Alégondine, who is a rare and wonderful blessing to Faërie."

Eli was finding it difficult to eat her delicious lunch, for the tale was both exciting and bewildering to her. Not least among its incredible details was the affection and acclaim for Alégondine. The King had met her, Eli knew, at Castle Davenia earlier this year, and the lovely Princess had been present, also, on the Day of Ævnad. But Eli had not, so far, heard her father laud her with such high praise, especially as he now proclaimed her as a *blessing* for his realm.

But it was Piv who could not contain himself, and exuded between bites of rich chestnut and cabbage *potage*, "Oh yes, yes! Such a blessing, not only for our wonderful kingdom but most especially for my darling Garo-lad! Oh, I am so happy for him, for him and his lady!"

The beauteous Rhynwanol was laughing at the giddy pixie, and her laughter was like a fountain of diamond-droplets.

"And does he know yet?" she inquired of Piv, when he had made a whizzing tour of the room and returned to his oversized bowl of soup. "Have you told Garo, or has his half-sister shared this news with him?"

Piv looked a little shyly at the King. "Ah no, my sweet stag-and-wolf-and-dragon lordling doesn't yet know, and I suppose it isn't *my* place ---- but I would have liked to!" he enthused.

Aulfrin chuckled as he shook his head. "I wish you could be the bearer of the news, dear Master Periwinkle. But I think it will be announced formally, by his sister, if you don't mind. It is a *very* important change of plans."

Piv nodded in agreement, though with a sigh. But Eli could not follow at all.

"Whatever *is* this change of plans?!" she exclaimed, smiling at all her family and also at the button-eyed little pixie, whose mouth and cheeks were now painted with green froth, the evidence of his drinking his soup as if it were a bowl of *café-au-lait*!

Alégondine gently placed her hand on Eli's arm, and smiled with her sublime air of peace and serenity. "My brother is freed from the bargain struck by our father Erreig with the Mage of Star Island, Eli. He will *not* be the next Sage-Hermit after Aulfrelas. I have offered myself in his place."

There was no way to stop them: the tears just streamed down Eli's face. All she could think of was her sister, Brocéliana. Her lover would *not* be taken from her in two years' time, to be forever sequestered on the sacred isle. They would be free to live out their love-story now. *Garo was free*!

It was many minutes before Eli could regain her composure. Jizay had come to her, and placed his head in her lap, and Ferglas had shaken his collar to make a jingling sea-shell overture to Alégondine's announcement.

"Are you happy, I mean are you willing to do this, do you do it freely?" inquired Eli at last, looking with such admiration and astonishment at the dark-skinned and shimmering fairy that Alégondine had to laugh.

"I'm very *very* happy," she confirmed. "I have always been a solitary fairy, and I was raised by the Sage-Hermit, you know. My education prepared me for the decision that I think he could always see coming. He is a *great* seer, the kind Aulfrelas; and I wonder if he was not testing the Dragon-Lord, just a little, by requiring his son of him. If he was, our father did not pass the test too gracefully!

"But I feel certain that both Aulfrelas and the Silkie-Queen Morliande knew that I would come back to Star Island. I had been chosen, most probably, even at my birth. Now I will take up my residence there and my new duties in the year 2012, as Garo would have done. I like that human-world date: the numbers add up to five! The present Sage-Hermit is devoted to the number seven, and Maelcraig was enamoured of thirteen; myself, I am partial to five: it is the number of the points of my ship's sail --- made for me by the sea-serpents; five are the notes in the scale of the *pentatone* --- in which I always sing; five is the number of the points of my Island home-to-be; and I was five years old when Aulfrelas swept me up into his arms and carried me away from Fantasie and into Quillir. Yes, my dear sister Eli, I am very happy. It will be an exciting age to come, and I am honoured to be the Sage-Hermit of the era when the Spiral of the Eleven Stars will fulfil the dreams of the Alliance."

"And another reason for celebration at this decision," added Aulfrin, "is that the former Mage, Maelcraig (who still resides often in my shee), is now no longer *opposed* to the union of Garo and Brocéliana. For until now, he saw the young Dragon-Lordling as the successor to Aulfrelas; and Maelcraig knew that Brocéliana had won the heart of Garo. He had seen this as a great disturbance and perturbation to the young Hermit-elect! He felt sure that, when the changeling-fairy-Princess returned, the gallant lover would follow his lady into the world and forsake his sacred duties. Now he has no need to seek to separate them. For Brocéliana will indeed go back when you return here, as I continue to hope you shall. But if Garo wishes to visit her there, that will not be a hindrance to the holy life and duties of the Hermit --- or should I say Hermit-ess?!"

Eli was quieter as she listened to Aulfrin pronounce these words. It was *not* really a solution for Brocéliana, that; and she knew it. And what she had *not* told her father was that her decision to return to her human-life was not merely because she felt she could do 'more good' there than here. It was also, and perhaps mainly, because she did not want to sunder Brocéliana from Garo... and from Faërie.

But she could say nothing of that to this company. She only continued to feel deep, deep joy for her half-sisters --- both of them.

****

The King and Queen stood with Eli and Alégondine at the open window, watching the display of the weaving and pulsating lights, like a huge halo, around the Great Trees. There was only the slightest drizzle of rain this afternoon, but all the fairies and creatures of Fantasie seemed to be dancing drunkenly! Jizay and Piv had gone down to join in the revelry and could be seen running, leaping and waltzing among the colourful host! Birds were chasing one another in riotous choreography to celebrate Rhynwanol's home-coming; while woodland animals, rabbits and mice, frogs, spiders and even a pair of very elegant tortoises were making a gay ballet on the lawns before the great Moon Tower.

Aulfrin exhaled with a sigh of satisfaction and deep delight.

"I will have my Queen *and* my Princess back to grace my realm now!" He then glanced at Eli, with just a tinge of concern.

"I have not told your mother that you are hesitating in your decision, my dear girl. But I feel her restraint about my statement, even as I pronounce it. Have you spoken of this…this dilemma?" He addressed both his wife and daughter, but it was the Queen who replied immediately.

"The third Visit of Eli is not yet drawn to its close," she smiled, almost winking at her daughter --- but only very discretely between them. "And we must not seek to influence her over-much. It is very important that children, that all those whom we love, be left free to choose their paths according to their own inner promptings. Eli must enjoy and continue to rediscover Faërie, for ten more days. Then she will know."

"You are ever my wise and noble Queen, my dear," Aulfrin murmured, bowing to her counsel and radiating his admiration for her in his eyes. "And I am glad that, although I must leave my daughter and my wife for a day or two, they will have the precious company of one another."

"You are leaving?" inquired Eli. "Is there some problem?"

"Not a problem, not at all; or at least I should hope not. The Heron-Fairy arrived early this morning with the news I was anticipating. Erreig has returned to Faërie, to Mermaid Island, where his great dragon was awaiting him. He has asked for an 'audience' with me, and I understand that Garo will also be there."

Eli smiled. She then asked, "Is Brocéliana to be present also? Or where is she now?"

"Ah, yes, you had expected them to be together of course. But I think that this should be a meeting between Dragon-Lords, Princes and Kings. Such a masculine conclave will have *easily* enough to discuss without adding romance to their agenda, at least for the moment!"

Aulfrin chuckled once again. "But I think the union of Garo and Brocéliana will come up in our discussions, in fact. However, I felt it better to invite the half-fairy damsel *here*, rather than *there*. She will be arriving tomorrow I should think. I know you will be pleased to see her again, for the strands of your two stories are closely knit, and your final decision --- which I agree I should not seek to influence --- is nonetheless an important subject for you and Brocéliana to broach. You must be reassured that she does not anticipate remaining here, and I know this to be her position, my Eli. But it will be good for you to hear this from her own lips, and I imagine Garo will return here with me after our meeting with his father --- for he shall learn of his change of fate and his new lease of freedom from his half-sister Alégondine here in Fantasie. At that time, you will be able to speak to all of them, and so put your mind at ease concerning the plans of the young lovers.

"I will fly to Leyano's Castle tomorrow morning, on Cynnabar. I hope to return with the half-moon overhead, on the evening of the 13th, in two days' time. You, Eli, and your dear mother, will no doubt explore together the oval of the City and enjoy these moments to recreate to your own bond of love, so long severed.

"When the subject of Erreig is at last distanced from my thoughts, we can all perhaps make our plans for the week or so remaining to Eli on this Visit. Of course, this will include a trip to the Dappled Woods and to the Prince Demoran, for he will be delighted to welcome his mother the Queen back to the realm and to his Princedom. And from there you will probably go directly to Scholar Owl Island. And after that adventure, we will all travel together to spend a day or so with Leyano, also, before ... the full moon."

Aulfrin's voice became a tinged with overtones of sorrow for a moment, like a shadow veiling the moonbeams which illuminate a silvery garden. But in only a moment he had breathed deeply and calmly, and laid his hand upon that of the Queen's, standing so resplendently beside him.

As they continued to enjoy the vista of Fantasie and the play of the swirling mists about the Great Trees, Jizay and Piv reappeared to urge Eli to come out onto the lawns and dance among the flowers with the other fairies and creatures celebrating the Queen's return. Eli invited Alégondine to join them, but the dusky fairy declined, saying that she had another engagement to fulfil.

Descending the grand staircase to the Tower's ground level with her two friends --- pixie and dog --- Eli suggested that, rather than mingling with the dizzy dancers just now, they wander off together for a tea at *The Tipsy Star*, but Piv crossed his arms in mock defiance of this plan.

"For a beer with a curious constellation-name, yes, nowhere better," he proclaimed, as the three of them stood before the great Entrance Doors of the Moon Tower, "but if it's *tea* you're thinking of --- with, I hope, a cake or two (I like the poppy-seeds ones best, drizzled with syrup from the maple trees) --- then I hasten to correct your choice, little Eli-een. *The Swooping Swallow* is the place for <u>that</u> sort of feast ... I mean high-tea."

He fluttered decidedly into the air and landed on Jizay's back. "Off we go!" he announced, and with both Eli and her hound of joy laughing, they proceeded to the cosy Inn along the southern walls of the City: Eli flying, and Jizay galloping happily beneath her with Piv astride him.

Knowing, now, that the first Gate of the Silver City was named Ioyeas, Eli stood and regarded it for a moment when they had arrived before the Inn. She knew that it had a corresponding note of music, and was also linked with one of the Great Trees, and with one of the Stones of the mysterious Circle. It was made in the form of a massive and rather Romanesque-arched double-door, in fact, with decorations of red and pale gold in waves and arabesques inlaid along the grain of its dark wood. Inscribed over its arch --- which appeared to be wrought of pure silver but could also have been a sort of shining grey branch --- was the motto of Faërie, in characters which Eli still could not read, though she knew the text from her Father having read it to her when they had arrived by the north-western Gate.

*You shall see the Moon forever full,
when you look with the eyes of the Sun.*

Ioyeas's doors were not closed but only very slightly ajar, and so she could *not* see beyond them down the pathway towards the Stone Circle, whose energies she could feel even from here. She had a strange urge to venture there once more --- almost as if she sensed that the mists around the megaliths would be filled with voices and messages, visions and faces. In the world, she would continue to have --- she expected --- the Silver Leaf and the Golden Rose with her, and thus she would have some means of communication with Faërie and with Rhynwanol and her father, and surely with Finnir too; and some contact with her true home would come to her when she played Róisín, undoubtedly. But at this moment she was keenly aware that a very great power, stronger than the Leaf or the Flower or the Harp of Barrywood, lurked there beyond the confines of Fantasie's walls; and it was beckoning to her and exciting her heart with curiosity and with longing, promising to speak to her from the depths of its ageless store of wisdom and magic regarding a special bond that could be forged, through it, to this beauteous kingdom.

But it was not the moment to venture there, she knew, and so she resisted the call of the Stones. Instead, together with her dear dog and her delightful pixie-friend she now turned to enter into the warmth of *The Swooping Swallow*. The wind was rising and the early evening was rapidly turning dark and chill, even in this protected and privileged City. This cosy haven was perfect and very welcoming, and tea was served according to Piv's detailed instructions to their host. As for Eli, she was very pleased to have the opportunity to talk confidentially with her friends.

"You *knew*, Piv? You knew that Alégondine had made this decision, this offer?"

"It was Bram who told me, by the threads of the mushrooms. Jizay was with me, last night, and we heard the news there in the White Garden, the closest to the secret Inner Garden. At first, we could hear the voices of *all* of the Great Ones, but only titbits of their conversation floated down to us, like flame-coloured leaves descending in pirouettes to join their brothers among the roots and toadstools. And that's what made me think of asking the fungus-folk, and as we were close to Bram, he spoke to us through them."

Jizay interjected, "We had gone there hoping to have confirmation of the rumours of the Queen's return. She was, it seems, already coming up the River Dragonfly, with the Princess Alégondine in her star-sailed barque. At the last repetition of the King's suit for her to return, later yester-eve, she must have been already nearly arrived! We had no trouble hearing about Rhynwanol's approach, for not only the Trees and toadstools, but all the flowers and stones, brooks and fountains of the three gardens were a-buzz with excitement! She has been long missed here."

Piv took up the tale once more.

"But then we heard the whispers regarding the Princess, hummed along the mushroom roads from the roots of Bram: *The new Sage-Hermit, she is coming to the City! The shape-shifter*

Garo, the brave and beautiful boy of the dragons, the disciple of Lord Hwittir, he will not *go to the Star! Instead, it will be the black flower, the Princess as dark as the hour before dawn, and as filled with promise of light. It will be Alégondine who shall become the Mage-Mother of our shee, and all the insects will sing, and all the sea-serpents will dance, and the Sun and the Moon will both do reverence to the Star, to the new Queen of Twilight and of Dawn...* That's what his roots were chanting!"

Eli poured steaming cups of tea for herself and the pixie, and a bowl of thin sheep's-cream with a dark rye biscuit was presented to Jizay. Periwinkle licked each of his tiny fingertips thoroughly, once he had eaten two or three of the little seed-cakes oozing with sticky maple-syrup. But as he looked back up at Eli, his bright eyes became a little sad.

"What's this that the King alluded to, my heart's Eli? He wondered if you will choose not to stay, if you will step back, forever, into the human-lands? But that isn't possible, is it? You're coming to us, and soon now? Why is he worried about that?"

Eli replaced her cup slowly on its rustic pottery saucer. She looked rather poignantly at her dear friend.

"I have to tell you, Piv, and I should have done so already. I'm sorry I couldn't find the moment or the words before this. But I'm *not* going to stay. I've decided to go back into the world, for the rest of my human life. I think I was always meant to, but I probably didn't share that notion with anyone, not even you, before I became a changeling babe. I seem to sense in my very heart a growing certainty, more *intuition* than memory, that long ago, in the Great Charm perhaps --- my, it's almost as if I'm beginning to remember it all as I tell you! --- that I had *already* conceived of this plan. It is, very strangely, as if it's starting to come back to me now as I speak. How odd! Yes, I can almost see myself talking to someone about it, but I can't quite recall who it was... And I said that I would become a changeling, but that I would choose to return to the world after that and not to Faërie, for reasons that were very clear to me even then. But I also said that, after my death as a woman, a bit like Lily, I would come to Faërie again. If I could…"

The pixie's face had gone quite white; even his usually apple-red cheeks had lost their glow. Jizay, also, had come to stand beside Eli, his head under her hand.

"And the reasons, if I comprehend your thoughts correctly," murmured the voice of her dear hound, silently but obviously quite clear to both his mistress and to Piv, "are, firstly, the good you believe you can do there --- especially with the Harp of Barrywood to aid you --- and, secondly, to allow your sister Brocéliana to remain here in Faërie, now with her beloved Garo beside her also."

Eli nodded, and so, eventually, did Periwinkle. And as he did so, his usually cheeky face became more thoughtful and serious. But he did not seem *sorrowful* any longer. A well of deep knowing was shining in his button eyes, and his bright green wings twitched like a cat flicking its tail to punctuate its most inscrutable thoughts. At last, one corner of his mouth turned upwards in a knowing grin, and he clicked his fingers.

"The Fourth Portal," he said slowly and almost as silently as Jizay's interior language. "You plan to come home by the Fourth Portal when you pass the human doorway of death, don't you, my Eli-sine? The mythical Portal that you think you and Peronne may have found, long ago. No fairy has *ever* done that! It is mad and more than courageous, and mighty and marvellous. It is just the sort of feat that Mélusine would set herself as challenge and goal. The Fourth Portal, oh my my! But you must *find* the Garnet Vortex for that. And there is the Key, so the legends say: I suppose it is the Black Key, and it must be given to the Keeper of the Veil of the Vortex."

Eli reached up, as if to tuck a dangling strand of hair behind her left ear, and she gently fingered the Flaming Crescent Moon ear-ring that hung there, invisible to all save Finnir, and the Lady Ecume, and the three twilight Queens who had blessed it and given it to her (and one of them was now gone into the night following twilight, and out into the dawn on the other side). One day, she hoped, Barrimilla, the 'Keeper' of whom Piv spoke, would also see the charm and grant her safe passage through his 'Veil'…

As Eli did not say anything more --- which Piv accepted philosophically, though there was still a hint of tears in his sparkling eyes.

Finally he added, "If you decide to choose that path, my Eli, then I will await you, always blessing you, always loving you, until you come home. For you will. If you have set yourself this feat to accomplish, then you will do it. For you are more Mélusine than ever you were Eli, in your heart of hearts. I *know* that you will succeed, even where no other fairy before you has ever done.

"I begin to recall certain riddling things you told me, before your transformation," continued Piv, while Eli sipped her tea in silence. "And, I also remember, you saw the Fourth Portal again in a vision, when you were in Leyano's Castle, on your last Visit, and I was with you. It came back to you then, almost as if it wanted to remind you of the pact you had made with it! I always had a hunch that you and your winged-horse had found that marvel in your far-flights, as I've said before.

"But my Eli, if you found it *there*, in the oceans of the Northern Seas, then it was when you were *here*, in Faërie, on this side. You'll be on the *other* side, on the human side, when you die. And as I said a moment ago," he added, one chubby finger now raised to emphasize his warning tone, "you would probably need the Black Key. Will you be given that, somehow, when you're back in the human world? Will the Lady Ecume bring it to you? Have you thought about all of this?!"

"The Black Key can open many things: doors and hidden chests, tombstone-passages and secret labyrinths. But there are other keys, too, and other tokens. And sometimes one key leads to another, as one twist in the path may lead to another turn. Do not fear for Eli, dear Master Periwinkle. She will have the key she needs and the door will open to her. She *will* return to Faërie. One day."

All three of them --- woman, pixie and hound --- turned to look at the speaker of these words. Though all three recognised their source. The voice was like a breeze in a forest, like birds roosting at dusk, like purple water reflecting the sunset light where harp-music is wafted over the waves from blue islands. It was the Queen Rhynwanol.

"Mother," Eli greeted her, standing. "Ah, and Aindel! Oh, how is this? Where is the King?"

Her brother smiled, and took Eli's hand to kiss it; a gesture that surprised her a little, but pleased her too. "He awaits us in his great Chamber of Seven Arches. Our mother excused herself to come and seek you --- knowing that you were to be found here. Well, not quite true, for we both thought you might have gone as far as the Stone Circle, for some reason. It was in your mind, was it not? No matter, this is a very good place to meet also! We are more like swallows, swooping with joy and love tonight, than we are cold Stones, however wise and magical!"

The fair, freckled face of the tall Prince was very merry as he added, "It is an enchanted date, the 11th of November, is it not, dear sister? We have our mother come back to her home and her King, and our half-sister welcomed in Fantasie and hailed as the new Hermit. What a wondrous day!"

"And now, let us rejoin my dear husband," said the sweet *violet* voice of the *violet* Queen. "We have yet more exciting news to give him, even before he hastens to Mermaid Island in the morning. Shall we all fly back, while Jizay runs, or *outruns* us?!"

She laughed, and with a happy bark from the golden hound, the company set off across the lawns and meadows, over the stream flowing from the fountain of Lysadel, and close by the

Gardens of the Trees --- already twinkling with the night-time display of their many lights and prisms, lanterns and dancing sparks of colour.

Eli could hardly believe the glory of flying like this, in company with her mother and brother and with the happy Piv coming and going to soar beside them for a moment, and then dipping down to race with Jizay or loop among the trees with owls or small grey bats, giants moths or green and gold fire-flies.

She found herself savouring each and every amazing instant of her life here, to keep as preciously as Lily's journal and Reyse's white rose, to relive in her memory during all the years to come.

****

The day, or rather the evening, became more and more wondrous for Eli. For when she and Jizay and the Queen Rhynwanol arrived in the great circular Council Chamber with its wide windows and its curtained central column of force and concealed light, they not only found Aulfrin and Alégondine, but yet another fairy.

Eli, closed her eyes as her smile grew and her heart bounded. When she opened them, he had come to her to kiss her hand as Aindel had done.

"Oh, Reyse, I am *so* happy to see you."

His smile was as radiant as hers, but he said nothing more than her name, as he inclined his head.

"My dear Reyse has only just arrived," beamed the King, clearly replete with happiness. "I have not even had time to hear how, or why exactly, he has come here, but --- as *chance* cannot be the cause --- I can only surmise that he was meant to share the joys of this extraordinary day with us!"

"He arrived at *my* invitation, Your Majesty. We have voyaged long and far together, and I count the Lord Reyse as one of my dearest friends --- though in recent centuries I have been more often in company with the Prince Finnir. But as the newly returned Queen bid me join you this evening, I took it upon myself to request the honour and the pleasure of Reyse's company also."

The King turned from Eli and his Queen, back to the doorway to see who spoke. Piv was hovering around the head and shoulders of a tall fairy. The pixie smiled rather excitedly, bubbling with curiosity, and then whizzed into the Chamber to stand close beside Jizay.

"I know your voice," Aulfrin murmured, speaking very slowly. "Who are you? You have voyaged with my dear friend, and with one of my sons, you say? I'm sure I know your voice…"

The perplexed monarch stepped up to the fair fairy, whose pale red-blond hair, tightly curled, was hanging loose this evening, shining with many delicate twisted cords of copper and the aquamarines held by them. The amber gems in his ears and beside his eyes caught the light of the many great candles in their brackets around the walls. And the colours of the aurora circling the Great Trees seemed to rush through the open arched windows to be reflected in his violet-blue regard. He certainly had the eyes of Rhynwanol.

Aindel did not need to reply to the King. For Aulfrin had now recognised the gems from Initiations many centuries before, the Initiations of his eldest son when he was eleven and seventeen. And there was no mistaking that his eyes were those of the Queen. With his transformation and the many years that had passed, the features in the kind and gentle face had altered somewhat, but he was --- indeed --- thoroughly recognisable to his father's bedazzled eyes.

The Queen Rhynwanol advanced, to stand beside her husband, laying a gentle hand on his trembling shoulder. The King could no longer see the face of the fairy before him, for his vision was veiled by his tears. But they were tears of pure and overwhelming joy.

"Timair!" he wept, repeating the name again and again as he took his son into his arms. "Timair, Timair, my son! But how is this possible? You died many centuries ago as the human-changeling you became. Have you stepped back through the doors of death, to render me this unhoped-for visit?"

Timair's voice was wavering with tears as well, but he answered, or began to answer, as best he could.

"My father, I will tell you all the details of the tale later, if you wish. But *no*, I am not on a visit to you from a human death in the mid-fourteenth century. For I was never Ardan, the changeling infant placed in the crib of Daireen. His mother had hidden the real Ardan away, to keep and raise as her own true child --- as he was. But I, my dearest father, by long design planned between myself and my grandparents, Morliande and Aulfrelas, as soon as I was placed in his cradle I was stolen away again and taken to the Sheep's Head Shee to be raised as *their* Prince. While the eldest child of King Tirrig and Queen Bowarry, Finnir the White, Finnir the Enchanted One, newborn and filled with light, *he* was placed in the crib in Ireland. The changeling-company of our Shee Mor took *that* royal fairy-babe, thinking him to be Ardan. And he has remained here, raised as your half-fairy son. But he is no half-fairy!"

Aulfrin had stepped back, only a pace, from Timair, listening to his words with eyes wide and heart pounding. But there was great and ecstatic joy mingled with his bewilderment and wonder.

Rhynwanol took up the tale. "I had been told, by your mother, the Silkie-Queen, of this plan, my Sovereign, my belovèd husband; but I was sworn to secrecy. For our son, Timair, had requested to interweave our clans thus, and his grand-parents had seen this as a high and noble project. All would have been revealed earlier, I believe, had not the Dragon-Lord troubled your realm with internal strife and division for many years, and then added the rash and ruinous affair which caused you to exile me. At that time, I chose to go to the Sheep's Head Shee, to be near our son."

There was a pause, while Aulfrin digested, it seemed to Eli, this news in all its complexity. But in only a moment her father pleased her by the proof that his effontery and his ego were both come well under his control now.

He shook his head at himself as he said, "It was my poor diplomacy and unwise delays in dealing with Erreig and his Sun-Singers --- as well as my arrogant response to that brief infidelity, wrought *by* Erreig --- which have caused this sorrow to haunt me for so many centuries. Since that distant time I have suffered the loss of both my son and my wife, when the truth could have been told me so much sooner, had I not been blinded by wrath and pride.

"Please forgive me, my Queen, and you also, my darling Timair. And thank you both, so much and so deeply, for coming back to me today."

****

As the gathering moved from the Chamber of Arches to the great Dining-Room, Periwinkle and Jizay hung back, and Eli stopped to remain with them as the others advanced down the hallway. Reyse waited for her, discreetly, just outside of the doorway.

Both hound and pixie seemed dazed. But in true fairy-fashion, they also seemed to wear expressions of a bemused desire to laugh at themselves.

"I feel I should have recognised Aindel as Timair, but I had never met the eldest Prince when he was young, nor put the pieces of the puzzle together when I had heard the tale of Ardan!" remarked Jizay softly, shaking his head. "Aindel I have seen on several occasions, here in Fantasie and in the Dappled Woods, and as we passed through Wineberry's Gate. I should have recognised the likeness to you, to your father, and even certain shared features with Demoran and Leyano … but I did not."

"I suppose he did not wish to be recognised," suggested Eli. "I imagine that a great Prince of Faërie has many magical powers at his finger-tips, when he needs them."

But it was Periwinkle who seemed the most astounded. He looked blankly before him, taking off his jaunty green cap to scratch his head.

"Oh my, oh my," he muttered, and he sat down, cross-legged, where he was. "Finnir is *not* the Prince Finnir, or rather he *is*, but not of here. And my Aindel, he *isn't* Aindel at all: my friend of moonlit magic and Seventh Gates, of Stone Circles and Cups of Light --- and cups of tea! He's not the Aindel-of-my-heart, he's the Prince Timair, who went away when he was only eighteen years old, who went into the world --- so the stories all said --- to King Aulfrin's Irish wife, Daireen. But I *knew* Timair, or I knew *of* him, for I was a young imp then, seven centuries ago. And I mourned his decision, the decision of Ardan, when he came home and then chose to go back…. Only it really *was* Ardan, that is a half-fairy human, and not the Ardan who was the changeling Timair…. For there was no changeling! Except for Finnir, but he was a changeling left by fairies and then stolen by fairies! But that's quite absurd… and that makes him the very highest Prince, the eldest son of the magical king and queen of the Sheep's Head Shee….only they're not really of that shee, for they come from far, far, far away. Oh my, oh my… I'm really so baffled."

And he put his tiny curly head in his hands, and started to cry.

"There, there, my darling Piv," Eli soothed. "Don't take it so hard, please! It's *all* alright now, and Aindel is still your friend, only you can call him by his real name at last. And our father is so happy, and I'm so happy too --- so relieved that he knows and that the secret is out in the open. I only found out about it recently too, on Samhain Eve, in fact. And I was as amazed as you!"

Piv suddenly looked up into Eli's eyes, and his were shining with another light now.

"Eli-een," he said, speaking slowly as if he were unwrapping a beautifully be-ribboned present, "this means that the Prince Finnir isn't your *brother* at all. We thought he was your half-brother, the child of Aulfrin and Daireen; but he's not! He's not related to you at all."

"And, in that case, there is no impediment to her falling in love with him," said Reyse's voice, very softly, from the doorway.

Piv turned his head with a jerk, and then he flew up straight into the air from where he sat, and spun off to fly once around Reyse's broad shoulders and then hover just before his face.

"Oh dear, oh dear *dear*," cried the pixie, starting to sob once again, "my sweet Lord Reyse! Oh but that would be so sad for you..."

The Eagle-Lord's clear brown eyes were opaque and dark, filled with a lightless resignation that Eli had rarely seen in them before. No glint of their golden rings sparkled from their depths. He repeated his words slowly.

"Yes, Eli is free now, as I have known for some time; but with this revelation today she is now free even in her father's eyes, free to fall in love with the Prince Finnir. Or perhaps she already has, and many years ago. It would seem, from what that dear friend --- a friend and companion in errantry even more beloved by me than by the fair Aindel, or rather Timair --- from what Finnir told me in private today, when I passed through his Portal, their love affair began during Eli's Great Charm. I was still undergoing the rigours of my *own* Great Charm, I expect --- for our times of trial and challenge overlapped, as you will recall my Lady Eli, by more than one hundred years; and I concluded mine in 1833.

"It was long before that, in 1599," he continued, as if musing, "ninety-nine years into my own Great Charm, when I raised and educated the flying-horse, Peronne, for the Princess, at her father's behest. She had not yet commenced her Charm then, and so her steed would be her companion throughout it. But for now, Peronne is not yet returned to Fantasie from Ireland, and so I have not been able to inquire more of him.

"Thus I have not discovered *exactly* when their vows were exchanged, but I would not think that they actually saw each other often, for in those days Finnir was busy with his guardian-ship of the Portal in Barrywood, and Eli was occupied with the completion of her Great Charm until 1958, shortly before her human adventure. But Finnir has told me that they found the opportunity, brief and clandestine though it was, to declare their love for one another and that they are bound by this troth and by profound and inviolate bonds.

"This great romance had to be kept a dark secret, of course, until the tidings of today were brought to light. And in the wake of this news, no doubt, the King will hasten to Barrywood to speak with the Prince whom he now knows is *not* his son, but whom he has loved as one for so many centuries. And he is probably as honoured and thrilled as his Queen to have the high Prince of the Sheep's Head as his foster-son and possibly his son-in-law to-be. For no one in all of Greater Faërie is the equal of that Prince. He is the most enchanted, and the most blessed and impressive, and certainly he is worthy of the love of a very great Princess, who will one day be his Queen."

Throughout this long speech, Eli's face had been gradually drained of colour, as Piv's had been earlier. And now her expression was one of deep confusion, and hesitation.

Reyse had stopped talking and was breathing quite quickly. But he had not looked directly at Eli during his monologue. Now Periwinkle had alighted on the floor at his feet, and had reached up a tentative hand, laying it gently on the Horse-Lord's knee. Jizay was standing near his mistress, but his gaze was on Reyse and his expression one of tenderness and concern.

Eli's eyes met Reyse's. They both looked unblinkingly into the other's, as they had done on the terrace of Gavenia's home in Fort William. Only this time, Eli finally found words to say.

"I don't know what love Mélusine feels in her heart, Reyse, because I'm *not* the Princess again yet, not fully. I can imagine that what you say is true, for I've recognised the bond that is between myself and Finnir when I have been with him. I can feel that something is there.

"But I am *Eli* at the moment. And I am choosing to remain Eli for as many more years of human life as I will be given to live in the world. I'm not staying here at the end of this Visit.

"I will be stepping through the Heart Oak to continue my life as Eli Penrohan. And so --- as you have previously requested --- I can't and won't make any statement or decision about Finnir now, because --- for the moment --- I only have the heart of a woman, a *human* woman. I'm not an enchanted Princess and I'm certainly in no position to even speculate on becoming Finnir's Queen while I am still Eli. I've realised, since my visit to Scotland in fact, that I *can't* know if Mélusine is in love, is still in love, until I *am* Mélusine once again, and that will be after my death, and it will depend on whether I succeed in finding and opening the Fourth Portal in order to return to Faërie."

It was Reyse's turn, now, to lose the ruddy colour of his cheeks, which had been very flushed by his earlier discourse. He walked the few steps to Eli, and he took both of her hands in his. He spoke with utter incredulity in his tone, and yet very gently.

"You're *sure* about this decision, Eli? You're going back, and not staying here after this third Visit? And you are going to try to return to Faërie *by the Fourth Portal*?!

"Eli, are you *sure*? This is very, *very* serious. By taking that one step back through the Heart Oak you are taking a very <u>wild</u> and irreversible step."

She said nothing, but she was not crying again. She held her head high, and her turquoise-green eyes were glinting with determination, firm with resolution.

But she could not find another word to say.

All she could do was to walk forward and lay her head, now, on Reyse's chest, as his arms encircled her back and pulled her tight against him, rather as Peronne had hugged her close with his noble head when they had first met again. She breathed very deeply, listening to Reyse's heart beating, feeling her own would burst.

And then she lifted her head slightly, just as he lowered his; and his brown eyes and her turquoise ones closed as their mouths came together in a long kiss.

****

Windy Hill Prayer

Chapter Seventeen:
The Eagle and the Unicorn

"*You're wearing* the moonstone pendant. You were *not* the last time we met, in Scotland. But you're wearing it tonight."

Eli nodded. Her arm was on Reyse's as they walked along the corridor to the Dining-Room.

"I have not known what to do with your gifts, all along. The pendant, and the white rose. For a while, I wore the moon- stone --- but I realised, with slight embarrassment, that it touched my heart, just where, I suppose, the moonstone I won in my second Initiation is set. You were with me at that time, were you not? It was passed with Half-Moon Horses."

"I was only guiding you for a small part of it," he replied softly, as they hesitated at the door of the brightly-lit room. "I had returned from my adventures in order to be your tutor on the White Willow Isles before your first Initiation --- when you were a head-strong and rather capricious child! --- but I had gone off again after that adventuring, with Finnir. I came back very briefly when you were hosted by the Half-Moon Horses, yes; but you were eighteen by then. And you had become very beautiful and very attractive to me. I did not stay long." There was a short silence.

"You wear moonstones also, in your ears," Eli remarked in a whisper.

Reyse looked deep into her eyes once more, smiling now, before they entered to take their places at the table.

"Yes, moonstones in my ears. And over *my* heart, a jasper. Set there by the eagles when I was twenty-one, in the year 821. On Samhain Eve. It is a royal-plume jasper, a jewel of stability and of dignity, allowing me to soar and to see, to look straight into the sun if I wish. The eagles assured me that it would also balance and sooth my oft-*soaring* emotions. But I cannot say that it is fulfilling that role just now."

A little laugh escaped Eli's lips, and Reyse's too. She released his arm as they went in to join the others.

****

The following morning, the Queen and Eli stood together on a high balcony of the King's Moon Tower, watching Aulfrin in flowing green cape and shining silver crown, gliding away on Cynnabar towards Treytherum, the Third Gate of Fantasie.

Below the balcony where mother and daughter stood, the elegant figure of Alégondine was crossing the diamond-shaped Entrance Court of the Tower. Her ample cloak of mysterious mauve billowed out from her shoulders in the crisp breeze; its hood was blown back, and the Princess's long black hair rippled out behind her like the mane of a wild horse.

"She is very lovely," sighed Eli, watching the dark fairy as if studying the illustration in a book of childhood wonder-tales. "It's still hard for me to believe that such miracles exist."

"Miracles such as beauty?" inquired Rhynwanol with a grin and a raised eyebrow.

Eli smiled back at her as they lingered on the balcony of the sitting-room where the two hounds awaited them. "I was thinking more of the incredible miracle of fairies in general, I suppose, and of all this kingdom --- with its flying-horses, mermaids, sea-serpents and even dragons. But I suppose I would consider beauty like Alégondine's a part of the miracle. For she is quite extraordinary."

"As are you, Mélusine," rejoined her mother. "I'm sorry, I should call you Eli for the time being. But I have missed saying the name of my daughter to her face for many centuries! It is such a delight to do so now."

Eli smiled more warmly as they both turned to go back into the bright room. But just as they were crossing the door-sill, a horse could be heard trotting into the Courtyard below. It was wearing bells on its light ribbon-reins, by the sound of it. Eli turned back to the balustrade.

"It's Brocéliana!" she said with delight. "She must have stayed last night at Shepherds' Lodge, to arrive so early here. I'll be so glad to see her."

The Queen rejoined Eli to look down into the Courtyard. Dozens of brown rabbits were scampering all around the prancing hooves of Brocéliana's chestnut mare --- just the same colour as her long, wavy hair undulating over her shoulders. She wore her cobalt-blue cloak embroidered with lavender and fine white motifs which blew open to reveal her pale green tunic and trousers. Behind her and her rabbit-company were two tea-beige deer; while another rider, obviously her attendant, brought up the rear on a large cream-coloured pony. He was playing on a long wooden flute, held sideways like a classical instrument, and hung over his horse's withers was Brocéliana's painted dulcimer, lightly wrapped in lacy cloth but clearly discernable through it.

"So this is your *other* half-sister." The Queen sighed with pleasure. "How like Lily she is! She radiates the same youthful and yet wise energy as her human mother. Well, Lily was not exactly *human*, or not fully so!" she added with a nod to Eli.

"I'm very glad that you knew Lily, my 'human mother' as well as Brocéliana's real one!" Eli confided to her *true* mother, as they watched Brocéliana dismount and then gaily walk up to the broad steps and the open doors of the King's Moon Tower. They sat down, now, to await her arrival in the cosy room.

"I was honoured to know Lily," resumed the Queen. "It's strange, is it not, how our lives sometimes present us with echoes or reflections to make us understand our *lessons*, and to open our hearts?! I was not a little jealous of Lily to start with, for I knew that Aulfrin had fallen deeply in love with her. But then I had to compare that to the burning jealousy that *he* had felt when my affair with Erreig was discovered. What is very healing now, for us both I think, is that we can come to know and love the children born from our respective 'illicit' unions. My husband now holds in high esteem the child of the Dragon-Lord, and I will now meet, and surely appreciate, the daughter of Lily and…Sean!"

Soon after the gracious Queen concluded, Brocéliana arrived at the door of the sitting-room, and both Jizay and Ferglas leapt to their feet to greet her. As the two hounds drew back from their enthusiastic good-mornings, the Queen extended her hand to the newcomer. Brocéliana covered her heart with a graceful gesture and a whispered "Your Majesty", inclining her head with a smile; and then she took the proffered hand as she looked up into the violet-blue eyes of Rhynwanol. The Queen was smiling radiantly, now, also. When she had released Brocéliana's hand, the two sisters embraced warmly.

"As I have just remarked to Eli," said the Queen, "you are the image of Lily. Your eyes are the same twilight blue, and filled with the same stars. And your features and face make me see her beauty, probably when she had your age. How old are you now, Brocéliana?"

"I am twenty-two, Your Majesty. And may I say the same, in some measure, of you and your beautiful daughter. For although Eli does not have eyes of a similar colour to either her mother or father, and she has hair more like the red locks of the King, she is in her fair face and regal carriage of form and figure certainly your child. There is no doubt that she is, even as a changeling-human for the moment, more the Princess

Mélusine and the daughter of the Queen of Faërie than she is the human Eli."

Rhynwanol led their guest to a soft settee draped with tapestry-fabric and scattered with autumn leaves in yellow and red.

"You are fair-spoken, and filled with gentleness, Brocéliana. I do not wonder that you arrive accompanied by rabbits and graceful does! And I do not wonder, either, that you have won the heart of Garo, Erreig's son who is --- as I have heard --- a brave and highly enchanted fairy. I hope I will have the joy of meeting him soon."

Brocéliana smiled very warmly, and said it could not be soon enough for her. But she knew that Garo was going, today, to an important meeting on Mermaid Island.

"Ah, well, *our* meeting is important too," Eli said, "because we have some news to give you, the Queen and myself."

The blue-eyed half-fairy looked expectantly from one to the other, smiling still.

The Queen spoke again now, and her voice was very maternal, and also rather like one young girl sharing a love-story with another, thought Eli.

"To begin with, I think, dear Brocéliana, I must say that you have probably been sensing a <u>threat</u> to your safety here: a certain menacing opposition to your love for Garo. Is that so?"

While her half-sister nodded slowly in accord with this fact, Eli interjected, "I felt it too, when I asked my harp, Clare, about coming back here for my last Visit. At that time, I had a sudden and alarming sense of some threat. I couldn't tell, then, if it were to our father or to myself. I think now that it was the opposition of Maelcraig to the love between yourself and Garo."

Her sister looked puzzled, but only for a moment.

"Maelcraig, the Sage-Hermit before Aulfrelas? He is known to my dear Garo; Maelcraig the Mauve he is called, I believe. And now I recall Garo saying that the Mage was not happy that he, as the next-in-line to that sacred role, should have fallen in love with me. But I thought he meant Aulfrelas."

"Ah, no, not at all," Rhynwanol assured her. "Your grandfather, the father of Aulfrin, is not at all discontented by your love for one another. But that is because he knew, all along it seems, that for Garo to woo you would pose no problem to the next Sage-Hermit. And now Maelcraig will know that also, and be at peace, and no longer in any way present a counter-force to your story together."

"But I don't understand," Brocéliana murmured, her smooth brow now wrinkled with confusion. "It surely *is* a problem for the next Sage-Hermit, and that is Garo. He *cannot* have a lady with him on Star Island. In any case, our love-story will be a short one ---- short but very beautiful, and I am so grateful to have even a fleeting joy with him --- for my dear sister returns to Faërie very soon now. And then I must go into the human-world from whence I came."

Her voice had fallen to a hushed timbre of sorrow, though she was certainly trying to compose herself and control her despair. She breathed deeply, and then resumed.

"As I say, I have felt a threat too, but I have not worried overmuch." Hesitating again, she finally repeated, clearly seeking to muster her courage, "I am grateful for even this short time that I have had with Garo, and soon Maelcraig will have nothing to reproach him for. I will be gone, and Garo will be free."

"He is free, now," whispered Eli, her hand taking that of her sister, and holding it tightly. "He *is* free."

"What do you mean?"

"My daughter," said the tender twilight-voice of the Queen, "my daughter by Erreig, Alégondine, *she* will be the next Sage-Hermit, not Garo. She has offered herself, with great happiness, in his place. Garo will *not* be required to go to Star Island."

The face of Brocéliana was pure poetry. It was transformed, in several stages, through shock, to dawning comprehension, to stupefaction, to wonderment and finally to overwhelming gratitude. She turned to Eli, sitting on one side of her, and threw her arms around her. And when she had released her sister she could not help hugging the Queen, on the other side of her on the settee, as well!

"Oh, but this is glorious: my dear Garo, he will be able to journey and to adventure --- it is what he loves most! And maybe he can even come into the world and visit me, for he has often gone to Norway, and to Iceland. And I can go to live wherever I wish, and then maybe I can see him sometimes…even though I won't be a fairy any more. It is wonderful, so much more wonderful than even our wildest dreams. I could never have seen him again once he was the Hermit on Star Island!"

There was a short pause, and then, very softly, Eli spoke.

"You will still be a fairy, my dear sister. And you will still be *in* Faërie, to share a long and blissful life with your belovèd Garo, I hope. For I have decided to return to my human life. You will not be required to leave here, for *I* am leaving --- at the full moon, in nine days from now. My decision is made."

The eyes of Brocéliana grew so wide that she seemed to resemble one of her attendant rabbits --- but one frozen with sudden shock and fear. She turned fully to Eli, and she clasped both her hands. Hers were trembling violently.

"Don't say that yet, Eli. Give yourself the time you should, the time you need, to decide such a thing. Don't do this *for me*!"

The beautiful, youthful, flower-like face of the half-fairy was awash with tears. Eli could hardly help crying with her. She dropped her hands and put her arms around her again, rocking her gently where they sat, both of them with closed, weeping eyes.

Eli spoke reassuringly and gently, but with composure in her tone of voice.

"I know, I know, I have another week or so to decide. But I don't even need that time. I have made my choice. And I'm sure that I'm not going to be swayed in my decision."

"Please wait, *please wait*," Brocéliana continued to plead in a whisper between her sobs. "Take the time given you, Eli, for it must be given for a reason. Take *all* the twenty-one days. You will know, with certainty, only at the full moon, I think. And whatever you decide then, I will accept it. But please don't make this decision too quickly. Don't pronounce it definitively now. Take your time, take *all* your time…*please*."

At last, Eli had to acquiesce, promising to consider her choice right up until the moment ordained for her to pass back through the Portal of the Heart Oak. Rhynwanol gave Eli a look which conveyed her full agreement with the young half-fairy's request, but which belied her own understanding of her daughter's decision.

Brocéliana seemed utterly overwhelmed by all she had heard, and looked like a faded flower in need of watering and a moment of respite from buffeting winds.

"I meant it to be only good news for you, my darling Brocéliana," Eli said, stroking her sister's tousled hair. "I've upset you more than pleased you, and that was not my intention!"

"I'm alright, my dear Eli. I'm just so glad you will wait, now, until the end of your Visit. And you know how over-joyed I am to learn of Garo's liberation from the 'bargain' struck by his father with Aulfrelas! That is **wonderful** news. And are you sure that Alégondine is contented in her choice? For that is as great a decision to take as yours, my sister. But, you know, somehow I can easily see that dark and mysterious Princess as a Mage. She seems to fit that role very well. She has always seemed to me to be a fairy like no other, so aloof and so *complete*, if you know what I mean."

"Yes, that is true," agreed the Queen. "She will, I think, be very wonderful as a Sage-Hermit; she will be the perfect fairy for that role which blends light and dark, just as twilight does. She is suited very well to the wild island of the Star and to all of its mysticism.

"Now you, both of you, must learn to what role and world *you* are suited: to which realm you shall belong. For you are both, at this time, part-fairy and part-woman. And you are both at cross-roads now. So keep your hearts open to Truth and Joy, and to Love. Then you, like Alégondine, will be sure to make the right choice of path.

"Now, let us go to our mid-day meal, and then I propose that we might have a little music. What do you think, my dear young ladies?"

They dined, the three of them, together. Even the two hounds did not join them, allowing them to enjoy being simply a feminine and very contented threesome for their lunch. And afterwards, they became a trio of musicians.

Making their way to the Queen's lovely Music Room, they played together --- Eli on Róisín and Brocéliana on the painted dulcimer, while the Queen sang in her sonorous mezzo-soprano twilight-blue voice as she played Gaëtanne --- and many airs gay and winsome, major and minor, dark and light were shared. And so beautiful was their music that it seemed that the very walls and all the nearby rooms vibrated ecstatically and harkened to this miniature chamber-orchestra of royal players.

****

"Come with me, Eli."

Reyse spoke very quietly. It was early evening, and he was walking with Eli around that part of the City beyond *The Tipsy Star*, between two of the slender Star Towers along the north-western wall of the oval. Eli and Jizay had left the Queen to a private moment in her Concocting Cell and Brocéliana to her relaxation and reflections in the library of the King's Tower. Ferglas had taken himself off to the King's private apartments, although Aulfrin had not yet returned to Fantasie from Mermaid Island.

Periwinkle and Reyse had been in each other's company since early morning; and Eli and her golden hound, coming from the King's Moon Tower, had found them near the Yellow Garden as they crossed the waving grass on their way to Lymeril. Now, having strolled for an hour or so together across these northern meadows, the pixie and Jizay galloped off once again ahead of Reyse and Eli.

"But I *am* with you!" chuckled Eli, as she continued to stroll by Reyse's side along the northern-most arc of the western walls of the City, admiring the many studios of artists and workshops of instrument-makers, the little rooms set aside for meditation and silence, the bakers and candle-makers, the pottery-wheels and the weaving looms, and even a purveyor of goat's cheese. This latest artisan was proud to explain to the delighted Eli that he made his cheeses *only* with the milk <u>given</u> him by the ladies of the Dancing Goat Plains, far in the southeast extreme of Karijan, when they had no use of it for their little ones.

"Sometimes," the charming cheese-maker recounted, "the does and nannies of the dancing goats continue to make milk, even after the kids are suckled; and they offer it to the fairies who sing to them. Well, I've always had an idea that those clever fairies --- oh in the southern parts, there, they are very cunning --- sing the milk right out of them! And then up into Sea-Horse Bay it comes, by dolphin and gull, and from there the cranes and storks, the swans and geese, they are kind enough to bring it to me here, flying low with their little bags and baskets held tight in their beaks, or ridden by small sprites who hold wooden jugs of milk and curd, up the Jolly Fairy River and the Shooting Star Lake, all across Mazilun. For the

King, he's partial to a bit of goat's cheese, and many of the folk here in the City too. But if the goats change their minds ---- and oh my, but goats can do so quickly! --- then there's none at all. So we must accept it when it comes to us, and enjoy it all the more!" Eli had giggled delightedly at his explications.

When they had walked on a little further, Reyse repeated his request.

"Come away with me, for a day or two, to visit your brother Demoran first, and then to restore the Amethyst Cloth to its place. I will be your gallant protector and companion for that mission, as I was when I bore the little Eli in her swaddling clothes to Dawn Rock. And we will have time to talk together, to be together, Eli, on our voyage --- before you … leave. Will you come, please?"

She stopped and looked at Reyse. So many mingled and muddled thoughts, and memories, and stirrings in her heart.

"Yes, alright," she said at last. "I'll ask my father tomorrow when he returns from Mermaid Island. I can't go without his leave. But I think he will agree."

"Thank you, my Lady Eli." A sudden gust of wind blew a flurry of red and butter-yellow leaves in a swirling, almost blinding, cascade around them. Laughing together, Reyse threw one side of his billowing cloak over Eli's shoulders, and held her close against him as they walked through the leaf-storm. They turned back, following what seemed to be the advice of the swirling leaves, to return to the King's Tower before nightfall.

Eli was climbing up to her own bedroom, high in one of the western turrets, when she met the Queen, descending a spiralling staircase from the floor above. The faint, spicy odours of her Concocting Cell still clung to her.

"You also have been to that sweet and pungent room, my daughter?" inquired Rhynwanol as they met and clasped hands. "I could feel your presence there. I am glad. You are not yet a Queen, but I think you will be one day. And already the Vase has opened itself to you, and you have heard wisdom from it, I deem."

Eli breathed deeply, savouring the lovely perfumes of exotic spices, as if she had just stepped into an ancient abbey hazy with incense-clouds of frankincense and myrrh. As the hypnotic image of chanting monks in black robes passed through her mind, she recalled the voice she had heard from the Vase, when she had visited that room with her father. The voice of her grand-mother, Morliande, explaining why brother and sister could not wed. But the strange poem had ended with an even stranger verse:

> *But hearken, my child, to your own heart.*
> *Can you and your love be torn apart?*
> *Magical beings have truth to impart;*
> *And to drink of love is the highest art.*
> *It may be that secrets shall come to light*
> *And you shall be aided in your plight.*
> *Believe, believe without respite,*
> *And seek for the sun in the moonlit night;*
> *Therein will lie your victory.*

The gentle voice of Rhynwanol followed fast on those words echoing in her memory. And so the watery and wistful tones of the Silkie-Queen were blended with the twilight-breeze cadences of her mother.

"Will you come with me there now?" It sounded almost like Reyse's request.

"To listen to the Queen's Head Vase? Because of my decision to return to the world?"

"I do not know what you might hear, if anything, today from the Vase. I simply invite you, for it occurs to me that it will be a pleasant place to share with you."

Eli did not hesitate long, as she regarded the tenderness in the violet eyes of the Queen. "Yes, I would like to go with you, if only to know the joy of visiting with you a place that is so close to your heart."

"Come, then!" And they returned up the spiralling stairs to the winding corridors.

They stepped, together, under the rather eerie arch of the doorway with its leafy heads and faces. Rhynwanol took Eli's hand, the one with the amethyst in its palm. The stone had not disappeared, and Eli had found that rather odd. But she imagined it would no longer be visible when she stepped back through the Portal on the 21st.

Out of the utter dimity of the curved corridor they came into the small, circular chamber, where the primitive-looking Vase reposed on its central table, exuding its glowing titian light.

The verse that had come back to her continued to replay itself in her mind, like a favourite song that one cannot stop humming inwardly. As they drew near to the Vase, the Queen seemed to hear it too.

"That is the voice of Morliande," she whispered. "Do you hear it, Eli? Ah, but yes --- it is coming from you and not from the Vase at all! *Seek for the sun in the moonlit night...* Yes. And indeed, you know already, that you will gain wisdom from your harping and already much truth has come to you from many magical beings.

"Do you hear other words, now?"

Slightly surprised that her mother could hear what was said to her, and even what was echoed inside her own head, Eli stepped up to the orange and yellow bouquet of light, sprinkled with flecks of white and red. She closed her eyes.

The scent of roses swept over the room like a breaking wave on a sun-drenched beach. Eli had opened her hands to either side of the Vase, and the palm where the amethyst was set was tingling and very warm.

Windy Hill Prayer

Return Gypsy, Princess, Artist, Queen ---
Your tears are the source of the rainbow's sheen;
Through spiralling waters when all is won
To the loving embrace of both Moon and Sun.

Where had Eli heard that verse before? But of course, yes! It was Piv who had told her that those words were written over her bier on Scholar Owl Island. He had recited them for her before she left Demoran's Castle to come here to Fantasie and then through Wineberry's Gate. Piv had said that she was both Moon-Dancer but also a Sun-Singer, and that such was the meaning of that verse, saying that she would be held in a loving embrace by both.

But now Eli was doubting that interpretation. She felt sure there was more to the riddle, and even to her own poem that had come to her again earlier this year, speaking of a gypsy's tent and an artist's garret.

I must go home.

I have been a liar.
I, who was so nobly born
In the tent of the gypsy.

I have been a thief.
Yes, the same,
Who was royally bred
In the artist's garret.

I must fly home.

I long to hide my face in my father's robes,
And weep and weep.

For here, among grey ghosts
Wandering in a daze-dance

Below the kittenish clouds,
My flight is hindered,
My path obscured.

I must ride home.
To the silver turrets of Fantasie
I must turn again my wind-horse-feet,

And homeward run,
To the arms of my moon
And my sun.

To the red and yellow banners
Of my pure beginnings.

It has begun.

The Queen's Head Vase had fallen silent, but not before Eli had heard all of her own poem, spoken by a voice that was at once hers, and *not* hers. Not who she was now, or yet. And it seemed that her mother had heard it too.

"Step back," whispered Rhynwanol, even more softly than before, but with greater urgency. "The light is too strong now."

Eli opened her eyes, and retreated a step or two, blinking. The Vase had become a fountain's spume of dancing light and colour, like a spout of water reflecting sun-and-moonlight and turning them both to rainbow iridescence. Immediately, as she stepped backwards from it, the fire-work phosphorescence was swallowed back into the Vase, and only the faintest warm glow remained, tickling the edges of the Queen's crown. The pottery eyes were still well and truly closed, but the mouth on the Vase was smiling serenely and broadly.

Neither she nor her mother moved or spoke for several moments. And both were breathing deeply, but not with any anxiety. Eli knew that she had been given keys to unlock many doors now, and clues to solve many riddles. But she could not put words or names on them. Not yet.

Rhynwanol caressed Eli's long, red hair with her slender, gentle fingers. When they had walked slowly out of the Concocting Cell and stood in the fresh, night air of the breezy landing at the head of the staircase once more, the Queen asked an odd question.

"I only *heard* the words in your human tongue, and did not see them in my mind," she began. "Is it : *Through spiralling waters when all is won – w.o.n.*, or is it *when all is one – o.n.e*?"

Eli looked searchingly at her. "I don't know," she replied, and added, "I only heard the words also, and I thought it was w-o-n. But then again it could be o-n-e. I don't know."

As they continued to remain there in silence for another minute or two, Eli recalled, in her mind, the final words of Wineberry to her:

Now you know, child of lilies and follower of unicorns. Now you know! You have sipped the wine, you cannot keep them apart any longer: **Night and light, moon and sun.** *No, no, nevermore apart! All is one, little Princess of the Rose, all is one… All is one, all…is…**one**!*

"Through spiralling waters, when all is…one," Eli repeated, inwardly. "I cannot keep them apart any longer. Night and light and moon and sun. To their loving embrace. I must fly home.

"It has begun."

****

It was not the *evening* of the following day, the 13th, when Aulfrin returned; it was early afternoon. All had gone well, and smoothly, and the King was in merry mood as he entered the small sitting-room with the ornate frog-and-fish pond at its centre. The dragon-lordling Garo, walking briskly just a few paces behind the King, was equally contented, if not quite so exuberant as the monarch.

When the Queen and Eli, Brocéliana and Alégondine had taken their seats around the tiled basin of green water, it was Garo who spoke, at a gestured invitation to do so from Aulfrin. His father had, he reported to the four ladies as well as the bright-eyed pixie *and* the two hounds, humbly presented his apology to the King, at least as regarded the theft of the Amethyst Cloth. He had then formally relinquished his amorous designs regarding the Queen (not mentioning those directed to Mélusine at all, Eli noted) and had announced that he was willing to leave Quillir and take up residence in the Shee of the Red-Eared Hart. With Vanzelle.

Periwinkle asked if Bawn had gone with him.

"Not for the moment," replied the King. "It seems that she considers her place to be in the Bay of Secrets where she has resided for many centuries, and she wishes to remain there. Erreig had spent a day or so already in her company, flying far and wide over Sea-Horse Bay with leaping *tursa* from the fjords of Norway cavorting in and out of the waves beneath them; and at the last he seemed to accept her decision with good grace. Leyano and Garo were happy with Bawn's choice also, as they have struck-up an almost *amicable* relationship with the great beast, and were glad to know that she would continue to preside over the great worms of Quillir.

"But now I must search for a replacement Dragon-Lord," remarked Aulfrin, shaking his head sadly and looking at his feet so as not to reveal the slight grin on his face. "Someone who, unlike Erreig, will swear allegiance to me as his Sovereign, and promise that he will do all in his power to ease the tensions in the clan of the Sun-Singers and win those of my subjects, once in league with Erreig, back into closer harmony with the Moon-Dancers. A true 'Lord of Quillir', as that high position *ought* to be fulfilled in my kingdom."

There was a faint breeze rustling through the pane-less windows, disturbing the vines of berries and rather dry leaves still clinging to their twisted stems. A sleepy goldfish poked its head out of the still, green water of the pond in the room's centre, and then slipped back to continue his autumnal afternoon nap. Brocéliana bit her lip and held her hands quite still on her lap, not daring to lift her eyes to look into those of her love. She breathed deeply, waiting for Alégondine to speak, but her face was quite flushed and she was sure that Garo was staring at her and not looking at the King or at the dusky Princess who now rose to face her half-brother.

At last, the lovely and serene voice of Alégondine resonated in the room, blending with the faint breeze. "I think that you would be well-suited to that role, my dear brother. Bawn has returned to the Bay of Secrets, but she is not able to be ridden by anyone but our father --- at least, not yet. And there are other dragons in Quillir, and Cats too, who will need to be governed and guided, as will the Sun-Singers. You are a shape-changer and a world-traveller, a friend of Stag and wolf and bear. You would make a fine Dragon-Lord to serve the King of the Shee Mor; but you will <u>not</u> be a fine Sage-Hermit, I'm afraid."

Garo's brows were furrowed in confusion at this speech, but he did not reply to his sister's words immediately. Instead, he looked from her indigo eyes to the sparkling emerald ones of the King, and then to those of the trembling Brocéliana, who could not help but lift her head to regard the face of her belovèd.

Garo, son of Erreig and of the silver-fairy Vanzelle, was gifted with subtlety and wisdom, and he had studied many mystical arts with the Great Ones of Faërie. And, as is true of any fairy, he could read and hear more in silences than was revealed in spoken sound. He turned back to his sister, and the deep wells of her profound and starlit eyes seemed to convey the revelation of her news to him before she could utter another word.

"*You* are going to be the next Sage-Hermit?" he whispered, almost as inaudibly as her disclosure of this fact had been made. "You have offered to go to Star Island in my place? I am ... *freed*?!"

"Yes", nodded the stately and shimmering fairy before him. "You are free, as I am in making this choice. Will you accept, now, the honour of becoming the Dragon-Lord of Quillir, in our father's stead? And in two years I will go, as you would have done, to Star Island, to take-up with great joy the wondrous role awaiting me there."

The handsome, rugged face of the brave Garo was streaked with tears, but his smile outshone the sparstones suspended from his pointed ears in their casings of gold. He knelt, first, before his sister, taking both her hands in his and laying his head upon them in reverence and gratitude.

Then he arose and turned and knelt before the King, and wordlessly --- but clearly to all present, including Eli --- he promised fealty and faithful service as Lord of Quillir.

Aulfrin, as silently as the young Dragon-Lord, responded with his acceptance and his delight; as Garo rose, the King extended his hand to Brocéliana, who left her place and came to stand beside her heart's love.

The bright peridots and emeralds sparkled as though they would burst from the delicate silver crown, as Aulfrin placed his daughter's hand in Garo's. Eli could not see the kiss shared by the couple, because joyous tears were filling her eyes. Her hand was joined to that of Piv, sitting on the arm of her chair and --- like her --- almost bursting with overwhelming sentimentality!

Eli could feel her mother radiating the same boundless happiness as the pixie, as she stood to embrace Brocéliana, just as if the young fairy were her own precious daughter.

****

Reyse had not been present for Alégondine's announcement to her brother, and it was towards the end of the afternoon when he reappeared in the Royal residence, and asked to see the King in private; for he wished to obtain permission to take Eli on the voyage he had proposed to her. Later still, about the twilight hour, the Eagle-Lord met Eli in the anti-chamber of one of the dining-halls for a gathering of all the guests before the evening meal. He stood near her and spoke in a confidential whisper.

"Your father is in full agreement that I go with you to the Dappled Woods, and from there to Scholar Owl Island. I told him we would be back in two or three days' time."

Eli looked a little sidelong at her champion, but good-humouredly.

"Are you trying to avoid my being here when Finnir arrives? Everyone seems to expect that he will come here tomorrow morning. Though I suppose my father is happy to have me replace the Cloth in my vault as soon as may be; and he will also be glad to talk in private with the enchanted fairy Prince, whom he now knows is *not* his son and so *not* my brother! I expect that he has some *sensitive* subjects to discuss with him. In fact, I have the impression that --- besides his considering it unwise for me to be with Finnir because we were half-siblings --- the King has a marked preference for *you* as my … *intended*!"

Eli and Reyse were served thin, fluted, crystal goblets of bubbly wine, pale yellow and flowery-fragrant --- very like an excellent champagne. When the attendant with ochre-feathered cap had moved away, Reyse clinked the rim of his goblet with Eli's.

"You may be right, my dearest Lady Eli, as regards *all* of your suspicions! I would like to have time with you before you meet with Finnir once again; it is urgent that the Cloth be restored to its place, and I would also agree that your fine father has always been somewhat favourable to my suit for his daughter's affection.

"There are clearly two camps, in fact, opposing one another in this delicate situation," he continued with a grin. "Certain wondrous ladies, mostly mauve-fairies I might add, are firmly united in their desire to see you become the next Queen of the Sheep's Head Shee. I learned this when I was in that shee this past August.

"There is a good deal of strife in that wind-buffeted island-realm, owing to the rather *foreign*, almost alien, nature of Finnir's parents. The Silkie-Queen and her daughter-in-law Rhynwanol are both of the opinion that the blending of Aulfrin's line with that of Tirrig and Biwarry's would sooth and reconcile many of the fairies there. One branch of that shee's population would like to see Dursol and Rhysianne return to their thrones, while another contingent is quite happy to have the new and incredibly enchanted beings as their rulers. It has become a rather a tense situation. But, as I say, four gentle-women --- Rhynwanol, Morliande, Lily (when she was there) and also the Queen Biwarry herself, the mother of the great Prince, are all convinced that you and Finnir, as the wedded monarchs of the Sheep's Head, would resolve all disputes and divisions and bring peace to that land.

"Your father, on the other hand, wise and wonderful fairy that he is and a close friend of mine for many hundreds of years, joins with one or two other extremely sensible fairies to form the camp of those who would be *very* happy to see you with *me*. You would not become a queen, it's true, because I am *not* a king; my shee, the Shee of the Dove, does not have a royal family. We might found one, of course, if we wished. But I am also very happy to welcome a *princess* --- purely and simply that and nothing more --- into my noble family. And into my loving arms."

Eli could not help but smile. Reyse's charm and persistence would soften anyone's heart, she thought.

"When do we leave?" she asked, after they had sipped their wine in unison.

"It is the half-moon tonight, and she is already high overhead. She will not set, though, until after the middle of this night is past. I have requested permission of your father to abscond with you after this *apéritif* together, arriving at your brother Demoran's Castle for a late supper. We go by flying-horse --- for I've also talked over these plans with Peronne of course, with whom I visited the Stone Circle earlier today. He had only returned late last night to the Shee Mor, by way of Finnir's (or Timair's) Portal. It's evident that he had greatly enjoyed his little hiatus with the *second* golden eagle and that fine bird's cousins in County Cork.

"But as Peronne is here in Fantasie, once more a flying-horse rather than a white-tailed sea-eagle, he is ready and willing to bear you off into the western winds in my company. We leave as soon as you can fling on your riding clothes and your royal-blue cape, my dear Lady."

"You have everything worked out, I see," Eli chided him, but her eyes were sparkling. "And does Demoran know that we're coming?"

"Corr-Seylestar was sent flitting over the King's Rise and into the Dappled Woods over an hour ago. Yes, the Prince of the Fair Stair will be aware of our plans well in advance of our arrival. And he will be glad to welcome us, *together*. He is among the wise fairies of the second camp."

"Is he?! Well," sighed Eli exaggeratedly, followed by a short laugh. "I had better say my farewells to my father and mother, Jizay and Piv. And to Brocéliana, Garo and Alégondine too. They will still all be here, I hope, when we return…"

Her farewell kisses concluded, and her attire changed, Eli joined Reyse once more, out on the high courtyard where both their steeds had flown up to receive their riders. Peronne was pawing happily at the marble-tiled ground --- impatient to set off, his grey coat and its partial white moon-motifs enhanced by the silver beams from the real half-moon poised over the turrets of the shadowy towers. Eli greeted him with a long embrace, both her arms wrapped around his arched neck.

Beside him was Reyse's winged-horse, an olive-green-eyed mare whom Eli had not met before.

Reyse introduced her as Habukaz, a glorious bay-leopard-appaloosa with creamy-yellow wings whose undersides were a rich gentian-blue; they were very similar in their play of colours to Peronne's wings, though the latter's were more an even mixture of these hues throughout. The horses seemed already to know each other well.

"She is absolutely exquisite," Eli enthused, stroking the mare's neck where mahogany-bay spots were artistically arranged on a background of vellum-white. "Why have I not seen her here with you before?"

Reyse helped Eli onto Peronne's broad back. "Habukaz usually remains in my own shee. You have, in fact, seen her once or twice --- in your former life here, my dearest Eli. But it is true that she comes with me rarely, and usually only for important adventures. She was with me when I was your tutor on the White Willow Isles, for I had been flying very far and free just before that. And about the same era as my interlude as your teacher, she accompanied me when I assisted your brother Leyano in his third Initiation, passed with falcons, eagles and holy white hawks. But *you* had not yet discovered, in those days, the joy of flight on horseback, and so my own winged-steed was not paramount in your concerns. You were more interested in unicorns, or so it appeared!"

Reyse had mounted Habukaz, and as his twinkling eyes glinted once more at Eli, his horse turned and broke into a canter towards the balustrade, leaping into the moonlit sky on her third stride.

"Come with *me*, Licorne!" he sang out over his shoulder with a laugh, as Eli and Peronne followed swiftly, running up a moon-beam, it seemed, and flying high over the northern walls and the turrets and banners of the King's Tower.

****

Demoran was, indeed, delighted to see them. They enjoyed a relaxed and intimate supper together, late that night. Most of the news seemed to be known to the inscrutable Prince: the Queen's return two days earlier, the revelation of Finnir's and Timair's true identities before the King, and even the deepening of Eli's own resolve to go back to the world after this Visit.

Eli shook her head at her middle brother with affection.

"It is nice, as you once confessed to me," she grinned, "very nice, that *someone* knows almost *everything* that's going on!"

"<u>Almost</u> is the key term there, I'm afraid," he retorted, looking rather seriously at her now. "I must admit that I had not imagined the change in Garo's fate with the amazing offer of our half-sister, Alégondine, to become the next Sage-Hermit. That is a solution born of love, no doubt about it. Well, that is where true solutions are always born.

"And though I knew our mother was sailing to the Silver City with her most exotic daughter, I did not expect her to go there *directly*. Still, she was no doubt eager to rediscover her husband and her home.

"Or, perhaps, she was hesitant to make any diversions to right or left of her path before consulting with the Queen's Head Vase..." he added, in a hushed tone.

Eli caught her brother's eye for a moment, but did not comment on his words. She turned back to gaze into the mingled orange, red and yellow flames of the fragrant fire before them. Reyse passed her a bowl of mulled apple-juice and then he and Demoran served bowls for themselves.

Numerous calico cats, as colourful as the dancing fire-figures in the hearth, snoozed about the room. On a cushion beside Eli was Ruilly, his thick grey fur glinting silver in the candle-and-chimney-light. His bright rabbit-eyes, ancient and merry, looked kindly and rather condescendingly at the visitors to this Castle, clearly *his* home as much as Demoran's!

He twitched his long white whiskers as he remarked, quietly and sweetly, "Solutions and love, ah me! Yes, there is love, long love, between the dark fairy Alégondine and her brother, and love also unites the twilight-Princess to her grand-parents, Aulfrelas the Serene and Morliande of the silkie-seal-folk. She bears a deep and fraternal love, too, for the great Prince Timair, who was oft accorded the honour of walking upon the bright Island of the Star, where the Princess will soon dwell. But the first love I mentioned is perhaps the deepest, for she bears a tender and laughing and leaping affection for her half-brother Garo, the darling of Hart and Great Tree and the sweetheart of the beauteous rabbit-friend Brocéliana. Ah, great and wide love she has, indeed indeed, and as far-reaching as her violet-voyages in an abalone-boat; for Alégondine will become the Mother-Mage --- our very own Abbess, might I suggest --- as the Alliance unites, closer and closer, the spiralling stars. Yes, yes, much love, and many loving solutions radiate from her."

Ruilly raised his tufted head a little further and regarded Eli squarely. "And *you* propose a loving solution too, bold Eli-élusine. Your great gift to young Brocéliana was to have a full two years more with her lover, before his duties stole him from her. But now, you can offer even greater joy to your sweet sister, for by your sacrifice --- if indeed you step back over the oaken heart-threshold under the toes of the two little owls --- she will have the long centuries of her fairy-life to live out her romance with the gallant Garo.

"Well and good, very good," continued the rabbit. But there was a chillier air in the room now, and Eli could not feel from whence it blew. "But you give to the young lovers with one hand, and with the other you will take the Princess Mélusine from the Alliance, for these years so crucial and so charged with change. Yes, I know, you can do wondrous good with your Harp of the Golden Rose, for healing and hope flow from her singing strings, it is true. But what would Mélusine do *here*, in the years ahead? And with *whom* would she unite her powers, becoming as radiant as a rainbow of soaring light stretched between the Sun and the Moon? Will your sister find joy in the wake of your sacrifice... such a great sacrifice made for her? She is as small and frail as a white moth on a stem of lavender; can she bear such a *burden* of love?

"I will suggest another *vision* of this 'solution' to you, Lady Eli of the unicorns and roses. Listen well to an old rabbit who has poked his long ears into the deepest burrows of this love-filled land of Faërie, and knows the secrets of mushrooms and dragons, Giant Cats and small Beltaine-birds. Listen, and consider well the fact that each quandary may attract myriad resolutions to itself."

And now Ruilly's furry voice became a sweetly chanted song:

> *Love's balance is two-fold: foot and wing,*
> *Days of laughter, nights of bliss;*
> *In music, both bass and treble sing,*
> *Now further, now closer: a tear, a kiss.*

> *Human heart needs human love,*
> *'Tis a gypsy-dance in stolen lands;*
> *While the highest marriage of fairy hearts*
> *Ah, that will wither in human hands!*

> *The moon-flower blooms in sacred ground,*
> *While a rose, unfading, travels far.*
> *When Sun-eyes see and Moon is round*
> *Will a path be cast from a bright sea-star?*

> *A door, a road, a treasure-chest:*
> *Have you the token to beg the key?*
> *With infinite Truth the heart is blest,*
> *So what prevents us to be free?*

> *A single Cloth, sundered and torn.*

A single heart, but loving two.
Restore the theft, the heart reborn
Will surely know what she must do.

So brief a time to grow and give;
A handful of years before the night
Beckons you back: will you not live
Each of those moments in love and light?

"Ah me..." sighed Ruilly, his lyrics' last line drifting off on the current of cool air that had come into the room, and now wafted out again. The fire blazed in its jolly dance, and the rabbit lazily scratched one long ear with a back paw.

He mumbled, somewhat sleepily, "The Lord Reyse here, he is a fine fairy; and he knows the world very well. Oh, and the Prince Finnir, of the royal family of the White Kangaroo Shee, he can charm purrs from the mightiest of the ferocious felines or a silver horn from the forehead of a horse! He is altogether magical, like the play of diamond-sun-stars on the waters of the Innumerable Falls. But to be his Queen, that would require a feat as enchanted as the phoenix-bird whose pyre is nothing more than a mass of yellow-blossomed mimosa! Can you match that feat, Rose Princess? Your destiny, they say, meanders with the horned-horses of the Glens; but though they walk on carpets of myriad years of silver-leaf-fall, can they be corralled in the oval of just *one* such Leaf?"

Eli had looked at Ruilly as he spoke, but now she returned her gaze to the fire, thinking of the yellow mimosa and the Silver Leaf, the ghostly unicorns and infinite blue of the Prince's eyes. The Black Key floated into her reverie, almost as incongruous --- she thought --- as when it had floated on the surface of the waters to be plucked from them by the webbed hand of the Lady Ecume. And then she saw, in a corner of her heart, Finnir's re-awakening and liberation, and the ghostly Chapel of Windy Hill in Reyse's vision.

"I can, I will, fulfil my destiny. Yes, wise Ruilly, I believe I will do so, even if I cannot see exactly what that destiny is, yet. I may be only a human now, but I am born a fairy; at times perhaps a gypsy, but I'm surely not a thief. As Finnir can turn a horse into a unicorn, so I can transform --- one day --- my human life back into its fairy one. And not by returning to Faërie through *his* Portal, but at the close of my full and long changeling-life by coming through wild waters and hidden paths. I *will* find my way, and achieve my phoenix-feat..."

It was not Ruilly who responded to Eli's soliloquy, it was the disembodied and perhaps imagined voice of her father: a memory of his voice reporting words from her mother. It was Rhynwanol's message which he had received, through his harp, to give to Eli before she went through the Gate of Wineberry:

All dreams are like Life itself, using symbols, often in poetic or riddling scenes, replacing one character or event with another --- not to confuse or to lie, but to draw you into deeper understanding of the heart's fragility... and of the heart's ultimate victory.

Eli found herself wondering if the Fourth Portal, as she was dreaming of it now, was merely a symbol of something else. If Finnir himself had been a symbol of something, and Leyano too, when she had seen them on the Island in Loch Eil. Had they *really* been there? Had that encounter been the 'real' one, or was her previous vision of it --- fearful and confused --- on the Hill of the Sun, just as 'real'? Had the tender and glorious kisses shared with Finnir in Gougane Barra been true, or a dream? Was everything just a symbol of something else?!

Would she, at the end of her human adventure, find her way home? Her sacrifice and her dream and her high, noble plans, were they --- all of them --- metaphors of other things, of other 'realities' invisible to her from where she now stood?

Unsure if Reyse or Ruilly or Demoran had heard the words of her mother that had seemed to ring so clearly through the shadowy room, Eli looked up from her rather trance-like gaze into the flames. Her eyes fell first on Reyse's. Now, in the firelight, the bright circles around his pupils were like molten gold. But his brown eyes were a little sad, sweetly sad and yet filled to overflowing with love.

Demoran rose and passed a short, yellow candle on a crystal saucer to Eli.

"This will light your path, like a sea-star, my dear sister --- only at this present moment it's only a very short and safe path, just leading you to the goal of a soft bed and a good night's sleep! Tomorrow Reyse will go with you to the Island where your sleeping fairy-form awaits the return of her sundered Cloth.

"But let your dreams *see it* as whole, and not torn in two. For as you have so well understood, all is a poem, each thing a symbol for another. But you must know, also, that there is an even greater Truth than that. It is that **all is one**. True of your Cloth, true of the well-spring of your deepest love, and even true of your tired and seemingly-divided heart. All is, in fact, one.

"Sweet dreams, little Moon-Dancer Eli. Good-night."

Eli took the candle, not able or desiring to say a word to either her brother or her champion. She inclined her head, with a little courteous nod, to the venerable rabbit. And she went to bed.

****

Reyse and Eli left Castle Davenia after a leisurely breakfast shared with Demoran and only two of his favourite cats, those --- in fact --- that had ridden with him in his *wyrm-char* when he had taken Eli to the Great Strand. Ruilly did not join them this morning. Demoran explained that the old rabbit was feeling as restless as the leaves in the swirling breezes, and so --- to quiet his mind --- he had gone to discuss the autumn plantations in the gardens with Vintig. Both the ancient fairy-groom and the almost equally ancient Ruilly would also be busy with the preparations for the infinitely complicated sleeping arrangements of the numerous rabbit-families in the Dappled Woods. Hundreds of warrens were being refurbished, enlarged and stocked with dry and comfortable bedding for the winter to come.

Coming out from the stables and gardens, Eli and Reyse decided to enjoy the rich colours of the autumn trees, riding by land rather than flying over the Woods for the forty or so miles of spectacular forest which lay to the north of the Castle. Peronne and Habukaz arched their wings closely around their riders, crossing the feathery tips over their croups. The large, strong-barbed flight-feathers of Peronne's great wings caressed Eli's thighs through her cloak as she twined her fingers in among the strands of his long mane while they walked or trotted along. The amethyst in her left palm was still visible and strangely comforting; it made her feel as though the Queen were with her and protecting her. The moonstone pendant dangled from its fine cord around her neck.

But she didn't need reminding that Reyse was with her.

Weaving in and around the boles of the trees, mostly not quite bare but adorned with clinging leaves in myriad gradations of warm hues, the two riders advanced almost side by side. Reyse's hood was pulled back from his handsome face, and Eli could sometimes watch him for a minute or two, before he felt her regard and turned to smile at her. His chestnut hair hung over his shoulders, resting on the mantle of his sage-green cloak; and his ear-points were now and then visible though his wavy locks, their glistening moonstones calling out to her pendant, and perhaps also to the one set invisibly in the skin over her heart.

Eli had not brought with her the journal of Lily, nor the Silver Leaf in fact. She had allowed the Leaf to remain in her bedchamber in Fantasie, close to the Rose on her harp's brow. In her shoulder-bag she carried the Amethyst Cloth, and Reyse's white rose. And quite forgotten at the bottom of the bag, the bamboo phial from Mama Ngeza.

It was well past mid-day when the riders and their great horses came out from the eaves of the last trees of the Dappled Woods. Another eighty miles lay before them now, over the rolling Star-Grazing Fields, to reach the cliffs which overlooked the Whale Race Sound and the Island of the Scholar Owls. The slightly swollen half-moon was already peeping over the low ridges of the distant Dog-Delight Hills. The couple picnicked under the arms of an oak which seemed to stretch its limbs into the crisp mid-November breeze and wiggle its fingers!

Now they would fly over the miles of rippling grass and the remaining star-flowers of these lands, and out over the Sound as well. Reyse came close to Eli as if ready to assist her, quite unnecessarily but with graceful courtesy, onto Peronne's back. Or so Eli thought. In fact, he first enveloped her in his cloak and his arms, and gently covered her flushed face with many tiny kisses, ending on her lips.

He stepped back --- as if nothing had happened, Eli thought to herself with an inward grin --- and said, "The Lady Eli now goes to the Princess Mélusine, or at least very near to her sleeping form. It is a strange moment for a changeling to draw close to their fairy-form, or so I have always heard said --- at least for a 'normal' changeling!

"Of course, for you tonight, this is not the moment of re-absorption, when the last vestige of the ghost of the human will fall back into the fairy, and re-animate her. But I imagine it will present a sensation that is surprising and fragile, a liminal hesitation wherein you will desire to be 'yourself' once more, a very strong urge to re-unite your *separated* selves; rather like the Cloth will wish it were not torn in two! Be prepared for that moment, my dear Eli. Be aware of it, and be ready."

She looked deeply into the brown and gold eyes of her companion. Then when she had mounted Peronne, with his gallant help, she kept her hand holding his for an instant longer. The ruby in his palm, the *Blarua Criha-Uval*, which he had said was 'powerful, rare and wonderful', touched the jewel still manifest in her own hand. Their joined hands glowed for a second, as if the colours were combining in an artist's palette, red and purple, making a soft aura of a rich burgundy shade --- as deep as the wine in the cup that had materialised among the black-berry bushes on the threshold of Wineberry's mountain-door.

"Garnet red," thought Eli. "Like the *blood-moon* (as it is often named), the garnet-red moon of a lunar eclipse, an eclipse as on the night of my human birth, when this same wonderful fairy had carried me as an infant across the Northern Seas. Like the Garnet Vortex, which I pray Finnir will help me to unlock with the key given us from the mysterious Barrimilla --- I suppose in return for the Flaming-Moon Ear-ring. Like the garnet gem-stone in my left ear-lobe, set there by Banvowha, the rainbow-fairy.

"What did I learn in that final Initiation? What wisdom was won then that the sleeping Mélusine knows, and Eli does not?

"Who *is* that fairy, the Mélusine that I am, that I will be, again --- I hope --- one day?

"And who am I *right now*?"

In steady flight, under the rising moon, Eli and Reyse arrived at Scholar Owl Island in roughly two hours. The sky was no longer a rich afternoon blue; it was the deep and twilight colour of shaggy cornflowers, and the few fast-floating clouds were tinged with a rosy, peachy gold. These were the two hues of the blossoms which had appeared in the chalice, the Dragon-Flower chalice, recalled Eli: yes, cornflowers and pinky-yellow roses --- just like these clouds.

They landed in a clearing among stately cedar trees, darkly clad in their foliage of intricate needles, smelling of sacred spices. In all of the trees were gigantic Owls, silver and black.

There must have been close to a hundred of these birds, watching them with a hushed and yet benevolent intensity.

They dismounted and walked deeper into the cedar grove, a miniature but towering forest *crowded* with Owls. Habukaz and Peronne followed close behind. And as they advanced, now one, now two, now ten or twenty of the great Owls took flight and whirred silently through the dark boughs on either side of them. Twilight had already given way to deep purple night, as if time had leapt forwards by several hours. But they had walked for only a short while, or so it seemed.

Eli could hear coastal waters again now, though they had left the southern shores of the Island far behind.

"We are already nearing the Cusp of the Heart Cockles," whispered Reyse, his hand holding hers. "I can hear the waves breaking and the spray hissing. We are nearly arrived at your vault."

They stepped out of the creaking cedars and onto a secluded lawn dotted with small, neat rose bushes --- unnaturally, for November, filled with buds and full-blown, fragrant flowers all gleaming white in the brilliant moonlight. Perhaps thirty or forty feet before them was a great and dim mound like a perfect dome, covered with long, blowing grasses and draped with trailing vines of heavily scented mauve flowers interspersed with long, pointed silver leaves.

Two distinct columns of trellised and interwoven branches --- or perhaps they were slender trees --- stood three feet apart, just in front of the dome. Climbing up and over these pedestals were dense growths of jasmine, and atop each sat a statuesque Owl, blinking at the visitors with huge orange eyes filled with reflected moonlight and sparkling stars.

Between the Owl-guardians was a slim, silver door. Tracery designs were carved onto its surface, but as one looked they moved and turned, coiled and uncoiled, crossed and separated. The door stood slightly ajar.

"Do you wish me to go in, and replace the Cloth on your body, Eli?" asked Reyse without speaking. "Or do you wish to go in yourself?"

In similar silent language, after a very deep breath, Eli replied...or rather asked:

"Could we go in together?"

She could feel Reyse's smile without being able to see his face, shadowed by his hood now. He tightened his grip on her hand, they stepped forward, and with her free hand Eli pushed open the animated door, which sang on its silver hinges like a multitude of chanting spiders.

Eleven Owls sat on golden branches protruding from the inner walls of the domed vault. As Eli's eyes adjusted to the dim light thrown from one large candle near the far wall, she saw that they were not branches, but tree roots, and not golden but rather a polished fawn-brown.

"There is surely a huge tree on the top of the mound," thought Eli, "to push such massive roots through the earth and stone and into this hallowed place." But she had not seen one.

Hallowed and holy this chamber surely seemed. It was like being in an abbey and a cathedral and a saint's-grotto and a crypt-sepulchre all at once. Like being under a waterfall or in a limitless desert, or like the soaring ecstasy of reposing on your back in a field of high grass and looking up into a starry sky with your true love lying beside you.

A bier of pale purple crystal stood in the room's centre. Mist hung around it like the swirling aurora of the Great Trees, only it was more restrained and less colourful. This mist was only mauve and white and silver, with tiny flecks of spinning gold twinkling in it, like minuscule metallic-hued butterflies. As she stood, with Reyse tall and strong and solid beside her, his warm hand firmly holding her trembling one, Eli saw the mist part --- just for an instant --- and she could discern a body lying on the crystal bed, wrapped like a chrysalis in mauve, in *amethyst* Cloths.

Another very deep breath, and Eli's eyes became fully accustomed to the faint light. She could see through all of the swirling mist now. She released Reyse's hand as she said, still wordlessly and in utter silence, just speaking with her heart:

"I'm going forward on my own from here, Reyse. I am strong enough. I can do it."

As soon as she had stepped away from him and towards her own sleeping form, the calligraphy on the wall or rounded ceiling beyond and above Mélusine became luminous and legible.

Return Gypsy, Princess, Artist, Queen ---
Your tears are the source of the rainbow's sheen;
Through spiralling waters when all is one
To the loving embrace of both Moon and Sun.

As Eli read the final line, she could hear Reyse's voice again, whispering still and soft inside her.

"You are my Sun and my Moon, Mélusine. As I am yours. *That* is the loving embrace…"

She did not turn, and she made no reply. For while she had read, she had reached her hand into the shoulder-bag and touched the Amethyst Cloth. And now, as she pulled it forth and held it up before the chrysalis-form of her own fairy-body, everything changed.

She was in an open field, sunny and warm, flower-filled and breezy. It was the Island in her vision and in the Scottish loch, but it was not. A dragon was perhaps wheeling away from her, a man or a knight or a king was perhaps standing nearby, but both were insignificant compared to this. Compared to the Truth of her wide-flung arms and her blowing red hair and her joyous laughter. She felt what it was to be simply and perfectly herself, and whole and complete. She felt victorious, and <u>alive</u>.

"All is one," she affirmed inwardly. "I am one, I am myself. **I am**…"

She held up the two pieces of the Amethyst Cloth before placing them on the shrouded body. But they were not two. Only one piece of Cloth was in her hand, complete and un-torn and whole. And she laid it in its place: on the scarce-breathing body of the Princess Mélusine. On her waiting self, on her true life, on the keeper of her deep wisdom and profound courage and invincible confidence and *joie-de-vivre*.

But no *body* was there. Or perhaps the vision was a dream of a kind of a body and the symbol of the Truth, too beautiful to hold its shape before the eyes of the human Eli.

Its fore-legs tucked under its petal-soft breast, its finely curved back extended over its comfortably bent hind-legs, its long and wavy mane draped prettily over its arched neck, its concave head with pointed ears and closed eyes and spiral silver horn, reposing peacefully on the crystal bier: a unicorn was all Eli saw. A sleeping unicorn.

All dreams are like Life itself, using symbols, often in poetic or riddling scenes, replacing one character or event with another --- not to confuse or to lie, but to draw you into deeper understanding of the heart's fragility… and of the heart's ultimate victory.

"My victory, the victory of my heart," repeated Eli to herself. "Although tonight it is my fragility, my heart's fragility --- it is *all my own*. My victory <u>will</u> be won, and all will be **one**. All *is* one, even now. I'm going forward on my own from here, Reyse. I am strong enough. I can do it."

She repeated that final phrase as if it were the refrain of a hymn. And then she spoke to the blurry vision before her, unicorn or princess or poem or dream:

"I promise you, will go back into the world, Mélusine. And I will live and die as Eli. And then I will return here. I will return to Faërie, when all is won. And when *all is one*."

****

Chapter Eighteen:
The Painted Dulcimer

A generous waxing moon was setting behind the domed mound, while Eli and Reyse, Peronne and Habukas walked along a pathway leading to the northern cove known as the Cusp of the Heart Cockles. As the narrow lane descended between banks of overgrown and shadowy rocks, the Cockle-Cusp came into view below them. Off the point of the extraordinary cove, Eli could just make out three tiny islets, like grey jewels placed on a wrinkled blue fabric; while farther out in the final reaches of Faërie's sea-borders was the Starfish Skellig, a moonlit pinnacle-finger of pale stone pointing heavenwards like a slender arrowhead.

"I wanted to show you the Cusp and its small islands, before we leave," Reyse's hushed voice whispered close in Eli's ear, like someone murmuring shyly in the midst of a solemn church service. "It's where Peronne and I flew from, fifty years ago; though on that occasion the night was stormier!"

"Reyse," asked Eli, her arm tight about his waist as they stood looking out over the bay, its writhing surface reflecting the dancing stars which were brightening now with the moon's departure. "Why did you say *that* to me, as I was replacing the Cloth? Why did you say that about the Sun and the Moon, and the loving embrace?"

He turned his face to hers, and his expression was amused and rather perplexed. "Say *what*?! I said nothing to you then, not at such a private and breathless moment, my dear Eli. I was suspended in timeless silence, as I supposed you were."

Eli was regarding him now, too, and their faces were very close. He continued, "I heard *your* voice, only in my heart, saying that you were strong enough to go on alone. I hoped you meant just to the bier of Mélusine, and not as regards other destinations and choices."

He was smiling, but Eli felt the anxiety in his voice.

"But you did not speak to me, after that? You did not call me by my fairy-name, and say that I was your Sun and Moon?"

He turned fully to face her now, and pulled his hood from his head; and then he lowered hers as well, with gentle fingers.

"My lovely Eli, I very rarely call you 'Mélusine', for you are not come back into her form and life again. And I didn't feel you tempted to merge with her in the vault, as I feared I might. Although I did *not* say the words you seemingly heard, perhaps I didn't need to. Maybe, quite simply, they came from your own heart.

"You are, indeed, my Sun and Moon, my sky of stars and my garden of roses. I think you know that very well, for I have been telling you as much, in perhaps less poetic words, for quite a long time now. But since you have chosen to become the changeling Eli, I have only made my loving declarations to Eli, and not to Mélusine. This evening I am with Eli --- *as* you are now, and *who* you are now. It is true, I am *also* in love with the Princess asleep on her bier of mauve crystal; but she is standing before me in another form tonight, and so it is as I find her at this *present moment* that I love her. I might add that I think that's the best way, the only way really, to love."

Eli, though still somewhat confused, felt also deeply touched, but nonetheless filled with questions. Had she invented that voice, or imagined Reyse saying those words to her? Or had she mistaken the voice to be that of her eagle-champion, when it was not? Was it *another* voice which had made that declaration?

Was it, in fact, because she had now met Finnir that she had projected *his* enchanted, imaginary presence into the scene, hearing a *phantom* message from him; and was that the reason why her sleeping self had taken on the appearance of a *unicorn*?

But whatever might be the explanation for the mysterious words and vision, of two things she felt sure. The first was that she would honour her vow to her true and magical fairy-self by going back into the world and by seeking to return to Faërie *after* her human life. She was utterly resolved now, and also sure that she --- as Mélusine --- had planned this to be her choice of paths.

But she was sure of a second thing also.

She was sure that Reyse was right. The only way to love is in the *present*, and to love the beloved as he or she is in this very moment, not who they might or might not become in another. She made a very firm pledge to herself now, to Eli and not to Mélusine. She promised herself that she would *never* --- especially in the years stretching before her in the world --- love an imagined projection of past or future; she would love, whenever she did love, only what was real and clear and *here*. She would never again fall in love with the ideas and illusions of what a person *might* be. She would only ever love their *truth*.

"Look!" whispered the Eagle-Lord, pointing out into the rough seas encircling the Starfish Skellig. "Another friend has come to support you in your mission here tonight!"

With his arm about her again, and both their long cloaks and their loose hair blowing out behind them from as they stood on the cliff ledge, Eli followed the direction of Reyse's extended arm. There, leaping through the deep blue waters just to the east of the far-off islands was a huge sea-serpent. Or was it? Did sea-serpents have wings?!

"What exactly *is* that?" Eli cried softly, squeezing herself closer to her companion and now laughing. "It's a most extraordinary beast, and a most *ridiculous* colour!"

"The Mauve Dragon, a very dear friend of yours, by all accounts," laughed Reyse with her now. "I have never met her, though I have heard many tales, for she is not only close to the Princess Mélusine, but to the Prince Finnir also. And yes, I must agree with you, that's quite an original colour, though very lovely, for a dragon --- even a sea-dragon!"

The marvellous winged-water-worm had surely seen them, for it flipped its glistening lavender-rose tail gleefully, and exhaled a luminous puff of pale yellow fire and deep red smoke into the cold night air. Both Eli and Reyse continued to laugh, and to hug, as they watched the Mauve Dragon swim in a series of leaping arcs, far-off to their right, finally disappearing around the contours of Scholar Owl Island, presumably heading back towards the mainland.

They mounted their flying-horses, ready to take to the skies and make their own way to Davenia's shores also, to return to Demoran's Castle in the Dappled Woods.

****

The moon had long ago set, oval and golden, when their two steeds came down to land in the dark gardens before the Castle's northern Entrance Door. When Habukaz and Peronne had wandered off to the elegant stables, the tired travellers walked silently up the steps, took hands for a moment, smiled as they looked deeply into one another's eyes, and then went to their beds to sleep --- perhaps not without various dreams visiting both --- for the few hours remaining of the night.

The morning of the 15th of November brought other arrivals to the Dappled Woods.

The Queen Rhynwanol was eager to see her middle son, with whom she had been very close before her banishment and also during the arduous months of his incarceration in the Red Hoopoe Mountain. She was a little perplexed that Demoran had not come to Fantasie on the 11th of November --- though he had been invited to do so --- to celebrate her home-coming to the Silver City. His mother had, therefore, decided that it behove her to go to him. And with her, at her warm request, had come Brocéliana.

Reyse and Eli were still sleeping soundly, and so even by mid-morning were not yet arisen. Thus the Queen and her gentle half-fairy companion, having set off from Fantasie very early, were greeted only by Vintig, several cats and the young fairy-in-waiting, Calenny. The Prince Demoran, explained the soft-spoken gardener-groom, had left the Castle the previous evening. He had, evidently, wished to watch the half-moon-set of middle-night from the shores of the Great Strand.

Rhynwanol, of late showing so clearly her returned cheerfulness and gaiety, became serious and thoughtful at his words, as though she had suddenly found herself in a dim and windowless room, offering no view of this morning's pale sky and its wispy cloud-forms. As she and Brocéliana made their way into the Entrance Hall and Calenny opened the door to the little sitting-room, laid for breakfast, the Queen addressed her words to Brocéliana in a low voice.

"I wonder, is my son very sorrowful or even embittered that I did not stop to greet him before all others --- when Alégondine and I sailed up the River Dragonfly from Kingfishers' Temple? We *could* have turned aside at the delta of the Turtle Shell Rivers, or sent word to him to come to those shores to meet us, it's true. But I had thought that he would surely come to Fantasie. Now, he must know that we were arriving here today, and yet he has chosen to absent himself by moon-watching from the wild western coasts! Ah me, I hope he is not brooding in bitterness."

Calenny had withdrawn, and Brocéliana looked lovingly at the violet-eyed Rhynwanol, watching her and waiting for her to take her place at the table before sitting, herself, opposite the Queen and allowing a faint smile to settle on her heart-shaped mouth.

"I had the privilege of coming to know the Prince Demoran, my half-brother, a little better when I last sojourned in this Castle, at the time of Eli's second Visit, in fact. I recall him telling me that he had known the sting of great and deep sorrow when you left this shee in 1367. But since that time he has lived many adventures, and learned much. He has become --- if I read the shining spirit-light of his eyes aright --- the bearer of a profoundly peaceful but nonetheless *light* heart. I do *not* think he retains any bitterness now, nor any anger, nor even much melancholy at all, in his fine character.

"He voyaged long and far, he confided in me," she added, "soon after that event, and he was yet very young --- only seventeen, I believe, then. Yes, I think that was the age he told me; he had only recently won the tender-blue tourmalines he wears in his ears, and *they* bore away much of his anguish and woe on their sweet azure currents of energy. He won those jewels in his second Initiation, did he not?"

The Queen nodded, gazing with interest and deep respect at the face of the beautiful young maiden before her. Brocéliana continued, pouring a cup of golden tea for her step-mother as she spoke.

"He was given them while hosted by small blue flowers, and blue-birds also, as I recall. And the gems were brought from a very distant shee, and presented to him... by his mother, by you."

The long, white fingers of Rhynwanol encircled her tea-cup as she placed it silently back onto its saucer and looked even more intently at Brocéliana's twilight-hued eyes. But now her gaze passed from the youthful fairy's eyes, to her ears.

"You bear tourmalines also, and like Demoran in your ear-lobes," whispered Rhynwanol. "I had not looked closely at them before; nor had I noticed the tiny points of clear quartz set beside your eyes --- even as Timair has nuggets of amber in that sacred and very unusual position."

Brocéliana smiled a little more broadly now. "I have gemstones which link me with several members of my fairy-family," she said slowly. "Even with you, Your beautiful Majesty. For embedded over my heart (at the completion of my second Initiation, when I was sixteen) is a lavender-pink kunzite, very like the gems which are set into your ears and those woven into the strands of your midnight-black hair."

The Queen opened her eyes wide, and then she closed them for an instant, as if allowing herself to see and feel, inwardly, the force of the stone set into Brocéliana's breast. When she opened them once again, her eyes were sparkling, and she too was wearing a smile.

"Indeed," she nodded. "I bear *lilac* kunzite gems, very like your *lavender* one. And I perceive that yours was awarded you by the sprites of the lavender-spikes, and by their attendant white moths. This confirms what I had already sensed: the grace and beauty you bear in your heart, a heart which is infinitely kind and loving. This is perhaps why Alégondine tells me that she sees you playing a vital role in the Alliance; for you are gifted with a 'universal' *tenderness* and the gentle strength which always accompanies that radiant attribute.

"But it is your pale, robin's-egg-blue tourmalines which intrigue me most," continued the Queen, as both women sipped their tea and shared a slice of rich nut-and-cardamom cake. "I can feel that they are with you since a very young age, from your first Initiation I would guess. But they do *not* come from the blue shee, the Shee of the Bull, whence I drew forth those bestowed upon my dear Demoran. From which shee *do* they come, and from what creatures, dear Brocéliana? For I cannot pinpoint the source or the host in my mind's eye."

"They were set there by *my* virtuous folk," replied an ancient and calm voice, before Borcéliana could do so.

Ruilly, the grey rabbit, had hopped up onto a cushioned stool and now peeped over the rim of the table, graciously inclining his head to the Queen, and then to the younger woman at his side.

"The Princess was indeed young, only eleven, when she came to us in Vivonny," he explained, languidly grooming his long whiskers with his soft fore-paws. "A blue fairy, or half-fairy, she clearly already was, with faint mists of *lavender*-blue light hung in the air about her chestnut red locks, and a deep kindness in her large eyes. Ah, as remarked one of my many wives, she had the eyes of a doe --- and they also blended mauve with blue, just like the twilight sky, as we all saw from the start! But she herself is *blue*, purely a blue fairy rather than a violet one --- so much is definitely clear.

"Furthermore, when she won her quartz-crystals --- and as you noted well, Your splendid Majesty, she bears them set *beside* those pretty eyes, which is a quite *rare* position -- she was with the rainbow-bees. So, you see, she shares with the Princess Mélusine a little of the guidance of blessed Banvowha too, in her education. But where Mélusine was all audacity and the mystical-magical fireworks of Sun and Moon, her more timid and modest sister here, she was the twinkle of star-reflections in a pool of deep water, its surface no more troubled than the heavens are by the song of a nightingale.

"And speaking of song," added the riddling rabbit, "I wonder have you brought your decorated instrument with you, my little Brocéliana? Yes?! Ah, I am glad of that. For I was ever and always *exceedingly* fond of your strumming and humming! And this day will warrant the blessing of your music, or I'm a hare!"

Ruilly accepted a small slice of cake from the gracious young fairy, and then he resumed. "Now, what may I say about the shining tourmalines, the sweet rabbit-jewels, in her ears?! Yes, yes, very like those of little Demoran they are, but indeed *not* from the Shee of the Bull who blows pastel-blue smoke-rings from his nostrils!" At that, Ruilly giggled at himself, and his tiny, bright eyes disappeared into the wrinkles and white-grey fur either side of his pink nose.

"Those of our Brocéliana," he resumed, "come from a nearer neighbour, the Shee of the Giddy Goats; oh but it is a shee still *far* away over the seas, almost lost in the laughing southern light which we can only see, sometimes, sparkling in the depths of the Heart Lakes near the coasts of Karijan. Strange and long-feathered birds had found and polished her blue gems for us, in their funny shee of capering *capricorni* and curled-up be-spectacled dormice. We besought them for our little blue girl-fairy, and we had them transported to the Shee Mor by dolphin and mermaid, and then overland and underland by rabbit-runner and our own shyly scuttling mice, and we gave them to her with our love and blessings.

"When the sleeping-late Princess, or the Lady Eli as she is still --- and seems set to remain for awhile more --- at last awakens, you shall play for us all perhaps? Yes, yes, a fitting tribute to her success and also a current of kindness to bear her forward to other horizons.

"Ah, but those caressing notes will not be for the Prince Demoran; not this morning, no. As you say, and rightly so, white-moth-maiden of the lavender-spikes, he has gone beyond and above <u>bitter</u> thoughts; but I do not agree that he has escaped the nets of sea-tears in his deepest heart. He has followed the lopsided moon to the long Strand, to beg her take his own sorrows to set with her into the sea-serpent swells. So he is not here this morning, not returned yet, to hear your music.

"He is making his way here though, rather slowly I would venture to add --- for I can hear the echoes of his cat-soft padding feet on the leaf-mould near to the Golden Water. He has left the bleak lands where the little green dragons have their warrens, so he is not far now. But why does he walk so sedately there, and whom does he dream may meet him and urge him homewards? Well, we cannot say. But perhaps her good and long-missed Majesty the Queen will take a swift *wyrm-char* from the chilly autumn Woods, or fly with her own glistening and dew-bespeckled wings, and go to speak with our dear Prince, and urge him homewards with hope and healing … if she believes, as I do, that he is rather sombre-hearted."

Ruilly began to nibble a corner of his slice of cardamom cake, and Rhynwanol breathed deeply, her violet eyes shining and seeming to look out across imaginary landscapes. Then she nodded, and rose slowly, gesturing to both her companions to remain where they were.

And she left the breakfast room.

****

Eli could hear the music before she entered the simple little Music Room beside the Library. She and Reyse had met in the otherwise empty breakfast room, quite late in the morning, and had hastily eaten a slice of cake and shared a pot of tea. But as no one else was there, they had returned to the Entrance Hall.

But then the notes had drifted out to them, across the Library, from the Music Room.

As they arrived two or three cats looked up from woven-rush rugs, as did Ruilly, lying with his paws tucked under his furry grey chest and facing Brocéliana from his place on a cushioned couch draped with flowery, faded purple tapestries. The serene half-fairy smiled, but she did not cease her playing as the couple seated themselves on soft armchairs either side of the rabbit.

The Painted Dulcimer. Eli had heard it in Leyano's Golden Sand Castle, but only in duets with Garo's *bodhrán* or in medley with other instruments. Now Brocéliana played many a haunting solo; and she hummed or chanted simple and sweet sounds --- rather than any distinct lyrics --- intertwined with the twinkling notes.

"This is not *healing* music" thought Eli. "It is *heavenly* music!"

When the tunes had ended and their last notes drifted away, like spring giving way to summer, Eli arose and went to her sister, kissing her auburn-haired head. Brocéliana smiled and greeted them both now.

"I understand, from Ruilly, that the quest you went on has been achieved. You have replaced your Cloth on your sleeping form once again; that is very good news. And today you have an aura of peacefulness all about you still, my dear sister. I'm glad that you had the Lord Reyse with you, too. Ruilly had told me that you would need an *eagle* as well as all the Owls, and --- he said too --- other creatures would be there, but I do not know which ones exactly. He is a riddler, as are all rabbits! Is that not true, dear Master Ruilly?"

The smug ball of grey fur did not reply, at least not directly. He chuckled, and then remarked, "That air you have just played would carry my little Méli-verses quite well, I think. We might set it to that music one day. Yes, the rhyme I chanted for you, dear Rose Princess and world-wanderer. Do you recall?

The moon-flower blooms in sacred ground,
While a rose, unfading, travels far.
When Sun-eyes see and Moon is round
Will a path be cast from a bright sea-star?

...A single Cloth, sundered and torn.
A single heart, but loving two.
Restore the theft, the heart reborn
Will surely know what she must do.

"Oh yes, yes, yes! The decorated wooden dulcimer-damsel could sing those wise words with her trembling strings, and the lavender-blue voice of her player could chant them also --- like a duo of heart and soul, eagle and unicorn, here and there... But she is quite right, it's all a riddle, all veiled in fog and mist and music and mirages. Just like life itself! Well, at least that's the way with rabbits, and our burrowing-and-bouncing lives. But you maybe have ears to hear the answers to my enigmas, though I must say that your little ears are very much shorter than mine!" He chortled to himself again, and seemed to fall asleep.

Eli shook her head, not sure whether to laugh or sigh. But as she hesitated between the two choices, her brother arrived at the door of the Music Room.

"Greetings, my dear sister," he intoned, serenely but as though tired, or at least drained of some energy or freed from some weary worry. "We have just returned, myself and my beauteous mother the Queen.

"Will you come and join us?" he smiled more warmly. "As you are now relieved of the Amethyst Cloth, so I am likewise unburdened, having deposited my own symbolic burdens in those blessed lands where the lunar-headlands look out towards the Great Strand. And, at last, our mother the Queen is here with me. What joy for me to welcome her to the Dappled Woods, and back to this shee which has longed for her for six centuries! Come upstairs into my Conversation Room, where she awaits you all three, and we will talk together."

Eli well-remembered this room, where she had been granted a vision of her mother the Queen through the window created by the Silver Leaf and her harp's Golden Rose. On that occasion, she had learned of the portion of the Amethyst Cloth being taken into the human-world by Erreig, and had been requested --- by her 'three mothers' --- to go after him and retrieve it. It seemed as though that dim scene of the shadowy Rhynwanol in her Castle in the Sheep's Head Shee had been shown her many years ago!

Eli smiled at how much less 'severe and impressive' the Queen seemed to her in person, and also at how different *she* felt since replacing the Cloth in her vault. Her quest was achieved; the torn Cloth was whole again and lay once more upon her sleeping form --- her own body, but which had appeared to her as a glorious unicorn. Her courage was bolstered and her resolve was firm and focused for the future. She surely had a 'heart reborn', as Ruilly's verses had predicted. And it was a heart that certainly knew 'what she must do'.

But she said nothing of these feelings at this time. She watched as Demoran lit the many stubby candles around the cosy little room and she and Reyse sat side by side on a settle just behind the low tiled-table where she had, when previously here, placed her various belongings. Brocéliana, the Painted Dulcimer cradled in her hands, sat on the three-legged stool which Eli had used when playing Roísín.

The Queen spoke to her son as she took her place near him, on a high-backed bench of carven oak roots.

"My dear Demoran, gentle lover of cats and birds, of humble blue forget-me-nots and mighty wise willows, our conversations --- especially those permitted us by dragon-egg-caskets and ice-cages, as well as those offered us today by virtue of wise rabbits and moon-sets! --- were ever rich in nourishment, and warmth, and heart-melodies. But here, finally, we sit side by side once again, able to touch hands as well as hearts, and to feel the dance of light between our eyes!"

As she spoke these words, her glinting violet eyes and the mottled green and golden ones of her son seemed to become united by a soft ray of starlight. Eli moved her hand slowly into Reyse's and their fingers interlaced.

"So *very* glad I am to feel again your closeness, my mother, and to have the graceful field of your vibrating love permeate my home. I have apologised that I did not come to the Silver City for the celebrations honouring your return there; but almost, now, I do not regret that choice --- somewhat *petulant* though I admit it may have seemed! For the thrill of our being truly together again *here*, in more intimate surroundings, suits me better, I think. And I am gladdened also to have Eli and

Reyse with us, and to see and feel their energies combined; and also it pleases me to have my half-sister Brocéliana once again in Castle Davenia."

"And the Painted Dulcimer," added Rhynwanol.

Demoran looked at this mother almost questioningly, but immediately he nodded. "Yes, the instrument of such insight and protection, healing and hope, taken by Aulfrin into the human-lands. For long years before that it was his loyal companion and counsellor; and more recently it has become a protector and a blessing for his half-human daughter here, and guided her on gentle paths as she studied with the Lady Ecume and others."

As the Queen nodded in her turn, Brocéliana began to softly strum the instrument, in such whispered tones that the music was hardly perceptible --- it was as diffused and milky as the light from the candles.

"You have fulfilled your quest, my dear Mélusine," continued Rhynwanol, turning to Eli and smiling her congratulations. "You have travelled far and retrieved the sundered Cloth in Scotland and then laid it, whole once more, on your own fairy-body on the Island of the Owls. And you have seen and heard much, and your heart has grown stronger and surer. Moreover, added to these worthy victories, there is another: there is a rolling wave of great love which I can sense in you, but its source is not clear to me. By the amethysts which bind us, my daughter --- even as I was enabled by the dragon-egg jewel to be in contact with Demoran while he was imprisoned --- I can perceive a new force of love within you since your mission to Scholar Owl Island. It intrigues me…

"I know that you, when still the Princess and indeed long years before her transformation, had pledged your heart to the Prince Finnir; for this reason, I cannot imagine that this swelling tide of tenderness I feel in you is for the Lord Reyse here, your noble and beloved tutor and champion, and your companion on your voyage to your vault. Though worthy many deem him to be of such love, what I feel now does not correspond to that interpretation."

At these words, her mother's voice became ever so slightly more severe and 'parental', to Eli's ears at any rate. But her tone softened again instantaneously.

"No, in fact, it is not love of a *romantic* nature at all, I think. It is like the love celebrated by the jewels of Brocéliana. It is a universal and all-embracing love. Perhaps it is the love you will need in the years ahead --- for the work and wonders you will affect among humankind."

The gentle music of the dulcimer continued to waft about the Conversation Room. The Queen nodded, and smiled at her daughter.

"If you will permit me," interjected Reyse --- and Eli was wondering if her 'champion and companion' was about to declare the depth of his devotion to her, here and now, before her mother! --- "I would like to tell you of some other energy I can feel in this room, for it is a very strong sensation, a marked presence and message, which I myself perceive."

The Queen turned to the noble fairy with an open and attentive regard, while both Demoran and Eli looked with some perplexity at Reyse. Brocéliana, curiously, did not falter in her playing, but seemed to nod her head as the Queen had done earlier, as if she --- too --- could sense the 'presence' to which the Eagle-Lord referred.

He said, "You speak of the all-embracing love needed for our fairy-work in the human-world: I am familiar with this, for I am often in those lands and have, for many centuries, tried to offer my assistance and support to our friends there. I work closely in that role with your two daughters, with Mowena and Malmaza, as you know."

Rhynwanol nodded once again, and she smiled. "Ah," she said in a hushed voice, "I feel the *presence* you speak of now too! Yes, they are here, my two fair daughters, in subtle ripples, in echoes of caring, in 'conversation' with us!"

Reyse resumed. "And there is more than that caring and closeness, I think, Your Majesty. I can feel an *invitation*."

Eli was more and more curious and puzzled. "Am I invited to work with them, in Scotland, Reyse?" she murmured, her hand still clasping his.

"No, not you, dear Eli." It was Demoran's voice. "I can feel it now, also. The Twins of the Stone Circle, yes, they are here in vibrations so soft and silent that it is like a breeze between the stars! But their offer is a beautiful one. Will you go, Brocéliana?"

Eli's eyes were wide with surprise and confusion. "The Twins are inviting *Brocéliana* to join them?" she asked, rather more loudly than she had intended.

The delicate fingers of the young half-fairy became still, remaining gracefully poised over the strings of the Painted Dulcimer on her lap. She was smiling, and the tiny points of quartz beside her deep blue eyes were sparkling like the stars Eli had seen in the cold night skies over Glencoe.

"Yes, I will," she acquiesced in her gentle voice. "I shall go to join them, willingly, and Garo will come too, from time to time. I think that we will be there together, and often, and in other lands, further and frostier. It is a splendid invitation! Garo has gone to the Stone Circle today, or at least that was his plan, and so it is perhaps their very conversation that the Lord Reyse has heard reiterated here.

"For my love and I discussed, yester-eve, our dreams of voyaging back and forth between the worlds, or of meeting there and working together. He is not very used to the *modern* world of mankind, and I have never yet ventured there; but if your kind daughters, dearest Queen, will befriend us --- at least in our first faltering steps --- I believe we will be able to do great good there. And perhaps, then, Eli will not feel that she must leave this kingdom of Faërie at all.

"I will be content to go back there and to rediscover my fully-human life," Brocéliana continued, "and if I can often have

Garo beside me, and have perhaps the charmed blessing of some of my memories left to me of these past fifty years here --- as he says may be possible --- then I am more than happy to return to the world as a human. For it was as a *human* babe that I was born to Lily, though I had the King of Faërie as my father!"

After a short and rather *intense* silence, it was Reyse who spoke again, now addressing the modest Brocéliana.

"I think it unlikely that Eli will change her mind, at least about her return to her human-life at the full moon."

He glanced, Eli half-thought, at the Queen Rhynwanol as he said this ---- but she was not sure.

He then continued, "But this does not counter your desire to go, with the brave Garo, to Scotland or to Ireland, to Iceland or to Norway and Finland, dear Brocéliana. Or further, should you wish! If you remain who and what you are here, you will be well-able to come and go as a royal half-fairy, as I have done in the many voyages I have made into that world; and with Garo's shape-changing skills you might even be visible to the humans as … wolf and rabbit, or in other guises --- who knows?!"

"And if you go there in human-form, as do the Twins," added Demoran, "then you can take the Painted Dulcimer with you. And its healing and helping, its sight and sensitivity, will be as much a blessing to you as they were to Sean Penrohan."

Brocéliana's expression was rather inscrutable, not unlike that so often worn by her father in fact. It was not easy to guess her thoughts as these suggestions were pronounced. She looked down at her dulcimer, and then she raised her twilight eyes to regard the Queen, and then Eli.

But she said nothing more, as yet.

****

Eli was pleased to take a leisurely mid-day stroll with Reyse, just the two of them.

Demoran remained in his Conversation Room with his mother, while Brocéliana rejoined Ruilly and they went to visit Vintig in the gardens, probably to further discuss the winter preparations for the rabbit community, as well as other matters dear to both their hearts.

As a flight of swans passed overhead, before the southern Entrance Doors of the Castle, Reyse proposed a walk to the Red Triskel Lake. Seemingly the swan-host was *en route* for the same destination --- their wide wings whining stridently and yet sweetly as they sailed through the bracing breeze. The music of the swan-flight made Eli's thoughts return to the whispered tones of Brocéliana's playing.

"What do you know of the Painted Dulcimer, Reyse?" she inquired as they crossed the sloping lawn and passed under the branches of the woods, where all the trees were rattling their colourful fingers of quivering autumn leaves.

"You should ask your sister," he replied, "for it has been hers for over forty years."

The couple walked either side of a silver-skinned birch and then, when they drew together again, they took hands.

"I will, when I have the chance, no doubt," she agreed. "But it probably has a very long story, stretching back well before it was the companion of Brocéliana, or even of Sean Penrohan."

"Then, even better than addressing your questions to the lavender-blue half-fairy, you might ask the Lady Ecume," suggested Reyse. "Though I do not know if you will be seeing her again on this Visit --- before you pass back through Finnir's Portal." There was a silence, as if Reyse was inviting Eli to redirect the conversation to that event, and what lay beyond it. But she did not wish to go there, just now, in her reflections.

"Did it actually *belong* to the ancient mermaid, or was she simply the music-teacher of Brocéliana?"

Reyse understood, quite clearly it seemed, that Eli was adamant about looking *backwards* at this moment, rather than peering into her future! He laughed briefly, and then continued, now linking Eli's arm through his and laying his hand over hers, so that his ruby and her amethyst were once again aligned. The pale claret-hued light that their union had emitted before shone gently once again, illuminating the over-laid hands.

"The wondrous mer-harper is not *only* a harper, it is true; and she plays --- very skilfully --- the dulcimer as well, though less often, I believe. She did, indeed, guide the child Brocéliana in her first year or two of study on it, or so I have heard, and thereafter your sister also went, occasionally, to the Castle of the Music-Makers on the southern coast of Mermaid Island. But I do not think that the Lady Ecume ever *possessed* the Painted Dulcimer, not as her own instrument. It was the charmed and healing voice of another fairy.

"It belonged to your grand-father, in fact, before it came to Aulfrin. It was the instrument of Aulfrelas when he had ceded his throne to his son but still remained in Davenia and Quillir --- before he went to Star Island. Or so the stories say."

"He was no longer the King for that entire century between 1200 and 1300, as I understand," nodded Eli. "And it was then that the Painted Dulcimer was his? How interesting. What else do the… 'stories' say, Reyse?"

"Well, they speak of the King *before* Aulfrelas, and how the Painted Dulcimer was created." Reyse was speaking lowly, in a tone at once reverent and suspenseful.

The Eagle-Lord took Eli by the hand once more as he led her over grass and leaf-mould thick with wild-cyclamen and they now approached the shores of the Red Triskel. The ground had risen gently as they walked, and their view of this, the south-western bank, was from a mounded hillock covered with hawthorn trees for the most part. One very old oak tree stood in their midst as well. The waters below them were the same colour as the *Blarua-Criha-Uval*, and the patterns of their three vortices of swirling cadmium-red were mesmerising to behold from here. The swans they had seen and heard earlier were gliding along the southern margins of the Lake, like a necklace of brilliant white pearls on the fringe of a crimson bodice. Eli gazed in wonderment, as Reyse resumed his tale.

There are many legends in Faërie, dearest Eli. Legends of kings and queens, of rainbows and mushrooms, rabbits and water-rats and swans and silkies, and even of humans protected by the wings of angelic doves. But I suppose the greatest of our mythologies and fireside tales tell of unicorns and of dragons.

And so one such legend recounts that in the time of Aulf the Mighty, a very great and very fierce dragon existed in this realm. I do not think that he lurks here still, but his mate remains. She is Bawn. But the male worm was much larger even than that mighty matriarch, by all accounts; he was white like her, but with dark wings as sombre as storm clouds. And he was untameable and wilder than a cyclone --- and he hated and feared humans.

It is told that he had ventured into the world, oh it would have been long before my birth, perhaps even before the human calendar marks its turning point with the coming of Christ. And thereafter, he harboured a deep distrust and distain of all things human, for those of 'your' race whom he had encountered were none too welcoming! When he came back to Faërie, wounded and maimed, he was wilder than ever; and at his return, in a tornado of spuming purple and orange flame, he hastened to come before the King Aulf.

Aulf the Mighty was a great traveller --- he has always been my hero, in a way! He had voyaged throughout the eleven shees, and back and forth between them and their corresponding human-lands, and he had even sailed over the oceans at the rim of creation and caught sight, so the legends say, of the blessed realms and the Islands of Youth, and of Beauty, and of Unmade Light. And he it was who bewailed, more than any other, the closure of the fairy-doors in the great Shee Mor, when the Sons of Míl had made war on the enchanted peoples --- as you have heard in the tale which was recounted to your

The Painted Dulcimer

Uncle Mor --- when those insensitive human warriors had hewn and burnt so many of the ancient oak trees in the lands of the myriad Portals, in Ireland especially.

Reyse paused, as if in respect for the dead, and in that moment the huge oak tree behind them creaked and groaned in the wind, as if keening or lamenting in its own cracked voice.

Yes, the wounded dragon-sire, Eagla-Anvash, presented himself before the king, in despair and distain and still in great pain, and he demanded that all of the Portals be sealed --- especially those in the shees linked to the Southern Hemisphere, for that was where he had lately been so grievously wounded. He insisted that all the dragon-slayers and hunters of even the smaller creatures be kept at bay and severed from the fairy-folk forever.

But Aulf refused, although he himself had seen much violence, even greater than that which the dragon had experienced. He refused to close the frontiers and the Portals, and he spoke to the seething Eagla-Anvash --- in such a calm voice that it enraged the ferocious beast even further --- of the seed of a royal idea: the tiniest of acorns in his kind thoughts, an acorn which had not yet even begun to burst its cap-like casing to take root and grow! It was a notion that all of the worlds he had visited could become --- one day --- a single kingdom, of fairies and of fairy-friends.

Eagla-Anvash was indignant and furious, calling this impossible, foolish and utterly unrealistic nonsense, the plot of a mad King. He vowed to hinder any such plan with all his might. He flew forth from the King's presence in disgust and flaming fury; and he was rarely if ever seen or heard of again, not even in tales or songs. But his lady-mate Bawn, and many of his off-spring, seemingly adopted his attitudes and his prejudices, and from that time many of the Sun-Singers became resolute in their determination to close the Portals of Faërie definitively.

But, alas, before the dragon left his brief audience with Aulf the Mighty, he had most mischievously and traitorously poisoned the King. His very breath, his fiery and sulphurous mouth-flames, were noisome and toxic. And Aulf fell into sickness and began to fade that very day.

*It was then that he was visited by the sires of the Golden Hounds, and they offered the monarch their help. Aulf was a great lover of all dogs, both blue and gold, and of all foxes and wolves, and also of the particular and wondrous trees especially beloved of the canines. The **dogwood** is very dear to the hounds of the Dog-Delight Hills, and branches of this tree were chosen for the dying King, and these the golden hounds brought to him. They instructed Aulf that he must fashion an instrument of this wood --- be it harp or flute or dulcimer --- and use its sweet sound to confound the curse of the malevolent worm, Eagla-Anvash.*

Thus, from the offering of the dogs and the dogwood trees of the yellow Hills, the Mighty Aulf, on his sickbed and resembling no more than a shadow-fairy, cut and shaped the various pieces of a dulcimer, an instrument which he had always desired to play.

His wife, the Silkie-Queen, came to his bedside, and as he fashioned his dulcimer, she painted its surfaces with tokens of peace and of heart's health, of the joy of the golden hounds and the far-seeing wisdom of the seals and the dolphins and the whale-fathers. She and he created, together, the Painted Dulcimer. And when the King played upon it, even for the very first time, it is said that he was instantly *healed and that the dragon-breath left him. Those poisoned fumes were replaced by air which had been blown into the few fragile strings and the light-coloured dogwood-body of the lovely little instrument from the four-corners of Greater Faërie.*

But the very sweetest of the sounds made by those winds and captured in the handiwork of Aulf were those notes which had whistled through the strange and exotic trees of the two shees in the far, far south. For the trees of those lands, in communion with the dogwoods of the rosy hills of the Shee Mor, felt that the music of the King and the 'acorn' of his dream for unity, would save them, most especially, from the scorn and hatred of the wounded dragon.

As soon as Aulf the Mighty was fully restored in health, and sound and strong once again, he sought a seedling of the mystical mimosa, from the Shee of the White Kangaroo. And he placed it in the Chapel of Windy Hill, together with many charms and blessings, and he hung the stars of the antipodes over it, to nourish its heart.

The Painted Dulcimer

The golden hounds he thanked with many words of praise and many regal gifts. And he and his seal-wise wife blessed the Painted Dulcimer also, naming it Heart-Healer and Forgetful-of-Fear, and claiming that it would remain in the royal family of the Shee Mor for all the ages to come, bringing health and confidence, seeing and soul-strength, hope and joy, to any who strummed it."

Eli was very quiet, her hand still in Reyse's, her heart beating like the thrumming rhythms of Garo's *bodhrán*, her eyes filled with dreams and stars and images both terrible and tremendous. After many minutes of silence had passed, savoured by both, Reyse spoke again.

"Let's return to the Castle of the Prince Demoran with our own wings, my Lady Eli. And after a light meal, we will replace that form of flight with another, and our fine horses will bear us back to Fantasie. The moon advances in her course and grows rounder and rounder. From the Silver City you must go to Leyano's island home for other farewells, but for today it is to your brother Demoran that you must bid 'good-bye' --- for now. The Queen, I think, flies back to her beloved husband later tonight.

"Come my Lady, for the wind will be at our backs and we will be blown across the tree-tops of the Dappled Woods like two dancing leaves!"

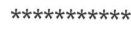

****

Windy Hill Prayer

Chapter Nineteen:
Revelations, Invitations and Reassurance

It was a blustery and bright late-afternoon, filled with the calls of migrating birds overhead and the rustling of playful and inquisitive foxes and hedgehogs through the drifts of fallen leaves, when Peronne and Habukaz landed, once again, within the oval of the City of Fantasie.

Reyse had invited Eli to take a glass or mug of something with him at *The Tipsy Star*, 'for old times' sake', as he put it. Eli had laughed, and assented to joining him in this sentimental gesture. Therefore their horses had alighted near the stream flowing from Lymeril, which then looped about a small coppice of creaking birches and 'young' oaks --- as Reyse remarked, saluting them --- of only a hundred years or so. Numerous squirrels and robins were playing in the trees, and tiny field mice under them, among the multi-coloured mushrooms.

The riders bid their horses farewell, and watched them trot off to return to the stables of the King's Moon Tower, while they walked across the meadows of fluttering grasses to the Inn. The high Star Tower behind it was blinking its shiny window-pane eyes in the sun whenever he peeped out from the fast-moving clouds. Inside there was a blazing fire in the grate of the huge fireplace at the base of the central stone pillar of the lopsided pub.

Eli and Reyse looked for a nook in one of the rather pointed angles of the room, more private than the other tables --- for there were many fairies here, enjoying the warmth and singing snatches of song as bright and gay as the autumn winds. But to their delight the last narrow angle they looked into was not utterly 'private'; it was occupied by a fairy whom they were very pleased to join. It was Timair.

Eli sat between her companion and her brother, and kissed the cheek of the latter. The amber in his ears and the be-jewelled copper cords wound about his longish, strawberry-blond hair all echoed the autumnal palette of nature, while his violet-blue eyes and the aquamarines clasped in the ruddy coils of their twisted cords made Eli think, for some reason, of the variety of blues in the Salmon Haven. And certainly his eyes made her feel just as calm and joyous.

"Timair," she ventured, a thought occurring to her, "I have a question for you."

"Please ask it, my dear Eli. Though I think I can guess what it is. Please don't worry; it wasn't lost!"

"You know *exactly* what I'm thinking!" she laughed. "Are we twins, or just brother and sister?!"

"The oldest and the youngest of our parents," he smiled. "Maybe that's the link, like a spiralling circle joining us mysteriously together! But about the moon-flower, which I *know* you have not found again where you tucked it back into your clothing: as I touched a gentle finger to the seam of your bodice, it came 'home' to me. You only needed her for your adventure, not forever. Some things are like that."

He winked at Reyse, which made Eli wrinkle her brows a little.

"I see, or think I do. I'm glad I didn't lose it by some error or because I was maladroit or disorganised."

"I would venture to guess that a precious flower given you by a fairy would *not* allow itself to fall prey to human error," retorted Timair, still with an eye on Reyse. "It would be unaffected by your clumsiness, as it is quite capable of looking after its *own* affairs!"

"Probably true of all flowers," interjected Reyse, returning the wink to Eli's brother. "Moon-flowers, unfading white roses, all enchanted flowers... They live their own lives and tend to their own business, but they also do what is best for you, when they can."

Eli joined in the gentlemen's laughter.

"Not only *white* roses, but golden ones too," added another laughing voice. A voice as soft and sweet and misty and slightly forest-green as the light from the thick, tinted windows of the Inn, falling in dapples and dusty pools on the rough wooden floor and tables. Another fairy had joined them, with a pair of chestnut-red squirrels hopping and playing about his feet, and then dashing outside once more, only to return in a moment to cavort among the table-legs.

"Greetings, Finnir," said Reyse, after a short --- and Eli thought a rather tense --- pause. But in an instant he was standing and placing his firm brown hand on his friend's shoulder. "When I saw Timair here, I assumed that *you* would be at your Portal still, albeit the King had thought that his *son* would now take up the honourable role of Guardian there."

"Hello, Reyse of my heart," said Finnir very warmly. "You are quite right that Timair will eventually take up such a role --- but not immediately. I remain the Guardian for the time being; but for these few days it is others of my comrades who are at the Heart Oak. I thought it would be appropriate to meet with the King *and* his true son; so I arrived here yesterday."

There was warmth, yes, but Eli could still feel the strain in the energy between Reyse and Finnir. Was she imagining it? Or was it that Finnir had been irritated not to find Eli waiting for him upon his arrival in the Silver City?

Both fairies sat down, Finnir facing them all across the triangular, polished table as the Inn-Keeper arrived with hot drinks and toasted cakes.

"Hmph," frowned Timair rather comically. "I wish we had *scones* here. I did enjoy them in Glengarriff, Eli. We must go back there together!" He smiled at her, and passed her a cake, taking one also for himself. "Oh dear, no, nothing like scones..." he shrugged.

Eli giggled at him. The 'missing piece in her puzzle', she had thought, when she first met him here months ago. He was just that. And how nice to have him here... with her 'two loves'. It seemed to dilute the strong energy in the air.

But jolly as he made her feel, it did not remove the shadow she felt in her heart. What did Finnir know, or sense, about her attraction to Reyse and how natural she felt in his company? If she created some sort of rivalry between them, what would that situation do to the centuries-old friendship of these two superb and noble fairies? And what *could* she, or *should* she, do about it all?

"You did not take Róisín to the Island, dearest Eli," Finnir commented, quite casually and not at all critically. "And no doubt it was best not to. You are radiant and musical enough without a harp from Barrywood, and your vault is --- for the moment --- still a place of soundlessness and sleep and shadow. And did you see your own harp, made from the Red Coral Tree? Or perhaps it was your gallant Reyse who entered, alone, to replace the Cloth. But I do not mean to interrogate you! Forgive me."

Finnir had surely seen an uncomfortable change in Eli's expression. But she exhaled, smiled, and steadied herself with a sip of her steaming beverage before replying.

"I went in myself, though Reyse crossed the threshold too. I didn't see the harp, no; I didn't even remember to look for it! It was, it's true, very dark and dim inside the domed-mound. But I replaced the Cloth on my sleeping form with my own hand, and it was a powerful and remarkable moment. I feel much stronger, and surer of myself, since then."

Timair wore a broad smile as his sister pronounced these words.

"And lighter, too, I imagine," he commented. "They do not know exactly *why* you left the token you did, or even what it contains, I think. But two Scholar Owls flew swiftly, yesterday, first to Demoran and then to myself here with our father and Finnir, to give the report that you had succeeded in your mission. The Owls mentioned the phial which you had deposited beside your bier, but they had not troubled you for any explanation regarding that act, before you departed with Reyse. They recognised where it had come from and will, of course, honour your gesture, and leave it exactly where you placed it."

Eli's face had gone blank, and then rather pale. She looked at Reyse.

"Did I leave a bamboo phial in my vault? I didn't even remember that it was still in my bag. When did I take it out, and what exactly did I do with it? I didn't mean to. Perhaps it fell out of its own accord…?"

Reyse looked quizzical, but then he explained, his voice steady and his words clear and deliberate. "As soon as you stepped forward, away from me, I heard you tell me --- in silence --- that you were strong enough to go on alone. A fact I never doubted," he added, with a slight smile. "But then you looked up, as if reading invisible writing in the air or on the far wall of the vault perhaps. And while you read, I saw you take a small length of bamboo, like a little phial, out of your bag --- quite deliberately I thought. I saw it, for an instant, in your moving hand, but I don't know if you drank from it, for your back was turned to me. After only a moment, you let it fall very gently --- it floated down like a dead leaf --- onto the ledge of amethyst crystal protruding from the base of your bier. And then you took out the Cloth."

Eli was staring at nothing, and hardly breathing. Why had she done this, and had she actually *chosen* to? Or was she guided, or influenced, or directed by another force? *Had* she drunk the 'love potion'?!

If she had, the first thing she had looked upon was <u>herself</u>. And, what's more, herself as a *unicorn*...! But then, of course, she had seen Reyse, when they had left the vault and gone back out into the moonlit night.

But maybe she had <u>not</u> drunk it at all, but merely left it there. For whom? For what moment in the future? Was it for her to drink, or to offer to another, when she returned in the years ahead? Was it maybe for another thief, such as Erreig, who might violate that hallowed place with evil intentions, and find himself --- instead --- in love?!

She could not know. And somehow she did not want to. She toyed with the thought of returning and retrieving the phial. Ridiculous. She would not. If she had taken it out while there, then *there* it would stay. Why such a firm decision not to return crossed her mind, she did not know. But she knew she *would* not, and *should* not, go back again on this Visit.

Bringing her eyes once more into normal focus, and her mood back into a rising contentment of being with these three fine fairies, she smiled and shook her head ... at herself. As she looked up, she caught the eye of Finnir.

His golden curls were playfully hiding ---or almost hiding --- the pearl in his forehead. The amber in his ear-points was also peeping in and out of his hair. It was a brighter amber than that of the richly-coloured jewels of Timair's ears and those which were set beside his violet eyes. But it was Finnir's eyes that, as ever, outshone all else. Eli was very much afraid that she would summon her wings out of her shoulders by mistake, in a desire to fly up and out into the innocent blue of that infinite sky!

"Periwinkle and Jizay will form a search-party to find us, and especially Eli, if we do not return to the palace soon," Timair warned, finishing the last cake with a disapproving shake of his head, but a smile to Eli. As they all stood to go, Finnir touched

Eli's arm very softly. She therefore walked more slowly, keeping well behind her brother and Reyse, so that Finnir could say a word to her privately.

"This evening I would like to speak with you, my dearest Eli. I leave Fantasie later tonight. Will you meet me in the Chamber of the Seven Arches?"

Eli nodded, and as she stood close beside him, she was flooded with memories of his kisses, of how he had looked on the threshold of his Portal on Samhain Eve --- an enchanted fairy-prince shining with power and mystery; and the breathless, but almost 'homely', feeling of standing before his Castle, his arms about her, and both of them gazing across the water to Windy Hill and its yellow-hearted chapel.

"I've only ever felt like this in very holy places," she said to herself, as she continued to look into his eyes, the two other fairies now waiting for them outside on the terrace of the Inn. "The only thing *at all* like being with Finnir is prayer. Real prayer, transporting prayer.

"He is the light of a million candles burning before the altar of Love itself," she thought; and then she laughed at herself, shaking her head at her penchant for exaggerated and ridiculously poetic metaphors for Finnir!

****

Their proposed meeting would be quite late, for the King had requested to see Finnir for a private conversation after he had arrived at the great Moon Tower. Jizay and Piv had kept Eli company while she waited, but they at last left --- when they heard Finnir approaching.

Only at first it was *not* Finnir, but Brocéliana.

"You have returned to the Silver City today also!" exclaimed Eli happily. "I'm glad, because I wanted very much to find a few minutes for us --- alone."

The sisters sat on a bench between two of the great, open arches which looked out onto the play of colours around the Great Trees. But the two women were content to look at one another, rather than at the glorious arboreal pageant of lights.

"Yes, the Queen will not be coming back here before late tonight, but I was eager to return before her and rejoin my dear Garo. And I was hoping, like you, to find a moment for us to speak in private, also, dear Eli," began Brocéliana.

The modest young fairy hesitated, changing her position slightly on the silken cushions of the bench. Eli laid a reassuring hand on her shoulder for a moment, then withdrew it in silence and simply smiled at her lovely sister.

Brocéliana continued, "I wanted to reiterate my plea that you *wait* to make your final decision, and that you don't sacrifice your return to this land *for me*. Truly, I could not bear that burden ... of *love*, I'm afraid. And I am, like Ruilly, not sure that you should take this dangerous and audacious step, traversing a human-death and hoping to return to Faërie by some secret path thereafter."

Eli was still smiling tenderly, but her green-blue eyes were sparkling, retaining still the glinting light of her resolve, even when mingled with compassion for her sister's worries.

"My dearest Brocéliana, I have been thinking about just these objections and concerns of yours. And here and now I can put your mind at ease, I think."

"Oh, Eli! I'm so glad: you mean that you *will* come back here, right away? I agree that you should. I know you have another few days to reflect, but you are the true and royal Princess of this realm; and you have so much to do here. I have been a part of the Alliance for only a few years, but Garo has been so for centuries, and Leyano too. Of course, I know them both better than I do Aindel --- I mean Timair --- and Alégondine is not very well-known to me either; but I am convinced that they **all** hold you in just as high esteem as I do, and they would surely say that Mélusine *must* be here, now as the Spiral of Stars grows brighter and stronger."

Eli's love for her sister was so intense that she almost wanted to take her in her arms. But she decided that would be too dramatic and, for her at any rate, there was *no* drama in this moment. She simply had to allow Brocéliana to see things from another perspective: a clearer and more correct one.

"Listen carefully to me, dearest girl. I have now replaced the Cloth in the vault where my fairy-body lies, as you know. And going to that hallowed place, well, it has truly changed me --- but not as it seems *you* are hoping. How can I put it? I saw and felt a *power* and a determination when I was there --- Mélusine's own power, I suppose it was --- and I knew, knew with every fibre of my being (even though I'm still only Eli) that these 'terrible decisions' which have haunted me since my first Visit, were all considered and decided long before I became a changeling at all. I know now that Mélusine had planned, all along, *not* to come back."

Brocéliana said nothing. Eli was not sure how to read her sister's incredulous expression; was it fear or hope or confusion, or a mixture of all three overlaid across her beautiful face, quite drained of colour for the moment.

Eli continued, speaking as calmly and *un*-dramatically as she could.

"As Eli, I had begun to entertain the idea that I could do some good in the world, now that I know about Faërie and especially as I have the magical Harp of Barrywood to use as a means to heal and help people. And then I added to this the notion that, by declining my right to return here and thereby allowing *you* to stay, I would be granting two extra years of joy --- and, I might add, of <u>service</u> to the Alliance --- to you and Garo. *Then* came the marvellous news that Alégondine would offer herself as the next Sage-Hermit, and so Garo was free; well, then I was over-joyed, for you and he would have all your lives together! My little 'sacrifice' for the sister I had grown to love so deeply, turned into a large and magnificent 'sacrifice'. And I was able to make it happily --- although with a certain underlying fear that I would surely miss Faërie, even though not regretting my decision.

"Now, follow closely, for this is the crux of the matter. I *then* learned that I could come back to Faërie *later*. Like your mother did, like Lily. Only in my case, I would come back to *stay* here, not to go on into the Light which follows a human death. I was given the means to find a way back here, in the style of our father's feat of passing through a human-death and voyaging by hidden passageways to arrive --- by his own will and courage --- once again in his kingdom."

The young half-fairy was wide-eyed, but nodding slightly, as if she began to understand, and even to believe.

"But it was still all rather fearful to me," Eli continued. "It seemed an outlandish risk and a very desperate scheme, almost a gamble or a far-fetched and wild dream." Eli paused, and she savoured, for herself in that moment, the faith and confidence she had won on Scholar Owl Island. For now she could shake her head at all of her previous thoughts, and her smile was sincere and confident.

"It's nothing like that, any of that, I find," she concluded. "I know it will all work out, and I *knew* it would long ago. I felt my *own* decision, Mélusine's decision and her absolute certainty, when I was there, inside the vault. I had *planned* this, and planned it *myself*, from the onset. I can't say that I know all of the details which I had considered as the Princess, or what I learned in the Great Charm; but I have the conviction that I am in control of this. It is, for some fundamental reason, absolutely *vital* that I remain in the world ---- just a few short decades at the most --- and then it is my *destiny* to find this extraordinary path to bring me home.

"It is a very nice side-effect of this entire plan, that I can heal people with harp-music, for I would love to do that. And it is even nicer that it means that you, my darling Brocéliana, can remain a fairy and stay here to live your love-story with your dear Garo. But I'm not doing it for *either* of those reasons <u>at all</u>. I'm doing it because of some greater and higher purpose: for my 'destiny', as I say, and perhaps even for the Alliance and --- more than that --- for Love itself. The ultimate outcome that I envisaged for this plan, this decision of mine, *that* I can't quite grasp or see yet; but I have, in some wonderful and unquestionable way, touched it again, touched just the hem of its garment. And yes, it is a garment woven of pure Love.

"So I'm **sure** now, and I will never question this step for any reason, ever again."

Finnir was standing at the doorway into the huge Council Chamber, his smile filling the room with vibrating light. Two or three creamy-beige squirrels climbed onto one of the window-ledges, their bright eyes shining and alert. And several swallows danced in the air just beyond them. Twilight was deepening, but the Tree-mists were painting the skies with glorious colours, richer than any sunset.

Brocéliana breathed very deeply, but she could not reply to Eli's discourse in words. She simply looked deeply into her sister's turquoise eyes for only a moment, her lips curved in a faint smile, and then she rose to go; but she stopped again to give Eli a long hug and a kiss on her forehead. The lovely young fairy-woman bowed slightly to the Prince, her smile becoming even broader, and then she left him and her sister alone.

"I could not help over-hearing your final words, and I found them very beautiful. And true. Your brush with the slumbering form of Mélusine has brought you great insight, and peace of mind, my belovèd...Eli."

Finnir had taken both her hands in his, and now kissed one of them, inclining his golden head over it and then, when he raised it again, making Eli catch her breath with the vastness of the universe in his incredible eyes.

She felt her head spinning, and had the urge to step back from him. It all seemed too much for her, suddenly. She swallowed and tried to find sensible, down-to-earth words to say to him, but she found herself floundering in a tide of energy sweeping all around her like churning water.

"I'm drowning," she heard herself say, but she did not think it was said aloud.

Finnir's expression changed to concern, and he quickly eased her away from the high window.

"Though you have seen with Mélusine's eyes, for a moment in her domed vault, and touched, as you say, 'the hem of the garment' of the pure Love you mentioned, I don't think you can withstand yet, as Eli, the merging of such energies as these. You were aligned between me and the window facing due south, the Arch of the Great Tree Selig."

Eli's breathing was becoming regular again, and Finnir sat with her on the bench where she and Brocéliana had been, between the southern Arch and the next window towards the east. Finnir explained, his smile reassuring and his hands still holding Eli's.

"Selig is the Great Tree with whom I am in closest communion, as you are with Bram and Rhadeg. But Selig is the first of the Trees, and he is aligned directly with the diamond-point of the King's Moon Tower, and resonating with the Great Gate of Fantasie in the south, Ioyeas."

"Ah yes," Eli nodded, "Piv explained it to me: the Gates and the Stones and Trees are numbered, corresponding to their notes of music, in the same criss-crossing order. Only with the Gates, number one is in the south, but with the Trees and the Stones number one is in a different place..."

"Exactly. And there is *no* tree in the south, not directly south," smiled the Prince. "The Gates criss-cross from south to north-west, north-east, due-west, due-east, south-west and south-east. But the Trees begin in the north, and then continue in the same pattern again, like the Gates. Your Tree-friends,

Rhadeg and Bram, are numbers three and four, linked with the Gates of those numbers. But the First Tree is facing the King's Moon Tower, and the First Stone is facing the Great Gates, in fact, in the north-east of the sacred Circle. It's quite complicated! I'm sorry if it's confusing to you --- for us it's easier, because we hear their notes of music even when we just look at them!" His laughter was gentle and buoyant, like music itself. But Eli was trying to follow the count, and feeling quite muddled.

"In any case, my darling," continued her love, "the problem is that you were in line with the potent energy of the first of the Trees, Selig, and his corresponding Arch, and you also had *me* on the other side of *you*, and behind me was the central pillar of this powerful room. You were caught in that current and --- while Mélusine would find such ecstasy normal and reviving --- Eli would be submerged by it and, as you said silently, she would certainly feel that she were drowning.

"But you are not drowned, nor will you be at the last. I am here, and I will be with you **then**. We will step through the Portal together, and the Garnet Vortex will be the spiralling horn of a unicorn, and we will ride him together. That is the legend of Faërie, the enchanted unicorn who may be ridden. Have you heard of that mythic tale on your Visits, or do you recall it?"

"I think Muscari referred to it, when she told me that some of the unicorns in the Glens of Barrywood were once real horses, and some were phantoms. She said that there was a legend of one of them being ridden. But, no, she didn't tell the whole tale to me. But I have seen Neya-Voun, your own horse, in the form of a unicorn, and you riding her…"

"Have you? Ah, that is very good! But as for the details of the legend and prophecy, they do not matter now, my love. You do not really need to remember the story, because it's *your* story. Yours and mine. You will fulfil the story; we will do so together. That was our vow and our plighted troth. You may not recall the legend or our promises yet, but Mélusine knows, and that is enough. Have faith, my dear Eli, for you will *be* that legend-come-to-life, in the years to come."

"It is hard, Finnir," she admitted, "very hard for me to live only on faith, I think. I feel like someone with amnesia. And it is so difficult for me to only half-feel and half-understand what is happening to me."

"It's what I wanted to talk to you about, in private, today, my Eli. We will not be alone, I suspect, when you come to the Portal to step back into the world for the last time, six days from now. And I wanted to speak my words of encouragement to you, just to you, today.

"I have requested, already, that you remain faithful to our love, and I asked that because I *know* it will be difficult, and perhaps *is* already. It is why I wanted us to have those moments of bliss in Gougane Barra in September, when I gave you Róisín. It was simply to give you some hope, some glimmer of what has already passed between us, and of what lies ahead. But it is only a very pale suggestion, like the light of a very distant star seen twinkling through the passing cloud-wrack.

"You knew that this would be your challenge, when we spoke --- well over fifty years ago --- of your adventure to come, your transformation into a changeling babe so that you could experience human-life in all of its colours and cares and tragedies and dreams. But you knew, then, that you would forget our love while a human, or keep it only as a longing ever-singing in your heart but in a language you would not understand.

"I, for my part, knew that you would most probably live *other* romances, while in the world of mankind. And that was difficult for me. At least we both realised that you would not bear children to another man, not as a changeling. I was happy about *that*, for I desire to be the father of all of your children!

"We contrived, between us, to have many tokens given back to you, when you would come here on your three Visits, so that you would return, finally, to await your 'death' with all the assurances of your plan's fulfilment in place. Thus you have the Silver Leaf and the Golden Flower, the Flaming Crescent Moon, and the Harp of Barrywood. And though you will not be able to see them with human eyes, the amethyst in your palm and the jewels in your ears and set over your heart, they will all remain with you and be very present in your awareness, and they will even shine softly at times or send out rays of warmth that you will be able to clearly feel.

"There is no way that I can explain to you, my heart's bride, what our love was or will be. It is kept, like a secret treasure, in the Princess's chrysalis-body. No words you could hear as a human would suffice, no delight or sensation in human relationships can be translated into the verity of that union we shared, and will share again.

"But I think you have also, now, been reminded of this by your fairy-self. Indeed, it was and is and will be the union of Sun and Moon, when all Light is one! You will see, then, with the heart and eyes of the Sun, and the Moon will be her true and ever-full self --- as you will be. For you will be embraced by both, when you find yourself once again, and forever, in *my* embrace, in our embrace."

Eli looked even more intensely at her Prince now. So, those words which she had heard in the vault, whispered in her heart, they *were* an echo of Finnir's voice.

"What a blessing," he added with a laugh, "that Erreig stole that Cloth, and that you had to go back to your vault! We had not planned that, and it has made a great and glorious difference, I think, to your determination and your peace-of-mind. But then, nothing arrives by <u>chance</u>, does it?"

There was a long and very sweet silence between them, an *other-worldly* silence, a moment of grace and a glimmer of their very ancient and very distant love. At least, that is how it felt to Eli.

Finally, Finnir spoke again.

"I leave this evening, my Lady, for I must go to the Caves of the White Cats."

Eli's eye-brows raised in alarm.

"No need to entertain any worries about that!" the golden-haired fairy assured her merrily. "I am on *very* good terms with Isck; he is a delightful feline, and I am fond of his kits too. But many changes are afoot. Bawn wishes to return to the Bay of Secrets, and Garo will take up residence in the White Dragon Fortress. Alégondine is to become the Hermit of the Star, but she will return --- for a while --- to her beauteous bower in the pine forests between the Beldrum Mountains and the sea. Though doubtless she will be more and more often on the sacred Island now, as she was as a child. Yes, there are many things happening in the province of Quillir!

"Of course, Isck is, himself, a king; and your father feels that it should be another *royal* fairy who delivers, quite ceremoniously, all of this information to him, as well as the news from the Silver City regarding *my* true identity and the return of Timair, as well as the home-coming of the Queen. All of this news should be brought to the monarch Isck by an 'official' emissary. As I will one day become the King of the Sheep's Head Shee and Timair will ascend to the throne of Aulfrin here in the Shee Mor, we thought it would be nice if we --- the two Princes for so long confounded --- bore the news to His Majesty the White Cat-King, though I would be surprised if he has not already heard much of it from Aulfrelas, or even from the squirrels of the Hazel-Nut Woods and his own wise-whiskered kits!

"After that, Timair and I will return to Barrywood, to be there for the day of the full moon and the passage of my Lady Eli through the Portal of the Heart Oak."

"I believe there is a suggestion of a little trip to Mermaid Island, to see my brother Leyano before that," Eli remarked.

"Ah yes, that is most likely. Your father the King will confirm all of his plans for your final days here when he dines with you tonight, I expect. You are invited to a late supper with him, as I understand: you and Jizay and Piv, Brocéliana and Garo. And Reyse, I think also."

Finnir stood before Eli and extended his hands to bring her to her feet also, and then he took her in his arms. He kissed her long and beautifully, as if his lips were full of music and his mouth could breathe into hers the perfumes of lilies and roses combined. Eli was wondering if she should not have remained seated to share that kiss, for she felt it might make her faint!

He looked deeply into her turquoise, shining eyes for another moment, before speaking again. It seemed that a mist like a thin, fleeting cloud passed across his face.

"It is good that you and the Eagle-Lord went together to the Island of the Owls; I am glad that you had his company, his protection and his guidance. I can feel, between you, a strong bond still --- for he has rendered great service to you at the time of your transformation, and in raising Peronne for you, and perhaps in many other ways. There is a shining light of devoted love which unites him to you; but I believe that it is the love of a soul-friend, an honourable and high admiration for a wondrous Lady felt by her champion --- the affection of a wise tutor for his gifted, but rather impetuous, student."

Finnir hesitated, and then added, softly, "I hope he has not touched your heart in any deeper ways, my betrothed. I know that he sought your love long years ago, and I also know that you refused him ... then."

Eli was still held in Finnir's arms, their faces close and the rippling energy of his body and of his incredible blue eyes making her tingle with breathless joy. But now she blinked and looked suddenly away from the view of that infinite sky. There was not really a tone of 'jealousy' in Finnir's voice, only of concern. It was certainly not that he sounded *possessive*, not really; only perhaps a little anxious or rather sad and somewhat frustrated, as though he realised that --- even with all his beautiful words --- he could *not* bring to full life again for her the love that he and she had shared. It was lost to her heart, for the time being. And like a man looking up at a rainbow while seated beside a friend who was blind, his heart was breaking just a little with the sting of a great beauty that Eli was unable to behold.

Very gently, Finnir touched Eli's left ear, fondling for an instant the Flaming-Moon pendant as he had in the woods of Gougane Barra, and then he allowed his hand to stray to her cheek and finally to her chin --- lifting her face a little so that he could kiss her just once more.

"I must now say my farewells to you, my dear love, until the moon swells and calls you back to me in a few days' time. But before we part, I have another message to give you."

"Timair and I were in the Stone Circle this mid-day. We met Garo and the Twins emerging from the swirling fog, but we did not stop to converse with them. For I felt a summons to venture into the central plain where the circular stream flows now one way, now another. I was called there by Aulfrelas, your grand-father. And while there, I heard his voice.

"He has asked to speak with you, Eli. And he has charged me to invite you --- when I leave this Chamber and you are quite alone here --- to approach the central column. I believe you will hear his voice there; and I think it will not feel like 'drowning', as the forceful alignment of energies here did earlier. I am sure you will be alright, for Aulfrelas is pure kindness and filled with profound wisdom. You do not feel nervous about fulfilling this request?"

Eli's eyes were wide, but she had a sudden vision which reassured her immediately. She was with Reyse before the golden embers of a little fire in the *Inn of the Smiling Salmon*, and they were listening to her father tell the tale of his subterranean adventures and his meeting with the Mushroom Lord. Aulfrin had said, in that account, that *kind and rich amber eyes... were before me*. Eli could clearly see such eyes now --- in her imagination or in her very heart --- and they were indeed very wise, and filled with love and kindness.

"No, I don't feel any fear or nervousness at all. I will do as you say, and I will be very happy to hear my grand-father's voice. "

Finnir smiled, and he bestowed one more delicate kiss on Eli's mouth, like a butterfly alighting on a flower and then fluttering off again. And so he left the Chamber of the Seven Arches.

****

It was surely almost the hour for the 'late supper' Finnir had mentioned. The night sky was dark but very starry, and the coloured mists of the Great Trees seemed to have become calm and thoughtful, humming in gentle blues and mauves, as if leaving the stage to the pulsating and dancing stars.

Feeling that she should be going to join the others soon now, Eli therefore did not hesitate. Once Finnir had departed, she approached the pillar at the Chamber's centre, covered by rich tapestries and yet always and ever exuding a vibration of power and bubbling life.

"*Mélusine...*" whispered a low, earthy, tender voice, when she had stopped a foot or so before the massive column.

Could she find, somewhere in her memories of Faërie, a recognition of those accents, that lulling sound? Had she heard her grand-father's voice when a Princess here? It was not dissimilar to Aulfrin's, in fact. But it sounded much, much older --- or was it eternally young? Yes, she thought now, it was the innocent and flower-like voice of a child.

"Draw apart the drapes, my dear one. The lights are sleepy and will not startle you, as they did once before --- ah no, they are purring like the tiniest kits of King Isck, curled up in their red-mounds, like baby birds in a cat-nest! Lift both of your hands and open the curtains just a little."

Eli's hands reached forward together, and her fingers delicately parted the heavy tapestries before her. A light like sweet treacle met her gaze, amber like the colour of the kind eyes she had glimpsed in her vision just before. But there were no eyes to see, only light. Buttery and warm, comfortable and soothing.

As she held the curtains open, only two or three inches, the summery yellow light seeped out into the room and diffused about her hands, making them feel like she had just plunged them into tepid water or that she were warming them before a turf fire. Now she descried filaments of magenta and ultramarine within the golden light, and then --- in a twinkling --- all the coloured glow was gone. Beyond the opening, like the crack in a great tree's trunk, was an inky blackness. But it was not disagreeable, either. It was like falling asleep, falling into a peaceful and rockabye-baby sleep. Eli suddenly had a fleeting but vivid memory of the cradle that Lily had painted for her as a new-born infant and where she had kept her dolls and toys when growing-up to girlhood: a dark wooden cradle decorated with crescent-moons and flying unicorns!

And then, out of the darkness, came the voice once more.

"You have been aided and guided, accompanied and protected, throughout your three Visits, my darling little Mélusine. But I beheld you in Scotland: ah, you were very strong there... and *almost* alone! Of course, your hound of joy was there, as a golden ghost. And your flying-horse was there, as an eagle. But, for many of those courageous steps over hill and mountain, into glen and forest, you were --- at heart --- simply with yourself.

"And so now I ask that you come and meet me, *alone*. Will you do that? Tomorrow is the 16th of the month, and those two numbers combined make *seven*. And I am very partial to the wondrous number seven! So I will meet you surrounded by *seven* benevolent beings: the seven mighty Stones. Will you come to the Stone Circle, tomorrow, and quite *alone*, my child?"

"Yes, Grand-father," Eli found herself whispering --- though she was not sure her whisper was uttered aloud at all. Perhaps it was in the 'silent language' that she used often with Jizay. "I will come tomorrow. When do you wish me to be in the Stone Circle?"

"Come when the sun is rising over the Silver City, when he is just above the heads of the Great Ones, the Seven Trees. And bring the white rose, please, that the Lord of the Eagles gave to you."

"Reyse's rose? Why then," she laughed, "I will not be alone!" It surprised her very much to hear herself make this comment, and moreover Eli knew that this time she had certainly spoken aloud. But Aulfrelas laughed with her --- and it was the most beautiful laughter she had ever heard in all of her life.

"Exactly, and that is the little puzzle I wish to pose you, my Mélusine. For when you come --- one day --- to the Fourth Portal, by red roads and yellow trees, by old age and new paths, by swirling water and garnet spirals, when you come home again --- you will be *quite alone*. But, at the same time, you will *not* be, I think.

"You are asking yourself, human Eli and bold Mélusine, if my words are a riddle, like the rhymes of Ruilly! Isn't that so? But, no, they are not, not really, not at all. Remember, all is *one*!

"It is not a *riddle*, only a puzzle. Like Life itself, like love can be, like all of our journeyings. But, as is often the case, the solution to this puzzle is obvious and very <u>reassuring</u>. Ah yes, we must speak together, you and I. Tomorrow. Tomorrow, my good and brave grand-daughter. The day of seven: it will be a day for *puzzles* --- and for solutions."

There was a silence, as if roosting birds who had been making the leaves and twigs chuckle and rustle had finally nestled down to sleep and had tucked their tiny heads under their wings.

"I will come tomorrow, to hear your puzzling words and your solutions and reassurances, Grand-father. I will come alone, and yet with a white rose --- so not *completely* alone! I will come at sunrise."

The heavy tapestry drapes eased themselves away from Eli's fingers and the opening closed like the petals of a flower at dusk. Eli turned from the quiet column and sighed; and then she went to her supper with fairies and friends and family, all of them very, very dear to her indeed.

****

Chapter Twenty:
The Stone Circle

Periwinkle and Jizay had evidently not been far from Eli, as she convened with her grand-father at the fringe of the Light (or the darkness) in the Chamber of the Seven Arches. As she made her way to her supper with her parents and Brocéliana and Reyse, they appeared from an adjoining room.

"My Eli-een," chimed the laughing pixie as he flew about her, "you are all quivering sun-haze! Is that because of your conversation with the Prince Finnir? Does *love* do that?! But no, it's something else," he added with a glint in his eye and a question in his high, piping voice. "You've spoken with someone else too... Aha, I can feel him, yes!"

Jizay's warm words resonated silently and clearly for them both to hear: "She has touched the curtains, and the tower's womb of Light has touched her, I sense."

Piv landed just before Eli's feet as she arrived at the threshold of the dining-room.

"I can clearly *feel* the presence you spoke with, for his folk are well-known to me. And you've been asked to make another voyage. It's not into the human-world, my Eli, is it?" the pixie asked, less gaily.

"As you perceived, she has met the Lord of the Mushrooms, Master Periwinkle; and I think he has, indeed, invited her to indulge in yet another adventure."

It was the voice of the King, relaxed and yet tinged with a rather quizzical tone. He had come to the door of the bright dining-room to extend his hand to his daughter and lead her to a place beside his shimmering dais at the head of the table.

Eli took his hand and entered the candle-lit room, nodding with a smile at her mother whose own throne was on the other side of the King's and elevated --- like his --- on the semi-transparent oval of light. Reyse was at the other side of the Queen, facing Eli. Piv, as usual, sat at his own 'place of honour' at the table's far end. Brocéliana was beside Eli, but across the table from her was another fairy.

"Greetings your Highness," he said, rising as Eli approached.

"Aytel! How nice to see you again. And how nice to see you … alive!" returned Eli, her smile sincere and welcoming.

As Aulfrin seated himself those standing did so also, with Jizay now at Eli's feet and Ferglas between the King and Queen.

"Yes, it is certainly good to see my brave Aytel in Fantasie once again, and to find him healed and whole. But he was already almost fully recovered when he departed from the Silver City in the summer, after his brush with Tintrac's and Tinna-Payst's deadly dragon-ire. Today he brought me tidings from his home in Barrywood; and it would seem that you too, my daughter, also have a message to relate. Jizay's remarks are quite true, as I heard him speaking them from just beyond the doorway. You have been summoned by the… *Mushroom Lord.*"

Here the questioning tone in the King's voice was evident once again, creating a strange effect in his expression --- but his confusion and hesitation were not in relation to the invitation itself. He continued now, and his brow was slightly furrowed.

"The Mushroom Lord, yes," he repeated softly. "I could feel his energy here as it seems Piv and Jizay could; and I could almost see his strange eyes once again as your hound spoke. Eyes so wide and round, a luminous orange --- or more a rich amber. Curious, large and kind. Yes, his presence in the

Council-Chamber is palpable in the lingering vibrations, even from here. But his words to you surprise me --- for he has invited you to go to ... Star Island. Is that not so?"

Eli took a sip from her chalice of pale purple wine, before she shook her head and looked intently at her father.

"Not Star Island, no. He asked me to go to the Stone Circle, early tomorrow morning, alone."

Aulfrin seemed slightly incredulous. "I felt him calling you to the Star, without a doubt. How strange. For, now, as I continue to perceive that summons, I clearly recognise --- in my heart --- that it could only be the Sage-Hermit, my father as I now know him to be, making the request I heard. No other being can offer an invitation to Star Island, and I felt sure that it was to that precise destination. But now you say it is to the sacred Stones, my dear Eli? Why am I hearing --- even still --- the pronouncement of the call to the Island of the Hermit?"

Suddenly the gems in his crown blazed with sparkling green fire, which as quickly died down once more to a forest-deep calm. The King's eyes had sparkled with the jewels, and now they were wide with comprehension.

"He, the *Mushroom Lord*, has invited you to Star Island because he ... *is* the Hermit!"

Brocéliana's eyes glinted a little, as did Reyse's, when the King pronounced these words. The Queen Rhynwanol wore a contented smile, soft and knowing.

Her husband continued, "They are the same? The gentle being who guided me through the underworld of fungus and quaking, gold-veined tunnels, he was my own *father*. The Sage-Hermit, *he* is the Lord of the Mushrooms?"

"He is of course, my good and great Majesty," confirmed Piv. "And if what you hear is true, then it's most likely that he's asked Eli to go to his Island *from* the Circle of the Stones. Oh, I know mushrooms who could tell you much more of your dear father, when he dons his mushy, mulchy cap and his sweetness and sagacity radiate out, long and lithe, through all the filaments of Faërie! Yes, yes; he is the Lord of the Fungi-folk, and he is the great Sage-Mage --- well, at least until the dark and delightful Alégondine will take up that role."

"But he did *not* mention my going to Star Island, only to the Stone Circle", objected Eli. "Might he really ask me to go further?"

Her father hesitated, occupied with his own thoughts, it would seem. But the Queen said, "You will know in the morning, my dear daughter. Allow it to unfold as it will. We hold the oars of our life's barque, but strangely enough we sail forward better when we merely allow them to feather the water's surface. It's nice to feel the contact with our path, but what delicious wisdom it is to be carried along by wise waves! The currents which cradle our life's little boat in their hands, they are like the fungus-filaments Piv speaks of, in a way: ever whispering and weaving knowledge across all the oceans, just as the mushrooms sing to unite all the roots and under-earth-river-ways, all the harmonics of nature's plucked harp-strings. The whale-fathers and dolphins, they would tell you much of that wave-wisdom and the guidance offered by the caring currents. And good Master Periwinkle, he holds as much knowing about the marvels and might of *mushrooms* under that green-cap of his as is to be found in all of Faërie, I think!"

Everyone smiled or laughed, even Piv. Though the pixie's giggling was blended with pride and gratitude at Rhynwanol's kind words of praise.

They began their meal in silence for a few moments, and Eli looked long at Reyse facing her (and almost studying her); he fingered his chalice and then lifted it slowly to his lips.

Did he know? Had he also heard the invitation of her grandfather, and Aulfrelas's addional request that she bring the unfading white rose with her? Reyse's walnut-brown eyes were filled with so many centuries of learning and loving, so many stories and voyages and heartfelt joys and sorrows, that Eli could not read where his thoughts were at this moment. The rings of gold around the centres of those deep eyes were mirroring the candle-light, but Eli did not know if their brightness included tender thoughts for her, or concern, or riddles even more puzzling than those of the Mushroom Lord!

When their meal had concluded, and all the company was standing about the table preparing to go to their night's rest, Aulfrin again brought up the subject of Eli's morning-meeting.

"You shall heed the summons of my father, dear girl, early tomorrow, as you say. And as your beauteous mother has said, you will then know if your invitation extends to the Star itself, as I predict. I am not *worried* for you, not at all. If it is the Sage-Hermit and Mushroom Lord who calls you to the Stone Circle, or beyond, then you shall be safe.

"Nonetheless, I feel the 'fatherly duty' to remind you of the intensity of that place, of the strong charge of its energy that caused you to lose your balance while astride Peronne on your last Visit, and of the even greater force of the Island in Holy Bay. Though her Sovereign, I have never set foot on the Star itself; and if you are permitted to do so --- and if you must be 'alone' as you say --- it is at once a great honour and a great peril.

"You will be protected, I know; but be wary, my dearest Eli. For you are more and more Mélusine with each Visit, it is true; but you are *Eli* at this time, still.

"And there is one other thing to be aware of," added her father --- and at this final warning, Eli could feel that Reyse had drawn closer to her where they stood, and his left hand gently touched her lower back. "The tidings which Aytel brought to me relate to that part of my realm also, near to the Star.

"To his woodland manor, deep among the trees of Barrywood, arrived messages from Brea and his hounds, who have ventured again into Quillir since Erreig's sojourn in the human-world. The doughty Brea offered to patrol the movements of dragons and Sun-Singers in the absence of their

Cheiftain over these past ten days. It seems likely that the Dragon-Lord left Star Island still in his phantom-form, for as such he was retained there by the Hermit. When I met with him three days ago, with Leyano and Garo, on Mermaid Island --- contrite and respectful as he was --- he did not *seem* to be a ghost; but then I suppose you had the same vision of him in Scotland --- solid and seemingly 'real'. That does not necessarily mean that he was in his true and complete fairy-body; for he is well-able to appear substantial to us all, even were he escaped from the Star as a wraith.

"There is un-easiness in Quillir, even among the Great Cats. My dear Queen, in her conversations with our son the Prince Demoran yesterday and earlier today, heard as much from him also --- for he and his own small cats are ever attentive and aware as regards the larger felines of the Southwest. Their whiskers wave at one another, as we say! Yes, there is anxiety in the mood of many Quillir-creatures --- cat and squirrel, bat and insect --- that Erreig is somehow not ... himself."

Aytel took up the explanations briefly: "We wonder, Your Highness, does the Dragon-Lord's fairy-body remain, even now, on Star Island; or has he somehow reclaimed it once again? In any case, even his 'subjects' and his winged-worms are not reassured, and I have come to give this news to your father the King, and with it I here and now remind you also of the warnings from the Prince Finnir --- who has left this evening with his Highness the Prince Timair to come before Isck, the King of Cats --- *Erreig is **not** to be trusted*. Ah, our bold Finnir knows well the vacillating and unpredictable character of the Dragon-Lord!"

"I reinforce Aytel's and Finnir's words to you now, my Eli," continued Aulfrin, "as an important warning to keep in mind if you must cross Quillir. Erreig *is not to be trusted*; he is wild and volatile, passionate and fearful. And, moreover, he bears the triple-charmed fire-opal *Gurtha*. That said, he is no match for the Sage-Hermit, I would say --- although he has evaded him and slipped from his Island sanctuary --- which is rather astounding, to say the least. But I urge you to beware, my sweet Eli. We do not think he has returned to the Shee Mor at this time, for he had proposed to go to the shee of the Lord Hwittir; and I hear nothing of his physical presence here in this realm from my harp or flute. But if he is a wraith he maybe has eluded even their perceptions, as he did those of Aulfrelas!"

"I wonder," interjected Reyse, speaking almost as if to himself, but close beside Eli and not far from the King, thus clearly audible to both, "if perhaps Eli will be given merely a *vision* from the Stone Circle, of the sacred Island. If her grand-father has requested her to visit him among the Stones, perhaps he does not intend to take her any further, save inwardly. For far from the Star, and above ground, he himself will surely be a vision or a mere voice there, also, and not substantial. Moreover, I find it an unlikely suggestion on the part of your father, the wise Aulfrelas, that she cross four-hundred miles of somewhat 'hostile' dragon-lands to go to the Star. And *alone* it would be so dangerous as to appear fool-hardy."

"I believe you are right, Reyse-of-my-heart," nodded the King. "And I am confident that all will be well. But we shall see when Eli returns to us after her meeting tomorrow what was solid and what ephemeral! And what wonders or wisdom were presented to her."

It was only as Eli ascended the spiral-staircase to her bed-chamber, with Jizay trotting before her, that she realised that Garo had not been at their dinner. Brocéliana had said nothing to her about him, though she imagined that the lovers had been together while she was occupied with Finnir and then with their grand-father. Now Piv had remained behind with the Queen and Brocéliana, while Aulfrin was busy exchanging a few more words with Aytel and Reyse as Eli had left the room. Where was Garo?

Hearing her thoughts, it seemed, Jizay spoke as they reached the bed-chamber with its minuscule fire glowing in the tiny grate from the room's corner.

"He is gone to Quillir also, the sun-stone Sun-Singer Garo. He left soon after Aytel arrived. Periwinkle and I were in the high courtyard when he flew off. His white wings were bright against the last crimson stains in the sunset sky; the rainbow labradorite --- or *spectrolite* I believe it is --- embedded in the back of his left shoulder was winking its own colours to the Great Trees. There were moths about us, many that had come here with Alégondine in fact. They said that it was to Quillir he had gone, and in haste. And they added that the dusky Princess had gone there too, leaving Fantasie in her sea-serpent-sailed boat to hasten back down the River Dragonfly earlier this evening, even as Aytel and Garo were exchanging news and making their decisions. For, as ever, she learns of her father's movements before all others, it is certain; her great moths are ever watchful of Erreig's wanderings, as she is of his worries and woes."

Eli did not really feel too reassured by any of this news. Before climbing into her hammock-bed, she slowly ran her hand over the upper curve of Roísín's golden form and then she caressed the Golden Flower also, with trembling fingers.

As for her *golden* hound, he looked long at her with his seal-black eyes --- but they were full of calm and confidence. Eli could not help thinking of Laurien, her 'imaginary dog' throughout her human childhood, who always befriended her with that same loyal and loving look of complicity.

****

Eli played her harp briefly, the Harp of Barrywood, very early the next morning. It wasn't even dawn yet; but she could not sleep any longer. And, as ever, she sought some insight, some guidance, some assurance from the notes of her instrument.

But Roísín said nothing to her of her coming adventure, neither was there any image or vision to suggest what might lie ahead. Instead, Eli saw Peronne.

So, replacing the Craigie tartan-blanket over her harp's contours, with a soft kiss on the Golden Flower and an even softer thought for Finnir before doing so, Eli and Jizay descended the many winding staircases to find the flying-horse in the elegant stables off the Entrance Court. He was expecting them.

"You must go alone," he said, rather than making any other greeting or 'good-morning'. "You must go ... *alone*, without me, but with the Lord Reyse's white rose in your pocket."

Eli nodded, coming closer to her dear steed and now running her hand slowly down his curved neck dappled with tiny moons. With her other hand she reached into her cloak's lining-pocket and touched the rose. It was moist with dew, still. Peronne continued.

"You were *alone* in Glen Etive, except for myself and Jizay, a moon-flower and a magical harp, the Rose and the Leaf --- and even a Dragon-Flower and a singing sailor at certain points in the journey. So, we may surmise that when one is *all alone*, it is sometimes amid a crowd!"

Eli actually laughed. Several other horses snorted in their dozing, and then lowered their heads once more in silent sleep. Eli noticed that Habukaz was in the stall beside Peronne's, and not asleep but following their hushed conversation with interest.

"That's true, my belovèd Peronne. I was not alone at all, in Scotland. I had the Cup of Light and the love of Lily, the mer-music of the Lady Ecume and the snow-blessing of the Lady Vanzelle. And there were two golden eagles besides you, my proud sea-eagle, and a white hawk."

"Very well that you remember all of that," Peronne intoned, nodding his great head slowly once or twice. In the mauve and lemony glint of breaking dawn, just peeping through the east-facing doorway, his flowery eyes were filled with constellations mirrored in indigo pools. "But you have not named one other of your companions, in fact. You have not said his name, only that of his disguise."

Eli turned to look down the long vaulted corridor of the great stables, because someone was approaching. "Oh," she exclaimed, trying to muffle her surprise and not disturb the other equines again. "Oh, Reyse, it's you!"

The Eagle-Lord walked noiselessly over the straw-strewn ground, bowed his head in greeting to his own horse, and then smiled as he caressed Peronne's slightly concave head and soft muzzle.

"Yes, it's me. I'm the character you forgot to name in your long list, except that you did name me, in fact, without really intending to."

Eli breathed very deeply, in happiness and in renewed confidence and as if basking in Reyse's love for her before setting off. She smiled, and nodded.

"The second golden eagle, that was you all along," she said.

He made a little offended grimace, but he grinned at the same time. "I was the *first* golden eagle, if you please, Lady Eli. The other eagle was surely the *second*!"

Laughing together now, as softly as they could, Eli offered her apologies. And then she asked, "And why are you here, dearest Reyse? I saw Peronne when I played my harp, and knew I should come here on my way to the Stone Circle. But I did not see you here too."

"Neither will you when... the time comes to be truly, utterly **alone**. But I will be there, all the same."

Reyse's face was more serious now. But his eyes were as starry as Peronne's. Eli raised both her eyebrows, but she did not ask anything else.

The tall fairy-lord lifted Eli's hand and kissed it. And then leaving all three of her dear companions, hound and horse and eagle, she drew her cloak tight about her in the chill breeze of

The Stone Circle

the dawning day, and left the King's Moon Tower to go to the Stone Circle.

Alone. Eli had not gone anywhere, it was true, *anywhere* outside of Fantasie on *any* of her Visits, entirely alone. It was a very, very nice sensation, she had to admit.

She glanced up at Selig, the first and most northerly of the Great Trees. Finnir's tree-friend. There was roughly a mile between where she stood on the outer steps of the Entrance Court and the first ring of the Gardens, vaguely yellow in the shy light. And it was further still to the ring of the huge Trees. But Selig dominated the sky, even from here.

Eli looked up at his massive and yet incredibly delicate arms and fingers, branches going up *and* down, and also outwards around the halo-loop of connecting branch-ways which danced with coloured mists.

"*La*, the note *la*," thought Eli. "Like the Great Gates in the South. That is the corresponding note of Selig, while Bram is four, so that's *re*, and Rhadeg, whom I can see as well from here, he's three so that a *do*." She wondered why these thoughts were coming to her now, this desire to hear which musical note went with which Tree. But she allowed the thoughts to come, and to develop.

"And the Stones have their numbers and notes, too. Let's see, Finnir said that the first Stone is in the *north-east*, looking towards the first Gate, towards Ioyeas. But then they go in the same criss-crossing order as the Trees and Gates do. Finnir seemed to suggest that fairies *hear* them rather than *see* them, the Gates and the Trees and probably the megaliths also.

"Well, I will try to understand why I'm so struck by these thoughts when I get there! For now, I need to walk across the oval of the Silver City to the first Gate, and then down to the Circle of Stones.

"Or do I need to walk?!"

A smile stole over Eli's lips as she called forth her *zephyrus*-wings, and drifted elegantly towards the Inner Garden for a moment, then veered to the east to pass before Rhadeg. She swooped over the Yellow Garden and also the Blue, then turned in her flight to cut back over the flowers of the White Garden just at the feet of Selig. They were all shiny and dewy, like the white rose in her pocket.

Continuing around the Gardens to the west and then to the south, she flew over the ring of the blue blossoms and bushes again now, passing Bram on her left. She breathed deeply, inhaling not just the pure air of Fantasie, but also the utter *glory* of flight and the lightness of her body as she navigated through the cool breezes. A tear-shaped pond or lake glimmered in the last light of the stars, about half-a-mile away to her right; a dim line of smallish trees, the eaves of a miniature wood, made a jagged and artistic backdrop to it. The moon had set long ago, and the sun --- on this side of the Garden --- was not yet present even in a gleaming promise of dawn.

Suddenly Eli could hear, in her heart, a ringing note of music. And she could see a colour. The note was a *fa#*, and its hue a sage-green: the colour which Finnir had chosen for the *fa*-strings on the Harp of Barrywood. "*Fa#*," she thought, "*fa#* --- that's the sixth note of the 'miraculous music' scale from *la* (and it's a sharp because we are really in the key of *sol*, as Piv explained to me). The Sixth Gate, Rhex, is the note *fa#* in the 'miraculous music'. I'm being called to fly **there**, and not to leave Fantasie by the Great Gates. I must leave by the Gate in the south-west, Rhex. I'm sure of it!"

Rhex stood between two of the eleven Star Towers of the City, the ninth and tenth. How, or why, Eli knew this, she could not imagine; but as she flew within sight of this Gate, which she had not yet seen on any of her Visits so far, the numbers came clearly to her mind. Just as the note of music and the colour had done several minutes ago.

The Stone Circle

"I'm becoming obsessed by all these *notes and numbers!*" she laughed to herself as she landed before the small, square, dark wooden Gate. "Nine and ten are nineteen, that's the Towers; and the Gate himself (*how* do I know it's a 'him'?! ... but I do!) is six. That all adds up to twenty-five, and two and five are **seven**. And *that's* why I'm here, and not at the first Gate. It's the preferred number of Aulfrelas.

"Oh dear, yes, I *am* obsessed with this numerical game!"

But when Eli approached the heavy door, crafted of deep brown fruit-wood and richly studded with intricate patterns of *chiastolite* or 'cross-stones' of greater size than she had ever before seen for this protective gem, she found that it was locked fast. An ornate golden handle was evident in its exact centre, but the door did not yield at all to gently pushing or pulling, and the handle did not turn.

Eli retracted her mauve and alizarin wings into her shoulders, and stood a little back from the sturdy door. No other fairies or animals seemed to be near, and it was eerily quiet. But slowly, very slowly, the dark wood of Rhex became lighter in colour, for the sun was at last rising over the tops of the two most southerly of the Great Trees, and a pale honey-tint was infusing the air.

And as he rose, the sun *sang* --- whether for Eli's ears only, or in her heart, or ringing like a church-bell across all of the Silver City, she could not tell. But the sound decidedly came from the sun, and it was one clear note. A *fa#*.

The golden handle twisted and uncurled, as if waking from sleep and stretching with a long yawn. Rhex creaked on his hinges, and swung outwards as the single note swelled to a crescendo and then ended abruptly. He stopped, and stood wide open where he was, affording Eli a view of the Stone Circle five miles down the sloping hillside. She glanced around her once again, but no one was near; however now there were birds singing a dawn-chorus from all of the trees and turrets and roof-tops. The single note was gone, but a million others had replaced it.

Eli drew a deep breath, and walked through the open Gate towards the distant megaliths swathed in dense fog.

****

She did not fly while approaching the Stone Circle, fearing that she might feel, again, the dizzying effect she had experienced on Peronne. She walked, but with a sure and steady gait.

"I'm not the same woman I was the last time I felt your energies, dear Stones," she said, calmly rather than at all defiantly, as she walked.

"We know," came a very audible, but extremely *silent*, reply. "We know, as does the Mage. If this were not so, you could not approach, nor could you enter here. But he does indeed bid you enter, Eli Penrohan. And so do we."

The voice was not a woolly one, like Wineberry's had been. It was not a chocolately-brown one like the interior and silent speech of Ferglas. But it was not cold, as Eli would have expected of this place. And it was a single and definable note of the musical scale as well: a rather melancholic *si*.

It sounded, she now thought, like the sound of speaking or singing into a glass jar, or a hollow tree-stump. It was an echoing and 'alive' sort of *si*-sound, not cold or frightening at all. But it was impressive and commanding.

And the megalith before her was very, very impressive, too.

"The first Stone is away to my left, facing the Gate of Ioyeas," she calculated quickly. "So this is the next Stone, to the north-west, the *second* note. Yes, the note is just that, a *si*. And what's more, I think I recognise this Stone," she added. "I was here with Aindel, I mean Timair. Garo walked out of the mist towards us, coming from between these two Stones, one and two, and the twins were with him."

The Stone Circle

No fear, none at all. She was not at all hesitant, only fascinated --- and a little impatient to meet her grand-father. She hummed, very softly, a *si*.

But nothing particular happened in response to the sound.

The fog was as dense as ever, almost a blanket of white cotton before her eyes. Above that curtain of thick, slowly undulating vapours it thinned to a fine mist, and higher the air was clear. As she looked up now, Eli could see the head of the Second Stone.

And it could see her. It was, unquestionably, staring down at her.

The pale grey rock-face was beautifully carved and decorated, and the Stone itself was immense. But more awesome that its beauty, or its magical and symbolic designs, or its size, was the fact that it was *alive*.

Eli had felt the power and majesty of mountains, the personality and properties of gemstones, the sublime and monumental artistry of a desert canyon or even the menace of an earth-quake fault or a slumbering volcano. But those were not like *this* aliveness.

This megalith was a creature of intelligence and sensitivity, of understanding and compassion, of unbending will and incalculable resistance, of ages and ages and ages of thought, of decision-making, of philosophising, of pondering. And as the Stone looked down upon her, Eli felt welcomed and accepted and respected. One noble being regarding another with infinite and very polite interest, tolerance, even communion.

"Hello," she whispered. Not shyly or too humbly, but not proudly either. Just in friendship and enjoying mutual respect. "Hello," she repeated a little more loudly.

"Hello," said a voice pitched to the note *si*, not interior or silently echoing in her heart, but a real voice. But it was *not* the voice of the Second Stone.

In the midst of the thick cloud of fog, right before her, were two eyes. Large and round, amber-orange and undeniably kind. And they blinked; and then Eli could see little lines at their corners, as if the owner of those eyes were smiling.

"Hello my child, I am Aulfrelas, your grand-father. It is so good of you to come to see me!"

It was the sort of greeting that any grand-father could offer to a visiting grand-child, and it was so homely and loving that it brought tears to Eli's eyes and laughter to her lips!

"Hello Grand-father. I am delighted to meet you."

"Now," continued the charming voice --- a warmer version of the same voice that Eli had heard behind the parted curtains of the central column in the Council-Chamber last night, but the same voice nonetheless --- "now, do come in, and we shall speak together."

Eli prepared herself to meet with the Mushroom Lord, as her father had described him in the rooty, stony and breathless darkness of the hidden passages winding from his Los Angeles graveyard to Eagle Abbey. Or, she thought, it may be that he will resemble Aulfrelas the former King, regal and fairy-winged and crowned, perhaps, with an oak-leaf garland-wreath!

Neither of these beings did she see. For she could *see* no one.

When she had passed through the wall of fog and come into the central plain or meadow wherein spun the strange, circling waters of the ring-like river enclosing the sacred Source, there was no one there at all. Even the amber eyes had disappeared. But the voice remained, and it was right beside her now. Childlike and very ancient, serene and rather joyfully excited, soothing and stately, intimate and infinite, watery and woody, serious and gay. It was a voice of endless opposites, of merging moods and extremes, of unity and peace.

"My dear child, tell me, how does it feel to come to this, hmm, remarkable and potent place *alone*? Are you at ease? Or are you a little timorous here?"

The Stone Circle

Eli walked slowly along beside the disembodied voice. They moved closer to the central Source and its crazy circle of deep waters going in both directions --- now one way, now the other. Eli began to follow the narrow water-course, at a good distance, slowly turning about the Source within it.

"I feel very happy, very peaceful, and well, rather independent and self-sufficient. It's quite nice *not* to need others to guide me, to explain things to me, all the time! I think that is maybe what I find the hardest part of coming back here on these Visits and re-discovering my true home and my true beginnings: the feeling of ignorance and of being incomplete, or a bit lost."

It felt so natural and familiar to speak with Aulfrelas like this, that Eli surprised herself by her candid and spontaneous remarks.

The gentle voice corrected her though. "It should be your 'pure beginnings', not your 'true' ones, I think. At least that was how you put it in your poem, was it not? I remember my dear Morliande bringing me a copy of those verses, oh several centuries back, I suppose it was. You'd written them for me in your pretty calligraphy, while you were an apprentice scribe in the scriptorium of Kitty Kyle. Do you recall? *...to the red and yellow banners of my pure beginnings.* It was a very nice line, I remember thinking at the time. Yes, I liked all the poem, in fact. Very apt, very honest. I do <u>so</u> admire honesty, you know."

Eli stopped and looked 'round at where the voice seemed to come from. Nothing was there, but she smiled at the fresh air nonetheless. And the soft breeze seemed to smile back at her. The meadow-lawn at her feet was very short and soft; and there were little flowers growing in pockets of pastel colours here and there, like children's candies hidden in the grass.

"I do too, Grand-father. I admire honesty, very much, and trust and also loyal love." Eli had the humbling sensation of not really having lived up to those qualities, not always anyway, in her own human life. She thought she had perhaps sounded rather haughty and imperious.

But her grand-father commented, before she could excuse herself, "Ah yes, noble character traits, those. Yes, yes, I couldn't agree more, my little one. And speaking of those qualities, did you bring the white rose, as I asked you to do?"

Without any apology, therefore, Eli reached into her pocket and extracted Reyse's gift. In the strange half-light of this place, surrounded by the massive heads of the Stones high over Eli's own and the veil of thick fog at ground-level, the white rose seemed the very brightest thing to be seen. It shone like a light and all its little droplets of dew sparkled like smoothly-cut diamonds.

"Ha!" exclaimed the gay and ancient voice. "There it is! Loyal love, trust, and honesty; you are quite right, my darling child --- they are the guiding beacons of our lives. And of our deaths sometimes too. Do you know the story of mine? Of my death, I mean to say? Oh, it was a very fine one, very fine, very enjoyable. But I wonder if 'death' is the right word."

"I have heard the tale of your body being swept away from the Great Strand. Demoran told it to me, on my first Visit home."

"Did he? Oh, I am so glad. A lovely lad is my grand-son Demoran, lovely. But you are not being very precise in your words. 'Swept away' indeed; I was swallowed, not swept!"

Eli started. "Swallowed?! By what, by whom? By a whale, like Jonah?"

The voice paused for the time it would take a head to shake, and then resumed. "Jonah? I do not know of that fairy, if fairy he was. But yes, of course, it *could* have been a whale --- for they are very helpful and accommodating creatures, as you shall one day see for yourself. But no, it was a sea-serpent. I am *very* fond of sea-serpents, and of seals, naturally. My other grand-daughter, who is not really of my blood you know but whom I love as a grand-daughter and whom I raised and taught --- ah, she will make as delightful and glorious a Sage-Hermit as anyone could wish for --- she loves sea-serpents too. She gets her excellent taste in aquatic wonders from me!" And here the voice broke into laughter like waves breaking on barnacled tide-pools and sea-weedy shores. Eli had to laugh too.

"Yes, it was a very kind sea-serpent who swallowed me, quite gently of course. He never intended to eat me! He bore me to Morliande in Silkie-Seal Bay where, according to long arrangement between us, I rested for many days and nights, under the waning moon and the smiling sun. It is rather tiring, dying, you know. But one soon recovers."

Eli raised an eyebrow, but continued to smile.

"Why did you ask me to bring the white rose with me, Grand-father?" she inquired.

"Why? Well, of course, for these very reasons we have just enumerated. For the honest, and trustworthy and loyal service he, the Eagle-Lord, shall offer you. Now, hearken well, my dear child.

"Iolar MacReyse Roic, he was given this rose by the bushes north of Fantasie, and they are the children of the rose-bushes with whom you worked so closely in your very first Initiation. A fine choice, I might add. You are, I am very pleased and proud to say, a Rose Princess. And she *is* the Princess, the beauteous Rose. What a splendid flower, is she not, the Rose? Pink ones or red, yellow or apricot orange --- like those that my predecessor Maelcraig so loved. He put those into the Cup of Purple Wine, you know. Very good idea, that. Well, all fairies love flowers, and flowers love fairies too. Where was I? Ah yes, roses. But there are other colours too. Let me see. There are golden roses, but they prefer to grow on harps. Haha! And then there are white ones. I'm very partial to *white* roses. Iolar MacReyse, maybe he knew that you had inherited that taste from me, as Alégondine did with sea-serpents. Well, who knows? But I thought, well, a white rose will be just the thing in your case. Because the whale-fathers, they are very romantic too, like MacReyse. He is very deeply in love with you; but I suppose you know that as well as I do..."

"What do the *whale-fathers* have to do with it, my dear Grand-father?" interrupted Eli, still in jocund tones. "They are not the creatures that swallowed you, as you said; but they were mentioned to me by another fairy and they gave me, oh what was it? *Ambergris*? I think that was it. Mama Ngeza, she put it into the phial of love-potion that she intended me to use to fall in love with Reyse, saying it was from the whale-fathers. But I've left the phial in my vault on Scholar Owl Island, and I don't think I've drunk it --- but, then again, perhaps I did..."

Eli realised she was rambling a bit now, in a style not unlike her grand-father's. She took a deep breath. And in her discourse's hiatus, Aulfrelas commented, "Yes you did. You drank at least *some* of it. Morliande was in the seas nearby, together with that adorable dragon --- you know, the one with mauve scales --- a great friend of my wife's. And they both said that you drank a little, and fell in love. But now, was it with Iolar MacReyse, or with yourself, or with Love in all its manifestations? Haha, ha! We must wait to know that!

"And I, personally, I think you did not drain the phial to the dregs. And if some remains, what will she do when she awakens, our slumbering Mélusine? Will she sip it upon reviving, and fall even more deeply in love --- and with whom? With what? Aha! Another of my puzzle-riddles, that. Now, where were we?

"Ah yes, the white rose."

Eli's head was spinning, but she remained silent now, and tried to follow the explanations of the air-borne voice beside her.

"Just as you so rightly suggested, a whale could indeed have swallowed me. One did not; but in your case it may prove the best idea. Possibly not to *swallow* you though; I think more to bear you and displace you, rather like one of the silkie-islands that my sweet wife can guide across the seas. I think that will be the most likely, yes. So, you will be buried with the white rose --- are you paying close attention? Yes, buried with the rose in your hands, because that will be the voice that will sing to the Eagle-Lord, that will be his signal --- rather like a trumpet-call but oh, so much more sweetly perfumed, so reverent and as silent as the stars --- don't you agree? And he will come to take you from your death-bed --- as he took you from your bier, when you were but a tiny changeling-infant. It's much the same feeling, you know, dying and being born as a tiny infant. He'll come, once more, with the sound and the smell of roses in the air, and he'll pass your body, as white as the rose, to the whale-fathers."

Eli was no longer smiling. Her eyes were as round and wide as those she had seen in the fog-wall.

"Reyse will take my body, when I die, to the whales?" she whispered.

"Yes, indeed. Just as you ordained. It was your idea, my dear Mélusine --- well, most of it. I must admit that I have added a touch, here and there, as has Morliande. And the Lady Ecume, she had quite a lot to say about it all, but more directly to you, as the Princess, when you were putting together all the pieces of your own bright riddle-puzzle-plan! Yes, yes; you worked very closely together on the whole project. So, the Eagle takes you to the whales, and the whales carry you to the kingfisher."

"To the ... *kingfisher*?" repeated Eli.

"Of course. To the Keeper of the Veil; to Barrimilla. You must present him with the Flaming Moon pendant, the ear-ring that you were given --- invisible to me, but I'm assured by my wife that you wear it always --- and so he will open the Portal, the Fourth Portal.

"And then, you will be quite **alone** --- ah and very contentedly so, I think, as we speak of it --- for the last and greatest moment."

Windy Hill Prayer

"To traverse the Garnet Vortex?" murmured Eli, her voice quite tremulous and her tone far from contented at all.

"I thought you said that you felt quite at ease here, and not at all nervous. You sound rather anxious, my child. There is no need to be, no need at all. You will be Mélusine again when you pass the Portal, as Sean became Aulfrin when he stepped over the threshold of the Portal of Dawn Rock. You will ride, with Finnir, the unicorn --- the spiralling horn of the legendary unicorn which is the Garnet Vortex. It is your destiny and your dream, your desire and your own joyful choice. Peronne will be there, on this side, because the Eagle-Lord will have told him that it is time.

"Do you understand now?"

"But I will be *dead*," Eli said, still in a soft voice but trying to sound bolder and less worried. "I will be dead, but alive enough to show a white rose to a whale and an enchanted, invisible ear-ring to a kingfisher? I will be dead, *and* alive? And I'll be on *that* side of the Portal, and then on *this* one? And in the oceans, and then riding a unicorn with Finnir and flying home on my winged-horse? All of that, at once?"

Another pause followed, this one long enough for Aulfrelas to shake his head even more amusedly.

"But naturally, my child. For all is one. *All is* **one**."

Eli was sure that both their encounter and their conversation were nearly at an end. She sighed, rather resignedly.

"Grand-father, I suppose I should I be going back now, back to the King's Moon Tower. They will be expecting me, I think."

"It does *not* matter, ever again, my dearest grand-daughter, what anyone anywhere *expects* of you! That is none of your affair at all, what they expect or not! But you are quite right, it is time to go now.

"But not to Fantasie and my son's Silver-Turreted Tower. No, no, not yet. It is time to go to my Island, for that is a very important part of our meeting and of my part in your ... *death*.

The very most important part, I'd venture to say --- but then, it was my idea, and it is really quite a good one. So, off to Star Island, for three days."

"Three days?!" cried Eli.

"Three days," confirmed the gentle, majestic, old and young voice of the Mushroom Lord.

****

Windy Hill Prayer

Chapter Twenty-One:
Many Islands, One Path

here is a merry Inn, smaller than *The Tipsy Star* or even *The Swooping Swallow*, not far from the two high poplar-trees which flank *Quatherum*, the Fourth Gate of the Silver City. Now, the poplars are on the exterior of the Gate, and the Inn is inside the oval of Fantasie; but it is, nonetheless, named *The Trembling Twosome* --- and the name refers to the two trees and their endlessly rustling and quivering leaves.

Eli had returned to the City by this Gate, singing a rollicking and resounding *re* as she flew, on Peronne, within sight of Quatherum and also of the *fourth* Moon Tower, which rises directly over the Gate. And, of course, she sent a warm 'hello' to Bram, the *fourth* Great Tree and her dear friend, though it was too far off, from the doors or windows of the Inn, to see him.

Reyse's leopard-bay-appaloosa Habukaz wandered among the high grasses and holly bushes nearby, with Peronne at her side. Jizay and Periwinkle had come from the King's Moon Tower to welcome Eli back to the City and the pixie was particularly happy to do so at the sign of the *Trembling Twosome*, owing --- he confessed --- to the 'airy-fairy oat-and-honey biscuits' they served with their steaming and frothy nut-milks. He wore a rather comical moustache of hot hazelnut-foam at the moment; while Jizay, sitting between his mistress and the pixie, had helped with the biscuits.

Piv, his mouth at last no longer too full to speak, asked both the travellers, "But I'm a bit muddled, for how is it *three* days, exactly, that you were gone, Eli-een? Do *you* make the count three, my Reyse-dear? She left on the morning of the 16th, and was gone all of the 17th, but now it's only the late-morning of the 18th. That's only *two* days in total, is it not? Am I being too *precise*?" he added with a giggle.

It was Reyse who began the explanations, but his tone was as light-hearted as the tiny fairy's. "It's not a question of precision, dear Piv; it's a question of tradition and terminology. Eli, like Lily, lived in the human-world and they were both used to --- and a part of --- the Judeo-Christian culture there. I fancy *myself*, when I'm there, more a Buddhist or even a Taoist! But I understand the way of counting, as a Christian would."

Periwinkle looked quite blank, so Eli continued. "It's like at the Christian festival of Easter, my dear Piv. You don't celebrate that here in Faërie, so let me explain: we say that Christ was 'in the tomb' for *three days*, but if you add the days up by 24-hour slices of time, it doesn't work at all. He was crucified on a Friday afternoon and laid in the tomb that evening; he was in the sepulchre --- or engaged in the harrowing of Hell, in fact --- on the Saturday; and at the break of dawn on the 'first day of the week', on Sunday, he had already risen from the dead. To many people, that seems like less than a day and a half; but it *touches* three distinct days: Friday and Saturday and Sunday. And so it's counted as **three days**.

"And, come to think of it, I believe that that was one of the 'ideas' that Aulfrelas added to his gift to me, *his* part in the charm. He wanted to make a reference to my Christian faith and to the ancient world's way of counting three days' time. He himself comes from that ancient epoch, in fact, so it's quite normal for him, most probably. When he agreed to keep me with him on Star Island for *three days*, it was simply that my presence there fell on three different dates."

Piv wiped away his gaudy milk-moustache, and squinted his eyes a little, as if working-out a complicated sum. "And you were *dead*, my precious Eli, while you were on Star Island?" he asked, slowly and still a little uncertainly.

"No, no, I wasn't dead; not this time. I was *saving* those three days for another occasion, when I *will* be 'dead'. You could say that I left those three days of my third Visit, still as Eli, on Star Island --- to be collected later. They are 'in the bank' --- oh, you won't understand that reference at all! They will be kept --- by my grand-father and after him by the next Sage-Hermit, Alégondine --- until I need them at the close of my human-life. For the Lady Ecume believes that the whales will require *four* days to take me to the Fourth Portal: one wherein I will be truly 'dead' as a human-being, and three more where I will be alive, still as Eli – but as the Eli I am now, on this Visit. You see, thanks to the Sage-Hermit, who will release these three days to me from Star Island, I will be able to voyage as Eli-the-changeling. Oh, it's all rather complicated! Do you understand, Piv?!"

Periwinkle nodded a little unconvincingly, for his eyes were very wide; and then they blinked once, rather like the Mushroom Lord's had done in the fog.

"And she will be **alone** then --- but not *utterly* alone." Reyse added these words with a very charming smile at Eli, snuggled beside him on the cushioned bench of the nook in The Trembling Twosome.

The pixie smiled now too. "You'll be with her, on her whale-journey, Reyse-of-my-heart? Just as you were this time?"

"Yes, indeed. This was my 'rehearsal', only without the whales!" laughed the loyal and trust-worthy fairy. "And this time I *answered the call of the white rose* to come to her on the shores of Star Island in my fairy-form, but next time --- far from there --- I'll be in my golden-eagle-guise, I expect. Or maybe even as an Irishman named Liam ... perhaps rowing alongside the whale-fathers in a little black *curragh*!" Eli joined in his laughter now. "But, yes indeed Piv, I'll be with her, until she comes to the Vortex. From there, she will be in other company."

"And so then, just like today and the voyage you've made together from Holy Bay this morning," nodded Piv, "Peronne will bear Eli and Habukaz will bear you?"

"Peronne will bear *Mélusine*," corrected Reyse. "She will become her true self as she arrives back in Faërie and is met by her flying-horse in the outer oceans of the far north. I will remain on the *other* side of the Portal --- without Habukaz, I'm afraid; and I'll find my way home from there. Or so I hope."

"But what happens to Mélusine's *true* body, in the vault, then?" Piv's voice was all perplexity and concern.

Now Jizay sighed rather philosophically, and commented, in silence, "I expect it will be transformed into another creature, if the legends speak the truth. And legends, somehow, always do. And when Mélusine and Peronne arrive at Scholar Owl Island, they will find that the Sun and the Moon have united in a single loving embrace, and that the Princess's two forms, her two lives --- human and fey, solid and subtle --- are come together into one."

"Both Mélusine and *Licorne*," whispered Reyse into her ear.

"All is one," murmured Eli in reply to him, and to her pixie-friend and golden hound. "Yes, I will be Mélusine *and* Licorne. For all will be, at last, one."

****

Early that afternoon, before their departure from the Silver City to go to Mermaid Island, Reyse and Eli stood on a modest balcony protruding from one of the silver turrets of the Royal Moon Tower. They would shortly be re-joined by the King and Queen, and by Periwinkle --- who had, all three, found that they had things to discuss in private following lunch.

As for Eli and Reyse, they had been happy *not* to discuss *anything*. It was enough to stand together, *alone* together, for this last hour in the City of Fantasie, looking out upon its autumn colours and savouring the vibrant breeze and the playful lights of the Great Trees.

Eli had tried to listen for the notes of the Trees, or of the Gates from afar, but she heard nothing particular. Just the hooting of owls, small and great --- some of them surely Scholar Owls --- and even what sounded like the melodious and plaintive song of a nightingale coming from the central Garden around the sacred Source, itself encircled, embraced and hallowed by the seven giants. Her thoughts extended to those *other* giants, too: the Stones, out of view and yet now permanently and forcefully etched in the memories of her Visits home.

She had, just before lunch, very briefly gone again to her mother's Concocting Cell, to see the Queen's Head Vase glowing on its little table --- though she had not felt moved to draw too near to it. And from there --- when she had been joined by her mother --- she had also returned to the Queen's Music Room, where the Harp of Barrywood had been carefully placed during her sojourn on Star Island. She and Rhynwanol had played a duet to delight Aulfrin when he came to look for them there; though, true to say, Eli had considered it a quartet, for Gaëtanne and Roísín were no mere 'instruments' but rather co-creators in the interpretation of the enchanted tunes!

She and both her parents had gone, *en route* to their dining-room, to the great Council Chamber of the Seven Arches and Eli had even approached the pulsating vibrations of the curtained column at its centre. But she did not dare to touch the tapestries again, uninvited; and so she simply and silently sent out a little message of thanks to her grand-father and to the Light in the Tower's 'womb'.

As all of these 'souvenirs' floated across Eli's mind, she turned to face Reyse; but she could still find no words to say to her companion and champion --- nothing to add to all of their shared voyages and adventures, quests and victories, tensions and trials as well as times of comfortable and natural tenderness.

As they regarded one another, the King and Queen arrived in the sitting-room behind the balcony, and with them not only Piv but Garo and Brocéliana also.

It was to the two young lovers that Eli addressed her words, warm and sincere: "Ah! I'm so glad that you've come in time, just before I must leave! I wanted to thank you so much, dear and amazing Garo, and you too my darling Moon-Child of Mermaids. You'd both flown away before I could say a word, so I am so pleased to see you again and so have the chance to express my gratitude!"

Garo bowed slightly, and Brocéliana came forward to kiss her sister's forehead, before she replied.

"We didn't have the right to actually *land* on Star Island, of course. We were only requested to take you as far as its shores!"

"And not even quite *that* far," laughed the sandy-haired, youthful Dragon-Lord. "I was very relieved to see the marvellous mermaid in Holy Bay below us. It was not simple for you to achieve steady flight with your own wings in the highly charged atmosphere surrounding the Star, and I knew that the Lady Ecume would help you to alight on the Island without wetting your feet. Well, *almost* without a little foot-bath! I think your short climb up the jagged point where she had chosen the *easiest* place of entry was quite wave-washed nonetheless!"

"Yes," laughed Eli, "I did have a bit of a scramble to get clear of the breakers chasing me up the tricky threshold of the Sage-Hermit's abode!"

Aulfrin's hand was on Garo's shoulder. "It is extremely convenient to have a shape-changer in the family, my boy. My thanks are joined to Eli's. But do I understand aright? The

Lord Hwittir made an appearance too, earlier, at the Stone Circle, was it?"

"Yes, my Liege, just at the moment when I and my Lady Brocéliana arrived, even before we had assumed our animal-forms. The great Stag appeared before us all --- in vision and voice only of course, as is his custom --- to give warning of Erreig's latest *caprice* to the Sage-Hermit, and to Eli. I can reassure you, Your Majesties, my sister Alégondine is already aware of our father's somewhat perfidious flight, by swift *tursa*, back over the eastern sea-leagues of your realm and into the waters beyond Sea-Horse Bay. But we have, as yet, still no news from her watchful-moths of his exact whereabouts, or of his intentions."

"At least he was *not* on the Star, as wraith or fairy, while Eli sojourned there," sighed the Queen. "That, at any rate, was a blessing. Truly, I am very grateful for the appearance of the Lord Hwittir beside the Stone's central Source, to alert us all to the threat of that *mischief-maker* returning to the Shee Mor.

"And," Rhynwanol continued, "I join my thanks to my husband's, and my compliments to you as shape-shifter, dear Garo --- and Brocéliana too!"

"Ah, my dearest Majesty," smiled the lovely half-fairy, "that is *not* a skill of mine, not yet! It was by Garo's gifts that I could take the form of a tiny white moth --- a suggestion offered by Alégondine, I might add. And it was a lovely way to travel, especially by dragon-flight! I was quite protected under one of Garo's silver scales. Though once or twice, I must admit, I peeped out to see the expression on Eli's face!"

All the company laughed, and Periwinkle flew once around the group, slapping his knees as he landed once again between Eli and Garo.

"Oh, I wish I could have seen it!" he chuckled in his piccolo-chiming tones. "My little Eli-sine flown across all the hundreds of miles of red and gold Quillir, past the Yellow Wren Mountain and all along the Rivers Silverfire and Luef! Dragons of all sizes and strengths must have been soaring about the Beldrum Mountains and scratching their crested-and-horned heads with wonder at the sight of that handsome worm ... and all the while not one of them guessing that the sleek and silver dragon speeding south like lightning was none other than my darling Garo; and that kneeling between his great, green wings was my little Eli!"

Garo laughed with them all, and bowed once more to Eli, accepting her renewed gratitude and Piv's applause with a hand over his heart.

"I think we were lucky," he concluded, "that my father's strange behaviour is causing such worry among the dragons and the bats and even in the clans of the Sun-Singers. They really don't know what he will do next, and so they seem to be holding their breath. And added to that was the blessing of having Finnir and Timair in the red-mounded courts of the King of Cats; for the presence of the two great Princes there created a focus for all the eyes of the province. The news they have taken to Isck regarding their criss-crossed identities will be circulating across the length and breadth of Quillir now, and made into Sun-Song and Cat-Ballad, Dragon-Chant and Lizard-Legend for many a year to come, I do not doubt!"

****

Brocéliana and Garo would not be coming to Mermaid Island, as they were to return to Quillir this evening, to the White Dragon Fortress which would now become their home. The loving farewells between Eli and the radiant couple were not sorrowful, but rather filled with hope and happiness, a confidence in all their shared dreams for the future of the Alliance of the Spiralling Stars. In any case, Eli was assured that the lovers would be venturing into the human-lands often over the coming years; and Eli's slight sorrow at today's parting was assuaged by thoughts of how and when they might next meet --- perhaps in Scotland, where Brocéliana would most probably go to work in company with the twins.

For their voyage to Sea-Horse Bay, Reyse rode Habukaz of course, with Róisín tied by the mauve Craigie tartan around her neck; while Eli and Piv were mounted together on Peronne, and the King had his grey-sorrel mare Cynnabar, with her russet and ochre wings. Rhynwanol took this occasion to ride a beautiful creature newly arrived in the royal stables, as her own winged-horse had returned to the Salley Woods and the Flying Horse Fields to the south of Aumelas-Pen when the Queen had been banished. That pale mouse-grey palfrey had become the matriarch-mare of many famous winged-colts and fillies since, but she had not yet been invited to return to Fantasie. And so, for this flight, Rhynwanol was seated on a young stallion, jet black with wings of silver and white and crimson feathers overlaid.

Ferglas and Jizay were also preparing to set forth; though their land-road would lead directly to the Castle at the rim of the Inward Sea just before the full moon, two nights from now. At that time, Finnir and Timair would also have returned from their audience with King Isck.

The company travelling by winged-horse broke their swift flight at mid-course, in the lands lying between the Shooting Star Lake and the great Forest of Barrywood which concealed the Unicorn Glens. Alighting in a verdant clearing, they paused to nibble on the fruits and nuts presented to them by local fairy-families, complemented by offerings from several squirrels and two very polite blackbirds --- bearing assorted tasty leaves and berries.

Their little snack was shared further with a tribe of dogs like great, shaggy wolves. Eli was told that these were the native canines of this wild region, running in small packs throughout the wide prairies and also under the trees of the enchanted forest. They had coats of roan-grey dotted with pale marigold-orange, and eyes of deep silver --- rather like Vanzelle's but deeper: more the colour of pewter. Many of the fairy-children sat astride their furry backs, stroking the wolves' noble heads and their pointed ears bordered with silky black hairs and studded with tiny tangerine-hued jewels right at their tips.

To the south --- over the plains of lush grasses decorated with many groups of angular stones --- far above and beyond the eaves of the Forest they could see the eastern arm of the majestic Turquoise Mountain range. The Feather Mountain and the White Hart Head already wore long veils of snow, halfway down their gleaming green-blue slopes. But most beautiful of all, at least to Eli, was the mysterious and almost endless line of tall, ancient and dark trees --- inviting rather than foreboding --- marking the borders of Barrywood.

Mists swirled around their trunks very like the perpetual fogs that enveloped the Stone Circle. The closest of the trees were easily eight or ten miles away, but even from so far, their intense alertness was palpable and almost heady. Eli knew, also, that she was surely feeling drawn to the spirit of Finnir, and his Castle looking out to Windy Hill --- far, far off in the depths of those Woods. Though the Prince himself was probably still in Quillir today...

As she stood, gazing across the plains to Barrywood, Reyse came suddenly and inexplicably into her mind. The thought of him, and especially of standing with him on the balcony earlier this afternoon and looking out over the Silver City of her true fairy-birth, fell into Eli's heart like a pebble into still water. She waited for the ripples to flow away and leave her again in peaceful contemplation --- but they did not.

Finally she turned, and saw that Reyse was watching her from where he stood beside Habukaz, who was herself engaged in conversation, it seemed, with two or three of the roan wolves. His expression was at once tender and troubled.

She walked back to join the company, as everyone prepared to take flight once more. Reyse held her regard for a moment;

and then without a word he exhaled slowly and completely, walked briskly to Habukaz, and was the first to take to the air.

The waxing gibbous moon was rising high before them, clearly reflected in the early evening blue of Sea-Horse Bay, as they flew down onto the northern lawns of Mermaid Island to land before the doors of Leyano's castle. The Prince was coming down the steps to greet them; while Pallaïs, dressed all in sea-shades, remained at the top of the staircase, but greeted Eli very warmly when they met at the great doors.

It was delightful to be reunited with Leyano, and Eli was looking forward to a wonderful evening with the gathered company of fairies. But before that, she asked if it would be possible to have a little time alone with her mother and father.

They sat close together, in an intimate room like a small study, high in one of the eastern towers with a view of Dawn Rock framed in the rounded window. Eli cleared her throat, and then breathed very deeply.

"I wondered," she began slowly, "I wondered if I should not have made a formal *appointment* to speak with you both in Fantasie, in the great Council Chamber perhaps, about the choice I have made, about staying here or…going back. I know you have understood my --- or rather Mélusine's --- *intention*, at least much more clearly since my days with Aulfrelas. But I realise that I haven't fully explained all of the details regarding my decision. I haven't told you what my journey to the Stones or to the Star *really* has given me. And I haven't declared, **officially**, my choice."

The face of Aulfrin, lately so much more relaxed and even more jovial than usual --- owning to the home-coming of his Queen --- became slightly sadder. His crown's emeralds grew dark, and his twinkling green eyes seemed to become cloudy. The Queen reached her hand to him, and their fingers intertwined.

"But then," continued Eli, a little nervously still, "I recalled that it was from Dawn Rock that I went *into* the human-lands as a baby; so I thought that maybe it was appropriate, after all, to tell you here."

The King opened his mouth slightly, as if he were going to speak; but instead he simply closed his eyes for a minute, as if keeping his tears in check, and remained silent. Rhynwanol nodded with a gentle smile of encouragement to her daughter, who now found the courage to continue.

"My dear and beloved parents, I want to thank you for everything: these three glorious Visits, my changeling-adventure, all of my wonderful life here in Faërie, spanning many centuries. But my decision is made, and was made long ago --- even before my transformation."

Aulfrin's face grew a little paler, but he did not interrupt Eli.

"Yes, well, I will explain. You see, as I've intimated to you before now, the thought was growing within me, since the spring really, that I might *not* come back here after this final Visit; it was tickling me from my very first three-week homecoming months ago. But it was only when I went to my vault on Scholar Owl Island that I truly *knew*. The certainty came to me there, undeniably and in such a wave of peace and acceptance and deep contentment, it was almost like meditating with the Smiling Salmon! I knew that, as Mélusine, I had already <u>decided</u>. This was *my plan*; it was what I intended to do all along. And even if I am not the Princess again yet, I now know that *she* knew. And I have utter faith in her --- I mean, in myself."

"What *exactly* did she know?" whispered Aulfrin slowly, at last able to speak, but only in a very hushed tone.

Eli almost wanted to cry, she felt such pathos in her father's voice; but she held firm.

"She knew that the adventure would not end here. It's only half completed. She had, from the start, decided… to do rather as you had done, my dear father: to leave her human life by the portal of a human 'death'. She intended, always, to come back, to return to Faërie --- but not right away. She still wants to do more, and she desires to *die* as a human. I can't know exactly why this was, and is, *so* important to her; but I am convinced that the most crucial part of all of this amazing experience is yet to come. And I want to go to the end, and find out why she conceived of this plan and put it in place.

"And I know that I *can* do so, and that I *can* come back. Because the Sage-Hermit will give me back the three days of this third Visit of mine which I have 'left' on Star Island. And in those three days, when they are returned to me after the first day of my human-death, I can come home."

Eli hesitated now. Having thought through how she would tell this to her father even when she was lingering on the sacred Isle, she still did not find her words coming just as she had meant them to. Instinctively, she very discreetly lifted her left hand to the side of her head and touched the Flaming-Moon Ear-ring where it dangled --- invisible to the King.

To her great relief, her mother took up the tale, and remarked, "Eli has been given a charmed gift, a *token*, my dear Aulfrin, by the Lady Ecume. It is not *quite* like the amber-token held by you, for it is not necessarily with the Black Key itself that this miracle will be made manifest. That sombre article is a key to use 'in great need and at the end of hope', so the Ancestors always said, and that is how we always characterise it.

"However, in Eli's case, hope shall *not be* at its end --- when the time comes! For she is a child of hope, the most daring and hopeful and high-dreaming of all of our children. And so she has been given *another* means to unlock a rather exceptional door. She is coming back to us, when she has traversed her human experience of dying, by the path of the Garnet Vortex."

Aulfrin's eyes had been fixed and staring, for a moment, as if he had been turned to ice. At the mention of the Garnet Vortex, he sat up a little straighter, as if in alarm.

Eli breathed deeply, and squared her shoulders. And then she took up her own explanations once again.

"Yes, my dear father, I will return to Faërie by the secret vortex and the Fourth Portal. I found it during my Great Charm --- Peronne and I found it, I am sure. Of course, we discovered it in Faërie, but I will find it on the other side too; I am confident of that. I will be guided there, in those three magical days which I have been accorded. And --- I will not be utterly alone."

Though his face was rather white, his voice was growing slightly warmer as he murmured, "I was not aware that it *truly* existed, though I have known all my long life of the myths which speak of it, like those of the Eleventh Gate of Fantasie. Naturally, I should have guessed that the legend of the Fourth Portal could not be founded, well, on *nothing*. But I never guessed that you, my daughter, had found where it lies."

His voice dropped to a hushed whisper. And then, as if speaking to himself, he added, "But of course: the legend speaks of a **unicorn** being ridden through the Vortex. It says that such a sign is to be shown only when the Fourth Portal can at last open inwards, *into* Faërie. It has never done so yet. It has only ever opened in the other sense, and that only in myth too!"

His voice rose slightly, but his eyes were still wide with wonder and not a little apprehension. "But you say you will not be alone. *Who* will help you, Eli?"

"A loyal and loving... friend, and also --- in the swirling waters --- the Keeper of the Veil," replied Eli.

"And myself and Morliande and the Lady Ecume," added the Queen. "We shall not be far, when the time comes."

"You, my dear, and the Great Ones you mention, may only be of assistance on *this* side, I imagine," Aulfrin reminded her. "No one can go *through* the tunnels and caverns of a human death *with* Eli. The paths through the shadowlands, and through the roaring Vortex, those she would have to traverse on *that* side, and unaccompanied."

Eli took another deep breath, but as she exhaled this time, she simply smiled, rather than speaking.

Aulfrin added, "In my case, I had the Mushroom Lord --- my own father as I now know him to be --- to help me, but not for *all* of the way. And I was going to one of the Shee Mor's three 'substantial' Portals. The Fourth is said to be phantom, and fluid. In legend it is like the Island of the Star of the White Seal, which is constantly moving and slipping into invisibility. I don't know if the Sage-Hermit (or Hermitess as will be the case soon) will be able to appear to you in the lands, or oceans, leading to *that* Portal, my dearest Eli. Evidently, it is on the other side of the human-world, in the hemisphere of the South Pole!"

"As for that," said Eli, her smile increasing by an act of will, but also by a strange mounting joy within her, "I wouldn't put it past Alégondine, or even the Lady Ecume or the Lord Hwittir, to appear --- if only in vision! Or even *others* of this astounding world that is my true home," she added, a little more softly.

"But above and beyond all of my helpers and guides, tokens and charms," she continued, "I now have something even more precious. Much more precious and important. I won't have my fairy-wings on the other side, but I will have other wings: those of my own certainty and *self*-confidence. I'll have wings of **faith**, faith in myself. I'll reach the Fourth Portal, as Eli, as a human; and I'll come through it and the Garnet Vortex as the Princess Mélusine. And I will do so because I *believe* ... in myself. I don't have any doubt about any of it, no doubt at all. For I do, at last, **believe** with all my heart."

There was a very long silence. At last, the King spoke, and as he did so, the emeralds and peridots of his crown began to glisten again, as did his eyes.

"No fairy has ever done such a thing. It is outlandish and ridiculously ambitious and wild and mad; it is *utter* folly...

"And that is why I must **agree** with you, Eli. For it is <u>exactly</u> the sort of *phoenix-feat* that Mélusine would conceive of, and that only Mélusine could achieve.

"You will be, as you always dreamed of being, a ghostly-unicorn turned 'real' --- or possibly riding one! You will rise from your Beltaine-like ritual of flame and water, out of your human-death-Portal, like a blue-priest-bird flying into and out of the great lake of Fantasie, like a branch blessed by the Great Trees materialising out of a fountain of diamond-light --- though it will be *garnet* light! Yes, it is perfect, and perfectly *you*. You have found the courage to be true to yourself, and to live the complex and exciting and original poem of your life to the last letter.

"My Queen, you are quite right --- this will not be the *end* of hope. It will be its beginning. Even now my hope is already *infinite*, and I am comforted and fully confident that our daughter will find her path back to us."

****

A very convivial meal was shared by all that evening, with enough *buicuri* to satisify even Piv.

After their supper, the high northern windows of the upper balcony were opened, and under the bright moon --- despite the chill of the evening --- the assembled company listened to a short but very sweet serenade, blown across the Bay from a distant rock where the Lady Ecume sat and played on the Harp of Seven Eyes. Then they gathered before a fine fire crackling in the grate in the comfortable room where the members of the Alliance had met in June; instruments were brought out and music was made far into the night.

Eli had Finnir's harp, naturally, and its Golden Rose shone and glinted in the firelight, but it was also lit from within with its own joyful soul. Aulfrin's silver flute sang a soprano line to complement Rhynwanol's strumming of a pretty dulcimer made of spruce and rose-wood, with carvings of tiny dolphins making the soundholes in the lower bout, and lilies in the upper. Leyano played his lovely lute, Pallaïs her golden-wood oboe, and Reyse was offered a slim, narrow harp: it was small and light, but with a bell-like sound which seemed to dance about the rounder and richer notes of Róisín. Piv did not play, but rather sang, his piccolo-voice at once both clear and deeply touching, very like the song of the nightingale in the Garden of the Great Trees. Though his lyrics were in the ancient pixie-tongue, their crystal-syllables were replete with melancholy and abundant hope combined.

The melodies subsided as the hour grew late, but before they all went to their beds, the King brought up the subject of Erreig.

"We may learn more from the two great Princes when we go to Barrywood tomorrow; but I must reiterate the persistence of this mystery. Where has the Dragon-Chieftain gone on his swift *tursa*, and why? You must be on your guard, my dearest Eli, when you step back into the land of mankind. For he may, perchance, follow you there --- or he may have gone there ahead of you."

"I would hazard a guess," observed Leyano, "that he is more likely to return to Quillir than to the world. I do not feel that he is 'hunting' Eli; though he might retain much curiosity about her. I have had no news, my father, about his exact whereabouts. But I have the intuition that he is torn between his love for Vanzelle and his plight of missing Bawn! His audacity and aggression, his affection and ambition, they should clearly be of concern to my dear sister; but I do not think he is ready to *confront* her again, not in this phase of her evolution as Eli Penrohan. For all he knows, she has simply decided to forsake her fairy-life and accept the finality of a human one. He cannot know of her ultimate goals or plans, at least so I believe."

"I am not so sure," remarked Periwinkle, shaking his head and making his yellow curls dance about his round face. "I think he has *many* ways of learning *many* things. He is not so skilled as I am in the language of mushrooms, it's true." Here the pixie raised his chin quite proudly. "Notwithstanding that, he has the means to perceive and to uncover much that is hidden or hinted-at. But I think my sweet Leyano is right in this: he is missing his white dragon-mount and wishes to return to the Bay of Secrets --- even if only to have news. For Bawn has the eyes of an eagle for sun-sight *and* far-sight, but she also has the sharp ears of a flying fox: the massive matriarch worm can capture sounds and signals, secrets and the subtle sighing of stars, and she can manoeuvre through the tangles of a labyrinthine-plot like a black bat can wheel between the spiky pinnacles of rock concealing the Dragons' Drink!"

It was now Eli's turn to grow pale, rather as her father had done earlier. But even in the midst of a rising trepidation she stopped short, and then she smiled. No, she found that --- in truth --- she was no longer afraid of Erreig at all.

"*I am greater, higher, more noble and more powerful than Erreig,*" she heard herself --- in memory --- proclaiming, here in this very Castle, to her father and to Leyano, on her second Visit.

And now, aloud, to all the company gathered about her, she said, "I have watched him and his petty ego fly off, like a dragon screeching away into the clear blue --- no longer turbulent --- skies. And I remained when he fled, with the knowledge that Finnir and Leyano, and then Reyse, were beside me and supporting me." Eli glanced at her brother and her champion as she pronounced these words. "But even just *on my own*, just upheld by my own knowledge of who and what I am, I was victorious in that moment. I'm not worried, for I no longer fear Erreig," she concluded.

Leyano regarded her with pride; Piv with deep devotion and her parents with incalculable love and relief. But it was Reyse's expression that touched her most. His eyes were dancing with smiles and summery light, as happy as the moment when she had opened wide her arms and relished the pure joy of that victory, on the Island in Loch Eil --- her hair streaming out and her laughter blending with the perfumes of the flowers and the tang of the sea-sweet breeze.

The Eagle-Lord lifted his chalice to her, as if offering a toast to her fine speech --- but Eli knew what his heart was celebrating, and hoping.

As the others, likewise, clinked and drank to Eli's affirmations, Reyse concluded, "Indeed, the fierce dragon has flown away from you, forever, I believe, Eli. I also saw that capricious ego cowed and heard the anguished screeching of the great worm as it wheeled away! I do not think that Erreig will ever seek to match wills with you again."

It wasn't until the following morning, the morning of the 19th of November, that Eli found herself alone with Leyano for a moment, sipping an early tea in the little room with the balcony looking out to the east, where they had shared their first moments of rediscovery of one another on her second Visit.

"Last night," her brother remarked, "You said that you had seen that *petty ego fly off, like a dragon screeching away into the clear blue skies.* And Reyse had reiterated your remark, saying that he, too, had witnessed the great worm wheeling away. His reference to that image made me wonder if you have perhaps *told* him of your encounter. You are, I know, very close to the Eagle-Lord, your protector and tutor, friend and...suitor, too, for many years; but I did not know that *anyone* had heard of that enchanted episode."

Leyano's placid Buddha-like smile and demeanour were, as ever, able to lull Eli into a warm relaxation, like floating on one's back in a tropical lagoon. But now she opened her eyes wide, placing her bowl of frothy tea on the sea-shell table.

She spoke very softly. "So you *were* there, you and Pallaïs, you were **not** a 'vision' --- and it was all 'real' and really *did* happen like that? But dear Leyano, Reyse **was** there too, at the end. He saw it. But perhaps you and Pallaïs had already departed…?"

"Reyse was not on the island, my dear sister! And we were both with you until the end --- when that occurred."

Eli felt increasingly perplexed.

"But at least you must have seen Erreig. He was not a vision…"

"Erreig? No, not at all. Erreig was not here either."

There was an abrupt silence.

"*Here*?! And when *what* occurred, exactly?" asked Eli, completely bewildered.

"When you were on the Island of Anéislis, here in Sea-Horse Bay, with the great dragon. When you sent the wild-worm streaming off like a puppy with its tail between its legs! It was here, my dear Eli, not more than seventy-five miles from where we sit. I thought it clear that you had recalled the true event, to have shared it with Reyse. Is that not what you were referring to?"

Eli felt herself slipping into **utter** confusion --- once again!

"What *is* this news, my dearest Leyano? Are there multiple events, or repetitions of this same encounter? I've seen the vision of that confrontation, or victory, or whatever it was, on more than one occasion, and so did Lily in fact. And then, when I went into the world, to Scotland, to reclaim the Amethyst Cloth from Erreig, it actually took place. Well, first the vision of it came to me again, very vividly; and then the actual scene was played out, on an island which appeared in Loch Eil. That, as I had been told just before, was the scene 'offered' to me, by the Lady Ecume. But what happened seemed at once a vision, and yet also so real, so deeply true. I actually *sailed* there with my Uncle Mor --- well, we sailed to that loch, but I think the island was a magical one called into being by Morliande --- but Morvan saw much of what happened too, as it *truly* took place, finally. We spoke about it; and he even saw Finnir there, I believe. Erreig left, vanquished I suppose you could say, and then Reyse was with me…"

Her calm and beautiful poet-brother, the Leo of Lily's miracle and the fair and noble Prince brought back from the brink of a mortal wound by the Dragon-Lord, shook his head with a chuckle.

"Ah, dreams and symbols, sonnets and ballads and epistles, Eli. We send our life's messages to ourselves, I think, over and over, practicing and playing them like a harpist does her favourite pieces or her most arduous scales and exercises. And sometimes we even have an audience for our recurring recitals, and even for our dress-rehearsals of them! It is clear, from what you say, that Reyse was somehow permitted to enter into the play of images that were recreated for you by the wondrous mer-harper, and of course it was meant to include Erreig while you were on your Scottish adventure, and it <u>did</u>. It is very touching and beautiful that we, myself and Pallaïs, took form in your imagination also.

"But it was not what I think you would term 'real', my sweet sister. It was still, and ever, a dream and a poem, a memory peeping through from Mélusine into Eli.

"I can show you Anéislis Island, if you like, where it truly happened, and that might help to bring the event into focus in your memory. It would make a nice little outing for us, before you leave. For I don't suppose that I'll get to see you again too often, during your remaining human years, not on the threshold of *this* Portal, at any rate --- unless you travel to California again! Yes, let's fly out over the infamous island, with our own wings, just for --- well --- a shared moment between you and me and my lady-love, and a little recollection of that poem-play!"

And so Leyano slipped out, for an instant, to invite his fair Pallaïs to join them, and then he led his incredulous and bemused sister onto the balcony; and in the rosy rays of the rising sun, they all three called forth their wings and soared low over Mermaid Island to the south. Eli descried the perfect little fairy-tale castle on the coast far beneath them, where they had gone on frazian ponies to hear the students of magical and healing music; and then they continued out over the wide waters to the south-east, far over the dolphin-dotted waves of the broad Bay. Perhaps fifty more miles of sea they crossed, and then, low and luscious, like a jade set into a variegated blue enamel background, an island appeared. Leyano glanced at his sister with a little nod, and they began their descent.

The fairy-couple flew down ahead of Eli, who took a moment to circle over the rather lozenge-shaped isle, gazing at it with one hand lifted before her mouth in amazement. She could recall having glimpsed it, in flight, when she had gone with Reyse and Piv and the King to look out upon Dizzy Dolphin Point. But on that occasion, they had seen it only from afar…

At last she alighted beside her brother and the blue sea-fairy. They all kept their great wings on their backs for several minutes, making them resemble a trio of glorious giant butterflies sunning themselves on a gigantic leaf. The island was not in full bloom now, but even in its winter-garb Eli could see its rich vegetation of bushes and tall, thick grasses, some with pale yellow or dark orange flowers, a little faded, still clinging to them. Beyond the shrubbery was the ochre-coloured clearing set upon a rounded hillock at the island's centre. But it was bare…

"I stood just there," mumbled Eli under her breath, gesturing with one hand while the other was now raised to hold down her wildly blowing red hair. "I stood there, and the dragon wheeled away, um, in *that* direction. And it was windy, like today, because my hair was blowing just as it is now --- and then I stretched out my arms, like this!"

"Yes, yes --- I remember it like that too," laughed Leyano. "And do you recall where <u>I</u> stood?"

Eli hesitated, but only for a second. "*There,*" she said firmly. "And you were in your armour, just as you were when you stood beside Bawn, in my vision on the Island in Loch Eil."

"I should hope I would be in my armour, with *that* particular dragon so near my home!" And he laughed more merrily still. "But here it was not Bawn, dear one. Not when the event *really* took place."

"Not Bawn?" repeated Eli, nonplussed, and then she asked, "Did I truly see Finnir, or was he a hallucination too?!"

"Of that, I can give you no assurance," replied Leyano, squinting a little with doubt. "You may have seen him, in the veritable scene here, but you never told me if you did. In his true fairy-body, I think, he was at his Portal and not here, in September of 1958."

"It was fifty-two years ago? It was while I was completing my Great Charm, then."

"Seven months *after* its completion. You ended your Great Charm on Imbolc of that year, the 1st of February. In September, you had come to see me to tell me about your desire to become a changeling. You had asked our father in mid-May, as I recall, and now you were ready to begin your preparations. Aulfrin was just making his preliminary visits into France, by way of Demoran's Portal, to find a suitable lady. And, by... *chance*, he found a queen! And you had come to Mermaid Island, to tell me of your decision.

"But while we were speaking in my Golden Sand Castle of your plans, you felt a presence, and a threat. That, in itself, was not surprising. As you had just completed three-hundred-and-thirty-three years of the most intense and enchanted work that a fairy can undertake, it is logical to suppose that certain 'forces' were, perhaps, arising to *challenge* you and your new-found strengths. In fact, whenever we take a step or two forward in our spiralling lives, this *must* occur. Every gain must be honed and refined, solidified and established if you like; every advancement and achievement must be put to the test, to become fully integrated into our being. At least, this is true in Faërie --- though I would be surprised if it were not the case in the human world also.

"Now, I have never dared the Great Charm, so I cannot really comment on what it might be like to live through that time of training and growth; in any case, we are talking of the Princess Mélusine, so I imagine it was even more extraordinary, dangerous, difficult and *crazy* than usual!" Here he winked at his sister, very much as he had in the room where the King's children were waiting for their father after his aerial battle with Erreig over the silver turrets of Fantasie in 1367.

"And so, on that blustery September day in 1958, we flew here together --- as we did today: Pallaïs and myself and you. I had only recently met my lovely sea-fairy sweetheart then, but she was ever a close companion of the Lady Ecume (who doubtless had also clearly felt both *your* presence in the Bay and --- as you had --- the menace and proximity of the dragon). Therefore, Pallaïs, who had likewise sensed an imminent and impending danger in the heightened energies of the sea-currents here, wished to be beside me --- in case we would be required, together, to challenge your adversary. Thus *both* of us accompanied you to your confrontation with the great reptile.

"If I'm not mistaken about the date, it was the 12th of September. I also recall, and quite vividly, that the moon was *not quite* new and hidden --- she was a frail and shy sickle of a waning moon-lash that was barely discernable --- but she had risen and was hung in the mid-morning azure sky, almost directly overhead. As the skies were windy and clear, she was visible, at least to fairies, positioned neatly over your head from where I was regarding you. I wonder, did the dragon see the moon also, and by that token did he thus *know* that the Princess Mélusine had heeded his summons. Or perhaps she herself had drawn him hither!

"Whether or not he saw that timorous moon, *you*, he certainly saw! And you, my dear sister, were **not** shy and timorous at all, as Eagla-Anvash flew up from the south and circled above this Island just as you have done today. And the cool skies became hot and dotted with red embers.

"Bawn's mate, the huge milk-white and shadowy-green-winged dragon-sire of the Beldrum Mountains --- exiled for long centuries in the isles of the volcanoes far in the south-eastern oceans --- roared through these skies, his crimson-tipped tail like a writhing serpent in his wake. He was alone, for he has never been ridden; not even the skilful Erreig could tame him, if indeed he ever tried. Without a doubt, Eagla-Anvash fully expected to find you here, and he was set on attack, or on hindering your choice of paths: he clearly wished to confound your decision to become a changeling.

"There are no creatures in Faërie, Eli, small or large, which are wholly malevolent or vile. But Eagla-Anvash is the closest I think we might come to a truly *vicious* dragon. But I am convinced that his determination to hinder you certainly had nothing to do with Erreig. The ferocious worm may have had an ancient and personal grudge against our royal family --- going back to Aulf the Mighty; that is possible. There are very old tales which tell of this dragon seeking to counter Aulf's complicity with the fairies of the farthest shees: those which had Portals opening into the antipodes of the human-lands. But if it was a grain of hatred sown in those mythic times which brought the massive worm here to meet you, or a more personal grudge against Mélusine, I cannot say. It is well known that he was ever redolently opposed to the passage of fairies back and forth into the world of mankind, and I have long wondered if Erreig's own opinions on that subject spring from his being in awe of the impressive Eagla-Anvash.

"In any case, I and Pallaïs watched, with great admiration and wonder I might add, as you wrestled in thought and spirit with the huge monster. He bears jewels, even as fairies win in their Initiations and wear encrusted or embedded in forehead or ear or hand, and his --- upon the crown of his head, at the base of his neck and also studded into his tail --- are immensely powerful ones. But those borne by the Princess Mélusine are remarkable also!

"Both of you --- using your jewels, your wills and your inner force --- fought one another with a play of exploding light, with fire and with wild wind-storms, with sublime moon-dancing and searing-hot sun-song. And a cunning and formidable *monster* Eagla-Anvash is, to be sure, both in mass and in mentality.

"But, at last, he was vanquished, and you victorious.

"It was obvious that this was something which you *had* to achieve, my amazing and audacious Eli. I would even go so far as to call it a 'rite-of-passage', set by Mélusine *for* Mélusine, before she could carry-out her transformation.

"It's really no wonder that you have seen it oft-replayed in vision, or dream, or that Lily felt it too. It was your *medal-of-honour*, won before you could continue onwards. And, now you mention it, I wonder if Finnir *was* implicated in that feat you achieved on the 12th of September in 1958. I don't know, myself, why he should have been --- but the idea came into my head and heart as I spoke, and he is present in my mind's eye, like a doubling of you in my vision when I call the scene to memory: yes, I can see Finnir too, now, even as we speak of the event.

"But I do not see the Lord Reyse there, either in my heart or in my imagination; and I feel certain that he was *not* here in the Shee Mor when the scene actually occurred. But only *you* know all the details, of course, my dear sister."

Eli inhaled deeply, and as she exhaled with a long sigh she confessed, "I *don't* know them all yet --- or again --- but I will. One day.

"Thank you, Leyano. Thank you for bringing me here, and for so many things that have been revealed to me by you, or near you, or because of you. You have played, I think, a very important role for me in all of my changeling-experience, and in the life of Lily, too."

Her brother stroked her blowing hair, and with a tender, tanned hand he gently caressed her face as well.

"It has been my privilege, my lovely sister. As it is my privilege to be your brother and to be a part of your legendary story.

"But for today, you are not quite a legend, just Eli Penrohan, and in that humble guise you must return to the world of humans, and leave this land of mad dragons! Come, we must return to Mermaid Island."

Nodding, as she sighed once again, Eli pushed her loose and billowing hair back from her eyes, and glanced up into the sweet blue of the morning sky, so reminiscent --- always to her --- of the shade of Finnir's astounding eyes.

With a sharp intake of breath, almost like a cry of alarm, she suddenly gripped Leyano's arm. At the same instant, Pallaïs stepped forward and reached her slender, white hand up and across Eli's face and then high out towards the heavens. From the sea-fairy's open palm a brilliant aquamarine emitted an instantaneous and very fine ray of pastel-blue light, only a shade paler than the sky itself. The peaceful shaft of protective light was directed to a distant form, sailing on a pathway of the eastern wind, but clearly aware of the three figures gathered on the tiny island far below him.

"Erreig," hissed Eli, under her breath. "That is *surely* Erreig!"

"I think you are correct." Leyano's drew forth once more his broad wings --- pale yellow like his own precious diamond, and veined in many intersecting lines of sea-green --- and he enveloped both Pallaïs and Eli as he spoke. "But he does not seem to be stopping here to trouble us. Look, he is increasing his speed now, as if to avoid the calm energies flowing up along the shaft of light from my belovèd's precious jewel."

"That is not Bawn he's riding, is it? It doesn't look like a dragon at all, at least from here. What in the world is it?" asked Eli, still rather shocked, but sounding less frightened now. "It's not Eagla-Anvash, surely; you said he could not be ridden…"

Pallaïs had lowered her arm and the streaming soft-blue light was called back into her palm. She was still looking up at the flying form, as Erreig and his mount diminished into the distance over the Morning Star Shoals, rosy and indistinct in the sea-haze of the western horizon.

Her voice, as musical as her pale oboe's, commented, "No, it is not the fierce Father of Dragons, and neither is it Bawn his lady-mate; it is a *tursa*, and an unusually great one. And flying high, for normally the *tursa* prefer to skim the sea's surface. The Chieftain Erreig has made a new friend, it would seem! I suppose they are headed to Quillir…"

"I hope that is their destination," Leyano reflected thoughtfully, "rather than seeking to lurk in the far foothills of the Turquoise Sisters, on the margins of Barrywood. But I think Finnir should be adverted, nonetheless, of our strange 'sighting' of this morning. We had better go back to my Castle, and arrange for a messenger to fly ahead of us to the enchanted Woods, even before our little company sets off this afternoon."

"Oh dear…" sighed Eli. "I hope Reyse was right, and my wave of confidence as well, and that I will have no further confrontations or problems with Erreig!"

Her brother glanced at her with concern, but he said, "No problem has arisen yet --- so we will remain optimistic and without undue worry; in fact, I would count it as a great blessing that we saw him passing. I doubt that he expected we would be here, so far south of my Castle! He probably hoped to pass quite unnoticed, and now we have an advantage because we have spotted him, and he us! I think he will be very careful, rather than reckless --- for he will certainly realise that the King will now be informed of his passage and his presence, and Finnir also. And that latter may generate more caution and hesitation in the Dragon-Lord's bold spirit than anything else!

"Come now, my dearest Eli, and with a light heart free of all worries. I am glad that you have, at least, revisited this place of your earlier exploits. But now, let us rejoin the others."

"Ah yes," Eli exclaimed. "We never said we were coming here; we didn't tell anyone. They'll be wondering what has happened to us!"

"*Nothing* would surprise any of those who know you, dear and wild Princess! And they will notice that we have all three gone together, so they will know that all is well. It's just that Piv will be getting hungry for lunch, and will probably have discovered the *buicuri* and finished my stock!"

Eli laughed with her darling brother, and his crimson-black eyes sparkled with tenderness for her. As she called forth her *zephyrus*-wings, she looked for a long, rather sentimental moment at Leyano and Pallaïs side by side; they were shining like the sun on the sea, in all the blues and whites and pale greens and diamond-yellows of the water and the Island of Anéislis.

Now all three took flight simultaneously, to go swiftly back to the Golden Sand Castle.

And very few *buicuri*, indeed, remained.

****

Windy Hill Prayer

Chapter Twenty-Two:
Morning Prayer

t was well into the afternoon when the four flying-horses and their five riders set off, sailing over the placid waters of the Bay to the coasts north of the Morning Star Shoals and south of the estuary of the Jolly Fairy River. Before their eyes, the solid blue-green mass of Barrywood's tall trees seemed to rise to meet them. Once over the coastal rock-pools, it was easily another thirty or thirty-five miles, in a graceful and sweeping curve over the dense forest, before they landed in the fore-court of the Castle.

Finnir and Timair were standing side by side on the broad steps; and Eli felt her heart over-flowing with the thrill of beholding them --- so handsome, so filled with love and light, so welcoming --- against the backdrop of flame-coloured ivies meandering over the silver-grey walls.

Gull-messengers had left Leyano's Castle long before the riders had. They had been dispatched by the Prince and the King Aulfrin, as soon as Eli had explained the sighting of Erreig far over Anéislis Island in the south of the Bay. The gulls had been sent to various destinations: firstly to avert Finnir, but also to take word to the Silver City and on to Corr-Seylestar. The Heron-Fairy would then relay the news to Demoran, while the gulls themselves would continue on to Alégondine, Garo and Brocéliana in Quillir. But, according to Aulfrin's intuition and the insights of the sea-harp of the Golden Sand Castle, it seemed most likely that Erreig was making for the Bay of Secrets, to be re-united with his beloved white dragon Bawn.

News was expected on the morrow, when the gulls returned, or when the moths of Alégondine would perhaps bring tidings. For now, there was nothing to do but wait, and to wonder about the recreant's next move.

That evening the company enjoyed a colourful meal of many autumn vegetables, toasted grains, spiced nuts, and goblets of forest-honey mead as dark as molasses.

The hopes and plans of the Alliance were alluded to in their conversations, but not debated or discussed at length. Aulfrin broached the subject of Eli remaining in touch with 'those she loved and who loved her', as he put it, throughout the remaining years of her life. It was to be her choice, of course, but the King hoped that she would be in frequent contact with Faërie at the *thresholds* of the Portals or by using the Silver Leaf and the Golden Flower.

Piv remarked that he would be happy to meet her at the doorsill of the Fair Stair, but he doubted if he would venture beyond it.

"My cousins who have done so, came back quite disappointed," he confessed. "Humans, they said, really do *not* understand mushrooms. I hope the Alliance will be able to re-educate them; but it is a long and patient kind of learning, and mankind seems to rush about a great deal, rather than going slow and steady. Don't they see how the fungus, and the snails too, progress? It's as clear as my cap-and-wings, there's nothing so wise as a toadstool or an interlace-snail, except the Smiling Salmon or the Great Trees themselves!"

Although Eli was not to be deprived of the *memories* of her three Visits --- as would be the case for an 'ordinary' changeling --- she could not hope to pass any of the Portals herself ever again. This was inscribed in the changeling-laws. She had now *formally renounced* the course of remaining in Faërie at the close

Morning Prayer

of her third Visit, and with the pronouncement of that decision she forfeited the right to come into the enchanted realm again while she lived. However, as in the case of the grand-father of Lily, she was welcome to come to the *doors or windows* of Faërie, by appointments granted her in communication with one of her harps --- as usual. This was a special gift or grace, accorded her in complicity with her guides and those who had supported her in both the Great Charm and her transformation: the Lady Ecume, Banvowha the rainbow-fairy, and her own grand-mother the Queen Morliande.

However, if the work of the Alliance should be furthered sufficiently during the years (or hopefully decades) remaining before Eli, then maybe **much greater** forms of exchange could be envisaged between mankind and fairy-folk. But even if such advances were made manifest, of course, Eli Penrohan remained a changeling. She was bound to respect the laws and limitations ordained by her status, until her death-day and then the 'liminal' period of three further magical days which her grand-father, Aulfrelas, has bestowed upon her.

Late in the evening, to Eli's immense joy, Ferglas and Jizay arrived, in company with several of the wolves that Eli had seen in the plains near Shooting Star Lake. They had passed through the Unicorn Glens together, and Jizay's eyes were dancing with wonder at all of the visions accorded them there. But he could put little more into even his profound and silent language than to say that he had passed through those lands only briefly before, when going to his interlude with Eli in the Dordogne farmhouse of Yves --- when he had had Finnir's help to pass the Portal of the Heart Oak and step into the body of the moribund puppy in Ireland whom Eli would find and save. He had returned to Faërie after that dog's 'death' by underground paths as blessed and eerie as those taken by the King to reach Eagle Abbey. But in all his strange adventures, Jizay affirmed, he had never seen such beauty or wonder as the sight of the myriad unicorns gathered in the glades near to the Portal now.

"They are awaiting the full moon," was all that Finnir would say. While Timair added, "As is Eli."

To this, very quietly, Reyse appended the remark: "As are we all." The King and Queen joined hands, as they nodded their smiling approval of this lovely statement. But Eli was not sure if Reyse was thinking of the fulfilment of the prophesy of Faërie's motto, or if his words were more personal and sentimental in nature.

****

Eli slept very soundly on the night of the 19th, but she awoke to a challenging and surprising day, at least in her own heart, on the 20th. She was to go through the Portal on the morning of the *next* day, the 21st of November, at the same hour as she had arrived.

According to her *original* plans, she should have been crossing the threshold on the 21st day, or night, counting from **Samhain Eve** at dusk. That would have been on *this* evening of the 20th, just before the moon showed herself; but because of Erreig's presence in Barrywood on Samhain Eve, she was now required to step through on the mid-morning of the 21st, when the moon had traversed the sky and had already set. But she *must* not see, or be seen by, the full moon. Officially, she should not *be in* Faërie during that night...

In fact, the moon would rise over the eastern horizon, beyond Sea-Horse Bay, in the afternoon --- though in Barrywood, where the trees were among the tallest and the forest the thickest in all of Faërie, she would not be visible until the dusk. As Aulfrin had explained, the **full moon** is not a single night, but --- in fact --- three. The second night is the actual and *complete* full moon, while the first and third are considered as part of that phase by the fairies, as the moon *appears* full and not oval. But Eli must not be seen by, nor herself behold, the moon on *any* of these nights.

Morning Prayer

It looked as though the moon would be concealed from view today, in any case, for the 20th dawned as fairies so love, with skies laden with rain and --- by late morning --- heavy downpours. Dancing ensued, of course, and Eli joined in with skill and delicious abandon. However, as the middle-day passed to early afternoon, the heavens cleared, and a clean-washed blue dome crowned Barrywood.

"My father Aulfrelas, the Sage-Hermit still for this time, is not here to ask," remarked the King, thoughtfully regarding the pretty sky, "but I would not be surprised if he would accord our dear Eli the leniency to be glimpsed by the moon in her *first* night of fullness. For Alégondine, his successor, sent back a message with the first of the gulls, intimating that a full moon which is hidden and veiled by cloud would probably be acceptable. The message contained (unfortunately) no clear report regarding Erreig's whereabouts --- for the giant moths were not the bearers of these reports --- but I felt cheered by this missal from the Twilight-Princess concerning Eli's dilemma. Unfortunately, this 'grace' extended from Star Island and its Hermits --- present and future --- does not seem to correspond to the clear skies we are offered at this moment."

"We may have another choice, my dear Majesty." Finnir's voice was as gentle as the sleepy eyes of the toffee-coloured squirrel cradled in his arms.

Aulfrin turned to him, where all the company stood on a high balcony of the Castle overlooking the Inward Sea and the imposing Island ten miles or so from the shore. "I miss your calling me 'father', my dear boy. Could you not continue, even though I am not the King Tirrig?!"

Finnir's laughter was as bright as the sunny expanse overhead. "I would be honoured, my dear *father*. For nearly seven hundred years I have used that privileged term for you, and I miss it also!"

"Excellent!" replied Aulfrin, "and what is this 'other choice', my *son*?"

"In the Chapel of Windy Hill, Eli will be on the other side of the vast realm of Faërie. It will be day and not night. There will be no moon."

"How is the Chapel on the *other side*?" inquired Piv, his head questioningly inclined, as was Jizay's also.

There was a brief pause, but before Finnir could reply, Reyse did so.

"The Chapel itself can be in one place or another," he said, speaking low. Eli glanced quickly and rather furtively at him, thinking of his own vision in the midst of the Whale Race Sound. But Reyse was not looking at Eli, but rather --- with all of the company --- out towards the isle in the Inward Sea, all shadowy greens with swirling mist at its shores, but crowned by the small white Chapel, its open doorway facing the Castle. Uncannily --- from so far away --- the mimosa tree growing within glowed like the 'million candles burning before the altar of Love itself': Eli's dramatic image for the energy she felt in Finnir's presence. Reyse continued, his words hushed and reverent.

"The inside of the Chapel of Windy Hill is not here, never fully here, not in this shee. Aulf the Mighty displaced its interior, with the help of Maelcraig --- then the Sage-Hermit --- so that the wattle-tree would thrive there. It is elsewhere; it is a bridge."

"A *bridge*?" echoed Eli.

"A bridge to *where*?" murmured Piv in similar hushed amazement.

Finnir answered, staring with the others at the brilliant yellow light framed by the distant doorway. "To my home, the White Kangaroo Shee. For wattles innumerable grow there, and in the vast lands into which our Portals open.

"Nine of the eleven shees of the Spiralling Stars," he continued, still speaking very softly and calmly, "have Portals which connect them to the human lands...in that world's *northern* hemisphere. But two of the shees have doorways which open into the *southern* one --- and my shee is one of them. A shee will always reflect the world to which it is linked, in the movements of sun and moon, and in the constellations of its stars also, to a great extent. If Eli is within the Chapel this evening, and all night, she will be in the **daytime** of *my* shee. And thus, there will be no moon, for it will have already set. It is already nearly **tomorrow** in the Shee of the White Kangaroo!"

Eli turned from gazing at the golden mimosa to smile, no longer incredulous but rather entranced, at Finnir --- who was now looking very intensely at her, and smiling broadly also. In the palpable silence which had followed his explanation, they continued to stare at one another and Eli could feel some memory tugging at her heart or mind. But like a dream fleeting too quickly to be caught, it slipped from her grasp and faded. She turned, now, to see Aulfrin and Rhynwanol grinning with dawning understanding at this curious proposal, and Piv was positively radiant.

"But it's *wonderful*!" he chirruped excitedly, sounding like a piping lark. "Oh, isn't it marvellous how marvellous it all is, when there is love?! Oh, it's true, it's true: love is always the solution; it always finds the solution! Oh, Finnir of the upside-down stars, can I come too?!"

Finnir was laughing, and so was Timair and the King and Queen, standing together on the balcony. Only Reyse seemed distant and detached. His expression was as shaded as his face when his dark hood was pulled up over his head. A pang of sympathy, or longing (or it might have been tenderness) shot through Eli's heart, pulling it in two directions at once.

But immediately she tightened her hands on the balustrade, and on the reins of her galloping thoughts. She nodded to Finnir.

He smiled, nodding back to her and to the King, who was also signalling his agreement with his deep green eyes and the shimmer of light escaping the emeralds and peridots of his crown. But Finnir had to disappoint Piv.

"I'm sorry, Master Periwinkle, but I think that it is only for Eli and myself to go there tonight. I hope you will understand..."

"Yes, yes, of course, only you two shall go," came Aulfrin's authoritative but serene voice. "Timair is the Prince-Guardian-apparent, yes, and I am the Sovereign even of Windy Hill, and Periwinkle is... well *Periwinkle*. But despite the claims of such august personages to certain privileges, the wattle-tree of my grand-sire Aulf the Mighty is more yours than ours, my dear son Finnir. You and it come from the same source of quivering light and myth and ancestral enchantment. I'm sorry, dear Periwinkle, and any other who would go to the sacred isle, but I decree that it shall only be granted to Eli and Finnir tonight."

Eli glanced, once more, at Reyse; but he had lowered his eyes from both the Chapel and from meeting hers.

They could not delay long, for the moon would shortly be rising over the treetops beyond the Castle's also very tree-like towers. Eli and Finnir donned their capes, which did not hinder them calling forth their own wings; and then they bid a good afternoon-and-night to the royal couple, Reyse and Piv, Timair and the two hounds.

They flew out over the waters of the Inward Sea, a rolling blue jewel --- here and there caressed by the wind into white lily-lace. Near the shores of both the mainland and the isle the waters were graced by several pairs of swans: some white, some charcoal-black.

As they landed, Finnir took Eli's hand in his, kissed it and held it for a moment against his breast. Her own heart was beating a polka, and all of her senses seemed heightened to the point of wishing to take flight like the rollicking swallows dashing about over Finnir's head. The Prince said nothing to her, but led her up the sloping path, winding between tall blowing grasses and dark flowers bowing to them in the breeze (among them several deep-purple Dragon-Flowers) and so they serpentined this side of the island until they came to the arched doorway of the Chapel. As Finnir ushered his Lady within, the skies darkened to an intense violet --- though whether it was the twilight-tint or another phenomenon, Eli was not sure --- and the Moon peeped over the hills along the eastern horizon, beyond which the Sage River flowed from the Inward Sea to the coasts of Sea-Horse Bay.

But Eli did not see the Moon, for she had already entered. And everything had changed.

A tiny candle burned on the modest altar and three windows, slender yet tall, gleamed with sunlight. The floor was earthen, and beside the pinkish altar raised on its circle of dark red stone, grew a beautiful little mimosa tree, half as high as the vaulted ceiling. Though seemingly constructed of cool white marble, the Chapel was well-warmed by the intense beams of sunshine pouring into it. Against one wall was a wide bench covered with rich, rough, rather primitive tapestries as bright as the petal-clothing of Mama Ngeza's miniature black sprites in the Fire-Bird Forest. There were strange paintings in reds and yellows on many of the walls: wild and wonderful animals, geometric or abstract patterns of dots and spirals, tiny and delicate moons and suns. And painted on the dome of the ceiling was a constellation of stars. Its form was rather like an elongated diamond, with four large stars marking the points, and a fifth --- somewhat smaller --- along one side.

"What is that?" asked Eli. "It reminds me of the flag of Australia!"

Finnir touched the pearl in his forehead as he regarded the pattern of stars.

"*Birubi*," he murmured. "At least, that is one of its names. My name, which I was given before my birth and before my exchange with Timair, and which I asked to be given in Aulfrin's shee when I was a child, is another of its names. In our Faërie-tongue, Finnir means Birubi. Yes, it means that beautiful and powerful star-formation, among other things."

Her love's clear blue eyes were filled with stars themselves. She could well understand the choice of name for him! Another question crossed her mind.

"Finnir, in your own shee, do you *look* the same?"

He turned his shining face back to smile at her. "Why do you ask that?" he laughed.

"I don't know; it just came to me. Uncle Mor said that your parents, the present King and Queen of the Sheep's Head Shee, they seem to be *made of light*; he said they did not really resemble 'people', not like the other fairies."

"Do you know, I think it is perhaps a very good question, in fact, my dearest Eli. Your Uncle Mor is a very clear-sighted human, it would seem; for to see *at all* the forms of Tirrig or Bowarry is not given to everyone. And when we go to live in that shee, myself and my belovèd Queen Mélusine, it is likely that we will be happy to vibrate as they do, and so we will appear to be made of light too."

"Are you… like an <u>angel</u>, then, Finnir?" enquired Eli now, almost nervously. She wondered what it would like to be married to an angel. The idea puzzled her, and terrified her a little too.

But Finnir laughed again. "No, no, my love. Angels and fairies are not at all the same. We cross paths, sometimes, and we can behold one another. But then even most animals, and many of the human children, can see angels very clearly --- as they can fairies. It is only *adult* humans that seem to have trouble perceiving them, or so the angels tell us.

"But I am not always in my form of light, or not only clothed with that. When I adventured with Reyse and Timair, long years ago, we went, all three of us, to the White Kangaroo Shee, and to that of the Dragon-Bats also --- the two shees opening into the Southern Hemisphere. And when I am in those, I am in my…*normal skin*, if you like. In that body, I am even darker skinned than Alégondine, and I have black --- but still very curly --- hair. But I have the same clear blue eyes, strangely enough!"

He laughed merrily. Eli was too surprised to do so, though. She was trying to imagine the tall, blond, fair-skinned Finnir with dark skin, a deeper shade than Erreig's, perhaps even like Mama Ngeza's. It was not so destabilising as trying to picture him as an angelic creature made of light; but it made her feel a little out of her depth, nonetheless. Well, like so much, she would have to await the moment when she became the Princess Mélusine once again, in order to experience and comprehend everything.

For the moment she was determined to remain *in* the moment. And it was glorious. The minuscule yellow pompoms of the wattle-tree were shining in the strong sunlight from the windows, strange birds and perhaps other foreign creatures were calling and cooing and clucking in the distance, and she was taking her place in Finnir's arms on the brightly draped bench, to wait through this night-turned-day. To doze, she imagined, and to talk, and hopefully to kiss occasionally.

As she settled herself on the bench, another sound could be distinguished among the animal and bird noises. It was that of water, but not the lapping of the Inward Sea beyond the Chapel's doorway. It was a gurgling sound, playful and poetic.

The small altar was made, Eli guessed, of crystal. It was impossibly large for such a precious-stone, but it resembled a single uncut formation of rose quartz. And the sound came from just behind it.

Eli now noticed (and she was certain it had not been there before) a trickling trail of pale green water flowing around the base of the altar, refreshing the roots of the wattle-tree before it tumbled down from the deep red dais and was absorbed into the earthen floor. And now, as she raised her eyes from the tiny rivulet, she saw a bird perched on the altar's rim.

It was a kingfisher. But only for a moment.

As Eli blinked in surprise, the bright turquoise-blue and persimmon-orange bird flew down and alighted on the dusty floor. As he did so, he became a fairy, about the same height as Corr-Seylestar and, like the Heron-Fairy, wearing a strange elongated head-dress in the form of a beak extending over his ancient face and glorious eyes. Those eyes were as turquoise as his feathers; they were the same hue as Eli's own eyes, but as round and kind and immeasurably deep as the Mushroom Lord's.

One bough of the mimosa tree fell just over his head, and he reached up and stroked it, as if it were a pet cat. A rain of yellow blossom floated down, but Eli could not see it land on the floor. It simply evaporated as it fell --- if indeed it *had* fallen at all! Finnir and Eli rose to greet their guest, and the Prince introduced him, though quite unnecessarily. Eli could have intoned the name herself.

"This is Barrimilla, my dearest Mélusine. He wished to give you his blessing before you return to this final chapter of your life in the world."

Eli was bemused and charmed and gratified. She inclined her head to the magical little fairy. "I am so thrilled to meet you, dearest Barrimilla. Thank you, for by appearing to me here in Windy Hill you give me great hope and force for the time ahead."

The bird-fairy's voice was piping and pleasing, full of high harmonics and as downy and gentle as the wattle-blossoms.

"You will replace all of your fears with joy, now, dear Mélusine, and with that *hope and force* you so sweetly speak of, until your soul bursts open into new life, and you come to meet me once again.

"I think you do not recall our first meeting, but you bid a hello to me across my threshold, ah perhaps a century ago! No matter that it is washed away in your human-haze; next time it will be a *very* joyous meeting on the watery-side of my swirling home. And it will be in fewer years than a hundred, I would guess, our next hello!"

Barrimilla chuckled, in musical tones exactly suited to his appearance and his merry and marvellous speaking voice.

"No doubt," agreed Eli, also laughing. "And you have assuaged what fears remained to me regarding that meeting. Just to hear you speak of it makes it already a more joyous thing to anticipate! Thank you."

"It has been my pleasure, Princess of the Flaming Moon," replied the Kingfisher-Fairy. "Now, live well and wisely on the other side, and pray fervently and with the certainty of gratification and success --- as if the eggs were already hatched and their little ones ready to fledge, as we say in my family! May the hope and force you have found in this white Chapel chirrup and sing in your heart for all the years to come!"

As he concluded, he immediately became --- once again --- a bird. He flew up into the bobbly branches of the mimosa tree, and he simply disappeared. But the pendant hanging from Eli's left ear grew hot and heavy for an instant; and then it was again as light as a tiny kingfisher's feather.

Returning to their bench, she and Finnir cuddled into one another's arms, speechlessly and happily. And not without several shared kisses. Eli slipped into a deep and peaceful sleep eventually; and she only awoke, still in Finnir's embrace, when the light had left the windows and was now only to be seen at the doorway. That sunlight was tentative and yet growing slowly bolder, glistening on the pale lavender waters of the Inward Sea.

It was dawn in the Shee Mor, and the moon over Aulfrin's kingdom had set. It was time to go the Portal of the Heart Oak.

****

Eli knew there was no way to make this moment less weighty than it was, less difficult in many respects, less important, less ultimate and irrevocable. She thought, once again, of Demoran's words, when she had stepped back over the invisible boundary of her two worlds at the close of her very first Visit:

All of our life's journey, long or short, is made up of this, my dear sister: stepping through doorways, out of one place or role or event or thought, and into the next. Sometimes we see where we're going, sometimes we think we know, and sometimes we have no idea really at all. But my advice is to never let your step falter, but to make it with courage and faith in Life and Love. For it is very good to always keep believing in Life and Love!

The difference for her, now, was that this was the conclusion of her *last* Visit. And there was no coming back, until she would come to the end of her human life. Her dear brother had sent word to the King last evening, by the gull who had met with the Heron-Fairy (and who had then continued on with him to the Dappled Woods) saying : *The Prince Demoran wished her a 'bon voyage' over the threshold, and that --- as she would presumably be living in France --- he invited her to come to the 'V'-shaped entrance to the Fair Stair in the woods of Ligugé at the Winter Solstice, where he would be able to meet with her.*

Finnir had told her, in a similar offer to that of Demoran's, that she could play Róisín for guidance (and to have the precise dates and times revealed to her) and come to Gougane Barra sometimes, where they could also meet. But he would not, he had reminded her, disobey her *own* decree as Mélusine: they could not touch on those occasions, which would only resemble the very real 'visions' accorded her by the Silver Leaf. And those could continue, too, allowing her to communicate with him at times, as well as with her father and mother. Finnir clearly had no intentions to do as Reyse, or even as Timair had alluded to: coming into the human-lands for a casual visit or a cup of tea together!

But Eli's own heart told her why she had put such physical limits in place, at least as concerned Finnir. Her union with the enchanted Prince, and her true and restored role as a Princess of Faërie, *must* remain in her future: it must be for her a beacon, a path of light on the waters before her, her dream, and --- as Barrimilla had said --- her fervent prayer. But Finnir would not, could not yet, be her *present*.

Not after she took this step.

It was fifty miles from the Castle of Barrywood to the Portal of the Heart Oak. She had made the journey, upon arriving for her third Visit, in a delicate little boat, floating down the River Barra while Finnir had played his harp to her. But now, she would go back on Peronne (rather than using her own wings), trotting and not flying. Finnir and Timair would accompany her, but the others were to come only *part of the way*. For the Portal lay in that part of Barrywood where the Unicorn Glens began and therefore it was governed by strict rules and laws.

Although it was not forbidden for the King or Queen, for even Piv to go there --- and Reyse passed in and out of the Heart Oak at will --- it was not a place to gather in a large company, or even in an extended family group. *Three* fairies could be present at once on the threshold, and *three* fairy animals, no more: that was the sacred rule and the limit set --- by the Portal itself, or by its twin grey-owl inhabitants perhaps. And so they would have to abide by that.

For the first leg of the journey they rode together: there were four flying-horses with wings laid gracious over the legs of their riders (Piv rode with Eli, while Reyse and the King and Queen were on their respective steeds). And now there were also wing-less horses, with Finnir on Neya-Voun and Timair on his own handsome strawberry-brindle stallion. Jizay and Ferglas loped along with them, weaving in and out of the shiny-grey or golden-skinned trees, over a carpet of un-withering fallen silver-white leaves. Many birds, among them swallows of course, perched among the branches or swooped hither and thither in short flights. Numerous beige or tan or light-red squirrels scampered about the path or up and down the trees to either side of it.

They were following, more or less, the winding circuit of the River Barra to their left, and when they had passed its most easterly loop and had turned towards the north-west, they drew to a halt. All the riders dismounted. It was the moment that Eli was dreading and yet which she knew she would cherish for all the years to come. Only she and the two Princes, together with their three steeds, would go on from here.

"You are held in the embrace of both Moon and Sun," said the King, unknowingly quoting Mélusine's own verse --- unless he had read it when on the Island of the Owls --- echoing very appropriately the calligraphy inscribed over her bier. "And their blessings lie generously upon you, my darling Eli. You have lived fifty impressive years in the human-realm already, showing the spirit and the soul of the fairy you are, without ever being aware of it. You have now been reminded of much; you have touched many memories of your former life here.

"I have never doubted, in roughly six-hundred-and-fifty years of knowing you, that you could do anything you chose to do. You begin, now, the most ambitious of all your challenges, perhaps even greater than the Great Charm itself. But I have *utter* confidence in you. And you have, forever, the love of your father with you."

"We wish you, my child," continued Rhynwanol, "a long life yet in the world. For you have much to accomplish, to learn, to share and to give. But we are, your father and I, and all of this your kingdom of Faërie, impatient also for your human-life's completion. We will be so happy to see you returning to us. But until that time, we shower you with the protection, the joy and the love of the Moon-Dancers and Sun-Singers of your true home. Farewell."

Morning Prayer

"Farewell," repeated Aulfrin, but he could not say more. He stood beside his Queen, and both of them were smiling and weeping.

Reyse stepped forward, and looked --- for a long moment --- into his friend Finnir's eyes. But there was no tension or jealousy or barrier between the two fairies; Eli could feel that. There was a friendship and a complicity stretching back over many centuries and that seemed to stretch forward into many more. They were both very wise, very ancient beings, and very enchanted --- though in *very* different ways. Finally Reyse continued another step or two and came before Eli.

"Where do you go, from here, Reyse?" she asked.

"I thought I would return to my own shee, by this Portal, in a few days' time. From West Cork I can go to Tipperary and the Portal there that leads to the Shee of the Dove. Rather as Peronne did recently, and in a similar guise!

"And, also like him, I may make a little trip to Scotland," he suggested, with a grin. "I wouldn't be surprised to find Morvan in Fort William, and I would enjoy another visit there. Gavenia has already done much, as a loyal and august member of the Craigie Clan and a devoted friend to your half-sisters, the fair twins; and she and your Uncle Mor will, no doubt, serve the Alliance more now that they are together. Two can always do more than one; and if they are also *in love*, they can work miracles."

There was a long silence --- but it did not feel uncomfortable to either of them.

"Farewell then, dear Reyse," Eli said at last, with no sadness in her voice, but with a good measure of affection. "And thank you ... for everything." They shared a smile, and Reyse kissed Eli's hand. The moonstone pendant, touching the other similar jewel invisibly embedded over her heart, was concealed under her clothing, and now tingled against her skin.

Eli's eyes overflowed with tears, and she could not control them, as she knelt and put her arms around Jizay's neck. Her hound of joy licked her face, and then he whispered --- in his silent voice, "I do not think you will need me now, in the years of adventures that lie ahead of you in that strange world. You will not require an invisible dog-friend or a rescued puppy with a fairy's light in his eye! For you are very strong now, and sure of your choice. If there comes a darker road than that which I can perceive from here, I will find a way to visit you; but I do not deem it will be necessary.

Then he added, "Good-bye, and may many blessings go with you, from all the creatures of Faërie!"

Ferglas stood not far off, and in his deep voice he added, "I join with Jizay in bestowing upon you all the benedictions of the hounds, both golden and blue. And may you run your course with a shining heart, unfaltering and with your eyes set on this fair realm, seeing its beauty and harmony everywhere so that you may better dream it into being in that foreign land."

"Farewell, my sweet mistress," Jizay reiterated, very softly.

As she rose, there was a blur of green wings, and little Piv was hovering before her. He wrapped his short arms tightly around her neck and kissed her cheek --- his own as wet with tears as hers.

"Good-bye, Eli-een, and be very good. Think of me whenever you see a mushroom or a water-rat or a snail --- even though I don't think the gallant gastropods have learned to do any interlace designs there. And at every birthday you pass as a human, every 13th of March --- well, and every 21st of June too, just for good measure --- I'll ring bell-flowers for you. Listen well, and I'm sure you'll hear me. And live a long time, and come home soon, hmm, ah, I mean not *too* soon; oh but it *must* be soon, for I shall miss you so much."

Eli squeezed the pixie in her arms, and she kissed his forehead just under his floppy little green cap.

She turned to Finnir and Timair now, and the three of them mounted their horses. Eli looked back, before they turned to go deeper into the woods, and tried very hard to smile and to see

Morning Prayer

clearly through her tears; for she wanted to crystallise this image, this incredible *tableau*, in her memory.

Her father, the 'King of the Fairies' --- as her crazy American harp-CD had told her --- with his sparkling emerald eyes and glittering filigree crown, his short red beard and his flowing cloak; her mother, the unimaginably beautiful violet Queen, with her pale skin and long bejewelled black hair and her robes of rhododendron petals and mauve gauze floating about her elegant form like mist and music; Jizay and Ferglas standing in a drift of silver leaves with Piv between them, one little hand on each dog's back and the eyes of all three gleaming with endless love and devotion.

And then Reyse. She looked last and longest at him. His weather-worn olive-green cloak was swept back over his wide shoulders, and the hood was pushed back too. His brown eyes with their gold circles were intense and deep and regal --- just like an eagle's, Eli thought --- and the moonstones in his ear-lobes and ear-points were shining and softly calling out to the one hanging over her heart. Reyse's curly brown hair hung just over his shoulders and his fine-boned, handsome, rugged, slightly lined face was held high. There was the hint of a smile on his lips, but only a hint.

Eli could hear his voice, though she was sure that he was not speaking audibly.

"Good-bye, Licorne. My heart is forever yours."

****

They had set off from the Castle this morning only shortly after dawn, but none too early it had been. For even now the way was still long, in and out of the trees, some slim and lithe while others were huge and hoary, tall and very ancient. But both Finnir and Timair knew the route well, and so they could lead Eli and Peronne at a trot or even a canter for the remaining miles. And by mid-morning, the three riders and the three fairy-horses had arrived at the Heart Oak.

Eli dismounted into her brother's strong arms. His fair, freckled face was aglow, warmed by his charming smile; his berry-blond hair was swept back, like Eli's deeper red tresses, and held at his neck. The aquamarines twined in their copper-threads peeped out among his curly locks and the amber beside his eyes and that of his ear-gems twinkled and gleamed. Those violet-blue eyes, so exactly like their mother's, harboured just one or two tears --- which trickled down onto his cheek, as did Eli's onto hers.

"Let's meet for a scone in Glengarriff one day soon, my darling sister, shall we? But I'm not going to travel again in your... what is it... your *car*? I will walk --- if I must avoid being seen flying --- from Gougane Barra, or from the Portal opening into Ahakista if I'm in the Sheep's Head; anything rather than getting into one of those metal cages again!

"But before then, here and now, I'll add my blessings, more seriously, too, my dear Eli. You have drunk of Wineberry's draught, you have glimpsed the Cup of Light, you have dared many feats worthy of song and story; but your finest gift and your greatest victory is to have been yourself, always and ever, whether you've been human or fairy. And always remember that you *are* both these beings, and that *all is one*. No need to look back with hesitation ever again, from any threshold, for you have gone beyond that. Sun and Moon, night and light, Eli and Mélusine. Many notes, but one music. All is one.

"Good-bye, my dear Eli-sine. Eleven stars, one spiral of love, be with you. Good-bye, for now."

He turned to his lovely brindle horse and untied the mauve tartan that held Róisín, placing the harp beside the Portal as Eli turned to her own great dapple-grey winged-horse. She wrapped her arms around Peronne's proud neck, and --- as he had done at their first meeting on Mermaid Island --- he lowered his head against her back and shoulder, pulling her closer to him.

"You have tasted flight again, my dear mistress. You will better recall, now, what it is to dance through the air! You have soared into the skies upon my back, and you have thrilled at the sensation of flying with your own wings. I savoured a new form of flight as an eagle in Scotland recently, as you have been granted these delights here in Faërie. But many more moments of delicious freedom await you, dear Moon-Dancer Mélusine; and they will take many different forms. The Lord Reyse 'taught' me, when I was a very young colt, and guided me as I spread my wings for the first time; but he did not give me my aerial ability and its innate joy. They were mine by nature; just as are your abilities and your own true joyous, infinite, eternal lightness.

"Fly well and dance through the heavens of all of your dreams and days to come, dearest Eli. And I will await you beyond the Garnet Vortex, when the time is ripe for new sky-paths to call you home. Farewell."

And now Finnir reached out his hand to Eli. And she stepped toward him.

"It may seem long, my love, the course of years and further human experiences which you have set yourself to traverse. But though they stretch to decades, made up of spiralling seasons, myriad colours and the endless music of creation, it is only a fleeting moment. But it is a moment of grace. You have chosen this, freely and with boundless courage and deep reflection. These years which lie at your feet are the fruit and flowers springing up out of your trials and victories in the Great Charm; they are your 'phoenix-feat', as you called them. You have drunk the purple wine, yes, as Timair says. And perhaps you have drunk the whale-fathers' potion of love from the black fairy, also! But you have little need of wine or charmed elixirs, for you are already in love, and deliciously drunken with true love's inebriating bliss! You are in love with

Life, with Creation, and also with *yourself* and the glory and gift of Being. You are indeed a rose and a unicorn, my Princess, my Queen."

Finnir reached up with his delicate, long-fingered hand --- the hand with the sapphire set into its back --- to touch Eli's left ear, and he gently fondled the Flaming-Crescent Moon hanging there.

"Look," he said, suddenly. "Look, they have come to add their blessings to ours, and to remind you that your true destiny awaits your return!"

Eli was falling heavenwards, once more, into the vastness of Finnir's eyes; but she turned now to where he was looking, for he was laughing like one of the innumerable silver waterfalls falling into the Lake of Gougane Barra, or into the Inward Sea of Faërie.

Among the boles of the thin golden-and-silver trees and between the massive trunks of the wrinkled and dark oaks, tip-toeing --- it seemed --- over the murmuring leaves, curled and luminous at their feet, were the creatures of the Glens.

Ten, twenty, perhaps even more were there: *unicorns*. They were only just visible on the threshold between the glade of the Heart Oak and their own mystical leaf-lands. Unicorns, white and proud --- just as when she had seen Neya-Voun transformed, with Finnir astride her --- with spirals of silver on their brows and hooves as golden as the trees, long manes of undulating white silk and coats as pristine as the radiant pearl in her Prince's forehead. Some were very misty and almost transparent, while others were solid and 'real', and many were whinnying or neighing in cadences like the 'miraculous music' that Eli had played for Wineberry.

"Unicorns!" Eli whispered, "Beautiful, amazing *unicorns!*"

Finnir's hand was laid lightly on her back, urging her to look, again, towards the Portal.

"It is time, my darling Mélusine. You must go. It is the hour."

Eli turned back to Finnir, and to the Portal of the Heart Oak. She could sense that the unicorns were gone, galloped off as silently as they had arrived.

"Good-bye, Finnir," she said. "Good-bye."

"Farewell, my Lady and my love."

Timair passed her harp into her hands. Eli looked up at the two grey owls in the dark, heart-shaped hollow just at the height of her head. They looked down at her and blinked once with their bead-like, orange eyes; and in a trice they flew forth into the woods.

Eli found herself high up in the palm created by the open hand of the various branches, but only for an instant. She stepped forward, with confidence and with joy and with all the determination she cold muster, into the gap at the back of the 'tree-throne'.

There was a light drizzle falling, and she pulled the mauve tartan blanket closer over her harp to keep it dry. She was still wearing a long, warm cloak, and so she also lifted its hood over *her* head, making sure that her shoulder-bag was tightly held in place under it. It held, still, Lily's journal, the Silver Leaf bookmark, and Reyse's white rose.

Behind her was a large and ancient oak tree. Its deeply lined and wrinkled bark was draped with many webs, but none contained singing spiders. Instead they were all hung with rainbow-glistening droplets like trembling jewels and prisms.

Rain and tears blended into one refreshing cascade down Eli's face as she walked away from the silent and solidly closed oak tree, off into the Irish woods. It was not even early afternoon here in Gougane Barra, for she had only been gone three hours from the time she had left on the morning of the 1st of November.

She would go back to her car and then to the Inn in Inchigeelagh, where she would have a pint and a warm meal. And perhaps, she mused --- as she headed towards the Lake through the green-shade and misty rain and the ranks of tall, mossy-toed trees --- perhaps she would begin to keep a journal herself, as Lily had. Not telling the tale of what *had* happened so far, but recounting what now lay *ahead* and what would happen in the years left to her here in the world.

For her adventure was far from over. She was certain that she would fulfil Mélusine's plans and see the dreams of the Alliance come true.

And when it came time for one life to fall away and another to burst into bloom, as Barrimilla had expressed it, she would find her way to the Garnet Vortex and the Fourth Portal. She had complete faith in that, and in herself.

Now, in this present moment, there was so much good to do, so much music to play, so much change to encourage, so much beauty to believe in.

"It is so good *to believe*," she repeated as she looked out over the Lake of Gougane Barra with its background of hillsides zebra-striped by countless cascades of water and dark, mysterious ravines among the gorse and heather.

The clouds were blowing past, and rays of sunlight were slanting down to illuminate the beautiful scene before her.

"*It is very good to believe*," she chanted again inwardly, glancing at the humble Oratory on its tiny promontory, sheltered by trees which cast dappled shadows onto the water as deep a turquoise as her own eyes. "To truly *believe* is nothing short of miraculous," she added. "And this world is sorely in need of miracles.

"God bless you, Lily, my little moon," she added, now speaking aloud --- though very softly, and whispered as she would a private and sacred prayer --- "and thank you for *all* you taught me, but especially for opening my heart to wonder and joy and faith ... and to boundless, fearless adventure. Because I believe that I have, with those gifts, found my Truth and at last I know where I *truly* belong. And I know what I must do, now, with the rest of my life, before I turn, at last, my wind-horse feet to the silver turrets and back to my pure beginnings.

"I will work, and wait --- and pray. My eyes are no longer 'wild' as in Liam's lines of love poetry; they are *open* now. And they are filled with the light of the Sun and with the magical glowing Moon ever-full. I will, one day, fly home to the red and yellow banners of Fantasie. I will return to Faërie. For, from today, I begin both my new life here and also my voyage home.

"Yes, it has begun."

****

Hic finitur liber tertius

This is the end of **Windy Hill Prayer**,
Book Three in the trilogy *Return to Faërie*

***

*May your life and all your loves
always spiral upwards,
growing from wonder to wonder.*

*May **joy** dwell deep within you,
but never so deep as to be out of reach.*

*And may you
believe
with all your heart.*

***

Three more notes in the music:

To mark the publication of this first edition of *Return to Faërie*, I wish to include a very personal little cadence, a trio of dedications:

***

To Michel:
my love and gratitude forever,
with hands and hearts joined

To Siobhán:
many blessings and thanks
to my beautiful soul-friend

To Giles:
my undying affection and many merry memories,
together with my profound apologies…

***

Jane Sullivan

Index of Characters

Moonrise

Aindel	301	Lady Ecume	89
Alégondine	53	Laurien	119
Annick	3	Leyano	52
Ardan	328	Liam	6
Aulf	239	Lord Hwittir	284
Aulfrelas	66	Maelcraig	232
Aulfrin	50	Maelys/Lily	14
Bawn	213	Mélusine	31
Belfina & Begneta	300	Morvan/Uncle Mor	43/105
Brocéliana	62		
Calenny	129	Muscari	246
Ceoleen	251	Mushroom Lord	239
Clare	58	Peronne	28
Colm	102	Piv/Periwinkle	261
Corr-Seylestar	269	Rapture	140
Daireen	328	Reyse	195
Demoran	34	Rhynwanol	64
Elfhea & Everil	321	Ruilly	133
Eli Penrohan	1	Sage-Hermit	53
Eochra	246	Sean Penrohan	14
Erreig	66	Sinéad	110
Ferglas	132	Timair	327
Fiach	140	Vanzelle	279
Finnir	52	Vintig	136
Garo	269	Violette	186
Gnome	282	Yann	42
Heron-Fairy	149	Yves	107
Hygga	283		
Jizay	29		
Kirik	211		

617

A Delicate Balance

Ævnad	372	Morliande	218
Artist of Kitty Kyle	355	Mowena & Malmaza	215
Aytel	182	Neya-Voun	187
Ban-Cocoilleen	339	Pallaïs	458
Banvowha	132	Rhadeg	257
Barrimilla	472	Tinna Payst & Tintrac	385
Bram	256	Wineberry	233
Brea	182		
Camiade (M & Mme)	40		

Windy Hill Prayer

Cynnabar	156		
Dinnagorm	161	Bowarry	358
Emile	10	Durnol	351
Finnhol-Og	338	Eagla-Anvash	507
Gaëtanne	260	Gavenia	371
Garv-Feyar	440	Habukaz	473
Janet	50	Rhysianne	351
King Isck	168	Roísín	76
Mama Ngeza	351	Tirrig	358
Mauve Dragon	286		

Maps

Due to the limitations imposed by the printing of this first edition, the following maps are presented only in black & white.

Map of Faërie – full

Detail north-east quarter
Detail south-east quarter
Detail north-west quarter
Detail south-west quarter

Map of the City of Fantasie

The full versions of the two maps in b&w are available for free download at www.return-to-faerie.com

Full-colour reproductions of the Map of Faërie and also the Map of the City of Fantasie are available to order from the **Return to Faërie** on-line shop:

https://www.zazzle.com/store/return_to_faerie

(please note that in this web-address the "e" of *faerie* has no umlaut !)

Other products and gift items associated with this book can also be found at the above address.

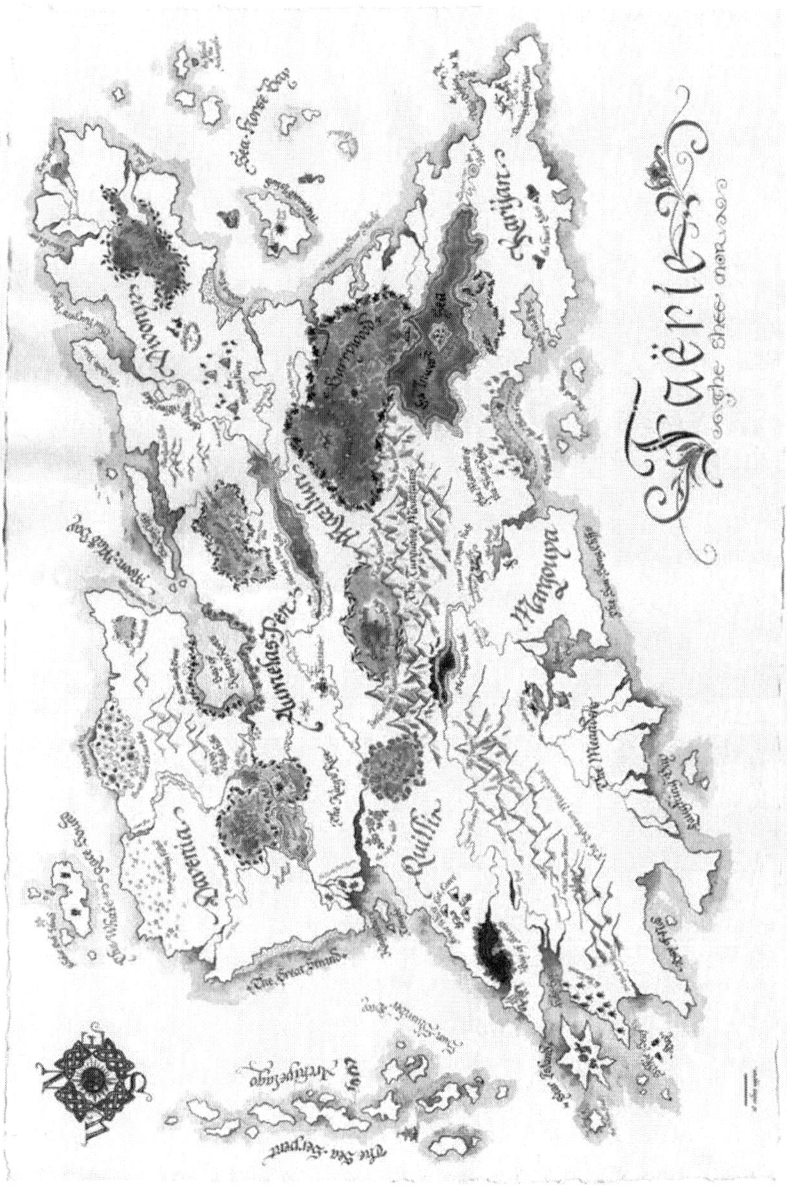
Faërie
Quillin
The Great Strand
The Sea-Serpent
Archipelago
Sea-Horse Bay
Moon-Mist Bay
The Turquoise Mountains

Sea-Horse Bay
Mermaid's Island
Morning Star Shoals
Barrywood
The Turquoise Mountains
Moon-Hag Bay
Blue Rangers' Bay

The Turquoise Mountains
White Hart Fields
the Inward Sea
Mauve Dragon Peak
The Marshes of the Flute Reeds
Blue Lizard Island
Margouya
the Shallows of the Blue Crabs
The Sun-Song Cliffs
The Crab Havens
Windy Word Bay
Karijan
the Heart Lakes
the Pearl
Dizzy Dolphin Point
Dancing Goat Plains
Faërie
The Shee Mor

The Great Strand
Archipelago
The Sea-Serpent
Bay of Knotty Roots

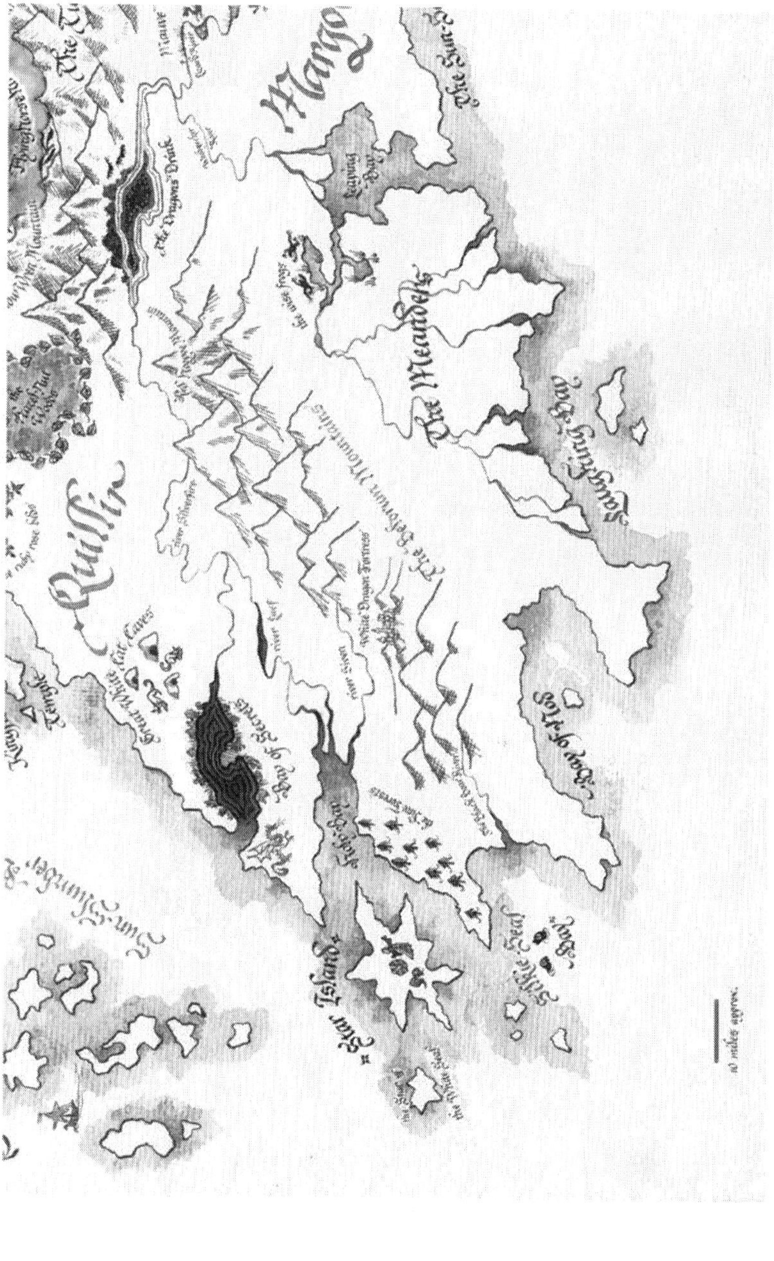

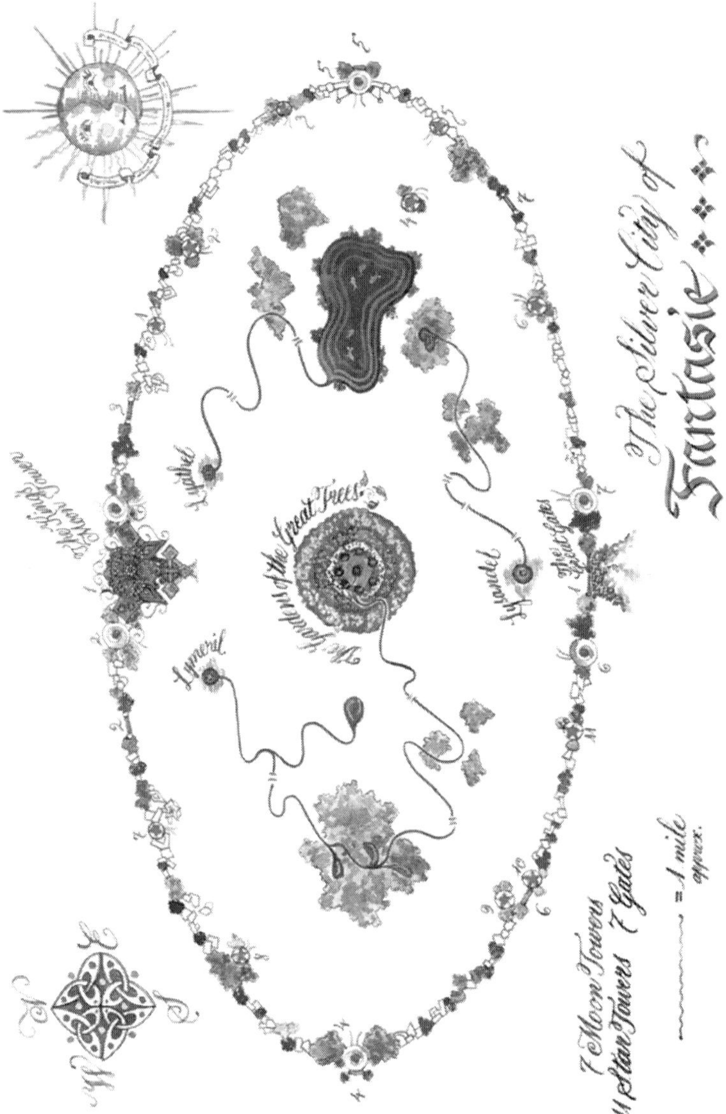

The Silver City of
Fantasie
The Gardens of the Great Trees
Lymeril
7 Moon Towers
11 Star Towers 7 Gates
= 1 mile
approx.

Printed in Great Britain
by Amazon